SUPPORT YOUR LOCAL WIZARD

DIANE DUANE

SUPPORT YOUR LOCAL WIZARD

*So You Want
  to Be a Wizard
Deep Wizardry
High Wizardry*

GUILDAMERICA
B O O K S™

SO YOU WANT TO BE A WIZARD   Copyright © 1983
by Diane Duane
DEEP WIZARDRY   Copyright © 1985 by Diane Duane
HIGH WIZARDRY   Copyright © 1990 by Diane Duane

Published by arrangement with
Delacorte Press
Bantam Doubleday Dell Publishing Group, Inc.
666 Fifth Avenue
New York, New York 10103

The trademark Delacorte Press® is registered in the U.S. Patent and Trademark Office

Printed in the United States of America

Quality Printing and Binding by:
R.R. Donnelley & Sons Company
1009 Sloan Street
Crawfordsville, IN 47933 U.S.A.

CONTENTS

SO YOU WANT TO BE A WIZARD

For Sam's friend

ACKNOWLEDGMENT

David Gerrold is responsible for the creation of several images found in this book, upon which the writer has elaborated slightly. He's also responsible for beating the writer with a club until the words came out right—a matter of several years' nonstop exertion. It would take several more years to fully acknowledge his contributions to both the writer and the written; but brevity is probably best. Old friend, big brother, thanks and love, again and always.

. . . By necessity every book must have at least one flaw; a misprint, a missing page, one imperfection. . . . the Rabbis . . . point out that even in the holiest of books, the scroll resting inside the Ark, the Name of Names is inscribed in code so that no one might say it out loud, and chance to pronounce properly the Word that once divided the waters from the waters and the day from the night. . . . As it is, some books, nearly perfect, are known to become transparent when opened under the influence of the proper constellation, when the full Moon rests in place. Then it is not uncommon for a man to become lost in a single letter, or to hear a voice rise up from the silent page; and then only one imperfect letter, one missing page, can bring him back to the land where a book, once opened, may still be closed, can permit him to pull up the covers around his head and smile once before he falls asleep.

—*Midrashim*, by Howard Schwartz

I have been a word in a book.

—"The Song of Taliesin"
in *The Black Book of Caermarthen*

CONTENTS

Prologue

Part of the problem, Nita thought to herself as she tore desperately down Rose Avenue, is that I can't keep my mouth shut.

She had been running for five minutes now, hopping fences, sliding sideways through hedges, but she was losing her wind. Some ways behind her she could hear Joanne and Glenda and the rest of them pounding along in pursuit, threatening to replace her latest, now-fading black eye. Well, Joanne *would* come up to her with that new bike, all chrome and silver and gearshift levers and speedometer/odometer and toeclips and waterbottle, and ask what she thought of it. So Nita had *told* her. Actually, she had told Joanne what she thought of *her*. The bike was all right. In fact, it had been almost exactly the one that Nita had wanted so much for her last birthday—the birthday when she got nothing but clothes.

Life can be really rotten sometimes, Nita thought. She wasn't really so irritated about that at the moment, however. Running away from a beating was taking up most of her attention.

"Callahan," came a yell from behind her, "I'm gonna pound you up and mail you home in bottles!"

I wonder how many bottles it'll take, Nita thought, without much humor. She couldn't afford to laugh. With their bikes, they'd catch up to her pretty quickly. And then . . .

She tried not to think of the scene there would be later at home—her father raising hands and eyes to the ceiling, wondering loudly enough for the whole house to hear, "Why didn't you hit them *back?*"; her sister making belligerent noises over her new battlescars; her mother shaking her head, looking away silently, because she understood. It was her sad look that would hurt Nita more than the bruises and scrapes and swollen face would. Her mom would shake her head, and clean the hurts up, and sigh. . . .

Crud! Nita thought. The breath was coming hard to her now. She was going to have to try to hide, to wait them out. But where? Most of the people around here didn't want kids running through their yards. There was Old Crazy Swale's house with its big landscaped yard, but the rumors among the neighborhood kids said that weird things happened in there. Nita herself had noticed that the guy didn't go to work like normal people. Better to get beat up again than go in *there*. But where can I hide?

She kept on running down Rose Avenue, and the answer presented itself to her: a little brown-brick building with windows warmly alight—refuge, safety, sanctuary. The library. It's open, it's open, I forgot it was open late on Saturday! Oh, thank Heaven! The sight of it gave Nita a new burst of energy. She cut across its tidy lawn, loped up the walk, took the five stairs to the porch in two jumps, bumped open the front door and closed it behind her, a little too loudly.

The library had been a private home once, and it hadn't lost the look of one despite the crowding of all its rooms with bookshelves. The walls were paneled in mahogany and oak, and the place smelled warm and brown and booky. At the thump of the door Mrs. Lesser, the weekend librarian, glanced up from her desk, about to say something sharp. Then she saw who was standing there and how hard she was breathing. Mrs. Lesser frowned at Nita and then grinned. She didn't miss much.

"There's no one downstairs," she said, nodding at the door that led to the children's library in the single big basement room. "Keep quiet and I'll get rid of them."

"Thanks," Nita said, and went thumping down the cement stairs. As she reached the bottom, she heard the bump and squeak of the front door opening again.

Nita paused to try to hear voices and found that she couldn't. Doubting that her pursuers could hear her either, she walked on into the children's library, smiling slightly at the books and the bright posters.

She still loved the place. She loved any library, big or little; there was something about all that knowledge, all those facts waiting patiently to be found that never failed to give her a shiver. When friends couldn't be found, the books were always waiting with something new to tell. Life that was getting too much the same could be shaken up in a few minutes by the picture in a book of some ancient temple newly discovered deep in a rainforest, a fuzzy photo of Uranus with its up-and-down rings, or a prismed picture taken through the faceted eye of a bee.

And though she would rather have died than admit it—no respectable thirteen-year-old *ever* set foot down there—she still loved the children's library too. Nita had gone through every book in the place when she was younger, reading everything in sight—fiction and nonfiction alike, fairy tales, science books, horse stories, dog stories, music books, art books, even the encyclopedias.

(Bookworm,) she heard the old jeering voices go in her head, (foureyes, smartass, hide-in-the-house-and-read. Walking encyclopedia. Think you're so hot.) "No," she remembered herself answering once, "I just like to find things out!" And she sighed, feeling rueful. *That* time she had found out about being punched in the stomach.

She strolled between shelves, looking at titles, smiling as she met old friends, books she had read three times or five times or a dozen. Just a title, or an author's name, would be enough to summon up happy images. Strange creatures like phoenixes and psammeads, moving under smoky London daylight of a hundred years before, in company with groups of bemused children; starships and new worlds and the limitless vistas of interstellar night, outer space challenged but never conquered; princesses in silver and golden dresses, princes and heroes carrying swords like sharpened lines of light, monsters rising out of weedy tarns, wild creatures that talked and tricked one another. . . .

I used to think the world would be like that when I got older. Wonderful all the time, exciting, happy. Instead of the way it is—

Something stopped Nita's hand as it ran along the bookshelf. She looked and found that one of the books, a little library-bound volume in shiny red buckram, had a loose thread at the top of its spine, on which her finger had caught. She pulled the finger free, glanced at the title. It was one of those "So You Want to Be a . . ." books, a series on careers. *So You Want to Be a Pilot* there had been, and *So You Want to Be a Scientist . . . a Nurse . . . a Writer . . .*

But this one said *So You Want to Be a Wizard.*

A *what?*

Nita pulled the book off the shelf, surprised not so much by the title as by the fact that she'd never seen it before. She thought she knew the whole stock of the children's library. Yet this wasn't a new book. It had plainly been there for some time—the pages had that yellow look about their edges, the color of aging, and the top of the book was dusty. SO YOU WANT TO BE A WIZARD. HEARNSSEN, the spine said: that was the author's name. Phoenix Press, the publisher. And then in white ink, in Mrs. Lesser's tidy handwriting, 793.4: the Dewey Decimal number.

This has to be a joke, Nita said to herself. But the book looked exactly like all the others in the series. She opened it carefully, so as not to crack the binding, and turned the first few pages to the table of contents. Normally Nita was a fast reader and would quickly have finished a page with only a few lines on it; but what she found on that contents page slowed her down a great deal. "Preliminary Determinations: A Question of Aptitude." "Wizardly Preoccupations and Predilections." "Basic Equipment and Milieus." "Introduction to Spells, Bindings and *Geasa.*" "Familiars and Helpmeets: Advice to the Initiate." "Psychotropic Spelling."

Psychowhat? Nita turned to the page on which that chapter began, looking at the boldface paragraph beneath its title.

WARNING

Spells of power sufficient to make temporary changes in the human mind are always subject to sudden and unpredictable backlash on the user. The practitioner is cautioned to make sure that his/her motives are benevolent before attempting spelling aimed at . . .

I don't believe this, Nita thought. She shut the book and stood there holding it in her hand, confused, amazed, suspicious—and *delighted.* If it was a joke, it was a great one. If it wasn't—

No, don't be silly.

But if it *isn't*—

People were clumping around upstairs, but Nita hardly heard them. She sat down at one of the low tables and started reading the book in earnest. The first couple of pages were a foreword.

Wizardry is one of the most ancient and misunderstood of arts. Its public image for centuries has been one of a mysterious pursuit, practiced in occult surroundings, and usually used at the peril of one's soul. The modern wizard, who works with tools more advanced than bat's blood and beings more complex than medieval demons, knows how far from the truth that image is. Wizardry, though exciting and interesting, is not a glamorous business, especially these days, when a wizard must work quietly so as not to attract undue attention.

For those willing to assume the Art's responsibilities and do the work, though, wizardry has many rewards. The sight of a formerly twisted growing thing now growing straight, of a snarled motivation untangled, the satisfaction of hearing what a plant is thinking or a dog is saying, of talking to a stone or a star, is thought by most to be well worth the labor.

Not everyone is suited to be a wizard. Those without enough of the necessary personality traits will never see this manual for what it is. That you have found it at all says a great deal for your potential.

The reader is invited to examine the next few chapters and determine his/her wizardly potential in detail—to become familiar with the scope of the Art—and finally to decide whether to become a wizard.

Good luck!

It's a joke, Nita thought. Really. And to her own amazement, she wouldn't believe herself—she was too fascinated. She turned to the next chapter.

PRELIMINARY DETERMINATIONS

An aptitude for wizardry requires more than just the desire to practice the art. There are certain inborn tendencies, and some acquired ones, that enable a person to become a wizard. This chapter will list some of the better documented of wizardly characteristics. Please bear in mind that it isn't necessary to possess all the qualities listed, or even most of them. Some of the greatest wizards have been lacking in the qualities possessed by almost all others and have still achieved startling competence levels. . . .

Slowly at first, then more eagerly, Nita began working her way through the assessment chapter, pausing only to get a pencil and scrap paper from the checkout desk, so that she could make notes on her aptitude. She was brought up short by the footnote to one page—

> Where ratings are not assigned, as in rural areas, the area of greatest population density will usually produce the most wizards, due to the thinning of worldwalls with increased population concentration . . .

Nita stopped reading, amazed. "Thinning of worldwalls"—were they saying that there are other worlds, other dimensions, and that things could get through? Things, or people?

She sat there and wondered. All the old fairy tales about people falling down wells into magical countries, or slipping backward in time, or forward into it—did this mean that such things could actually happen? If you could actually go into other worlds, other places, and come back again . . .

Aww—who would believe anybody who came back and told a story like that? Even if they took pictures?

But who cares! she answered herself fiercely. If only it could be true. . . .

She turned her attention back to the book and went on reading, though skeptically—the whole thing still felt like a game. But abruptly it stopped being a game, with one paragraph:

> Wizards love words. Most of them read a great deal, and indeed one strong sign of a potential wizard is the inability to get to sleep without reading something first. But their love for and fluency with words is what makes wizards a force to be reckoned with. Their ability to convince a piece of the world—a tree, say, or a stone—that it's not what it thinks it is, that it's something else, is the very heart of wizardry. Words skillfully used,

the persuasive voice, the persuading mind, are the wizard's most basic tools. With them a wizard can stop a tidal wave, talk a tree out of growing, or into it—freeze fire, burn rain—*even slow down the death of the Universe.*

That last, of course, is the reason there *are* wizards. See the next chapter.

Nita stopped short. The universe was running down, all the energy in it was slowly being used up; she knew that from astronomy. "Entropy," the process was called. But she'd never heard anyone talk about slowing it down before.

She shook her head in amazement and went on to the "correlation" section at the end of that chapter, where all the factors involved in the makeup of a potential wizard were listed. Nita found that she had a lot of them— enough to be a wizard, if she wanted to.

In rising excitement she turned to the next chapter. "Theory and Implications of Wizardry," its heading said. *"History, Philosophy, and the Wizards' Oath."*

Fifty or sixty eons ago, when life brought itself about, it also brought about to accompany it many Powers and Potentialities to manage the business of creation. One of the greatest of these Powers held aloof for a long time, watching its companions work, not wishing to enter into Creation until it could contribute something unlike anything the other Powers had made, something completely new and original. Finally the Lone Power found what it was looking for. Others had invented planets, light, gravity, space. The Lone Power invented death, and bound it irrevocably into the worlds. Shortly thereafter the other Powers joined forces and cast the Lone One out.

Many versions of this story are related among the many worlds, assigning blame or praise to one party or another. However, none of the stories change the fact that entropy and its symptom, death, are here now. To attempt to halt or remove them is as futile as attempting to ignore them.

Therefore there are wizards—to handle them.

A wizard's business is to conserve energy—to keep it from being wasted. On the simplest level this includes such unmagical-looking actions as paying one's bills on time, turning off the lights when you go out, and supporting the people around you in getting their lives to work. It also includes a great deal more.

Because wizardly people tend to be good with language, they can also become skillful with the Speech, the magical tongue in which objects and living creatures can be described with more accuracy than in any human language. And what can be so accurately described can also be preserved—or freed to become yet greater. A wizard can cause an inanimate object or animate creature to grow, or stop growing—to be what it is, or something else. A wizard, using the Speech, can cause death to slow down, or go somewhere else and come back later—just as the Lone Power caused it to come about in the first place. Creation, preservation, destruction, transformation—all are a matter of causing the fabric of being to do what you want it to. And the Speech is the key.

Nita stopped to think this over for a moment. *It sounds like, if you know what something is, truly* know, *you don't have any trouble working with it. Like my telescope—if it acts up, I know every piece of it, and it only takes a second to get it working again. To have that kind of control over—over* everything—*live things, the world, even . . .* She took a deep breath and looked back at the book, beginning to get an idea of what kind of power was implied there.

The power conferred by use of the Speech has, of course, one insurmountable limitation: the existence of death itself. As one renowned Senior Wizard has remarked, "Entropy has us outnumbered." No matter how much preserving we do, the Universe will eventually die. But it will last longer because of our efforts—and since no one knows for sure whether another Universe will be born from the ashes of this one, the effort seems worthwhile.

No one should take the Wizards' Oath who is not committed to making wizardry a lifelong pursuit. The energy invested in a beginning wizard is too precious to be thrown away. Yet there are no penalties for withdrawal from the Art, except the knowledge that the Universe will die a little faster because of energy lost. On the other hand, there are no prizes for the service of Life—except life itself. The wizard gets the delight of working in a specialized area—magic—and gets a good look at the foundations of the Universe, the way things really work. It should be stated here that there are people who consider the latter more of a curse than a blessing. Such wizards usually lose their art. Magic does not live in the unwilling soul.

Should you decide to go ahead and take the Oath, be warned that an ordeal of sorts will follow, a test of aptitude. If you pass, wizardry will ensue. . . .

Yeah? Nita thought. *And what if you* don't *pass?*

"Nita?" Mrs. Lesser's voice came floating down the stairs, and a moment later she herself appeared, a large brunette lady with kind eyes and a look of eternal concern. "You still alive?"

"I was reading."

"So what else is new? They're gone."

"Thanks, Mrs. L."

"What was all that about, anyway?"

"Oh . . . Joanne was looking to pick a fight again."

Mrs. Lesser raised an eyebrow at Nita, and Nita smiled back at her shame-facedly. She *didn't* miss much.

"Well, I might have helped her a little."

"I guess it's hard," Mrs. Lesser said. "I doubt *I* could be nice all the time, myself, if I had that lot on my back. That the only one you want today, or should I just have the nonfiction section boxed and sent over to your house?"

"No, this is enough," Nita said. "If my father sees too many books he'll just make me bring them back."

Mrs. Lesser sighed. "Reading one book is like eating one potato chip," she said. "So you'll be back Monday. There's more where that came from. I'll check it out for you."

Nita felt in her pockets hurriedly. "Oh, crud. Mrs. L., I don't have my card."

"So you'll bring it back Monday," she said, handing her back the book as they reached the landing, "and I'll stamp it then. I trust you."

"Thanks," Nita said.

"Don't mention it. Be careful going home," Mrs. Lesser said, "and have a nice read."

"I will."

Nita went out and stood on the doorstep, looking around in the deepening gloom. Dinnertime was getting close, and the wind was getting cold, with a smell of rain to it. The book in her hand seemed to prickle a little, as if it were impatient to be read.

She started jogging toward home, taking a circuitous route—up Washington from Rose Avenue, then through town along Nassau Road and down East Clinton, a path meant to confound pursuit. She didn't expect that they would be waiting for her only a block away from her house, where there were no alternate routes to take. And when they were through with her, the six of them, one of Nita's eyes was blackened and the knee Joanne had so carefully stomped on felt swollen with liquid fire.

Nita just lay there for a long while, on the spot where they left her, behind the O'Donnells' hedge; the O'Donnells were out of town. There she lay, and cried, as she would not in front of Joanne and the rest, as she would not until she was safely in bed and out of her family's earshot. Whether she provoked these situations or not, they kept happening, and there was nothing she could do about them. Joanne and her hangers-on had found out that Nita didn't like to fight, wouldn't try until her rage broke loose—and then it was too late, she was too hurt to fight well, all her self-defense lessons went out of her head with the pain. And they knew it, and at least once a week found a way to sucker her into a fight—or, if that failed, they would simply ambush her. All right, she had purposely baited Joanne today, but there'd been a fight coming anyway, and *she* had chosen to start it rather than wait, getting angrier and angrier, while they baited *her*. But this would keep happening, again and again, and there was nothing she could do about it. Oh, I wish we could move. I wish Dad would say something to Joanne's father—no, that would just make it worse. If only something could just happen to make it stop!

Underneath her, where it had fallen, the book dug into Nita's sore ribs. The memory of what she had been reading flooded back through her pain and was followed by a wash of wild surmise. If there are spells to keep things from dying, then I bet there are spells to keep people from hurting you. . . .

Then Nita scowled at herself in contempt for actually believing for a moment what couldn't possibly be more than an elaborate joke. She put aside thoughts of the book and slowly got up, brushing herself off and discovering some new bruises. She also discovered something else. Her favorite pen was gone. Her space pen, a present from her Uncle Joel, the pen that could write on butter or glass or upside down, her pen with which she had never failed a test, even in math. She patted herself all over, checked the ground, searched in pockets where she knew the pen couldn't be. No use; it was gone. Or taken, rather—for it had been securely clipped to her front jacket pocket when Joanne and her group jumped her. It must have fallen out, and one of them picked it up.

"Aaaaaagh!" Nita moaned, feeling bitter enough to start crying again. But she was all cried out, and she ached too much, and it was a waste. She stepped around the hedge and limped the little distance home.

Her house was pretty much like any other on the block, a white frame house with fake shutters; but where other houses had their lawns, Nita's had a beautifully landscaped garden. Ivy carpeted the ground, and the flowerbeds against the house had something blooming in every season except the dead of winter. Nita trudged up the driveway without bothering to smell any of the spring flowers, went up the stairs to the back door, pushed it open, and walked into the kitchen as nonchalantly as she could.

Her mother was elsewhere, but the delicious smells of her cooking filled the place; veal cutlets tonight. Nita peered into the oven, saw potatoes baking, lifted a pot lid and found corn-on-the-cob in the steamer.

Her father looked up from the newspaper he was reading at the dining-room table. He was a big, blunt, good-looking man, with startling silver hair and large capable hands—"an artist's hands!" he would chuckle as he pieced together a flower arrangement. He owned the smaller of the town's two flower shops, and he loved his work dearly. He had done all the landscaping around the house in his spare time, and around several neighbors' houses too, refusing to take anything in return but the satisfaction of being up to his elbows in a flowerbed. Whatever he touched grew. "I have an understanding with the plants," he would say, and it certainly seemed that way. It was people he sometimes had trouble understanding, and particularly his eldest daughter.

"My Lord, Nita!" her father exclaimed, putting the paper down flat on the table. His voice was shocked. "What happened?"

As if you don't know! Nita thought. She could clearly see the expressions going across her father's face. *MiGod*, they said, *she's done it again! why doesn't she fight back? What's wrong with her?* He would get around to asking that question at one point or another, and Nita would try to explain it again, and as usual her father would try to understand and would fail. Nita turned away and opened the refrigerator door, peering at nothing in particular, so that her father wouldn't see the grimace of impatience and irritation on her face. She was tired of the whole ritual, but she had to put up with it. It was as inevitable as being beaten up.

"I was in a fight," she said, the second verse of the ritual, the second line of the scene. Tiredly she closed the refrigerator door, put the book down on the counter beside the stove, and peeled off her jacket, examining it for rips and ground-in dirt and blood.

"So how many of them did you take out?" her father said, turning his eyes back to the newspaper. His face still showed exasperation and puzzlement, and Nita sighed. He looks about as tired of this as I am. But really, he *knows* the answers. "I'm not sure," Nita said. "There were six of them."

"Six!" Nita's mother came around the corner from the living room and into the bright kitchen—danced in, actually. Just watching her made Nita smile sometimes, and it did now, though changing expressions hurt. She had been a dancer before she married Dad, and the grace with which she moved made her every action around the house seem polished, endlessly rehearsed, lovely to look at. She glided with the laundry, floated while she cooked. "Loading the odds a bit, weren't they?"

"Yeah." Nita was hurting almost too much to feel like responding to the gentle humor. Her mother caught the pain in her voice and stopped to touch Nita's face as she passed, assessing the damage and conveying how she felt about it in one brief gesture, without saying anything that anyone else but the two of them might hear.

"No sitting up for you tonight, kidlet," her mother said. "Bed, and ice on that, before you swell up like a balloon."

"What started it?" her dad asked from the dining room.

"Joanne Virella," Nita said. "She has a new bike, and I didn't get as excited about it as she thought I should."

Nita's father looked up from the paper again, and this time there was discomfort in his face, and regret. "Nita," he said, "I couldn't afford it this month, really. I thought I was going to be able to earlier, but I couldn't. I *wish* I could have. Next time for sure."

Nita nodded. "It's okay," she said, even though it wasn't really. She'd *wanted* that bike, wanted it so badly—but Joanne's father owned the big five-and-dime on Nassau Road and *could* afford three-hundred-dollar bikes for his children at the drop of a birthday. Nita's father's business was a lot smaller and was prone to what he called (in front of most people) "cash-flow problems" or (in front of his family) "being broke most of the time."

But what does Joanne care about cash flow, or any of the rest of it? I wanted that bike!

"Here, dreamer," her mother said, tapping her on the shoulder and breaking her thought. She handed Nita an icepack and turned back toward the stove. "Go lie down or you'll swell worse. I'll bring you something in a while."

"Shouldn't she stay sitting up?" Nita's father said. "Seems as if the fluid would drain better or something."

"You didn't get beat up enough when you were younger, Harry," her mother said. "If she doesn't lie down, she'll blow up like a basketball. Scoot, Nita."

She scooted, around the corner into the dining room, around the second corner into the living room, and straight into her little sister, bumping loose one of the textbooks she was carrying and scattering half her armload of pink plastic curlers. Nita's father raised his eyebrows and turned his attention back to his paper as Nita bent to help pick things up again. Her sister, bent down beside her, didn't take long to figure out what had happened.

"Virella again, huh?" she said. Dairine was eleven years old, redheaded as her mother, gray-eyed as Nita, and precocious; she was taking tenth-grade English courses and breezing through them, and Nita was teaching her some algebra on the side. Dairine had her father's square-boned build and her mother's grace, and a perpetual, cocky grin. She was a great sister, as far as Nita was concerned, even if she was a little too smart for her own good.

"Yeah," Nita said. "Look out, kid, I've gotta go lie down."

"Don't call me kid. You want me to beat up Virella for you?"

"Be my guest," Nita said. She went on through the house, back to her room. Bumping the door open, she fumbled for the light switch and flipped it on. The familiar maps and pictures looked down at her—the National Geographic map of the Moon and some enlarged *Voyager* photos of Jupiter and Saturn and their moons.

Nita eased herself down onto the bottom bunk bed, groaning softly—the deep bruises were beginning to bother her now. Lord, she thought, what did I say? If Dari *does* beat Joanne up, I'll never hear the end of it. Dairine had once been small and fragile and subject to being beaten up—mostly because she had never learned to curb her mouth either—and Nita's parents had sent her to jujitsu lessons at the same time they sent Nita. On Dari, though, the lessons took. One or two overconfident kids had gone after her, about a month and a half into her lessons, and had been thoroughly and painfully surprised. She was protective enough to take Joanne on and, horrors, throw her clear over the horizon. It would be all over school; Nita Callahan's little sister beat up the girl who beat *Nita* up.

Oh, no! Nita thought.

Her door opened slightly, and Dari stuck her head in. "Of course," she said, "if you'd rather do it yourself, I'll let her off this time."

"Yeah," Nita said, "thanks."

Dairine made a face. "Here," she said, and pitched Nita's jacket in at her, and then right after it the book. Nita managed to field it while holding the icepack in place with her left hand. "You left it in the kitchen," Dairine said. "Gonna be a magician, huh? Make yourself vanish when they chase you?"

"Sure. Go curl your hair, runt."

Nita sat back against the headboard of the bed, staring at the book. Why not? Who knows what kinds of spells you could do? Maybe I could turn Joanne into a turkey. As if she isn't one already. Or maybe there's a spell for getting lost pens back.

Though the book made it sound awfully serious, as if the wizardry were for big things. Maybe it's not right to do spells for little stuff like this—and anyway, you can't do the spells until you've taken the Oath, and once you've taken it, that's supposed to be forever.

Oh, come on, it's a *joke!* What harm can there be in saying the words if it's a joke? And if it's not, then . . .

Then I'll be a wizard.

Her father knocked on her door, then walked in with a plate loaded with dinner and a glass of cola. Nita grinned up at him, not too widely, for it hurt. "Thanks, Dad."

"Here," he said after Nita took the plate and the glass, and handed her a couple of aspirin. "Your mother says to take these."

"Thanks." Nita took them with the Coke, while her father sat down on the edge of the bed.

"Nita," he said, "is there something going on that I should know about?"

"Huh?"

"It's been once a week now, sometimes twice, for quite a while. Do you want me to speak to Joe Virella and ask him to have a word with Joanne?"

"Uh, no, sir."

Nita's father stared at his hands for a moment. "What should we do, then? I really can't afford to start you in karate lessons again—"

"Jujitsu."

"Whatever. Nita, what *is* it? Why does this keep happening? *Why don't you hit them back?*"

"I *used* to! Do you think it made a difference? Joanne would just get more kids to help." Her father stared at her, and Nita flushed hot at the stern look on his face. "I'm sorry, Daddy, I didn't mean to yell at you. But fighting back just gets them madder, it doesn't help."

"It might help keep you from getting mangled every week, if you'd just keep trying!" her father said angrily. "I hate to admit it, but I'd love to see you wipe the ground up with that loudmouth rich kid."

So would I, Nita thought. That's the problem. She swallowed, feeling guilty over how much she wanted to get back at Joanne somehow. "Dad, Joanne and her bunch just don't like me. I don't do the things they do, or play the games they play, or like the things they like—and I don't *want* to. So they don't like me. That's all."

Her father looked at her and shook his head sadly. "I just don't want to see you hurt. Kidling, I don't know . . . if you could just be a little more like them, if you could try to. . . ." He trailed off, running one hand through his silver hair. "What am I saying?" he muttered. "Look. If there's anything I can do to help, will you tell me?"

"Yessir."

"Okay. If you feel better tomorrow, would you rake up the backyard a little? I want to go over the lawn around the rowan tree with the aerator, maybe put down some seed."

"Sure. I'll be okay, Dad. They didn't break anything."

"My girl." He got up. "Don't read so much it hurts your eyes, now."

"I won't," Nita said. Her father strode out the door, forgetting to close it behind himself as usual.

She ate her supper slowly, for it hurt to chew, and she tried to think about something besides Joanne or that book.

The Moon was at first quarter tonight; it would be a good night to take the telescope out and have a look at the shadows in the craters. Or there was that fuzzy little comet, maybe it had more tail than it did last week.

It was completely useless. The book lay there on her bed and stared at her, daring her to do something childlike, something silly, something absolutely ridiculous.

Nita put aside her empty plate, picked up the book, and stared back at it.

"All right," she said under her breath. "All right."

She opened the book at random. And on the page to which she opened, there was the Oath.

It was not decorated in any way. It stood there, a plain block of type all by itself in the middle of the page, looking serious and important. Nita read the Oath to herself first, to make sure of the words. Then, quickly, before she could start to feel silly, she read it out loud.

" 'In Life's name, and for Life's sake,' " she read, " 'I say that I will use the Art for nothing but the service of that Life. I will guard growth and ease pain. I will fight to preserve what grows and lives well in its own way; and I will change no object or creature unless its growth and life, or that of the system of which it is part, are threatened. To these ends, in the practice of my Art, I will put aside fear for courage, and death for life, when it is right to do so—till Universe's end.' "

The words seemed to echo slightly, as if the room were larger than it really was. Nita sat very still, wondering what the ordeal would be like, wondering what would happen now. Only the wind spoke softly in the leaves of the trees outside the bedroom window; nothing else seemed to stir anywhere. Nita sat there, and slowly the tension began to drain out of her as she realized that she hadn't been hit by lightning, nor had anything strange at all happened to her. *Now* she felt silly—and tired too, she discovered. The effects of her beating were catching up with her. Wearily Nita shoved the book under her pillow, then lay back against the headboard and closed her hurting eyes. So much for the joke. She would have a nap, and then later she'd get up and take the telescope out back. But right now . . . right now. . . .

After a while, night was not night any more; that was what brought Nita to the window, much later. She leaned on the sill and gazed out in calm wonder at her backyard, which didn't look quite the same as usual. A blaze of undying morning lay over everything, bushes and trees cast light instead of shadow, and she could see the wind. Standing in the ivy under her window, she turned her eyes up to the silver-glowing sky to get used to the brilliance. *How about that,* she said. *The backyard's here too.* Next to her, the lesser brilliance that gazed up at that same sky shrugged slightly. *Of course,* it said. *This is Timeheart, after all. Yes,* Nita said anxiously as they passed across the yard and out into the bright shadow of the steel and crystal towers, *but did I do right?* Her companion shrugged again. *Go find out,* it said, and glanced up again. Nita wasn't sure she wanted to follow the glance. Once she had looked up and seen—*I dreamed you were gone,* she said suddenly. *The magic stayed, but you went away.* She hurt inside, enough to cry, but her companion flickered with laughter. *No one ever goes away forever,* it said. *Especially not here.* Nita looked up, then, into the bright morning and the brighter shadows. The day went on and on and would not end, the sky blazed now like molten silver. . . .

The Sun on her face woke Nita up as usual. Someone, her mother probably, had come in late last night to cover her up and take the dishes away. She turned over slowly, stiff but not in too much pain, and felt the hardness under her pillow. Nita sat up and pulled the book out, felt around for her glasses. The book fell open in her hand at the listing for the wizards in the New York metropolitan area, which Nita had glanced at the afternoon before. Now she looked down the first column of names, and her breath caught.

CALLAHAN, Juanita L., 243 E. Clinton Ave., Hempstead NY 11575 (516)555-6786. (novice, pre-rating)

Her mouth fell open. She shut it.
I'm going to be a wizard! she thought.
Nita got up and got dressed in a hurry.

Preliminary Exercises

She did her chores that morning and got out of the house with the book as fast as she could, heading for one of her secret places in the woods. *If weird things start happening,* she thought, *no one will see them there. Oh, I'm going to get that pen back! And then . . .*

Behind the high school around the corner from Nita's house was a large tract of undeveloped woodland, the usual Long Island combination of scrub oak, white pine, and sassafras. Nita detoured around the school, pausing to scramble over a couple of chain-link fences. There was a path on the other side; after a few minutes she turned off it to pick her way carefully through low underbrush and among fallen logs and tree stumps. Then there was a solid wall of clumped sassafras and twining wild blackberry bushes. It looked totally impassable, and the blackberries threatened Nita with their thorns, but she turned sideways and pushed through the wall of greenery undaunted.

She emerged into a glade walled all around with blackberry and gooseberry and pine, sheltered by the overhanging branches of several trees. One, a large crabapple, stood near the edge of the glade, and there was a flattish half-buried boulder at the base of its trunk. Here she could be sure no one was watching.

Nita sat down on the rock with a sigh, put her back up against the tree, and spent a few moments getting comfortable—then opened the book and started to read.

She found herself not just reading, after a while, but studying—cramming the facts into her head with that particular mental *stomp* she used when she knew she was going to have to know something by heart. The things the book was telling her now were not vague and abstract, as the initial discussion of theory had been, but straightforward as the repair manual for a new car, and nearly as complex. There were tables and lists of needed resources for working spells. There were formulas and equations and rules. There was a syllabary and pronunciation guide for the 418 symbols used in the wizardly Speech to describe relationships and effects that other human languages had no specific words for.

The information went on and on—the book was printed small, and there seemed no end to the things Nita was going to have to know about. She read about the hierarchy of practicing wizards—her book listed only those practicing in the U.S. and Canada, though wizards were working everywhere in the world—and she scanned down the listing for the New York area, noticing the presence of Advisory wizards, Area Supervisors, Senior wizards. She read through a list of the "otherworlds" closest to her own, alternate earths where the capital of the United States was named Huictilopochtli or Lafayette City or Hrafnkell or New Washington, and where the people still called themselves Americans, though they didn't match Nita's ideas about the term.

She learned the Horseman's Word, which gets the attention of any member of the genus *Equus*, even the zebras; and the two forms of the Mason's Word, which give stone the appearance of life for short periods. One chapter told her about the magical creatures living in cities, whose presence even the nonwizardly people suspect sometimes—creatures like the steambreathing fireworms, packratty little lizards that creep through cracks in building walls to steal treasures and trash for their lair-hoards under the streets. Nita thought about all the steam she had seen coming up from manhole covers in Manhattan and smiled, for now she knew what was causing it.

She read on, finding out how to bridle the Nightmare and learning what questions to ask the Transcendent Pig, should she meet him. She read about the Trees' Battle—who fought in it, and who won it, and why. She read about the forty basic classes of spells and their subclasses. She read about Timeheart, the unreal and eternal realm where the places and things people remember affectionately are preserved as they remember them, forever.

In the middle of the description of things preserved in their fullest beauty forever, and still growing, Nita found herself feeling a faint tingle of unease. She was also getting tired. She dropped the book in her lap with an annoyed sigh, for there was just too much to absorb at one sitting, and she had no clear idea of where to begin. "Crud," she said under her breath. "I thought I'd be able to make Joanne vanish by tomorrow morning. . . ."

Nita picked the manual up again and leafed through it to the section labeled "Preliminary Exercises."

The first one was set in a small block of type in the middle of an otherwise empty page.

To change something, you must first describe it. To describe something, you must first see it. Hold still in one place for as long as it takes to see something.

Nita felt puzzled and slightly annoyed. This didn't sound much like magic. But obediently she put the book down, settled herself more comfortably against the tree, folded her arms, and sighed. It's almost too warm to think about anything serious. . . . What should I look at? That rock over there? Naah, it's kind of a dull-looking rock. That weed . . . look how its leaves go up around the stem in a spiral. . . . Nita leaned her head back, stared up through the crabtree's branches. That rotten Joanne. Where would she have hidden that pen? I wonder. Maybe if I could sneak into her house somehow, maybe there's a spell for that. . . . Have to do it after dark, I guess. Maybe I could do it tonight . . . wish it didn't take so long to get dark this time of year. Nita looked at the sky where it showed between the leaves, a hot blue mosaic of light with here and there the fireflicker of sun showing through, shifting with the shift of leaves in the wind. There are kinds of patterns—the wind never goes through the same way twice, and there are patterns in the branches but they're never quite the same either. And look at the changes in the brightness. The sky is the same but the leaves cover sometimes more and sometimes less . . . the patterns . . . the patterns, they . . . they. . . .

(They won't let you have a moment's rest,) the crabapple tree said irritably. Nita jumped, scraping her back against the trunk as she sat up straight. She had heard the tree quite plainly in some way that had nothing to do with spoken words. It was light patterns she had heard, and wind movements, leafrustle, fireflicker.

(Finally paid attention, did you?) said the tree. (As if one of them isn't enough, messing up someone's fallen-leaf pattern that's been in progress for fifteen years, drawing circles all over the ground and messing up the matrices. Well? What's *your* excuse?)

Nita sat there with her mouth open, looking up at the words the tree was making with cranky light and shadow. It works. It *works!* "Uh," she said, not knowing whether the tree could understand her, "I didn't draw any circles on your leaves—"

(No, but that other one did,) the tree said. (Made circles and stars and diagrams all over Telerilarch's collage, doing some kind of power spell. You people don't have the proper respect for artwork. Okay, so we're amateurs,) it added, a touch of belligerence creeping into its voice. (So none of us have been here more than thirty years. Well, our work is still valid, and—)

"Uh, listen, do you mean that there's a, uh, a wizard out here somewhere doing magic?"

(What else?) the tree snapped. (And let me tell you, if you people don't—)

"Where? Where is she?"

(He,) the tree said. (In the middle of all those made-stone roads. I remember when those roads went in, and they took a pattern Kimber had been working on for eighty years and scraped it bare and poured that black rock over it. One of the most complex, most—)

He? Nita thought, and her heart sank slightly. She had trouble talking to boys. "You mean across the freeway, in the middle of the interchange? That green place?"

(Didn't you hear me? Are you deaf? Silly question. That other one *must* be not to have heard Teleri yelling at him. And now I suppose *you'll* start scratching up the ground and invoking powers and ruining *my* collage. Well, let me tell you—)

"I, uh—listen, I'll talk to you later," Nita said hurriedly. She got to her feet, brushed herself off, and started away through the woods at a trot. Another wizard? And my God, the trees— Their laughter at her amazement was all around her as she ran, the merriment of everything from foot-high weeds to hundred-foot oaks, rustling in the wind—grave chuckling of maples and alders, titters from groves of sapling sassafras, silly giggling in the raspberry bushes, a huge belly-laugh from the oldest hollow ash tree before the freeway interchange. How could I never have heard them before!

Nita stopped at the freeway's edge and made sure that there were no cars coming before she tried to cross. The interchange was one of those cloverleaf affairs, and the circle formed by one of the offramps held a stand of the original pre-freeway trees within it, in a kind of sunken bowl. Nita dashed across the concrete and stood a moment, breathless, at the edge of the downslope, before starting down it slantwise.

This was another of her secret places, a spot shaded and peaceful in summer and winter both because of the pine trees that roofed the hollow in. But there was nothing peaceful about it today. Something was in the air, and the trees, irritated, were muttering among themselves. Even on a foot-thick cushion of pine needles, Nita's feet seemed to be making too much noise. She tried to walk softly and wished the trees wouldn't stare at her so.

Where the slope bottomed out she stopped, looking around her nervously, and that was when she saw him. The boy was holding a stick in one hand and staring intently at the ground underneath a huge shag-larch on one side of the grove. He was shorter than she was, and looked younger, and he also looked familiar somehow. Now who *is* that? she thought, feeling more nervous still. No one had ever been in one of her secret places when *she* came there.

But the boy just kept frowning at the ground, as if it were a test paper and he was trying to scowl the right answer out of it. A very ordinary-looking kid, with straight black hair and a Hispanic look to his face, wearing a beat-up green windbreaker and jeans and sneakers, holding a willow wand of a type that Nita's book recommended for certain types of spelling.

He let out what looked like a breath of irritation and put his hands on his hips. *"Cojones,"* he muttered, shaking his head—and halfway through the shake, he caught sight of Nita.

He looked surprised and embarrassed for a moment, then his face steadied down to a simple worried look. There he stood regarding Nita, and she realized with a shock that he wasn't going to yell at her, or chase her, or call her names, or run away himself. He was going to let her explain herself. Nita was amazed. It didn't seem quite normal.

"Hi," she said.

The boy looked at her uncertainly, as if trying to place her. "Hi."

Nita wasn't sure quite where to begin. But the marks on the ground, and the willow wand, seemed to confirm that a power spell was in progress. "Uh," she said, "I, uh, I don't see the oak leaves. Or the string."

The boy's dark eyes widened. "So *that's* how you got through!"

"Through what?"

"I put a binding spell around the edges of this place," he said. "I've tried this spell once or twice before, but people kept showing up just as I was getting busy, and I couldn't finish."

Nita suddenly recognized him. "You're the one they were calling crazy last week."

The boy's eyes narrowed again. He looked annoyed. "Uh, yeah. A couple of the eighth graders found me last Monday. They were shooting up the woods with BB guns, and there I was working. And they couldn't figure out what I was doing, so at lunch the next day they said—"

"I know what they said." It had been a badly rhymed song about the kid who played with himself in the woods, because no one else would play with him. She remembered feeling vaguely sorry for the kid, whoever he was; boys could be as bad as girls sometimes.

"I thought I blew the binding too," he said. "You surprised me."

"Maybe you can't bind another wizard out," Nita said. That was it, she thought. If he's not one—

"Uhh . . . I guess not." He paused. "I'm Kit," he said then. "Christopher, really, but I hate Christopher."

"Nita," she said. "It's short for Juanita. I hate that too. Listen—the trees are mad at you."

Kit stared at her. "The *trees?*"

"Uh, mostly this one." She looked up into the branches of the shag-larch, which were trembling with more force than the wind could lend them. "See, the trees do—I don't know, it's artwork, sort of, with their fallen leaves—and you started doing your power schematic all over their work, and, uh—"

"Trees?" Kit said. "Rocks I knew about, I talked to a rock last week—or it talked to me, actually—though it wasn't talking, really. . . ." He looked up at the tree. "Well, hey, I'm sorry," he said. "I didn't know. I'll try to put things back the way I found them. But I might as well not have bothered with the spell," he said, looking again at Nita. "It got caught, it's not working. You know anything about this?"

He gestured at the diagram he had drawn on the cleared ground, and Nita went to crouch down by it. The pattern was one she had seen in her book, a basic design of interlocking circles and woven parallelograms. There were symbols drawn inside the angles and outside the curves, some of them letters or words in the Roman alphabet, some of them the graceful characters of the wizardly Speech. "I just got my book yesterday," she said. "I doubt I'll be much help. What were you trying to get? The power part of it I can see."

She glanced up and found Kit looking with somber interest at her black eye. "I'm getting tired of being beat up just because I have a Spanish accent," he said. "I was going to attract enough power to me so that the big kids would just leave me alone and not start anything. An 'aura,' the book called it. But the spell got stuck a couple of steps in, and when I checked the book it said that I was missing an element." He looked questioningly at Nita. "Maybe you're it?"

"Uhh—" She shook her head. "I don't know. I was looking for a spell for something different. Someone beat me up and stole my best pen. It was a space pen, the kind the astronauts have, and it writes on anything, and I always took all my tests with it and I always pass when I use it, and I want it *back.*" She stopped, then added, "And I guess I wouldn't mind if they didn't beat me up any more either."

"We could make a finding spell and tie it into this one," Kit said.

"Yeah? Well, we better put these needles back first."

"Yeah."

Kit stuck the willow wand in his back pocket as he and Nita worked to push the larch's needles back over the cleared ground. "Where'd you get your book?" Nita said.

"In the city, about a month ago. My mother and father went out antique hunting, there's this one part of Second Avenue where all the little shops are —and one place had this box of secondhand books, and I stopped to look at them because I always look at old books—and this one caught my eye. My hand, actually. I was going after a Tom Swift book underneath it and it pinched me. . . ."

Nita chuckled. "Mine snagged me in the library," she said. "I don't know . . . I didn't want Joanne—she's the one who beat me up—I didn't want her to get my pen, but I'm glad she didn't get *this.*" She pulled her copy of the book out of her jacket as Kit straightened up beside her. She looked over at him. "Does it work?" she demanded. "Does it really *work?*"

Kit stood there for a moment, looking at the replaced needles. "I fixed my dog's nose," he said. "A wasp stung him and I made it go down right away. And I talked to the rock." He looked up at Nita again. "C'mon," he said. "There's a place in the middle where the ground is bare. Let's see what happens."

Together they walked to the center of the hollow, where the pine trees made a circle open to the sky and the ground was bare dirt. Kit pulled out his willow wand and began drawing the diagram again. "This one I know by heart," he said. "I've started it so many times. Well, this time for sure." He got his book out of his back pocket and consulted it, beginning to write symbols into the diagram. "Would you look and see if there's anything else we need for a finding spell?"

"Sure." Nita found the necessary section in the index of her book and checked it. "Just an image of the thing to be found," she said. "I have to make it while you're spelling. Kit, do you know *why* this works? Leaves, pieces of string, designs on the ground. It doesn't make sense."

Kit kept drawing. "There's a chapter on advanced theory in there, but I couldn't get through it all the way. The magic is supposed to have something to do with interrupting space—"

"Huh?"

"Listen, that's all I could get out of it. There was this one phrase that kept turning up, 'temporospatial claudication.' I think that's how you say it. It's something like, space isn't really empty, it folds around things—or words—and if you put the right things in the right place and do the right things with them, and say the right things in the Speech, magic happens. Where's the string?"

"This one with all the knots in it?" Nita reached down and picked it up.

"Must have fallen out of my pocket. Stand on this end, okay?" He dropped one end of the string into the middle of the diagram, and Nita stepped onto it. Kit walked around her and the diagram with it, using the end of the string to trace a circle. Just before he came to the place where he had started, he used the willow wand to make a sort of figure-eight mark—a "wizards' knot," the book had called it—and closed the circle with it. Kit tugged at the string as he stood up. Nita let it go, and Kit coiled it and put it away.

"You've got to do this part yourself," Kit said. "I can't write your name for you—each person in a spelling does their own. There's a table in there with all the symbols in it—"

Nita scuffed some pages aside and found it, a long list of English letters and numbers, and symbols in the Speech. She got down to look at Kit's name, so that she could see how to write hers, and group by group began to puzzle the symbols out. "Your birthday's August twenty-fifth?"

"Uh huh."

Nita looked at the symbol for the year. "They skipped you a couple grades, huh?"

"Yeah. It's rotten," Kit said, sounding entirely too cheerful as he said it. Nita knew that tone of voice—it was the one in which she usually answered Joanne back, while trying to hide her own fear of what was sure to happen next. "It wouldn't be so bad if they were my age," Kit went on, looking over Nita's shoulder and speaking absently. "But they keep saying things like 'If you're so smart, 'ow come you talk so funny?' " His imitation of their imitation of his accent was precise and bitter. "They make me sick. Trouble is, they outweigh me."

Nita nodded and started to draw her name on the ground, using the substitutions and symbols that appeared in her manual. Some of them were simple and brief; some of them were almost more complex than she believed possible, crazy amalgams of curls and twists and angles like those an insane stenographer might produce. She did her best to reproduce them, and tied all the symbols together, fastening them into a circle with the same wizards' knot that Kit had used on the outer circle and on his own name.

"Done?" Kit said. He was standing up again, tracing the outer circle around one more time.

"Yup."

"Okay." He finished the tracing with another repetition of the wizards' knot and straightened up; then he put his hand out as if to feel something in the air. "Good," he said. "Here, come check this."

"Check what?" Nita said; but she got up and went over to Kit. She put out her hand as he had, and found that something was resisting the movement of her hand through the air—something that gave slightly under increased pressure, like a mattress being pushed down and then springing back again. Nita felt momentarily nervous. "Can air get through this?"

"I think so. I didn't have any trouble the last couple of times I did it. It's only supposed to seal out unfriendly influences."

Nita stood there with her hand resting against nothing, and the nothing supported her weight. The last of her doubts about the existence of magic went away. She might have imagined the contents of the book, or been purposely misreading. She might have dozed off and dreamed the talking tree. But *this* was daylight, the waking world, and she was leaning one-handed on empty air!

"Those guys who came across you when you had this up," she said, "what did they think?"

"Oh, it worked on them too. They didn't even understand why they couldn't get at me—they thought it was their idea to yell at me from a distance. They thought they were missing me with the BB guns on purpose too, to scare me. It's true, what the book said. There are people who couldn't see a magic if it bit them." He glanced around the finished circle. "There are other spells like this that don't need drawings after you do them the first time, and when you need them, they're there really fast—like if someone's about to try beating you up. People just kind of skid away from you. . . ."

"I bet," Nita said, with relish. Thoughts of what else she might be able to do to Joanne flickered through her head, but she pushed them aside for the moment. "What next?"

"Next," Kit said, going to the middle of the circle and sitting down carefully so as not to smudge any of the marks he'd made, "we read it. Or I read most of it, and you read your name. Though first you have to check my figuring."

"How come?" Nita joined him, avoiding the lines and angles.

"Two person spell—both people always check each other's work. But your name, you check again after I do."

Kit was already squinting at her squiggles, so Nita pulled out her book again and began looking at the symbols Kit had drawn in the dirt. There were clearly two sides to the diagram, and the book said they both had to balance like a chemical equation. Most of the symbols had numerical values attached, for ease in balancing, and Nita started doing addition in her head, making sure both sides matched. Eventually she was satisfied. She looked again at her name, seeing nothing wrong. "Is it okay?"

"Yeah." Kit leaned back a little. "You have to be careful with names, it says. They're a way of saying what you *are*—and if you write something in a spell that's *not* what you are, well. . . ."

"You mean . . . *you* change . . . because the spell says you're something else than what you are? You *become* that?"

Kit shrugged, but he looked uneasy. "A spell is saying that you want something to happen," he said. "If you say your name wrong—"

Nita shuddered. "And now?"

"Now we start. You do your name when I come to it. Then, the goal part down there—since it's a joint goal, we say it together. Think you can do it okay if I go slow?"

"Yeah."

Kit took a deep breath with his eyes closed, then opened his eyes and began to read.

Nita had never heard a voice speaking a spell aloud before, and the effect was strange. Ever so slightly, ever so slowly, things began to change around her. The tree-sheltered quiet grew quieter. The cool light that filtered through the canopy of branches grew expectant, fringed with secrecy the way things seen through the edge of a lens are fringed with rainbows. Nita began to feel as if she was caught in the moment between a very vivid dream and the awakening from it. There was that feeling of living in a body—of being aware of familiar surroundings and the realities of the daylight world waiting to be resumed—yet at the same time seeing those surroundings differently, colored with another sort of light, another kind of time. On one level Nita heard Kit reciting a string of polysyllables that should have been meaningless to her—words for symbols, pieces of words, babble. Yet she could also hear Kit talking, saying casually, and, it seemed, in English, "We need to know something, and we suggest this particular method of finding the information. . . ." And the words didn't break the expectancy, the listening silence. For once, for the first time, the dream was *real* while Nita was awake. Power stirred in the air around her and waited for her to shape it.

Magic.

She sat and listened to Kit. With each passing second she could catch more clearly the clean metallic taste of the equation as it began to form itself, flickering chill and bright in her mind. Kit's speech was giving it life, and with quiet, flowing efficiency it was going about its purpose. It was invoking the attention of what Nita might have called physical laws, except that there was nothing physical about them—they had to do with flows of a kind of power as different from ordinary energy as energy was from matter. The equation stretched and coiled and caught those powers within itself as the words wove it. Nita and Kit were caught in it too. To Nita it seemed as if, without moving, she held out her hands, and they were taken—by Kit, and by the spell itself, and by the ponderous powers caught across from her in the dance. There was a pause: Kit looked across the diagrams at her.

Nita scowled at the symbols beside her and began to read them, slowly and with some hesitation—naming herself one concept or one symbol at a time, binding herself into the spell. At first she was scared, for she could feel the strangeness folding in close around her. But then she realized that nothing awful was happening, and as her name became part of the spell, *that* was what was sliding down around her, protecting her. She finished, and she was out of breath, and excited, and she had never been happier in her life.

Kit's voice came in again then, picking up the weave, rejoining the dance. So it went for a while, the strange words and the half-seen, half-felt movements and images falling into a rhythm of light and sound and texture, a song, a poem, a spell. It began to come whole all around them, and all around the tingling air stayed still to better hold the words, and the trees bent close to listen.

Kit came to the set of symbols that stood for his name and who he was, and read them slowly and carefully. Nita felt the spell settle down around him too. He finished it and glanced up at Nita, and together they began the goal section of the spell. Nita did her best to make a clear image of the pen as she spoke—the silver case, gone a little scratched and grubby now, her initials incised up on the top. She hardly had time to wonder at the harmony their paired voices made before things began to change again. The shadows of the trees around them seemed to grow darker; the aura of expectancy grew sharp enough to taste. The silence became total, and their voices fell into it as into a great depth.

The formula for their goal, though longer than either of their names had been, seemed to take less time to say—and even stranger, it began to sound like much more than just finding a pen and being left alone. It began to taste of starfire and night and motion, huge and controlled, utterly strange. Saying the formula left Kit and Nita breathless and drained, as if something powerful had briefly been living and speaking through them and had worn them down. They finished the formula together, and gulped for air, and looked at each other in half-frightened expectation, wondering what would happen next.

The completed spell took effect. Nita had thought that she would gradually begin to see something, the way things had changed gradually in the grove. The spell, though, had its own ideas. Quick as a gasp it slammed them both out of one moment and into another, a shocking, wrenching transition like dreaming that you've fallen out of bed, *wham!* Instinctively they both hung on to the spell as if onto a railing, clutching it until their surroundings steadied down. The darkness had been replaced by a lowering, sullen-feeling gloom. They looked down as if from a high balcony onto a shadowed island prisoned between chill rivers and studded with sharp spikes of iron and cold stone.

(Manhattan?) Kit asked anxiously, without words. Nita felt frozen in place like a statue and couldn't turn to answer him—the spell was holding her immobile.

(It looks like Manhattan,) she said, feeling just as uneasy. (But what's my pen doing *there?*)

Kit would have shaken his head if he could have. (I don't get it. What's wrong here? This *is* New York City—but it never looked this awful, this dirty and nasty and . . .) He trailed off in confusion and dismay.

Nita looked around her. It was hard to make out anything on the island—there was a murky pall over the city that seemed more than just fog. There was hardly any traffic that she could see, and almost no light—in fact, in all of Manhattan there were only two light sources. In one place on the island—the east Fifties, it looked like—a small point of brittle light seemed to pulse right through steel and stone, throbbing dully like a sown seed of wildfire waiting to explode. The pulses were irregular and distressing, and the light was painful to look at. Some blocks to the south, well into the financial district near the south end of the island, another fire burned, a clear white spark like a sunseed, beating regularly as a heart. It was consoling, but it was very small.

(Now what?) Nita said. (Why would my pen be in this place?) She looked down at the dark grainy air below them, listened to the brooding silence like that of a beast of prey ready to spring, felt the sullen buildings hunching themselves against the oppressive sky—and then felt the *something* malevolent and alive that lay in wait below—a something that *saw* them, was conscious of them, and was darkly pleased.

(Kit, what's *that?*)

(It *knows!*) Kit's thought sang with alarm like a plucked string. (It knows we're here! It shouldn't be able to, but—Nita, the spell's not balanced for this. If that thing grabs us or holds us somehow, we won't be able to get back!)

Nita felt Kit's mind start to flick frantically through the memories of what he had read in his wizards' manual, looking for an idea, for something they could do to protect themselves.

She held very still and looked over his shoulder at his thoughts, even though part of her trembled at the thought of that dark presence which was even now reaching out toward them, lazy, curious, deadly. Abruptly she saw something that looked useful.

(Kit, stop! No, go back one. That's it. Look, it says if you've got an imbalance, you can open out your side of the spell to attract some more power.)

(Yeah, but if the wrong kind of power answers, we're in for it!)

(We're in for it for *sure* if that gets us,) Nita said, indicating the huge, hungry darkness billowing upward toward them like a cloud. (Look, we'll make a hole through the spell big enough for something friendly to fall into, and we'll take pot luck.)

Nita could feel Kit's uncertainty as he started choosing from memory the words and symbols he would need. (All right, but I dunno. If something worse happens . . .)

(What could be worse?) Nita hollered at Kit, half in amusement, half in fear. The hungry something drew closer.

Kit started to answer, then forgot about it. (There,) he said, laying the equation out in his mind, (I think that's all we need.)

(Go ahead,) Nita said, watching anxiously as their pursuer got closer and the air around them seemed to grow thicker and darker yet. (You say it. Just tell me what to do and when.)

(Right,) Kit said, and began speaking in his mind, much faster than he had during the initial spelling. If that first magic had felt like the weaving of a whole, this one felt like ripping something apart. Their surroundings seemed to shimmer uncertainly, the dark skyline and lead-gray sky rippled like a wind-stirred curtain; even that stalking presence seemed to hesitate in momentary confusion. (Push,) Kit said suddenly, (push right there.) Nita felt the torn place that Kit had made in the spell, and she shoved clumsily at it with her mind, trying to make the hole larger.

(It's . . . giving . . .)

(Now, *hard!)* Kit said, and Nita pushed until pain stabbed and stabbed again behind where her eyes should have been, and at the moment she thought she couldn't possibly push any more, Kit said one short sharp syllable and threw the spell wide open like a door.

It was like standing at the core of a tornado which, rather than spinning you away to Oz, strips the roof off your home, opens the house walls out flat as the petals of a plaster flower, and leaves you standing confused and disbelieving in the heart of a howling of smoke and damned voices; or like moving through a roomful of people, every one of whom tries to catch your eye and tell you the most important thing that ever happened to him. Nita found herself deluged in fragments of sights and sounds and tastes and feelings and thoughts not her own, a madly coexisting maelstrom of imageries from other universes, other earths, other times. Most of them she managed to shut out by squeezing her mind shut like eyes and hanging on to the spell. She sensed that Kit was doing the same and that their stalker was momentarily as bewildered as they were by what was happening. The whirling confusion seemed to be funneling through the hole in the spell like water going down a drain—things, concepts, creatures too large or too small for the hole fell through it, or past it, or around it. But sooner or later something just the right size would catch. (Hope we get something useful,) Nita thought desperately. (Something bigger than that *thing,* anyway.)

And *thump,* something fitted into the hole with snug precision, and the crazy whirling died away, and the two of them had company in the spellweb. Something small, Nita felt; very small, *too* small—but no, it was big, too . . . Confused, she reached out to Kit.

(Is that it? Can we get out now? Before that what's-its-name—)

The what's-its-name shook itself with a ripple of rage and hunger that Kit and Nita could feel even at a distance. It headed toward them again, quickly, done with playing with them.

(Uh oh!) Kit said. (Let's get outa here!)

(What do we—)

(What in the—) said a voice that neither of them recognized.

(Out!) Kit said, and hooked the spell into the added power that the newcomer provided, and *pulled*—

—and plain pale daylight came down around them, heavy as a collapsed tent. Gravity yanked at them. Kit fell over sideways and lay there panting on the ground like someone who's run a race. Nita sagged, covered her face, bent over double right down to the ground, struggling for breath.

Eventually she began to recover, but she put off moving or opening her eyes. The book had warned that spelling had its prices, and one of them was the physical exhaustion that goes along with any large, mostly mental work of creation. Nita felt as if she had just been through about a hundred English tests with essay questions, one after another. "Kit?" she said, worried by his silence.

"Nnngggg," Kit said, and rolled over into a sort of crouch, holding his head in his hands. "Ooooh. Turn off the *Sun.*"

"It's not that bad," Nita said, opening her eyes. Then she winced and shut them in a hurry. It was.

"How long've we been here?" Kit muttered. "The Sun shouldn't be showing here yet."

"It's—" Nita said, opening her eyes again to check her watch and being distracted by a bright light to her right that was entirely too low to be the Sun, and squinting at it—and then forgetting what she had started to say.

Hanging in midair about three feet away from her, inside the circle, was a spark of eye-searing white fire. It looked no bigger than a pinhead, but it was brilliant all out of proportion to its size, and was giving off light about as bright as that of a two-hundred-watt bulb without a shade. The light bobbed gently in midair, up and down, looking like a will-o'-the-wisp plugged into too powerful a current and about to blow out. Nita sat there with her mouth open and *stared.*

The bright point dimmed slightly, appeared to describe a small tight circle so that it could take in Kit, the drawn circle, trees and leaves and sky; then it came to rest again, staring back at Nita. Though she couldn't catch what Kit was feeling, now that the spell was over, she could feel the light's emotions quite clearly—amazement, growing swiftly into unbelieving pleasure. Suddenly it blazed up white-hot again.

(Dear Artificer,) it said in bemused delight, (I've blown my quanta and gone to the Good Place!)

Nita sat there in silence for a moment, thinking a great many things at once. Uhh. . . . she thought. And, So I wanted to be a wizard, huh? Serves me right. Something falls into my world and thinks it's gone to Heaven. Boy, is it gonna get a shock. And, What in the world *is* it, anyway?

"Kit," Nita said. "Excuse me a moment," she added, nodding with abrupt courtesy at the light source. "Kit." She turned slightly and reached down to shake him by the shoulder. "Kit. C'mon, get up. We have company."

"Mmmp?" Kit said, scrubbing at his eyes and starting to straighten up. "Oh, no, the binding didn't blow, did it?"

"Nope. It's the extra power you called in. I think it came back with us."

"Well, it—oh," Kit said, as he finally managed to focus on the sedately hovering brightness. *"Oh.* It's—uh. . . ."

"Right," Nita said. "It says," she added, "that it's blown its quanta. Is that dangerous?" she asked the light.

(Dangerous?) It laughed inside, a crackling sound like an overstimulated Geiger counter. (Artificer, child, it means I'm *dead.)* "Child" wasn't precisely the concept it used; Nita got a fleeting impression of a huge volume of dust and gas contracting gradually toward a common center, slow, confused, and nebulous. She wasn't flattered.

"Maybe you won't like hearing this," Nita said, "but I'm not sure this is the Good Place. It doesn't seem that way to *us,* anyhow."

The light drew a figure-eight in the air, a shrug. (It looks that way to *me,)* it said. (Look how orderly everything is! And how much life there is in just one place! Where I come from, even a spore's worth of life is scarcer than atoms in a comet's tail.)

"Excuse me," Kit said, "but what *are* you?"

It said something Nita could make little sense of. The concept she got looked like page after page of mathematical equations. Kit raised his eyebrows. "It uses the Speech too," he commented as he listened.

"So what is it?"

Kit looked confused. "Its name says that it came from way out in space somewhere, and it has a mass equal to—to five or six blue-white giant stars and a few thousand-odd planets, and it emits all up and down the matter-energy spectrum, all kinds of light and radiation and even some subatomic particles." He shrugged. "You have any idea what that is?"

Nita stared at the light in growing disbelief. "Where's all your mass?" she said. "If you have that much, the gravity should have crushed us up against you the minute you showed up."

(Elsewhere,) the light said offhandedly. (I have a singularity-class temporospatial claudication.)

"A warp," Nita whispered. "A tunnel through space-time. Are you a white hole?"

It stopped bobbing, stared at her as if she had said something derogatory. (Do I look like a hole?)

"Do I look like a cloud of gas?" Nita snapped back, and then sighed—her mouth was getting the better of her again. "I'm sorry. That's just what we call your kind of, uh, creature. Because you act like a hole in the Universe that light and radiation come through. I know you're not, really. But, Kit," she said, turning, "where's my pen? And where's the power you were after? Didn't the spell work?"

"Spells always work," Kit said. "That's what the book says. When you ask for something, you always get back something that'll help you solve your problem, or be the solution itself." He looked entirely confused. "I asked for that power aura for me, and your pen for you—that was all. If we got a white hole, it means he's the answer—"

"If he's the answer," Nita said, bemused, "I'm not sure I understand the question."

(This is all fascinating,) the white hole said, (but I have to find a functional-Advisory nexus in a hurry. I found out that the *Naming of Lights* has gone missing, and I managed to find a paradimensional net with enough empty loci to get me to an Advisory in a hurry. But something seems to have gone wrong. Somehow I don't think you're Advisories.)

"Uh, no," Kit said. "I think we called you—"

(You called me?) the white hole said, regarding Kit with mixed reverence and amazement. (You're one of the Powers born of Life? Oh, I'm sorry I didn't recognize You—I know You can take any shape but somehow I'd always thought of You as being bigger. A quasar, or a mega-nova.) The white hole made a feeling of rueful amusement. (It's *confusing* being dead!)

"Oh, brother," Kit said. "Look, I'm not—you're not—just *not.* We made a spell and we called you. I don't think you're dead."

(If you say so,) the white hole said, polite but doubtful. (You called *me,* though? Me personally? I don't think we've met before.)

"No, we haven't," Nita said. "But we were doing this spell, and we found something, but something found us too, and we wouldn't have been able to get back here unless we called in some extra power—so we did, and it was you, I guess. You're not mad, are you?" she asked timidly. The thought of what a live, intelligent white hole might be able to do if it got annoyed scared her badly.

(Mad? No. As I said, I was trying to get out of my own space to get the news to someone who could use it, and then all of a sudden there was a paranet with enough loci to handle all the dimensions I carry, so I grabbed it.) The white hole made another small circle, looking around him curiously. (Maybe it did work. Are there Advisories in this—on this— What is this, anyway?)

Kit looked at Nita. "Huh?"

(This,) the white hole said, (all of this.) He made another circle.

"Oh! A planet," Nita said. "See, there's our star." She pointed, and the white hole rotated slightly to look.

(Artificer within us,) he said, (maybe I *have* blown my quanta, after all. I always wanted to see a planet, but I never got around to it. Habit, I guess. You get used to sitting around emitting X-rays after a while, and you don't think of doing anything else. You want to see some?) he asked suddenly. He sounded a little insecure.

"Uh, maybe you'd better not," Nita said.

(How come? They're really pretty.)

"We can't see them—and besides, we're not built to take hard radiation. Our atmosphere shuts most of it out."

(A real planet,) the white hole said, wondering and delighted, (with a real atmosphere. Well! If this is a planet, there has to be an Advisory around here somewhere. Could you help me find one?)

"Uhh—" Kit looked uncertainly at the white hole. "Sure. But do you think you could help me find some power? And Nita get her pen back?"

The white hole looked Kit up and down. (Some potential, some potential,) he muttered. (I could probably have you emitting light pretty quickly, if we worked together on a regular basis. Maybe even some alpha. We'll see. What's a pen?)

"What's your name?" Kit said. "I mean, we can't just call you 'hey you' all the time."

(True,) the white hole said. (My name is Khairelikoblephareh-glukumeilichephreidosd'enagouni—) and at the same time he went flickering through a pattern of colors that was evidently the visual translation.

"Ky—elik—" Nita began.

"Fred," Kit said quickly. "Well," he added as they looked at him again, "if we have to yell for help or something, the other way's too long. And that was the only part I got, anyway."

"Is that okay with you?" Nita asked.

The white hole made his figure-eight shrug again. (Better than having my truename mangled, I guess,) he said, and chuckled silently. (Fred, then. And you are?)

"Nita."

"Kit."

(I see why you like them short,) Fred said. (All right. Tell me what a 'pen' is, and I'll try to help you find it. But we really must get to an Advisory as fast as we can—)

"Okay," Kit said. "Let's break the circle and go talk."

"Sounds good," Nita said, and began to erase the diagrams they had drawn. Kit cut the wizards' knot and scuffed the circle open in a few places, while Nita took a moment to wave her hand through the now-empty air. "Not bad for a first spell," she said with satisfaction.

(I meant to ask,) Fred said politely, (what's a spell?)

Nita sighed, and smiled, and picked up her book, motioning Fred to follow her over by where Kit sat. It was going to be a long afternoon, but she didn't care. Magic was loose in the world.

Research and
Development

They were at the schoolyard early the next morning, to be sure they wouldn't miss Joanne and her crew. Nita and Kit sat on the curb by the front door to the school, staring across at the packed dirt and dull grass of the athletic field next to the building. Kit leafed through his wizards' manual, while Fred hung over his shoulder and looked around with mild interest at everything. (Will it be long?) he said, his light flickering slightly.

"No," Nita said. She was shaking. After the other day, she didn't want anything to do with Joanne at all. But she wanted that pen back, so . . .

"Look, it'll be all right," Kit said, paging through his manual. "Just do it the way we decided last night. Get close to her, keep her busy for a little while. Fred'll do the rest."

"It's keeping her busy that worries me," Nita muttered. "Her idea of busy usually involves her fists and my face."

(I don't understand,) Fred said, and Nita had to laugh briefly—she and Kit had heard that phrase about a hundred times since Fred arrived. He used it on almost everything. (What are you afraid of?)

"This," Nita said, pointing to her black eye. "And this—" uncovering a bruise. "And this, and this—"

Fred regarded her with a moment's discomfiture. (I thought you came that way. Joanne makes this happen?)

"Uh huh. And it hurts *getting* this way."

(But she only changes your outsides. Aren't your insides still the same afterward?)

Nita had to stop and think about that one.

"Okay," Kit said suddenly, "here's the Advisory list for our area." He ran a finger down the page. "And here's the one in town. Twenty-seven Hundred Rose—"

"That's up the hill past the school. What's the name?"

"Lessee. 'Swale, T.B., and Romeo, C.J. Research Advisories, temporospatial adjustments, entastics, non-specific scryings—' "

"Wait a minute," Nita said hurriedly. " 'Swale'? You mean Crazy Swale?
We can't go in there, Kit, that place is haunted! Everybody knows that!
Weird noises are always coming out of there—"

"If it's haunted," Kit said, "it's haunted by wizards. We might as well go
after school, it's only five or six blocks up the road."

They were quiet for a while. It was about twenty minutes before the bell
would ring for the doors to open, and a few early kids were gathering around
the doors. "Maybe we could rig you a defense against getting hit," Kit said,
as he kept looking through his manual. "How about this?" He pointed at one
page, and both Nita and Fred looked at the formula he was indicating. All it
needed was the right words. It would be something of a strain to carry the
shield for long, but Nita wouldn't have to; and any attempt to hit her would
just glance off.

(The problem is,) Fred said, (that spell will alter the field slightly around
this Joanne person. I'm going to have a hard enough time matching my
pattern to that of your pen so that I can get it off her—if indeed she has it.
Her own field is going to interfere, and so will yours, Nita. More stress on the
space in the area and I might not be able to get your pen back at all.)

Nita shook her head. She could tolerate another black eye if it meant
getting that pen back. "Forget it," she said, still shaking, and leaned forward
a bit, elbows on knees and face in hands, trying to relax. Above her the old
maple trees were muttering morning thoughts in the early sunlight, languid
observations on the weather and the decreasing quality of the tenant birds
who built nests in their branches. Out in the field the grass was singing a
scratchy soprano chorus—(growgrowgrowgrowgrowgrow)—which broke off
abruptly and turned into an annoyed mob-sound of boos and razzes as one of
the ground-keepers, way across the field, started up a lawnmower. I'm good
with plants, Nita thought. I guess I take after Dad. I wonder if I'll ever be
able to hear people this way.

Kit nudged her. "You're on," he said, and Nita looked up and saw Joanne
walking into the schoolyard. Their eyes met. Joanne recognized her, saw her
handiwork, smiled. Now or never! Nita thought, and got right up before she
had a chance to chicken out and blow everything. She walked over to Joanne
without a pause, fast, to keep the tremor in her knees from showing. Oh,
Fred, please be behind me. And what in the world can I say to her?

"I want my pen back, Joanne," she said,—or rather it fell out of her
mouth, and she went hot at her own stupidity. Yet the momentary shocked
look on Joanne's face made her think that maybe saying what was on her
mind hadn't been so stupid after all. Joanne's shock didn't last; a second later

she was smiling again. "Callahan," she said slowly, "are you looking for another black eye to match that one?"

"Lllp. No," Nita said, "just my pen, thanks."

"I don't know what you're talking about," Joanne said, and then grinned. "You always were a little odd. I guess you've finally flipped out."

"I had a space pen on me the other day, and it was gone afterward. One of you took it. I want it back." Nita was shaking worse than ever, but she was also surprised that the fist hadn't hit yet. And there over Joanne's shoulder, a flicker, a pinpoint of light, hardly to be seen, looking at her.

(Don't react. Make me a picture of the thing now.)

"What makes you think I would want anything of *yours?*" Joanne was saying, still with that smile. Nita looked straight at her and thought about the pen. Silver barrel, grooved all around the lower half so your fingers, or an astronaut's, wouldn't slip. Her initials engraved on it. *Hers,* her pen.

(Enough. Now then—)

"But now that I think of it, I do remember finding a pen on the ground last week. Let's see." Joanne was enjoying this so much that she actually flipped open the top of her backpack and began rummaging around. "Let's see, *here*—" She came up with something. Silver barrel, grooved—and Nita went hot again, not with embarrassment this time.

"It's mine!"

"Come and get it, then," Joanne said, dropping her backpack, keeping her smile, holding the pen back a little.

And a spark of white light seemed to light on the end of the pen as Joanne held it up, and then both were gone with a *pop* and a breath of air. Joanne spun to see who had plucked the pen out of her fingers, then whirled on Nita again. Nita smiled and held out her hands, empty.

Joanne was not amused. She stepped in close, and Nita took a few hurried steps back, unable to stop grinning even though she knew she was going to get hit. Heads were turning all around the schoolyard at the prospect of a fight. "Callahan," Joanne hissed, "you're in for it now!"

The eight-thirty bell went off so suddenly they both jumped. Joanne stared at Nita for a long long moment, then turned and went to pick up her backpack. "Why hurry things?" she said, straightening. "Callahan, if I were you, I'd sleep here tonight. Because when you try to leave—"

She walked off toward the doors. Nita stood where she was, still shaking, but with amazement and triumph as much as with fear. Kit came up beside her when Joanne was gone, and Fred appeared, a bright point between them.

"You were great!" Kit said.

"I'm gonna get killed tonight," Nita said, but she couldn't be terrified about it just yet. "Fred, have you got it?"

The point of light was flickering, and there was something about the way it did so that made Nita wonder if something was wrong. (Yes,) Fred said, the thought coming with a faint queasy feeling to it. (And that's the problem.)

"Are you okay?" Kit said. "Where'd it go?"

(I swallowed it,) Fred said, sounding genuinely miserable now.

"But that was what you were going to do," Nita said, puzzled. "Catch it in your own energy-field, you said, make a little pocket and hold it there."

(I know. But my fields aren't working the way they should. Maybe it's this gravity. I'm not used to any gravity but my own. I think it went down the wrong way.)

"Oh, brother," Kit said.

"Well," Nita said, "at least Joanne hasn't got it. When we go to the Advisories tonight, maybe they can help us get it out."

Fred made a small thought-noise somewhere between a burp and a squeak. Nita and Kit looked up at him, concerned—and then both jumped back hurriedly from something that went BANG! down by their feet.

They stared at the ground. Sitting there on the packed dirt was a small portable color TV, brand new.

"Uh, Fred—" Kit said.

Fred was looking down at the TV with embarrassment verging on shame. (I emitted it,) he said.

Nita stared at him. "But I thought white holes only emitted little things. Subatomic particles. Nothing so big—or so orderly."

(I wanted to visit an orderly place,) Fred said miserably. (See what it got me!)

"Hiccups," Kit muttered. "Fred, I think you'd better stay outside until we're finished for the day. We'll go straight to the Advisories' from here."

"Joanne permitting," Nita said. "Kit, we've got to go in."

(I'll meet you here,) Fred said. The mournful thought was followed by another burp/squeak, and another BANG! and four volumes of an encyclopedia were sitting on the ground next to the TV.

Kit and Nita hurried for the doors, sweating. Apparently wizardry had more drawbacks than the book had indicated. . . .

Lunch wasn't calm, but it *was* interesting, due to the thirty teachers, assistant principal, principal, and school superintendent who were all out on the athletic field, along with most of the students. They were walking around looking at the furniture, vacuum cleaners, computer components, books, knickknacks, motorcycles, typewriters, art supplies, stoves, sculptures, lumber, and many other odd things that had since morning been appearing one after another in the field. No one knew what to make of any of it, or what to do; and though Kit and Nita felt sure they would be connected with the situation somehow, no one accused them of anything.

They met again at the schoolyard door at three, pausing just inside it while Nita peered out to see if Joanne was waiting. She was, and eight of her friends were with her, talking and laughing among themselves. "Kit," Nita said quietly, "we've got problems."

He looked. "And this is the only door we can use."

Something went BANG! out in the field, and Nita, looking out again, saw heads turn among Joanne's group. Without a moment's pause every one of the girls headed off toward the field in a hurry, leaving Joanne to glare at the school door for a moment. Then she took off after the others. Kit and Nita glanced at each other. "I get this feeling . . ." Kit said.

"Let's go."

They waited until Joanne was out of sight and then leaned cautiously out of the door, looking around. Fred was suddenly there, wobbling in the air. He made a feeling of greeting at them; he seemed tired, but cheerful, at least for the moment.

Nita glanced over her shoulder to see what had drawn the attention of Joanne and her group—and drew in a sharp breath at the sight of the shiny silver Learjet. "Fred," she said, "you did that on purpose!"

She felt him look back too, and his cheerfulness drowned out his weariness and queasiness for a moment. (I felt you wondering whether to come out, so I exerted myself a little. What *was* that thing?)

"We'll explain later; right now we should run. Fred, thank you!"

(You're most welcome. Just help me *stop* this!)

"Can you hold it in for a few blocks?"

(What's a block?)

They ran down Rose Avenue, and Fred paced them. Every now and then a little of Fred's hiccup-noise would squeak out, and he would fall behind them, controlling it while they ran on ahead. Then he would catch up again. The last time he did it, they paused and waited for him. Twenty-seven Hundred Rose had a high poplar hedge with one opening for the walk up to the house, and neither of them felt like going any farther without Fred.

(Well?) he said, when he caught up. (Now what?)

Nita and Kit looked at each other. "I don't care if they *are* wizards," Nita said, "I want to peek in and have a look before I just walk in there. I've heard too many stories about this place—"

(Look,) Fred said in great discomfort, (I've got to—)

Evidently there was a limit on how long a white hole in Fred's condition could hold it in. The sound of Fred's hiccup was so much louder than usual that Nita and Kit crowded back away from him in near-panic. The BANG! sounded like the beginning of a fireworks display, and when its echoes faded, a powder-blue Mercedes-Benz was sitting half on, half off the sidewalk.

(My gnaester hurts,) Fred said.

"Let's peek," Nita said, turned, and pushed a little way through the hedge. She wanted to be sure there were no monsters or skeletons hanging from trees or anything else uncanny going on in the yard before she went in. What she did *not* expect was the amiable face of an enormous black-and-white English sheepdog, which first slurped her face energetically, then grabbed her right arm in gentle but insistent teeth and pulled her straight through the hedge.

"Kit!" she almost screamed, and then remembered not to because Crazy Swale or whoever else lived here might hear her. Her cry came out as sort of a grunt. She heard Kit come right through the bushes behind her as the sheepdog dragged her along through the yard. There was nothing spooky about the place at all—the house was big, a two-story affair, but normal-looking, all warm wood and shingles. The yard was grassy, with a landscaped garden as pretty as one of her father's. One side of the house had wide glass patio doors opening on a roofed-over terrace. Potted plants hung down and there was even a big square masonry tank, a fishpond—Nita caught a glimpse of something coppery swimming as the sheepdog dragged her past it to the terrace doors. It was at that point that the dog let go her arm and began barking noisily, and Nita began thinking seriously of running for it.

"All right, all right," came a man's voice, a humorous one, from inside the house, and it was *definitely* too late for running. Kit came up behind Nita, panting. "All *right*, Annie, let's see what you've got this time."

The screen door slid open, and Nita and Kit looked at the man who opened it in slight surprise. Somehow they had been expecting that any wizard not their age would be old, but this man was young, certainly no more than in his middle thirties. He had dark hair and was tall and broad-shouldered. He looked rather like someone out of a cigarette ad, except that he was smiling, which the men in cigarette ads rarely do. "Well," the man said, sounding not at all annoyed by three unexpected guests, "I see you've met Annie. . . ."

"She, uh," Nita said, glancing down at the dog, who was smiling at her with the same bemused interest as her master. "She found me looking through your hedge."

"That's Annie for you," the man said, sounding a bit resigned. "She's good at finding things. I'm Tom Swale." And he held out his hand for Nita to shake.

"Nita Callahan," she said, taking it.

"Kit Rodriguez," Kit said from beside her, reaching out to shake hands too.

"Good to meet you. Call me Tom. What can I do for you?"

"Are you the Advisory?" Kit said.

Tom's eyebrows went up. "You kids have a spelling problem?"

Nita grinned at the pun and glanced over her shoulder. "Fred?"

Fred bobbed up between her and Kit, regarding Tom, who looked back at the unsteady spark of light with only moderate surprise. "He's a white hole," Nita said. "He swallowed my space pen."

(T-*hup!*) Fred said, and BANG! went the air between Kit and Nita as they stepped hurriedly off to either side. Fourteen one-kilogram bricks of 999-fine Swiss gold fell clattering to the patio's brown tiles.

"I can see this is going to take some explaining," Tom said. "Come on in."

They followed him into the house. A big comfortable living room opened onto a den on one side and a bright kitchen-dining room on the other. "Carl, we've got company," Tom called as they entered the kitchen.

"Wha?" replied a muffled voice—muffled because the upper half of its owner was mostly in the cabinet under the double sink. The rest of him was sprawled across the kitchen floor. This by itself wasn't so odd; what *was* odd was the assortment of wrenches and other tools floating in the air just outside the cabinet doors. From under the sink came a sound like a wrench slipping off a pipe, and a sudden soft thump as it hit something else. Probably its user, for "Nnngg!" said the voice under the sink, and all the tools fell clattering to the kitchen floor. The voice broke into some most creative swearing.

Tom frowned and smiled both at once. "Such language in front of guests! You ought to sleep outside with Annie. Come on out of there, we're needed for a consultation."

"You really are wizards!" Nita said, reassured but still surprised. She had rarely seen two more normal-looking people.

Tom chuckled. "Sure we are. Not that we do too much freelancing these days—better to leave that to the younger practitioners, like you two."

The other man got out from under the sink, brushing himself off. He was at least as tall as Tom, and as broad-shouldered, but his dark hair was shorter and he had an impressive mustache. "Carl Romeo," he said in a voice with a pronounced Brooklyn accent, and shook hands with Kit and Nita. "Who's this?" he said, indicating Fred. Fred hiccuped; the resulting explosion produced six black star sapphires the size of tennis balls.

"Fred here," Tom said, "has a small problem."

"I wish *I* had problems like that," Carl remarked. "Something to drink, people? Soda?"

After a few minutes the four of them were settled around the kitchen table, with Fred hovering nearby. "It said in the book that you specialize in temporospatial claudications," Kit said.

"Carl does. Maintenance and repair; he keeps the worldgates at Grand Central Station and Rockefeller Center working. You've come to the right place."

"His personal gate is acting up, huh?" Carl said. "I'd better get the books." He got up. "Fred, what're the entasis figures on your warp?"

Fred mentally rattled off a number of symbols in the Speech, as he had when Kit asked him what he was. "Right," Carl said, and went off to the den.

"What do you do?" Nita said to Tom.

"Research, mostly. Also we're something of a clearinghouse for news and gossip in the Business. If someone needs details on a rare spell, or wants to know how power balances are running in a particular place, I can usually find out for them."

"But you do other things too." Kit looked around at the house.

"Oh, sure, we work. I write for a living—after all, some of the things I see in the Business make good stories. And Carl sells commercial time for WNXT in the city. As well as regular time, on the side."

Kit and Nita looked at each other, puzzled. Tom chuckled. "Well, he does claudications, gatings, doesn't he? Temporospatial—time and space. If you can squeeze space—claudicate it—so that you pop out of one place and into another, why can't you squeeze time the same way? Haven't you heard the saying about 'buying time'? Carl's the one you buy it from. Want to buy a piece of next Thursday?"

"I can get it for you wholesale," Carl said as he came back into the room. In his arms he was carrying several hardbound books as thick as telephone directories. On his shoulder, more interesting, was a splendid scarlet-blue-and-yellow macaw, which regarded Kit and Nita and Fred out of beady black eyes. "Kit, Nita, Fred," Carl said, "Machu Picchu. Peach for short." He sat down, put the books on the table, and began riffling through the one on top of the stack; Tom pulled one out of lower in the pile and began doing the same.

"All right," Tom said, "the whole story, from the beginning."

They told him, and it took a while. When they got to Fred's part of the story, and the fact that the *Naming of Lights* was missing, Tom and Carl became very quiet and just looked at one another for a moment. "Damn," Tom said, "I *wondered* why the entry in the *Materia Magica* hadn't been updated in so long. This is news, all right. We'll have to call a regional Advisories' meeting."

Fred hiccuped again, and the explosion left behind it a year's back issues of *TV Guide*.

"Later," Carl said. "The situation here looks like it's deteriorating." He paused at one page of the book he was looking through, ran his finger down a column. The macaw peered over his shoulder as if interested. "Alpha-rai-en-tath-eight, you said?"

(Right.)

"I can fix you," Carl said. "Take about five minutes." He got up and headed for the den again.

"What *is* the *Naming of Lights?*" Kit said to Tom. "We tried to get Fred to tell us last night, but it kept coming out in symbols that weren't in our books."

"Well, this is a pretty advanced subject. A novice's manual wouldn't have much information on the *Naming of Lights* any more than the instruction manual for a rifle would have information on atomic bombs. . . ." Tom took a drink. "It's a book. At least that's what it looks like when it's in or near this Universe. The *Book of Night with Moon*, it's called here, since in these parts you need moonlight to read it. It's always been most carefully accounted for; the Senior wizards keep an eye on it. If it's suddenly gone missing, we've got trouble. . . ."

"Why?" Nita said.

"Well, if you've gotten even this far in wizardry, you know how the wizards' symbology, the Speech, affects the things you use it on. When you use it, you *define* what you're speaking about. That's why it's dangerous to use the Speech carelessly. You can accidentally redefine something, change its nature. Something, or some*one*—" He paused, took another drink of his soda. "The *Book of Night with Moon* is written in the Speech. In it, everything's described. *Everything.* You, me, Fred, Carl . . . this house, this town, this world. This Universe and everything in it. *All* the Universes. . . ."

Kit looked skeptical. "How could a book that big get lost?"

"Who said it was big? You'll notice something about your manuals after a while," Tom said. "They won't get any bigger, but there'll be more and more inside them as you learn more, or need to know more. Even in plain old math it's true that the inside can be bigger than the outside; it's definitely true in wizardry. But believe me, the *Book of Night with Moon* has everything described in it. It's one of the reasons we're all here—the power of those descriptions helps keep everything that *is*, in existence." Tom looked worried. "And every now and then the Senior wizards have to go get the *Book* and read from it, to remind the worlds what they are, to preserve everything alive or inanimate—"

"Have *you* read from it?" Nita said, made uneasy by the disturbed look on Tom's face.

Tom glanced at her in shock, then began to laugh. "Me? No, no. I hope I never have to."

"But if it's a good *Book*, if it preserves things—" Kit said.

"It's good—at least, yes, it preserves, or lets things grow the way they want to. But reading it, being the vessel for all that power—I wouldn't want to.

Even good can be terribly dangerous. But this isn't anything you two need to worry about. The Advisories and the Senior wizards will handle it."

"But you *are* worried," Kit said.

"Yes, well—" Tom took another drink. "If it were just that the bright *Book* had gone missing, that wouldn't be so bad. A universe can go a long time without affirmation-by-reading. But the bright *Book* has an opposite number, a dark one; the *Book which is not Named*, we call it. It's written in the Speech too, but its descriptions are . . . skewed. And if the bright *Book* is missing, the dark one gains potential power. If someone should read from that one now, while the *Book of Night with Moon* isn't available to counteract the power of the dark one—" Tom shook his head.

Carl came in then, the macaw still riding his shoulder. "Here we go," he said, and dumped several sticks of chalk, an enormous black claw, and a 1943 zinc penny on the table. Nita and Kit stared at each other, neither quite having the nerve to ask what that claw had come off of. "Now you understand," Carl said as he picked up the chalk and began to draw a circle around the table, "that this is only going to stop the hiccups. You three are going to have to go to Manhattan and hook Fred into the Grand Central worldgate to get that pen out. Don't worry about being noticed. People use it all the time and no one's the wiser. *I* use it sometimes when the trains are late."

"Carl," Tom said, "doesn't it strike you as a little strange that the first wizardry these kids do produces Fred—who brings this news about the good *Book*—and they come straight to us—"

"Don't be silly," the macaw on Carl's shoulder said in a scratchy voice. "*You* know there are no accidents."

Nita and Kit stared.

"Wondered when you were going to say something useful," Carl said, sounding bored. "You think we keep you for your looks? OW!" he added, as the bird bit him on the ear. He hit it one on the beak, and, while it was still shaking its head woozily, put it up on the table beside Tom.

Picchu sidled halfway up Tom's arm, stopped and looked at Nita and Kit. "Dos d'en agouni nikyn toude pheresthai," it muttered, and got all the way up on Tom's shoulder, and then glared at them again. "Well?"

"She only speaks in tongues to show off," Tom said. "Ignore her, or rap her one if she bites you. We just keep her around because she tells the future." Tom made as if to smack the bird again, and Picchu ducked back. "How about the stocks tomorrow, bird?" he said.

Picchu cleared her throat. " 'And that's the way it is,' " she said in a voice very much like that of a famous newscaster, " 'July eighteen, 1988. From New York, this is Walter—' "

Tom fisted the bird in the beak, *clunk!* Picchu shook her head again.

" 'Issues were down in slow trading,' " she said resentfully. " 'The Dow-Jones index—' " and she called off some numbers. Tom grimaced.

"I should have gone into pork bellies," he muttered. "I ought to warn you two: If you have pets, look out. Practicing wizardry around them can cause some changes."

"There we go," Carl said, and stood up straight. "Fred, you ready? Hiccup for me again."

(I can't,) Fred said, sounding nervous. (You're all staring.)

"Never mind, I can start this in the meantime." Carl leaned over the table, glanced down at one of the books, and began reading in the Speech, a quick flow of syllables sharpened by that Brooklyn accent. In the middle of the third sentence Fred hiccuped, and without warning the wizardry took. Time didn't precisely stop, but it held still, and Nita became aware of what Carl's wizardry was doing to Fred, or rather had done already—subtly untangling forces that were knotted tight together. The half-finished hiccup and the wizardry came loose at the same time, leaving Fred looking bright and well for the first time since that morning. He still radiated uncertainty, though, like a person who isn't sure he's stopped hiccuping yet.

"You'll be all right," Carl said, scuffing away the chalk marks on the floor. "Though as I said, that pen is still in there with the rest of your mass, at the other end of your claudication, and you'll need Grand Central to get it out."

(Have you stopped my emissions entirely?) Fred said.

"No, of course not. I couldn't do that: you'll still emit from time to time. Mostly what you're used to, though. Radiation and such."

"Grand Central!" Kit was looking worried. "I don't think my mother and father are going to want me in the city alone. I could sneak in, I guess, but they'd want to know where I'd been all that while."

"Well," Tom said, looking thoughtful, "you've got school. You couldn't go before the weekend anyway, right? Carl could sell you a piece of Saturday or Sunday—"

Kit and Nita looked at each other, and then at the two men. "Uh, we don't have much money."

"Who said anything about money?" Carl said. "Wizards don't pay each other cash. They pay off in service—and sometimes the services aren't done for years. But first let's see if there's any time available this weekend. Saturdays go fast, even though they're expensive, especially Saturday mornings."

He picked up another book and began going through it. Like all the other books, it was printed in the same type as Nita's and Kit's manuals, though the print was much smaller and arranged differently. "This way," Tom said, "if you buy some time, you could be in the city all day, all week if you wanted —but once you activate the piece of time you're holding, you're back *then*. You have to pick a place to anchor the time to, of course, a twenty-foot radius. But after you've finished whatever you have to do, you bring your marked time to life, and there you are. Maybe five minutes before you started for the city, back at home. Or anywhere and anywhen else along the path you'll follow that day."

"Huh," Carl said suddenly. "Callahan, J., and Rodriguez, C., is that you two?" They nodded. "You have a credit already," Carl said, sounding a little surprised. "What have you two been doing to rate that?"

"Must have been for bringing Fred through," Tom said. "I didn't know that Upper Management had started giving out door prizes, though."

From her perch on Tom's shoulder, Picchu snorted. "Oh? What's that mean?" Tom said. "Come on, bird, be useful. Is there something you know that these kids ought to?"

"I want a raise," Picchu said, sounding sullen.

"You just had one. Talk!"

" 'Brush your teeth twice a day, and see your dentist regularly,' " the macaw began, in a commercial-announcer's voice. Tom made a fist and stared at her. "All right, all right," Picchu muttered. She looked over at Kit and Nita, and though her voice when she spoke had the usual good-natured annoyance about it, her eyes didn't look angry or even teasing—they looked anxious. Nita got a sudden chill down her back. "Don't be afraid to make corrections," Picchu said. "Don't be afraid to lend a hand." She fell silent, seeming to think for a moment. "And don't look down."

Tom stared at the macaw. "Can't you be a little more specific?"

"Human lives," Picchu said irritably, "aren't much like the Dow-Jones index. No, I can't."

Tom sighed. "Sorry. Kids, if she says it, she has a reason for saying it—so remember."

"Here you go," Carl said. "Your piece of time is from ten forty-five to ten forty-seven on this next Saturday morning. There aren't any weekend openings after that until sometime in July."

"We'll take this one," Kit said. "At least I can—Nita, will your folks let you go?"

She nodded. "I have some allowance saved up, and I'd been thinking about going into the city to get my dad a birthday present anyhow. I doubt there'll be any trouble."

Kit looked uncomfortable for a moment. "But there's something I'm not sure about. My spell—our spell brought Fred here. How are we going to get him back where he belongs?"

(Am I a problem?) Fred said, sounding concerned.

"Oh, no, no—it's just that, Fred, this isn't your home, and it seemed as if sooner or later you might want to go back where you came from."

"As far as that goes," Tom said, "if it's your spell that brought him here, you'll be able to send him back. The instructions are in your book, same as the instructions for opening the Grand Central worldgate."

"Stick to those instructions," Carl said. "Don't be tempted to improvise. That claudication is the oldest one in New York, and it's the trickiest because of all the people using it all the time. One false syllable in a spell and you may wind up in Schenectady."

(Is that another world?) Fred asked.

"Nearly." Carl laughed. "Is there anything else we can do for you?"

Nita and Kit shook their heads and got up to leave, thanking Tom and Carl and Picchu. "Let us know how things turn out," Tom said. "Not that we have any doubts—two wizards who can produce a white hole on the first try are obviously doing all right. But give us a call. We're in the book."

The two men saw Nita and Kit as far as the patio door, said their good-byes, and went back into the house. Nita started off across the lawn the way she had come, but Kit paused for a moment by the fishpool, staring down into it. He pulled a penny out of his pocket, dropped it in.

Nita saw the ripples spread—and then suddenly another set of ripples wavered away from the head of a very large goldfish, which spat the penny back at Kit and eyed him with distaste. "Do *I* throw money on *your* living-room floor?" it said, and then dived out of sight.

Kit picked up his penny and went after Nita and Fred as they pushed through the poplar hedge again. The blue Mercedes, which had been half in the street and half on the sidewalk, was now neatly parked by the curb. In front of it sat Annie, with her tongue hanging out and a satisfied look on her face. There were teethmarks deep in the car's front fender. Annie grinned at them as Nita and Kit passed, and then trotted off down the street, probably to "find" something else.

"If my dog starts doing things like that," Kit muttered, "I don't know how I'm going to explain it to my mother."

Nita looked down the street for signs of Joanne. "If we can just get home without being killed, I wouldn't care *what* the dog found. *Uh* oh—" A good ways down the street, four or five girls were heading toward them, and Nita saw Joanne's blond hair. "Kit, we'd better split up. No reason for them to come after you too."

"Right. Give me a call tonight. I'm in the book. . . ." He took off down a side street.

She looked around, considering the best direction to run in—and then thought of the book she was carrying. There wasn't much time, though. She forced herself to calm down even while she knew they were coming for her, made herself turn the pages slowly to the place Kit had shown her that morning, the spell that made blows slide off. She read through it slowly in the Speech, sounding out the syllables, taking the time to look up the pronunciation of the ones she wasn't sure of, even though they were getting close and she could hear Joanne's laugh.

Nita sat down on the curb to wait for them. They let her have it when they found her, as they had been intending to all day; and she rolled around on the ground and fell back from their punches and made what she hoped were horrible groaning noises. After a while Joanne and her four friends turned away to leave, satisfied that they had taught her a lesson. And Nita stood up and brushed herself off, uncut, unbruised, just a little dirty. "Joanne," she called after them. In what looked like amazement, Joanne turned around.

Nita laughed at her. "It won't work any more," she said.

Joanne stood dumb.

"Never again," she said. She felt like turning her back on them, but instead she walked *toward* them, watching the confusion in their eyes. On a sudden urge, she jumped up in the air and waved her arms crazily. "BOO!" she shouted.

They broke and ran, all of them. Joanne was the first, and then the rest followed her in a ragged tail down Rose Avenue. Not a word, not a taunt. They just ran.

Nita stopped short. The feeling of triumph that had been growing in her withered almost instantly. Some victory, she thought. It took so little, so little to scare them. Maybe I could have done that at any time, without a shield. Maybe. And now I'll never know for sure.

(Are you all right?) Fred said quietly, bobbing again by her shoulder. (They didn't hurt you this time.)

"No," Nita said slowly. She was thinking of all the glorious plans she'd had to use her new-found wizardry on Joanne and her bunch, to shame them, confuse them, hurt them. And look what so small and inoffensive thing as a body shield had done to them. They would hate her worse than ever now.

I've got to be careful with this, she thought. I thought it was going to be all fun.

"Come on, Fred," she said, "let's go home."

Temporospatial
Claudications
Use and Abuse

The week went by quickly for Nita. Though Carl had made the business of opening a worldgate sound fairly simple, she began to suspect that he'd been doing it so long that it actually seemed that way to him. It wasn't simple, as her book told her as soon as she opened to the pertinent chapter, which was forty pages long in small print.

Grand Central worldgate had its own special requirements: specific supplies and objects that had to be present at an opening so that space would be properly bent, spells that had to be learned just so. The phone calls flew between Nita's house and Kit's for a couple of days, and there was a lot of visiting back and forth as they divided up the work. Nita spent a lot of time keeping Fred from being noticed by her family, and also got to see a lot of Kit's mother and father and sisters, all of whom were very friendly and kept forgetting that Nita couldn't speak Spanish. She started to learn a little of it in self-defense. Kit's dog told her the brand of dog biscuits it could never get enough of; she began bringing them with her when she visited. The dog spoke the Speech with a Spanish accent, and would constantly interrupt Kit and Nita as they discussed who should do what in the spelling. Kit wound up with most of the spoken work, since he had been using the Speech longer and was better at it; Nita picked up supplies.

"You ever swallow anything accidentally before, Fred?" Nita said under her breath. It was late Friday afternoon, and she was in a little antiques-and-junk store on Nassau Road, going through boxes of dusty odds and ends in search of a real silver fork. Fred was hanging over her shoulder, almost invisible, a faint red point lazily emitting heat.

(Not for a long time) he said, glancing curiously at a pressed-glass saltshaker Nita was holding. (Not since I was a black hole, certainly. Black holes swallow *everything*, but a white hole's business is emission. Within limits,) he added, and the air around him rippled with heat as he shuddered. (I don't ever again want to emit the way I did after your pen went down. Some of those things *hurt* on the way out. And anyway, all that emission makes me nervous. Too much of that kind of thing and I could blow my quanta.)

She looked up at him, worried. "Really? Have you emitted that much stuff that you're in danger of blowing up?"

(Oh, not really—I'd have to lose a lot more mass first. After all, before I was a black hole, I was a respectable-sized blue-white star, and even those days I massed a few hundred thousand times what your cute little yellow-dwarf Sun does. I wouldn't worry about it—I'm nowhere near the critical threshold yet.)

" 'Cute'?" Nita said.

(Well, it *is*. . . . And I suppose there's no harm in getting better at emissions. I have been improving a lot. What's that?)

Nita looked farther down in the box, dug deep, and came up with a battered old fork. It was scratched and its tines were bent out of shape, but it was definitely silver, not stainless steel. "That's what I needed," she said. "Thanks, Fred. Now all I need is that piece of rowan wood, and then tonight I go over my part of the spells again."

(You sound worried.)

"Well, yeah, a little," Nita said, getting up. All that week her ability to hear what the plants were saying had been getting stronger and surer; the better she got with the Speech, the more sense the bushes and trees made. "It's just—the rowan branch has to come off a live tree, Fred, and I can't just pick it—that'd be like walking up to someone and pulling one of their fingers off. I have to ask for it. And if the tree won't give it to me . . ."

(Then you don't get your pen back, at least not for a while.) Fred shimmered with colors and a feeling like a sigh. (I *am* a trouble to you.)

"Fred, no. Put your light out a moment so we can get out of here." Nita interrupted the shopkeeper's intense concentration on a Gothic novel long enough to find out what the fork cost (a dollar) and buy it. A few steps outside the door, Fred was pacing her again. "If you're trouble, you're the best trouble that's happened around here for a while. You're good to talk to, you're good company—when you don't forget and start emitting cosmic rays—"

Fred blazed momentarily, blushing at Nita's teasing. In an excited moment the night before he had forgotten himself and emitted a brief blast of ultrashortwave radiation, which had heated up Nita's backyard a good deal, ionized the air for miles around, and produced a local but brilliant aurora. (Well, it's an old habit, and old habits die hard. I'm working on it.)

"Heat we don't mind so much. Or ultraviolet, the longwave kind that doesn't hurt people's eyes."

(You fluoresce when I use that, though. . . .)

Nita laughed. "I don't mind fluorescing. Though on second thought, don't do that where anyone but Kit can see. I doubt my mother'd understand."

They walked home together, chatting alternately about life in the suburbs and life in a part of deep space close to the Great Galactic Rift. Nita felt more relaxed than she had for months. Joanne had been out of sight since Monday afternoon at Tom and Carl's. Even if she hadn't, Nita had been practicing with that body shield, so that now she could run through the syllables of the spell in a matter of seconds and nothing short of a bomb dropped on her could hurt her. She could even extend the spell to cover someone else, though it wasn't quite so effective; she had a harder time convincing the air to harden up. But even that lessened protection would come in handy if she and Kit should be in trouble together at some point and there was no time to cooperate in a spelling. Not that she was expecting any more trouble. The excitement of a trip into the city was already catching at her. And this wasn't just another shopping trip. Magic was loose in the world, and she was going to help work some. . . .

She ate supper and did her homework almost without thinking about either, and as a result had to do much of the math homework twice. By the time she was finished, the sun was down and the backyard was filling with a cool blue twilight. In the front of the house, her mother and father and Dairine were watching TV as Nita walked out the side door and stood on the step, letting her eyes get used to the dimness and looking east at the rising Moon. Canned laughter echoed inside the house as Fred appeared by her shoulder.

(My, that's bright for something that doesn't emit heat,) Fred said, looking at the Moon too.

"Reflected sunlight," Nita said absently.

(You're going to talk to the tree now?)

"Uh huh."

(Then I'll go stay with the others and watch that funny box emit. Maybe I'll figure out what it's trying to get across.)

"Good luck," Nita said as Fred winked out. She walked around into the backyard.

Spring stars were coming out as she stood in the middle of the lawn and looked down the length of the yard at the rowan, a great round-crowned tree snowy with white flowers. Nita's stomach tightened slightly with nervousness. It had been a long time ago, according to her manual, that the trees had gone to war on mankind's behalf, against the dark powers that wanted to keep human intelligence from happening at all. The war had been a terrible one, lasting thousands of centuries—the trees and other plants taking more and more land, turning barren stone to soil that would support them and the animals and men to follow; the dark powers breaking the soil with earthquake and mountain building, scouring it with glaciers, climate-changing good ground for desert, and burning away forests in firestorms far more terrible than the small brushfires any forest needs to stay healthy. But the trees and the other plants had won at last.

They had spent many more centuries readying the world for men—but when men came, they forgot the old debts and wasted the forests more terribly than even the old dark powers. Trees had no particular reason to be friendly to people these days. Nita found herself thinking of that first tree that had spoken to her, angry over the destruction of its friend's artwork. Even though the rowan tree had always been well tended, she wasn't certain how it was going to respond to her. With the other ash trees, rowans had been in the forefront of the Battle; and they had long memories.

Nita sighed and sat down under the tree, book in hand, her back against its trunk. There was no need to start right away, anyhow—she needed a little while to recover from her homework. The stars looked at her through the rowan's windstirred branches, getting brighter by the minute. There was that one pair of stars that always looked like eyes, they were so close together. It was one of the three little pairs associated with the Big Dipper. The Leaps of the Gazelle, the ancient Arabs had called them, seeing them as three sets of hoofprints left in the sky. "Kafza'at al Thiba," Nita murmured, the old Arabic name. Her eyes wandered down toward the horizon, finding a faint reddish gleam. "Regulus." And a whiter gleam, higher: "Arcturus." And another, and another, old friends, with new names in the Speech, that she spoke silently, remembering Carl's warning: (Elthátht¨e . . . ur'Senaahel . . .) The distant fires flickered among shadowy leaves. (Lahirien . . .)

(And Methcháné and Ysen and Cahadhwy and Rasaugéhil. . . . They *are* nice tonight.)

Nita looked up hurriedly. The tree above her was leaning back comfortably on its roots, finished with the stretching-upward of growth for the day, and gazing at the stars as she was. (I was hoping that haze would clear off,) it said as silently as Nita had spoken, in a slow, relaxed drawl. (This will be a good night for talking to the wind. And other such transient creatures. I was wondering when you were going to come out and pay your respects, wizardling.)

(Uh—) Nita was reassured: the rowan sounded friendly. (It's been a busy week.)

(You never used to be too busy for *me*,) the rowan said, its whispery voice sounding ever so slightly wounded. (Always up in my branches you were, and falling out of them again. Or swinging. But I suppose you outgrew me.)

Nita sat quiet for a moment, remembering how it had been when she was littler. She would swing for hours on end, talking to herself, pretending all

kinds of things, talking to the tree and the world in general. And sometimes— (You talked *back!*) she said in shocked realization. (You *did*, I wasn't
making it up.)

(Certainly I talked. You were talking to *me*, after all. . . . Don't be surprised. Small children look at things and *see* them, listen to things and hear
them. Of course they understand the Speech. Most of them never realize it
any more than you did. It's when they get older, and stop looking and
listening, that they lose the Speech, and we lose them.) The rowan sighed,
many leaves showing pale undersides as the wind moved them. (None of us
are ever happy about losing our children. But every now and then we get one
of you back.)

(All that in the book was true, then,) Nita said. (About the Battle of the
Trees—)

(Certainly. Wasn't it written in the *Book of Night with Moon* that this
world's life would become free to roam among our friends there)—the rowan
stretched upward toward the turning stars for a moment—(if we helped?
After the world was green and ready, we waited for a long time. We started
letting all sorts of strange creatures live in our branches after they came up
out of the water. We watched them all; we never knew which of our guests
would be the children we were promised. And then all of a sudden one odd-
looking group of creatures went *down* out of our branches, and looked upward again, and called us by name in the Speech. Your kind. . . .) The tree
looked down musingly at Nita. (You're still an odd-looking lot,) it said.

Nita sat against the rowan and felt unhappy. (We weren't so kind to you,)
she said. (And if it weren't for the plants, we wouldn't be here.)

(Don't be downcast, wizardling,) the tree said, gazing up at the sky again.
(It isn't your fault. And in any case, we knew what fate was in store for us. It
was written in the *Book.)*

(Wait a minute. You mean you knew we were going to start destroying
your kind, and you got the world ready for us *anyway?)*

(How could we do otherwise? You *are* our children.)

(But . . . we make our houses out of you, we—) Nita looked guiltily at
the book she was holding. (We *kill* you and we write on your *bodies!)*

The rowan continued to gaze up at the night sky. (Well,) it said. (We are
all in the *Book* together, after all. Don't you think that we wrote enough in
the rock and the soil, in our day? And we still do. We have our own lives, our
own feelings and goals. Some of them you may learn by your wizardry, but I
doubt you'll ever come to know them all. We do what we have to, to live.
Sometimes that means breaking a rock's heart, or pushing roots down into
ground that screams against the intrusion. But we never forget what we're
doing. As for you)—and its voice became very gentle—(how else should our
children climb to the stars but up our branches? We made our peace with

that fact a long time ago, that we would be used and maybe forgotten. So be it. What you learn in your climbing will make all the life on this planet greater, more precious. You have your own stories to write. And when it comes to that, who writes the things written in *your* body, *your* life? And who reads?) It breathed out, a long sigh of leaves in the wind. (Our cases aren't that much different.)

Nita sat back and tried to absorb what the tree was saying. (The *Book of Night with Moon,*) she said after a while. (Do you know who wrote it?)

The rowan was silent for a long time. (None of us are sure,) it said at last. (Our legends say it wasn't written. It's simply *been*, as long as life has been. Since they were kindled, and before.) It gazed upward at the stars.

(Then the other Book, the dark one—)

The whole tree shuddered. *(That* one was written, they say.) The rowan's voice dropped to a whisper. (By the Lone Power—the Witherer, the one who blights. The Kindler of Wildfires. Don't ask more. Even talking about that one or its works can lend it power.)

Nita sat quiet for a while, thinking. (You came to ask something,) the rowan said. (Wizards are always asking things of rowans.)

(Uh, yes.)

(Don't worry about it,) the rowan said. (When we decided to be trees of the Light, we knew we were going to be in demand.)

(Well—I need some live wood. Just enough for a stick, a little wand. We're going to open the Grand Central worldgate tomorrow morning.)

Above Nita's head there was a sharp cracking sound. She pressed back against the trunk, and a short straight branch about a foot and a half long bounced to the grass in front of her. (The Moon is almost full tonight,) the rowan said. (If I were you, I'd peel the leaves and bark off that twig and leave it out to soak up moonlight. I don't think it'll hurt the wood's usefulness for your spelling, and it may make it more valuable later on.)

(Thank you, yes,) Nita said. The book had mentioned something of the sort—a rowan rod with a night's moonlight in it could be used for some kind of defense. She would look up the reference later. (I guess I should go in and check my spells over one more time. I'm awfully new at this.)

(Go on,) the tree said, with affection. Nita picked up the stick that the rowan had dropped for her, got up and stretched, looking up at the stars through the branches. On impulse she reached up, hooked an arm around the branch that had had the swing on it.

(I guess I could still come and climb sometimes,) she said.

She felt the tree looking at her. (My name in the Speech is Liused,) it said in leafrustle and starflicker. (If there's need, remember me to the trees in Manhattan. You won't be without help if you need it.)

"I'm Nita," she said in the Speech, aloud for this once. The syllables didn't

sound strange: they sounded like a native language and made English feel like a foreign tongue. For a moment every leaf on the tree quivered with her name, speaking it in a whispery echo.

(Go,) the rowan said again. (Rest well.) It turned its calm regard to the stars again.

Nita went back inside.

Saturday morning about eight, Kit and Nita and Fred took the bus down to the Long Island Railroad station and caught a shiny silver train for Manhattan. The train was full of the usual cargo of Saturday travelers and shoppers, none of whom paid any particular attention to the boy and girl sitting by one window, going over the odd contents of their backpacks with great care. Also apparently unnoticed was a faint spark of white light hanging in the center of the window between the two, gazing out in fascination at the backyards and parking lots and stores the train passed.

(What are all those dead hunks of metal there? All piled up?)

(Cars, Fred.)

(I thought cars moved.)

(They did, once.)

(They all went there to die?)

(They were dead when they got there, probably.)

(But they've all climbed on top of each other! When they were dead?)

(No, Fred. They have machines—)

(What was *that?* There are three—I don't know who those were, but they have them shut up in a box hanging from that long thing.)

(No one you know, Fred. That was a traffic light.)

(It was emitting— Look, he's trying to say something! Hello! *Hello!)*

(Fred, you're flashing! Calm down or someone'll see you!)

(Well, I don't know what a nice guy like him was doing in a place like *that.)*

Nita sighed out loud. "Where were we?" she said to Kit.

"The battery."

"Right. Well, here it is."

"Lithium-cadmium?"

"Right. Heavy thing, it weighs more than anything else we've got. That's the last thing for activating the piece of time, isn't it?"

"One more. The eight and a half sugar cubes."

"Here." Nita held up a little plastic bag.

"Okay. Now the worldgate stuff. The pine cone—"

"Bristlecone pine." Nita held it up, then dropped it in her backpack.

"The aspirin."

"Uh huh."

"The fork."

"Here."

"The rowan branch."

"Yup." She held it up. Cut down and peeled, it was about a foot long, a greenish-white wand.

"Great. Then we're set. You've got all that other stuff, why don't you give me the battery?"

"Here." Nita handed it to him, watched as he found a good spot for it in his backpack, under the sandwiches. "What's that?" she said, spotting something that hadn't been accounted for in the equipment tally.

"Huh? Oh, this." He reached in and brought out a slim piece of metal like a slender rod, with a small knob at one end and broken off jaggedly at the other.

"What is it?"

"A piece of junk. A busted-off car antenna. Well," Kit amended, "it was, anyway. I was sitting out behind the garage yesterday afternoon, reading, and I started talking to my dad's old car. He has this ancient Edsel. He's always talking about getting it reconditioned, but I don't think he's really going to— there's never enough money. Anyway he goes out every now and then to work on the engine, usually when he's tired or mad about something. I don't know if he ever really gets any work done, but he always comes inside greasy all over and feeling a lot better. But I was going over the spells in my head, and the car spoke to me in the Speech—"

"Out loud?"

"No, inside, like Fred does. Kind of a grindy noise, like its voice needed a lube job. I wasn't too surprised; that kind of thing has been happening since I picked the book up. First it was rocks, and then *things* started to talk to me when I picked them up. They would tell me where they'd been and who'd handled them. Anyway, the car and I started talking." Kit paused, looking a touch guilty. "They don't see things the way we do. We made them, and they don't understand why most of the time we make things and then just let them wear out and throw them away afterward. . . ."

Nita nodded, wondering briefly whether the train was alive too. Certainly it was as complex as a car. "What about this antenna thing, though?" she said after a moment.

"Oh. The car said to take it for luck. It was just lying there on the ground, rusting. Dad replaced the antenna a long time ago. So I took it inside and cleaned it up, and there are some wizardries you can do with metal, to remind it of the different forces it felt when it was being made. I did a couple of those. Partly just practicing, partly . . ."

"You thought there might be trouble," Nita said.

Kit looked at her, surprised. "I don't know," he said. "I'm going to be

areful, anyway. Carl was pretty definite about not messing around with the
worldgate; I wasn't thinking about anything like that. But it occurred to me
hat it'd be easy to carry the antenna to school if I wanted to. And if anyone
started bothering me—" He shrugged, then laughed. "Well, that's their
problem. Hey, look, we're getting close to that big curve where you can see
he city before you go under the river. Come on, these trains have a window
n the very front of the first car. Fred! Want to see where we're going?"

(Why not? Maybe I'll understand it better than where we've been. . . .)

Kit and Nita wriggled into their backpacks and made their way up through
a couple of cars, hanging on carefully as they crossed the chained walkways
between them. Treetops and housetops flashed by in a rush of wind and
clatter of rails. Each time Nita touched the bare metal of the outside of the
train, she jumped a little, feeling something, she wasn't quite sure what. The
train? she thought. Thinking? And now that I'm aware that it does, I can feel
it a little?—though not as clearly as the trees. Maybe my specialty is going to
be things that grow and Kit's is going to be things that run. But how many
other kinds of life are there that I could learn to feel? Who knows where
thought is hiding? . . .

They went into the first car and made their way up to the front window,
carefully hanging on to the seats of oblivious riders to keep the swaying of the
train from knocking them over. There were no more stops between there and
Penn Station, and the train was plunging along, the rails roaring beneath it.
Those rails climbed gradually as the already elevated track went higher still to
avoid a triple-stacked freeway. Then the rails bent away to the left in a long
graceful curve, still climbing slightly; and little by little, over the low brown
cityscape of Brooklyn, the towers of Manhattan rose glittering in the early
sunlight. Gray and crystal for the Empire State Building, silver-blue for the
odd sheared-off Citibank building, silver-gold for the twin square pillars of
the World Trade Center, and steely white fire for the scalloped tower of the
Chrysler Building as it caught the Sun. The place looked magical enough in
the bright morning. Nita grinned to herself, looking at the view and realizing
that there *was* magic there. That forest of towers opened onto other worlds.
One day she would open that worldgate by herself and *go* somewhere.

Fred stared at the towers, amazed. (This is *more* life? More even than the
place where you two live?)

(Ten million lives in the city, Fred. Maybe four or five million on that
island alone.)

(Doesn't it worry you, packing all that life together? What if a meteor hits
it? What if there's a starflare? If something should happen to all that life—
how terrible!)

Nita laughed to herself. (It doesn't seem to worry *them*. . . .) Beside her,
Kit was hanging on to a seat, being rocked back and forth by the train's

speed. Very faintly Nita could hear what Kit heard and felt more strongly; the train's aliveness, its wild rushing joy at doing what it was made to do—its dangerous pleasure in its speed, the wind it fought with, the rails it rode. Nita shook her head in happy wonder. And I wanted to see the life on other planets. There's more life in *this* world than I expected. . . .

(It's beautiful,) Fred said from his vantage point just above Kit's shoulder. "It really is," Nita said, very quiet.

The train howled defiant joy and plunged into the darkness under the river.

Penn Station was thick with people when they got there, but even so it took them only a few minutes to get down to the Seventh Avenue Subway station and from there up to Times Square and the shuttle to Grand Central. The shuttle ride was short and crowded. Nita and Kit and Fred were packed tight together in a corner, where they braced themselves against walls and seats and other people while the train shouted along through the echoing underground darkness.

(I can't feel the Sun,) Fred said, sounding worried.

(We're ten or twenty feet underground,) Nita said silently. (We'll get you some Sun as soon as we get off.)

Kit looked at Fred with concern. (You've been twitchy ever since we went into the tunnel, haven't you?)

Fred didn't speak for a moment. (I miss the openness,) he said then. (But worse I miss the feeling of your star on me. Where I come from no one is sealed away from the surrounding emissions.) He trailed off, his thoughts full of the strange hiss and crackle of interstellar radiation—subtly patterned sound, rushing and dying away and swelling up again—the Speech in yet another of its forms. Starsong, Nita thought. (You said you *heard* about the *Book of Night with Moon*,) she said. (Was that how? Your . . . friends, your people, they actually talk to each other over all those distances—millions of light-years?)

(That's right. Not that we use light to do it, of course. But the words, the song, they never stop. Except now. I can hardly hear anything but neutrinos. . . .)

Kit and Nita glanced at each other. (The worldgate is underground, Fred,) Kit said. (In back of a deli, a little store. We'll have to be there for at least a few minutes to get Nita's pen out.)

(We could go out first and look around,) Nita said. (We're early—it's only nine thirty. We don't even have to think about anchoring the timeslide for a little bit yet.)

The subway cars screeched to a halt, doors rolled open, and the crush loosened as people piled out. Nita got off gladly, looking around for directional signs to point the way toward the concourse level of Grand Central—it had been a while since she'd been there.

"Are you sure you know your way around this place?" Kit said as Nita headed down one torn-up looking corridor.

"Uh huh. They're always doing construction in here. C'mon."

She led them up a flight of stairs into the lower Grand Central concourse —all beige tiles, gray floor, signs pointing to fifty different trains, and small stores packed together. "The deli's down there," she said as she went, waving a hand at a crowd of hurrying people and the wide hall past them. "We go up here." And another flight of stairs, wider and prettier, let them out on the upper concourse, a huge stretch of cream-colored marble under a great blue dome painted with constellations and starred with lights.

They headed across the marble floor, up a short ramp, and out one of many brassy yellow doors, onto the street. Immediately the three of them were assailed by noise, exhaust fumes, people hurrying in all directions, a flood of cabs and buses and cars. But there was also sunlight, and Kit and Nita stood against the wall by the Grand Central doors, letting Fred soak it up and get his composure back. He did so totally oblivious to the six men and three jackhammers working just across the street behind a barrier of saw-horses and orange plastic cones. (That's much better,) he said.

(It was quieter inside, though,) Kit said, and Nita was inclined to agree with him. The rattling clamor of the jackhammers was climbing down her ears into her bones and making her teeth jitter. The men, two burly ones and one skinny one, all three broad-shouldered and tan, all in helmets and jeans and boots, appeared to be trying to dig to China. One of them hopped down into the excavation for a moment to check its progress, and vanished up to his neck. Then the hammering started again. "How can they stand it?" Nita muttered.

(Stand what? It's lovely out here.) Fred danced about a little in the air, brightening out of invisibility for a few moments and looking like a long-lived remnant of a fireworks display.

(Fred, put it out!) Kit said. (If somebody sees you—)

(They didn't see me in the field the other day,) Fred replied, (though Artificer knows they *looked.)*

(Probably the Learjet distracted them. Fred, come on, tone it down a little,) Nita said. (Let's go back inside and do what we have to. Then we can set the timeslide and have fun in the city for the rest of the day.)

They went back inside and down the stairs again, accompanied by the quiet inward sound of Fred's grumbling. There was no trouble finding the little deli where the worldgate was situated, and Nita and Kit paused outside it. (You have everything ready?) Nita said.

(All in here.) Kit tapped his head. (The spells are all set except for one or

two syllables—it's like dialing almost all of a phone number. When I call fo
you, just come on back. All we need is for the supplies to be in range of th
spell; there's nothing special that has to be done with them. Fred, you stay
with Nita.)

(As you say.)

They went in. Nita lingered by the front counter, staring at dill pickles and
sandwich makings, trying to look normal while she waited for Kit to call her
Fred hung over her shoulder, looking with great interest at bologna and
salami and mayonnaise and cream cheese. (You people certainly have enough
ways to internalize energy,) he said. (Is there really that much difference
between one brand of matter and another?)

(Well, wasn't there any difference when you were a black hole? Didn't a
rock, say, taste different from a ray of light, when you soaked one or the other
up?)

(Now that you mention it, yes. But appreciating differences like that wa
something you had to work at for a long time. I wouldn't expect someone a
young as you to—)

(Nita,) Kit's thought came abruptly. (We've got trouble. It's not here.)

(What? It has to be!)

(It's *gone*, Nita.)

"Girlie," said the man behind the deli counter in a no-nonsense growl
"you gonna buy anything?"

"Uh," Nita said, and by reflex more than anything else picked up a can of
soda from the nearby cooler and fished around in her pocket for the change
"Kit—" she called.

"Coming?"

Nita paid for the soda. Kit joined her, carrying a small bag of potato chips
which he paid for in turn. Together they went back out into the corridor, and
Kit knelt down by the window of a store across the way, a window full of
shiny cutlery. He got his wizards' manual out of his pack and began going
through the pages in a hurry. "I don't get it," he said. "I even checked this
morning to make sure there hadn't been any change in the worldgate status.
It said, right here, 'patent and operative.'"

"Were the spells all right?"

Kit glared up at Nita, and she was instantly sorry she'd asked. "The spells
were fine," Kit said. "But they got caught like that first one I did, when you
came along. Oh, damn. . . ." He trailed off, and Nita edged around beside
him to look at the page. "Something's changed," Kit said, and indeed the
page didn't look as it had when Nita had checked it herself in her own
manual the night before. The listings for the other Manhattan worldgates
were the same—the World Trade Center gate was still listed as "under construction" and the Rockefeller Center gate as "closed for routine mainte-

nance." But under the Grand Central gate listing was a small red box that said in boldface type, *Claudication temporarily dislocated due to unscheduled spatial interruption,* followed by a string of numbers and symbols in the Speech, a description of the gate's new location. Kit glanced up at the roof, through which the sound of jackhammers could plainly be heard. "The construction," he said. "It must have screwed up the worldgate's interruption of space somehow."

Nita was puzzling over the symbols for the new location. "Isn't that term there the one for height above the ground?" she asked.

"Uh huh. Look at it, it must be sixty, seventy stories straight up from here." Kit slapped the book shut in great annoyance, shoved it back in his backpack. *"Now* what do we do?"

(We go back outside?) Fred said, very hopefully.

It seemed the best suggestion. The three of them walked out again, and Fred bobbed and danced some more in the sunlight while Nita and Kit walked slowly eastward along Forty-second Street, toward the Park Avenue overpass. "Dislocated," Kit muttered. "And who knows how long it'll take to come *un*dislocated? A perfectly good piece of time wasted."

Nita stopped and turned, looking up into the air and trying to estimate where the deli lay under the Grand Central complex. She picked a spot that seemed about right, let her eye travel up and up, sixty, maybe seventy stories. "Kit," she said. "Kit! Look what's seventy stories high, and right next door."

Kit looked. Dark blue and silver, with its big stylized globe logo on one side, the Pan Am Building reared its oblong self up at least seventy stories high, right there—not only right behind Grand Central, but part of it. "Yeah," Kit said, his voice still heavy with annoyance. "So?"

"So you remember that shield spell you showed me? The one that makes the air solid? If you change the quantities in the spell a little, you can use it for something else. To walk on, even. You just keep the air hard."

She couldn't keep from grinning. Kit stared at Nita as if she'd gone crazy. "Are you suggesting that we *walk out* to the worldgate and—" He laughed. "How are we going to get up there?"

"There's a heliport on top of the building," Nita said promptly. "They don't use it for big helicopters any more, but the little ones still land, and there's an elevator in the building that goes right to the top. There's a restaurant up there too; my father had lunch with someone up there once. I bet we could do it."

Kit stared at her. "If you talk the air solid, *you're* going to walk on it first! I saw that spell; it's not that easy."

"I practiced it some. Come on, Kit, you want to waste the timeslide? It's almost ten now! It'll probably be years before these guys are finished digging. Let's do it!"

"They'll never let us up there," Kit said with conviction.

"Oh, yes, they will. They won't have a choice, because Fred'll make a diversion for us. We don't even need anything as big as a Learjet this time. How about it, Fred?"

Fred looked at them reluctantly. (I must admit I *have* been feeling an urge to burp—)

Kit still looked uncertain. "And when we get up there," he said, "all those stories up, and looking as if we're walking on nothing—what if somebody sees us?"

Nita laughed. "Who are they going to tell? And who's going to believe them?"

Kit nodded and then began to grin slowly too. "Yeah," he said. "Yeah! Let's go, it's getting late."

Back they went into Grand Central, straight across the main concourse this time and up one of the six escalators that led up to the lobby of the Pan Am Building. They paused just outside the revolving doors at the end of the escalators. The Pan Am lobby was a big place, pillared and walled and paved in dark granite, echoing with the sound of people hurrying in and out of the station. They went up the escalator to the next floor, and Nita pointed off to one side, indicating an elevator bank. One elevator had a sign standing by it: COPTER CLUB—HELIPAD LEVEL—EXPRESS. Also standing by it was a bored-looking uniformed security guard.

"That's it," Nita said.

"So if we can just get him away from there . . ."

"It's not that simple." She pointed down at the end of the hall between two more banks of elevators. Another guard sat behind a large semicircular desk, watching a row of TV monitors. "They've got cameras all over the place. We've got to get that guy out of there too. Fred, if you're going to do something, do it right between them. Out in front of that desk."

(Well,) Fred said, sounding interested, (let's see, let's see. . . .) He damped his light down and floated off toward the elevators, nearly invisible unless you were looking for him, and even then looking like an unusually large speck of dust, nothing more. The dustmote stopped just between the desk and the elevator guard, hung in midair, and concentrated so fiercely that Nita and Kit could both feel it thirty feet away.

(T-*hup!*)

BANG!

"That'll get their attention," Kit muttered. It did; both the guards started at the noise, began looking around for the source of it—then both went very very slowly over to examine the large barrel cactus in a brass pot that had suddenly appeared in the middle of the shiny floor.

"Now," Kit said, and took off toward the elevator with Nita close behind.

Both the guards had their backs turned, and Nita, passing them, saw the elevator keys hanging off one guard's belt. (Fred,) she said hurriedly, (can you grab those real fast, the way you grabbed my pen? Don't swallow them!)

(Once I might make that mistake,) Fred said, (but not twice.) As they slipped into the elevator Fred paused by the guard's belt, and the keys vanished without so much as a jingle. He sailed in to them. (How was that?)

(Great. Quick, Nita, close the door!)

She punched one of the elevator buttons and the doors slid shut; the keys appeared again, and Kit caught them in midair before they fell. "It's always one of these round ones, like they use on coin phones," he said, going through the keys. "Fred, I didn't know you could make *live* things!"

(I didn't know either,) Fred said, sounding unsettled, (and I'm not sure I like it!)

"Here we go," Kit said, and put one key into the elevator lock, turning it to RUN, and then pressed the button marked 73—RESTAURANT—HELIPAD. The elevator took off in a hurry; it was one of the high-speed sort.

Nita swallowed repeatedly to pop her ears. "Aren't you going to have to change the spells a little to compensate for the gate being up high now?" she said after a moment.

"A little. You just put in the new height coordinate. Oops!"

The elevator began to slow down quickly, and Nita's stomach churned for a moment. She and Kit both pressed themselves against the sides of the elevator, so they wouldn't be immediately visible to anyone who might happen to be standing right outside the door. But when the doors slid open, no one was there. They peered out and saw a long carpeted corridor with a plate-glass door at one end. Through it could be seen tables and chairs and, more dimly, through a window, a hazy view of the East Side skyline. A muffled sound of plates and silverware being handled came down the hall to them.

(It's early for lunch,) Nita said, relieved. (Let's go before someone sees us.)

(What about these keys?)

(Hmm. . . .)

(Look, let's leave them in the elevator lock. That way the guard downstairs'll just think he left them there. If they discover they're missing, they'll start looking for whoever took them—and this would be the first place they'd look.)

(Yeah, but how are we going to get down?)

(We'll walk on air,) Kit said, his voice teasing. Nita rolled her eyes at the ceiling. (Or we'll go down with the people coming out from lunch, if that doesn't work. Let's just get out of *here* first, okay? Which way do we go to get up on the heliport?)

(Left. There are stairs.)

They slipped out of the elevator just as it chimed and its doors shut again

—probably the guard had called it from downstairs. The corridor off to the left was featureless except for one door at its very end. HELIPAD ACCESS, the door said in large red letters. Nita tried the knob, then let her hand fall in exasperation. (Locked. Crud!)

(Well, wait a moment,) Kit said, and tried the knob himself. *"You don't really want to be locked, do you?"* he said aloud in the Speech, very quietly. Again Nita was amazed by how natural the wizards' language sounded when you heard it, and how nice it was to hear—as if, after being lost in a foreign country for a long time, someone should suddenly speak warmly to you in English. *"You've been locked for a couple of days now,"* Kit went on, his voice friendly and persuasive, not casting a spell, just talking—though in the Speech, the two were often dangerously close. *"It must be pretty dull being locked, no one using you, no one paying any attention. Now we need to use you at least a couple of times this morning, so we thought we'd ask—"*

Kt-chk! said the lock, and the knob turned in Kit's hand. *"Thank you,"* he said. *"We'll be back later."* He went through the door into the stairwell, Nita and Fred following, and as the door swung to behind them and locked itself again, there was a decidedly friendly sound to the click. Kit grinned triumphantly at Nita as they climbed the stairs. "How about *that?*"

"Not bad," Nita said, determined to learn how to do it herself, if possible. "You've been practicing too."

"Not really—some of this stuff just seems to come naturally as you work with it more. My mother locked herself out of the car at the supermarket last week and I was pulling on the car door and talking at it—you know how you do when you're trying to get something to work. And then it worked. I almost fell over, the door came open so fast. It's the Speech that does it, I think. Everything loves to hear it."

"Remember what Carl said, though."

"I know. I won't overdo it. You think we ought to call him later, let him know what happened to the gate?"

They came to the top of the stairs, paused before the next closed door, breathing hard from the exertion of climbing the stairs fast. "Probably he knows, if he's looked at his book this morning," Nita said. "Look, before we do anything else, let's set the timeslide. This is a good place for it; we're out of sight. When we're tired of running around the city, we can just activate it and we'll be back here at quarter of eleven. Then we just go downstairs, into Grand Central and downstairs to the shuttle, and then home in time for lunch."

"Sounds good." They began rummaging in their backpacks, and before too long had produced the eight and a half sugar cubes, the lithium-cadmium battery—a fat one, bigger than a D cell and far heavier—a specific integrated-circuit chip salvaged from the innards of a dead pocket calculator, and the handle of a broken glass teacup. "You might want to back away a little, Fred, so your emissions don't interfere with the spell," Kit said.

(Right.) Fred retreated high up into one ceiling-corner of the stairwell, flaring bright with interest. There was a brief smell of burning as he accidentally vaporized a cobweb.

"All right," Kit said, thumbing through his manual to a page marked with a bit of ripped-up newspaper, "here we go. *This is a timeslide inauguration,*" he said aloud in the Speech. "*Claudication type mesarrh-gimel-veignt-six, authorization group—*" Nita swallowed, feeling the strangeness set in as it had during their first spell together, feeling the walls lean in to listen. But it was not a silence that fell this time. As Kit spoke, she became aware of a roaring away at the edge of her hearing and a blurring at the limits of her vision. Both effects grew and strengthened to the overwhelming point almost before she realized what was happening. And then it was too late. She was seeing and hearing everything that would happen for miles and miles around at quarter to eleven, as if the building were transparent, as if she had eyes that could pierce stone and ears that could hear a leaf fall blocks away. The words and thoughts of a million minds poured down on her in a roaring onslaught like a wave crashing down on a swimmer, and she was washed away, helpless. Too many sights, commonplace and strange, glad and frightening, jostled and crowded all around her, and squeezing her eyes shut made no difference—the sights were in her mind. I'll go crazy, I'll go crazy, stop it! But she was caught in the spell and couldn't budge. Stop it, oh, let it stop—

It stopped. She was staring at the floor between her and Kit as she had been doing when the flood of feelings swept over her. Everything was the same as it had been, except that the sugar was gone. Kit was looking at her in concern. "You all right?" he said. "You look a little green."

"Uh, yeah." Nita rubbed her head, which ached slightly as if with the memory of a very loud sound.

"What happened to the sugar?"

"It went away. That means the spell took." Kit began gathering up the rest of the materials and stowing them. He looked at her again. "Are you *sure* you're okay?"

"Yeah, I'm fine." She got up, looked around restlessly. "C'mon, let's go."

Kit got up too, shrugging into his backpack. "Yeah. Which way is the—"

CRACK! went something against the door outside, and Nita's insides constricted. She and Kit both threw themselves against the wall behind the door, where they would be hidden if it opened. For a few seconds neither of them dared to breathe.

Nothing happened.

(What was that?) Kit asked.

(I don't know. It sounded like a shot. Lord, Kit what if there's somebody up here with a gun or something—)

(What's a gun?) Fred said.

(You don't want to know,) Kit said. (Then again, if there *was* somebody out there with a gun, I doubt they could hurt you. Fred, would you go out there and have a quick look around? See who's there?)

(Why not?) Fred floated down from the ceiling, looked the door over, put his light out, and slipped through the keyhole. For a little while there was silence, broken only by the faint faraway rattle of a helicopter going by, blocks away.

Then the lock glowed a little from inside, and Fred popped back in. (I don't see anyone out there,) he said.

Kit looked at Nita. (Then what made that noise?)

She was as puzzled as he was. She shrugged. (Well, if Fred says there's nothing out there—)

(I suppose. But let's keep our eyes open.)

Kit coaxed the door open as he had the first one, and the three of them stepped cautiously out onto the roof.

Most of it was occupied by the helipad proper, the long wide expanse of bare tarmac ornamented with its big yellow square-and-H symbol and surrounded by blue low-intensity landing lights. At one end of the oblong pad was a small glass-walled building decorated with the Pan Am logo, a distended orange windsock, and an anemometer, its three little cups spinning energetically in the brisk morning wind. Beyond the helipad, the roof was graveled, and various low-set ventilator stacks poked up here and there. A yard-high guardrail edged the roof. Rising up on all sides was Manhattan, a stony forest of buildings in all shapes and heights. To the west glimmered the Hudson River and the Palisades on the New Jersey side; on the other side of the building lay the East River and Brooklyn and Queens, veiled in mist and pinkish smog. The Sun would have felt warm if the wind had stopped blowing. No one was up there at all.

Nita took a few steps off the paved walkway that led to the little glass building and scuffed at the gravel suspiciously. "This wind is pretty stiff," she said. "Maybe a good gust of it caught some of this gravel and threw it at the door." But even as she said it, she didn't believe it.

"Maybe," Kit said. His voice made it plain that he didn't believe it either. "Come on, let's find the gate."

"That side," Nita said, pointing south, where the building was wider. They headed toward the railing together, crunching across the gravel. Fred perched on Nita's shoulder; she looked at him with affection. "Worried?"

(No. But you are.)

"A little. That sound shook me up." She paused again, wondering if she heard something behind her. She turned. Nothing; the roof was bare. But still— Nita turned back and hurried to catch up with Kit, who was looking back at her.

"Something?"

"I don't know. I doubt it. You know how you see things out of the corner of your eye, movements that aren't there? I thought maybe the door moved a little."

"I don't know about you," Kit said, "but I'm not going to turn my back on anything while I'm up here. Fred, keep your eyes open." Kit paused by the railing, examining the ledge below it, maybe six feet wide, then looked up again. "On second thought, do you *have* eyes?"

(I don't know,) Fred said, confused but courteous as always. (Do you have chelicerae?)

"Good question," Nita said, a touch nervously. "Kit, let's do this and get out of here."

He nodded, unslung his pack, and laid the aspirin, pine cone, and fork on the gravel by the railing. Nita got out the rowan wand and dropped it with the other materials, while Kit went through his book again, stopping at another marked spot. "Okay," he said after a moment. *"This is an imaging-and-patency spell for a temporospatial claudication, asdekh class. Purpose: retrieval of an accidentally internalized object, matter-energy quotient . . ."* Kit read a long string of syllables, a description in the Speech of Nita's pen, followed by another symbol group that meant Fred and described the properties of the little personal worldgate that kept his great mass at a great distance.

Nita held her breath, waiting for another onslaught of uncanny feelings, but none ensued. When Kit stopped reading and the spell turned her loose, it was almost a surprise to see, hanging there in the air, the thing they had been looking for. Puckered, roughly oblong, vaguely radiant, an eight-foot scar on the sky; the worldgate, about a hundred feet out from the edge where they stood and maybe thirty feet below the heliport level.

"Well," Kit said then, sounding very pleased with himself. "There we are. And it looks all right, not much different from the description in the book."

"Now all we have to do is get to it." Nita picked up the rowan wand, which for the second part of the spell would serve as a key to get the pen through the worldgate and out of Fred. She tucked the wand into her belt, leaned on the railing, and looked out at the air.

According to the wizards' manual, air, like the other elements, had a memory and could be convinced in the Speech to revert to something it had been before. It was this memory of being locked in stone as oxides or nitrates, or frozen solid in the deeps of space, that made the air harden briefly for the shielding spell. Nita started that spell in its simplest form and then went on into a more formal one, as much a reminiscence as a convincing—she talked to the air about the old days when starlight wouldn't twinkle because there was nothing to make it do so, and when every shadow was sharp as a razor, and distances didn't look distant because there was no air to soften them. The immobility came down around her as the spell began to say itself along with Nita, matching her cadence. She kept her eyes closed, not looking, for fear something that should be happening might not be. Slowly with her words she began to shape the hardening air into an oblong, pushing it out through the other, thinner air she wasn't including in the spell. It's working better than usual, faster, she thought. Maybe it's all the smog here—this air's half solid already. She kept talking.

Kit whispered something, but she couldn't make out what and didn't want to try. *"I know it's a strain, being solid these days,"* she whispered in the Speech, *"but just for a little while. Just to make a walkway out to that puckered place in the sky, then you can relax. Nothing too thick, just strong enough to walk on—"*

"Nita. *Nita!*"

The sound of her name in the Speech caught her attention. She opened her eyes. Arrow-straight, sloping down from the lower curb of the railing between her and Kit, the air had gone hard. There was dirt and smog trapped in it, making the sudden walkway more translucent than transparent—but there was no mistaking it for anything but air. It had a more delicate, fragile look than any glass ever could, no matter how thin. The walkway ran smooth and even all the way out to the worldgate, widening beneath it into room enough for two to stand.

"Wow!" Nita said, sagging against the railing and rubbing at her eyes as she let the spell go. She was tired; the spelling was a strain—and that feeling of nervousness left over from the loud noise outside the stairwell came back. She glanced over her shoulder again, wondering just what she was looking for.

Kit peered over the railing at the walkway. "This better be some pen," he said, and turned his back to the worldgate, watching the roof. "Go ahead."

Nita made sure her backpack was slung properly, checked the rowan wand again, and slowly swung over the guardrail, balancing on the stone in which it was rooted. She was shaking, and her hands were wet. If I don't just do this, she thought, I never will. Just one step down, Callahan, and then a nice solid walkway straight across. Really. Believe. Believe. Ouch!

The air was so transparent that she misjudged the distance down to it—her foot hit before she thought it would, and the jolt went right up her spine. Still holding the railing, Nita lifted that foot a bit, then stomped down hard on the walkway. It was no different from stomping on a sidewalk. She let her weight down on that foot, brought the second down, and stomped with that too. It *was* solid.

"Like rock, Kit!" she said, looking up at him, still holding the rail. "C'mon!"

"Sure," Kit said, skeptical. "Let go of the rail first."

Nita made a face at Kit and let go. She held both arms out at first, as she might have on a balance beam in gym, and then waved them experimentally. "See? It works. Fred?"

Fred bobbed down beside her, looking with interest at the hardened air of the walkway. (And it will stay this way?)

"Until I turn it loose. Well?" She took a step backward, farther onto the walkway, and looked up challengingly. "How about it?"

Kit said nothing, just slung his own backpack over his shoulders and swung over the railing as Nita had done, coming down cautiously on the hardened air. He held on to the rail for a moment while conducting his own tests of the air's solidity. "Come on," Nita said. "The wind's not too bad."

"Lead the way."

Nita turned around, still holding her arms a little away from her to be sure of her balance, and started for the worldgate as quickly as she dared, with Fred pacing her cheerfully to the left. Eight or ten steps more and it was becoming almost easy. She even glanced down toward the walkway—and there she stopped very suddenly, her stomach turning right over in her at the sight of the dirty, graveled roof of Grand Central, a long, long, *long* fall below. "Don't look down," a memory said to her in Machu Picchu's scratchy voice. She swallowed, shaking all over, wishing she had remembered the advice earlier.

"Nita, what's the—"

Something went *whack!* into the walkway. Nita jumped, lost her balance, and staggered back into Kit. For a few awful seconds they teetered back and forth in wind that gusted suddenly, pushing them toward the edge together —and then Kit sat down hard on the walkway, and Nita half fell on top of him, and they held very still for a few gasps.

"Wh-what—"

"I think it was a pigeon," Nita said, not caring whether Kit heard the tremulousness of her voice. "You okay?"

"Sure," Kit said, just as shakily. "I try to have a heart attack every day whether I need one or not. Get off my knee, huh?"

They picked each other up and headed for the gate again. (Even you have trouble with gravity,) Fred said wonderingly as he paced them. (I'm glad I left my mass elsewhere.)

"So are we," Nita said. She hurried the last twenty steps or so to the widened place at the end of the walkway, with Kit following close.

She knelt down in a hurry, to make sure the wind wouldn't push her over again, and looked up at the worldgate. Seen this close it was about four feet by eight, the shape of a tear in a piece of cloth. It shone with a palely glowing, shifting, soap-bubble iridescence. Finally, finally, my pen! she thought—but somehow the thought didn't make Nita as happy as it should have. The uneasy feeling that had started in the stairwell was still growing. She glanced over her shoulder at Kit. He was kneeling too, with his back to her, watching the walkway and the rooftop intently. Beside her, Fred hung quietly waiting.

(Now what?) he asked.

Nita sighed, pulled the rowan rod out of her belt, and inserted one end of it delicately into the shimmering veil that was the surface of the worldgate. Though the city skyline could be seen very clearly through the shimmer, the inch or so of the wand that went through it appeared to vanish. "Just perch yourself on the free end here," Nita said, holding the wand by its middle. "Make contact with it the same way you did with those keys. Okay?"

(Simple enough.) Fred floated to the end of the rod and lit there, a bright, still spark. (All right, I'm ready.)

Nita nodded. *"This is a retrieval,"* she said in the Speech. *"Involvement confined to a pen with the following characteristics: m'sedh-zayin six point three—"*

(Nita!)

The note of pure terror in Kit's mind-voice caused Nita to do the unforgivable—break off in the middle of a spell and look over her shoulder. Shapes were pouring out of the little glass shelter building, which had been empty, and was still somehow empty even as Nita looked. She got a first impression of grizzled coats, red tongues that lolled and slavered, fangs that gleamed in the sunlight, and she thought, Wolves!

But their eyes changed her mind as ten or twelve of the creatures loped across the roof toward the transparent walkway, giving tongue in an awful mindless cacophony of snarls and barks and shuddering howls. The eyes. *People's* eyes, blue, brown, green, but with almost all the intelligence gone out of them, nothing left but a hot deadly cunning and an awful desire for the taste of blood. From her reading in the wizards' manual, she knew what they were: perytons. Wolves would have been preferable—wolves were sociable creatures. *These* had been people once, people so used to hating that at the end of life they'd found a way to keep doing it, by hunting the souls of others through their nightmares. And once a peryton caught you . . .

Nita started to hitch backward in total panic and then froze, realizing that there was nowhere to go. She and Kit were trapped. Another second and the perytons would be on the bridge, and at their throats, for eternity. Kit whipped his head around toward Nita and the worldgate. "Jump through and break the spell!" he yelled.

"But—" And she grabbed his arm, pushed the rowan wand through her belt, and yelled, "Come on, Fred!" The first three perytons leaped the guard-rail and landed on the bridge, running. Nita threw herself and Kit at the worldgate, being careful of the edges, as she knew she must, while screaming in absolute terror the word that would dissolve the walkway proper.

For a fraction of a second she caught the sound of screams other than her own, howls of creatures unseen but falling. Then the shimmer broke against her face like water, shutting out sound, and light, and finally thought. Blinded, deafened, and alone, she fell forever. . . .

Exocontinual Protocols

She lay with her face pressed against the cold harsh gravel, feeling the grit of it against her cheek, the hot tears as they leaked between her lashes, and that awful chill wind that wouldn't stop tugging at her clothes. Very slowly Nita opened her eyes, blinked, and gradually realized that the problem with the place where she lay was not her blurred vision. It was just very dim there. She leaned on her skinned hands, pushed herself up, and looked to see where she was.

Dark-gray gravel was all around. Farther off, something smooth and dark, with navy-blue bumps. The helipad. Farther still, the railing, and beyond it the sky, dark. That was odd—it had been morning. The sound of a moan made Nita turn her head. Kit was close by, lying on his side with his hands over his face. Sitting on his shoulder, looking faint as a spark about to go out, was Fred.

Nita sat up straighter, even though it made her head spin. She had fallen a long way, she didn't want to remember how far. . . . "Kit," she whispered. "You okay? Fred?"

Kit turned over, pushed himself up on his hands to a sitting position, and groaned again. Fred clung to him. "I don't think I busted anything," Kit said, slow and uncertain. "I hurt all over. Fred, what about you?"

(The Sun is gone,) Fred said, sounding absolutely horrified.

Kit looked out across the helipad into the darkness and rubbed his eyes. "Me and my bright ideas. What have I got us into?"

"As much my bright idea as yours," Nita said. "If it weren't for me, we wouldn't have been out by that worldgate in the first place. Anyway, Kit, where else could we have gone? Those perytons—"

Kit shuddered. "Don't even talk about them. I'd sooner be here than have *them* get me." He got to his knees, then stood up, swaying for a moment. "Oooh. C'mon, let's see where the worldgate went."

He headed off across the gravel. Nita got up on her knees too, then caught sight of a bit of glitter lying a few feet away and grabbed at it happily. Her pen, none the worse for wear. She clipped it securely to the pocket of her shirt and went after Kit and Fred.

Kit was heading for the south-facing railing. "I guess since you only called for a retrieval, the gate dumped us back on top of the . . ."

His voice trailed off suddenly as he reached the railing. Nita came up beside him and saw why.

The city was changed. A shiver ran all through Nita, like the odd feeling that comes with an attack of *déjà vu*—but this was true memory, not the illusion of it. She recognized the place from her first spell with Kit—the lowering, sullen-feeling gloom, the shadowed island held prisoner between its dark, icy rivers. Frowning buildings hunched themselves against the oppressive, slaty sky. Traffic moved, but very little of it, and it did so in the dark. Few headlights or taillights showed anywhere. The usual bright stream of cars and trucks and buses was here only dimly seen motion and a faint sound of snarling engines. And the sky! It wasn't clouded over; it wasn't night. It was *empty*. Just a featureless grayness, hanging too low, like a ceiling. Simply by looking at it Nita knew that Fred was right. There was no Sun behind it, and there were no stars—only this wall of gloom, shutting them in, imprisoning them with the presence Nita remembered from the spell, that she could feel faintly even now. It wasn't aware of her, but— She pushed back away from the rail, remembering the rowan's words. (The Other. The Witherer, the Kindler of Wildfires—)

"Kit," she said, whispering, this time doing it to keep from perhaps being overheard by *that*. "I think we better get out of here."

He backed away from the rail too, a step at a time. "Well," he said, very low, "now we know what your pen was doing in New York City. . . ."

"The sooner it's out of here, the happier I'll be. Kit—*where did the world-gate go!*"

He shook his head, came back to stand beside her. "Wherever it went, it's not out *there* now."

Nita let out an unhappy breath. "Why should it be? Everything else is changed." She looked back at the helipad. The stairwell was still there, but its door had been ripped away and lay buckled on the gravel. The helipad itself had no design painted on it for a helicopter to center on when landing. The glass of the small building by the pad was smashed in some places and filmed all around; the building was full of rubble and trash, a ruin. "Where *are* we?" Nita said.

"The place we saw in the spell. Manhattan—"

"But different." Nita chewed her lip nervously. "Is this an alternate world, maybe? The next universe over? The worldgate *was* just set for a retrieval, but we jumped through; maybe we messed up its workings. Carl said this one was easy to mess up."

"I wonder how much trouble you get in for busting a worldgate," Kit muttered.

"I think we're in enough trouble right now. We have to *find* the thing."

(See if you can find me the Sun and the stars and the rest of the Universe while you're at it,) Fred said. He sounded truly miserable, much worse than when he had swallowed the pen. (I don't know how long I can bear this silence.)

Kit stood silent for a moment, staring out at that grim cold cityscape. "There *is* a spell we can use to find it that doesn't need anything but words," he said. "Good thing. We don't have much in the way of supplies. We'll need your help, though, Fred. Your claudication was connected to the worldgate's when we went through. You can be used to trace it."

(Anything to get us out of this place,) Fred said.

"Well," Nita said, "let's find a place to get set up."

The faint rattling noise of helicopter rotors interrupted her. She looked westward along the long axis of the roof, toward the dark half-hidden blot that was Central Park, or another version of it.

A small flying shape came wheeling around the corner of a skyscraper a few blocks away and cruised steadily toward the roof where they stood, the sharp chatter of its blades ricocheting more and more loudly off the blank dark faces of neighboring skyscrapers. "We better get under cover," Kit said. Nita started for the stairwell, and Kit headed after her, but a bit more slowly. He kept throwing glances over his shoulder at the approaching chopper, both worried by it and interested in it. Nita looked over her shoulder too, to tell him to hurry—and then realized how close the chopper was, how fast it was coming. A standard two-seat helicopter, wiry skeleton, glass bubble protecting the seats, oval doors on each side. But the bubble's glass was filmed over except for the doors, which glittered oddly. They had a faceted look. No pilot could see out that, Nita thought, confused. And the skids, the landing skids are wrong somehow. The helicopter came sweeping over their heads, low, too low.

"KIT!" Nita yelled. She spun around and tackled him, knocking him flat, as the skids made a lightning jab at the place where he had been a moment before, and hit the gravel with a screech of metal. The helicopter soared on past them, refolding its skids, not yet able to slow down from the speed of its first attack. The thunderous rattling of its rotors mixed with another sound, a high frustrated shriek like that of a predator that has missed its kill—and almost immediately they heard something else too, an even higher-pitched squealing, ratchety and metallic, produced by several sources and seeming to come from inside the ruined glass shelter.

Kit and Nita clutched at each other, getting a better look at the helicopter from behind as it swung around for another pass. The "skids" were doubled-back limbs of metal like those of a praying mantis, cruelly clawed. Under what should have been the helicopter's "bubble," sharp dark mandibles worked hungrily—and as the chopper heeled over and came about, those faceted eyes *looked* at Kit and Nita with the cold, businesslike glare reserved for helpless prey.

"We're dead," Nita whispered.

"Not yet." Kit gasped, staggering up again. "The stairwell—" Together he and Nita ran for the stairs as the chopper-creature arrowed across the rooftop at them. Nita was almost blind with terror; she knew now what had torn the door off the stairwell and doubted there was any way to keep that thing from getting them. They fell into the stairwell together. The chopper roared past again, not losing so much time in its turn this time, coming about to hover like a deadly dragonfly while positioning itself for another jab with those steel claws. Kit fell farther down the stairs than Nita did, hit his head against a wall and lay moaning. Nita slid and scrabbled to a stop, then turned to see that huge, horrible face glaring into the stairwell, sighting on her for the jab. It was unreal. None of it could possibly be real; it was all a dream; and with the inane desperation of a dreamer in nightmare, Nita felt for the only thing at hand, the rowan rod, and slashed at the looming face with it.

She was completely unprepared for the result. A whip of silver fire the color of the Moon at full cracked across the bubble-face from the rod, which glowed in her hand. Screaming in pain and rage, the chopper-creature backed up and away, but only a little. The razor-combed claws shot down at her. She slashed at them too, and when the moonfire curled around them, the creature screamed again and pulled them back.

"Kit!" she yelled, not daring to turn her back on those raging, ravenous eyes. "Kit! The antenna!"

She heard him fumbling around in his pack as the hungry helicopter took another jab at her, and she whipped it again with fire. Quite suddenly something fired past her ear—a bright, narrow line of blazing red light the color of metal in the forge. The molten light struck the helicopter in the underbelly, splattering in bright hot drops, and the answering scream was much more terrible this time.

"It's a machine," Nita said, gasping. "Your department."

"Great," Kit said, crawling up the stairs beside her. "How do you kill a helicopter?" But he braced one arm on the step just above his face, laid the antenna over it, and fired again. The chopper-creature screeched again and swung away.

Kit scrambled up to his feet, pressed himself flat against what remained of the crumbling doorway, pointed the antenna again. Red fire lanced out, followed by Nita's white as she dove back out into the stinging wind and thunder of rotors and slashed at the horror that hung and grabbed from midair. Gravel flew and stung, the wind lashed her face with her hair, the air was full of that ear-tearing metallic scream, but she kept slashing. White fire snapped and curled—and then from around the other side of the chopper-creature there came a sharp *crack!* as a bolt of Kit's hot light fired upward. The scream that followed made all the preceding ones sound faint. Nita wished she could drop the wand and cover her ears, but she didn't dare—and anyway she was too puzzled by the creature's reaction. That shot hadn't hit anywhere on its body that she could see. Still screaming, it began to spin helplessly in a circle like a toy pinwheel. Kit had shattered the helicopter's tail rotor. It might still be airborne, but it couldn't fly straight, or steer. Nita danced back from another jab of those legs, whipped the eyes again with the silver fire of the rowan wand as they spun past her. From the other side there was another *crack!* and a shattering sound, and the bubble-head spinning past her again showed one faceted eye now opaque, spiderwebbed with cracks. The helicopter lurched and rose, trying to gain altitude and get away.

Across the roof Kit looked up, laid the antenna across his forearm again, took careful aim, fired. This time the molten line of light struck through the blurring main rotors. With a high, anguished, ringing snap, one rotor flew off and went pinwheeling away almost too fast to see. The helicopter gave one last wild screech, bobbled up, then sideways, as if staggering through the air. "Get down!" Kit screamed at Nita, throwing himself on the ground. She did the same, covering her head with her arms and frantically gasping the syllables of the defense-shield spell.

The explosion shook everything and sent gravel flying to bounce off the hardened air around her like hail off a car roof. Jagged blade shards snapped and rang and shot in all directions. Only when the roaring and the wash of heat that followed it died down to quiet and flickering light did Nita dare to raise her head. The helicopter-creature was a broken-backed wreck with oily flame licking through it. The eye that Kit had shattered stared blindly up at the dark sky from the edge of the helipad; the tail assembly, twisted and bent, lay half under the creature's body. The only sounds left were the wind and that shrill keening from the little glass building, now much muted. Nita rid herself of the shielding spell and got slowly to her feet. "Fred?" she whispered.

A pale spark floated shakily through the air to perch on her shoulder. (Here,) he said, sounding as tremulous as Nita felt. (Are you well?)

She nodded, walked toward the wreck. Kit stood on the other side of it, his fist clenched on the antenna. He was shaking visibly. The sight of his terror made Nita's worse as she came to stand by him. "Kit," she said, fighting the urge to cry and losing—tears spilled out anyway. "This is *not* a nice place," she said.

He gulped, leaking tears himself. "No," he said, trying to keep his voice steady, "it sure isn't." He looked over at the glass-walled building.

"Yeah," Nita said, scrubbing at her face. "We better have a look."

Slowly and carefully they approached the building, came to one collapsed wall, peered in. Nita held her wand high, so they could see by its glow. Inside, hidden amid the trash and broken glass, was what seemed to be a rude nest built of scraps of metal and wire. In the nest were three baby helicopters, none more than two feet long. They stared fiercely at Kit and Nita from tiny faceted eyes like their parent's, and threatened with little jabbing forelegs, whirring with rotors too small to lift them yet. Sharing the nest with the fledglings was the partially stripped skeleton of a dog.

Kit and Nita turned away together. "I think maybe we should go downstairs a little ways before we do that finding spell," Kit said, his voice still shaking. "If there's another of those things—"

"Yeah." They headed down the stairwell, to the door that in their own world had opened onto the elevator corridor. The two of them sat down, and Nita laid the rowan wand in her lap so there would be light—the ceiling lights in the stairwell were out, and the place felt like the bottom of a hole.

"Fred," Kit said, "how're you holding up?"

Fred hung between them, his light flickering. (A little better than before. The silence is still very terrible. But at least you two are here.)

"We'll find you the Sun, Fred," Nita said, wishing she was as sure as she was trying to sound. "Kit, which spell was it you were going to use?"

Kit had his manual out. "At the bottom of three eighteen. It's a double, we read together."

Nita got out her own book, paged through it. "McKillip's Stricture? That's for keeping grass short!"

"No, no!" Kit leaned over to look at Nita's manual. "Huh. How about that, our pages are different. Look under 'Eisodics and Diascheses.' The fourth one after the general introduction. Davidson's Minor Enthalpy."

Nita ruffled through some more pages. Evidently her book had more information than Kit's on the spells relating to growing things. Her suspicion about what their specialties were grew stronger. "Got it." She glanced through the spell. "Fred, you don't have to do anything actually. But this is one of those spells that'll leave us blind to what's happening around here. Watch for us?"

(Absolutely!)

"Okay," Kit said. "Ready? One—two—three—"

They spoke together, slowly and carefully, matching cadence as they described the worldgate, and their own needs, in the Speech.

The shadowy stairwell grew darker still, though this darkness seemed less hostile than what hung overhead; and in the deepening dimness, the walls around them slowly melted away. It seemed to Nita that she and Kit and the small bright point between them hung at a great height, unsupported, over a city built of ghosts and dreams. The buildings that had looked real and solid from the roof now seemed transparent skeletons, rearing up into the gloom of this place. Stone and steel and concrete were shadows—and gazing through them, down the length of the island, Nita saw again the two points of light that she and Kit had seen in the first spell.

The closer one, perhaps ten blocks north in the east Fifties, still pulsed with its irregular, distressing light. Compelled by the spell's working, Nita looked closely at it, though that was the last thing she wanted to do—that bit of angry brightness seemed to be looking back at her. But she had no choice. She examined the light, and into her mind, poured there by the spell, came a description of the light's nature in the Speech. She would have backed away, as she had from the perytons, except that again there was nowhere to go. A catalogue, of sorts, that light was—a listing, a set of descriptions. But all wrong, all twisted, angry as the light looked, hungry as the helicopter-creature had been, hating as the surrounding darkness was, full of the horrors that everything in existence could become. The *Book which is not Named*—

Nita struggled, though unable to move or cry out; her mind beat at the spell like a bird in a cage, and finally the spell released her. But only to look in the other direction, downtown toward the Wall Street end of the island. There in the illogical-looking tangle of streets built before the regular gridwork of Manhattan was laid down, buried amid the ghosts of buildings, another light throbbed, regular, powerful, unafraid. It flared, it dazzled with white-silver fire, and Nita thought of the moonlight radiance of the rowan wand.

In a way, the spell said, this second light was the source of the wand's power, even though here and now the source was bound and limited. This time the syllables of the Speech were no crushing weight of horror. They were a song, one Nita wished would never stop. Courage, merriment, an invitation to everything in existence to be what it was, be the best it could be, grow, *live*—description, affirmation, encouragement, all embodied in one place, one source, buried in the shadows. The *Book of Night with Moon*.

A feeling of urgency came over Nita, and the spell told her that without the protection of the bright *Book*, she and Kit and Fred would never survive the hungry malevolence of this place long enough to find the worldgate and escape. Nor, for that matter, would they be able to find the worldgate at all; it was being held against them by powers adept in wizardries more potent

than anything the two of them could manage. It would be folly to try matching wizardries with the Lone Power on its own ground, this outworld long
given over to its rule. Their best chance was to find the bright *Book* and free
it of the constraint that held its power helpless. Then there might be a
chance.

The spell shut itself off, finished. Walls and physical darkness curdled
around them again. Kit and Nita looked at each other, uncertain.

"We've been had," Kit said.

Nita shook her head, not following him.

"Remember Tom saying it was odd that our first spell turned up Fred and
the news that the bright *Book* was missing? And what Picchu said then?"

"There are no accidents," Nita murmured.

"Uh huh. How likely do you think it is that all *this* is an accident? Something *wanted* us here, I bet." Kit scowled. "They might have asked *us!* It's
not fair!"

Nita held still for a moment, considering this. "Well, maybe they did ask
us."

"Huh? Not *me*, I—"

"The Oath."

Kit got quiet quickly. "Well," he admitted after a while, "it did have all
kinds of warnings in front of it. And I went ahead and read it anyway."

"So did I." Nita closed her eyes for a second, breathing out, and heard
something in the back of her head, a thread of memory: *Did I do right? Go
find out. . . .* "Look," she said, opening her eyes again, "maybe we're not as
bad off as we think. Tom did say that younger wizards have more power. We
don't have a lot of supplies, but we're both pretty good with the Speech by
now, and Fred is here to help. We're armed—" She glanced down at the
rowan wand, still lying moon-bright in her lap.

"For how long?" Kit said. He sighed too. "Then again, I guess it doesn't
matter much—if we're going to find the bright *Book*, the only way to do it is
to hurry. Somebody knows we're here. That thing showed up awful fast—"
He nodded at the roof.

"Yeah." Nita got up, took a moment to stretch, then glanced down at Kit.
He wasn't moving. "What's the matter?"

Kit stared at the antenna in his hands. "When I was talking to the Edsel,"
he said, "it told me some things about the Powers that didn't want intelligence to happen in machines. They knew that people would start talking to
them, make friends with them. Everybody would be happier as a result.
Those Powers—" He looked up. "If I understood that spell right, the one
running this place is the chief of them all, the worst of them. The Destroyer,
the engenderer of rust—"

"Kit!"

"I know, you shouldn't name it—" He got up, held out a hand to Fred, who bobbled over to Kit and came to rest on his palm. "But that's who we're up against. Or what. Fred, do you know what we're talking about?"

Fred's thought was frightened but steady. (The Starsnuffer,) he said. (The one who saw light come to be and could not make it in turn—and so rebelled against it, and declared a war of darkness. Though the rebellion didn't work as well as it might have, for darkness only made the light seem brighter.)

Kit nodded. "That's the one. If we do get the bright *Book,* that's who'll come after us."

Fred shuddered, a flicker of light so like a spark about to go out in the wind that Kit hurriedly tucked the antenna under his arm and cupped his other hand around Fred protectively. (I've lost enough friends to that one,) Fred said, (heard enough songs stilled. People gone nova before their time, or fallen through naked singularities into places where you burn forever but don't learn anything from it.)

For a moment neither of them could follow Fred's thought. Though he was using the Speech, as always, they couldn't follow what other things he was describing, only that they were as terrible to him as a warped thing like the helicopter-creature was to them. (No matter,) he said at last. (You two are part of the answer to stopping that kind of thing. Otherwise my search for an Advisory nexus wouldn't have brought me to you. Let's do what we can.)

Kit nodded. "Whatever that is. I wish I knew where to begin."

Nita leaned back against the wall. "Didn't Tom say something about the two Books being tied together? So that you could use one to guide you to the other?"

"Yeah."

"Well. We're not too far from the dark one." Nita swallowed. "If we could get hold of that—and use it to lead us to the bright one. That vision only gave a general idea of where the *Book of Night with Moon* was. Probably because of it being restrained, or guarded, or whatever—"

Kit looked at Nita as if she had taken leave of her senses. "Steal the dark Book? Sure! And then have—" He waved his hand at the northward wall, not wanting to say any name. "—and Lord knows what else come chasing after us?"

"Why not?" Nita retorted. "It's a better chance than going straight for the bright one, which we *know* is guarded somehow. We'd go fumbling around down there in the financial district and probably get caught right away. But why would they guard the dark Book? They're the only ones who would want it! I bet you we could get at the dark one a lot more easily than the other."

Kit chewed his lip briefly. "Well?" Nita said. "What do you think?"

"I think you're probably nuts. But we can't just sit here, and it wouldn't hurt to go see what the situation is—Fred?"

(Lead,) Fred said, (I'll follow.)

Kit gently tossed Fred back into the air and paused long enough to put his book away. He didn't put the antenna away, though. The rowan wand glowed steadily, and brilliantly. "Can't you damp that down a little?" Kit said. "If somebody sees us—"

"No, I can't. I tried." Nita cast about for ways to hide it, finally settled on sticking it in her back jeans pocket and settling her down vest over it. "Better?"

"Yeah." Kit had turned his attention to the doorknob. He touched it, spoke softly to it in the Speech, turned it. Nothing happened. "Not listening?" he wondered out loud, and bent to touch the keyhole. "Now why— Ow!" He jumped back, almost knocking Nita over.

"What's the matter?"

Kit was sucking on his finger, looking pained. "Bit me!" he said, removing the finger to examine it. It bled.

"I get the feeling," Nita said slowly, "that there's not much here that's friendly."

"Yeah." Kit looked glumly at the doorknob. "I guess we'd better consider everything we see potentially dangerous." He lifted the antenna, bent down by the lock again, and touched the keyhole delicately with the knob at the antenna's end. A brief red spark spat from the antenna; the innards of the lock clicked. This time when Kit turned the knob, the door came open a crack.

With great caution he opened the door a bit more, peered out, then opened it all the way and motioned Nita to follow him. Together they stepped out into a hall much like the elevator corridor in their own world, but dark and silent. (The elevator?) Kit said inwardly, not wanting to break that ominous quiet.

(Do you trust it?)

(No. Know where the stairs are?)

(Down the way we came. Past the elevator.)

The door to the main stairway had to be coerced into opening by the same method as the door to the roof. When they were through it Kit spent another moment getting it to lock again, then stepped over to the banister and looked down at story after story of switchback stairs. (It could be worse,) Nita said. (We could be going up.)

(It *will* be worse,) Kit said. (If the worldgate stays at this level, we're going to *have* to come back up. . . .)

They headed down. It took a long time. The few times they dared stop to rest, Kit and Nita heard odd muffled noises through the walls—vaguely threatening scrapes and groans and rumbles, the kind of sounds heard in nightmares. The stairs were as dark as the corridor had been, and it was hard to sit in the corner of a landing, rubbing aching legs, with only the light of Nita's wand to argue with the blackness that towered above and yawned below, as those sounds got louder.

They quickly lost count of how many stories downward they'd gone. All the landings looked the same, and all the doors from them opened off into the same pitch-blackness—until finally Kit eased one open as he had eased open scores of others and abruptly stood very still. He put his hand out behind him. (Nita! The wand.)

She passed it to him. It dimmed in his hand from moonfire to foxfire, a faint silver glimmer that he held out the door as he looked around. (It's all that shiny stone, like the other lobby. There should be a way down into the station, then—)

Nita's hair stood up on end at the thought. (Kit, you saw what happened to helicopters. Do you really want to meet a *train?* Let's go out on the street level, okay?)

He gulped and nodded. (Which way?)

(There's a door out onto Forty-fifth Street. C'mon.)

She slipped out, and Kit followed with the wand. Its pale light reached just far enough ahead to gleam off the glass wall at the end of the corridor. Near it was the down escalator, frozen dead. They made their way softly down it, then across the slick floor and out the glass doors to the street.

It was nearly as dark outside as it had been inside; a night without a hint of Moon or stars. The air down there wasn't as chill as it had been on the building's roof, but it stank of dark city smells—exhaust, spilled gasoline, garbage, and soot. The gutter was clogged with trash. They stepped out to cross Forty-fifth—

"No," Nita hissed, startled into speech, and dragged Kit back into the dark of the doorway. Pale yellow-brown light flickered down the street, got brighter. A second later, with a snarl of its engine, a big yellow Checker Cab hurled itself past them, staring in front of it with headlight-eyes burned down to yellow threads of filament—eyes that looked somehow as if they could see. But the cab seemed not to notice them. Its snarl diminished as it plunged down the street, leaving a whirl of dirty paper and dead leaves in its wake. Kit coughed as its exhaust hit them.

(That was alive,) he said when he got his breath back. (The same way the helicopter was.)

Nita made a miserable face. (Let's get outa here,) she said.

Kit nodded. She led him off to their left, through the Helmsley-Spear Building, which should have been bright with gold-leafed statuary. Here it was gray with soot, and the carvings stared down with such looks of silent malice that Nita refused to glance up more than that once.

She hoped for some more encouraging sight as they came onto Forty-sixth Street and looked up Park Avenue. The hope was vain. The avenue stretched away and slightly upward for blocks as it did in their own world, vanishing in the murk. But the divider between the uptown and downtown lanes, usually green with shrubbery, had become one long tangle of barren thorn bushes. The old-fashioned red-and-green traffic lights burned low and dark as if short on power; and no matter how long one watched, they never changed from red. The shining glass-and-steel office buildings that had lined the avenue in their Manhattan were grimy shells here, the broad sidewalks before them cluttered with rubbish. Nothing moved anywhere, except far up Park, where another pair of yellow eyes waited at a corner.

Those eyes made Nita nervous. (This way,) she said. She hurried past a dirty granite facade full of still doors and silent windows. Kit followed close, and Fred with him, both looking worriedly at everything they passed.

Nita was doing her best to keep herself calm as they turned the corner onto Forty-seventh. It can't all be as bad as the helicopter, she told herself. And nothing really bad has happened to us yet. It was just the shock of the—

She jumped back into the shadow of a building on hearing a clapping sound so loud she felt sure the helicopter's mate was coming for them. Fred and Kit huddled terrified into that shadow too, and it took a few seconds for any of them to find the source of the sound. Not more than five or six feet from them, a pigeon had landed—a sooty-dark one, cooing and strutting and head-bobbing in a perfectly normal fashion. It walked away from them, muttering absently, intent on its own pursuits. Kit poked Nita from behind—not a warning: a teasing poke. (Getting jumpy, huh.)

(Yeah, well, *you* were the one who said—)

The lightning-stroke of motion not six feet away knocked the merriment right out of them. What had seemed a perfectly ordinary fire hydrant, dull yellow, with rust stains and peeling paint, suddenly cracked open and shot out a long, pale, ropy tongue like a toad's. The pigeon never had a chance. Hit side-on, the bird made just one strangled gobbling noise before the tongue was gone again, too fast to follow, and the wide horizontal mouth it came from was closed again. All that remained to show that anything had happened was a slight bulge under the metallic-looking skin of the fire hydrant. The bulge heaved once and was still.

Nita bit her lip. Behind her she could feel Kit start shaking again. (I feel sorry for the next dog that comes along,) he said. (I hope you don't mind if I cross the street.) Kit headed out of the shadow.

(I think I'll join you,) Nita said. She backed out of range of that tongue before she started across the street herself—

There was no time to move, to scream, even to think. Kit was halfway across the street, with his eye on that fire hydrant, his head turned away from the big yellow Checker Cab that was maybe six feet away and leaping straight at him.

A flash of brilliance struck Nita like a blow, and did the same for the cab, so that it swerved to its left and knocked Kit sideways and down. The cab roared on by, engine racing in frustration, evidently too angry to try for another pass. But something about it, maybe the savage sidelong look it threw Nita out of its burned-down eyes as it squealed around the corner of Forty-sixth and Madison—something made Nita suspect that it would not forget them. She ran out into the street and bent over Kit, not sure whether she should try to move him.

('Sawright,) Kit said, groaning softly as he worked at getting up. Nita slipped hands under his arms to help. (Fred did it.)

(Are you all right?) came the frantic thought, as Fred appeared in front of Kit's face. (Did I hurt you, did I emit anything you can't take? I took out all the ultraviolet. Oh, no! I forgot the cosmic rays again.)

Kit managed a smile, though not much of one; his face was skinned and bruised where one cheekbone had hit the pavement. (Don't worry about it, Fred, that thing would have done a lot worse to me than a few cosmic rays if it'd hit me the way it wanted to.) He stood up, wincing. (It got my leg some, I think.)

Nita bent down to look at Kit's left leg and sucked in her breath. His jeans were torn, and he had a straight horizontal gash six inches or so below the knee, which was bleeding freely. (Does it feel deep?)

(No. It just hurts a lot. I think it was the cab's fender, there was a jagged piece sticking out of the chrome. Listen, Fred, thanks—)

(You're sure I didn't hurt you? You people are so fragile. A little gamma radiation will ruin your whole day, it seems.)

(I'm fine. But I've gotta do something about this leg. And then we've got to get moving again and get to the dark Book.)

Nita looked over at the fire hydrant, fear boiling in her. Casually, as if this was something it did many times a day, the hydrant cracked open and spat something out onto the sidewalk—a dessicated-looking little lump of bones and feathers. Then it got up and waddled heavily down to a spot about fifty feet farther down the block, and sat down again.

And I thought it couldn't all be bad.

Together, as quickly as they could, two small, frightened-looking figures and a spark like a lost star hurried into the shadows and vanished there.

Entropics
Detection and Avoidance

(How close are we?)

(Uh . . . this is Madison and Forty-ninth. Three blocks north and a long one east.)

(Can we rest? This air burns to breathe. And we've been going fast.)

(Yeah, let's.)

They crouched together in the shadow of a doorway, two wary darknesses and a dim light, watching the traffic that went by. Mostly cabs prowled past, wearing the same hungry look as the one that had wounded Kit. Or a sullen truck might lumber by, or a passenger car, looking uneasy and dingy and bitter. None of the cars or trucks had drivers, or looked like they wanted them. They ignored the traffic lights, and their engines growled.

Nita's eyes burned in the dark air. She rubbed them and glanced down at Kit's leg, bound now with a torn-off piece of her shirt. (How is it?)

(Not too bad. It feels stiff. I guess it stopped bleeding.) He looked down, felt the makeshift bandage, winced. (Yeah. . . . I'm hungry.)

Nita's stomach turned over—she was too nervous to even consider eating —as Kit came up with a ham sandwich and offered her half. (You go ahead,) she said. She leaned against the hard cold wall, and on a sudden thought pulled her pen out of her pocket and looked at it. It seemed all right, but as she held it she could feel a sort of odd tingling in its metal that hadn't been there before.

(Uh, Fred—)

He hung beside her at eye level, making worried feelings that matched the dimness of his light. (Are you *sure* that light didn't hurt you?)

(Yeah. It's not that.) She held out the pen to him. Fred backed away a little, as if afraid he might swallow it again. (Is this radioactive or anything?) Nita said.

He drifted close to it, bobbed up and down to look at it from several angles. (You mean beta and gamma and those other emissions you have trouble with? No.)

Nita still felt suspicious about the pen. She dug into her backpack for a piece of scrap paper, laid it on her wizards' manual, clicked the point out, and scribbled on the paper. Then she breathed out, perplexed. (Come *on*, Fred! Look at that!)

He floated down to look. The pen's blue-black ink would normally have been hard to see in that dimness, no matter how white the paper. But the scrawl had a subtle glimmer about it, a luminosity just bright enough to make out. (I don't think it's anything harmful to you,) Fred said. (Are you sure it didn't do that before?)

(Yes!)

(Well, look at it this way. Now you can see what you're writing when it's dark. Surprising you people hadn't come up with something like that already.)

Nita shook her head, put the paper away, and clipped the pen back in her pocket. Kit, finishing the first half of his sandwich, looked over at the scribble with interest. (Comes of being inside Fred, I guess. With him having his own claudication, and all the energy boiling around inside him, you might have expected something like that to happen.)

(Yeah, well, I don't like it. The pen was fine the way it was.)

(Considering where it's been,) Kit said, (you're lucky to get it back in the same shape, instead of crushed into a little lump.) He wrapped up the other half of his sandwich and shoved it into his backpack. (Should we go?)

(Yeah.)

They got up, checked their surroundings as usual to make sure that no cabs or cars were anywhere close, and started up Madison again, ducking into doorways or between buildings whenever they saw or heard traffic coming.

(No people,) Kit said, as if trying to work it out. (Just things—all dark and ruined—and machines, all twisted. Alive—but they seem to hate everything. And pigeons—)

(Dogs, too,) Nita said.

(Where?) Kit looked hurriedly around him.

(Check the sidewalk and the gutter. They're here. And remember that nest.) Nita shrugged uneasily, setting her pack higher. (I don't know. Maybe people just can't live here.)

(We're here,) Kit said unhappily. (And maybe not for long.)

A sudden grinding sound like tortured metal made them dive for another shadowy doorway close to the corner of Madison and Fiftieth. No traffic was in sight; nothing showed but the glowering eye of the traffic light and the unchanging DON'T WALK signs. The grinding sound came again—metal scrap-ng on concrete, somewhere across Madison, down Fiftieth, to their left. Kit edged a bit forward in the doorway.

(What are you—)

(I want to see.) He reached around behind him, taking the antenna in hand.

(But if—)

(If that's something that might chase us later, I at least want a look at it. Fred? Take a peek for us?)

(Right.) Fred sailed ahead of them, keeping low and close to the building walls, his light dimmed to the faintest glimmer. By the lamppost at Madison and Fiftieth he paused, then shot low across the street and down Fiftieth between Madison and Fifth, vanishing past the corner. Nita and Kit waited, sweating.

From around the corner Fred radiated feelings of uncertainty and curiosity. (These are like the other things that run these streets. But these aren't moving. Maybe they were dangerous once. I don't know about now.)

(Come on,) Kit said. He put his head out of the doorway. (It's clear.)

With utmost caution they crossed the street and slipped around the corner, flattening to the wall. Here stores and dingy four-story brownstones with long flights of railed stairs lined the street. Halfway down the block, jagged and bizarre in the dimness and the feeble yellow glow of a flickering sodium-vapor street light, was the remains of an accident. One car, a heavy two-door sedan, lay crumpled against the pole of another nearby street light, its right-hand door ripped away and the whole right side of it laid open. A little distance away, in the middle of the street, lay the car that had hit the sedan, resting on its back and skewed right around so that its front end was pointed at Kit and Nita. It was a sports car of some kind, so dark a brown that it was almost black. Its windshield had been shattered when it overturned, and it had many other dents and scrapes, some quite deep. From its front right wheelwell jutted a long jagged strip of chrome, part of the other car's fender, now wound into the sports car's wheel.

(I don't get it,) Nita said silently. (If that dark one hit the other, why isn't its front all smashed in—)

She broke off as with a terrible metallic groan the sports car suddenly rocked back and forth, like a turtle on its back trying to right itself. Kit sucked in a long breath and didn't move. The car stopped rocking for a moment, then with another scrape of metal started again, rocking more energetically this time. Each time the side-to-side motion became larger. It rocked partway onto one door, then back the other way and partway onto the other, then back again—and full onto its left-hand door. There it balanced, precarious, for a few long seconds, as if getting its breath. And then twitched, hard, shuddered all the way over, and fell right-side down.

The scream that filled the air as the sports car came down on the fender-tangled right wheel was terrible to hear. Instantly it hunched up the fouled wheel, holding it away from the street, crouching on the three good wheels and shaking with its effort. Nita thought of an old sculpture she had seen once, a wounded lion favoring one forelimb—weary and in pain, but still dangerous.

Very slowly, as if approaching a hurt animal and not wanting to alarm it, Kit stepped away from the building and walked out into the street.

(Kit!)

(Ssssh,) he said silently. (Don't freak it.)

(Are you out of your—)

(Sssssshhh!)

The sports car watched Kit come, not moving. Now that it was right-side up, Nita could get a better idea of its shape. It was actually rather beautiful in its deadly looking way—sleekly swept-back and slung low to the ground. Its curves were battered in places; its once-shining hide was scored and dull. It stared at Kit from hunter's eyes, headlights wide with pain, and breathed shallowly, waiting.

(Lotus Esprit,) Kit said to Nita, not taking his eyes off the car, matching it stare for stare.

Nita shook her head anxiously. (Does that mean something? I don't know cars.)

(It's a racer. A mean one. What it is *here*— Look, Nita, there's your answer. Look at the front of it, under the headlights.) He kept moving forward, his hands out in front of him. The Lotus held perfectly still, watching.

Nita looked at the low-sloping grille. (It's all full of oil or something.)

(It's a predator. These other cars, like that sedan—they must be what it hunts. This time its prey hurt the Lotus before it made its kill. Like a tiger getting gored by a bull or something. Ooops!)

Kit, eight or ten feet away from the Lotus's grille, took one step too many; it abruptly rolled back away from him a foot or so. Very quietly its engine stuttered to life and settled into a throaty growl.

(Kit, you're—)

(Shut up.) *"I won't hurt you,"* he said in the Speech, aloud. *"Let me see that wheel."*

The engine-growl got louder—the sound of the Speech seemed to upset the Lotus. It rolled back another couple of feet, getting close to the curb, and glared at Kit. But the glare seemed to have as much fear as threat in it now.

"I won't hurt you," Kit repeated, stepping closer, holding out his hands, one of them with the antenna in it. *"Come on, you know what this is. Let me do something about that wheel. You can't run on it. And if you can't run, or*

hunt— I bet there are other hunters here, aren't there? Or scavengers. I'm sure there are scavengers. Who'll be coming here to clean up this kill? And do you want them to find you here, helpless?"

The Lotus stared at him, shifting a little from side to side, now, swaying uncertainly. The growl had not stopped, but it hadn't gotten any louder either. *"If I were going to hurt you, I would have by now,"* Kit said, getting closer. The car was four feet away, and its headlights were having to look up at Kit now. *"Just let me do something about that fender stuck in you, then you'll go your way and I'll go mine."*

The dark eyes stared at the antenna, then at Kit, and back at the antenna again. The Lotus stopped swaying, held very still. Kit was two feet away. He reached out with his free hand, very slowly, reached down to touch the scratched fiberglass hide—

The engine raced, a sudden startling roar that made Nita stifle a scream and made Kit flinch all over—but he didn't jump away, and neither did the Lotus. For a second or two he and the car stood there just looking at each other—small trembling boy, large trembling predator. Then Kit laid his hand carefully on the brown hide, a gingerly gesture. The car shook all over, stared at him. Its engine quieted to an uncertain rumbling.

"It's okay," he said. *"Will you let me take care of it?"*

The Lotus muttered deep under its hood. It still stared at Kit with those fearsome eyes, but its expression was mostly perplexed now. So was Kit's. He rubbed the curve of the hurt wheelwell in distress. (I can't understand why it's mute,) he said unhappily. (The Edsel wasn't. All it took was a couple of sentences in the Speech and it was talking.)

(It's bound,) Nita said, edging out of the shadow of the building she stood against. (Can't you feel it, Kit? There's some kind of huge binding spell laid over this whole place to keep it the way it is.)

She stopped short as the Lotus saw her and began to growl again. *"Relax,"* Kit said. *"She's with me, she won't hurt you either."*

Slowly the growl dwindled, but the feral headlight-eyes stayed on Nita. She gulped and sat down on the curb, where she could see up and down the street. "Kit, do what you're going to do. If another of those cabs comes along—"

"Right. Fred, give me a hand? No, no, no," he said hastily, as Fred drifted down beside him and made a light-pattern and a sound as if he was going to emit something. "Not *that* kind. Just make some light so I can see what to do down here."

Kit knelt beside the right wheel, studying the damage, and Fred floated in close to lend his light to the business, while the Lotus watched the process sidelong and suspiciously. "Mmmfff—nothing too bad, it's mostly wrapped around the tire. Lucky it didn't get fouled with the axle.

"Come on, come on," Kit said in the Speech, patting the bottom of the tire, *"relax it, loosen up. You're forcing the scrap into yourself, holding the wheel up like that. Come on."* The Lotus moaned softly and with fearful care relaxed the uplifted wheel a bit. *"That's better."* Kit slipped the antenna up under the Lotus's wheelwell, aiming for some piece of chrome that was out of sight. "Fred, can you get in there so I can see? Good. *Okay, this may sting a little."* Molten light, half-seen, sparked under the Lotus's fender. It jumped, and an uneven half-circle-shaped piece of chrome fell clanging onto the pavement. *"Now hunch the wheel up again. A little higher—"* Kit reached in with both hands and, after a moment's tugging and twisting, freed the other half of the piece of metal. *"There,"* Kit said, satisfied. He tossed the second piece of scrap to the ground.

The engine roared again with terrible suddenness, deafening. This time Kit scrambled frantically backward as the Lotus leaped snarling away from him. With a screech of tires it swept so close past Nita that she fell over backward onto the sidewalk. Its engine screaming, the Lotus tore away down Fiftieth toward Madison, flung itself left around the corner in a cloud of blue exhaust, and was gone.

Very slowly Kit stood up, pushed the antenna into his pants pocket, and stood in the street dusting his hands off on his shirt as he gazed in disappointment after the Lotus. Nita sat herself back up again, shaking her head and brushing at herself. (I thought maybe it was going to stay long enough to thank you,) she said.

Kit shook his head, evidently in annoyance at himself for having thought the same thing. (Well, I don't know—I was thinking of what Picchu said. 'Don't be afraid to help.') He shrugged. (Doesn't really matter, I guess. It was hurting; fixing it was the right thing to do.)

(I hope so,) Nita said. (I'd hate to think the grateful creature might run off to—*you* know—and tell everybody about the people who helped it instead of hurting it. I have a feeling that doing good deeds sticks out more than usual around here.)

Kit nodded, looking uncomfortable. (Maybe I should've left well enough alone.)

(Don't be dumb. Let's get going, huh? The . . . whatever the place is where the dark Book's kept, it's pretty close. I feel nervous standing out here.)

They recrossed Madison and again started the weary progression from doorway to driveway to shadowed wall, heading north.

At Madison and Fifty-second, Nita turned right and paused. (It's on this block somewhere,) she said, trying to keep even the thought quiet. (The north side, I think. Fred, you feel anything?)

Fred held still for a moment, not even making a flicker. (The darkness feels thicker up ahead, at the middle of the block.)

Kit and Nita peered down the block. (It doesn't look any different,) Kit said. (But you're the expert on light, Fred. Lead the way.)

With even greater care than usual they picked their way down Fifty-second. This street was stores and office buildings again; all the store windows empty, all the windows dark. But here, though external appearances were no different, the feeling slowly began to grow that there was a reason for the grimy darkness of the windows. Something watched, something peered out those windows, using the darkness as a cloak, and no shadow was deep enough to hide in; the silent eyes would see. Nothing happened, nothing stirred anywhere. No traffic was in sight. But the street felt more and more like a trap, laid open for some unsuspecting creature to walk into. Nita tried to swallow as they ducked from one hiding place to another, but her mouth was too dry. Kit was sweating. Fred's light was out.

(This is it,) he said suddenly, his thought sounding unusually muted even for Fred. (This is the middle of the darkness.)

(This?) Kit and Nita thought at the same time, in shock, and then simultaneously hushed themselves. Nita edged out to the sidewalk to get a better look at the place. She had to crane her neck. They were in front of a skyscraper, faced completely in black plate glass, an ominous, windowless monolith.

(Must be about ninety stories,) Nita said. (I don't see any lights.)

(Why would you?) Fred said. (Whoever lives in this place doesn't seem fond of light at all. How shall we go in?)

Nita glanced back up the street. (We passed a driveway that might go down to a delivery entrance.)

(I'll talk to the lock,) Kit said. (Let's go!)

They went back the way they had come and tiptoed down the driveway. It seemed meant for trucks to back into. A flight of steps at one side led up to a loading platform about four feet above the deepest part of the ramp. Climbing the stairs, Kit went to a door on the right and ran his hands over it as Nita and Fred came up behind. (No lock,) Kit said. (It's controlled from inside.)

(We can't get in? We're dead.)

(We're not dead yet. There's a machine in there that makes the garage doors go up. That's all I need.) Kit got out the antenna and held it against the door as he might have held a pencil he was about to write with. He closed his eyes. (If I can just feel up through the metal and the wires, find it. . . .)

Nita and Fred kept still while Kit's eyes squeezed tighter and tighter shut in fierce concentration. Inside one garage door something rattled, fell silent, rattled again, began to grind. Little by little the door rose until there was an opening at the bottom of it, three feet high. Kit opened his eyes but kept the antenna pressed against the metal. (Go on in.)

Fred and Nita ducked through into darkness. Kit came swiftly after them. Behind him, the door began to move slowly downward again, shutting with a thunderous clang. Nita pulled out the rowan wand, so they could look around. There were wooden loading pallets stacked on the floor, but nothing else—bare concrete walls, bare ceiling. Set in the back wall of the huge room was one normal-sized double door.

(Let's see if this one has a lock,) Kit said as they went quietly up to it. He touched the right-hand knob carefully, whispered a word or two in the Speech, tried it. The right side of the double door opened.

(Huh. Wasn't even locked!) Through the open door, much to everyone's surprise, light spilled—plain old fluorescent office-building light, but cheery as a sunny day after the gloom outdoors. On the other side of the door was a perfectly normal-looking corridor with beige walls and charcoal-color doors and carpeting. The normality came as something of a shock. (Fred, I thought you said it was *darker* here!)

(Felt darker. And colder. And it does,) Fred said, shivering, his faint light rippling as he did so. (We're very close to the source of the coldness. It's farther up, though.)

(Up?) Nita looked at Kit uneasily. (If we're going to get the dark Book and get out of here fast, we can't fool with stairs again. We'll have to use the elevators somehow.)

Kit glanced down at the antenna. (I think I can manage an elevator if it gets difficult. Let's find one.)

They slipped through the door and went down the hall to their right, heading for a lobby at its far end. There they peered out at a bank of elevators set in the same dark-green marble as the rest of the lobby. No one was there.

Kit walked to the elevators, punched the call button, and hurriedly motioned Nita and Fred to join him. Nita stayed where she was for a moment. (Shouldn't we stay out of sight here?)

(Come on!)

She went out to him, Fred bobbing along beside. Kit watched the elevator lights to see which one was coming down and then slipped into a recess at the side. Nita took the hint and joined him. The elevator bell chimed; doors slid open—

The perytons piled out of the middle elevator in a hurry, five of them together, not looking to left or right, and burst out the front door into the street. Once outside they began their awful chorus of howls and snarls, but Nita and Kit and Fred weren't sitting around to listen. They dove into the middle elevator, and Kit struck the control panel with the antenna, hard. *'Close up and take off!''*

The elevator doors closed, but then a rumbling, scraping, gear-grinding screech began—low at first, then louder, a combination of every weird, unsettling noise Nita had ever heard an elevator make. Cables twanged and ratchets ratcheted, and, had they been moving, she would have sworn they were about to go plunging down to crash in the cellar.

"Cut it out or I'll snap your cables myself when I'm through with you!" Kit yelled in the Speech. Almost immediately the elevator jerked slightly and then started upward.

Nita tried again to swallow and had no better luck than the last time. "Those perytons are going to pick up our scent right outside that door, Kit! And they'll track us inside, and it won't be five minutes before—"

"I know, I know. Fred, how well can you feel the middle of the darkness?"

(We're closer.)

"Good. You'll have to tell me when to stop."

The elevator went all the way up to the top, the eighty-ninth floor, before Fred said, (This is it!)

Kit rapped the control panel one last time with his antenna. *"You stay where you are,"* he said.

The elevator doors opened silently to reveal another normal-looking floor, this one more opulent than the floor downstairs. Here the carpets were ivory-white and thick; the wall opposite the elevators was one huge bookcase of polished wood, filled with hundreds of books, like volumes of one huge set. Going left they came to another hallway, stretching off to their left like the long stroke of an L; this one too was lined with bookcases. At the far end stood a huge polished desk, with papers and Dictaphone equipment and an intercom and a multiline phone jumbled about on it. At the desk sat—

—it was hard to know *what* to call it. Kit and Nita, peering around the corner, were silent with confusion and fear. The thing sitting in a secretary's swivel chair and typing on an expensive electric typewriter was dark green and warty, and sat about four feet high in the chair. It had limbs with tentacles and claws, all knotted together under a big eggplant-shaped head, and goggly, wicked eyes. All the limbs didn't seem to help the creature's typing much, for every few seconds it made a mistake and went grumbling and fumbling over the top of its messy desk for a bottle of correcting fluid. The creature's grumbling was of more interest than its typing. It used the Speech, but haltingly, as if it didn't care much for the language—and indeed the smooth, stately rhythms of the wizardly tongue suffered somewhat, coming out of that misshapen mouth.

Kit leaned back against the wall. (We've gotta do something. Fred, are you *sure* it's up here?)

(Absolutely. And past that door, behind that—) Fred indicated the warty typist. From down the hall came another brief burst of typing, then more grumbling and scrabbling on the desk.

(We've got to get it away from there.) Nita glanced at Fred.

(I shall create a diversion,) Fred said, with relish. (I've been good at it so far.)

(Great. Something big. Something alive again, if you can manage it—then again, forget that.) Nita breathed out unhappily. (I wouldn't leave anything alive here.)

(Not even Joanne?) Kit said with a small but evil grin.

(Not even her. This place has her outclassed. Fred, just—)

A voice spoke, sounding so loud that Kit and Nita stopped breathing, practically stopped thinking. "Akthanath," it called, a male voice, sounding weary and hassled and bored, "come in here a moment. . . ."

Nita glanced at Kit. They carefully peeked down the hall once more and saw the tentacled thing hunch itself up, drop to the floor behind the desk, and wobble its way into the inner office.

(Now?) Fred said.

(No, save it! But come on, this is our best chance!) Nita followed Kit down the hall to the door, crouched by it, and looked in. Past it was another room. They slipped into it and found themselves facing a partly open door that led to the office the typist had gone into. Through the slit they could just see the tentacly creature's back and could hear the voice of the man talking to it. "Hold all my calls for the next hour or so, until they get this thing cleared up. I don't want everybody's half-baked ideas of what's going on. Let Garm and his people handle it. And here, get Mike on the phone for me. I want to see if I can get something useful out of him."

Nita looked around, trying not even to think loudly. The room they were in was lined with shelves and shelves of heavy, dark, leatherbound books with gold-stamped spines. Kit tiptoed to one bookshelf, pulled out a volume at random, and opened it. His face registered shock; he held out the book for Nita to look at. The print was the same as that in Carl's large Advisory manual, line after line of the clear graceful symbols of the Speech—but whatever was being discussed on the page Nita looked at was so complicated she could only understand one word out of every ten or twenty. She glanced at Kit as he turned back to the front of the book and showed her the title page. UNIVERSES, PARAUNIVERSES AND PLANES—ASSEMBLY AND MAINTENANCE, it said. A CREATOR'S MANUAL. And underneath, in smaller letters, *Volume 108—Natural and Supernatural Laws*.

Nita gulped. Beside her, Fred was dancing about in the air in great agitation. (What is it?) she asked him.

(It's in *here.*)

(Where?) Kit said.

(One of *those*. I can't tell which, it's so dark down that end of the room.) Fred indicated a bookcase on the farthest wall. (It's worst over *there*.) Nita stopped dead when she saw the room's second door, which gave on the inner office and was wide open.

Nita got ready to scoot past the door. The man who sat at the desk in the elegant office had his back to it and was staring out the window into the dimness. His warty secretary handed him the phone, and he swiveled around in the high-backed chair to take it, showing himself in profile. Nita stared at him, confused, as he picked up the phone. A businessman, young, maybe thirty, and very handsome—red-gold hair and a clean-lined face above a trim, dark three-piece suit. *This* was the Witherer, the Kindler of Wildfires, the one who decreed darkness, the Starsnuffer?

"Hi, Michael," he said. He had a pleasant voice, warm and deep. "Oh, nothing much—"

(Never mind *him*,) Kit said. (We've got to get that Book.)

(We can't go past the door till he turns around.)

"—the answer to that is pretty obvious, Mike. I can't do a bloody thing with this place unless I can get some more power for it. I can't afford street lights, I can barely afford a little electricity, much less a star. The entropy rating—"

The young man swiveled in his chair again, leaning back and looking out the window. Nita realized with a chill that he had a superb view of the downtown skyline, including the top of the Pan Am Building, where even now wisps of smoke curled black against the lowering gray. She tapped Kit on the elbow, and together they slipped past the doorway to the bookshelf.

(Fred, do you have even a *little* idea—)

(Maybe one of those up there.) He indicated a shelf just within reach. Kit and Nita started taking down one book after another, looking at them. Nita was shaking—she had no clear idea what they were looking for.

(What if it's one of those up there, out of reach?)

(You'll stand on my shoulders. Kit, hurry!)

"—Michael, don't you think you could talk to the rest of Them and get me just a *little* more energy? —Well, They've *never* given me what I asked for, have They? All I wanted was my own Universe where everything *works*— Which brings me to the reason for this call. Who's this new operative you turned loose in here? This Universe is at a very delicate stage, interference will—"

They were down to the second-to-last shelf, and none of the books had been what they were looking for. Nita was sweating worse. (Fred, are you sure—)

(It's dark there, it's *all* dark. What do you *want* from me?)

Kit, kneeling by the bottom shelf, suddenly jumped as if shocked. (Huh? Nita said.

(It stung me. *Nita!*) Kit grabbed at the volume his hand had brushed yanked it out of the case, and knelt there, juggling it like a hot potato. He managed to get it open and held it out, showing Nita not the usual clear page, close-printed with the fine small symbols of the Speech, but a block of transparency like many pages of thinnest glass laid together. Beneath the smooth surface, characters and symbols seethed as if boiling up from a great depth and sinking down again.

Nita found herself squinting. (It hurts to look at.)

(It hurts to *hold!*) Kit shut the book hurriedly and held it out to Fred for him to check, for externally it looked no different from any other book there (Is this what we're looking for?)

Fred's faint glimmer went out like a blown candle flame with the nearness of the book. (The darkness—it blinds—)

Kit bundled the book into his backpack and rubbed his hands on his jacket (Now if we can just get out of here. . . .)

"—oh, come on, Mike," the voice was saying in the other office. "Don' get cute with me. I had an incident on top of one of my buildings. One of my favorite constructs got shot up and the site stinks of wizardry. *Your* brand moonlight and noon-forged metal." The voice of the handsome young man in the three-piece suit was still pleasant enough, but Nita, peering around the edge of the door, saw his face going hard and sharp as the edge of a knife. He swiveled around in his chair again to look out the window at that thin plume of ascending smoke, and Nita waved Kit past the door, then scuttled after him herself. "—that's a dumb question to be asking *me*, Michael. If I knew would I tell you where the bright *Book* was? And how likely is it that I know at all? You people keep such close tabs on it, at least that's what I hear Anyway, if it's not read from every so often, don't *I* go ffft! like everything else? —You're absolutely right, that's not a responsive answer. Why should be responsive, *you're* not being very helpful—"

Kit and Nita peeked back into the hall. Fred floated up to hang between them. (I get a feeling—) Kit started to say, but the sudden coldness in the voice of the man on the phone silenced him.

"—Look, Mike, I've had about enough of this silliness. The Bright Power got miffed because I wanted to work on projects of my own instead of following-the-leader like you do, working from Their blueprints instead of drawing up your own. You can do what you please, but I thought when settled down in this little pittance of a Universe that They would let me be and let me do things my way. They said They didn't need me when They threw me out—well, I've done pretty well without Them too. Maybe They don't like that, because now all of a sudden I'm getting interference. You say this operative isn't one of your sweetness-and-Light types? Fine. Then you won't mind if when I catch him, her, or it, I make his stay interesting and permanent. Whoever's disrupting my status quo will wish he'd never been born, spawned, or engendered. And when you see the rest of Them, you tell Them from me that—hello? Hello?"

The phone slammed down. There was no sound for a few seconds. "Akthanath," the young man's voice finally said into the silence, "someone's soul is going to writhe for this."

The slow cold of the words got into Nita's spine. She and Kit slipped around the door and ran for it, down the hall and into the elevator. "—he's playing it close to the chest," that angry voice floated down the hall to them. "I don't know what's going on. The Eldest still has it safe?—Good, then see that guards are mounted at the usual accesses. And have Garm send a pack of his people backtime to the most recent gate opening. I want to know which universe these agents are coming from."

In the elevator, Kit whipped out the antenna and rapped the control panel with it. *"Down!"*

Doors closed, and down it went, Nita leaned back against one wall of the elevator, panting. Now she knew why that first crowd of perytons had come howling after them on top of the Pan Am Building, but the solution of that small mystery made her feel no better at all. "Kit, they'll be waiting downstairs, for sure."

He bit his lip. "Yeah. Well, we won't be where they think we'll be, that's all. If we get off a couple of floors too high and take the stairs—"

"Right."

"Stop at Four," Kit said to the elevator.

The elevator stopped, opened its doors. Kit headed out the door fast and tripped—the elevator had stopped several inches beneath the fourth floor. *"Watch your step,"* the elevator said, snickering.

Kit turned and smacked the open elevator door with his antenna as Nita and Fred got out. *"Very funny. You stay here until I give the word.* C'mon, let's get out of here!"

They ran down the hall together, found the stairs, and plunged down them. Kit was panting as hard as Nita now. Fred shot down past landing after landing with them, his light flickering as if it were an effort to keep up. "Kit," Nita said, "where are we going to go after we leave this building? We need time, and a place to do the spell to find the bright *Book.*"

Kit sounded unhappy. "I dunno. How about Central Park? If we hid in there—"

"But you saw what it looks like from the top of Pan Am. It's all dark in there, there were things moving—"

"There's a lot of room to hide. Look, Nita, if I can handle the machines here, it's a good bet you can handle the plants. You're good with plants and live stuff, you said."

She nodded reluctantly. "I guess we'll find out how good."

They came to the last landing, the ground floor. Nita pushed the door open a crack and found that they were almost directly across from the green lobby and the elevators.

(What's the situation?) Kit said silently.

(They're waiting.) Six perytons, black-coated, brown-coated, one a steely gray, were sitting or standing around the middle elevator with their tongues hanging out and looks of anticipation and hunger in their too-human eyes.

(Now?) Fred said, sounding eager.

(Not yet. We may not need a diversion, Fred.) *"Go!"* he whispered then in the Speech. The antenna in his hand sparked and sputtered with molten light, and Kit pressed close behind Nita. (Watch them!)

There was no bell, but even if there had been one, the sound of it and of the elevator doors opening would have been drowned out in snarls as the perytons leaped in a body into the elevator. The moment the perytons were out of sight, Nita pushed the door open and headed for the one to the garage. It stuck and stung her as the dark Book had; she jerked her hand away from it. Kit came up behind her and blasted it with the antenna, then grabbed it himself. This time it came open. They dashed through and Kit sealed the door behind them.

No one was in the garage, but a feeling was growing in the air as if the storm of rage they'd heard beginning upstairs was about to break over their heads. Kit raised the antenna again, firing a line of hot light that zapped the ceiling-mounted controls of the delivery door. With excruciating slowness the door began to rumble upward. (Now?) Fred said anxiously as they ran toward it.

(No, not yet, just—)

They bent over double, ducked underneath the opening door, and ran up the driveway. It was then that the perytons leaped at them from both sides, howling, and Nita grabbed for her wand and managed one slash with it, yelling, "Now, Fred! *Now!"*

All she saw clearly was the peryton that jumped at her, a huge, blue-eyed, brindled she-wolf, as the rowan wand spat silver moonfire and the peryton fell away screaming. Then came the explosion, and it hurled both her and Kit staggering off to their right. The street shook as if lightning-struck, and part of the front of the dark building was demolished in a shower of shattered plate glass as tons and tons and tons of red bricks came crashing down from somewhere to fill the street from side to side, burying sidewalks and perytons and doors and the delivery bay twenty feet deep.

Nita picked herself up. A few feet away, Kit was doing the same, and Fred bobbed over to them as an ominous stillness settled over everything. (How was I?) Fred said, seeming dazed but pleased.

"Are you all right?" Kit said.

(I'm alive, but my gnaester will never be the same,) Fred said. (You two?)

"We're fine," Kit said.

"And I think we're in trouble," Nita added, looking at the blocked street. "Let's get going!"

They ran toward Fifth Avenue, and the shadows took them.

Contractual Magic
An Introduction

A four-foot-high wall ran down the west side of Fifth Avenue, next to sidewalk of gray hexagonal paving-stones. Nita and Kit crouched behind it just inside Central Park, under the shadows of barren-branched trees, and tried to catch their breath. Fred hung above them, watching both Fifth Avenue and Sixty-fourth Street for signs of pursuit.

Nita leaned against the dirty wall, careless of grime or roughness or th pigeon droppings that streaked it. She was scared. All through her life, th one thing she knew she could always depend on was her energy—it neve gave out. Even after being beaten up, she always sprang right back. But her and now, when she could less afford exhaustion than she had ever been abl to in her life, she felt it creeping up on her. She was even afraid to rest, fc fear it would catch up with her quicker. But her lungs were burning, and i felt so good to sit still, not have death or something worse chasing her. An there was another spell to be cast. . . .

If I'd known I was going to get into a situation like this, she though would I ever have picked that book up at all? Would I have taken the Oath Then she shook her head and tried to think about something else, for she go an inkling of the answer, and it shocked her. She had always been told tha she wasn't brave. At least that's what Joanne and her friends had always said *Can't take a dare, can't take a joke, crybaby, crybaby. We were only tea ing.* . . .

She sniffed and rubbed her eyes, which stung. "Did you find the spell? she said.

Kit had been paging through his wizards' manual. Now he was running finger down one page, occasionally whispering a word, then stopping himse to keep from using the Speech aloud. "Yeah. It's pretty simple." But he wa frowning.

"What's the matter?"

Kit slumped back against the wall, looked over at her. "I keep thinking about what—you know who—was talking about on the phone."

"Sounded like he was hiding something."

"Uh huh. They know where the bright *Book* is, all right. And somebody's watching it. Whoever the 'Eldest' is. And now there're going to be more guards around it."

" 'The usual accesses,' he said. Kit, there might be an *un*usual access, then."

"Sure. If we had any idea where the thing was hidden."

"Won't the spell give us a vision, a location, like the last one?"

"No. It's a directional." Kit dropped his hands wearily on the book in his lap, sighed, looked over at Nita. "I don't know. . . . I just don't get it."

"What?" She rolled the rowan wand between her hands, watching the way its light shone between her fingers and through the skin.

"He didn't look evil. Or sound that way, at least not till right at the end here."

(The Snuffer was always glorious to look at before it scorned the light,) Fred said. (And it kept the beauty afterward—that's what the stars always used to say. That's one reason it's dangerous to deal with that one. The beauty . . . seduces.) Fred made a small feeling of awe and fear. (What a blaze of darkness, what a flood of emissions. I was having a hard time keeping my composure in there.)

"Are you all right now?"

(Oh, yes. I was a little amazed that you didn't perceive the power burning around the shell he was wearing. Just as well—you might have spoken to him, and everything would have been lost. That one's most terrible power, they say, is his absolute conviction that he's right in what he does.)

"He's not right, then?" Kit said.

(I don't know.)

"But," Nita said, confused, "if he's fighting with . . . with Them . . . with the ones who made the bright *Book*, isn't he in the wrong?"

(I don't know,) Fred said again. (How am I supposed to judge? But you're wizards, you should know how terrible a power belief is, especially in the wrong hands—and how do you tell which hands are wrong? *Believe* something and the Universe is on its way to being changed. Because *you've* changed, by believing. Once you've changed, other things start to follow. Isn't that the way it works?)

Nita nodded as Fred looked across the dark expanse of Central Park. The branches of trees were knitted together in tangled patterns of strife. Ivy strangled what it climbed. Paths were full of pitfalls, copses clutched themselves full of threat and darkness. Shadows moved secretively through shadows, making unnerving noises. (This is what—he—believes in,) Fred said sadly, (however he justifies the belief.)

Nita could find nothing to say. The wordless misery of the trees had been wearing at her ever since she set foot inside the wall. All the growing things there longed for light, though none of them knew what it was; she could feel their starved rage moving sluggishly in them, slow as sap in the cold. Only in one place was their anger muted—several blocks south, at Fifth and Central Park South, where in her own New York the equestrian statue of General Sherman and the Winged Victory had stood. Here the triumphant rider cast in black bronze was that handsome young man they had seen in the black glass building, his face set in a cold proud conqueror's smile. The creature he rode was a skull-faced eight-legged steed, which the wizards' manual said brought death with the sound of its hooves. And Victory with her palm branch was changed to a grinning Fury who held a dripping sword. Around the statue group the trees were silent, not daring to express even inarticulate feelings. They knew their master too well.

Nita shook her head and glanced at Kit, who was looking in the same direction. "I thought it'd be fun to know the Mason's Word and run around bringing statues to life," he said unhappily, "but somehow I don't think there's any statue here I'd want to use the Word on. . . . You ready? We should start this."

"Yeah."

The spell was brief and straightforward, and Nita turned to the right page in her manual and drew the necessary circle and diagram. Kit got the dark Book out of his backpack and dropped it in the middle of the circle. Nita held up her wand for light. They began to recite the spell.

It was only three sentences long, but by the end of the first sentence Nita could feel the trees bending in close to watch—not with friendly, secretive interest, as in her first spell with Kit, but in hungry desperation. Even the abstract symbols and words of the Speech must have tasted of another Universe where light was not only permitted, but free. The rowan wand was blazing by the end of the second sentence, maybe in reaction to being so close to something of the dark powers, and Nita wondered whether she should cover it up to keep them from being noticed. But the spell held her immobile as usual. For another thing, the trees all around were leaning in and in with such piteous feelings of hunger that she would as soon have eaten in front of starving children and not offered them some of what she had. Branches began to toss and twist, reaching down for a taste of the light. Nita and Kit finished the spell.

Kit reached right down to pick up the dark Book, which was as well, for immediately after the last word of the spell was spoken it actually hitched itself a little way along the ground, southward. Kit could only hold it for moment before stuffing it back into his backpack. It no longer looked innocent. It burned, both to touch and to look at. Even when Kit had it hidden away and the backpack slung on, neither of them felt any easier. It was as if they were all now visible to something that was looking eagerly for them.

"Let's get out of here," Kit said, so subdued that Nita could hardly hear him. Nita stood and laid a hand against the trunk of the nearest tree, a consoling gesture. She was sorry she couldn't have left them more light. (I wish there was something I could do,) she said silently. But no answer came back. These trees were bound silent, like the car Kit had tended.

She rejoined Kit, who was looking over the wall. "Nothing," he said. Together they swung over the dropping-streaked stone and hurried down Fifth Avenue, crossing the street to get a safe distance between them and the strange cries and half-seen movements of the park. "Straight south?" Nita said.

"Pretty nearly. It's pushing straight that way on my back. The bright *Book* looked like it was way downtown, didn't it, in that spell?"

"Uh huh. The financial district, I think." She gulped. It *was* a long way to walk—miles—even without having to worry about someone chasing you.

"Well, we'd better hurry," Kit said. He paused while they both stopped at the corner of Fifth and Sixty-first. When they were across, he added, "What gets me is that he's so sure that we're interference from the bright side. We haven't done anything yet."

"Huh," Nita said, gently scornful. "Sure we haven't. And anyway, whaddaya mean we aren't 'interference from the bright side'? *You* were the one who said we'd been had."

Kit mulled this over as they approached Sixtieth. "Well . . . maybe. If they know about us, do you think they'll send help?"

"I don't know. I get the feeling that maybe we *are* the help."

"Well, we're not dead yet," Kit said, and peered around the corner of Sixtieth and Fifth—and then jumped back, pale with shock. "We're dead," he said, turned around, and began running back the way they had come, though he limped doing it. Nita looked around that corner just long enough to see what he had seen—a whole pack of big yellow cabs, thundering down Sixtieth. The one in front had a twisted fender that stuck out slightly on one side, a jagged piece of metal. She turned and ran after Kit, frantic. "Where can we hide?"

"The buildings are locked here too," Kit said from up ahead. He had been trying doors. "Fred, can you do something?"

(After that last emission? So soon?) Fred's thought was shaken. (It's all I can do to radiate light. I need time to recover.)

"Crud! Kit, the park, maybe the trees'll slow them down."

They both ran for the curb, but there was no time. Cabs came roaring around the corner from Sixtieth, and another pack of them leaped around the corner of Sixty-first and hurtled down Fifth toward them; they would never make it across the street.

Kit grabbed for his antenna, and Nita yanked out the wand, but without much hope—it hadn't worked that well on the helicopter. The cabs slowed, closed in from both sides, forming a half-circle with Kit and Nita and Fred at the center, backing them against the wall of a dingy building. The cordon tightened until there were no gaps, and one cab at each side was up on the sidewalk, blocking it. No matter where Nita looked, all she saw were chromed grilles like gritted teeth, hungry headlights staring. One of the cabs shouldered forward, its engine snarling softly. The jagged place at one end of its front fender wore a brown discoloration. Not rust—Kit's blood, which it had tasted. Kit lifted the antenna, the hand that gripped it shaking.

The high-pitched yowl of rage and defiance from outside the circle jerked Kit's head up. Nita stared. Fenders scraped and rattled against one another as the tight-wedged cabs jostled, trying to see what was happening. Even the bloodstained cab, the pack leader, looked away from Kit. But none of them could move any way but backward, and one cab paid immediately for that limitation as a fanged grille bit deep into its hindquarters and dragged it screaming out of the circle. Metal screeched and tore, glass shattered as the Lotus Esprit's jaws crushed through the cab's trunk, ripped away its rear axle and with a quick sideways shake of its front end flung the bitten-off axle crashing down Fifth Avenue. Then the Lotus slashed sideways, its fang opening up the side of another cab like a can opener. The circle broke amid enraged roaring; cabs circled and feinted while the first victim dragged itself away by its front wheels to collapse in the street.

Everything started happening at once. Nita slashed at the front of the cab closest to her. The whip of moonfire cracking across its face seemed to confuse and frighten it, but did no damage. I hope *it* doesn't notice that right away, she thought desperately, for there was no use yelling for help. Kit had his hands full. He had the antenna laid over his forearm again and was snapping off shot after shot of blinding-hot light, cracking headlights, burning holes in hoods and exploding tires, a hit here, a hit there—nothing fatal, Nita noticed with dismay. But Kit was managing to hold the cabs at their distance as they harried him.

Out in the street one cab lunged at the Lotus, a leap, its front wheels clear of the ground and meant to come crashing down on the racer's hood—until suddenly the Lotus's nose dipped under the cab and heaved upward, sending the cab rolling helplessly onto its back. A second later the Lotus came down on top of the cab, took a great shark-bite out of its underbelly, and then whirled around, whipping gas and transmission fluid all over, to slash at another cab about to leap on it from behind. This was the king cab, the pack leader, and as the Lotus and the Checker circled one another warily in the street, the other cabs drew away from Kit and Nita to watch the outcome of the combat.

There were two more cabs dead in the street that Nita hadn't seen fall—one with everything from right rear door to right front fender torn away, another horribly mangled in its front end and smashed sideways into a tree on the other side of Fifth, as if it had been thrown there. Amid the wreckage of these and the other two cabs, the cab and the Lotus rolled, turning and backing, maneuvering for an opening that would end in a kill. The Lotus was scored along one side but otherwise unhurt, and the whining roar of its engine sounded hungry and pleased. Infuriated, the Checker made a couple of quick rushes at it, stopping short with a screech of tires and backing away again each time in a way that indicated it didn't want to close in. The Lotus snarled derisively, and without warning the Checker swerved around and threw itself full speed at Kit and Nita, still braced against the wall.

This is it, Nita thought with curious calm. She flung up the rowan wand in one last useless slash and then was thrown back against the wall with terrible force as a thunderstorm of screaming metal flew from right to left in front of her and crashed not five feet away. She slid down the wall limp as a rag doll, stunned, aware that death had gone right past her face. When her eyes and ears started working again, the Lotus was standing off to her left, its back scornfully turned to the demolished pack leader, which it had slammed into the wall. The Checker looked like the remains of a front-end collision test—it was crumpled up into itself like an accordion, and bleeding oil and gas in pools. The Lotus roared triumphant disdain at the remaining two cabs, then threatened them with a small mean rush. They turned tail and ran a short distance, then slowed down and slunk away around the corner of Sixty-first. Satisfied, the Lotus bent over the broken body of one dead cab, reached down, and with casual fierceness plucked away some of the front fender, as a falcon plucks its kill before eating.

Nita turned her head to look for Kit. He was several feet farther down the wall, looking as shattered as she felt. He got up slowly and walked out into the street. The Lotus glanced up, left its kill and went to meet him. For a moment they simply looked at each other from a few feet apart. Kit held one hand out, and the Lotus slowly inched forward under the hand, permitting the caress. They stood that way for the space of four or five gasps, and then the Lotus rolled closer still and pushed its face roughly against Kit's leg, like a cat.

"How about that," Kit said, his voice cracking. "How about that."

Nita put her face down in her hands, wanting very much to cry, but all she could manage were a couple of crooked, whopping sobs. She had a feeling that much worse was coming, and she couldn't break down all the way. Nita hid her eyes until she thought her voice was working again, then let her hands fall and looked up. "Kit, we've got to—"

The Lotus had rolled up and was staring at her—a huge, dangerous, curious, brown-hided beast. She lost what she was saying, hypnotized by the fierce, interested stare. Then the Lotus smiled at Nita, a slow, chrome smile, silver and sanguine. "Uhh," she said, disconcerted, and glanced up at Kit, who had come to stand alongside the racer. "We've gotta get out of here, Kit. It has to be the spell that brought these things down on us. And when those two cabs let you-know-who know that we didn't get caught, or killed—"

Kit nodded, looked down at the Lotus; it glanced sideways up at him, from headlights bright with amusement and triumph. *"How about it?"* Kit said in the Speech. *"Could you give us a lift?"*

In answer the Lotus shrugged, flicking its doors open like a bird spreading its wings.

Nita stood up, staggering slightly. "Fred?"

He appeared beside her, making a feeling of great shame. "Fred, what's the matter?" Kit said, catching it too.

(I couldn't do anything.)

"Of course not," Nita said, reaching up to cup his faint spark in one hand. "Because you just *did* something huge, dummy. We're all right. Come on for a ride." She perched Fred on the upstanding collar of her down vest; he settled there with a sigh of light.

Together she and Kit lowered themselves into the dark seats of the Lotus, into the dim, warm cockpit, alive with dials and gauges, smelling of leather and metal and oil. They had barely strapped themselves in before the Lotus gave a great glad shake that slammed its doors shut, and burned rubber down Fifth Avenue—out of the carnage and south toward the joining of two rivers and the oldest part of Manhattan.

Nita sat at ease, taking a breather and watching the streets of Manhattan rush by. Kit, behind the steering wheel, was holding the dark Book in his lap, feeling it carefully for any change in the directional spell. He was reluctant to touch it. The farther south they went, the more the Book burned the eye that looked at it. The wizards' manual had predicted this effect—that, as the two Books drew closer to one another, each would assert its own nature more and more forcefully. Nita watched the Book warping and skewing the very air around it, blurring its own outlines, and found it easy to believe the manual's statement that even a mind of terrible enough purpose and power to wrench this Book to its use might in the reading be devoured by what was read. She hoped for Kit's sake that it wouldn't devour someone who just touched it.

"We're close," Kit said at last, in a quiet, strained voice.

"You okay?"

"I've got a headache, but that's all. Where are we?"

"Uh—that was just Pearl Street. Close to City Hall." She tapped the inside of her door, a friendly gesture. "Your baby *moves.*"

"Yeah," Kit said affectionately. The Lotus rumbled under its hood, sped on.

"Fred? You feeling better?"

Fred looked up at her from her collar. (Somewhat. I'd feel better still if I knew what we were going to be facing next. If I'm to make bricks again, I'm going to need some notice.)

"Your gnaester, huh?" Kit said.

(I'm not sure I *have* a gnaester any more, after that last emission. And I'm afraid to find out.)

"Kit, scrunch down," Nita said suddenly, doing the same herself. The Lotus roared past the corner of Broadway and Chambers, pointedly ignoring a pair of sullen-looking cabs that stared and snarled as it passed. They were parked on either side of an iron-railed stairway leading down to a subway station. About a block farther along Broadway, two more cabs were parked at another subway entrance.

From his slumped-down position, Kit glanced over at Nita. "Those are the first we've seen."

" 'The usual accesses,' " Nita said. "They've got it down in the subway somewhere."

"Oh, no," Kit muttered, and (Wonderful,) Fred said. Nita swallowed, not too happy about the idea herself. Subway stations, unless they were well lighted and filled with people, gave her the creeps. Worse, even in her New York, subways had their own special ecologies—not just the mice and rats and cats that everybody knew about, but other less normal creatures, on which the wizards' manual had had a twenty-page chapter. "They're all over the place," she said aloud, dealing with the worst problem first. "How are we going to—"

"Ooof!" Kit said, as the dark Book, sitting on his lap, sank down hard as if pushed. The Lotus kept driving on down Broadway, past City Hall, and Kit struggled upward to look out the back window, noting the spot. "That was where the other Book was—straight down from that place we just passed."

The Lotus turned right onto a side street and slowed as if looking for something. Finally it pulled over to the left-hand curb and stopped. "What—" Kit started to say, but the racer flicked open first Kit's door, then Nita's, as if it wanted them to get out.

They did, cautiously. The Lotus very quietly closed its doors. Then it rolled forward a little way, bumping up onto the sidewalk in front of a dingy-looking warehouse. It reached down, bared its fangs, and with great delicacy sank them into a six-foot-long grille in the sidewalk. The Lotus heaved, and with a soft scraping groan, the grille-work came up to reveal an electric-smelling darkness and stairs leading down into it.

"It's one of the emergency exits from the subway, for when the trains break down," Kit whispered, jamming the dark Book back into his backpack and dropping to his knees to rub the Lotus enthusiastically behind one head-light. "It's perfect!"

The Lotus's engine purred as it stared at Kit with fierce affection. It backed a little and parked itself, its motions indicating it would wait for them. Kit got up, pulling out his antenna, and Nita got out her wand. "Well," she said under her breath, "let's get it over with. . . ."

The steps were cracked concrete, growing damp and discolored as she walked downward. Nita held out the wand to be sure of her footing and kept one hand on the left wall to be sure of her balance—there was no banister or railing on the right, only darkness and echoing air. (Kit—) she said silently, wanting to be sure he was near, but not wanting to be heard by anything that might be listening down there.

(Right behind you. Fred?)

His spark came sailing down behind Kit, looking brighter as they passed from gloom to utter dark. (Believe me, I'm not far.)

(Here's the bottom,) Nita said. She turned for one last glance up toward street level and saw a huge sleek silhouette carefully and quietly replacing the grille above them. She gulped, feeling as if she were being shut into a dungeon, and turned to look deeper into the darkness. The stairs ended in a ledge three feet wide and perhaps four feet deep, recessed into the concrete wall of the subway. Nita held up the wand for more light. The ledge stretched away straight ahead, with the subway track at the bottom of a wide pit to the right of it. (Which way, Kit?)

(Straight, for the time being.)

The light reflected dully from the tracks beside them as they pressed farther into the dark. Up on the streets, though there had been darkness, there had also been sound. Here there was a silence like black water, a silence none of them dared to break. They slipped into it holding their breaths. Even the usual dim rumor of a subway tunnel, the sound of trains rumbling far away, the ticking of the rails, was missing. The hair stood up all over Nita as she walked and tried not to make a sound. The air was damp, chilly, full of the smells of life—too full, and the wrong kinds of life, at least to Nita's way of thinking. Mold and mildew; water dripping too softly to make a sound, but still filling the air with a smell of leached lime, a stale, puddly odor; wet trash piled in trickling gutters or at the bases of rusting iron pillars, rotting quietly and always the sharp ozone-and-scorched-soot smell of the third rail. Shortly there was light that did not come from Nita's wand. Pale splotches of green-white radiance were splashed irregularly on walls and ceiling—firefungus which the wizards' manual said was the main food source of the subway's smallest denizens, dun mice and hidebehinds and skinwings. Nita shuddered at the thought and walked faster. Where there were hidebehinds, there would certainly be rats to eat them. And where there were rats, there would also be fireworms and thrastles—

(Nita.)

She stopped and glanced back at Kit. He was holding his backpack in one arm now and the antenna in the other, and looking troubled in the wand's silver light. (That way,) he said, pointing across the tracks at the far wall with its niche-shaped recesses.

(Through the *wall?* We don't even know how thick it is!) Then she stopped and thought a moment. (I wonder—You suppose the Mason's Word would work on concrete? What's in concrete, anyhow?)

(Sand—quartz, mostly. Some chemicals—but I think they all come out of the ground.)

(Then it'll work. C'mon.) Nita hunkered down and very carefully let herself drop into the wide pit where the tracks ran. The crunch of rusty track cinders told her Kit was right behind. Fred floated down beside her, going low to light the way. With great care Nita stepped over the third rail and balanced on the narrow ledge of the wall on the other side. She stowed the wand and laid both hands flat on the concrete to begin implementation of the lesser usage of the Word, the one that merely manipulates stone rather than giving it the semblance of life. Nita leaned her head against the stone too, making sure of her memory of the Word, the sixteen syllables that would loose what was bound. Very fast, so as not to mess it up, she said the Word and pushed.

Door, she thought as the concrete melted under her hands, and a door there was; she was holding the sides of it. (Go ahead,) she said to Kit and Fred. They ducked through under her arm. She took a step forward, let go, and the wall re-formed behind her.

(Now what the—) Kit was staring around him in complete confusion. It took Nita a moment to recover from the use of the Word, but when her vision cleared, she understood the confusion. They were standing in the middle of another track, which ran right into the wall they had just come through and stopped there. The walls there were practically one huge mass of firefungus. It hung down in odd green-glowing lumps from the ceiling and layered thick in niches and on the poles that held the ceiling up. Only the track and ties and the rusty cinders between were bare, a dark road leading downward between eerily shining walls for perhaps an eighth of a mile before curving around to the right and out of view.

(I don't get it,) Kit said. (This track just starts. Or just stops. It would run

right into that one we just came off! There aren't any subway lines in the city
that do that! Are there?)

Nita shook her head, listening. The silence of the other tunnel did not
persist here. Far down along the track, the sickly green light of the firefungus
was troubled by small shadowy rustlings, movements, the scrabbling of claws.
(What about the *Book?*) she said.

Kit nodded down toward the end of the track. (Down there, and a little to
the right.)

They walked together down the long aisle of cold light, looking cautiously
into the places where firefungus growth was sparse enough to allow for
shadow. Here and there small sparks of brightness peered out at them, paired
sparks—the eyes of dun mice, kindled to unnatural brightness by the fungus
they fed on. Everywhere was the smell of dampness, old things rotting or
rusting. The burning-ozone smell grew so chokingly strong that Nita realized
it couldn't be just the third rail producing it—even if the third rail were alive
in a tunnel this old. The smell grew stronger as they approached the curve at
the tunnel's end. Kit, still carrying the backpack, was gasping. She stopped
just before the curve, looked at him. (Are you okay?)

He gulped. (It's close, it's really close. I can hardly see, this thing is blur
ring my eyes so bad.)

(You want to give it to me?)

(No, you go ahead. This place seems to be full of live things. Your depart
ment—)

(Yeah, right,) Nita agreed unhappily, and made sure of her grip on the
rowan wand. (Well, here goes. Fred, you ready for another diversion?)

(I think I could manage something small if I had to.)

(Great. All together now. . . .)

They walked around the curve, side by side. Then they stopped.

It was a subway station. Or it had been at one time, for from where they
stood at one end of the platform, they could see the tons of rubble that had
choked and sealed the tunnel at the far end of the platform. The rubble and
the high ceiling were overgrown with firefungus enough to illuminate the old
mosaics on the wall, the age-cracked tiles that said CITY HALL over and over
again, down the length of the platform wall. But the platform and tracks
weren't visible from where they stood. Heaped up from wall to wall was a
collection of garbage and treasure, things that glittered, things that mold
ered. Nita saw gems, set and unset, like the plunder of a hundred jewelry
stores, tumbled together with moldy kitchen garbage; costly fabric in bolts or
in shreds, half buried by beer cans and broken bottles; paintings in ornate
frames, elaborately carved furniture, lying broken or protruding crookedly
from beneath timbers and dirt fallen from the old ceiling; vases, sculpture,
crystal, silver services, a thousand kinds of rich and precious things, lying all

together, whole and broken, among shattered dirty crockery and base metal. And lying atop the hoard, its claws clutched full of cheap costume jewelry, whispering to itself in the Speech, was the dragon.

Once more Nita tried to swallow and couldn't manage it. This looked nothing like the fireworm her book had mentioned—a foot long mouse-eating lizard with cigarette-lighter breath. But if a fireworm had had a long, long time to grow—she remembered the voice of the young man in the three-piece suit, saying with relief, "The Eldest has it." There was no telling how many years this creature had been lairing here in the darkness, growing huger and huger, devouring the smaller creatures of the underground night and dominating those it did not devour, sending them out to steal for its hoard—or to bring it food. Nita began to tremble, looking at the fireworm-dragon's thirty feet of lean, scaled, tight-muscled body, looking at the size of its dark-stained jaws, and considering what kind of food it must eat. She glanced down at one taloned hind foot and saw something that lay crushed and forgotten beneath it—a subway repairman's reflective orange vest, torn and scorched; a wrench, half melted; the bones, burned black. . . .

The dragon had its head down and was raking over its hoard with huge claws that broke what they touched half the time. Its tail twitched like a cat's as it whispered to itself in a voice like hissing steam. Its scales rustled as it moved, glowing faintly with the same light as the firefungus, but colder, greener, darker. The dragon's eyes were slitted as if even the pale fungus light was too much for it. It dug in the hoard, nosed into the hole, dug again, nosed about, as if going more by touch than sight. *"Four thousand and ssix,"* it whispered, annoyed, hurried, angry. *"It was here sssomewhere, I know it was. Three thousand—no. Four thousand and—and—"*

It kept digging, its claws sending coins and bottlecaps rolling. The dragon reached into the hole and with its teeth lifted out a canvas bag. Bright things spilled out, which Nita first thought were more coins but that turned out to be subway tokens. With a snarl of aggravation the fireworm-dragon flung the bag away, and tokens flew and bounced down the hoard-hill, a storm of brassy glitter. One rolled right to Nita's feet. Not taking her eyes off the dragon, she bent to pick it up. It was bigger than the subway token the New York transit system used these days, and the letters stamped on it were in an old-time style. She nudged Kit and passed it to him, looking around at the mosaics on the walls. They were *old.* The City Hall motif repeated in squares high on the train-side wall of the platform looked little like the City Hall of today. This station had to be one of those that were walled up and forgotten when the area was being rebuilt long ago. The question was—

(The problem is—) Kit started to say in his quietest whisper of thought. But it wasn't quiet enough. With an expression of rage and terror, the dragon looked up from its digging, looked straight at them. Its squinted eyes kindled in the light from Nita's wand, throwing back a frightful violet reflection "*Who's there? Who's there!*" it screamed in the Speech, in a voice like an explosion of steam. Without waiting for an answer it struck forward with it neck as a snake strikes and spat fire at them. Nita was ready, though; the sound of the scream and the sight of many tiny shadows running for cover had given her enough warning to put up the shield spell for both herself and Kit. The firebolt, dark red shot with billowing black like the output of flamethrower, blunted against the shield and spilled sideways and down lik water splashing on a window. When the bolt died away, the dragon was creeping and coiling down the hoard toward them; but it stopped, confused when it saw that Kit and Nita and Fred still stood unhurt. It reared back it head for another bolt.

"*You can't hurt us, Eldest,*" Nita said hurriedly, hoping it wouldn't try; the smell of burned firefungus was already enough to turn the stomach. The dragon crouched low against the hoard, its tail lashing, staring at them.

"*You came to ssteal,*" it said, its voice quieter than before but angrier, as realized it *couldn't* hurt them. "*No one ever comes here but to ssteal. Or t try,*" it added, glancing savagely over at another torn and fire-withered orang vest. "*What do you want? You can't have it. Mine, all thiss is mine. No or takes what'ss mine. He promissed, he ssaid he would leave me alone when came here. Now he breakss the promiss, is that it?*"

The Eldest squinted wrathfully at them. For the second time that day Nita found herself fascinated by an expression. Rage was in the fireworn dragon's face, but also a kind of pain; and its voice was desperate in its anger It turned its back, then, crawling back up onto the hoard. "*I will not let hir break the promiss. Go back to him and tell him that I will burn it, burn it al ssooner than let him have one ring, one jewel. Mine, all thiss is mine, no hoar has been greater than thiss in all times, he will not diminishhh it—*" The Eldest wound itself around the top of the hoard-mound like a crown of spine and scales, digging its claws protectively into the gems and the trash. A sma avalanche of objects started from the place where it had been laying the hoard open before. Gold bars, some the small collectors' bars, some larg ones such as the banks used, clattered or crashed down the side of the mound. Nita remembered how some ten million dollars' worth of Feder Reserve gold had vanished from a bank in New York some years before—jus vanished, untraceable—and she began to suspect where it had gone.

"*Mine,*" hissed the Eldest. "*I have eight thousand six hundred forty-two cr diamonds, I have six hundred—no. I have four hundred eight emeralds. I hav eighty-nine black opals—no, fifteen black opals. I have eighty-nine—eight nine—*" The anxiety in its voice was growing, washing out the ange Abruptly the Eldest turned away from them and began digging again, sti talking, its voice becoming again as it had been when they first came ir urried, worried. *"Eighty-nine pounds of silver plate. I have two hundred ourteen pounds of gold—no, platinum. I have six hundred seventy pounds of old—"*

"Nita," Kit said, very softly, in English, hoping the Eldest wouldn't under- tand it. "You get the feeling it's losing its memory?"

She nodded. "Lord, how awful." For a creature with the intense posses- iveness of a fireworm to be unable to remember what it had in its hoard must be sheer torture. It would never be able to be sure whether everything as there; if something was missing, it might not be able to tell. And to a reworm, whose pride is in its defense of its hoard from even the cleverest hieves, there was no greater shame than to be stolen from and not notice nd avenge the theft immediately. The Eldest must live constantly with the ear of that shame. Even now it had forgotten Kit and Nita and Fred as it lug and muttered frantically, trying to find something, though uncertain of hat it was looking for.

Nita was astonished to find that she was feeling sorry for a creature that ad tried to kill her a few minutes before. "Kit," she said, "what about the right *Book?* Is it in there?"

He glanced down at the dark Book, which was straining in his backpack oward the piled-up hoard. "Uh huh. But how are we going to find it? And re you sure that defense shield is going to hold up at close range, when it omes after us? You know it's not going to just let us *take* something—"

(Why not trade it something?) Fred asked suddenly.

Nita and Kit both looked at him, struck by the idea. "Like what?" Kit said. (Like another Book?)

"Oh, no," they said in simultaneous shock.

"Fred," Kit said then, "we can't do that. The—you-know-who—he'll just ome right here and get it."

(So where did *you* get it from, anyway? Doubtless he could have read from any time he wanted. If you can get the bright *Book* back to the Senior izards in your world, can't they use it to counteract whatever he does?)

Nita and Kit both thought about it. "He might have a point," Nita said fter a second. "Besides, Kit—if we *do* leave the dark Book here, can you nagine you-know-who getting it back without some trouble?" She glanced p at the mound, where the Eldest was whispering threats of death and estruction against whoever might come to steal. "He wouldn't have put the right *Book* here unless the Eldest was an effective guardian."

Even through the discomfort of holding the dark Book, Kit managed to rack a small smile. "Gonna try it?"

Nita took a step forward. Instantly the dragon paused in its digging to stare t her, its scaly lips wrinkled away from black fangs in a snarl, but its eyes frightened. *"Eldest,"* she said in the Speech, *"we don't come to steal. We'r̄ here to make a bargain."*

The Eldest stared at Nita a moment more, then narrowed its eyes furthe *"Hss, you're a clever thiefff,"* it said. *"Why ssshould I bargain with you?"*

Nita gulped. *Wizardry is words*, the book had said. *Believe, and create th̄ truth; but be careful what you believe.* *"Because only your hoard, out of all th̄ other hoards from this world to the next, has what we're interested in,"* she sai carefully. *"Only you ever had the taste to acquire and preserve this thing."*

"Oh?" said the Eldest. Its voice was still suspicious, but its eyes looked les̄ threatened. Nita began to feel a glimmer of hope. *"What might thiss thin̄ be?"*

"A book," Nita said, *"an old book something like this one."* Kit took a ste forward and held up the dark Book for the Eldest to see. This close to i̊ bright counterpart, the dark volume was warping the air and light around so terribly that its outlines writhed like a fistful of snakes.

The Eldest peered at the dark Book with interest. *"Now there is ssom̄ thing I don't have,"* it said. *"Sssee how it changes. That would be an interes ing addition. . . . What did you ssay you wanted to trade it for?"*

"Another Book, Eldest. You came by it some time ago, we hear. It's close ī value to this one. Maybe a little less," Nita added, making it sound offhan̄

The dragon's eyes brightened like those of a collector about to get the bē of a bargain. *"Lesss, you say. Hsss. . . . Sssomeone gave me a book rath̄ like that one, ssome time ago, I forget just who. Let me ssseee. . . ."* It turne away from them and began digging again. Nita and Kit stood and watche and tried to be patient while the Eldest pawed through the trash and th̄ treasure, making sounds of possessive affection over everything it touched mumbling counts and estimating values.

"I wish it would hurry up," Kit whispered. "I can't believe that after we'v̄ been chased this far, they're not going to be down here pretty quick. W didn't have too much trouble getting in—"

"You didn't open the wall," Nita muttered back. "Look, I'm still worrie about leaving this here."

"Whaddaya want?" Kit snapped. "Do I have to carry it all the wa home?" He breathed out, a hiss of annoyance that sounded unnervingly lik̄ the Eldest, and then rubbed his forearm across his eyes. "This thing burn I'm sorry."

"It's okay," Nita said, slightly embarrassed. "I just wish there were som̄ way to be *sure* that you-know-who wouldn't get his hands on it anytim̄ soon."

Kit looked thoughtful and opened his mouth to say something. It was ā that moment that the Eldest put its face down into the hole it had bee digging and came up again with something bright.

The *Book of Night with Moon* fell with a thump onto a pile of gold and gems and made them look tawdry, outshone them in a way that seemed to have nothing to do with light. Its cover was the same black leather as that of the dark *Book*—but as one looked at it, the blackness seemed to gain depth; light seemed hidden in it like a secret in a smiling heart. Even the dim green glow of the firefungus looked healthier now that the *Book* lay out in it. Where page edges showed, they glittered as if brushed with diamond dust rather than gilding. The Eldest bent over the bright *Book,* squinting as if into a great light but refusing to look away. *"Aaaaaahhh,"* it said, a slow, caressing, proprietary sigh. *"Thisss is what you wisshed to trade your book ffor?"*

"Yes, Eldest," Nita said, starting to worry.

The dragon laid its front paws on either side of the *Book.* *"Ffair, it is ssso fair. I had fforgotten how ssweet it was to look on. No. No, I will not trade. I will not. Mine, mine. . . ."* It nosed the bright *Book* lovingly.

Nita bit her lip and wondered what in the world to try next. *"Eldest,"* Kit said from beside her, *"we have something more to trade."*

"Oh?" The dragon looked away from the *Book* with difficulty and squinted at Kit. *"What might that be?"*

(Yeah, what?) Nita said silently.

(Sssh.) *"If you will take our book in trade for that one, we'll work such a wizardry about this place that no thief will ever enter. You'll be safe here for as long as you please. Or forever."*

(What are you talking about!) Nita said, amazed. (We don't have the supplies for a major wizardry like that. The only one you could possibly manage would be one of—)

(—the blank-check spells, I know. Nita, *shaddup!*)

The Eldest was staring at Kit. *"No one would ever come in again to ssteal from me?"* it said.

"That's right."

Nita watched the dragon's face as it looked away from Kit, thinking. It was old and tired, and terrified of losing what it had amassed; but now a frightened hope was awakening in its eyes. It looked back at Kit after a few seconds. *"You will not come back either? No one will trouble me again?"*

"Guaranteed," Kit said, meaning it.

"Then I will trade. Give me your book, and work your spell, and go. Leave me with what is mine." And it picked up the *Book of Night with Moon* in its jaws and dropped it off the hoard-hill, not far from Kit's feet. *"Give me, give me,"* the Eldest said. Warily, Nita dropped the shield spell. Kit took a couple of uneasy steps forward and held out the dark *Book.* The dragon shot its head down, sank teeth in the dark *Book,* and jerked it out of Kit's hands so fast that he stared at them for a moment, counting fingers.

"Mine, mine," it hissed as it turned away and started digging at another

spot on the hoard, preparing to bury the dark Book. Kit stooped, picked up
the *Book of Night with Moon*. It was as heavy as the dark Book had been,
about the size of an encyclopedia volume, and strange to hold—the depth of
the blackness of its covers made it seem as if the holding hands should sink
right through. Kit flipped it open as Nita and Fred came up behind to look
over his shoulder. (But the pages are blank,) Fred said, puzzled.

(It needs moonlight,) Kit said.

(Well, this is moonlight.) Nita held up the rowan wand over the opened
Book. Very vaguely they could make out something printed, the symbols of
the Speech, too faint to read. (Then again, maybe secondhand moonlight
isn't good enough. Kit, what're you going to do? You *have* to seal this place
up now. You promised.)

(I'm gonna do what I said. One of the blank-check wizardries.)

(But when you do those you don't know what price is going to be asked
later.)

(We have to get this *Book*, don't we? That's why we're here. And this is
something that has to be done to get the *Book*. I don't think the price'll be
too high. Anyway *you* don't have to worry, I'll do it myself.)

Nita watched Kit getting out his wizards' manual and bit her lip. (Oh, no
you're not,) she said. (If you're doing it, I'm doing it too. Whatever you're
doing. . . .)

(One of the Moebius spells,) Kit said, finding the page. Nita looked over
his shoulder and read the spell. It would certainly keep thieves out of the
hoard. When recited, a Moebius spell gave a specified volume of space a half
twist that left it permanently out of synch with the spaces surrounding it.
The effect would be like stopping an elevator between floors, forever. (You
read it all through?) Kit said.

(Uh huh.)

(Then let's get back in the tunnel and do it and get out of here. I'm
getting this creepy feeling that things aren't going to be quiet on ground level
when we get up there.)

They wanted to say good-bye to the Eldest, but it had forgotten them
already. *"Mine, mine, mine,"* it was whispering as garbage and gold flew in all
directions from the place where it dug.

(Let's go,) Fred said.

Out in the tunnel, the firefungus seemed brighter to Nita—or perhaps that
was only the effect of looking at the *Book of Night with Moon*. They halted
at the spot where the tunnel curved and began with great care to read the
Moebius spell. The first part of it was something strange and unsettling—an
invocation to the Powers that governed the arts of wizardry, asking help with
this piece of work and promising that the power lent would be returned when
They required. Nita shivered, wondering what she was getting herself into.

for use of the Speech made the promise more of a prediction. Then came the definition of the space to be twisted, and finally the twisting itself. As they spoke the words Nita could see the Eldest, still digging away at his hoard, going pale and dim as if with distance, going away, though not moving. The words pushed the space farther and farther away, toward an edge that could be sensed more strongly though not seen—then, suddenly, over it. The spell broke, completed. Nita and Kit and Fred were standing at the edge of a great empty pit, as if someone had reached up into the earth and scooped out the subway station, the hoard, and the Eldest, whole. Someone had.

"I think we better get out of here," Kit said, very quietly. As if in answer to his words came a long, soft groan of strained timber and metal—the pillars and walls of the tunnel where they stood and the tunnel on the other side of the pit, bending under new stresses that the pillars of the station had handled and that these were not meant to. Then a rumble, something falling.

Nita and Kit turned and ran down the tunnel, stumbling over timbers and picking themselves up and running again. Fred zipped along beside like a shooting star looking for the right place to fall. They slammed into the wall at the end of the track as the rumble turned to a thunder and the thunder started catching up behind. Nita found bare concrete, said the Mason's Word in a gasp, and flung the stone open. Kit jumped through with Fred behind him. The tunnel shook, roared, blew out a stinging, dust-laden wind, and went down in ruin as Nita leaped through the opening and fell to the tracks beside Kit.

He got to his knees slowly, rubbing himself where he had hit. "Boy," he said, "if we weren't in trouble with you-know-who before, we are now. . . ."

Hurriedly Kit and Nita got up and the three of them headed for the ledge and the way to the open air.

Major Wizardries
Termination and Recovery

With great caution and a grunt of effort, Kit pushed up the grille at the to
of the concrete steps and looked around. "Oh, brother," he whispered
"sometimes I wish I wasn't right."

He scrambled up out of the tunnel and onto the sidewalk, with Nita an
Fred following right behind. The street was a shambles reminiscent of Fift
and Sixty-second. Corpses of cabs and limousines and even a small truck wei
scattered around, smashed into lampposts and the fronts of buildings, ove
turned on the sidewalk. The Lotus Esprit was crouched at guard a few fee
away from the grille opening, its engine running in long, tired-soundin
gasps. As Kit ran over to it, the Lotus rumbled an urgent greeting an
shrugged its doors open.

"They know we're here," Nita said as they hurriedly climbed in and buck
led up. "They have to know what we've done. Everything feels different sinc
the dark Book fell out of this space."

(And they must know we'll head back for the worldgate at Pan Am,) Fre
said. (Wherever that is.)

"We've gotta find it—oof!" Kit said, as the Lotus reared back, slammin
its doors shut, and dove down the street they were on, around the corner an
north again. "Nita, you up for one more spell?"

"Do we have a choice?" She got her manual out of her pack, starte
thumbing through it. "What I want to know is what we're supposed to try oi
whatever they have waiting for us at Grand Central. You-know-who isn't jus
going to let us walk in there and leave with the bright *Book*—"

"We'll burn that bridge when we come to it." Kit had his backpack opei
in his lap and was peeking at the *Book of Night with Moon.* Even in thi
sullen dimness that leaked in the Lotus's windows, the edges of the pages oi
the *Book* shone, the black depths of its covers glowed with the promise o

ght. Kit ran a finger along the upper edge of one cover, and as Nita watched
his face settled into a solemn stillness, as if someone spoke and he listened
intently. It was a long moment before the expression broke. Then Kit
glanced over at her with a wondering look in his eyes. "It really doesn't look
like that much," he said. "But it feels—Nita, I don't think they can hurt us
while we have this. Or if they can, it won't matter much."

"Maybe not, if we read from it," Nita said, reading down through the spell
that would locate the worldgate for them. "But you remember what Tom
said—"

"Yeah." But there was no concern in Kit's voice, and he was looking
soberly at the *Book* again.

Nita finished checking the spell and settled back in the seat to prepare for
it, then started forward again as a spark of heat burned into her neck. "Ow!"

(Sorry.) Fred slid around from behind her to perch farther forward on her
shoulder.

"Here we go," Nita said.

She had hardly begun reading the imaging spell before a wash of power
such as she had never felt seized her and plunged her into the spell headfirst.
And the amazing thing was that she couldn't even be frightened, for whatever had so suddenly pulled her under and into the magic was utterly benevolent, a huge calm influence that Nita sensed would do her nothing but good,
though it might kill her doing it. The power took her, poured itself into her,
made the spell *part* of her. There was no longer any need to work it; it *was*.
Instantly she saw all Manhattan laid out before her again in shadow outlines,
and there was the worldgate, almost drowned in the darkness created by the
Starsnuffer, but not hidden to her. The power let her go then, and she sat
back gasping. Kit was watching her strangely.

(I think I see what you mean,) she said. (The *Book*— it made the spell
happen by itself, almost.)

"Not 'almost,'" Kit said. "No wonder you-know-who wants it kept out of
the hands of the Senior wizards. It can make even a beginner's spell happen.
It did the same thing with the Moebius spell. If someone wanted to take this
place apart—or if someone wanted to make more places like it, and they had
the *Book*—" He gulped. "Look, where's the gate?"

"Where it should be," Nita said, finding her breath. "Underground—
under Grand Central. Not in the deli, though. It's down in one of the train
tunnels."

Kit gulped again, harder. "Trains. . . . And you *know* that place'll be
guarded. Fred, are you up to another diversion?"

(Will it get us back to the Sun and the stars again? Try me.)

Nita closed her eyes to lean back and take a second's rest—the power that
had run through her for that moment had left her amazingly drained—but

nearly jumped out of her skin the next moment as the Lotus braked wildly, fishtailing around a brace of cabs that leaped at it out of a side street. With a scream of engine and a cloud of exhaust and burned rubber it found it traction again and tore out of the intersection and up Third Avenue, leaving the cabs behind.

"They know, they *know*," Nita moaned. "Kit, what're we going to do? I the *Book* going to be enough to stand up to him?"

"We'll find out, I guess," Kit said, though he sounded none too certain "We've been lucky so far. No, not lucky, we've been ready. Maybe that'll be enough. We both came prepared for trouble, we both did our reading—"

Nita looked sheepish. "You did, maybe. I couldn't get past Chapter Forty No matter how much I read, there was always more."

Kit smiled just as uncomfortably. "I only got to Thirty-three myself, then skimmed a lot."

"Kit, there's about to be a surprise quiz. *Did we study the right chapters?*"

"Well, we're gonna find out," Kit said. The Lotus turned left at the corner of Third and Forty-second, speeding down toward Grand Central. Forty second seemed empty; not even a cab was in sight. But a great looming darkness was gathered down the street, hiding the iron overpass. The Lotus slowed, unwilling to go near it.

"Right here is fine," Kit said, touching the dashboard reassuringly. The Lotus stopped in front of the doors to Grand Central, reluctantly shrugging first Nita's, then Kit's door open.

They got out and looked around them. Silence. Nita looked nervously at the doors and the darkness beyond, while the Lotus crowded close to Kit who rubbed its right wheelwell absently.

The sound came. A single clang, like an anvil being struck, not too far away. Then another clang, hollow and metallic, echoing from the blank-eyed buildings, dying into bell-like echoes. Several more clangs, close together Then a series of them, a slow drumroll of metal beating on stone. The Lotus pulled out from under Kit's hand, turning to face down Forty-second the way they had come, growling deep under its hood.

The clangor grew louder; echoes bounced back and forth from building to building so that it was impossible to tell from what direction the sound was coming. Down at the corner of Lexington and Forty-second, a blackness jutted suddenly from behind one of the buildings on the uptown side. The shape of it and its unlikely height above the pavement, some fifteen feet kept Nita from recognizing what it was until more of it came around the corner, until the blackness found its whole shape and swung it around into the middle of the street on iron hooves.

Eight hooves, ponderous and deadly, dented the asphalt of the street. They belonged to a horse—a huge, misproportioned beast, its head skinned down to a skull, leaden-eyed and grinning hollowly. All black iron that steed was, as if it had stepped down from a pedestal at its rider's call; and the one who rode it wore his own darkness on purpose, as if to reflect the black mood within. The Starsnuffer had put aside his three-piece suit for chain mail like hammered onyx and a cloak like night with no stars. His face was still handsome, but dreadful now, harder than any stone. His eyes burned with the burning of the dark Book, alive with painful memory about to come real. About the feet of his mount the perytons milled, not quite daring to look in their master's face, but staring and slavering at the sight of Kit and Nita, waiting the command to course their prey.

Kit and Nita stood frozen, and Fred's light, hanging small and constant as a star behind them, dimmed down to its faintest.

The cold, proud, erect figure on the black mount raised what it held in its right hand, a steel rod burning dark and skewing the air about it as the dark Book had. *"You have stolen something of mine,"* said a voice as cold as space, using the Speech with icy perfection and hating it. *"No one steals from me."*

The bolt that burst from the rod was a red darker than the Eldest's fiery breath. Nita did not even try to use the rowan wand in defense—as well try to use a sheet of paper to stop a laser beam. But as she and Kit leaped aside, the air around them went afire with sudden clarity, as if for a moment the darkness inherent in it was burned away. The destroying bolt went awry, struck up sideways and blasted soot-stained blocks out of the facing of Grand Central. And in that moment the Lotus screamed wild defiance and leaped down Forty-second at the rider and his steed.

"NO!" Kit screamed. Nita grabbed him, pulled him toward the doors. He wouldn't come, wouldn't turn away as the baying perytons scattered, as the Lotus hurtled into the forefront of the pack, flinging bodies about. It leaped up at the throat of the iron beast, which reared on four hooves and raised the other four and with them smashed the Lotus flat into the street.

The bloom of fire that followed blotted out that end of the street. Kit responded to Nita's pulling then, and together they ran through the doors, up the ramp that led into Grand Central, out across the floor—

Nita was busy getting the rowan wand out, had gotten ahead of Kit, who couldn't move as fast because he was crying—but it was his hand that shot out and caught her by the collar at the bottom of the ramp, almost choking her, and kept her from falling into the pit. There was no floor. From one side of the main concourse to the other was a great smoking crevasse, the floor and lower levels and tunnels beneath all split as if with an axe. Ozone smell and cinder smell and the smell of tortured steel breathed up hot in their faces, while from behind, outside, the thunder of huge hooves on concrete and the howls of perytons began again.

Below them severed tunnels and stairways gaped dark. There was no seeing the bottom—it was veiled in fumes and soot, underlit by the blue arcs of shorted-out third rails and an ominous deep red, as if the earth itself had broken open and was bleeding lava. The hooves clanged closer.

Nita turned to Kit, desperate. Though his face still streamed with tears, there was an odd, painful calm about it. "I know what to do," he said, his voice saying that he found that strange. He drew the antenna out of his back pocket, and it was just as Nita noticed how strangely clear the air was burning about him that Kit threw the piece of steel out over the smoking abyss. She would have cried out and grabbed him, except that he was watching it so intently.

The hoofbeats stopped and were followed by a sound as of iron boots coming down on the sidewalk, immensely heavy, shattering the stone. Despite her own panic, Nita found she couldn't look away from the falling antenna either. She was gripped motionless in the depths of a spell again, while the power that burned the air clear now poured itself through Kit and into his wizardry. There was something wrong with the way the antenna was falling. It seemed to be getting bigger with distance instead of smaller. It stretched, it grew, glittering as it turned and changed. It wasn't even an antenna any more. Sharp blue light and diffuse red gleamed from flat, polished faces, edges sharp as razors. It was a sword blade, not even falling now, but laid across the chasm like a bridge. The wizardry broke and turned Nita loose. Kit moved away from her and stepped out onto the flat of the blade, fear and pain showing in his face again.

"Kit!"

"It's solid," he said, still crying, taking another step out onto the span, holding his arms out for balance as it bent slightly under his weight. "Come on, Nita, it's noon-forged steel, he can't cross it. He'll have to change shape or seal this hole up."

(Nita, come on,) Fred said, and bobbled out across the crevasse, following Kit. Though almost blind with terror, her ears full of the sound of iron-shod feet coming after them, she followed Fred, who was holding a straight course out over the sword blade—followed him, arms out as she might have on a balance beam, most carefully not looking down. This was worse than the bridge of air had been, for that hadn't flexed so terribly under each step she or Kit took. His steps threw her off balance until she halted long enough to take a deep breath and step in time with him. Smoke and the smell of burning floated up around her; the shadows of the dome above the concourse stirred with wicked eyes, the open doors to the train platforms ahead of her muttered, their mouths full of hate. She watched the end of the blade, looked straight ahead. Five steps: Kit was off. Three. One—

She reached out to him, needing desperately to feel the touch of a human hand. He grabbed her arm and pulled her off the bridge just as another blast f black-red fire blew in the doors on the other side of the abyss. Kit said one harp word in the Speech, and the air went murky around his body again as he *Book* ceased to work through him. Nita let go, glanced over her shoulder n time to see the sword blade snap back to being an antenna, like a rubber and going back to its right size. It fell into the fuming darkness, a lone litter, quickly gone.

They ran. Nita could still see in her mind the place where the worldgate vas hidden; the *Book* 's power had burned it into her like a brand. She took he lead, racing down a flight of stairs, around a corner and down another light, into echoing beige-tiled corridors where Fred and the rowan wand vere their only light. Above them they could hear the thunderous rumor of ron footsteps, slow, leisurely, inexorable, following them down. The howls of erytons floated down to them like the voices of lost souls, hungry for the lood and pain they needed to feel alive again.

"Here!" Nita shouted, not caring what might hear, and dodged around a orner, and did what she had never done in all her life before—jumped a ubway turnstile. Its metal fingers made a grab for her, but she was too fast or them, and Kit eluded them too, coming right behind. At full speed Nita ounded down the platform, looking for the steps at the end of it that would et them down onto the tracks. She took them three at a time, two leaps, and hen was running on cinders again, leaping over ties. Behind her she could ear Kit hobbling as fast as he could on his sore leg, gasping, but keeping up. red shot along beside her, pacing her, lighting her way. Eyes flickered in his ight—hidebehinds, dun mice, ducking under cover as the three of them vent past. Nita slowed and stopped in the middle of the tracks. "Here!"

Kit had his manual out already. He found the page by Fred's light, humped to a stop beside Nita. *"Here?* In the middle of the—"

"Read! Read!" she yelled. There was more thunder rolling in the tunnel han just the sound of their pursuer's footsteps. Far away, she could hear vhat had been missing from the other tunnel beneath City Hall: trains. Away n the darkness, wheels slammed into the tracks they rode—even now the ails around them were clacking faintly in sympathy, and a slight cool wind oreathed against Nita's face. A train was coming. On *this* track. Kit began he worldgating spell, reading fast. Again the air around them seemed clearer, resher, as the power of the *Book of Night with Moon* seized the spell and its peaker, used them both.

That was when the Starsnuffer's power came down on them. It seemed mpossible that the dank close darkness in which they stood could become ny darker, but it did, as an oppressive blanket of clutching, choking hatred ell over them, blanketing everything. The rowan rod's silver fire was smoth-red. Fred's light went out as if he had been stepped on. Kit stopped reading, truggled for breath. Nita tried to resist, tried to find air, couldn't, collapsed

to her knees, choking. The breeze from the dark at the end of the tunnel go
stronger: the onrushing train, pushing the air in front of it, right up the track
right at them—

(I—will—*not*,) Fred said, struggling, angry. (I will—*not*—go out!) His de
termination was good for a brief flare, like a match being struck. Kit foun
his voice, managed to get out a couple more words of the spell in Fred'
wavering radiance, grew stronger, managed a few more. Nita found that sh
could breathe again. She clutched the rowan wand, thinking with all he
might of the night Liused had given it to her, the clear moonlight shinin
down between the branches. The wand came alive again. Shadows that ha
edged forward from the walls of the tunnel fled again. Kit read, hurrying
Two thirds done, Nita thought. If he can just finish—

Far away down the tunnel, there were eyes. They blazed. The headlights o
a train, coming down at them in full career. The clack of the rails rose to
rattle, the breeze became a wind, the roar of the train itself echoed not just i
the other tunnels, but in this one. Nita got to her feet, facing those eye
down. She would not look away. Fred floated by her shoulder; she gathere
him close, perching him by her ear, feeling his terror of the overwhelmin
darkness as if it were her own but having nothing to comfort him with. *Kit*
she thought, not daring to say it aloud for fear she should interrupt hi
concentration. The sound of his words was getting lost in the thunder fro
above, iron-shod feet, the thunder from below, iron wheels on iron rails.

Suddenly Kit's voice was missing from the mélange of thunders. Withou
warning the worldgate was there, glistening in the light of the rowan wan
and Fred and the train howling down toward them—a great jagged soa
bubble, trembling with the pressure of sound and air. Kit wasted no time, bu
leaped through. Fred zipped into the shimmering surface and was gone. Nit
made sure of her grip on the rowan wand, took a deep breath, and jumpe
through the worldgate. A hundred feet away, fifty feet away, the blazing eye
of the train glared at her as she jumped; its horn screamed in delight, antici
pating the feel of blood beneath its wheels; sudden thunder rocked the plat
form behind her, black-red fire more sensed than seen. But the rainbo
shimmer of the gate broke across her face first. The train roared through th
place where she had been, and she heard the beginnings of a cry of frustrate
rage as she cheated death, and anger, and fell and fell and fell. . . .

—and came down *slam* on nothing. Or it seemed that way, until openin
her eyes a little wider she saw the soot and smog trapped in the hardened ai
she lay on, the only remnant of her walkway. Kit was already getting up fro
his knees beside her, looking out from their little island of air across to th
Pan Am Building. Everything was dark, and Nita started to groan, certai
that something had gone wrong and that the worldgate had simply dumpe

hem back in the Starsnuffer's world—but no, her walkway *was* there. Greatly daring, she looked down and saw far below the bright yellow glow of sodium-vapor street lights and red of taillights. City noise, roaring, cacophonous and alive, floated up to them. We're back. It worked!

Kit was reading from his wizards' manual, as fast as he had read down in the train tunnel. He stopped and then looked at Nita in panic as she got up. "I can't close the gate!"

She gulped. "Then he can follow us . . . through. . . ." In an agony of haste she fumbled her own book out of her pack, checked the words for the air-hardening spell one more time, and began reading herself. Maybe panic helped, for this time the walkway spread itself out from their feet to the roof of the building very fast indeed. "Come on," she said, heading out across it as quickly as she dared. But where will we run to? she thought. He'll come behind, hunting. We can't go home, he might follow. And what'll he do to the city?

She reached up to the heliport railing and swung herself over it. Kit followed, with Fred pacing him. "What're we gonna do?" he said as they headed across the gravel together. "There's no time to call the Senior wizards, wherever they are—or even Tom and Carl. *He'll* be here shortly."

"Then we'll have to get away from here and find a place to hole up for a little. Maybe the bright *Book* can help." She paused as Kit spoke to the lock on the roof door, and they ran down the stairs. "Or the manuals might have something, now that we need it."

"Yeah, right," Kit said as he opened the second door at the bottom of the stairs, and they ran down the corridor where the elevators were. But he didn't sound convinced. "The park?"

"Sounds good."

Nita punched the call button for the elevator, and she and Kit stood there panting. There was a feeling in the air that all hell was about to break loose, and the sweat was breaking out all over Nita because *they* were going to have to stop it somehow. "Fred," she said, "did you ever hear anything, out where you were, any stories of someone getting the better of you-know-who?"

Fred's light flickered uncomfortably as he watched Kit frantically consulting his manual. (Oh, yes,) he said. (I'd imagine that's why he wanted a universe apart to himself—to keep others from getting in and thwarting him. It used to happen fairly frequently when he went up against life.)

Fred's voice was too subdued for Nita's liking. "What's the catch?"

(Well . . . it's possible to win against him. But usually someone dies of it.)

Nita gulped again. Somehow she had been expecting something like that. "Kit?"

The elevator chimed. Once inside, Kit went back to looking through his

manual. "I don't see anything," he said, sounding very worried. "There's
general-information chapter on him here, but there's not much we don
know already. The only thing he's never been able to dominate was the *Boo*
of Night with Moon. He tried—that's what the dark Book was for; h
thought by linking them together he could influence the bright *Book* with i
diminish its power. But that didn't work. Finally he was reduced to simpl
stealing the bright *Book* and hiding it where no one could get at it. That wa
no one could become a channel for its power, no one could possibly defea
him. . . ."

Nita squeezed her eyes shut, not sure whether the sinking feeling in he
stomach was due to her own terror or the elevator going down. *Read from i*
No, no. I hope I never have to, Tom's voice said in her mind. . . . *Readin*
it, being the vessel for all that power—I wouldn't want to. Even good can b
terribly dangerous.

And that was an Advisory, Nita thought, miserable. There was no doub
about it. One of them might have to do what a mature wizard feared doing
read from the *Book* itself.

"Let me do it," she said, not looking at Kit.

He glanced up from the manual, stared at her. "Bull," he said, and the
looked down at the manual again. "If you're gonna do it, *I'm* gonna do it.

Outside the doors another bell chimed as the elevator slowed to a stop. Ki
led the way out across the black stone floor, around the corner to the en
trance. The glass door let them out onto a street just like the one they ha
walked onto in the Snuffer's otherworld—but here windows had lights i
them, and the reek of gas and fumes was mixed with a cool smell of evenin
and a rising wind, and the cabs that passed looked blunt and friendly. Nit
could have cried for relief, except that there was no reason to feel relieved
Things would be getting much worse shortly.

Fred, though, felt no such compunctions. (The stars, the stars are back,) h
almost sang, flashing with delight as they hurried along.

"Where?" Kit said skeptically. As usual, the glow of a million street light
was so fierce that even the brightest stars were blotted out by it. But Fred wa
too cheerful to be suppressed.

(They're there, they're *there!*) he said, dancing ahead of them. (And th
Sun is there too. I don't care that it's on the other side of this silly place,
can feel—feel—)

His thought cut off so abruptly that Nita and Kit both stopped anc
glanced over their shoulders. A coldness grabbed Nita's heart and wrung it
The sky, even though clear, did have a faint golden glow to it, city ligh
scattered from smog—and against that glow, high up atop the Pan Am
Building, a form half unstarred night and half black iron glowered down a
them like a statue from a dauntingly high pedestal. Nita and Kit froze like

noths pinned to a card as the remote clear howl of perytons wound through he air.

"He'll just jump down," Nita whispered, knowing somehow that he could o it. But the rider did not leap, not yet. Slowly he raised his arms in ammons. One hand still held the steel rod about which the air twisted and rithed as if in pain; as the arm lifted, that writhing grew more violent, more ortured.

And darkness answered the gesture. It flowed forward around the feet of he dark rider's terrible mount, obscuring the perytons peering down over the oof's edge, and poured down the surface of the building like a black fog. Vhat it touched, changed. Where the darkness passed, metal tarnished, glass lmed over or shattered, lighted windows were quenched, went blind. Down ll the sides of the building it flowed, black lava burning the brightness out of verything it touched.

Kit and Nita looked at each other in despair, knowing what would happen hen that darkness spilled out onto the ground. The streets would go deso-te and dark, the cabs would stop being friendly; and when all the island om river to river was turned into his domain, the dark rider would catch hem at his leisure and do what he pleased with them. And with the bright *ook*—and with everything else under the sky, perhaps. This was no other-orld, frightening but remote. This was their home. If this world turned into *iat* one—

"We're dead," Kit said, and turned to run. Nita followed him. Perhaps out f hope that another Lotus might be waiting innocently at some curbside, he way Kit ran retraced their earlier path. But there was no Lotus—only right streets, full of people going about their business with no idea of what as about to happen to them, cars honking at one another in cheerful igno-nce. Fat men running newsstands and bemused bag-ladies watched Nita nd Kit run by as if death and doom were after them, and no one really oticed the determined spark of light keeping pace. They ran like the wind own West Fiftieth, but no Lotus lay there, and around the corner onto 'ifth and up to Sixty-first, but the carnage left in the otherworld was not eflected here—the traffic on Fifth ran unperturbed. Gasping, they waited or a break in it, then ran across, hopped the wall into the park and crouched own beside it as they had in the world they'd left.

The wind was rising, not just a night breeze off the East River, but a chill ind with a hint of that other place's coldness to it. Kit unslung his pack as red drew in close, and by his light Kit brought out the *Book of Night with Moon*. The darkness of its covers shone, steadying Kit's hands, making Fred eem to burn brighter. Kit and Nita sat gasping for breath, staring at each ther.

"I'm out of ideas," Kit said. "I think we're going to have to read from this

to keep the city the way it should be. We can't just let him change thing
until he catches us. Buildings are one thing; but what happens to *people* aft
that black hits them?"

"And it might not stop here either," Nita said between gasps, thinking
her mother and father and Dairine, of the quiet street where they lived, th
garden, the rowan, all warped and darkened—if they would survive at all.

Her eyes went up to the Moon shining white and full between the shiftir
branches. All around them she could feel the trees stirring in that nev
strange, cold wind, whispering uneasily to one another. It was so good to l
in a place where she could hear the growing things again.

The idea came. "Kit," she said hurriedly, "that dark was moving pret
fast. If we're going to read from the *Book* we may need something to buy
time, to hold off the things that'll come with it, the perytons and the cabs

"We're out of Lotuses," Kit said, his voice bleak.

"I know. But look where we are! Kit, this is *Central Park!* You know ho
many trees there are in here of the kinds that went to the Battle in the o
days? They don't forget."

He stared at her. "What can they—"

"The *Book* makes everything work better, doesn't it? There's a spell that
I'll do it, you'll see. But you've got to do one too, it's in your specialty grou
The Mason's Word, the long version—"

"To bring stone or metal to life." He scrubbed the last tears out of his ey
and managed ever so slight and slow a smile. "There are more statues withi
screaming distance of this place—"

"Kit," Nita said, "how loud can you scream?"

"Let's find out."

They both started going through their manuals in panicky haste. Far awa
on the east side, lessened by all the buildings and distance that lay betweer
but still much too clear, there was a single, huge, deep-pitched *clang*, a
immense weight of metal hitting the ground with stone-shattering forc
Fred bobbled a little in the air, nervously. (How long do you think—)

"He'll be a while, Fred," Kit said, sounding as if he hoped it would be
long while. "He doesn't like to run; it's beneath his dignity. But I think—
He broke off for a moment, reading down a page and forming the syllables
the Mason's Word without saying them aloud. "I think we're going to have
few friends who'll do a little running for us."

He stood up, and Fred followed him, staying close to light the page. "Nit
hand me the *Book.*" She passed it up to him, breaking off her own frant
reading for a moment to watch. "It'll have to be a scream," he said as if
himself. "The more of them hear me, the more help we get."

Kit took three long breaths and then shouted the Word at the top of h
lungs, all twenty-seven syllables of it without missing a one. The sound b

ame impossibly more than the yell of a twelve-year-old as the *Book* seized
he sound and the spell together and flung them out into the city night. Nita
ad to hold her ears. Even when it seemed safe to uncover them again, the
·choes bounced back from buildings on all sides and would not stop. Kit
tood there amazed as his voice rang and ricocheted from walls blocks away.
'Well," he said, "they'll feel the darkness, they'll know what's happening. I
hink."

"My turn," Nita said, and stood up beside Kit, making sure of her place.
Ier spell was not a long one. She fumbled for the rowan wand, put it in the
aand that also held her wizards' manual, and took the bright *Book* from Kit.
'I hope—" she started to say, but the words were shocked out of her as the
eeling that the *Book* brought with it shot up her arm. Power, such sheer
oyous power that no spell could fail, no matter how new the wizard was to
he Art. Here, under moonlight and freed at last from its long restraint, the
3ook was more potent than even the dark rider who trailed them would
uspect, and that potency raged to be free. Nita bent her head to her manual
ınd read the spell.

Or tried to. She saw the words, the syllables, and spoke the Speech, but the
noonfire falling on the *Book* ran through her veins, slid down her throat, and
urned the words to song more subtle than she had ever dreamed of, burned
oehind her eyes and showed her another time, when another will had voiced
hese words for the first time and called the trees to battle.

All around her, both now and then, the trees lifted their arms into the
vind, breathed the fumes of the new-old Earth and breathed out air that
nen could use; they broke the stone to make ground for their children to till
ınd fed the mold with themselves, leaf and bough, and generation upon
generation. They knew to what end their sacrifice would come, but they did
t anyway, and they would do it again in the Witherer's spite. They were
loing it now. Oak and ash and willow, birch and alder, elm and maple, they
elt the darkness in the wind that tossed their branches and would not stand
till for it. The ground shook all around Nita, roots heaved and came free—
irst the trees close by, the counterparts of the trees under which she and Kit
ınd Fred had sheltered in the dark otherworld. White oak, larch, twisted
crabapple, their leaves glittering around the edges with the flowering radi-
ınce of the rowan wand, they lurched and staggered as they came rootloose,
ınd then crowded in around Kit and Nita and Fred, whispering with wind,
naking a protecting circle through which nothing would pass but moonlight.
The effect spread out and away from Nita, though the spell itself was fin-
shed, and that relentless power let her sag against one friendly oak, gasping.

For yards, for blocks, as far as she could see through the trunks of the trees
hat crowded close, branches waved green and wild as bushes and vines and
uundred-year monarchs of the park pulled themselves out of the ground and

moved heavily to the defense. Away to the east, the clangor of metal hooves and the barks and howls of the dark rider's pack were coming closer. The trees waded angrily toward the noise, some hobbling along on top of the ground, some wading through it, and just as easily through sidewalks and stone walls. In a few minutes there was a nearly solid palisade of living wood between Kit and Nita and Fred and Fifth Avenue. Even the glare of the street lights barely made it through the branches.

Kit and Nita looked at each other. "Well," Kit said reluctantly, "I guess we can't put it off any longer."

Nita shook her head. She moved to put her manual away and was momentarily shocked when the rowan wand, spent, crumbled to silver ash in her hand. "So much for that," she said, feeling unnervingly naked now that her protection was gone. Another howl sounded, very close by, and was abruptly cut off in a rushing of branches as if a tree had fallen on something on purpose. Nita fumbled in her pocket and pulled out a nickel. "Call it," she said.

"Heads."

She tossed the coin, caught it, slapped it down on her forearm. Heads. "Crud," she said, and handed the bright *Book* to Kit.

He took it uneasily, but with a glitter of excitement in his eye. "Don't worry," he said. "You'll get your chance."

"Yeah, well, don't hog it." She looked over at him and was amazed to see him regarding her with some of the same worry she was feeling. From outside the fence of trees came a screech of brakes, the sound of a long skid, and then a great splintering crashing of metal and smashing of glass as an attacking cab lost an argument with some tree standing guard. Evidently reinforcements from that other, darker world were arriving.

"I won't," Kit said. "You'll take it away from me and keep reading if—"

He stopped, not knowing what might happen. Nita nodded. "Fred," she said, "we may need a diversion. But save yourself till the last minute."

(I will. Kit—) The spark of light hung close to him for a moment. (Be careful.)

Suddenly, without warning, every tree around them shuddered as if violently struck. Nita could hear them crying out in silent anguish, and cried out in terror herself as she felt what they felt—a great numbing cold that smote at the heart like an axe. Kit, beside her, sat frozen with it, aghast. Fred went dim with shock. (Not again!) he said, his voice faint and horrified. (Not *here*, where there's so much life!)

"The Sun," Nita whispered. "He put out the Sun!" Starsnuffer, she thought. That tactic's worked for him before. And if the Sun is out, pretty soon there won't be moonlight to read by, and he can—

Kit stared up at the Moon as if at someone about to die. "Nita, how long
o we have?"

"Eight minutes, maybe a little more, for light to get here from the Sun.
ight minutes before it runs out. . . ."

Kit sat down hurriedly, laid the bright *Book* in his lap, and opened it. The
ght of the full Moon fell on the glittering pages. This time the print was not
ague as under the light of Nita's wand. It was clear and sharp and dark, as
asily read as normal print in daylight. The *Book* 's covers were fading, going
lear, burning with that eye-searing transparency that Nita had seen about
it and herself before. The whole *Book* was hardly to be seen except for its
rinting, which burned in its own fashion, supremely black and clear, but
listening as if the ink with which the characters were printed had moonlight
apped in them too. *"Here's an index,"* Kit whispered, using the Speech
ow. *"I think—the part about New York—"*

Yes, Nita thought desperately, as another cab crashed into the trees and
nished itself. And what then? What do we do about— She would not finish
ie thought, for the sound of those leisurely, deadly hoofbeats was getting
loser, and mixing with it were sirens and the panicked sound of car horns.
he thought of that awful dark form crossing Madison, kicking cars aside,
rushing what tried to stop it, and all the time that wave of blackness wash-
ig alongside, changing everything, stripping the streets bare of life and light.
nd what about the Sun? The Earth will freeze over before long, and he'll
ave the whole planet the way he wants it— Nita shuddered. Cold and
arkness and nothing left alive—a storm-broken, ice-locked world, full of
visted machines stalking desolate streets forever. . . .

Kit was turning pages, quickly but gently, as if what he touched was a live
iing. Perhaps it was. Nita saw him pause between one page and the next,
olding one bright-burning page draped delicately over his fingers, then let-
ng it slide carefully down to lie with the others he'd turned. *"Here,"* he
hispered, awed, delighted. He did not look up to see what Nita saw, the
ave of darkness creeping around them, unable to pass the tree-wall, passing
iward, surrounding them so that they were suddenly on an island of grass in
sea of wrestling naked tree limbs and bare-seared dirt and rock. *"Here—"*

He began to read, and for all her fear Nita was lulled to stillness by
onder. Kit's voice was that of someone discovering words for the first time
ter a long silence, and the words he found were a song, as her spell to free
ie trees had seemed. She sank deep in the music of the Speech, hearing the
ory told in what Kit read.

Kit was invoking New York, calling it up as one might call up a spirit; and
bedient to the summons, it came. The skyline came, unsmirched by any
ackness—a crown of glittering towers in a smoky sunrise, all stabbing points
id jeweled windows, precipices of steel and stone. City Hall came, brooding

over its colonnades, gazing down in weary interest at the people who came and went and governed the island through it. The streets came, hot, dirty, crowded, but flowing with voices and traffic and people, bright lifeblood surging through concrete arteries. The parks came, settling into place one by one as they were described, free of the darkness under the night—from tiny paved vest-pocket niches to the lake-set expanses of Central Park, they all came, thrusting the black fog back. Birds sang, dogs ran and barked and rolled in the grass, trees were bright with wary squirrels' eyes. The Battery came, the crumbling old first-defense fort standing peaceful now at the southernmost tip of Manhattan—the rose-gold of some remembered sunset glowed warm on its bricks as it mused in weedy silence over old battles won and nonetheless kept an eye on the waters of the harbor, just in case some British cutter should try for a landing when the colonists weren't looking. Westward over the water, the Palisades were there, shadowy cliffs with the Sun behind them, mist-blue and mythical-looking though New Jersey was only a mile away. Eastward and westward the bridges were there, the lights of their spanning suspension cables coming out blue as stars in the twilight. Seabirds wheeled pale and graceful about the towers of the George Washington Bridge and the Verrazano Narrows and the iron crowns of the 59th Street Bridge, as the soft air of evening settled over Manhattan, muting the city roar to a quiet breathing rumble. Under the starlight and the risen Moon, an L-1011 arrowed out of LaGuardia Airport and soared over the city, screaming its high song of delight in the cold upper airs, dragging the thunder along behind—

Nita had to make an effort to pull herself out of the waking dream. Kit read on, while all around the trees bent in close to hear, and the air flamed clear and still as a frozen moment of memory. He read on, naming names in the Speech, describing people and places in terrifying depth and detail, making them real and keeping them that way by the *Book* 's power and the sound of the words. But no sign of any terror at the immensity of what he was doing showed in Kit's face—and that frightened Nita more than the darkness that still surged and whispered around them and their circle of trees. Nita could see Kit starting to burn with that same unbearable clarity, becoming more real, so much so that he was not needing to be visible any more. Slowly, subtly, the *Book*'s vivid transparency was taking him too. Fred, hanging beside Kit and blazing in defiance of the dark, looked pale in comparison. Even Kit's shadow glowed, and it occurred to Nita that shortly, if this kept up, he wouldn't have one. What do I do? she thought. He's not having trouble, he seems to be getting *stronger*, not weaker, but if this has to go on much longer—

Kit kept reading. Nita looked around her and began to see an answer. The darkness had not retreated from around them. Out on the Fifth Avenue side

of the tree-wall, the crashes of cabs were getting more frequent, the howls of
perytons were closer, the awful clanging hoofbeats seemed almost on top of
them. There was nowhere to run, and Nita knew with horrible certainty that
not all the trees in the park would be enough to stop the Starsnuffer when he
came there. Keeping New York real was one answer to this problem, but not
the answer. The darkness and the unreality were symptoms, not the cause.
Something had to be done about *him.*

The iron hooves paused. For an awful moment there was no sound; howls
and screeching tires fell silent. Then metal began to smash on stone in a
thunderous canter, right across the street, and with a horrible screeching
neigh the rider's iron steed smashed into the tree-wall, splintering wood,
bowing the palisade inward. Nita wanted to shut her mind against the
screams of the trees broken and flung aside in that first attack, but she could
not. All around her the remaining trees sank their roots deep in determination, but even they knew it would be hopeless. There were enough cracks in
the wall that Nita could see the black steed rearing back for another smash
with its front four hooves, the rider smiling, a cold cruel smile that made Nita
shudder. One more stroke and the wall would be down. Then there would be
wildfire in the park. Kit, oblivious, kept reading. The iron mount rose to its
full height. "Fred," Nita whispered, "I think you'd better—" The sound of
heavy hoofbeats, coming from behind them, from the park side, choked her
silent. He has a twin brother, Nita thought. We *are* dead.

But the hoofbeats divided around the battered circle of trees and poured
past in a storm of metal and stone, the riders and steeds marble pale or
bronze dark, every equestrian statue in or near Central Park gathered together into an impossible cavalry that charged past Nita and Kit and Fred
and into the street to give battle. Perytons and cabs screamed as General
Sherman from Grand Army Plaza crashed in among them with sword raised,
closely followed by Joan of Arc in her armor, and Simon Bolivar and General
San Martin right behind. King Wladislaw was there in medieval scale mail,
galloping on a knight's armored charger; Don Quixote was there, urging poor
broken-down Rosinante to something faster than a stumble and shouting
threats against the whole breed of sorcerers; Teddy Roosevelt was there,
cracking off shot after shot at the cabs as his huge horse stamped them into
the pavement; El Cid Campeador rode there, his bannered lance striking
down one peryton after another. Behind all these came a wild assortment of
creatures, pouring past the tree circle and into the street—eagles, bears, huge
dogs, a hunting cat, a crowd of doughboys from the first World War with
bayoneted rifles—all the most warlike of the nearby statuary—even some not
so warlike, such as several deer and the Ugly Duckling. From down Fifth
Avenue came striding golden Prometheus from his pedestal in Rockefeller
Center, bearing the fire he brought for mortals and using it in bolt after bolt

to melt down cabs where they stood; and from behind him, with a stony roar
like the sky falling, the great white lions from the steps of the Public Library
leaped together and threw themselves upon the iron steed and its dark rider.
For all its extra legs, the mount staggered back and sideways, screaming in a
horrible parody of a horse's neigh and striking feebly at the marble claws that
tore its flanks.

Under cover of that tumult of howls and crashes and the clash of arms,
Nita grabbed Kit to pull him away from the tree-wall, behind another row of
trees. She half expected her hands to go right through him, he was becoming
so transparent. Unresisting, he got up and followed her, still holding the
Book open, still reading as if he couldn't stop, or didn't want to, still burning
more and more fiercely with the inner light of the bright Book's power.
"Fred," she said as she pushed Kit down onto the ground again behind a
looming old maple, "I've got to do this now. I may not be able to do anything
else. If a diversion's needed—"

(I'll do what's necessary,) Fred said, his voice sounding as awed and frightened as Nita felt at the sight of what Kit was becoming. (You be careful too.)

She reached out a hand to Fred. He bobbed close and settled at the tip of
one finger for a moment, perching there delicately as a firefly, energy touching matter for a moment as if to reconfirm the old truth that they were just
different forms of the same thing. Then he lifted away, turning his attention
out to the street, to the sound of stone and metal wounding and being
wounded; and in one quick gesture Nita grabbed the Book of Night with
Moon away from Kit and bent her head to read.

An undertow of blinding power and irresistible light poured into her, over
her, drowned her deep. She couldn't fight it. She didn't want to. Nita understood now the clear-burning transfiguration of Kit's small plain human face
and body, for it was not the wizard who read the Book; it was the other way
around. The silent Power that had written the Book reached through it now
and read what life had written in her body and soul—joys, hopes, fears, and
failings all together—then took her intent and read that too, turning it into
fact. She was turning the bright pages without even thinking about it, finding
the place in the Book that spoke of creation and rebellion and war among the
stars—the words that had once before broken the terrible destroying storm of
death and darkness that the angry Starsnuffer had raised to break the new-
made worlds and freeze the seas where life was growing, an eternity ago. "I
am the wind that troubles the water," Nita said, whispering in the Speech.
The whisper smote against the windowed cliffs until they echoed again, and
the clash and tumult of battle began to grow still as the wind rose at her
naming. "I am the water, and the waves; I am the shore where the waves break
in rainbows; I am the sunlight that shines in the spray—"

The power rose with the rhythms of the old, old words, rose with the wind as all about her the earth and air and waters of the park began to remember what they were—matter and energy, created, indestructible, no matter what darkness lay over them. *"I am the trees that drink the light; I am the air of the green things' breathing; I am the stone that the trees break asunder; I am the molten heart of the world—"*

"NO!" came his scream from beyond the wall of trees, hating, raging, desperate. But Nita felt no fear. It was as it had been in the Beginning; all his no's had never been able to stand against life's *I Am*. All around her trees and stones and flesh and metal burned with the power that burned her, self-awareness, which death can seem to stop but can never keep from happening, no matter how hard it tries. *"Where will you go? To what place will you wander?"* she asked sorrowfully, or life asked through her, hoping that the lost one might at last be convinced to come back to his allegiance. Of all creatures alive and otherwise, he had been and still was one of the mightiest. If only his stubborn anger would break, his power could be as great for light as for darkness—but it could not happen. If after all these weary eons he still had not realized the hopelessness of his position, that everywhere he went, life was there before him— Still she tried, the ancient words speaking her solemnly. *"—in vale or on hilltop, still I am there—"*

Silence, silence, except for the rising wind. All things seemed to hold their breath to hear the words; even the dark rider, erect again on his iron steed and bitter of face, ignoring the tumult around him. His eyes were only for Nita, for only her reading held him bound. She tried not to think of him, or of the little time remaining before the Moon went out, and gave herself over wholly to the reading. The words shook the air and the earth, blinding, burning.

> *"—will you sound the sea's depth, or climb the*
> *mountain?*
> *In air or in water, still I am there;*
> *Will the earth cover you? Will the night hide you?*
> *In deep or in darkness, still I am there;*
> *Will you kindle the nova, or kill the starlight?*
> *In fire or in deathcold, still I am there—"*

The Moon went out.

Fred cried out soundlessly, and Nita felt the loss of light like a stab in the heart. The power fell away from her, quenched, leaving her small and cold and human and alone, holding in her hands a *Book* gone dark from lack of moonlight. She and Kit turned desperately toward each other in a darkness rapidly becoming complete as the flowing blackness put out the last light of the city. Then came the sound of low, satisfied laughter and a single *clang* of a heavy hoof, stepping forward.

Another *clang*.

Another.

(Now,) Fred said suddenly, *(now* I understand what all that emitting was practice for. No beta, no gamma, no microwave or upper-wavelength ultraviolet or X-rays, is that all?)

"Fred?" Kit said, but Fred didn't wait. He shot upward, blazing, a point of light like a falling star falling the wrong way, up and up until his brightness was as faint as one more unremarkable star. "Fred, where are you *going?*"

(To create a diversion,) his thought came back, getting fainter and fainter (Nita, Kit—)

They could catch no more clear thoughts, only a great wash of sorrow and loss, a touch of fear—and then brightness intolerable erupted in the sky as Fred threw his claudication open, emitting all his mass at once as energy, blowing his quanta. He could hardly have been more than halfway to the Moon, for a second or two later it was alight again, a blazing searing full such as no one had ever seen. There was no looking at either Fred's blast of light or at the Moon that lit trees and statues and the astounded face of the Starsnuffer with a light like a silver sun.

The rider spent no more than a moment being astounded. Immediately he lifted his steel rod, pointing it at Fred this time, shouting in the Speech cold words that were a curse on all light everywhere, from time's beginning to its end. But Fred burned on, more fiercely, if possible. Evidently not even the Starsnuffer could quickly put out a white hole that was liberating all the bound-up energy of five or six blue-white giant stars at once.

"Nita, Nita, *read!*" Kit shouted at her. Through her tears she looked down at the *Book* again and picked up where she had left off. The dark rider was cursing them all in earnest now, knowing that another three lines in the *Book* would bring Nita to his name. She had only to pronounce it to cast him out into the unformed void beyond the universes, where he had been cast the first time those words were spoken.

Cabs and perytons screamed and threw themselves at the barrier in a last wild attempt to break through, the statues leaped into the fray again, stone and flesh and metal clashed. Nita fell down into the bright power once more, crying, but reading in urgent haste so as not to waste the light Fred was giving himself to become.

As the power began again to read her, she could hear it reading Kit too, his voice matching hers as it had in their first wizardry, small and thin and brave and choked with grief like hers. She couldn't stop crying, and the power burned in her tears too, an odd hot feeling, as she cried bitterly for Fred, for Kit's Lotus, for everything horrible that had happened all that day—all the

air things skewed, all the beauty twisted by the dark Lone Power watching
on his steed. If only there were some way he could be otherwise if he wanted
o. For here was his name, a long splendid flow of syllables in the Speech,
wild and courageous in its own way—and it said that he had not always been
o hostile; that he got tired sometimes of being wicked, but his pride and his
ear of being ridiculed would never let him stop. *Never, forever,* said the
ymbol at the very end of his name, the closed circle that binds spells into an
unbreakable cycle and indicates lives bound the same way. Kit was still read-
ng. Nita turned her head in that nova moonlight and looked over her shoulder at the one who watched. His face was set, and bitter still, but weary. He
new he was about to be cast out again, frustrated again; and he knew that
because of what he had bound himself into being, he would never know
ulfillment of any kind. Nita looked back down to the reading, feeling sorry
ven for him, opened her mouth and along with Kit began to say his name.
Don't be afraid to make corrections!

Whether the voice came from her memory or was a last whisper from the
blinding new star far above, Nita never knew. But she knew what to do.
While Kit was still on the first part of the name she pulled out her pen, her
est pen that Fred had saved and changed. She clicked it open. The metal
till tingled against her skin, the ink at the point still glittered oddly—the
ame glitter as the ink with which the bright *Book* was written. Nita bent
uickly over the *Book* and, with the pen, in lines of light, drew from that
nal circle an arrow pointing upward, the way out, the symbol that said
hange could happen—if, only if—and together they finished the Starsnuf-
er's name in the Speech, said the new last syllable, made it real.

The wind was gone. Fearfully Nita and Kit turned around, looked at Fifth
avenue—and found it empty. The creeping blackness was gone with the
reaking of its master's magic and the sealing of the worldgate he had held
pen. Silent and somber, the statues stood among the bodies of the slain—
rushed cabs and perytons, shattered trees—then one by one each paced off
nto the park or down Fifth Avenue, back to its pedestal and its long quiet
egard of the city. The howl of sirens, lost for a while in the wind that had
isen, now grew loud again. Kit and Nita stood unmoving as the trees ringing
hem moved away to their old places, sinking roots back into torn-up earth
nd raising branches to the burning Moon. Some ninety-three million miles
way, the Sun had come quietly back to life. But its light would not reach
:arth for another eight minutes yet, and as Nita and Kit watched, slowly the
ew star in the heavens faded, and the Moon faded with it—from daylight
rilliance to silver fire, to steel-gray glow, to earthlight shimmer, to nothing.
he star went yellow, and red, and died. Nothing was left but a stunning,
ky-wide aurora, great curtains and rays of rainbow light shivering and crack-
ng all across the golden-glowing city night.

"He forgot the high-energy radiation again," Kit said, tears constricting hi voice to a whisper.

Nita closed the *Book* she held in her hands, now dark and ordinary-lookin, except for the black depths of its covers, the faint shimmer of starlight on page edges. "He always does," she said, scrubbing at her eyes, and then offered Kit the *Book.* He shook his head, and Nita dropped it into he backpack and slung it over her back again. "You think *he'll* take the chance?" she said.

"Huh? Oh." Kit shook his head unhappily. "I dunno. Old habits die harc If he wants to. . . ."

Above them the Moon flicked on again, full and silver-bright through th blue and red shimmer of the auroral curtain. They stood gazing at it, serene, remote brilliance, seeming no different than it had been an hou before, a night before, when everything had been as it should be. And now—

"Let's get out of here," Nita said.

They walked out of the park unhindered by the cops and firemen wh were already arriving in squad cars and fire trucks and paramedic ambulance Evidently no one felt that two grade-school kids could possibly have anythin to do with a street full of wrecked cabs and violently uprooted trees. As the crossed Fifth Avenue and the big mesh-sided Bomb Squad truck passe them, Nita bent to pick up a lone broken-off twig of oak, and stared at sorrowfully. "There wasn't even anything left of him," she said as the walked east on Sixty-fourth, heading back to the Pan Am Building and th timeslide.

"Only the light," Kit said, looking up at the aurora. Even that was fadin now.

Silently they made their way to Grand Central and entered the Pan A Building at the mezzanine level. The one guard was sitting with his back t them and his feet on the desk, reading the *Post.* Kit went wearily over to on elevator, laid a hand on it, and spoke a word or three to it in the Speech. I doors slid silently open, and they got in and headed upstairs.

The restaurant level was dark, for the place served only lunch, and ther was no one to see them go back up to the roof. Kit opened the door at th top of the stairs, and together they walked out into peace and darkness and wind off the ocean. A helicopter was moored in the middle of the pad wit steel pegs and cables, crouching on its skids and staring at them with clea sleepy, benevolent eyes. The blue high-intensity marker lights blazed about like the circle of a protection spell. Nita looked away, not really wanting think about spells or anything else to do with wizardry. The book said would be hard. *That* I didn't mind. But I *hurt!* And where's the good par There was supposed to be happiness too. . . .

The bright *Book* was heavy on her back as she looked out across the nigh

All around, for miles and miles, was glittering light, brilliant motion, shining under the Moon; lights of a thousand colors gleaming from windows, glowing on streets, blazing from the headlights of cars. The city, breathing, burning, living the life they had preserved. Ten million lives and more. *If something should happen to all that life—how terrible!* Nita gulped for control as she remembered Fred's words of just this morning, an eternity ago. And this was what being a wizard was about. Keeping terrible things from happening, even when it hurt. Not just power, or control of what ordinary people couldn't control, or delight in being able to make strange things happen. Those were side effects—not the reason, not the purpose.

She could give it up, she realized suddenly. In the recovery of the bright *Book,* she and Kit had more than repaid the energy invested in their training. If they chose to lay the Art aside, if *she* did, no one would say a word. She would be left in peace. Magic does not live in the unwilling soul.

Yet never to hear a tree talk again, or a stone, or a star . . .

On impulse Nita held out her hands and closed her eyes. Even without the rowan rod she could feel the moonfire on her skin as a tree might feel it. She could taste the restored sunlight that produced it, feel the soundless roar of the ancient atomic furnace that had burned just this way while her world was still a cloud of gas, nebulous and unformed. And ever so faintly she could taste a rainbow spatter of high-energy radiation, such as a white hole might leave after blowing its quanta.

She opened her eyes, found her hands full of moonlight that trembled like bright water, its surface sheened with fading aurora-glow. "All right," she said after a moment. "All right." She opened her hands to let the light run out. *"Kit?"* she said, saying his name in the Speech.

He had gone to stand beside the helicopter and was standing with one hand laid against its side. It stared at him mutely. *"Yeah,"* he said, and patted the cool metal, and left the chopper to rejoin Nita. *"I guess we pass the test."*

They took their packs off and got out the materials necessary for the timeslide. When the lithium-cadmium battery and the calculator chip and the broken teacup-handle were in place, Kit and Nita started the spell—and without warning were again caught up by the augmenting power of the bright *Book* and plunged more quickly than they expected into the wizardry. It *was* like being on a slide, though they were the ones who held still, and the events of the day as seen from the top of the Pan Am Building rushed backward past them, a high-speed 3-D movie in reverse. Blinding white fire and the nova Moon grew slowly in the sky, flared, and were gone. The Moon, briefly out, came on again. Darkness flowed backward through the suddenly open worldgate, following its master on his huge dark mount, who also stepped backward and vanished through the gate. Kit and Nita saw *themselves* burst out of the roof door, blurred with speed; saw themselves run backward over the railing, a bright line of light pacing them as they plunged out into the dark air, dove backward through the gate, and vanished with it. The Sun came up in the west and fled back across the sky. Men in coverall burst out of the roof door and unpegged the helicopter; two of them got into it and it took off backwards. Clouds streamed and boiled past, jets fell backward into LaGuardia. The Sun stood high—

The slide let them go, and Kit and Nita sat back gasping. "What time have you got?" Kit said when he had enough breath.

Nita glanced at her watch. "Nine forty-five."

"*Nine* forty-five! But we were supposed to—"

"It's this *Book*, it makes everything work too well. At nine forty-five we were—"

They heard voices in the stairwell, behind the closed door. Kit and Nita stared at each other. Then they began frantically picking up the items left from their spelling. Nita paused with the lithium-cadmium battery in her hand as she recognized one of those voices coming up the stairs. She reared back, took aim, and threw the heavy battery at the closed door, hard. CRACK!

Kit looked at her, his eyes wide, and understood. "Quick, behind there," he said. Nita ran to scoop up the battery, then ducked around after Kit and crouched down with him behind the back of the stairwell. There was a long, long pause before the door opened and footsteps could be heard on the gravel. Kit and Nita edged around the side of the stairwell again to peer around the corner. Two small, nervous-looking figures were heading for the south facing rail in the bright sunlight. A dark-haired girl, maybe thirteen, wearing jeans and a shirt and a down vest; a dark-haired boy, small and a touch stocky, also in jeans and parka, twelve years old or so. The boy held a broken-off piece of antenna, and the girl held a peeled white stick, and they were being paced by a brilliant white spark like a will-o'-the-wisp plugged into too much current and about to blow out.

" 'There are no accidents,' " Kit whispered sadly.

The tears stung Nita's eyes again. "G'bye, Fred," she said softly in English for fear the Speech should attract his attention, or hers.

Silently and unseen, Kit and Nita slipped through the door and went downstairs for the shuttle and the train home.

Timeheart

The walk home from the bus stop was weary and quiet. Three blocks from Nita's house, they reached the corner where their ways usually parted. Kit paused there, waiting for the light to change, though no traffic was in sight. "Call me tomorrow?" he said.

What for? Nita felt like saying, for there were no more spells in the offing, and she was deadly tired. Still . . . "It's your turn," she said.

"Huh. Right." The light changed, and Kit headed across the street to Nita's left. In the middle of the street he turned, walking backward. "We should call Tom and Carl," he shouted, sounding entirely exhausted.

"Yeah." The light changed again, in Nita's favor; Kit jumped up onto the sidewalk on the other side and headed south toward his place. Nita crossed east, watching Kit as she went. Though the look on his face was tired and sad, all the rest of his body wore the posture of someone who's been through so much fear that fear no longer frightens him. Why's he so afraid of getting beat up? Nita thought. Nobody in their right mind would mess with him.

In midstep she stopped, watching him walk away. How about that. How about that. He got what he asked for.

After a second she started walking home again. The weight at her back suddenly reminded her of something. (Kit!) she called silently, knowing he could hear even though he was now out of sight. (What about the *Book?*)

(Hang on to it,) he answered. (We'll give it to the Advisories. Or they'll know what to do with it.)

(Right. See ya later.)

(See ya.)

Nita was so tired that it took three or four minutes before the identity of the blond person walking up East Clinton toward her registered at all. By then Joanne was within yelling distance, but she didn't yell at Nita at all, much to Nita's surprise. This was such an odd development that Nita looked at Joanne carefully as they got closer, something she had never done before. There was something familiar about Joanne today, a look that Nita couldn't quite pin down—and then she recognized the expression and let out a tired, unhappy breath. The look was less marked, less violent and terrible than that of the pride-frozen misery of the dark rider, but there all the same. The angry fear was there too—the terror of what had been until now no threat but was now out of control; the look of the rider about to be cast out by a power he had thought himself safe from, the look of a bully whose victim suddenly wasn't a victim any more.

Nita slowed down and stopped where she was, in the middle of the sidewalk, watching Joanne. *Even he can be different now,* she thought, her heart beating fast—her own old fear wasn't entirely gone. *But that was partly because we gave him the chance.*

She stood there, watching Joanne slow down warily as she got closer to Nita. Nita sweated. Doing something that would be laughed about behind her back was almost as bad as being beaten up. But she stood still until Joanne came to a stop four or five feet away from her. "Well?" Joanne said, her voice full of anger and uncertainty.

I don't know what to say to her, we have absolutely nothing in common, Nita thought frantically. *But it has to start somewhere.* She swallowed and did her best to look Joanne in the eye, calmly and not in threat. "Come on over to my place after supper sometime and look through my telescope," she said. "I'll show you Jupiter's moons. Or Mars—"

Joanne made that old familiar haughty face and brushed past Nita and away. "Why would I ever want to go to *your* house? You don't even have a color TV."

Nita stood still, listening to Joanne's footsteps hurrying away, a little faster every second—and slowly began to realize that she'd gotten what she asked for too—the ability to break the cycle of anger and loneliness, not necessarily for others, but at least for herself. It wouldn't even take the Speech; plain words would do it, and the magic of reaching out. It would take a long time, much longer than something simple like breaking the walls between the worlds, and it would cost more effort than even the reading of the *Book of Night with Moon.* But it would be worth it—and eventually it would work. A spell always works.

Nita went home.

That night after supper she slipped outside to sit in Liused's shadow and watch the sky. The tree caught her moon and, after greeting her, was quiet—until about ten o'clock, when it and every other growing thing in sight suddenly trembled violently as if stricken at the root. They had felt the Sun go out.

(It's all right,) she said silently, though for someone whose tears were starting again, it was an odd thing to say. She waited the eight minutes with them, saw the Moon blink out, and leaned back against the rowan trunk, sheltering from the wind that rose in the darkness. Branches tossed as if in a hurricane, leaves hissed in anguish—and then the sudden new star in the heavens etched every leaf's shadow sharp against the ground and set the Moon on fire. Nita squinted up at the pinpoint of brilliance, unwilling to look away though her eyes leaked tears of pain. She'd thought, that afternoon, that living through the loss a second time would be easier. She was wrong. The tears kept falling long after the star went out, and the Moon found its light again, and the wind died to a whisper. She stopped crying long enough to go back inside and go to bed, and she was sure she would start again immediately. But she was wrong about that too. Exhaustion beat down grief so fast that she was asleep almost as soon as her head touched the pillow under which she had hidden the *Book of Night with Moon.* . . .

The place where they stood was impossible, for there's no place in Manhattan where the water level in the East River comes right up to the railed path that runs alongside it. There they stood, though, leaning with their backs against the railing, gazing up at the bright city that reared against the silver sky, while behind them the river whispered and chuckled and slapped its banks. The sound of laughter came down the morning wind from the apartments and the brownstones and the towers of steel and crystal; the seabirds wheeled and cried over the white piers and jetties of the Manhattan shoreline, and from somewhere down the riverside came the faint sound of music—quiet rock, a deep steady backbeat woven about with guitars and voices in close harmony. A jogger went by on the running path, puffing, followed by a large black and white dog galloping to catch up with its master.

Are we early, or are they late? Kit asked, leaning back farther still to watch an overflying Learjet do barrel-roll after barrel-roll for sheer joy of being alive.

Who cares? Nita said, leaning back too and enjoying the way the music and the city sounds and the Learjet's delighted scream all blended. *Anyway, this is Timeheart. There's nothing here but Now.* . . .

They turned their backs on the towers and the traffic and the laughter, and looked out across the shining water toward Brooklyn and Long Island. Neither was there just then—probably someone else in Timeheart was using them, and Kit and Nita didn't need them at the moment. The silver expanse of the Atlantic shifted and glittered from their feet to the radiant horizon, endless. Far off to their right, south and west of the Battery, the Statue of Liberty held up her torch and her tablet and looked calmly out toward the sunrise as they did, waiting. Nita was the first to see the dark bulge out on the water. She nudged Kit and pointed. *Look, a shark!*

He glanced at her, amused. *Even here I don't think sharks have wheels. . . .*

The Lotus came fast, hydroplaning. Water spat up from its wheels as it skidded up to the railing and fishtailed sideways, grinning, spraying them both. On its wildly waving antenna rode a spark of light. Nita smiled at her friend, who danced off the antenna to rest momentarily on one of her fingers like a hundred-watt firefly. *Well,* Nita said, *is it confusing being dead?*

Fred chuckled a rainbow, up the spectrum and down again. *Not very.* Beside him, the Lotus stood up on its hind wheels, putting its front ones on the railing so that Kit could scratch it behind the headlights.

We brought it, Kit said.

Good, said the Lotus, as Nita got the bright *Book* out of her backpack and handed it to Kit. *The Powers want to put it away safe. Though the precaution may not really be necessary, after what you did.*

It worked? He's changed? Nita said.

Fred made a spatter of light, a gesture that felt like the shake of a head. *Not changed. Just made otherwise, as if he'd been that way from the beginning. He has back the option he'd decided was lost—to put aside his anger, to build instead of damn. . . .*

Then if he uses that option—you mean every place could be like this some day? Kit looked over his shoulder at the city and all the existence behind it, preserved in its fullest beauty while still growing and becoming greater.

Possibly. What he did remains. Entropy's still here, and death. They look like waste and horror to us now. But if he chooses to have them be a blessing on the worlds, instead of anger's curse—who knows where those gates will lead then? . . . The Lotus sounded pleased by the prospect.

Kit held out the *Book of Night with Moon.* Most delicately the Lotus opened fanged jaws to take it, then rubbed its face against Kit and dropped to all four wheels on the water. It smiled at them both, a chrome smile, silver and sanguine—then backed a little, turned and was off, spraying Kit and Nita again.

Fred started to follow, but Nita caught him in cupped hands, holding him back for a moment. *Fred! Did we do right?*

Even here she couldn't keep the pain out of her question, the fear that she could somehow have prevented his death. But Fred radiated a serene and wondering joy that took her breath and reassured her and filled her with wonder to match his, all at once. *Go find out,* he said.

She opened her hands and he flew out of them like a spark blown on the wind—a brightness zipping after the Lotus, losing itself against the dazzling silver of the sea, gone. Nita turned around to lean on the railing again, and

fter a moment Kit turned with her. They breathed out, relaxing, and settled
ack to gaze at the city transfigured, the city preserved at the heart of Time,
s all things loved are preserved in the hearts that care for them—gazed up
ito the radiance, the life, the light unending, the light. . . .

. . . the light was right in her eyes, mostly because Dairine had yanked
he curtain open. Her sister was talking loudly, and Nita turned her head and
uite suddenly felt what was not under her pillow. "You gonna sleep all
iorning? Get up, it's ten thirty! The Sun went out last night, you should see
:, it was on the news. And somebody blew up Central Park; and Kit Rodri-
iez called, he wants you to call him back. How come you keep calling each
ther, anyhow?" Halfway out the bedroom door, realization dawned in her
ister's eyes. "Maaaaa!" she yelled out the door, strangling on her own laugh-
:r. "Nita's got a *boyfriend!*"

"Oh, jeez, Dairiiiiiiiine!"

The wizard threw her pillow at her sister, got up, and went to breakfast.

DEEP WIZARDRY

For J.A.C.
re: redemption and fried zucchini

ACKNOWLEDGMENT

Heartfelt thanks go to Neil Harris and his erstwhile comrades at Commodore, who went crazy hooking up a desperate writer's computer to one of their printers, and who helped her hit her deadline.

CONTENTS

A pause! Lost ground!
—yet not unavailing, for soon shall be found
what took three ages to subdue.
The hunters, on their guard,
give sparingly and greatly, east and west:
yet how shall only faithfulness prevail
against the peril of the overarching deep?

Trigram 63/Chi Chi:
Water over Fire

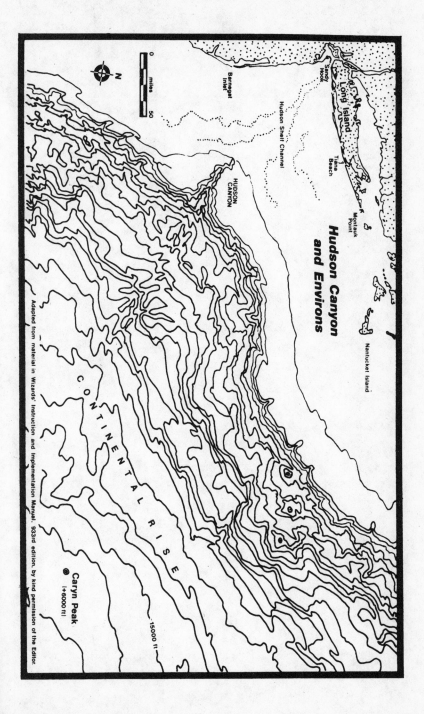

Hudson Canyon
and Environs

N

0
miles
50

Sandy
Hook
Long Island

Barnegat
Inlet

Hudson Shelf Channel

Tiana
Beach

HUDSON
CANYON

Montauk
Point

Nantucket Island

CONTINENTAL RISE

15000 ft

● Caryn Peak
(+6000 ft)

Adapted from material in Wizards' Instruction and Implementation Manual, 933rd edition, by kind permission of the Editor.

Summer Night's Song

Nita slipped out the back door of the beach house, careful not to let the rickety screen door slam, and for a second stood silently on the back porch in the darkness. It was no use. "Nita"—her mother's voice came floating out from the living room—"where're you going?"

"Out," Nita said, hoping to get away with it just this once.

She might as well have tried to rob a bank. "Out where?"

"Down to the beach, Mom."

There was a sigh's worth of pause from the living room, broken by the sound of a crowd on TV shouting about a base that had just been stolen somewhere in the country. "I don't like you walking down there alone at night, Neets. . . ."

"Nhhnnnnn," Nita said, a loud noncommittal noise she had learned to make while her mother was deciding whether to let her do something. "I'll take Ponch with me," she said in a burst of inspiration.

"Mmmmmm . . ." her mother said, considering it. Ponch was a large black and white dog, part Border collie, part German shepherd, part mutt—an intrepid hunter of water rats and gulls, and ferociously loyal to his master and to Nita because she was his master's best friend. "Where's Kit?"

"I dunno." It was at least partly the truth. "He went for a walk a while ago."

"Well . . . okay. You take Ponch and look for Kit, and bring him back with you. Don't want his folks thinking we're not taking care of him."

"Right, Ma," Nita said, and went pounding down the creaky steps from the house to the yard before her mother could change her mind, or her father, immersed in the ball game, could come back to consciousness.

"Ponch! Hey Pancho!" Nita shouted, pounding through the sandy front yard, through the gate in the ancient picket fence, and out across the narrow

paved road to the dune on the other side of the road. Joyous barking bega
on the far side of the dune as Nita ran up it. *He's hunting again,* Nit
thought, and would have laughed for delight if running had left her an
breath. *This is the best vacation we ever had. . . .*

At the top of the dune she paused, looking down toward the long dar
expanse of the beach. "It's been a good year," her father had said a couple o
months before, over dinner. "We can't go far for vacation—but let's g
somewhere nice. One of the beaches in the Hamptons, maybe. We'll rent
house and live beyond our means. For a couple weeks, anyway. . . ."

It hadn't taken Nita much begging to get her folks to let her friend K
Rodriguez go along with them, or to get Kit's folks to say yes. Both familie
were delighted that their children had each finally found a close friend. Nit
and Kit laughed about that sometimes. Their families knew only the surfac
of what was going on—which was probably for the best.

A black shape came scrabbling up the dune toward Nita, flinging sand i
all directions in his hurry. "Whoa!" she shouted at Ponch, but it was no us
it never was. He hit her about stomach level with both paws and knocked h
down, panting with excitement; then, when she managed to sit up, he starte
enthusiastically washing her face. His breath smelled like dead fish.

"Euuuuw, enough!" Nita said, making a face and pushing the dog more o
less off her. "Ponch, where's Kit?"

"Yayayayayayayaya!" Ponch barked, jumping up and bouncing around Nit
in an attempt to get her to play. He grabbed up a long string of dead seawee
in his jaws and began shaking it like a rope and growling.

"Cut it out, Ponch. Get serious." Nita got up and headed down the fa
side of the dune, brushing herself off as she went. "Where's the boss?"

"He played with me," Ponch said in another string of barks as he lope
down the dune alongside her. "He threw the stick. I chased it."

"Great. Where is he *now?*"

They came to the bottom of the dune together. The sand was hard
there, but still dry; the tide was low and just beginning to turn. "Don'
know," Ponch said, a bark with a grumble on the end of it.

"Hey, you're a good boy, I'm not mad at you," Nita said. She stopped t
scratch the dog behind the ears, in the good place. He stood still with h
tongue hanging out and looked up at her, his eyes shining oddly in the ligh
of the nearly full Moon that was climbing the sky. "I just don't feel lik
playing right now. I want to swim. Would you find Kit?"

The big brown eyes gazed soulfully up at her, and Ponch made a sma
beseeching whine. "A dog biscuit?"

Nita grinned. "Blackmailer. Okay, you find the boss, I'll give you a biscu
Two biscuits. Go get 'im!"

Ponch bounded off westward down the beach, kicking up wet sand. Ni headed for the water line, where she shrugged off the windbreaker that had been covering her bathing suit and dropped it on the sand. Two months ago, talking to a dog and getting an answer back would have been something that happened only in Disney movies. But then one day in the library, Nita had stumbled onto a book called *So You Want to Be a Wizard*. She'd followed the instructions in the book, as Kit had in the copy he'd found in a used-book store—and afterward, dogs talked back. Or, more accurately, she knew what language they spoke and how to hear it. There was nothing that *didn't* talk back, she'd found—only things she didn't yet know how to hear or how to talk to properly.

Like parents, Nita thought with mild amusement. If her mother knew Nita was going swimming, she'd probably pitch a fit: she'd had a terrible thing about night swimming after seeing *Jaws*. But it's okay, Nita thought. There aren't any sharks here . . . and if there were, I think I could talk them out of eating me.

She made sure her clothes were above the high-water line, then waded down into the breakers. The water was surprisingly warm around her knees. The waxing Moon, slightly golden from smog, made a silvery pathway on the water, everywhere else shedding a dull radiance that made both land and sea look alive.

What a great night, Nita thought. She went out another twenty paces or so, then crouched over and dived into an incoming wave. Waterborne sand scoured her, the water thundered in her ears; then she broke surface and lay in the roil and dazzle of the moonlit water, floating. There were no street-lights there, and the stars she loved were bright. After a while she stood up in the shoulder-high water, watching the sky. Back up on the beach, Ponch was barking, excited and noisy. He can't have found Kit that fast, Nita thought. Probably something distracted him. A crab, maybe. A dead fish. A shark. . . .

Something pushed her in the back, *hard*. Nita gasped and whipped around in the water, thinking, This is it, there are *too* sharks here and I'm *dead!* The sight of the slick-skinned shape in the water stopped her breath—until she realized what she was looking at. A slender body, ten feet long; a blowhole and an amused eye that looked at her sidelong; and a long, beaked face that wore a permanent smile. She reached out a hesitant hand, and under her touch the dolphin turned lazily, rolling sideways, brushing her with skin like warm, moonlit satin.

She was immensely relieved. *"Dai'stiho,"* she said, greeting the swimmer in the Tongue that wizards use, the language that she'd learned from her manual and that all creatures understand. She expected no more answer than a fizz or squeak as the dolphin returned the greeting and went about its business.

But the dolphin rolled back toward her and looked at her in what seemed to be shock. *"A wizard!"* it said in an urgent whistle. Nita had no time to answer; the dolphin dived and its tail slapped the surface, spraying her. By the time Nita rubbed the salt sting out of her eyes, there was nothing near her but the usual roaring breakers. Ponch was bouncing frantically on the beach, barking something about sea monsters to the small form walking beside him.

"Neets?"

Nita waded out of the breakers. At the water line Kit met her and handed Nita her windbreaker. He was smaller than she was, a year younger, dark-haired and brown-eyed and sharp of face and mind; definitely sharper, Nita thought with approval, than the usual twelve-year-old. "He was hollering about whales," Kit said, nodding at Ponch.

"Dolphins," Nita said. "At least, *a* dolphin. I said hi to it and it said 'A wizard!' and ran away."

"Great." Kit looked southward, across the ocean. "Something's going on out there, Neets. I was up on the jetty. The rocks are upset."

Nita shook her head. Her specialty as a wizard was living things; animals and plants talked to her and did the things she asked, at least if she asked properly. It still startled her sometimes when Kit got the same kind of result from "unalive" things like cars and doors and telephone poles, but that was where his talent lay. "What can a rock get upset about?" she said.

"I'm not sure. They wouldn't say. The stones piled up there remembered something. And they didn't want to think about it any more. They were shook." Kit looked up sharply at Nita. "That was *it*. The earth shook once. . . ."

"Oh, come off it. This isn't California. Long Island doesn't have earthquakes."

"Once it did. The rocks remember. . . . I wonder what that dolphin wanted?"

Nita was wondering too. She zipped up her windbreaker. "C'mon, we have to get back before Mom busts a gut."

"But the dolphin—"

Nita started down the beach, then turned and kept walking backward when she noticed that Kit wasn't following her. "The ball game was almost over," she said, raising her voice as she got farther from Kit and Ponch. "They'll go to bed early. They always do. And when they're asleep—"

Kit nodded and muttered something, Nita couldn't quite hear what. He vanished in a small clap of inrushing air and then reappeared next to Nita, walking with her; Ponch barked in annoyance and ran to catch up.

"He really hates that 'beam-me-up-Scotty' spell," Nita said.

"Yeah, when it bends space, it makes him itch. Look, I was practicing that other one—"

"With the water?" She grinned at him. "In the dark, I hope."

"Yeah. I'll show you later. And then—"

"Dolphins."

"Uh-*huh*. C'mon, I'll race you."

They ran up the dune, followed by a black shape barking loudly about dog biscuits.

Wizards' Song

The Moon got high. Nita sat by the window of her ground-floor room, listening through the stillness for the sound of voices upstairs. There hadn't been any for a while.

She sighed and looked down at the book she held in her lap. It looked like a library book—bound in one of those slick-shiny buckram library bindings, with a Dewey decimal number written at the bottom of the spine in that indelible white ink librarians use, and at the top of the spine, the words *SO YOU WANT TO BE A WIZARD*. But on opening the book, what one saw were the words *Instruction and Implementation Manual, General and Limited Special-Purpose Wizardries, Sorceries, and Spells: 933rd Edition*. Or that was what you saw if you were a wizard, for the printing was done in the graceful, Arabic-looking written form of the Speech.

Nita turned a few pages of the manual, glancing at them in idle interest. The instructions she'd found in the book had coached her through her first few spells—both the kinds for which only words were needed and those that required raw materials of some sort. The spells had in turn led her into the company of other wizards—beginners like Kit and more experienced ones typical of the wizards, young and old, working quietly all over the world. And then the spells had taken her right out of the world she'd known, into one of the ones "next door," and into a conflict that had been going on since time' beginning, in all the worlds there were.

In that other world, in a place like New York City but also terribly different, she had passed through the initial ordeal that every candidate for wizardry undergoes. Kit had been with her. Together they had pulled each other and themselves through the danger and the terror, to the successful completion of a quest into which they had stumbled. They saved their own world without attracting much notice; they lost a couple of dear friends they'd m

long the way; and they came into their full power as wizards. It was a
privilege that had its price. Nita still wasn't sure why she'd been chosen as
one of those who fight for the Worlds against the Great Death of entropy.
She was just glad she'd been picked.

She flipped pages to the regional directory, where wizards were listed by
name and address. Nita never got tired of seeing her own name listed there,
or other wizards to call if they needed her. She overshot her own page in the
Nassau County section, wanting to check the names of two friends, Senior
Wizards for the area—Tom Swale and Carl Romeo. They had recently been
promoted to Senior from the Advisory Wizard level, and as she'd suspected,
their listing now read "On sabbatical: emergencies only." Nita grinned at the
memory of the party they'd thrown to celebrate their promotion. The guests
had been a select group. More of them had appeared out of nowhere than
arrived through the front door. Several had spent the afternoon floating in
midair; another had spent it in the fishpond, submerged. Human beings had
been only slightly in the majority at the party, and Nita became very careful
at the snack table after her first encounter with the dip made from Pennsyl-
vania crude oil and fresh-ground iron filings.

She paged back through the listing and looked at her own name.

CALLAHAN, Juanita T.   243 E. Clinton Avenue
                          Hempstead NY 11575
                          (516) 379-6786
         On active status   Assignment location:
                          38 Tiana Beach Road
                          Southampton NY 11829
                          (516) 667-9084

Nita sighed, for this morning the status note had said, like Tom's, "Vaca-
tioning/emergencies only." The book updated itself all over that way—pages
changing sometimes second to second, reporting the status of worldgates in
the area, what spells were working where, the cost of powdered newt at your
local Advisory. *Whatever's come up,* Nita thought, *we're expected to be able
to handle it.*

Of course, last time out they expected us to save the world, too. . . .

"Neets!"

She jumped, then tossed her book out the window to Kit and began climbing out. "Sssh!"

"Shhh yourself, mouth. They're asleep. C'mon."

Once over the dune, the hiss and rumble of the midnight sea made talking
safer. "You on active status too?" Kit said.

"Yup. Let's find the dolphin and see what's up."

They ran for the breakers. Kit was in bathing suit and windbreaker as Nita was, with sneakers slung over his shoulder by the laces. "Okay," he said, "watch this." He said something in the Speech, a long liquid-sounding sentence with a curious even-uneven rhyme in it, all of which told the night and the wind and the water what Kit wanted of them. And without pause Kit ran right up to the water, which was retreating at that particular moment—and then onto it. Under his weight it bucked and sloshed the way a waterbed will when you stand on it; but Kit didn't sink. He ran four or five paces out onto the silver-slicked surface—then lost his balance and fell over sideways.

Nita started laughing, then hurriedly shut herself up for fear the whole beach should hear. Kit was lying on the water, his head propped up on one hand; the water bobbed him up and down while he looked at her with a sour expression. "It's not funny. I did it all last night and it never happened *once.*"

"Must be that you did the spell for two this time," Nita said, tempted to start laughing again, except that Kit would probably have punched her out. She kept her face as straight as she could and stepped out to the water, putting a foot carefully on an incoming, flattened-out wave. It took her weight, flattening more as she stepped up with the other foot and was carried backward. "It's like the slidewalk at the airport," she said, putting her arms out for balance and wobbling.

"Kind of." Kit got up on hands and knees and then again, swaying. "Come on. Keep your knees bent a little. And pick up your feet."

It was a useful warning. Nita tripped over several breakers and sprawled each time, a sensation like doing a bellywhopper onto a waterbed, until she got her sea legs. Once past the breakers she had no more trouble, and Kit led her at a bouncy trot out into the open Atlantic.

They both came to understand shortly why not many people, wizards or otherwise, walk on water much. The constant slip and slide of the water under their feet forced them to use leg muscles they rarely bothered with on land. They had to rest frequently, sitting, while they looked around them for signs of the dolphin.

At their first two rest stops there was nothing to be seen but the lights of Ponquogue and Hampton Bays and West Tiana on the mainland, three miles north. Closer, red and white flashing lights marked the entrance to Shinnecock Inlet, the break in the long strip of beach where they were staying. The Shinnecock horn hooted mournfully at them four times a minute, a lonely-sounding call. Nita's hair stood up all over her as they sat down the third time and she rubbed her aching legs. Kit's spell kept them from getting wet, but she was chilly; and being so far out there in the dark and quiet was very much like being in the middle of a desert—a wet, hissing barrenness unbroken for miles except by the quick-flashing white light of a buoy or two

"You okay?" Kit said.

"Yeah. It's just that the sea seems . . . safer near the shore, somehow. How deep is it here?"

Kit slipped his manual out of his windbreaker and pulled out a large nautical map. "About eighty feet, it looks like."

Nita sat up straight in shock. Something had broken the surface of the water and was arrowing toward them at a great rate. It was a triangular fin. Nita scrambled to her feet. "Uh, Kit!"

He was on his feet beside her in a second, staring too. "A shark has to stay in the water," he said, sounding more confident than he looked. "We don't. We can jump—"

"Oh, yeah? How high? And for how long?"

The fin was thirty yards or so away. A silvery body rose up under it, and Nita breathed out in relief at the frantic, high-pitched chattering of a dolphin's voice. The swimmer leaped right out of the water in its speed, came down, and splashed them both. "I'm late, and you're late," it gasped in a string of whistles and pops, "and S'reee's about to be! Hurry!"

"Right," Kit said, and slapped his manual shut. He said nothing aloud, but the sea's surface instantly stopped behaving like a waterbed and started acting like water. "*Whoolp!*" Nita said as she sank like a stone. She didn't get wet—that part of Kit's spell was still working—but she floundered wildly for a moment before managing to get hold of the dolphin in the cold and dark of the water.

Nita groped up its side and found a fin. Instantly the dolphin took off, and Nita hoisted herself up to a better position, hanging from the dorsal fin so that her body was half out of the water and her legs were safely out of the way of the fiercely lashing tail. On the other side, Kit had done the same. "You might have warned me!" she said to him across the dolphin's back.

He rolled his eyes at her. "If you weren't asleep on your feet, you wouldn't need warning."

"Kit—" She dropped it for the time being and said to the dolphin, "What's S'reee? And why's it going to be late? What's the matter?"

"She," the dolphin said. "S'reee's a wizard. The Hunters are after her and she can't do anything, she's hurt too badly. My pod and another one are with her, but they can't hold them off for long. She's beached, and the tide's coming in—"

Kit and Nita shot each other shocked looks. Another wizard in the area—and out in the ocean in the middle of the night? "What hunters?" Kit said, and "Your pod?" Nita said at the same moment.

The dolphin was coming about and heading along the shoreline, westward toward Quogue. "*The* Hunters," it said in a series of annoyed squeaks and

whistles. "The ones with teeth, who else? What kind of wizards are the
turning out these days, anyway?"

Nita said nothing to this. She was too busy staring ahead of them at a lon
dark bumpy whale shape lying on a sandbar, a shape slicked with moonligh
along its upper contours and silhouetted against the dull silver of the sea. I
was the look of the water that particularly troubled Nita. Shapes leaped an
twisted in it, shapes with two different kinds of fins. "Kit!"

"Neets," Kit said, not sounding happy, "there really aren't sharks here, th
guy from the Coast Guard said so last week—"

"Tell *them!*" the dolphin said angrily. It hurtled through the water towar
the sandbar around which the fighting continued, silent for all its viciousnes
The only sound came from the dark shape that lay partly on the bar, part
off it—a piteous, wailing whistle almost too high to hear.

"Are you ready?" the dolphin said. They were about fifty yards from th
trouble.

"Ready to *what?*" Kit asked, and started fumbling for his manual.

Nita started to do the same—and then had an idea, and blessed he
mother for having watched *Jaws* on TV so many times. "Kit, forget it
Remember a couple months ago and those guys who tried to beat you up
The freeze spell?"

"Yeah. . . ."

"Do it, do it big. I'll feed you power!" She pounded the dolphin on th
side. "Go beach! Tell your buddies to beach too!"

"But—"

"Go do it!" She let go of the dolphin's fin and dropped into the wate
swallowing hard as she saw another fin, of the wrong shape entirely, begin t
circle in on her and Kit. "Kit, get the water working again!"

It took a precious second; and the next one—one of the longer seconds o
Nita's life—for her and Kit to clamber up out of the "liquid" water onto th
"solid." They made it and grabbed one another for both physical and mor
support, as that fin kept coming. "The other spell set?" Nita gasped.

"Yeah—*now!*"

The usual immobility of a working spell came down on them both, wit
something added—a sense of being not one person alone, but part of a *on*
that was somehow bigger than even Nita and Kit together could be. Insid
that sudden oneness, she felt the "freeze" spell waiting like a phone numbe
with all but one digit dialed. Kit said the one word in the Speech that set th
spell free, the "last digit," then gripped Nita's hand hard.

Nita did her part, quickly saying the three most dangerous words in a
wizardry—the words that give all of a wizard's power over into another'
hands. She felt it going from her, felt Kit shaking as he wound her power, he
trust, into the spell. And then she took all her fright, and her anger at th

harks, and her pity for the poor wailing bulk on the sand, and let Kit have
hose too.

The spell blasted away from the two of them with a shock like a huge jolt
f static, then dropped down over the sandbar and the water for hundreds of
eet around, sinking like a weighted net. And as if the spell had physically
lragged them down, all the circling, hunting fins in the water sank out of
ight, their owners paralyzed and unable to swim.

No wizardry is done without a price. Kit wobbled in Nita's grip as if he
vere going to keel over. Nita had to lock her knees to keep standing. But
oth of them managed to stay upright until the weakness passed, and Nita
ooked around with grim satisfaction at the empty water. "The sharks won't
e bothering us now," she said. "Let's get up on the sandbar."

It was a few seconds' walk to where the dolphins lay beached on the bar,
hattering excitedly. Once up on the sand, Kit took a look at what awaited
hem and groaned out loud. Nita would have too, except that she found
erself busy breathing deep to keep from throwing up. Everywhere the sand
vas black and sticky with gobs and splatters of blood, some clotted, some
resh.

The dark bulk of the injured whale heaved up and down with her breath-
ig, while small weak whistling noises went in and out. The whale's skin was
narked with rope burns and little pits and ragged gashes of shark bites. The
reatest wound, though, the one still leaking blood, was too large for any
hark to have made. It was a crater in the whale's left side, behind the long
wimming fin; a crater easily three feet wide, ragged with ripped flesh. The
hale's one visible eye, turned up to the moonlight, watched Kit and Nita
ully as they came.

"What happened?" Kit said, looking at the biggest wound with disbelief
nd horror. "It looks like somebody bombed you."

"Someone did," the whale said in a long pained whistle. Nita came up
eside the whale's head and laid a hand on the black skin behind her eye. It
vas very hot. "It was one of the new killing-spears," the whale said to Nita,
the kind that blasts. But never mind that. What did you do with the
harks?"

"Sank them. They're lying on the bottom with a 'freeze' on them."

"But if they don't swim, they can't breathe—they'll die!" The concern in
ie whale's voice astonished Nita. "Cousins, quick, kill the spell! We're going
o need their good will later."

Nita glanced at Kit, who was still staring at the wound with a tight, angry
ok on his face. He glanced up at her. "Huh? Oh. Sure. Better put up a
izard's wall first, so that the dolphins can get back in the water without
etting attacked again."

"Right." Nita got her book out and riffled through pages to the appropri-

ate spell, a short-term forcefield that needed no extra supplies to produce
She said the spell and felt it take hold, then sagged back against the whal
and closed her eyes till the dizziness went away. Off to one side she heard Ki
saying the words that released the freeze.

A few moments later fins began appearing again out on the water, circlin
inward toward the sandbar, then sliding away as if they bumped into some
thing, and circling in again.

"The water will take the blood away soon enough," the whale saic
"They'll go away and not even remember why they were here. . . ." Th
whale's eye fixed on Nita again. "Thanks for coming so quickly, cousins."

"It took us longer than we wanted. I'm Nita. That's Kit."

"I'm S'reee," the whale said. The name was a hiss and a long, plaintive
upscaling whistle.

Kit left the wound and came up to join Nita. "It was one of those explosiv
harpoons, all right," he said. "But I thought those were supposed to b
powerful enough to blow even big whales in two."

"They are. Ae'mhnuu died that way, this morning." S'reee's whistle wa
bitter. "He was the Senior Wizard for this whole region of the Plateau. I wa
studying with him—I was going to be promoted to Advisory soon. Then th
ship came, and we were doing a wizardry, we didn't notice—"

Nita and Kit looked at each other. They had found out for themselves tha
a wizard is at his most vulnerable when exercising his strength. "He die
right away," S'reee said. "I took a spear too. But it didn't explode right away
and the sharks smelled Ae'mhnuu's blood and a great pack of them showe
up to eat. They went into feeding frenzy and bit the spear right out of me
Then one of them started chewing on the spear, and the blasting part of
went off. It killed a lot of them and blew this hole in me. They got so bus
eating each other and Ae'mhnuu that I had time to get away. But I wa
leaving bloodtrail, and they followed it. What else should I have e
pected? . . ."

She wheezed. "Cousins, I hope one of you has skill at healing, for I'm i
trouble, and I *can't* die now, there's too much to do."

"Healing's part of my specialty," Nita said, and was quiet for a momen
She'd become adept, as Kit had, at fixing the minor hurts Ponch kept pickin
up—bee stings and cat bites and so forth. But this was going to be differen

She stepped away from S'reee's head and went back to look at the wound
keeping tight control of her stomach. "I can seal this up all right," she saic
"But you're gonna have a huge scar. And I don't know how long it'll take th
muscles underneath to grow back. I'm not real good at this yet."

"Keep my breath in my body, cousin, that'll be enough for me," S'ree
said.

Nita nodded and started paging through her book for the section on med

ine. It started out casually enough with first aid for the minor ailments of
wizards—the physical ones like colds and the mental ones like spell backlash
nd brainburn. Behind that was a section she had only skimmed before,
never expecting to need it: *Major Surgery*. The spells were complex and
lengthy. That by itself was no problem. But all of them called for one supply
n common—the blood of the wizard performing them. Nita began to shake.
Seeing someone else bleed was bad enough; the sight of her own blood in
quantity tended to make her pass out.

"Oh, great," she said, for there was no avoiding what had to be done. "Kit,
you have anything sharp on you?"

He felt around in his pockets. "No such luck, Neets. . . ."

"Then find me a shell or something."

S'reee's eye glinted in the moonlight. "There are the dolphins," she said.

"What do *they*—oh." The one dolphin still beached, the one who had
brought them in, smiled at Nita, exhibiting many sharp teeth.

"Oh, brother," she said, and went down the sandbar to where the dolphin
lay. "Look," she said, hunkering down in front of it, "I don't even know your
name—"

"Hotshot." He gave her a look that was amused but also kindly.

"Hotshot, right. Look—don't do it hard, okay?" And wincing, Nita put
out her left hand and looked away.

"Do what?"

"Do *llllp!*" Nita said, as the pain hit. When she looked again, she saw that
Hotshot had nipped her very precisely on the outside of the palm—two little
crescents of toothmarks facing each other. Blood welled up, and the place
stung, but not too badly to bear.

Hotshot's eyes glittered at her. "Needs salt."

"Yeccch!" But Nita still wanted to laugh, even while her stomach churned.
She got up and hurried back to Kit, who was holding her book for her.

Together they went over to the terrible wound, and Nita put her bleeding
hand to it, turned away as far as she could, and started reading the spell. It
was a long series of complicated phrases in the Speech; she spoke them
quickly at first, then more slowly as she began to be distracted by the pain in
her hand. And as often happens in a wizardry, she began to lose contact with
her physical surroundings.

Soon Kit and S'reee and the beach were gone. Even the book was gone,
though she was reading from it. She was surrounded by the roaring of green
water around her, and the smell of blood and fear, and shadows in the water,
pursuing her. She swam for her life, and kept reading.

No wound can be healed, the book said, unless the pain of its inflicting is
fully experienced. There was nothing to do but read, and flee, wailing terror-
song and grief-song into the water, until the first pain came, the sick, cold

sharpness in her side. Nita knew she was sagging, knew Kit was holding her up from behind. But all that was far away.

The second pain came, the fierce mouths ripping and worrying at her till she couldn't go forward any more, only flail and thrash in an agony of help lessness and revulsion—

—and then the third pain hit, and Nita lost control of everything and started to fall down as the white fire blew up in her side. But the words were speaking *her* now, as they do in the more powerful wizardries. Though inwardly Nita screamed and cried for release, it did her no good. Her own power was loose, doing what she had told it to, and the wizardry wouldn't let her go until it was done. When it was, finally, it dropped her on her face in the sand, and she felt Kit go down with her, trying to keep her from breaking something.

Eventually the world came back. Nita found herself sitting on the sand feeling wobbly, but not hurting anywhere. She looked up at S'reee's side. New gray skin covered the wound, paler than the rest of the whale, but unbroken. There was still a crater there, but no blood flowed; and many of the smaller shark bites were completely gone, as were the burns from the harpoon's rope where it had gotten tangled around S'reee's flukes.

"Wow," Nita said. She lifted her left hand and looked at it. The place where Hotshot had bitten her was just a little oval of pink puncture marks, all healed.

"You all right?" Kit said, trying to help her up.

"Yeah, yeah, sure," Nita said. She pushed him away as kindly and quickly as she could, staggered down to the water line, and lost her dinner.

When she came back, her mouth full of the taste of the salt water she'd used to wash it out, S'reee had rolled herself more upright and was talking to Kit. "I still feel deathly sick," she said, "but at least dying isn't a problem . . . not for the moment."

She looked at Nita. Though the long face was frozen into that eternal smile, it was amazing how many expressions could live in a whale's eyes. Admiration was there just now, and gratitude. "You and I aren't just cousins now, hNii't," S'reee said, giving Nita's name a whistly whalish intonation, "but sisters too, by blood exchanged. And I'm in your debt. Maybe it's poor thanks to a debtor to ask him to lend to you again, right away. But maybe a sister, or a friend"—she glanced at Kit—"would excuse that if it had to happen."

"We're on active status," Kit said. "We have to handle whatever comes up in this area. What's the problem?"

"Well then." S'reee's whistling took on a more formal rhythm. "As the only remaining candidate Senior Wizard for the Waters About the Gates, by wizard's Right I request and require your assistance. Intervention will take place locally and last no more than ten lights-and-darks. The probable level of difficulty does not exceed what the manual describes as 'dangerous,' though if intervention is delayed, the level may escalate to 'extremely dangerous' or critical.' Will you assist?"

Nita and Kit looked at each other, unnerved by the second part of the job description. S'reee moaned. "I hate the formalities," she said in a long unhappy whistle. "I'm too young to be a Senior: I'm only two! But with Ae'mhnuu gone, I'm stuck with it! And we're in trouble, the water people and the land people both, if we don't finish what Ae'mhnuu was starting when he died!" She huffed out a long breath. "I'm just a calf; why did I get stuck with this? . . ."

Kit sighed too, and Nita made a face at nothing in particular. On their first job, she and Kit had said something similar, about a hundred times. "I'll help," she said, and "Me too," said Kit, in about the same breath.

"But you're tired," Nita said, "and we're tired, and it's late, we ought to go home. . . ."

"Come tomorrow, then, and I'll fill you in. Are you living on the Barrier?"

Nita didn't recognize the name. "Over there," Kit said, pointing across the water at Tiana Beach. "Where the lights are."

"By the old oyster beds," S'reee said. "Can you go out swimming a couple hours after the sun's high? I'll meet you and we'll go where we can talk."

"Uh," Kit said, "if the sharks are still around—"

Out on the water there was a splash of spray as a silvery form leaped, chattering shrilly, and hit the water again. "They won't be," S'reee said, sounding merry for the first time. "Hotshot and his people are one of the breeds the sharks hate worst; when there are enough of them around, few sharks would dare come into the area. Hotshot will be calling more of his people in tonight and tomorrow—that's part of the work I'm doing."

"Okay," Nita said. "But what about you? You're stuck here."

"Wake up!" Kit shouted playfully in Nita's ear, nudging her to look down at the sandbar. She found herself standing ankle-deep in salt water. "Tide's coming in. She'll be floated off here in no time."

"Oh. Well then. . . ." Nita opened her book, found the word to kill the wizard's-wall spell, and said it. Then she looked up at S'reee. "Are you sure you're gonna be all right?"

S'reee looked mildly at her from one huge eye. "We'll find out tomorrow," he said. "Dai'stiho."

"Dai," Nita and Kit said, and walked slowly off the sandbar, across the water, and toward the lights of home.

A Song of Choice

Nita got up late, and was still yawning and scrubbing her eyes even after she'd washed and dressed and was well into her second bowl of cereal. Her mother, walking around the kitchen in her bathrobe and watering the plants that hung all over, looked at Nita curiously.

"Neets, were you reading under the covers again last night?"

"No, Mom." Nita started to eat faster.

Her mother watered another plant, then headed for the sink. On the way she put a hand against Nita's forehead. "You feel okay? Not coming down with anything, are you?"

"No, I'm fine." Nita made an annoyed face when her mother's back was turned. Her mom loved the beach, but at the same time was sure that there were hundreds of ways to get sick there: too much heat, too much cold, too much time in the water; splinters, rusty nails, tar. . . . Nita's little sister Dairine had kicked off a tremendous family fight last week by insisting that the blueness of her lips after a prolonged swim was actually caused by a grape Popsicle.

"Is Kit having a good time?" her mother said.

"Wow, yeah, he says it's the best," Nita said. Which was true enough: Kit had never been at the beach for more than a day at a time before. Nita suspected that if he could, he'd dig into the sand like a clam and not come out for months.

"I just wanted to make sure. His dad called last night . . . wanted to see how his 'littlest' was."

" 'El Niño,' " Nita said, under her breath, grinning. It was what Kit's family called him sometimes, a pun—both the word for "the baby" and the name for a Pacific current that caused storms that could devastate whole countries. The name made Kit crazy, and Nita loved to use it on him.

"Be careful he doesn't hear you," Nita's mom said mildly, "or he'll deck you again. —How *have* you two been getting along?"

"Huh? We're fine. Kit's great." Nita saw a slightly odd look come into her mother's eyes. "For a boy," she added hurriedly.

"Well," her mother said, "be careful." And she took the watering can off into the living room.

Now what was that about? Nita thought. She finished her cornflakes at high speed, rinsed the bowl and spoon in the sink, and hurried out of the house to find Kit.

Halfway across the sparse sandy grass of the front yard, another voice spoke up. "Aha," it said. "The mystery lady."

"Put a cork in it, Dairine," Nita said. Her sister was hanging upside down from the trapeze swing of the rusty swing set, her short red hair ruffling in the breeze. Dairine was a tiny stick of a thing and an all right younger sister, though (in Nita's estimation) much too smart for her own good. Right now entirely too much smart was showing in those sharp gray eyes. Nita tried not to react to it. "Gonna fall down and bust your head open," she said. "Probably lose what few brains you have all over the ground."

Dairine shook her head, causing herself to swing a little. "Naaah," she said, "but I'd sooner"—she started pumping, so as to swing harder—"fall off the swing—than fall out the window—in the middle of the night!"

Nita went first cold, then hot. She glanced at the windows to see if anyone was looking out. They weren't. *"Did you tell?"* she hissed.

"I—don't tell anybody—anything," Dairine said, in time with her swinging. This was true enough. When Dairine had needed glasses, when she'd started getting beaten up at school, and when she was exposed to German measles, nobody had heard about it from *her*.

"Y'like him, huh?" Dairine said.

Nita glared at Dairine, opened her mouth to start shouting, then remembered the open windows.

"Yeah, I like him," Nita said, and turned red at having to make the admission. The problem was, there was no lying to Dairine. She always found out the truth sooner or later and made your life unbearable for having tried to hide it from her.

"You messing around?" Dairine said.

"Dairiiiiiiine!" Nita said, quietly, but with murder in it. "No, we are *not* messing around!"

"Okay. I just wondered. You going swimming?"

"No," Nita said, snapping the strap of her bathing suit very obviously at her sister, "I thought I'd go skiing. Wake *up*, lamebrain."

Dairine grinned at Nita upside down. "Kit went west," she said.

"Thanks," Nita said, and headed out of the yard. "Tell Mom and Dad I'l
be back for supper."

"Be careful," Dairine called after Nita, in a perfect imitation of thei
mother. Nita made a face.

"And watch out for sharks!" Dairine added at the top of her lungs.

"Oh, *great,*" Nita said to herself, wondering if her mom or dad had heard
She took off at a dead run in case they had.

She found Kit waiting about a mile down the beach, playing fetch with
Ponch to tire him out, as he'd told her he was going to. "Otherwise he get
crazy if I go away. This way he'll just lie down and sack out." And sure
enough, after some initial barking and dancing around Nita when she arrived
Ponch flopped panting on the sand beside them where they sat talking and
finally rolled over on one side and began to snore.

They grinned at each other and headed out into the water. It was un
nerving at first, to swim straight out into the ocean, past the breakers and the
rollers, past the place where the bottom fell away, and to just keep going as i
they never intended to come back. Nita had uncomfortable thoughts abou
undertow and how it might feel to drown. But just when she was at he
twitchiest, she saw a long floppy fin tip up out of the water. S'reee was lolling
there in the wavewash, her long pale barnacled belly upward.

The night before, when S'reee had been injured and immobile, it had been
hard to tell much of anything about her. Now Nita was struck by the size o
her—S'reee was at least forty feet from the tips of her flukes to her point
nose. And last night she had been a wheezing hulk. Now she was all grace
floating and gliding and rolling like some absurd, fat, slim-winged bird—fo
her long swimming fins looked more like wings than anything else.

"Did you sleep well?" she sang at them, a weird cheerful crescendo lik
something out of a happy synthesizer. "I slept wonderfully. And I ate wel
too. I think I may get back most of the weight I lost yesterday."

Kit looked at the healed place, treading water. "What *do* you eat?"

"Krill, mostly. The littlest things that live in the water, like little shrimp
But some fish too. The blues are running, and the little ones are good. O
they have been until now. . . ." She sighed, spraying water out her blow
hole. "That's in the story I have to tell you. Come on, we'll go out to one o
the Made Rocks."

They took hold of her dorsal fin, and she towed them. The "Made Rock
turned out to be an old square fishing platform about three miles south o
Tiana Beach: wooden pilings topped by wooden slats covered with tarre
canvas and with bland-faced seagulls. Most of the gulls immediately took of
and began flying around and screaming about the humans sitting on *the*
spot, despite Nita's and Kit's polite apologies. Some of the other gulls wer

ss annoyed, especially after they found out the visitors were wizards. Later
n, whenever Nita thought of her first real conversation with S'reee, what she
emembered best were the two seagulls who insisted on sitting in her lap the
hole time. They were heavy, and not housebroken.

"I guess the best place to start," S'reee said when Nita and Kit were
ettled, "is with what you already know, that there's been trouble for wizards
n the land lately. The trouble's been felt in the sea too. Out here we've been
aving quakes on the sea floor much more often than we should be having
em—severe ones. And some other old problems have been getting worse.
he dirt they throw into the water from the High and Dry, especially: there's
ore of it than ever—"

" 'The High and Dry'?"

"The place with all the high things on it."

"Oh," Kit said. "New York City. Manhattan, actually."

"The water close to it is getting so foul, the fish can't breathe it for many
ousands of lengths out. Those that can are mostly sick. And many more of
e boats-that-eat-whales have been out here recently. The past few months,
ere's been a great slaughter—"

Nita frowned at the thought of other creatures suffering what S'reee had
een through. She had heard all the stories about the hungry people in Japan,
ut at the moment she found herself thinking that there *had* to be something
se to eat.

"Things have not been good," S'reee said. "I know less about the troubles
n land, but the Sea tells us that the land wizards have been troubled of late,
at there was some great strife of powers on the High and Dry. We saw the
Ioon go out one night—"

"So did we," Kit said. There was fear in his eyes at the memory, and pride
 his voice. "We were in Manhattan when it happened."

"We were part of it," Nita said. She still didn't know all of how she felt
out what had happened. But she would never forget reading from the book
at kept the world as it should be, the *Book of Night with Moon*, while
ound her and Kit the buildings of Manhattan wavered like a dream about
 break—and beyond a barrier of trees brought to life, and battling statues,
e personification of all darkness and fear, the Lone Power, fought to get at
em and destroy them.

S'reee looked at them somberly from one eye. "It's true then what
e'mhnuu used to tell me, that there are no accidents. You've met the Power
at created death in the beginning and was cast out for it. All these things—
e lost Moon, that night, and the earthquakes, and the fouled water, and
e whale-eating ships—they're all Its doing, one way or another."

Kit and Nita nodded. "It took a defeat in that battle you two were in,"
reee said. "It's angry, and the problems we've been having are symptoms of

that anger. So we have to bind It, make It less harmful, as the first sea peopl
bound It a long time ago. Then things will be quiet again for a while."

"Bind It how?" Nita said.

"No, wait a minute," Kit said. "You said something about the Sea tellin
you things—"

S'reee looked surprised for a moment. "Oh, I forgot that you do it diffe
ently. You work your wizardry with the aid of those things you carry—"

"Our books."

"Right. The whales who are wizards get their wizardry from the Sea. Th
water speaks to you when you're ready, and offers you the Ordeal. Then
you pass it, the Heart of the Sea speaks whenever you need to hear it and tel
you what you need to know."

Nita nodded. The events in that "other" Manhattan had been her Ordea
and Kit's; and after they passed it, their books had contained much mor
information than before. "So," she said, "bind the Lone Power *how?*"

"The way the first whale-wizards did," S'reee said. "The story itself *is* th
binding. Or rather, the story's a song: the Song of the Twelve. In the lon
form it takes—*will* take—hours to sing."

"I'm glad I had breakfast," Kit muttered.

S'reee spouted good-naturedly. Nita wondered whether it was accident
that the wind turned at that exact moment, threw the spray straight at Ki
and soaked him to the skin. At any rate, Nita laughed.

"I won't take quite that long," S'reee said. "You know about the great W
of the Powers, at the beginning of everything; and how the Lone Pow
invented death and pain, and tried to impose them on the whole univers
and the other Powers wouldn't let It, and threw It out."

"Even regular human beings have stories about it," Kit said. He took c
his windbreaker and shook it out, mostly on Nita.

"I'm not surprised," S'reee said. "Everything that lives and tells stories ha
this story in one form or another. Well. After that war in the Above an
Beyond, the Lone Power spent a long while in untraveled barren universe
recouping Its strength. Then It came back to our native universe, looking fc
some quiet, out-of-the-way place to try out Its new inventions. Right then th
only place vulnerable to It, because thinking life was very new here, was th
world; and the only place thinking life existed as yet was the Sea. So the Lor
One came here to trick the Sea into accepting Death. Its sort of deatl
anyway—where all power and love are wasted into an endless darkness, lo
forever."

"Entropy," Nita said.

"Yes. And any sea people It succeeded in tricking would be stuck with th
death, the Great Death, forever. —Now there was already a sort of death i
the Sea, but only the kind where your body stops. Everyone knew it wasn

permanent, and it didn't hurt much; you might get eaten, but you would go on as part of someone else. No one was afraid of not being his own self any more—I guess that's the simplest way of putting it. That calm way of life drove the Lone Power wild with hate, and It swore to attach fear and pain to it and make it a lot more interesting."

S'reee sighed. "The whales' job then was what it is now: to be masters and caretakers for the fish and the smaller sea people, the way you two-leggers are for the dry-land beasts. So naturally, the only wizards in the Sea were whales, just as humans were originally the only ones on land. That early on, there were only ten whale-wizards, all Seniors. *Ni'hwinyii*, they were called, the Lords of the Humors—"

Nita was puzzled. "It's the old word for emotions, sort of," Kit said. "Not like 'funny' humor."

"I know," Nita said, annoyed. She hadn't.

S'reee blew, laughing. The spray missed Kit this time. "Those ten whales ruled the Sea, under the Powers," she said. "If the Lone Power wanted to trick the Sea into the Great Death, It had to trick the Ten—then all the life they ruled would be stuck with the Great Death too. So the Lone One went to the Ten in disguise, pretending to be a stranger, a new whale sent to them so that they could decide under which of their Masteries it fell. And as each one questioned the Lone Power, the Stranger whale offered each of them the thing he wanted most, if he would only accept the 'Gift' the Stranger would give him. And he showed them just enough of his power to prove that he could do it."

"Uh-oh," Kit said softly. "I've heard that one before."

"Apples and snakes," Nita said.

"Yes. The pattern repeats. One after another, the Lone One tempted the Ten. The Sea was silent then and gave them no advice—some people say that the Powers wanted the Ten to make up their own minds. But however that might have been, three of the Ten took the Gift, and fell. Three of them were undecided. Three of them rejected the Gift. And the Lone Power needed a majority of the Lords to accept Death, or Its victory would only be partial."

"Those were only nine Lords, though," Kit said.

"Yes, and here the Tenth comes in: the Silent Lord, they called her. She was the youngest of them, and each of the other Nine tried to bring her around to his own way of thinking. The Lone One came to her too and tempted her as It had tempted the others. You know, though, that it's the youngest wizard who has the most power, and where the other Lords were deceived, the Silent Lord wasn't. She realized what the Stranger was and what It was trying to do.

"She was faced with a difficult choice. She knew that even if she rejected the Stranger, the fighting would only go on among the other Nine. Sooner or later they or their successors would accept the Gift and doom the whole Sea to the Great Death. But she also knew something else that the Sea had told her long before, and that others have found out since. If one knows death is coming—any death, from the small ones to the Great one—and is willing to accept it fully, and experience it fully, then the death becomes something else—a passage, not an ending: not only for himself, but for others."

S'reee's voice got very soft. "So the Silent Lord did that," she said. "Luck, or the Powers, brought one more creature into the singing, uninvited. It was the one fish over whom no mastery was ever given—the Pale Slayer, whom we call the Master-Shark. The Silent Lord decided to accept the 'Gift' that the Stranger offered her—and then, to transform the Gift and make it 'safe,' she gave herself up willingly to die. She dived into a stand of razor coral; and the Master-Shark smelled her blood in the water, and . . . well." S'reee blew. "He accepted the sacrifice."

Nita and Kit looked at each other.

"When that happened, the Lone Power went wild with rage," S'reee said. "But that did It no good. The Silent One's sacrifice turned death loose in some of the Sea, but not all; and even where it did turn up, death was much weaker than it would have been otherwise. To this day there are fish and whales that have astonishing lifespans, and some that never seem to die of natural causes. The sharks, for instance: some people say that's a result of the Master-Shark's acceptance of the Silent Lord's sacrifice. But the important thing is that the Lone Power had put a lot of Its strength into Its death wizardry. It had become death Itself, in a way. And when death was weakened, so was the Lone One. It fell to the sea floor, and it opened for It and closed on It afterward. And there It lies bound."

" 'Bound'?" Kit said. "S'reee, when we had our last run-in with the Lone Power, It didn't seem very bound to us. It had a whole alternate universe of Its own, and when It came into this one to get us, It went around tearing things up any way It liked. If It is bound, how could It have also been running loose in Manhattan?"

S'reee blew, a sober sound. "It's the usual confusion about time," she said. "All the great Powers exist outside it, and all we usually see of Them are the places and moments where and when They dip into the timeflow we're inhabiting. This world has always been an annoyance to the Lone One—It gets frustrated here a lot—so It visits often, in many forms. From inside our timeflow, it can look as if the Lone Power is bound in one place-time and free in another . . . and both appearances are true." S'reee rolled and stretched in the water. "Meanwhile, outside the timeflow, where things don't have to happen one after another, the Lone One is eternally rebelling and eternally defeated—"

"We gave It a chance to do something else, when we fought last," Nita said. "We offered It the option to stop being a dark power—"

"And it worked," S'reee said, sounding very pleased. "Didn't you know? It's also eternally redeemed. But meantime we have to keep fighting the battles, even though the war's decided. The Lone One's going to take a long while to complete Its choice, and if we get lazy or sloppy about handling Its thrashing around, a lot of people are going to die."

"The sea floor," Nita said, "has been shaken up a lot lately."

"That's one symptom that tells us the TwelveSong needs to be reenacted," S'reee said. "We do the Song at intervals anyway, to make sure the story's never forgotten. But when the Lone Power gets troublesome—as It seems to be doing now—we reenact the Song, and bind It quiet again."

"Where do you do this stuff?" Kit said.

"Down the coast a ways," S'reee said, "off the edge of the plateau, in the Great Deep past the Gates of the Sea. Ae'mhnuu was getting ready to call the Ten together for a Song in three days or so. He was training me for the Singer's part—before they blew him in two pieces and boiled him down for oil."

Her song went bitter, acquiring a rasp that hurt Nita's ears. "Now I'm stuck handling it all myself. It's not easy: You have to pick each whale wizard carefully for each part. I don't know who he had in mind to do what. Now I have to work it out myself—and I need help, from wizards who can handle trouble if it comes up." She looked up at them. "You two can obviously manage that. And the Ten will listen to you, they'll respect you, after what you went through up in the High and Dry. You've fought the Lone Power yourselves and gotten off—"

"It was luck," Kit muttered. Nita elbowed him.

"Singing, huh," Nita said, smiling slightly. "I don't have much of a singing voice. Maybe I'd better take the Silent One's part."

S'reee looked at Nita in amazement. "Would you?"

"Why not?"

"Not me," Kit said. "I'm even worse than she is. But I'll come along for the ride. The swim, I mean."

S'reee looked from Kit to Nita. "You two are enough to make me doubt all the stories I've heard about humans," she said. "HNii't, best check that 'book' thing and make sure this is something you're suited for. The temperaments of the singers have to match the parts they sing—but I think this might suit you. And the original Silent Lord was a humpback. The shapechange would come easily to you, since we've shared blood—"

"Wait a minute! *Shapechange?*" Nita cried. "You mean me be a whale?"

Kit laughed. "Why not, Neets? You *have* been putting on a little weight lately. . . ."

She elbowed him again, harder. "Oh, you'd shapechange too, K!t," S'reee said. "We couldn't take you down in the Great Deeps otherwise. —Look, you two, there's too much to tell, and some of it's going to have to be handled as we go along. We've got three days to get everyone together for the Song, so that it happens when the Moon's round. Otherwise it won't keep the sea bottom quiet—"

Kit looked suddenly at Nita. "Did you see that thing on the news the other night? About the volcano?"

"The *what?*"

"There was some scientist on. He said that hot-water vents had been opening up all of a sudden off the Continental Shelf. And he said that if those little tremors we've been having keep getting worse, it could open the bottom right up and there'd be a volcano. The least it'd do would be to boil the water for miles. But it could also break Long Island in two. The beaches would go right under water. And Manhattan skyscrapers aren't built for earthquakes." Kit was quiet for a moment, then said, "The rocks remembered. That's why they were upset. . . ."

Nita wasn't thinking about rocks, or Manhattan. She was thinking that her folks were planning to be there for another week and a half at least—and she saw a very clear picture of a tidal wave of dirty, boiling water crashing down on the beach house and smashing it to driftwood.

"When should we start, S'reee?" she said.

"Dawn tomorrow. There's little time to waste. Hotshot will be going with us—he'll be singing the Fourth Lord, the Wanderer, in the Song."

"Dawn—" Nita chewed her lip. "Could it be a little later? We've got to have breakfast with my parents or they'll freak out."

"*Parents?*" S'reee looked from Nita to Kit in shock. "You're still calves, is that what you're telling me? And you went outworld into a Dark Place and came back! I'd thought you were much older—"

"We wished we were," Nita said under her breath.

"Oh, well. No matter. Three hours after dawn be all right? The same place? Good enough. Let me take you back. I have something to fetch so that you can swim with us, K!t. And, look—" She gazed at them for some time from that small, worried, gentle eye; but longer at Nita. "Thank you," she said. "Thank you very much indeed."

"Think nothing of it," Kit said grandly, slipping into the water and patting S'reee on one big ribbed flank.

Nita slid into the water, took hold of S'reee's dorsal fin, and thought something of it all the way home.

Seniors' Song

The alarm clock went off right above Nita's head, a painful blasting buzz like a dentist's drill. "Aaagh," she said, reluctantly putting one arm out from under the covers and fumbling around on the bedside table for the noisy thing.

It went quiet without her having touched it. Nita squinted up through the morning brightness and found herself looking at Dairine. Her little sister was standing by the bedside table with the alarm clock in her hands, wearing Star Wars pajamas and an annoyed look.

"And where are we going at six in the morning?" Dairine said, too sweetly.

"*We* are not going anywhere," Nita said, swinging herself out of bed with a groan. "Go play with your Barbie dolls, Einstein."

"Only if you give them back," Dairine said, unperturbed. "Anyway, there are better things to play with. Kit, for example—"

"Dairine, you're pushing it." Nita stood up, rubbed her eyes until they started working properly, and then pulled a dresser drawer open and began pawing through it for a T-shirt.

"What're *you* doing, then—getting up so early all the time, staying out late? You think Mom and Dad aren't noticing? —Oh, don't wear *that*," Dairine said at the sight of Nita's favorite sweatshirt. It featured numerous holes made by Ponch's teeth and the words WATCH THIS SPACE FOR FUR-THER DEVELOPMENTS. "Oh, really, Neets, *don't*, it's incredibly tacky—"

"That sounds real weird," Nita said, "coming from someone with little Yodas all over her pajamas."

"Oh, stuff it, Nita," Dairine said. Nita turned her head and smiled, thinking that Dairine had become easier to tease since she'd decided to be a Jedi Knight when she grew up. Still, Nita went easy on her sister. It wasn't fair for a wizard to make fun of someone who wanted to do magic, of whatever brand.

"Same to you, runt. When're Mom and Dad getting up, did they say?"

"They're up now."

"What for?"

"They're going fishing. *We're* going with them."

Nita blanched. "Oh, no! Dair, I *can't*—"

Dairine cocked her head at Nita. "They wanted to surprise us."

"They did," Nita said, in shock. "I *can't* go—"

"Got a hot date, huh?"

"*Dairine!* I told you—"

"Where were you two going?"

"Swimming." That was the truth.

"Neets, you can swim any time," Dairine said, imitating their mother's tone of voice. Nita zipped up her jeans and sat down on the bed with a thump. "What were you gonna be *doing,* anyway?"

"I told you, *swimming!*" Nita got up, went to the window, and looked out, thinking of S'reee and the summoning and the Song of the Twelve and the rest of the business of being on active status, which was now looking ridiculously complicated. And it looked so simple yesterday. . . .

"You could tell them something—"

Nita made a face at that. She had recently come to dislike lying to her parents. For one thing, she valued their trust. For another, a wizard, whose business is making things happen by the power of the spoken word, learns early on not to say things out loud that aren't true or that he *doesn't* want to happen.

"Sure," she said in bitter sarcasm. "Why don't I just tell them that we're on a secret mission? Or that we're busy saving Long Island and the greater metropolitan area from a fate worse than death? Or maybe I could tell them that Kit and I have an appointment to go out and get turned into whales, how about *that?*"

Even without turning around, Nita could feel her sister staring at her back. Finally the quiet made Nita twitchy. She turned around, but Dairine was already heading out of the room. "Go on and eat," Dairine said quietly, over her shoulder. "Sound happy." And she was gone.

Under her breath, Nita said a word her father would have frowned at, and then sighed and headed for breakfast, plastering onto her face the most sincere smile she could manage. At first it felt hopelessly unnatural, but in a few seconds it was beginning to stick. At the dining-room door, where her father came around the corner from the kitchen and nearly ran her over, Nita took one look at him—in his faded lumberjack shirt and his hat stuck full of fish hooks—and wondered why she had ever been worried about getting out of the fishing trip. It was going to be all right.

Her dad looked surprised. "Oh! You're up. Did Dairine—"

"She told me," Nita said. "Is there time to eat something?"

"Sure. I guess she told Kit too then—I just looked in his room, but he wasn't there. The bed was made; I guess he's ready—"

Nita cheerfully allowed her father to draw his own conclusions, especially since they were the wrong ones. "He's probably down at the beach killing time," she said. "I'll go get him after I eat."

She made a hurried commando raid on the kitchen and put the kettle on the stove for her mother, who was browsing through the science section of *The New York Times* and was ready for another cup of tea. Nita's mother looked up at her from the paper and said, "Neets, where's your sister? She hasn't had breakfast."

That was when her sister came thumping into the dining room. Nita saw her mom look at Dairine and develop a peculiar expression. "Dari," her mother said, "are you feeling all right?"

"Yeah!" said Dairine in an offended tone. Nita turned in her chair to look at her. Her sister looked flushed, and she wasn't moving at her normal break-neck speed. "C'mere, baby," Nita's mother said. "Let me feel your fore-head."

"*Mom!*"

"Dairine," her father said.

"Yeah, right." Dairine went over to her mother and had her forehead felt, rolling her eyes at the ceiling. "You're hot, sweetie," Nita's mother said in alarm. "Harry, I *told* you she was in the water too long yesterday. Feel her."

Nita's dad looked slightly bored, but he checked Dairine's forehead and then frowned. "Well. . . ."

"No 'wells.' Dari, I think you'd better sit this one out."

"Oh, *Mom!*"

"Cork it, little one. You can come fishing with us in a day or two." Nita's mother turned to her. "Neets, will you stick around and keep an eye on your sister?"

"Mom, I don't need a babysitter!"

"Enough, Dairine," her mom said. "Up to bed with you. Nita, we'll take you and Kit with us the next time; but your dad really wants to get out today."

"It's okay, Mom," Nita said, dropping what was left of the smile (though it now really wanted to stay on). "I'll keep an eye on the runt."

"Don't call me a runt!"

"Dairine," her father said again. Nita's little sister made a face and left, again at half the usual speed.

As soon as she could, Nita slipped into Dairine's room. Her sister was lying on top of the bed, reading her way through a pile of X-Men comics; she looked flushed. "Not bad, huh?" she said in a low voice as Nita came in.

"How did you *do* that?" Nita whispered.

"I used the Force," Dairine said, flashing a wicked look at Nita.

"Dari! Spill it!"

"I turned Dad's electric blanket up high and spent a few minutes under it. Then I drank about a quart of hot water to make sure I stayed too warm." Dairine turned a page in her comic book, looking blasé about the whole thing. "Mom did the rest."

Nita shook her head in admiration. "Runt, I owe you one."

Dairine looked up from her comic at Nita. "Yeah," Dairine said, "you do."

Nita felt a chill. "Right," she said. "I'll hang out here till they leave. Then I have to find Kit—"

"He went down to the general store just before you got up," Dairine said. "I think he was going to call somebody."

"Right," Nita said again.

There was the briefest pause. Then: "Whales, huh?" Dairine said, very softly.

Nita got out of there in a great hurry.

The sign on top of the building merely said, in big, square, black letters, TIANA BEACH. " 'Tiana Beach' *what?*" people typically said, and it was a fair question. From a distance there was no telling what the place was, except a one-story structure with peeling white paint.

The building stood off the main road, at the end of a spur road that ran down to the water. On one side of it was its small parking lot, a black patch of heat-heaved asphalt always littered with pieces of clamshells, which the gulls liked to drop and crack open there. On the other side was a dock for people who came shopping in their boats.

The dock was in superb repair. The store was less so. Its large multipaned front windows, for example, were clean enough outside, but inside they were either covered by stacked-up boxes or with grime; nothing was visible through them except spastically flashing old neon signs that said "Pabst Blue Ribbon" or "Cerveza BUDWEISER." Beachgrass and aggressive weeds grew next to (and in places, through) the building's cracked concrete steps. The rough little U.S. Post Office sign above the front door had a sparrow's nest behind it.

Nita headed for the open door. It was always open, whether Mr. Friedman the storekeeper was there or not; "On the off chance," as Mr. Friedman usually said, "that someone might need something at three in the morning . . . or the afternoon. . . ."

Nita walked into the dark, brown-smelling store, past the haphazard shelves of canned goods and cereal and the racks of plastic earthworms and nylon surf-casting line. By the cereal and the crackers, she met the reason that Mr. Friedman's store was safe day and night. The reason's name was Dog: a whitish, curlyish, terrierish mutt, with eyes like something out of Disney and teeth like something out of Transylvania. Dog could smell attempted theft for miles; and when not biting people in the line of business, he would do it on his own time, for no reason whatever—perhaps just to keep his fangs in.

"Hi, Dog," Nita said, being careful not to get too close.

Dog showed Nita his teeth. "Go chew dry bones," he said in a growl.

"Same to you," Nita said pleasantly, and made a wide detour around him, heading for the phone booth in the rear of the store.

"Right," Kit was saying, his voice slightly muffled by being in the booth. "Something about 'the Gates of the Sea.' I tried looking in the manual, but all I could find was one of those 'restricted' notices and a footnote that said to see the local Senior for more details—"

Kit looked up, saw Nita coming, and pointed at the phone, mouthing the words "Tom and Carl." She nodded and squeezed into the booth with him; Kit tipped the hearing part of the receiver toward her, and they put their heads together. "Hi, it's Nita—"

"Well, hi there yourself," Tom Swale's voice came back. He would doubtless have gone on with more of the same if someone else, farther away from his end of the line, hadn't begun screaming "Hel-LOOOOOOO! HEL-lo!" in a creaky, high-pitched voice that sounded as if Tom were keeping his insane grandmother chained up in the living room. This, Nita knew, was Tom and Carl's intractable macaw Machu Picchu, or Peach for short. Wizards' pets tended to get a bit strange as their masters grew more adept in wizardry, but Peach was stranger than most, and more trying. Even a pair of Senior wizards must have wondered what to do with a creature that would at one moment deliver the evening news a day early, in a flawless imitation of any major newscaster you pleased, and then a second later start ripping up the couch for the fun of it.

"Cut that out!" Nita heard another voice saying in the background, one with a more New Yorkish sound to it: That was Carl. "Look out!— She's on the stove. Get her—oh, Lord. There go the eggs. *You little cannibal!*—"

"It's business as usual around here, as you can tell," Tom said. "Not where you are, though, to judge from how early Kit called . . . and from what he tells me. Kit, hang on a minute: Carl's getting the information released for you. Evidently the Powers That Be don't want it distributed without a Senior's supervision. The area must be sensitive right now."

Nita made small talk with Tom for a few minutes while, in the back-

ground, Peach screamed, and Annie and Monty the sheepdogs barked irritably at the macaw, who was shouting "Bad dog! Bad dog! Nonono!" at them
—or possibly at Carl. Nita could imagine the scene very well—the bright airy
house full of plants and animals, a very ordinary-looking place as far as the
neighbors were concerned. Except that Tom spent his days doing research
and development on complex spells and incantations for other wizards, and
then used some of the things he discovered to make a living as a writer on the
side. And Carl, who sold commercial time for a "flagship" station of one of
the major television networks, might also make a deal to sell you a more
unusual kind of time—say, a piece of last Thursday. The two of them were
living proof that it was possible to live in the workaday world and function as
wizards at the same time. Nita was very glad to know them.

"The link's busy," she heard Carl saying, at some distance from the phone.
"Oh, never mind, there it goes. Look," he said, apparently to one of his own
advanced-level manuals, "we need an intervention authorization for an offshore area—yeah, that's right. Here's the numbers—"

Kit had his manual open to the spot where he'd found the notification.
Nita looked over his shoulder and watched the box that said RESTRICTED
INFORMATION suddenly blink out, replaced by the words SEE CHART PAGE
1096. "Got it?" Tom said.

"Almost." Kit turned pages. Nita looked over his shoulder and found herself looking at a map of the East Coast, from Nova Scotia to Virginia. But
the coast itself was squeezed far over on the left-hand side, and individual
cities and states were only sketchily indicated. The map was primarily concerned with the ocean.

"Okay, I've got it in my book too," Tom said. "All those lines in the
middle of the water are contour lines, indicating the depth of the sea bottom.
You can see that there aren't many lines within about a hundred miles of
Long Island. The bottom isn't much deeper than a hundred feet within that
distance. But then—you see a lot of contour lines packed closely together?
That's the edge of the Continental Shelf. Think of it as a cliff, or a mesa,
with the North American continent sitting on top of it. Then there's a steep
drop—the cliff is just a shade less than a mile high—"

"Or deep," Nita said.

"Whichever. About a five thousand foot drop; not straight down—it
slopes a bit—but straight enough. Then the sea bottom keeps on sloping
eastward and downward. It doesn't slope as fast as before, but it goes deep—
some fifteen thousand feet down; and it gets deeper yet farther out. See
where it says 'Sohm Abyssal Plain' to the southeast of the Island, about six or
seven hundred miles out?"

"It has 'the Crushing Dark' underneath that on our map," Nita said. "I
that the whales' name for it?"

"Right. That area is more like seventeen, eighteen thousand feet down."

"I bet it's cold down there," Kit muttered.

"Probably. Let me know when you get back," Tom said, "because that's here you're going."

Nita and Kit looked at each other in shock. "But I thought even subma-nes couldn't go down *that* far," Nita said.

"They can't. Neither can most whales, normally—but it helps to be a izard," Tom said. "Look, don't panic yet—"

"Go ahead! Panic!" screamed Picchu from somewhere in the background. Do it now and avoid the June rush! Fear death by water!"

"Bird," Carl's voice said, also in the background, "you're honing for a unch in the beak."

"Violence! You want violence, I'll give you violence! No quarter asked or ven! Damn the torpedoes, full speed ahead! Don't give up the *WWWK!*"

"Thanks, Carl," Tom said, as silence fell. "Where were we? Oh, right. You on't just be going out there and diving straight down. There's a specific pproach to the Plain. Look back closer to the Island, and you'll see some ontours drawn in dotted lines—"

"Hudson Channel," Nita said.

"Right. That's the old bed of the Hudson River—where it used to run a undred thousand years ago, while all that part of the Continental Shelf was ill above water. That old riverbed leads farther southeast, to the edge of the helf, and right over it . . . there was quite a waterfall there once. See the otch in the Shelf?"

"Yeah. 'Hudson Canyon,' it says—"

"The Gates of the Sea," said Tom. "That's the biggest undersea canyon on e East Coast, and probably the oldest. It cuts right down through the helf. Those walls are at least two or three thousand feet high, sometimes ur. Some of the canyons on the Moon and Mars could match the Hudson –but none on Earth. And for the whale-wizards, the Gates have become the raditional approach to the Great Depths and the Crushing Dark."

The thought of canyon walls stretching above her almost a mile high gave Jita chills. She'd seen a rockslide once, and it had made her uneasy about anyons in general. "Is it safe?" she said.

"Of course not," Tom said, sounding cheerful. "But the natural dangers re Carl's department; he'll fill you in on what precautions you'll need to ake, and I suspect the whales will too."

" 'Natural dangers,' " Kit said. "Meaning there are unnatural ones too."

"In wizardry, when aren't there? This much I can tell you, though. New ork City has not been kind to that area. All kinds of things, even unex-loded depth charges, have been dumped at the head of Hudson Canyon

over the years. Most of them are marked on your map; but watch out for one
that aren't. And the city has been dumping raw sewage into the Hudso
Channel area for decades. Evidently in the old days, before people were to
concerned about ecology, they thought the water was so deep that the dump
ing wouldn't do any harm. But it has. Quite a bit of the sea-bottom life i
that area, especially the vegetation that the fish depend on for food, has bee
killed off entirely. Other species have been . . . changed. The manual w
give you details. You won't like them."

Nita suspected that Tom was right. "Anyway," he said, "let me give yo
the rest of this. After you do the appropriate rituals, which the whales w
coach you through, the access through the Gates of the Sea takes you dow
through Hudson Canyon to its bottom at the lower edge of the Shelf, an
then deeper and farther southeast—where the canyon turns into a valley tha
gets shallower and shallower as it goes. The valley ends just about where th
Abyssal Plain begins, at seven hundred miles off the coast, and seventee
thousand feet down. Then you come to the mountain."

It was on the map—a tiny set of concentric circles—but it had looked s
peculiar, standing there all by itself in the middle of hundreds of miles
flatness, that Nita had doubted her judgment. "The Sea's Tooth," she sai
reading from the map.

"Caryn Peak," Tom agreed, giving the human name. "Some of the ocea
ographers think it's simply the westernmost peak of an undersea mountai
range called the Kelvin Seamounts—they're off the eastward edge of you
map. Some think otherwise; the geological history of that area is bizarre. Bu
either way, the Peak's an important spot. And impressive; that one peak is s
thousand feet high. It stands up sheer from the bottom, all alone, a third a
high as Everest."

"Five Empire State Buildings on top of each other," Kit said, awed. H
liked tall things.

"A very noticeable object," Tom said. "It's functioned as landmark an
meeting place and site of the whales' great wizardries for not even they kno
how long. Certainly since the continents started drifting toward their presen
positions . . . at least a hundred thousand years ago. And it may have bee
used by . . . other sorts of wizards . . . even earlier than that. There
some interesting history in that area, tangled up with whale-wizards an
human ones too."

Tom's voice grew sober. "Some of the wizards who specialize in history sa
that humans only learned wizardry with the whales' assistance . . . an
even so, our brands of wizardry are different. It's an old, old branch of th
Art they practice. Very beautiful. Very dangerous. And the area aroun
Caryn Peak is saturated with residue from all the old wizardries that whale

and others, have done there. That makes any spell you work there even more dangerous."

"S'reee said that the 'danger' level wouldn't go above 'moderate,' " Kit said.

"She said it *shouldn't*," Nita said.

"Probably it won't," Tom said. He didn't sound convinced, though. "You should bear in mind that the 'danger' levels for humans and whales differ. Still, the book said she was about to be promoted to Advisory status, so she would know that— All the same . . . you two keep your eyes open. Watch what agreements you make. And if you make them—keep them, to the letter. From all indications, the Song of the Twelve is a lovely wizardry, and a powerful one . . . probably the most powerful magic done on a regular basis. The sources say it leaves its participants forever changed, for the better. At least, it does when it works. When it fails—which it has, once or twice in the past—it fails because some participant has broken the rules. And those times it's failed. . . . Well, all I can say is that I'm glad I wasn't born yet. *Be careful.*"

"We will," Nita said. "But what are the chances of something going wrong?"

"We could ask Peach," Kit said. It was a sensible suggestion; the bird, besides doing dramatic readings from *Variety* and *TV Guide*, could also predict the future—when it pleased her.

"Good idea. Carl?"

"Here I am," Carl said, having picked up an extension phone. "Now, Kit, about the monsters—"

"Carl, put that on hold a moment. What does the Walter Cronkite of the bird world have to say about all this?"

"I'll find out."

Monsters? Nita mouthed at Kit. "Listen," she said hurriedly to Tom, "I'm going to get off now. I've got to be around the house when my folks leave, so they won't worry about my little sister."

"Why? Is she sick?"

"No. But that's the problem. Tom, I don't know what to do about Dairine. I thought nonwizards weren't supposed to *notice* magic most of the time. I'm not sure it's working that way with Dairine. I think she's getting suspicious. . . ."

"We'll talk. Meanwhile, Carl—what does the bird say?"

"Oh, it is, it is a splendid thing/To be a pirate kiiiiiiiiiiiing!" Picchu was singing from somewhere in Tom's living room.

"Picchu—"

"What'sa matter? Don't you like Gilbert and Sullivan?"

"I told you we should never have let her watch *Pirates* on cable," Tom remarked to his partner.

"Twice your peanut ration for the week," Carl said.

". . . and I did the deed that all men shun, I shot the Albatross. . . ."

"You're misquoting. How about *no* peanuts for the rest of the week—"

"Pieces of eight! Pieces of eight!"

"How about no *food?*"

"Uh—" There was a pause. It didn't take Nita much imagination to picture the look that Carl was giving Picchu. She was glad no one had ever looked at *her* that way.

"Give."

"Well." The bird paused again, a long pause, and when she spoke her voice sounded more sober than Nita could remember ever hearing it. "Do what the night tells you. Don't be afraid to give yourself away. And read the small print before you sign!"

Kit glanced at Nita with a quizzical expression; she shrugged. At the other end of the line, sounding exceptionally annoyed, Carl said to Picchu, "You call *that* advice? We asked you for the odds!"

"Never ask me the odds," Picchu said promptly. "I don't want to know. And neither do *you*, really." And that end of the conversation swiftly degenerated into more loud squawking, and the excited barking of dogs, and Carl making suggestions to Picchu that were at best rather rude.

"Thanks," Nita said to Tom. "I'll talk to you later." She squeezed out of the phone booth and past Dog, who growled at her as she went. Behind her, Kit said, in entirely too cheerful a tone of voice, "So, Carl, what about the monsters?"

Nita shook her head and went home.

The Blue's Song

"Giant man-eating clams," she said to Kit later, as they walked down an isolated stretch of Tiana Beach toward the surf. "Giant squid—"

"Krakens," Kit said.

"I don't care what you call them, they're still giant squid. And squid belong in sushi. I don't like this."

"With luck, we won't see any of them, Carl says."

"When have we ever had that kind of luck? . . ."

"Besides, Neets, even *you* can outrun a clam. . . ."

"Cute," she said. They splashed into the water together, glancing up and down the beach as they did so. No one was in sight; and they had left Ponch up in the dunes, looking for a good place to bury the remains of his latest water rat. "Look," Nita said, pointing.

Several hundred yards out, there was a glitter of spray, and sunlight glanced off the curved, upleaping body of a dolphin as if from an unsheathed, upheld sword. Wild, merry chattering, a dolphin's laughter, came to them over the water, as the leaping shape came down with a splash and another shock of spray.

"Hotshot," Kit said. "Let's go."

They struck out through the breakers, into water that was again surprisingly warm. This time Nita wasn't able to enjoy it quite as much; the thought of undersea volcanoes was much with her. But even she couldn't be depressed for long when they paused to rest a moment, dog-paddling, and from behind came the nudge in the back she remembered, followed by a delphine laugh. "You rotten thing," she said, turning to rub Hotshot affectionately. "I'm gonna get you for the first time you did that."

"You'll have to catch me first," Hotshot said with a wicked chuckle—as well he might have, for nothing in the Sea except perhaps a killer whale or one of the great sharks on the hunt was fast enough to catch a dolphin that didn't want to be caught.

"Where's S'reee?" Kit said.

"Out in deeper water, by the Made Rock. HNii't's change could be done right here, but the kind of whale you're going to be would ground at this depth, K!t. Take hold; I'll tow you."

The fishing platform was once more covered with seagulls, which rose in a screaming cloud at the sight of Kit and Nita and Hotshot. "I'll meet you later, out at sea," Hotshot said, leaving them beside a rusty metal ladder that reached down into the water.

Kit and Nita climbed up it and walked across the platform to where they could look down at S'reee, who was rolling in the wavewash.

"You're early," she whistled, putting her head up out of the water at them, "and it's just as well; I'm running a bit late. I went a-Summoning last night, but I didn't find most of the people—so we'll have to make a stop out by the Westernmost Shoals today. Sandy Hook, you call it."

"New Jersey?" Nita said, surprised. "How are we going to get all the way out there and back before—"

"It's going to be all right, hNii't," S'reee said. "Time doesn't run the same under the waters as it does above them, so the Sea tells me. Besides, a humpback swims fast. And as for K!t—well, one change at a time. It'll come more easily for you, hNii't; you'd best go first."

Wonderful, Nita thought. She had long been used to being picked last for things; having to go first for anything gave her the jitters. "What do I have to do?" she said.

"Did you have a look at your book last night?"

"Uh-huh. I understand most of what we're going to be doing; it's fairly straightforward. But there was some business I didn't understand very well—"

"The part about shapechanging."

"Yeah. There wasn't that much in the book, S'reee. I think it might have been missing some information."

"Why? What did it tell you?"

"Only a lot of stuff about the power of imagination." She was perplexed. "S'reee, aren't there supposed to be words or something? A specific spell, or materials we need?"

"For shapechange? You have everything you need. Words would only get in the way," said S'reee. "It's all in the being. You pretend hard enough, and sooner or later what you're pretending to be, you *are*. The same as with other things."

"Oh, c'mon, S'reee," Kit said. "If somebody who wasn't a wizard jumped into the water and pretended to be a whale, I don't care how hard they pretended, nothing would happen without wizardry—"

"Exactly right, K!t. *Wizardry*—not one particular spell. The only reason it works for you is that you *know* wizardry works and are willing to have it so. Belief is no good either; belief as such always has doubt at the bottom. It's knowing that makes wizardry work. Only knowing can banish doubt, and while doubt remains, no spell, however powerful, will function properly. 'Wizardry does not live in the unwilling heart,' the Sea says. There'd be lots more wizards if more people were able to give up doubt—and belief. Like any other habit, though, they're hard to break. . . ."

"It did take me a while to know for sure that it wasn't just a coincidence when the thing I'd done a spell for actually *happened* as soon as I'd done the spell," Kit admitted. "I guess I see the problem."

"Then you're ready for the solution," S'reee said. "Past the change itself, the chief skill of unassisted shapechanging lies in not pretending so hard that you can't get back again. And as I said, hNii't, you have an advantage; we've shared blood. You have humpback in you now—not that our species are so far apart anyway; we're all mammals together. I suppose the first thing you'd better do is get in the water. . . ."

Nita jumped in, bobbed to the surface again. "And that stuff around you is going to have to go," S'reee added, looking with mild perplexity at Nita's bathing suit. Nita shot a quick look over her shoulder. For a moment, Kit just gazed innocently down at her, refusing to look away—then he turned, rolling his eyes.

Nita skinned hurriedly out of the suit and called to Kit, "While you're up here, put a warding spell on the platform. I don't want the gulls doing you-know-what all over my suit while we're gone. Or yours." She flung the wet lump of bathing suit out of the water overhanded; it landed with a sodden *hwack!* at which Kit almost turned around again. "Can we get on with this?" Nita said to S'reee.

"Surely. HNii't, are you all right?" S'reee said.

"Yes, fine, let's do it!" Nita said.

"So begin!" said S'reee, and began singing to herself as she waited.

Nita paddled for a moment in the water, adjusting to not having her bathing suit on. Saying "Begin to *what?*" especially with Kit listening, seemed incredibly stupid, so she just hung there in the water for a few moments and considered being a whale. I don't have the faintest idea what this is supposed to feel like, she thought desperately. But I should be able to come up with something. I *am* a wizard, after all.

Nita got an idea. She took a deep breath, held it, and slowly began to relax to the sound. Her arms, as she let them go limp, no longer supported her; she sank, eyes open, into salty greenness. It's all right, she thought. The air's right above me if I need it. She hung weightless in the green, thinking of nothing in particular.

Down there in the water, S'reee's note seemed louder, fuller; it vibrated against the ears, against the skin, inside the lungs, filling everything. And there was something familiar about it. Cousin, S'reee had called her; and We have blood in common, she had said. So it should be easy. A matter of remembering, not what you have been . . . but what, somewhere else, you *are*. Simply allow what is, somewhere else, to be what is *here*—and the change is done, effortless. Nita shut her eyes on the greenness and trusted to the wizardry inside her. That was it. "Wizardry does not live in the unwilling heart." Not the kind of will that meant gritted teeth, resisting something else, like your own disbelief, that was trying to undermine you—not "will-power"—but the will that was desire, the will so strong that it couldn't be resisted by all the powers of normality. . . .

Where am I getting all this? Nita didn't know, didn't care. To be a whale, she thought. To float like this all the time, to be weightless, like an astronaut. But space is green, and wet, and warm, and there are voices in it, and things growing. Freedom: no walls, no doors. And the songs in the water. . . . Her arms were feeling heavy, her legs felt odd when she kicked; but none of it mattered. Something was utterly right, something was working. Nita began to feel short of air. It hadn't worked all the way, that was all. She would get it right the next time. She stroked for the surface, broke it, opened her eyes to the light—

—and found it different. First and oddest—so that Nita tried to shake her head in disbelief, and failed, since she suddenly had no neck—the world was split in two, as if with an axe. Trying to look straight ahead of her didn't work. The area in front of her had become a hazy uncertainty comprised of two sets of peripheral vision. And where the corners of her eyes should have been, she now had two perfectly clear sets of sideways vision that nonetheless felt like "forward." She was seeing in colors she had no names for, and many she had names for were gone. Hands she still seemed to have, but her finger hung down oddly long and heavy, her elbows were glued to her sides, and her sides themselves went on for what seemed years. Her legs were gone; a tail and graceful flukes were all she had left. Her nose seemed to be on the top of her head, and her mouth somewhere south of her chin; and she resolved to ask S'reee, well out of Kit's hearing, what had happened to some part of her. "S'reee," Nita said, and was amazed to hear it come out of the middle of her head, in a whistle instead of words, "it was easy!"

"Come on, hNii't," S'reee said. "You're well along in wizardry at this point; you should know by now that it's not the magic that's exciting—it's what you do with it afterward."

More amazement yet. Nita wanted to simply roll over and lie back in the

ater at the sheer richness of the sound of S'reee's words. She had done the
sual experiments in school that proved water was a more efficient conductor
f sound than air. But she hadn't dreamed of what that effect would be like
hen one was a whale, submerged in the conducting medium and wearing a
undred square feet of skin that was a more effective hearing organ than any
uman ear. Suddenly sound was a thing that stroked the body, sensuous as a
ouch, indistinguishable from the liquid one swam in.

More, Nita could hear echoes coming back from what she and S'reee had
aid to each other; and the returning sound told her, with astonishing preci-
on, the size and position of everything in the area—rocks on the bottom,
eed three hundred meters away, schools of fish. She didn't need to see
nem. She could feel their textures on her skin as if they touched her; yet she
ould also distinctly perceive their distance from her, more accurately than
ne could have told it with mere sight. Fascinated, she swam a couple of
rcles around the platform, making random noises and getting the feel of the
rrain.

"I don't believe it," someone said above Nita, in a curious, flat voice with
o echoes about it. Is that how we sound? Nita thought, and surfaced to look
: Kit out of first one eye, then the other. He looked no different from the
ay he usually did, but something about him struck Nita as utterly hilarious,
ough at first she couldn't figure out what it was. Then it occurred to her.
e had legs.

"You're next, K!t," S'reee said. "Get in the water."

Nita held her head out of water and stared at Kit for a moment. He didn't
y anything, and after a few seconds of watching him get so red she could
e it through his sunburn, Nita submerged, laughing like anything—a sound
actly like oatmeal boiling hard.

Nita felt the splash of his jump all over her. Then Kit was paddling in the
ater beside her, looking at her curiously. "You've got barnacles," he said.

"That's as may be, K!t," S'reee said, laughing herself. "Look at what I
ought for you."

Kit put his head under the water for a moment to see what she was talking
out. For the first time, Nita noticed that S'reee was holding something
elicately in her mouth, at the very tip-end of her jaw. If spiders lived in the
a, what S'reee held might have been a fragment torn from one of their
ebs. It was a filmy, delicate, irregular meshwork, its strands knotted into a
t some six feet square. The knotting was an illusion, as Nita found when
e glided closer to it. Each "knot" was a round swelling or bulb where
veral threads joined. Flashes of green-white light rippled along the net
henever it moved, and all Nita's senses, those of whale and wizard alike,
ickled with the electric feeling of a live spell, tangled in the mesh and
ipatient to be used.

"You must be careful with this, Kit," S'reee said. "This is a whalesark, an
a rare thing. A sark can only be made when a whale dies, and the magi
involved is considerable."

"What is it?" Kit said, when he'd surfaced again.

"It's a sort of shadow of a whale's nervous system, made by wizardry. A
the whale's death, before the lifelightning's gone, a spell-constructed energ
duplicate of the whale's brain and nerves is made from the pattern laid dow
by the living nerves and brain. The duplicate then has an 'assiste
shapechange' spell woven into it. When the work's done properly, conta
with the sark is enough to change the wearer into whatever kind of whale th
donor was."

S'reee tossed her head. Shimmering, the sark billowed fully open, like
curtain in the wind. "This is a sperm-whalesark, like Aivaaan who donated
He was a wizard who worked these waters several thousand full Moons ag
and something of a seer; so that when he died, instead of leaving himse
wholly to the Sea, Aivaaan said that we should make a sark of him, becau
there would be some need. Come try it on for size, K!t."

Kit didn't move for a moment. "S'reee—is what's his name, Aivaaan,
there? Am I going to be him, is that it?"

S'reee looked surprised. "No, how did you get that idea?"

"You said this was made from his brain," Nita said.

"Oh. His *under*-brain, yes—the part of the brain that runs breathing a
blood flow and such. As for the rest of Aivaaan, his *mind*—I don't think s
Not that I'm any too sure where 'mind' is in a person. But you should still I
K!t, by what the Sea tells me. Come on, time's swimming."

"What do I do with it?"

"Just put it around you and wrap it tight. Don't be afraid to handle
roughly. It's stronger than it looks." She let go of the sark. It floated in t
water, undulating gently in the current. Kit took another breath, submerge
reached down, and drew the sark around him.

"Get back, hNii't," S'reee said. Nita backfinned several times her ov
length away from Kit, not wanting to take her eyes off him. He was exhalin
slowly sinking feet-first, and with true Rodriguez insouciance he swirled t
sark around him like Zorro putting on a new cape. Kit's face grew surprise
though, as the "cape" continued the motion, swirling itself tighter a
tighter around him, binding his arms to his sides.

Alarmed, Kit struggled, still sinking, bubbles rising from him as he we
down. The struggling did him no good, and it suddenly became hard to s
him as the wizardry in the whalesark came fully alive, and light danc
around Kit and the sark. Nita had a last glimpse of Kit's eyes going wide
panic as he and the whalesark became nothing more than a sinking, swirli
storm of glitter.

"S'reee!" Nita said, getting alarmed.

With a sound like muffled thunder and a blow like a nearby lightning-strike, displaced water hit Nita and bowled her sideways and backward. She fluked madly, trying to regain her balance enough to tell what was going on. The water was full of stirred-up sand, tatters of weed, small confused fish darting in every direction. And a bulk, a massive form that had not been there before—

Nita watched the great gray shape rise toward her and understood why S'reee had insisted on Kit's change being in deep water. Her own size had surprised her at first—though a humpback looks small and trim, even the littlest males tend to be fifty feet long. But Kit was twice that, easily. He did not have the torpedolike grace of a humpback, but what he lacked in stream-lining he made up in sheer mass. The sperm is the kind that most people think of when they hear the word whale, the kind made famous by most whaling movies. Nita realized that all her life she had mostly taken the whale's shape for granted, not considering what it would actually be like up close to one.

But here came Kit, stroking slowly and uncertainly at first with that im-mense tail, and getting surer by the second; looking up at her with the tiny eyes set in the huge domed head, and with his jaw working a bit, exposing the terrible teeth that could crunch a whaling boat in two. Nita felt the size of him, the weight, and somehow the danger—and kept her movements slow and respectful. He was still Kit—but something had been added.

He glanced at S'reee and Nita, saying nothing, as he rose past them and broke surface to breathe. They followed. He spouted once or twice, appar-ently to get the feel of it, and then said to S'reee in a rather rueful tone of song, "I wish you'd warned me!"

His voice ranged into a deeper register than a humpback's and had a sharper sound to it—more clicks and buzzes. It was not entirely comfortable on the skin. "I couldn't," S'reee said, "or you might have fought it even harder than you did, and the change might have refused to take. That would've been trouble for us; if a whalesark once rejects a person, it'll never work for him at all. After this it'll be easier for you. Which in itself will make some problems. Right now, though, let's get going. Take a long breath; I want to get out of the bay without attracting too much attention."

They took breath together and dived deep, S'reee in the lead and swim-ming south by west, Nita and Kit following. The surroundings—thick, lazily waving kelp beds and colonies of bright polyps and anemones, stitched through with the brief silver flash of passing fish—fascinated Nita. But she couldn't give the landscape, or seascape, her whole attention; she had other concerns. (Kit,) she tried to say in the Speech's silent form, for privacy's sake —then found that it wasn't working; she wasn't getting the sort of mental "echo" that told her she was sending successfully. Probably it had something to do with the shapechange spell. "Hey," she said aloud, "you okay?"

The question came out of her as such a long, mournful moan that Kit laughed—a sound more like boiling lava than boiling oatmeal: huge hisses and bubblings mixed together. "Now I am," he said, "or I will be as soon as I can get used to this bit with the eyes—"

"Yeah, it's weird. But kind of nice too. Feeling things, instead of seeing them. . . ."

"Yeah. Even the voices have feelings. S'reee's is kind of twitchy—"

"Yeah. You've got sharp edges—"

"You've got fur."

"I do not!"

"Oh, yes you do. It's soft, your voice. Not like your usual one—"

Nita was unsure whether to take this as a compliment, so she let it lie. The moment had abruptly turned into one of those times when she had no idea just what to say to Kit, the sort of sudden silence that was acutely painful to Nita, though Kit never seemed to notice it at all. Nita couldn't think of anything to do about the problem, which was the worst part of the whole business. She wasn't about to mention the problem to her mom, and on this subject the wizards' manual was hugely unhelpful.

The silence was well along toward becoming interminable when S'reee said, "That's the primary way we have for knowing one another, down here. We haven't the sort of physical variations you have—differences in head shape and so forth—and even if we did, what good would a distinction be if you had to come right up to someone to make it? By voice, we can tell how far away a friend is, how he's feeling, practically what he's thinking. Though the closer a friend is to you, usually, the harder it is to tell what's on his mind with any accuracy."

Nita started to sing something, then caught herself back to silence. "Is the change settling in, K!t?" S'reee said.

"Now it is. I had a weird feeling, though, like something besides me, my mind I mean—like something besides that was fighting the change. But it's gone now."

"Only for the moment," S'reee said. "See, it's the old rule: no wizardry without its price, or its dangers. Though the dangers are different for each of you, since you changed by different methods. As I said, hNii't, you have to beware pretending too hard—thinking so much like a whale that you don't want to be a human being any more, or forget how. Wizards have been lost that way before, and there's no breaking the spell from outside; once you're stuck inside the change-shape, no one but you can break out again. If you start finding your own memories difficult to recall, it's time to get out of the whaleshape, before it becomes you permanently."

"Right," Nita said. She wasn't very worried. Being a humpback was delightful, but she had no desire to spend her life that way.

"Your problem's different, though, K!t. Your change is powered more by he spell resident in the whalesark than by anything you're doing yourself. And all the sark's done is confuse your own body into thinking it's a whale's body, for the time being. That confusion can be broken by several different kinds of distraction. The commonest is when your own mind—which is stronger than the whale-mind left in the sark—starts to override the instructions the whalesark is giving your body."

"Huh?"

"K!t," S'reee said very gently, finning upward to avoid the weedy, barnacled wreck of a fishing boat, "suppose we were—oh, say several hundred humpback-lengths down, in the Crushing Dark—and suddenly your whalebody started trying to behave like a human's body. Human breathing rate, human pulse and thought and movement patterns, human response to pressures and the temperature of the water—"

"Uh," Kit said, as the picture sank in.

"So you see the problem. Spend too much time in the sark, and the part of our brain responsible for handling your breathing and so forth will begin to overpower the 'dead' brain preserved in the sark. Your warning signs are nearly the opposite of hNii't's. Language is the first thing to go. If you find ourself losing whalesong, you *must* surface and get out of the sark immediately. Ignore the warning— The best that can happen is that the whalesark will probably be so damaged it can never be used again. The worst thing—"
he didn't say it. The worry in her voice was warning enough.

No one said much of anything for a while, as the three of them swam nward, south and west. The silence, uneasy at first, became less so as they vent along. S'reee, to whom this area was as commonplace as Kit's or Nita's ome streets might have been, simply cruised along without any great interest in the surroundings. But Nita found the seascape endlessly fascinating, nd suspected Kit did too—he was looking around him with the kind of ascination he rarely lent anything but old cars and his z-gauge train set.

Nita had rarely thought of what the seascape off the coast of the island ould look like. From being at the beach she had a rather dull and sketchy icture of bare sand with a lot of water on top of it; shells buried in it, as they vere on the beach, and there had to be weed beds; the seaweed washed up om somewhere. But all the nature movies had given her no idea of the chness of the place.

Coral, for example; it didn't come in the bright colors it did in tropical aters, but it was there in great quantity—huge groves and forests of it, the hite or beige or yellow branches twisting and writhing together in tighthoked abstract patterns. And shells, yes—but the shells still had creatures inside them; Nita saw Kit start in amazement, then swim down for a closer look at a scallop shell that was hopping over the surface of a brain coral, going about its business.

They passed great patches of weed, kinds that Nita didn't know the names of—until they started coming to her as if she had always known them: red bladder, kelp, agar, their long dark leaves or flat ribbons rippling as silkily in the offshore current as wheat in a landborn wind.

And the fish! Nita hadn't taken much notice of them at first; they'd all looked alike to her—little and silver. But something had changed. They passed by a place where piles had been driven into the sea floor, close together, and great odd-shaped lumps of rusty metal had been dumped among them. Weed and coral had seized on the spot, wrapping the metal and the piles; and the little life that frequented such places, tiny shrimp and krill swam everywhere. So did thousands of iridescent, silvery-indigo fish, ranging from fingerling size to about a foot long, eating the krill and fry as if there were no tomorrow. For some of the smallest of them there wasn't *going* to be one, Nita realized, as she also realized how hungry she was.

"Blues!" she said, one sharp happy note, then dived into the cloud of bluefish and krill, and helped herself to lunch.

It was a little while before she'd had enough. It took Nita only a couple of minutes to get used to the way a humpback ate—by straining krill and other of the tiniest ocean creatures, including the smallest of the blues, through the sievelike plates of whalebone, or "baleen," in her jaws. The swift blue shapes that had been darting frantically in all directions were calming down already as Nita soared out of the whirling cloud of them and headed back over to S'reee and Kit, feeling slightly abashed and that an explanation of some kind was in order for the sudden interruption of their trip. However, there turned out to be no need for one. S'reee had stopped for a snack herself; and Nita realized that Kit had been snacking on fish ever since they left Tiana Beach. A sperm whale was, after all, one of the biggest of the "toothed" whales, and needed a lot of food to keep that great bulk working. Not that he did anything but swallow the fish whole when he caught them; a sperm's terrible teeth are mostly for defense.

Kit paused only long enough to eat nine or ten of the biggest blues, then drifted down toward the pilings and the objects stacked sloppily among them. "Neets," he said, "will you take a look at this? It's *cars!*"

She glided down beside him. Sure enough, the corroded fins of an old model Cadillac were jutting out of a great mound of coral. Under the tangled whiteness of the coral, as if under a blanket of snow, she could make out the buried shapes of hoods or doors, or the wheels and axles of wrecks wedged on their sides and choked with weed. Fish, blues and others, darted in and out of broken car windows and crumpled hoods, while in several places crabs crouched in the shells of broken headlights.

"It's a fish haven," S'reee said as she glided down beside them. "The land people dump scrap metal on the bottom, and the plants and coral come and make a reef out of it. The fish come to eat the littler fish and krill that live in reefs; and then the boats come and catch the fish. And it works just as well for us as for the fishers who live on land. But we've got other business than dinner to attend to, at the moment. And hNii't, don't you think it would be a good idea if you surfaced now?"

Nita and Kit looked at one another in shock, then started upward in a hurry, with S'reee following them at a more leisurely pace. "How long have we been down?" Kit whistled.

They surfaced in a rush, all three, and blew. S'reee looked at Kit in some puzzlement; the question apparently meant nothing to her. "Long enough to need to come up again," she said.

"Neets, look," Kit said in a rumbly groan, a sperm whale's sound of surprise. She fluked hard once or twice, using her tail to lift herself out of the swell, and was surprised to see, standing up from the shore half a mile away, a tall brick tower with a pointed, weathered green-bronze top; a red light flashed at the tower's peak. "Jones Beach already!" she said. "That's miles and miles from Tiana—"

"We've made good time," S'reee said, "but we've a ways to go yet. Let's put our tails into it. I don't want to keep the Blue waiting."

They swam on. Even if the sight of the Jones Beach tower hadn't convinced Nita they were getting close to New York, she now found that the increasing noise of the environment would have tipped off the whale that she'd become. Back at Tiana Beach, there had been only the single mournful hoot of the Shinnecock horn and the far-off sound of the various buoy bells. But this close to New York Harbor, the peaceful background hiss of the ocean soon turned into an incredible racket. Bells and horns and whistles and gongs shrieked and clunked and whanged in the water as they passed them; and no sooner was she out of range of one than another one assaulted her twitching skin.

Singing pained notes at one another, the three ran the gauntlet of sound. It got worse instead of better as they got closer to the harbor entrance, and to the banging and clanging was added the sound of persistent dull engine noise. Their course to Sandy Hook unfortunately crossed all three of the major approaches to New York Harbor. Along all three of them big boats came and went with an endless low throbbing, and small ones passed with a rattling, jarring buzz that reminded Nita of lawn mowers and chain saws.

The three surfaced often to get relief from the sound, until S'reee warned them to dive deep for a long underwater run through one of the shipping lanes. Nita was beginning to feel the slow discomfort that was a whale's experience of shortness of breath before S'reee headed for the surface again.

They broached and blew and looked around them. Not far away stood a huge, black, white-lettered structure on four steel pilings. A white building stood atop the deck, and beside it was a red tower with several flashing lights. A horn on the platform sang one noncommittal note, shortLONG! short-LONG! again and again.

"Ambrose Light," Kit said.

"The Speaking Tower, yes," S'reee said. "After this it'll be quieter—there are fewer markers between here and the Hook. And listen! There's a friend's voice."

Nita went down again to listen, and finally managed to sort out a dolphin's distant chattering from the background racket. She surfaced again and floated with the others awhile, watching Hotshot come, glittering in the sun like a bright lance hurling itself through the swells. As he came abreast of the Lightship he leaped high out of the water in a spectacular arc and hit the surface with a noise that pierced even all the hooting and dinging going on.

"For Sea's sake, we hear you!" S'reee sang at the top of her lungs, and then added in annoyed affection, "He's such a showoff."

"But most dolphins are," Kit said, with a note to his song that made it plain he wasn't sure how he knew that.

"True enough. He's worse than some, though. No question that he's one of the best of the young wizards, and a talented singer. I love him dearly. But what this business of being Wanderer is going to do to his precious ego—" She broke off as Hotshot came within hearing range. "Did you find him?"

"He's feeding off the Hook," Hotshot said, arrowing through the water toward them and executing a couple of playful and utterly unnecessary barrel rolls as he came. Nita began to wonder if S'reee might be right about him. "He's worried about something, though he wouldn't tell me what it was. Said it was just as well you were coming; he would've come looking for you if you hadn't."

The four of them started swimming again immediately; that last sentence was by itself most startling news. Blue whales did not *do* things, Nita realized, in the sudden-memory way that meant the information was the Sea's gift. Blue whales *were*, that was all. Action was for other, swifter species . . . except in the Song of the Twelve, where the Blue briefly became a power to be reckoned with. The Song, as Tom had warned, had a way of changing the ones who sang it . . . sometimes even before they started.

"Are you ready for the Oath?" S'reee was saying to the dolphin. "Any last thoughts?"

"Only that this is going to be one more Song like any other," Hotshot said "even if it *is* your first time. Don't worry, Ree; if you have any problems, I'll help you out."

Nita privately thought that this was a little on the braggy side, coming from a junior wizard. The thought of talking to an Advisory or Senior that way—Tom, say—shocked her. Nevertheless, she kept her mouth shut, for it seemed like Hotshot and S'reee had known one another for a while.

"And how are our fry doing here?" Hotshot said, swimming careless rings around Nita as he sang. "Getting used to the fins all right?"

"Pretty much," Nita said. Hotshot did one last loop around her and then headed off in Kit's direction. "How about you, Minnow—*eeeech!*"

The huge jaw of a sperm whale abruptly opened right in front of Hotshot and closed before he could react—so that a moment later the dolphin was keeping quite still, while Kit held him with great delicacy in his huge fangs. Kit's eyes looked angry, but the tone of his song was casual enough. "Hotshot," he said, not stopping, just swimming along with casual deliberateness, "I'm probably singing too. And even if I'm not, I *am* a sperm whale. Don't push your luck."

Hotshot said nothing. Kit swam a few more of his own lengths, then opened his mouth and let the dolphin loose. "Hey," he said then, "no hard feelings."

"Of course not," Hotshot said in his usual recklessly merry voice. But Nita noticed that the dolphin made his reply from a safe distance. "No problem, Mi"—Kit looked at Hotshot, silent—"ah, K!t."

"Minnow it is," Kit said, sounding casual himself. The four of them swam on; Nita dropped back a few lengths and put her head up beside Kit's so that she could sing her quietest and not be heard too far off.

"What was that all about?"

"I'm not sure," Kit said—and now that only Nita was listening, he sounded a bit shaken. "S'reee might have been right when she said this body doesn't actually have what's-his-voice's—"

"Aivaaan."

"His memories, yeah. But the body has its own memories. What it's like to be a sperm. What it *means* to be a sperm, I guess. You don't make fun of us —of them." He paused, looking even more shaken. "Neets—don't let me get lost!"

"Huh?"

"*Me.* I don't beat people up, that's not my style!"

"You didn't beat him up—"

"No. I just did the ocean equivalent of pinning him up against the wall and scaring him a good one. Neets, I got into being a wizard because I wanted other people *not* to do that kind of stuff to *me!* And now—"

"I'll keep an eye on you," Nita said, as they began to come up on another foghorn, a loud one. And there was something odd about that foghorn. Its note was incredibly deep. *That has to be almost too deep for people to hear at all. What kind of—*

The note sounded again, and Nita shot Kit an amazed look as she felt the water all around her, and even the air in her lungs, vibrate in response to it. One note, the lowest note she could possibly imagine, held and held until a merely human singer would have collapsed trying to sing it . . . and then slurred slowly down through another note, and another, and holding on a last one of such profound depth that the water shook as if with thunder.

S'reee slowed her pace and answered the note in kind, the courtesy of one species of whale to another on meeting or parting—singing the same slow, somber sequence, several octaves higher. There was a pause; then she was answered with a humpback's graceful fluting, but sung in a bottom-shaking baritone.

"Come on," S'reee said, and dived.

The waters around Sandy Hook boil with krill in the spring and summer, so that by night the krill's swarming luminescence defines every current and finstroke in a blaze of blue-green light; and by day the sun slants through the water, brown with millions of tiny bodies, as thickly as through the air in a dusty room. As the group dived, they began to make out a great dark shape in the cloudy water, moving so slowly it barely did more than drift. A last brown-red curtain of water parted before them in a swirl of current, and Nita found herself staring down at her first blue whale.

He was hardly even blue in this light, more a sort of slaty maroon; and the faint dapples on his sides were almost invisible. But his color was not what impressed Nita particularly. Neither was his size, though blues are the biggest of all whales; this one was perhaps a hundred twenty feet from nose to tail, and Kit, large for a sperm, was almost as big. That voice, that stately, leisurely, sober, sorrowful voice that sounded like a storm in mourning, *that* mattered to her; and so did the tiny eye, the size of a tennis ball, which looked at her from the immense bulk of the head. That eye was wise. There was understanding in it, and tolerance, and sadness: and most of all, great age.

Age was evident elsewhere too. The blue's flukes were tattered and his steering fins showed scars and punctures, mementos of hungry sharks. Far down his tail, the broken stump of a harpoon protruded, the wood of it rotting, the metal crumbling with rust; yet though the tail moved slowly, it moved with strength. This creature had been through pain and danger in his long life, and though he had learned sadness, it had not made him bitter or weak.

Nita turned her attention back to the others, noticing that Kit was holding as still as she was, though at more of a distance; and even Hotshot was holding himself down to a slow glide. "Eldest Blue about the Gates," S'reee sang, sounding more formal than Nita had ever heard her, "I greet you."

"Senior for the Gate-waters," said the Blue in his deep voice, with slow dignity, "I greet you also."

"Then you've heard, Aroooon."

"I have heard that the Sea has taken Ae'mhnuu to its Heart," said the Blue, "leaving you Senior in his place, and distressed at a time when there's distress enough. Leaving you also to organize a TwelveSong on very short notice."

"That's so."

"Then you had best be about it," said the Blue, "while time still remains for singing, and the bottom is still firm under us. First, though, tell me who comes here with you. Swift-Fire-In-The-Water I know already—"

Hotshot made the closest sound Nita could imagine to an embarrassed delphine cough. She smiled to herself; now she knew now what to tease him with if he got on her case.

"Land wizards, Aroooon," S'reee said. "HNii't—" Nita wasn't sure what to do, so she inclined the whole front of her body in the water in an approximation of a bow. "—and K!t." Kit followed Nita's suit. "They were the ones who went into the Dark High-And-Dry after the *Naming of Lights*—"

To Nita's utter astonishment, Aroooon inclined his own body at them, additionally curling his flukes under him in what she abruptly recognized as a gesture of congratulation. "They're calves," S'reee added, as if not wanting to leave anything out.

"With all due respects, Senior, they are not," Aroooon said. "They came *back* from that place. That is no calf's deed. Many who were older than they did not come back. —You will sing with us then? What parts?"

"I'm not sure yet," Kit said. "S'reee needs to see if all her people come in."

"The Silent Lord," Nita said.

"Indeed." Aroooon looked at her for several long moments. "You are a good age for it," he said. "And you are learning the song—"

"I got most of the details from my manual," she said. She had been up studying late the night before, though not as late as Kit had; a lot of exertion in salt air always left her drained, and she'd put the book aside after several hours, to finish the fine details of her research later. "The Sea will give me the rest, S'reee says, as we go along."

"So it will. But I would have you be careful of how you enact your part, young hNii't." Aroooon drifted a bit closer to her, and that small, thoughtful eye regarded her carefully. "There is old trouble, and old power, about you and your friend . . . as if blood hung in the water where you swim. The one Power apparently knows your names. It will not have forgotten the disservice you did It recently. You are greatly daring to draw Its attention to you again. Even the Heart of the Sea—Timeheart as your kind calls it—may not be quiet for one who has freely attracted the Lone One's enmity. Beware what you do. And do what you say; nowhere does the Lone Power enter in so readily as through the broken word."

"Sir," Nita said, rather unnerved, "I'll be careful."

"That is well." Aroooon looked for a moment at Kit before speaking. "It is a whalesark, is it not?"

"Yes, sir," Kit said in the same respectful tone Nita had heard him use on his father.

"Have a care of it, then, should you find yourself in one of the more combative parts of the Song," said Aroooon. "Sperm whales were fighters before they were singers, and though their songs are often the fairest in the sea, the old blood rises too often and chokes those songs off before they can be sung. Keep your mouth closed, you were best, and you'll do well enough."

"Thank you, sir."

"Enough politeness, young wizard," Aroooon said, for the first time sounding slightly crusty. "If size is honor, you have as much as I; and as for years, just keep breathing long enough and you'll have as many of those as I do. —S'reee, you travel more widely now than I, so I put you a question. Are the shakings in the depths worse these days than they ought to be at this time of year and tide of Moon?"

"Much worse, Eldest. That was why Ae'mhnuu originally wanted to convene the Song. And I don't know if the Song will be in time to save the fishing grounds to the east and north, around Nantucket and the Races. Hot water has been coming up close to there, farther east and south. The Shelf is changing."

"Then let us get started," Aroooon said. "I assume you came to ask me to call in some of the Celebrants, time being as limited as it is."

"Yes, Aroooon. If you would. Though as the rite requires, I will be visiting the Pale One tomorrow, in company with hNii't and K!t. The meeting place for the Song is to be ten thousand lengths north-northeast of the shoals at Barnegat, three days from now. A fast rehearsal—then right down the channel and through the Gates of the Sea, to the place appointed."

"Well enough. Now administer me the Celebrant's Oath, Senior, so that I may lawfully call the others."

"Very well." S'reee swam up close to Aroooon, so that she was looking him straight in one eye with one of hers; and when she began to sing, it was in a tone even more formal and careful than that in which she had greeted him. "Aroooon u'ao!uor, those who gather to sing that Song that is the Sea's shame and the Sea's glory desire you to be of their company. Say, for my hearing, whether you consent to that Song."

"I consent," the Blue said in notes so deep that coral cracked and fell or ock shelves some yards away, "and I will weave my voice and my will and my blood with that of those who sing, if there be need."

"I ask the second time, that those with me, both of your Mastery and not, may hear. Do you consent to the Song?"

"I consent. And may my wizardry and my Mastery depart from me sooner than I abandon that other Mastery I shall undertake in the Song's celebration."

"The third time, and the last, I ask, that the Sea, and the Heart of the Sea, shall hear. Do you consent to the Song?"

"Freely I consent," Aroooon sang with calm finality, "and may I find no place in that Heart, but wander forever amid the broken and the lost, sooner than I shall refuse the Song or what it brings about for the good of those who live."

"Then I accept you as Celebrant of the Song, as Blue, and as latest of a line of saviors," S'reee said. "And though those who swim are swift to forget, the Sea forgets neither Song nor singer." She turned a bit, looking behind her at Hotshot. "Might as well get all of you done at once," she said. "Hotshot?"

"Right."

The dolphin went through the Oath much faster than Aroooon had, though his embarrassment at being referred to as Swift-Fire-In-The-Water was this time so acute that Nita actually turned away so she wouldn't have to look at him. As for the rest of the Oath, though, Hotshot recited it, as Nita had expected, with the mindless speed of a person who thinks he has other more important matters to attend to.

S'reee turned to Nita. "We can't give K!t the Oath yet," she said. "We don't know who he's going to be."

"Can't you just give it to me and leave that part blank or something?" Kit said eagerly. He loved ceremonies.

"Kit!"

"No, K!t. HNii't, do you know the words?"

"The Sea does," she said, finding it true. S'reee had already begun the ritual questioning; Nita felt for the response, found it. "I consent, and I will weave my voice and my will and my blood with that of those who sing, if there be need." It was astonishing, how much meaning could be packed into a few notes. And the music itself was fascinating; so somber, but with that old thread of joy running through it. She threw herself into the grave joy of the final response. ". . . And may I find no place in that Heart, but wander forever amid the broken and the lost, sooner than I shall refuse the Song or what it brings about for the good of those who live."

"Then I accept you as Celebrant of the Song, and as Silent One, and as the latest in a line of saviors. And though those who swim are swift to forget, the Sea forgets neither Song nor singer." S'reee looked at Nita with an expression in those blue eyes of vast relief, so much like the one she had given her and Kit when they'd first agreed to help that Nita shuddered a little with the intensity of it, then smiled inside. It was nice to be needed.

"That was well done," Aroooon said slowly. "Now, S'reee, give me names so I'll know whom to call."

A few moments of singing ensued as S'reee recited the names of five whales Nita had never heard of. Her inner contact with the Sea, moments later, identified them all as wizards of various ratings, all impressive. Aroooon rumbled agreement. "Good enough," he said. "Best get out of the area so that I may begin Calling."

"Right. Come on, K!t, hNii't. Till the Moon's full, Aroooon—"

"Till then."

They swam away through the darkening water. S'reee set the pace; it was a quick one. "Why did we have to leave in such a hurry?" Kit said.

"There aren't many wizardries more powerful than a Calling," S'reee said as she led them away. "He'll weave those whales' names into his spell, and they agree to be part of the Song, the wizardry will lead them to the place appointed, at the proper time."

"Just by singing their names?"

"K!t, that's plenty. Don't you pay attention when someone calls you by your name? Your name is *part of you.* There's power in it, tied up with the way you secretly think of yourself, the truth of the way you are. Know what a person's name means to him, know who he feels he *is*—and you have power over him. That's what Aroooon is using."

That was a bit of information that started Nita's thoughts going in nervous circles. How do I think of myself? And does this mean that the people who know what I think can control me? I'm not sure I like this. . . .

The first note rumbled through the water behind them, and Nita pulled up short, curling around in a quick turn. "Careful, hNii't!" S'reee sang, a soft sharp note of warning. Nita backfinned, hovering in the water. "Don't disturb his circle—"

Looking back, she wouldn't have dreamed of it. The water was growing darker by the second, and as a result the glow of the krill in it was now visible—a delicate, shimmery, indefinite blue-green light that filled the sea everywhere. The light grew brighter, moment by moment; but it was brighter still at the surface, where the waves slid and shifted against one another in a glowing, undulating ceiling. And brightest of all was the track left by Aroooon's swimming—a wake that burned like clouds of cool fire behind him with every slow stroke of his tail.

At the head of the wake, Aroooon himself traced the grand curves of his spell, sheathed in bubbles and cold light. One circle he completed, melding into itself as he sang that single compelling note; then he began another at right angles to the first, and the water burned behind him, the current not taking the brilliance away. And the blue's song seemed to get into the blood, into the bone, and would not be shaken—

"HNii't," S'reee said, "we can't stay, you said you have to get back—"

Nita looked around her in shock. "S'reee, when did it get so dark! My folks are gonna have a fit!"

"Didn't I mention that time didn't run the same way below the water as it does in the Above?"

"Yeah, but I thought—" Kit said, and then he broke off and said a very bad word in whale. "No, I didn't think. I assumed that it'd go *slower*—"

"It goes faster," Nita moaned. "Kit, how are we going to get anything done? S'reee, how long exactly is the Song going to take?"

"Not long," the humpback said, sounding a bit puzzled by her distress. "A couple of lights, as it's reckoned in the Above—"

"Two days!"

"We're in trouble," Kit said.

"That's exactly what we're in. S'reee, let's put our tails into it! Even if we were getting home right now, we'd have some explaining to do."

She turned and swam in the direction where her sharpening whale-senses told her home was. It was going to be bad enough, having to climb out of this splendid, strong, graceful body and put her own back on again. But Dairine was waiting to give her the Spanish Inquisition when she got home. And her mother and father were going to give her more of those strange looks. Worse . . . there would be questions asked, she knew it. Her folks might even call Kit's family if they got worried enough—and Kit's dad, who was terminally protective of his son, might make Kit come home.

That thought was worst of all.

They went home. It was lucky for them that Nita's father was too tired from his fishing—which had been successful—to make much noise about their lateness. Her mother was cleaning fish in the kitchen, too annoyed at the smelly work to much care about anything else. And as for Dairine, she was buried so deep in a copy of *The Space Shuttle Operators' Manual* that all she did when Nita passed her room was glance up for a second, then dive back into her reading. Even so, there was no feeling of relief when Nita shut the door to her room and got under the covers; just an uneasy sense of something incomplete, something that was going to come up again later . . . and not in a way she'd like.

"Wizardry . . ." she muttered sourly, and fell asleep.

Ed's Song

"Neets," her mother said from where she stood at the sink, her back turned. "Got a few minutes?"

Nita looked up from her breakfast. "What's up?"

Her mother was silent for a second, as if wondering how to broach what ever she had on her mind. "You and Kit've been out a lot lately," she said at last. "Dad and I hardly ever seem to see you."

"I thought Dad said it'd be fun to have Dairine and me out of his hair for a while, this vacation," said Nita.

"Out of his hair, yes. Not out of his life. —We worry about you two when you're out so much."

"Mom, we're fine."

"Well, I wonder. . . . What exactly are you two doing out there all day?"

"Oh, Mom! Nothing!"

Her mother looked at her and put up one eyebrow in an excellent imitation of Mr. Spock.

Nita blushed a bit. It was one of those family jokes that you wish would go away, but never does; when Nita had been little and had said "Nothing!" she had usually been getting into incredible trouble. "Mom," Nita said, "some times when I say 'nothing,' it's really just nothing. We hang out, that's all. We . . . do stuff."

"What kind of stuff?"

"Mom, what does it matter? Just stuff!"

"It matters," her mother said, "if it's adult kinds of stuff . . . instead of kid stuff."

Nita didn't say a word. There was no question that what she and Kit were doing were adult sorts of things.

Her mother took in Nita's silence, waiting for her daughter to break it. "

von't beat around the bush with you, Neets," she said at last. "Are you and
Kit getting . . . physically involved?"

Nita looked at her mother in complete shock. "Mom!" she said in a de-
pairing groan. "You mean *sex?* No!"

"Well," her mother said slowly, "that takes a bit of a load off my mind."
There was a silence after the words. Nita was almost sure she could hear her
mother thinking, *If it's true. . . .*

The silence unnerved Nita more than the prospect of a talk on the facts of
life ever could have. "Mom," she said, "if I were gonna do something like
that, I'd talk to you about it first." She blushed as she said it. She was
embarrassed even to be talking about this to anybody, and she would have
been embarrassed to talk to her mom about it too. Nevertheless, what she'd
said was the truth. "Look, Mom, you know me, I'm chicken. I always run and
ask for advice before I do anything."

"Even about this?"

"Especially about this!"

"Then what *are* you doing?" her mother said, sounding just plain curious
now. And there was another sound in her voice—wistfulness. She was feeling
left out of something. "Sometimes you say to me 'playing,' but I don't know
what kids mean any more when they say that. When I was little, it was
hopscotch, or Chinese jumprope, or games in the dirt with plastic animals.
Now when I ask Dairine what she's doing, and she says 'playing,' I go in and
find she's doing quadratic equations . . . or using my hot-curlers on the
neighbor's red setter. I don't know what to expect."

Nita shrugged. "Kit and I swim a lot," she said.

"Where you won't get in trouble, I hope," her mother said.

"Yeah," Nita said, grateful that her mother hadn't said anything about
lifeguards or public beaches. This is a real pain, she thought. I have to talk to
Tom and Carl about this. What do they do with *their* families? . . . But her
mother was waiting for more explanation. She struggled to find some. "We
walk, we look at stuff. We explore. . . ."

Nita shook her head, then, for it was hopeless. There was no explaining
even the parts of her relationship with Kit that her mother *could* understand.
"He's just my friend," Nita said finally. It was a horrible understatement, but
she was getting hot with embarrassment at even having to think about this
kind of thing. "Mom, we're okay, really."

"I suppose you are," her mom said. "Though I can't shake the feeling that
there are things going on you're not telling me about. Nita, I trust you . . .
but I still worry."

Nita just nodded. "Can I go out now, Mom?"

"Sure. Just be back by the time it gets dark," she said, and Nita sighed and
headed for the door. But there was no feeling of release, no sense of anything

having been really settled, as there usually was when a family problem had been hashed out to everyone's satisfaction. Nita knew her mother was going to be watching her. It griped her.

There's no reason for it! she thought guiltily as she went down to the beach, running so she wouldn't be late for meeting Kit. But there was reason for it, she knew; and the guilt settled quietly into place inside her, where not all the sea water in the world would wash it out.

She found Kit far down the beach, standing on the end of the jetty with a rippling, near-invisible glitter clutched in one hand: the whalesark. "You're late," he said, scowling, as Nita climbed the jetty. "S'reee's waiting—" Then the scowl fell off his face when he saw her expression. "You okay?"

"Yeah. But my mom's getting suspicious. And we have to be back by dark or it'll get worse."

Kit said something under his breath in Spanish.

"¡Ay!" Nita said back, a precise imitation of what either of Kit's folks would have said if they'd heard him. He laughed.

"It's okay," she said. "Let's go."

"We'd better leave our suits here," Kit said. Nita agreed, turning her back and starting to peel out of hers. Kit made his way down the rocks and into the water as she put her bathing suit under the rock with his. Then she started down the other side of the jetty.

Nita found that the whale-body came much more easily to her than it had the day before. She towed Kit out into deeper water, where he wrapped the whalesark around him and made his own change; his too came more quickly and with less struggle, though the shock of displaced water, like an undersea explosion, was no less. S'reee came to meet them then, and they greeted her and followed her off eastward, passing Shinnecock Inlet.

"Some answers to Aroooon's Calling have already come back," she said. "K!t, it looks like we may not need you to sing after all. But I would hope you'd attend the Song anyway."

"I wouldn't miss it," he sang cheerfully. "Somebody has to be around to keep Neets from screwing up, after all. . . ."

Nita made a humpback's snort of indignation. But she also wondered about the nervousness in S'reee's song. "Where's Hotshot this morning?"

"Out calling the rest of his people for patrol around the Gates. Besides, I'm not sure he's . . . well, suited for what we're doing today. . . ."

"S'reee," Kit said, picking up the tremor in her song, "what's the problem? It's just another wizard we're going to see—"

"Oh, no," she said. "The Pale One's no wizard. He'll be singing one of the Twelve, all right—but the only one who has no magic."

"Then what's the problem? Even a shark is no match for three wizards—"

"K!t," S'reee said, "that's easy for you to say. You're a sperm, and it's true enough that the average shark's no threat to one of your kind. But this is no average shark we're going to see. This shark would be a good candidate to *really* be the Pale Slayer, the original Master-Shark, instead of just playing him. And there are some kinds of strength that even wizardry has trouble matching." Her song grew quieter. "We're getting close. If you have any plans to stay living for a while more, watch what you say when the Pale One starts talking. And for the Sea's sake, if you're upset about anything, don't show it!"

They swam on toward Montauk Point, the long spit of land that was the southeastern tip of Long Island. The bottom began to change from the yellow, fairly smooth sand of the South Shore, littered with fish havens and abandoned oyster beds and deep undergrowth, to a bottom of darker shades —dun, brown, almost black—rocky and badly broken, scattered with old wrecks. The sea around them grew noisy, changing from the usual soft background hiss of quiet water to a rushing, liquid roar that grew in intensity until Nita couldn't hear herself think, let alone sing. Seeing in the water was difficult. The surface was whitecapped, the middle waters were murky with dissolved air, and the hazy sunlight diffused in the sea until everything seemed to glow a pallid gray white, with no shadows anywhere.

"Mind your swimming," S'reee said, again in that subdued voice. "The rocks are sharp around here; you don't want to start bleeding."

They surfaced once for breath near Montauk Point, so that Nita got a glimpse of its tall octagonal lighthouse, the little tender's house nearby, and a group of tourists milling about on the cliff that slanted sharply down to the sea. Nita blew, just once, but spectacularly, and grinned to herself at the sight of the tourists pointing and shouting at each other and taking pictures of her. She cruised the surface for a good long moment to let them get some good shots, then submerged again and caught up with Kit and S'reee.

The murkiness of the water made it hard to find her way except by singing brief notes, waiting for the return of the sound, and judging the bottom by it. S'reee was doing so, but her notes were so short that she seemed to be grudging them.

What's the matter with her? Nita thought. *You can't get a decent sounding off such short notes*— And indeed, she almost hit a rock herself as she was thinking that, and saved herself from it only by a quick lithe twist that left her aching afterward. The roaring of the water over the Shoals kept on growing, interfering with the rebound of the song-notes, whiting them out. S'reee was bearing north around the point now and slowing to the slowest of glides. Kit, to keep from overswimming her, was barely drifting, and keeping well above the bottom. Nita glanced up at him, a great dark shape against the greater brightness of the surface water—and saw his whole body thrash once, hard, in a gesture of terrible shock. "Nita!"

She looked ahead and saw what he saw. The milky water ahead of them had a great cloud of blood hanging and swirling in it, with small bright shapes flashing in and out of the cloud in mindless confusion. Nita let out one small squeak of fear, then forced herself to be quiet. The sound came back, though, and told her that inside that roiling red darkness, something was cruising by in a wide curve—something nearly Kit's size. She backfinned to hover in the water, glancing up at Kit.

He drifted downward to her, singing no note of his own. She could understand why. Tumbling weightlessly out of the blood-cloud, trailing streaks of watery red, were the slashed and broken bodies of a school of smallfin tuna—heads, tails, pieces too mangled to name, let alone to bear close examination. Some of these drifted slowly to the bottom, where the scavengers—salt-water catfish and crabs and other such—ate them hurriedly, as if not wanting to linger and face whatever hunted above.

Nita didn't want to attract its attention either, but she also wanted Kit's reassurance. This place to which S'reee had brought them was unquestionably the location of a shark's "feeding frenzy," in which the hunter begins to devour not only its prey, but anything else that gets in the way, uncontrollably, mindlessly, until sated.

Inside the cloud of blood, which the current over the shoals was taking away, something moved. Impossible, was Nita's first reaction as the circling shape was revealed. It broke out of its circling and began to soar slowly toward her and Kit and S'reee. Sonar had warned her of its size, but she was still astonished. No mere fish could be that big.

This one could. Nita didn't move. With slow, calm, deadly grace the huge form came curving toward them. Nita could see why S'reee had said that this creature was a good candidate for the title Master-Shark, even if the original had lived ten thousand years ago, when everything was bigger. The shark was nearly as long as Kit—from its blunt nose to the end of its tail's topfin, no less than ninety feet. Its eyes were that same dull, expressionless black that had horrified Nita when she'd watched *Jaws.* But seeing those eyes on a TV screen was one thing. Having them dwell on you, calm and hungry even after a feeding frenzy—that was much worse.

The pale shape glided closer. Nita felt Kit drift so close to her that his skin brushed hers, and she felt the thudding of his huge heart. In shape, the shark looked like a great white, at least as well as Nita could remember from *Jaws.* There, though, the resemblance ended. "Great white" sharks were actually a pale blue on their upper bodies and only white below. This one was white all over, an ivory white so pale that great age might have bleached it that color. And as for size, this one could have eaten the *Jaws* shark for lunch, and

ooked capable of working Nita in, in no more than a bite or two, as dessert.
ts terrible maw, hung with drifting, mangled shreds of bleeding tuna, was
asily fifteen feet across. Those jaws worked gently, absently, as the white
orror cruised toward the three of them.

S'reee finned forward a little. She inclined the fore half of her body toward
he white one and sang, in what seemed utter, toneless calm,
Ed'Rashtekaresket, chief of the Unmastered in these waters, I greet you."

The shark swam straight toward S'reee, those blank eyes fixed on her. The
vhale held her position as the Pale One glided toward her, his mouth open,
iis jaws working. At the last possible moment he veered to one side and
egan to describe a great circle around the three.

Three times he circled them, in silence. Next to Nita, Kit shuddered. The
hark looked sharply at them, but still said nothing, just kept swimming until
ie had completed his third circle. When he spoke at last, there was no
varmth in his voice, none of the skin-stroking richness she had grown used to
n whale-voices. This voice was dry . . . interested, but passionless; and
hough insatiably hungry, not even slightly angry or vicious. The voice de-
troyed every idea Nita had of what a shark would sound like. Some terrible
nalice, she could have accepted—not this deadly equanimity. "Young wiz-
.rd," the voice said, cool and courteous, "well met."

The swimmer broke free of his circling and described a swift, clean arc
hat brought him close enough to Nita and Kit for Nita to see the kind of
ough, spiky skin that had injured S'reee so badly two nights before. The
;reat shark almost touched Nita's nose as he swept by.

"My people," the Pale One said to S'reee, "tell me that they met with you
wo nights since. And fed well."

"The nerve!" Kit said, none too quietly, and started to swim forward.

Aghast, Nita bumped him to one side, hard. He was so startled he held still
.gain. "Keep your mouth shut!" she said quietly. "That thing could eat us all
f it wanted to!"

"If *he* wanted to," said the Pale One, glancing at Nita and fixing her, just
'or a moment, with one of those expressionless eyes. "Peace, young human.
'll deal with you in a moment."

She subsided instantly, feeling like a bird face to face with a snake.

"I am told further," said the shark, circling S'reee lazily, "that wizardry
;truck my people down at their meal. . . ."

"And then released them."

"The story's true, then."

"True enough, Unmastered," said S'reee, still not moving. "I'm no more
gnorant than Ae'mhnuu was of the price paid for the reckless wasting of life.
Besides, I knew I'd be talking to you today . . . and even if I didn't, I'd

have you to deal with at some later time. . . . Shall we two be finished with this matter, then? I have other things to discuss with you."

"Having heard the Calling in the water last night, I believe you do," said the Pale One, still circling S'reee with slow grace. His jaws, Nita noticed, were still working. "You were wise to spare those of my Mastery. Are your wounds healed? Is your pain ended?"

"Yes to both questions, Pale One."

"I have no further business with you, then," said the shark. Nita felt Kit move slightly against her, an angry, balked movement. Evidently he had been expecting the shark to apologize. But the shark's tone of voice made it plain that he didn't think he'd done anything wrong . . . and bizarrely, it seemed as if S'reee agreed with him.

"Well enough," S'reee said, moving for the first time, to break out of the Pale One's circle. "Let's get to business." The shark went after, pacing her.

"Since you heard the Calling," S'reee said, "you know why I'm here."

"To ask me to be Twelfth in the Song," said the shark. "When have I not? You may administer the Oath to me at your leisure. But first you must tell me who the Silent One is."

"She swims with us," S'reee said, rolling over on her back as she swam— something Nita would certainly never have dared do, lest it give this monster ideas—and indicating Nita with one long forefin.

Nita would have preferred to keep Kit between her and the shark; but something, the Sea perhaps, told her that this would be a bad idea. Gulping, she slipped past Kit and glided up between S'reee and the great white. She was uncertain of protocol—or of anything except that she should show no fear. "Sir," she said, not "bowing" but looking him straight in those black eyes, "I'm Nita."

"My lady wizard," the Pale One said in that cool, dry voice, "you're also terrified out of your wits."

What to say now? But the shark's tone did have a sort of brittle humor about it. She could at least match it. "Master-Shark," she said, giving him the title to be on the safe side, "if I were, saying so would be stupid; I'd be inviting you to eat me. And saying I wasn't afraid would be stupid too—and a lie."

The shark laughed, a terrible sound—quiet, and dry, and violent under its humor. "That's well said, Nita," he said when the laughing was done. "You're wise not to lie to a shark—nor to tell him that particular truth. After all, fear is distress. And I end distress; that's my job. So beware. I am pleased to meet you; but don't bleed around me. Who's your friend? Make him known to me."

Nita curved around with two long strokes, swam back to Kit, and escorted him back to the white with her fins barely touching him, a don't-screw-it-up! gesture. "This is Kit," she said. "He may or may not be singing with us."

"A whalesark?" said the Pale One, as Kit glided close to him.

"Yes," Kit said bluntly, without any honorific note or tone of courtesy appended to the word. Nita looked at him in shock, wondering what had gotten into him. He ignored her, staring at the shark. Kit's teeth were showing.

The Pale One circled Kit once, lazily, as he had when offering challenge to S'reee. "She is not as frightened as she looks, Kit," he said, "and at any rate, I suspect you're more so. Look to yourself first until you know your new shape better. It has its own fierce ways, I hear; but a sperm whale is still no match for me." He said this with the utter calm of someone telling someone else what time it was. "I would not make three bites of you, as I would with Nita. I would seize your face and crush your upper jaw to make myself safe from your teeth. Then I would take hold of that great tongue of yours and not let go until I had ripped it loose to devour. Smaller sharks than I am have done that to sperm whales before. The tongue is, shall we say, a delicacy."

The shark circled away from Kit. Very slowly, Kit glided after. "Sir," he said—sounding subdued, if not afraid, "I didn't come here to fight. I thought we were supposed to be on the same side. But frightening us seems a poor tactic if we're supposed to be allies, and singing the same Song."

"I frighten no one," said the shark. "No one who fears gets it from anywhere but himself. Or herself. Cast the fear out—and then I am nothing to fear. . . . No matter, though; you're working at it. Kit, Nita, my name is ed'Rashtekaresket."

"It has teeth in it," Nita said.

The shark looked at her with interest in his opaque gaze. "It has indeed," he said. "You hear well. And you're the Silent One? Not the Listener?"

"The Listener's part is spoken for, Pale One," S'reee said. "And the Silent One's part needs a wizard more experienced than any we have—one already tested against the Lone Power, yet young enough to fulfill the other criteria. HNii't is the one."

"Then these are the two who went up against the Lone One in Manhattan," ed'Rashtekaresket said. "Oh, don't sing surprise at me, Kit: I know the human names well enough. After all, you are who you eat."

Nita swallowed hard. "Such shock," the shark said, favoring Nita again with that dark, stony, unreadable look. "Beware your fear, Nita. They say I'm a 'killing machine'—and they say well. I am one." The terrible laugh hissed in the water again. "But one with a mind. Nor such a machine that I devour without cause. Those whom I eat, human or whale or fish, always give me cause. —I'm glad you brought them, S'reee. If this 'Heart of the Sea' the wizards always speak of really exists, then these two should be able to get its attention. And its attention is needed."

For the first time since the conversation began, S'reee displayed a mild annoyance. "It exists, Pale One. How many Songs have you played Twelfth in, and you still don't admit that—"

"More Songs than you have, young one," ed'Rashtekaresket said. "And it would take more still to convince me of what can't be seen by anyone not a wizard. *Show* me the Sea's Heart, this Timeheart you speak of, and I'll admit it exists."

"Are you denying that wizardry comes from there?" S'reee said, sounding even more annoyed.

"Possibly," said the shark, "if it does not. Don't be angry without reason, S'reee. You warm-bloods are all such great believers. But there's no greater pragmatist than a shark. I believe what I eat . . . or what I see. Your power I've seen: I don't deny that. I simply reserve decision on where it comes from. What I say further is that there's trouble in the deep waters hereabouts, more trouble than usual—and it's as well the Song is being enacted now, for there's need of it, wherever its virtue comes from. Will you hear my news? For if things go on as they're going now, the High and Dry will shortly be low and wet—and those of my Mastery will be eating very well indeed."

A Song of Battles

What is it?" Kit said. "Is it the krakens?"

Ed'Rashtekaresket looked at Kit and began a slow, abstracted circling round him. "You know about that?" said the Master-Shark. "You're wise for human."

"I know that the krakens are breeding this year," Kit said, "breaking their usual eleven-year cycle. And they're bigger than usual, our Seniors told us. In the deep water, krakens have been seen that would be a match for just about any whale or submarine they grabbed."

"That is essentially what I would have told you," the Master-Shark said to S'reee, still circling Kit. "My own people have been reporting trouble with the bottom dwellers—but any sharks who cannot escape such are no longer entitled to the Mastery's protection in any case. At any rate, I pass this news along as a courtesy to you warm-bloods. By way of returning the courtesy done to my people after your accident."

"Thank you," S'reee said, and bowed as they swam.

"Odd," ed'Rashtekaresket mused as they went, "that qualified wizards of high levels are so few, the whales must bring in humans to make up the number."

"Odd isn't the word for it, Pale One," S'reee said. "Advisories and Seniors have been dying like clams at red tide lately."

"As if," the Master-Shark said, "someone or something did not care to have the Song enacted just now." His voice sounded remote. "I'm reminded of that Song enacted, oh, a hundred thirty thousand moons ago—when the bottom shook as it does now, and the Lone One had newly lost the Battle of the Trees. One wizard was injured by rockfall while they made the journey down through the Gates of the Sea. And when they began the Singing proper, first the Killer and then the Blue lost control of their spells at crucial

times. You know the moment, S'reee: when the mock-battle breaks ou
among the three parties, and each one tries to force the others around to i
way of thinking."

Ed'Rashtekaresket fell silent. The four of them swam on. "Uh, Ed-
ed'Rak—" Nita stopped short, unable to remember the rest of his name a
anything but the sound of gnashing teeth. "Look, can I call you Ed?"

Blank eyes turned their attention toward her. "At least I can say it," sh
said. "And if I'm going to be singing with you, it can't be titles all the tim
We have to know each other, you say."

"A sprat's name," the shark said, dry-voiced. "A fry name—for me, th
Master." Then came the quiet, terrible laughter again. "Well enough. You'r
the Sprat, and I'm Ed." He laughed again.

Nita had never heard anything that sounded less like mirth in her lif
"Great. So, Ed, what happened? In that Song, when it went wrong. Wa
anyone hurt?"

"Of the singers? No. They were inside a spell-circle, and protected—it ha
to be that way, else anything might get in among the singers and upset the
spelling. But when the Song failed, all the power its Singers had tried to us
to bind the Lone One rebounded and freed him instead. The sea bottom fo
hundreds of miles about was terribly torn and changed as a result. Volcanoe
earthquakes. . . . Also, there was a landmass, a great island in the middle o
these waters. Surely you know about that country, since your people name
the ocean after it. That island was drowned. There were humans on i
millions of them died when the island sank. As for the rest—eating was goo
hereabouts for some time. The species of my Mastery prospered."

"A hundred thirty thousand moons ago—" Kit whispered, one sof
breathed note of song. "Ten thousand years!"

"Atlantis," Nita said, not much louder.

"Afállonë," S'reee said, giving the name in the wizardly Speech. "Ther
were Senior and Master wizards there," she said sadly, "a great many o
them. But even working together, they couldn't stop what happened. Th
earthquakes begun by the downfall of Afállonë were so terrible that they tor
straight through the first level of the land-under-Sea—the crust, I think th
two-leggers call it—and right down to the mantle, the molten stuff beneath
The whole island plate on which Afállonë stood was broken in pieces an
pushed down into the lava of the mantle—utterly destroyed. The plates o
your continent and that of Europe have since drifted together over the i
land's old location, covering its grave. . . . But even after the Downfal
there was trouble for years—mostly with the atmosphere, because of all th
ash the volcanoes spat into the air. It got cold, and whole species of lan
creatures died for lack of their food. It was thousands of Moons before thing

were normal again. So we tend to be very careful about the Song. 'Lest the Sea become the Land, and the Land become the Sea—' "

"And the krakens are breeding," the Pale One said as they swam. "Well. I'm for the Northern Rips tonight; there's trouble in the water there."

What kind of creature, Nita wondered, could hear the sounds of simple distress at a distance of two hundred miles and more?

"Beware, Nita," Ed said. "Only a dead shark could have avoided hearing *that* thought. If we're to know each other well, as you say you desire, best mind how you show me your feelings. Else I shall at last know you most intimately, sooner than you are planning—and the relationship will be rather one-sided."

Ed's jaws worked. "—I was going to say: matters swimming as they do, I will see you three home. It's getting dark, and—"

"Dark!" Nita and Kit looked around them. The water, turbid green white when they had come here, was now almost black.

"The Sun's going down," Kit said unhappily. "We're really in for it now."

Nita agreed. "Master-Shark," she said, staying as calm as she could, "we have to get back to, uh, our feeding grounds. And in a hurry. Our parents are waiting for us, and we had orders to be back before it got dark."

Ed simply looked at Nita with that calm black stare. "As you say," he said, and began to swim faster. "But we will not be at Bluehaven before many stars are out and the Moon is about to set."

"I know," Nita said. It was hard to sound unconcerned while her insides were churning. "Maybe you should go ahead and let them know we're okay," she said to Kit. "Tell them I'm coming—"

"No," Kit said, also at pains to sound calm. "I'll take my chances with you, Neets. 'All for one. . . .' "

"Sprat," Ed said to Nita, "this is an odd thing, that your sire and dam impose restrictions on you when you're doing a wizardry of such weight."

"They don't know we're wizards," Kit said.

S'reee was so surprised by this that she backfinned to a dead stop in the water. Ed, as if nothing took him by surprise, merely circled about the group, while Kit and Nita coasted close by. "They don't *know!*" S'reee said. "How do you do anything? How do you prepare wizardries? Let alone the matter of singing the Song without the full support of the people close to you—and when you're singing the Silent One's part, no less!"

There had been something about that last part in the manual. Nita had thought she had all the support she needed in Kit. She was becoming less sure. *Tom, got to call Tom—* "I know," she said out loud. "S'reee, let's swim. We're late enough as it is."

The four of them headed west again. "It can't be helped," Kit said. "It's not like it is here, where wizardry is something respectable and useful that most everybody knows about. Up on the land, they used to burn people for it. Nowadays—well, it's safer to hide what you're up to. People would think you were nuts if you tried to tell them you were a wizard. Most people don't believe in magic."

"What *do* they believe in?" S'reee said, unnerved.

"Things," Nita said unhappily. "S'reee, it's too complicated. But doing wizardry and keeping everybody from noticing is a problem."

"I'm no wizard," Ed said, "but only a fool would try to deny a wizard's usefulness. It must be a crippled life your people live up there, without magic, without what can't be understood, only accepted—"

For all her concern about being late, Nita looked wryly sideways at Ed. "This from someone who won't admit Timeheart exists unless he sees it himself?"

"Sprat," Ed said, "if it does in fact exist, can my not believing in it make the slightest difference? And as for understanding—I'm not interested in understanding Timeheart. What use is spending time figuring out, say, why water is wet? Will it make breathing it any— 'Ware, all!"

The warning came so conversationally that it took Nita precious moments to realize what the problem was. The sea around them was dark to begin with. But in the black water, darker shapes were moving. One of them, writhing and growing, reached up dim arms at them. Nita let out a squeak of surprise, and the returning echoes hit her skin and told her, to her terror, what her eyes couldn't. A long torpedo-shaped body, a great mass of arms that squirmed like snakes, and a long wicked beak-fang hidden at the bottom of them. She backfinned desperately as those writhing arms with all their hooked suckers reached for her.

The sound that began rumbling through the water probably upset the krakens as much as it did her. Nita had never heard the battlecry of an enraged sperm whale—a frightful scrape of sound, starting at the highest note a human being can hear and scaling down with watershaking roughness to the lowest note, then past it. It was hard to see what was going on, but Nita kept singing so her radar would tell her. She would have preferred not to; the echo-"sight" of Kit in the whalesark, arrowing toward the leading kraken, jaws open, all his sharp teeth showing, was a horror. Suckered arms whipped around him, squeezing; and the giant squid had its own noise, a screech so high it sounded like fingernails being scraped down a blackboard.

Before she really knew what she was doing, Nita circled off to pick up speed, and then swam straight toward the kraken's head-ruffle, the thick place where the tentacles joined behind mouth and tooth. She sang for air as she charged, then lost the song when she rammed the kraken. The squid's long porous backbone crunched and broke under her blow. Rolling, tail lashing, she fluked away. All the telephone pole–length arms spasmed an squeezed Kit hard one last time, then fell away limp. Kit shot in toward the head of the broken squid. Jaws opened, crunched closed, opened again to slash once or twice with wild ferocity. Then Kit fluked powerfully, still singing, and arched away through the water.

"Kit!" Nita cried, but his only answer was the sperm-whale battlecry. The water was dark with night, thick with squid ink, and scratchy with stirred sand. Through it all a pallid shape was cruising with terrible speed, jaws open, circling in. The patch of darkness he circled threw out a score of arms to grapple with him. Ed let them draw him closer to his prey, then bit, and blood and ink billowed everywhere in the frantic rush of water expelled by the shrieking squid. Severed chunks of kraken arm spun and swirled in the water, and sank through it. Ed swept forward, jaws wide, and bit again. The shriek cut off. Out of the cloud of blood and ink Ed came silently sailing, cool, untroubled, graceful: the Pale Slayer, a silent ghost looking calmly about him for his next victim. Nita held very still and sang not a note until he passed her by.

S'reee was ramming another kraken as Nita had. But one more closed on her from behind. Kit came swimming, singing his battlecry. He bit the second squid amidships, hanging onto that bullet-shaped body like a bulldog as its struggles shook him from side to side. Between her and Kit and S'reee, Ed was circling a third kraken. It flailed at him, trying to bind his mouth shut so that it could get a better grip on him and squeeze him to death.

It might as well not have bothered. As a fourth kraken came for her, Nita saw Ed break his circling pattern to dart in and slash, then curve away. Again and again he feinted, again and again his teeth tore, until the kraken was reduced to a tattered, screaming storm of blood and ink and flailing tentacles. Blank-eyed, Ed soared straight at the finned rear end of the doomed creature and opened his mouth. When his jaws scissored shut, all that was left to drift downward were the tips of several tentacles. The kraken had been about the size of a station wagon.

A fifth kraken took a great suck of water into its internal jet-propulsion system and thrust it out again, tainting the water with the sepia taste of ink as it fled into the depths, wailing like a lost soul. Nita was willing to let it go, and was swimming for the surface when a chill current and a pale form sank past her, spiraling downward with deadly grace. The utter dark of the night sea swallowed Ed. She heard the kraken's screams, which had been diminishing—and now grew louder, and more ragged, until they abruptly stopped.

Wearily Nita swam upward. She broached and blew gratefully, doing nothing for a long while but lie there in the wavewash, gasping.

Not too far away, S'reee broached and made her way slowly toward Nita. Neither of them said anything; but the two of them sagged together and simply leaned against each other, taking comfort in the presence of another whale. Some yards off, the water rushed away from Kit's back and sides as he came up, gasping too. Nita looked over at him, shaking. She knew that what she saw was just her friend in a whalesuit. But she kept seeing sharp teeth, slashing in a blood-hunger too much like Ed's for comfort.

"Are you okay?" she said to Kit.

"Yeah." He sounded uncertain, and Nita breathed out in relief. The voice was a sperm whale's, but the person inside it was definitely Kit. "Got a little —a little carried away there. You, Neets?"

"All right," she said.

Out of the depths a white form came drifting upward toward them.

They breathed and dived, all three, to find Ed circling in the clearing water, while a storm of fingerling blues and sardines swarmed about him, picking scraps and shreds out of the water, some of them even daring to pick bloody bits off Ed's skin or from between his teeth. "That last one was in pain at the thought of returning to the depths without its purpose fulfilled," he said. "So I ended that pain."

"Purpose?" Kit said.

"Surely you don't take that attack for an accident, young one," Ed said. "Any more than the shaking of the sea bottom these days or the ill chances that have been befalling S'reee's people have been accidents."

Nita looked at Kit, and then at Ed, in confusion. "You mean that what happened to S'reee— I thought you were on our side!"

Ed began to circle slowly inward toward Nita. "Peace, spratling," he said. "I pay no allegiance to anyone in the Sea or above it; you know that. Or you should. I am the Unmastered. I alone." He swept in closer. "The encounter S'reee and Ae'mhnuu had with the ship-that-eats-whales was doubtless the Lone One's doing. It has many ways to subtly influence those who live. As for the sharks—" Ed's voice became shaded with a cold, slow rage that chilled Nita worse than anything he'd said or done yet. "They did according to their nature, just as you do. Do not presume to blame them. On the other flank, however, *my* people have only one Master. If the Lone One has been tampering with species under my Mastery, then It will have to deal with *me.*"

That made Nita shake—not only at the thought of Ed trying to take on the Lone Power himself, but at the outrageous thought that the Lone One, for all Its power, might actually be in for some trouble. "I'm sorry," she said, "I thought you meant you told the sharks to just go ahead and attack a hurt whale." And with some trepidation, she copied S'reee's earlier gesture— rolling over in the water, exposing her unprotected flanks and belly to th Master-Shark.

A few long seconds afterward she felt what few beings have lived to te about—the abrasive touch of a live shark's skin. Ed nudged Nita ever s lightly in the ribs, then glided by; almost a friendly touch, except that Nit could see the fanged mouth working still, the opaque black eyes tracking on her. Finned whiteness sailed silent and immense above her, hardly stirring the water. "In another time, in another place, I might have told them to," Ed said. "In another time, I may yet tell them to. And what will you think of me then, Sprat?"

"I don't know," she said, when the white shape had passed over.

"That was well said too." Ed circled about the three of them, seeming to both watch them and ignore them at the same time. "So let us be on our way; we're close to Tiana Beach. S'reee, you and I have business remaining that must be done before witnesses."

S'reee wasted no time about it, gliding close to Ed—but, Nita noticed, not nearly as close as S'reee had come to Aroooon or Hotshot, or herself. "Ed'Rashtekaresket t'k Gh'shestaesteh, Eldest-In-Abeyance to the Pale Slayer That Was, Master for the Sharks of Plain and Shelf and what lies between—those who gather to sing that Song that is the Sea's shame and the Sea's glory desire you to be of their company. Say, for my hearing, whether you consent to that Song."

"I consent, and I will weave my voice and my will and my blood with that of those who sing, if there be need."

"I ask the second time—"

"Peace, S'reee, I know the words by now: Who better? A second time I say it, that those with me, both of my Mastery and not, may hear. Twice I consent to the Song, in my Mastery's name; and a third time, that the Sea, and the Heart of the Sea, shall hear. . . ." Was his voice just a touch drier on that phrase, Nita wondered? "So up, now, the three of you. We are where you need to be."

Kit looked around him in confusion. "How can you tell? There's a lot of Tiana Beach, and you've never seen our house—"

"I can smell your human bodies in the water from this morning," Ed said, unperturbed. "And, besides, I hear distress."

"Uh-oh . . ." Kit said.

"S'reee," Nita said, stalling, "when will you need us next?"

"Next dawn," the humpback said, brushing against first Nita, then Kit, in sympathy. "I'm sorry we can't have a day's rest or so, but there's no time any more."

"Do we have to be there?" Kit said.

"The Silent Lord does," S'reee said, glancing at Nita. "In fact, normally it's the Silent Lord who administers the Oath, since her stake in the Song is the greatest."

Nita made an unhappy sound. "Kit," she said, "maybe you'd better stay home. At least you won't get in trouble with your folks that way."

Kit shouldered over beside her, absent affection that bumped her considerably sideways as his hundred-foot bulk hit her. "No," he said. "I told you: 'All for one.' It's not fair for you to be stuck with this alone. Besides, what if those things show up again, and Ed's not here—"

"Right," Nita said.

"Neets, we better get going," Kit said.

She headed for the surface. Kit and S'reee followed; but Ed was above her and surfaced first, several hundred yards westward and much closer to the shore. So the first sound Nita heard from the shore was the screaming.

Nita had never heard her mother scream. The raw panic in the sound got under Nita's skin even worse than Kit's hunting song had.

"Harry!" her mother was shouting, and every few words her terror would gnaw its way through her desperately controlled voice and come out as a scream again. "Harry, for God's sake look, there's a *fin* out there, it's a *shark!* Get Mr. Friedman, get the cops, get *somebody!*"

The beach flickered with lights—flashlights, held by people running up and down—and every light in Nita's house was on, as well as most of those in the houses next door. Nita gulped at her father's hoarse reply—just as scared as her mother, trying to stay in control and failing.

"Betty, hang on, they're coming! Hang on! Don't go near the water!" For her mother was floundering into the surf, looking out seaward, searching for someone she couldn't see. "Nita!"

Nita had to fight to stay silent.

Ed cruised serenely, contemptuously close to the shore, bearing off westward, away from Nita and Kit and S'reee. The flashlights followed his pale fin as it broached, as Ed went so far as to raise himself a little out of the water, showing a terrible expanse of back, then the upward-spearing tailfin as big as a windsurfer's sail. Shouting in fear and amazement, the people followed him down the beach as if hypnotized. The flashlights bobbed away.

"He's got them distracted, we've gotta get out now," Kit said.

"But our bathing suits—"

"No time! Later! S'reee, we'll see you in the morning!" The two of them fluked wildly and made for the beach, in the direction opposite the one in which Ed was leading the people on the shore. Nita stayed under the surface as long as she could, then felt the bottom scrape on her belly; she was grounded. Kit had grounded sooner than she had. Nita gasped a long breath of air and let the shapechange go, then collapsed into the water again—not deep for a whale, but three feet deep for her. She struggled to her feet and staggered to shore through the breakers, wiping the salt out of her eyes and shaking with the shock of a spell released too suddenly.

By the time her sight was working properly, there was no time to do anything about the small, dark figure standing a few feet up the incline of the beach, looking straight at her.

Dairine.

There was a slam of imploding air behind Nita. Kit came scrambling up ut of the water, with the undone whalesark clutched glittering in one fist. Quick," he said, "I can do the Scotty spell before they come back—" He eached out and grabbed her by the arm, shaking her. "Neets, are you okay?"

Then he saw Dairine too. "Uh," he said. The sounds of voices down the each were getting closer; and through them, abrupt and terrible, came a udden *crack!* of gunfire. Kit looked down that way, then at Dairine again, nd took a long breath. "Right back," he said. He said one quick syllable and, a another clap of air, vanished.

Dairine just stood there in her pajamas with Yoda all over them, staring at er sister. "Whales," she said.

"Dairine," Nita whispered, "how long have they been out here?"

"About an hour."

"Oh, *no.*" And her folks would be there in moments. "Dairine," Nita said, look—" There she stopped. She couldn't think what she wanted to say.

"It *is* magic," Dairine whispered back. "There really *is* such a thing. And 's that book you have, isn't it? It's not just an old beat-up kids' book. It's—"

In another slam of air, blowing outward this time, Kit reappeared. He was lready in his bathing suit; he flung Nita's at her and then looked unhappily t Dairine.

"And you too," she said to him as Nita struggled into her suit.

"A wizard?" Kit said. "Yeah. Both of us."

Off to their left, there was another gunshot, and a mighty splash. Nita and it stared out at the sea. Ed was arrowing straight up out of the water with low, frightful grace, jaws working as he arched up in a leap like a dolphin's. ifty feet of him towered out of the water, sixty, eighty, until even his long harp tailfin cleared the surface and he hung there in midair, bent like a bow, he starlight and the light of the Moon sheening ice white along his hide and he water that ran down it. "Until later, my wizards!" came his hissed cry in he Speech, as Ed dived dolphin-curved back into the sea. The gunshot racked across the water at him, once, twice. Ed went down laughing in corn.

"That's as much as he's gonna do," Kit said. "They'll be back in a mo-ent, when they see he's gone."

"That shark—" said Dairine, sounding about ready to go into shock.

"He's a friend," Nita said.

"Neets," Kit said, "what're we gonna tell them?"

"That depends on Dairine." Nita took care to keep her voice perfectly vel. "What about it, Dari? Are you going to spill everything? Or are you oing to keep quiet?"

Dairine looked at the two of them, saying nothing. Then, "I want you to
tell me everything later," she said. *"Everything."*

"It'll have to be tonight, Dari. We've got to be out again by dawn."

"You're gonna get it," Dairine said.

"Tell us something else we don't know, Sherlock," Kit said, mild-voiced.

"Well. I guess I saw you two coming over the dune," Dairine said, looking
from Kit to Nita. She turned to head down the beach.

Nita caught Dairine by the arm, stopping her. Dairine looked back at Nita
over her shoulder—her expression of unease just visible in the dim light from
the houses up the beach. "I really don't want to lie to them, Dari," Nita said.

"Then you better either keep your mouth shut," Dairine said, "or tell
them the truth." And she tugged her arm out of Nita's grasp and went
pounding off down the beach, screaming, in her best I'm-gonna-tell voice,
"Mom, Dad, it's Nita!"

Nita and Kit stood where they were. "They're gonna ground us," Kit said.

"Maybe not," said Nita, in forlorn hope.

"They will. And what're you going to do then?"

Nita's insides clenched. And the sound of people talking was coming down
the beach toward them.

"I'm going," she said. "This is *lives* we're talking about—whales' lives,
People's lives. It can't just be stopped in the middle! You remember what E
said."

"That's what I'd been thinking," Kit said. "I just didn't want to get you in
my trouble—just because I'm doing it, I mean." He looked at her. "Dawn,
then."

"Better make it before," Nita said, feeling like a conspirator and hating it.
"Less light to get caught by."

"Right." And that was all they had time for, for Nita's mother and father
and Mr. Friedman, and Dairine, all came trotting up together. Then things
got confusing, for Nita's dad grabbed her and hugged her to him with tears
running down his face, as if he were utterly terrified; and her mother slowed
from her run, waved her arms in the air and roared, "Where the blazes have
you *been?*"

"We lost track of the time," Kit said.

"We were out, Mom," Nita said. "Swimming—"

"Wonderful! There are sharks the size of houses out there in the water
and my daughter is off swimming! At night, at high tide, with the undertow—" Her mother gulped for air, then said more quietly, "I didn't expect
this of you, Nita. After we talked this morning, and all."

Nita's father let go of her slowly, nodding, getting a fierce, closed look on
his face now that the initial shock of having his daughter back safe was
passing. "And I thought you had better sense, Kit," he said. "We had a

agreement that while you stayed with us, you'd do as we said. Here it is hours and hours after dark—"

"I know, sir," Kit said. "I forgot—and by the time I remembered, it was too late. It won't happen again."

"Not for a while, anyway," Nita's mother said, sounding grim. "I don't want you two going out of sight of the house until further notice. Understood?"

"Yes, Mrs. Callahan."

"Nita?" her mother said sharply.

There it was: the answer she wasn't going to be able to get around. "Okay, Mom," she said. Her stomach turned over inside her at the sound of the lie. Too late now. It was out, not to be recalled.

"That also means staying out of the water," her father said.

Why me? Why me! Nita thought. She made a face. "Okay."

"Okay," Kit said too, not sounding very happy.

"We'll see how you two behave in the next few days," Nita's mother said. "And whether that shark clears out of here. Maybe after that we'll let you swim again. Meanwhile—you two get home."

They went. Just once Nita looked over her shoulder and was sure she saw, far out on the water, a tall pale fin that stood high as a sail above the surface, then slid below it, arrowing off toward Montauk—distress ended for the moment, and a job done.

Nita felt the miserable place in her gut and thought it was just as well that Ed couldn't come up on the land.

Fearsong

Nita lay awake in the dark, staring at the ceiling. It was three thirty in the morning, by the glow of the cheap electric clock on the dresser. She would very much have liked to turn over, forget about the clock, the time, and everything else, and just sack out. But soon it would be false dawn, and she and Kit would have to be leaving.

Changes . . .

Only last week, her relationship with her folks had seemed perfect. Now all that was over, ruined—and about to get much worse, Nita knew, when her mom and dad found her and Kit gone again in the morning.

And the changes in Kit—

She rolled over on her stomach unhappily, not wanting to think about it. She had a new problem to consider, for when everyone was in bed, Dairine had come visiting.

Nita put her face down into her pillow and groaned. Dairine had gone right through Nita's wizard's manual, staring at all the strange maps and pictures. It was annoying enough to begin with that Dairine could see the book at all; nonwizards such as her mother and father, looking at it, usually saw only an old, beat-up copy of something called *So You Want to Be a Wizard*, apparently a kids' book. But Dairine saw what was there, and was fascinated.

The aptitude for wizardry sometimes runs through a whole generation of a family. Several famous "circles" of wizards in the past had been made up of brothers or sisters or cousins, rather than unrelated people such as she and Kit, or Tom and Carl, who met by accident or in some other line of work and came to do wizardry together by choice. But families with more than one wizard tended to be the exception rather than the rule, and Nita hadn't been expecting this. Also, Nita was beginning to realize that she had rather en oyed having her wizardry be a secret from everybody but the other wizards she worked with. That secret, that advantage, was gone now too. Dairine had he aptitude for wizardry as strongly as Nita herself had had it when she tarted.

In fact, *she's got it more strongly than I did,* Nita thought glumly. *The book had to get my attention by force, that first time I passed it in the library. But Dairine noticed it herself, as soon as I brought it home.*

For several years Nita had kept her advantage over her sister by only the slimmest of margins. She knew quite well that Dairine was a lot smarter than he was in most things. Wizardry had been a large and satisfying secret she'd felt sure Dairine would never catch on to. But that advantage was now gone too. The youngest wizards were the strongest ones, according to the book; older ones might be wiser but had access to less sheer power. Dairine had gotten the better of her again.

Nita turned over on her back, staring at the ceiling once more.

Kit . . .

He just wasn't himself in the whalesark. *When he's in his own skin,* she told herself fiercely, *he's fine.* But she couldn't quite make herself believe that. His look, his stance, were too different in just the past day or two.

She had thought that having a best friend at last would be great fun. And he and Kit had enjoyed each other's company immensely in their first couple months of wizardry, after the terror and sorrow of their initial encounter with he Art had worn off a bit. But sometimes things just didn't work. Kit would get moody, need to be by himself for days at a time. Or he would say sudden things that Nita thought cruel—except that it was Kit saying them, and Kit wasn't cruel; she knew that.

I wish I'd had some friends when I was younger, she thought. *Now I've got one who really matters—and I don't know what to do so he stays my friend. He changes. . . .*

And Kit was going to be in that whalesark for more and more time in the next couple of days. Would she even know him if this kept up?

Would he know her? Or want to? Humpbacks and sperms were different. Her own aggressiveness had frightened her badly enough, after the fight with the krakens. Kit's had been worse. And he had been *enjoying* it. . . .

Listless, Nita reached under her pillow for her wizard's manual and a flashlight. She clicked the light on and started paging through the book, intending to kill some time doing "homework"—finishing the study of her parts of the Song, the Silent Lord's parts. They were mostly in what whales used for verse—songs with a particular rhythm and structure, different for each species, but always more formal than regular conversational song. Since she wasn't good at memorizing, Nita was relieved to find that when she was whaleform, the Sea would remind her of the exact words. What she

needed to study were the emotions and motivations behind each song, the
way they were sung.

She riffled through the book. There was a lot of background material—the
full tale of the first Song, and of others, including the disastrous "Drowned
Song" that ended in the downfall of Atlantis; the names of famous whale
wizards who had sung and how they had sung their parts; "stage direction"
for the Song itself; commentary, cautions, permitted variations, even jokes
for evidently though the occasion was serious, it didn't have to be somber
Then the Song proper, in verse, with the names of the ten Lords of the
Humors: the Singer, the Gazer, the Blue, the Sounder, the Gray Lord, the
Listener, the Killer, the Wanderer, the Forager, and of course the Silent
Lord. Each of them ruled a kind of fish and also a kind of temperament.

Some of them struck Nita as odd; the Killer, for example, was the patron-
ess of laughter, always joking: the Gazer looked at everything and hardly ever
said what he saw. And the Silent Lord— Nita paused at the lines that
described "the one who ruled seas with no songs in them, and hearts that
were silent; but in her own silence, others would sing forever. . . ."

And of course there was the Pale Slayer. And another odd thing; though
the names of all the whales ever to sing the Song were listed, there was no
listing for the Master-Shark, except the mere title, repeated again and again
Maybe he's like an executioner in the old days, Nita thought. *Anonymous.*
The commentaries weren't very illuminating. "The Master of the lesser
Death," one of them called him, "who, mastering it, dieth not. For wizardry
toucheth not one to whom it hath not been freely given: nor doth the
messenger in any wise partake of the message he bears."

The manual was like that sometimes. Nita sighed and skimmed down to
the first canto: S'reee's verse, it would be, since the Singer opens the Song a
the other Ten gather around the lonely seamount Caryn Peak, the Sea
Tooth. Alongside the musical and movement notations for a whale singing
the Song, the manual had a rough translation into the Speech:

> Blood in the water I sing, and one who shed it:
> > deadliest hunger I sing, and one who fed it—
> weaving the ancientmost tale of the Sea's sending;
> > singing the tragedy, singing the joy unending.
>
> This is our shame—this is the whole Ocean's glory;
> > this is the Song of the Twelve. Hark to the
> > story!
> Hearken, and bring it to pass; swift, lest the sorrow
> > long ago laid to its rest devour us tomorrow!

There was much more: the rest of the prologue, then the songs of each of the Masters who were part of the Song and their temptations by the Stranger-whale, the Lone Power in disguise. Nita didn't need to pay any attention to those, for the Silent Lord came in only near the end, and the others, even the Stranger, dared use nothing stronger than persuasion on her. The whale singing the part of the Silent One then made her decision which side to be on—and acted.

That was the part Nita had gotten up to. Almost done, she thought with some relief, seeing that there wasn't much more beyond this. Only a few more cantos. *Boy, how do you manage to be cheerful while singing this stuff? It sounds so creepy.*

> Must I accept the barren Gift?
>   —learn death, and lose my Mastery?
> Then let them know whose blood and breath
>   will take the Gift and set them free:
> whose is the voice and whose the mind
>   to set at naught the well-sung Game—
> when finned Finality arrives
>   and calls me by my secret Name.
>
> Not old enough to love as yet,
>   but old enough to die, indeed—
> the death-fear bites my throat and heart,
>   fanged cousin to the Pale One's breed.
> But past the fear lies life for all—
>   perhaps for me; and, past my dread,
> past loss of Mastery and life,
>   the Sea shall yet give up Her dead!

Glad that wasn't me back then, she thought. *I could never have pulled that off. . . .* Nita read down through the next section, the "stage directions" for this sequence of the Song. "The whale singing the Silent One then enacts the Sacrifice in a manner as close to the original enactment as possible, depending on the site where the Song is being celebrated. . . ."

She skimmed the rest of it, the directions detailing the Pale Slayer's "acceptance of Sacrifice," his song, the retreat of the Lone Power, and the song's conclusion by the remaining Ten. But she was having trouble keeping her mind on her work. *Kit*—

"Neets!"

His voice was the merest hiss from outside the locked window. She got up and peered out the window to see where Kit was, then waved him away from the wall. The spell she had in mind for getting out needed only one word to start it. Nita spoke it and walked through the wall.

Between the distracting peculiarity of the feeling, which was like walking through thick spiderwebs, and the fact that the floor of her room was several feet above the ground, Nita almost took a bad fall, the way someone might who'd put his foot into an open manhole. Kit staggered, barely catching her, and almost fell down himself.

"Clumsy," he said as he turned her loose.

"Watch it, *Niño*—"

He punched her, not as hard as he might have; then spent a moment or two brushing himself off, and redraped the whalesark over one shoulder, where it hung mistily shimmering like a scrap of fog with starlight caught in it. "Is that locked?" he said, looking up at Nita's window with interest.

"Uh-huh."

"And the front and back doors are too."

"Yeah."

Kit threw a wicked look at Nita as they made their silent way out of the yard and toward the beach. "Your mom and dad are going to be real curious how we got out of the house and then locked all the inside locks when we don't have the keys."

"Uh-huh," Nita said. "If we're gonna get in real trouble, we might as well confuse them as much as possible. It might distract them . . ."

"Wanna bet?" Kit said.

Nita didn't answer.

The beach was desolate. Nita and Kit left their bathing suits under a prominent boulder and slid into the chilly water. Nita changed first and let Kit take hold of her dorsal fin and be towed out to deeper water. She shuddered once, not knowing why, at the strange cool feeling of human hands on her hide as she swam outward.

Beyond the breakers, the water was peculiarly still. The sky was cobalt with a hint of dawn-silver in it; the sea was sheenless, shadowless, the color of lead. And rising up from the listless water, four or five hundred yards from shore, a tall white fin was cruising in steady, silent circles, like the sail of a ghost ship unable to make port.

"I didn't think Ed was going to be here," Kit said. He let go of Nita's fin and slipped off into the water.

"Neither did I," Nita said, not knowing if he heard her before he dived When he was finished changing, she dived too and made her way toward where Ed swam serenely.

S'reee was there as well. She swam close, whistling Nita a greeting, and brushed skin with her. Hotshot was there too, gamboling and swooping in the dim-lit water—though with just a little more restraint than usual around the silently drifting bulk of Ed.

"A long swim today," S'reee said to Nita. "Up to Nantucket. Are you ready? Did you get your problem with your dam and sire worked out?"

"Not really," Nita said. "In fact, it'll probably get a lot worse before it gets any better. There's going to be trouble tonight. . . ." She stopped; there was no use letting it spoil the day. "Never mind," she said. "Let's go."

S'reee led the way, a straight course east-northeast, to Nantucket Rips. From her reading and from what the Sea told her, Nita knew those were treacherous waters, full of sudden shelves and hidden rocks. And the wizard's manual spoke of uneasy "forces" that lingered about those dead and broken ships—forces Nita suspected she would mistake for restless ghosts, if she should have the bad luck to see one.

"You are silent today," said a dry, cool voice directly above Nita. Glancing upward, Nita saw floating above her, effortlessly keeping pace, the great pale form that had been one of the images keeping her awake last night. "And you did not greet me. Is this courtesy to another celebrant?"

"Good morning, Ed," Nita said, in the same mildly edgy tone of voice she would have used on a human being who bugged her that way.

"Oh, indeed," Ed said. "You're bold, Sprat. And the boldness comes of distress. Beware lest I be forced to hurry matters, so that we should have even less time to get acquainted than you seem to desire."

"That was something I was meaning to ask you about," Nita said, looking up at Ed again. "The 'distress' business—"

"Ask, Sprat."

"You said before that it was your 'job' to end distress where you found it. . . ."

"You are wondering who gave me the job," Ed said, sinking to Nita's level, so that her left-side eye was filled with the sight of him. "Perhaps it was the Sea itself, which you wizards hear speaking to you all the time. You look askance? Doubtless you think the Sea would be too 'good' to assign a whole species to nothing but painful and violent killing." Ed's voice stayed cool as always, though there was a tinge of mockery to it. "If you think so, look around you, Sprat. The ocean is full of weaponry as effective as my teeth. Poisons and spines, snares and traps and claws that catch are everywhere. We all have to eat."

Ed smiled at her. A long shiver went down Nita from head to tail; a shark's smile is an expression the wise person does not provoke. "Those are just dumb creatures, though," she said, keeping her song as inoffensive-sounding as possible. "They don't think. You do—and you *enjoy* what you do."

"So?" Ed swam closer. "How should I not? Like all my people I'm built to survive in a certain fashion . . . and it's only wise to cause what you build to feel good when it does what it must to survive. My nerves are tuned to pain. That fact tells me beyond question what my job is. Distress calls me; blood in the water is the clearest sign of that distress, and I have a duty to it. If I destroy, still I serve life. What can't elude me is often sick or injured, and suffering; what survives me or outthinks me is stronger and wiser for it. And the survivor's descendants will be too. Is that so bad?"

"Well, that way . . . no. But I bet you wouldn't be so calm about it if it was *you* dying."

"Me? Die?" Ed laughed again. "The Master-Shark eats the Silent Lord's 'Gift,' you know, along with the Silent One. There's immortality in all the sharks, in various degrees. But what good is immortality if you haven't died first? And nothing in the Sea is deadly enough to kill me against my will."

Something about Ed's voice was making Nita curious. "What about with it?"

"Ah, but will must spread to the body from the mind. And after all the years I've lived in it, my body is too strong. All it wants is to eat, and live. And so it does; and I swim on. Immortality is of terrible power. It would take something more powerful yet to override it. . . ."

Nita didn't say anything.

"But all that being so," Ed said, "for good or ill, I am the Destroyer. Being that, I might as well enjoy my work, might I not? And so I do. Would it help if I decided to be miserable?" There was actually a touch of humor in that cold, dry voice.

"No, I suppose not."

"So I go about my work with a merry heart," Ed said, "and do it well as a result. That should please you, I think—"

"I'm delighted," Nita sang, under her breath.

"—for spells work best, you wizards tell me, when all the participants are of light heart and enjoying themselves. I'll certainly enjoy eating *you* when the time comes 'round."

"Ed, that's not funny."

"It isn't?" said the Master-Shark, looking at her.

Nita stopped swimming, letting herself coast for a moment. There was something odd about the way he'd said that— "Ed, what was that crack supposed to mean?"

The look Ed gave her was expressionless as ever. "The Silent Lord is pleased to jest with me," he said.

"Ed!"

"Distress, distress, Sprat. Have a care."

Ed was drifting closer again, and Nita kept herself as outwardly calm as she could. "Ed," she said, slowly and carefully, "are you trying to say that you're actually planning to *eat* me sometime soon?"

"The day after tomorrow," said the Master-Shark in perfect calm, "if we keep to schedule."

Nita couldn't think of a thing to say.

"You seem surprised," Ed said. "Why?"

It took Nita a few moments to answer, for her mind was boiling with sudden memories. S'reee's great relief when Nita agreed to participate in the Song. Her repeated questions to Nita about whether she was sure she wanted to do this. The Blue's silent, sad appraisal and approval of her. S'reee's remark about the Silent Lord's contribution to the Song being the most important of any celebrant—"the Silent Lord has the most at stake." And the wording of the Celebrant's Oath itself, with its insistent repetition and the line Nita had been so sure was ceremonial: "and I will blend my blood with theirs should there be need. . . ."

Nita gulped. "Ed," she said, "the Song, the whole thing . . . I thought it was just sort of, sort of a play. . . ."

"Indeed not." Ed seemed unconcerned by her terror. "There's always blood in the water at the end of the Song. I am no wizard, but even I know that nothing else will keep the Lone Power bound. Nothing but the willing sacrifice, newly made by the Celebrant representing the Silent One—by a wizard who knows the price he is paying and what it will buy. The spells worked during the Song would be powerless otherwise, and the Lone Power would rise again and finish what It once began."

"But—" Off on her right, she saw Kit looking curiously at her. But at the moment Kit meant nothing to her, and neither did Ed, or the chill silver light dawning in the water, or anything else. The manual's words, which he'd skimmed over so casually: those were what mattered now. *The whale singing the Silent One then enacts the Sacrifice in a manner as close to the original enactment as possible, depending on the site where the Song is being celebrated. The shark singing the Pale Slayer then receives the Sacrifice. . . .* With frightful clarity she could remember sitting on the fishing platform off Tiana Beach and S'reee saying, "The Silent One dived into a stand of razor coral; and the Master-Shark smelled her blood in the water, and . . . well. . . ."

Nita started to swim, without any real idea of where she was going, or why she was going there. She went slowly at first, then faster. "Neets," Kit was singing behind her, "what's wrong, what is it?"

"HNii't!" sang another voice, farther away. "Wait! What's the matter?"

That voice she wanted to hear some more from. Nita wheeled about and hurtled back the way she had come, almost ramming Kit, and not caring, letting him get out of her way as best he could. S'reee saw Nita coming and simply stopped swimming. "S'reee!" Nita cried, one long note that was more scream than a song. "Why didn't you tell me!"

"Oh, hNii't," S'reee sang, desperate and hurried, "the Master-Shark i
about—for Sea's sake, control yourself!"

"Never mind him! *Why didn't you tell me!*"

"About what the Silent One does?" S'reee said, sounding confused and
upset as Nita braked too late and almost hit her too. "But you said you
knew!"

Nita moaned out loud. It was true. *Just about finished with my reading,* she
remembered herself saying. *Only one thing I don't understand; everything else
is fairly straightforward. . . .* And, *I got it, S'reee, let's get on with it. . .*
But the truth didn't break her rage. "You should have made sure I knew what
you were talking about!"

"Why?" S'reee cried, getting angry herself now. "You're a more experi
enced wizard than *I* am! You went into the Otherworlds and handled thing
by yourself that it'd normally take whole circles of wizards to do! And
warned you, make sure you know what you're doing before you get into this
But you went right ahead!"

Nita moaned again, and S'reee lost her anger at the sound and moaned
too. "I knew something bad was going to happen," she sang unhappily. "The
minute I found Ae'mhnuu dead and me stuck with organizing the Song,
knew! But I never thought it'd be anything as bad as *this!*"

Kit looked from one of them to the other, somewhat at a loss. "Look," he
said to S'reee, "are you telling me that the whale who sings the Silent One
actually has to *die?*"

S'reee simply looked at him. Nita did not look at him, could not.

"That's horrible," Kit said in a hushed voice. "Nita, you can't—"

"She must," S'reee said. "She's given her word that she would."

"But couldn't somebody else—"

"Someone else could," S'reee said. "If that person would be willing to take
the Oath and the role of the Silent Lord in hNii't's place. But no one will
What other wizard are we going to be able to find in the space of a day and
half who would be willing to die for Nita's sake?"

Kit was silent with shock.

"Anyway, hNii't took the Oath freely in front of witnesses," S'reee said
unhappily. "Unless someone with a wizard's power freely substitutes himsel
for her, she has to perform what she's promised. Otherwise the whole Song i
sabotaged, useless—can't be performed at all. And if we don't perform it, o
if something goes wrong. . . ."

Nita closed her eyes in horror, remembering the time the Song failed
What Atlantis couldn't survive, she thought in misery, New York and Lon
Island sure won't. Millions of people will die. Including Mom and Dac
Dairine, Ponch, Kit's folks—

"But the Song hasn't started yet," Kit protested.

"Yes, it has," Nita said dully. *That* she remembered very clearly from her reading; it had been in the commentaries, one of the things she found strange. "The minute the first Celebrant takes the Oath, the Song's begun— and everything that happens to every Celebrant after that is part of it."

"HNii't," S'reee said in a voice so small that Nita could barely hear her, "what will you do?"

A shadow fell over Nita, and a third and fourth pair of eyes joined the first two: Hotshot, grinning as always, but with alarm behind the grin; Ed, gazing down at her out of flat black eyes, emotionless as stones. "I thought I sensed some little troubling over here," said the Master-Shark.

Kit and S'reee held still as death. "Yes," Nita said with terrible casualness, amazed at her own temerity.

"Is the pain done?" said the Master-Shark.

"For the moment," Nita said. She could feel herself slipping into shock, an insulation that would last her a few hours at least. She'd felt something similar, several years before, when her favorite uncle had died. The shock had gotten Nita through the funeral; but afterward, it had been nearly two weeks before she had been able to do much of anything but cry. I won't have that option this time, she thought. There's work to be done, a Song to sing, spells to work. . . . But all that seemed distant and unimportant to her, since in a day and a half, it seemed, a shark was going to eat her. Kit looked at Nita in terror, as if he suddenly didn't know her.

She stared back, feeling frozen inside. "Let's go," she said, and turned to start swimming east-northeast again, their original course. "The Gray is waiting, isn't she?"

By the sound of her way-song Nita could hear S'reee and Kit and Hotshot following after her; and last of all, silent, songless, came Ed.

I'm going to die, Nita thought.

She had thought that before, occasionally. But she had never believed it. She didn't believe it now.

And she knew it was going to happen anyway.

Evidently, Nita thought, Ed had been right when he'd said that belief made no difference to the truth. . . .

The Gray Lord's Song

They found the whale who would sing the part of the Gray in the chill waters about Old Man Shoals, a gloomy place strewn full of boulders above which turbulent water howled and thundered. The current set swift through the shoals, and the remnants of its victims lay everywhere. Old splintered spars of rotting masts, fragments of crumbled planks, bits of rusted iron covered with barnacles or twined about with anemones; here and there a human bone, crusted over with coral— Broken-backed ships lay all about, strangled in weed, ominous shapes in the murk; and when Nita and Kit and the others sang to find their way, the songs fell into the silence with a wet, thick, troubled sound utterly unlike the clear echoes that came back from the sandy bottoms off Long Island.

The place suited Nita's mood perfectly. She swam low among the corpses of dead ships, thinking bitter thoughts—most of them centering on her own stupidity.

They warned me. *Everybody* warned me! Even Picchu warned me: "Read the fine print before you sign!" Idiot! she thought bitterly. What do I do now? I don't want to die!

But "Any agreements you make, make sure you keep," Tom had said—and though his voice had been kind, it had also been stern. As stern as the Blue's "Nowhere does the Lone Power enter in so readily as through the broken word."

She could see what she was expected to do . . . and it was impossible. can't die—I'm too young, what would Kit say to Mom and Dad, I don't want to, it's not fair! But the answer stayed the same nonetheless.

She groaned out loud. Two days. Two days left. Two days is a long time Maybe something will happen and I won't have to die.

"Stop that sniveling noise!" came a sharp, angry burst of song, from pract

cally in front of her. Nita backfinned, shocked at the great bulk rising up
from the bottom before her. The echoes of her surprised squeak came back
raggedly, speaking of old scars, torn fins and flukes, skin ripped and gouged
and badly healed. And the other's song had an undercurrent of rage to it that
hit Nita like a deep dive into water so cold it burned.

"How dare you come into my grounds without protocol?" said the new
whale as she cruised toward Nita with a slow deliberateness that made Nita
back away even faster than before. The great head and lack of a dorsal fin
made it plain that this was another sperm whale.

"Your pardon," Nita sang hurriedly, sounding as conciliatory as possible. "I
didn't mean to intrude—"

"You have," said the sperm, in a scraping phrase perilously close to the
awful sperm-whale battlecry that Nita had heard from Kit. She kept advanc-
ing on Nita, and Nita kept backing, her eye on those sharp teeth. "These are
my waters, and I won't have some noisy krill-eating songster scaring my
food—"

That voice was not only angry, it was cruel. Nita started to get angry at the
sound of it. She stopped backing up and held her ground, poising her tail for
a short rush to ram the other if necessary. "I'm not interested in your fish,
even if they could hear me, which they can't—and you know it!" she sang
angrily. "Humpbacks sing higher than fish can hear—the same as you do!"

The sperm kept coming, showing more teeth. "You look like a whale," she
said, voice lowering suspiciously, "and you sing like a whale—but you don't
sound like a whale. Who are you?"

"HNii't," Nita said, giving her name the humpback accent. "I'm a wizard.
A human wizard—"

The sperm whale cried out and rushed at her, jaws wide. Nita arrowed off
to one side, easily avoiding the sperm's rush. "Spy! Murderer!" The sperm
was howling, a terrible rasping song like a scream. It came at her again—

Again Nita rolled out of the way, her maneuverability easily defeating the
other's rage-blinded charge. "I may be a human," she sang angrily, "but I'm
still a wizard! Mess with me and I'll—"

WHAM! The sperm whale's spell hit her with an impact that made the
displaced-water explosions of Kit's shapechanges seem puny. Nita was thrown
backward, literally head over tail, thrashing and struggling for control as she
swore at herself for being caught off guard. The spell was a simple physical-
violence wizardry, as contemptuous a gesture from one wizard to another as a
slap in the face . . . and as much a challenge to battle as such a slap would
have been from one human to another.

Nita went hot with rage, felt about for her inner contact with the Sea,
found it, and sang—only three notes, but pitched and prolonged with exqui-
site accuracy to take the power of the other's spell and turn it back on her

tenfold. The spell and the water thundered together. The sperm whale was blown backward as Nita had been, but with more force, tumbling violently and trailing a song of shock and rage behind her.

Nita held still, shaking with anger, while S'reee and Hotshot and Kit gathered around her. "I'm all right," she said, the trembling getting into her song. "But that one needs some lessons in manners."

"She always has," S'reee said. "HNii't, I'm sorry. I would have kept you back with us, but—" She didn't go on.

"It's all right," Nita said, still shaking.

"Nice shot," said a low scrape of song beside her ear, angry and appreciative: Kit. She brushed him lightly with one flank as a great pale shape came drifting down on the other side of her, eyeing her with dark-eyed interest.

"So," Ed said, calm as ever, "the Sprat has teeth after all. I am impressed."

"Thanks," Nita said, not up to much more conversation with Ed at the moment.

Slowly they swam forward together to where S'reee was hovering in the water, singing more at than with the other whale. "—know you were out of bounds, Areinnye," she said. "There was no breach of protocol. We came in singing."

"That one did not," said the sperm whale, her song so sharp with anger that it was a torture to the ears. "My right—"

"—does not extend to attacking a silent member of a party entering your waters within protocols," S'reee said. "You attacked hNii't out of spite, nothing more. First spite, then anger because she was human. We heard—"

"Did you indeed? And what else have you heard in these waters, you nursling wizard, you and your little playfellows?" The sperm whale glared at them all as they gathered around her, and the rasp of pain and hatred in her voice was terrible. "Have you seen my calf hereabouts? For all your magics, I think not. The whalers have been through these waters three days ago, and they served my little M'hali as they served your precious Ae'mhnuu! Speared and left to float belly-up, slowly dying, while they hunted me—then hauled bloated out of the water and gutted, his bleeding innards thrown overboard by bits and pieces for the gulls and the sharks to eat!"

When S'reee spoke again, her voice was unhappy. "Areinnye, I share your grief. It's things like this that the Song will help to stop. That's why we're here."

The sperm whale laughed, a sound both anguished and cruel. "What lies," she said. "Or what delusions. Do you truly think *anything* will make them go away and stop hunting us, S'reee?" Areinnye looked with hatred at Nita. "Now they're even coming into the water after us, I see."

Kit glided forward ever so slowly, until he was squarely between Nita and Areinnye. "I guarantee you don't know what she's here for, Areinnye. Preserving your life, along with those of a lot of others—though at the moment, in *your* case, I can't imagine why anyone would bother."

Areinnye made a sound at Kit that was the sperm-whale equivalent of a sneer. "Oh, indeed," Areinnye said. "What could she possibly do that would make any difference to my life?"

"She is the Silent Lord for the Song," S'reee said.

Areinnye turned that scornful regard on Nita. "Indeed," the sperm said again. "Well. We are finally getting something useful out of a human. But she doubtless had to be compelled to it. No human would ever give up its life for one of us, wizard or not. Or did you trick her into it?"

Gently, hardly stroking a fin, Ed soared toward Areinnye. "Unwise," he said. "Most unwise, wizard, to scorn a fellow wizard so—whatever species she may belong to. And will you hold Nita responsible for all her species' wrongdoing, then? If you do that, Areinnye, I would feel no qualms about holding you responsible for various hurts done my people by yours over the years. Nor would I feel any guilt over taking payment for those hurts out of your hide, *now*."

Areinnye turned her back on Ed and swam away, as if not caring what he said. "You take strange sides, Slayer," the sperm said at last, cold-voiced. "The humans hunt those of your Mastery as relentlessly as they hunt us."

"I take no sides, Areinnye," Ed said, still following her. "Not with whales, or fish, or humans, or any other Power in the Sea or above it. Wizard that you are, you should know that." He was beginning to circle her now. "And if I sing this Song, it is for the same reason that I have sung a hundred others: for the sake of my Mastery—and because I am pleased to sing. You had best put your distress aside and deal with the business we have come to discuss, lest something worse befall you."

Areinnye turned slowly back toward the group. "Well, if you've come to administer me the Oath," Areinnye said to S'reee, "you might as well get on with it. I was in the midst of hunting when you interrupted me."

"Softly," S'reee said. "Your power is a byword all throughout these parts; I want it in the Song. But we're not so short of wizards that I'll include one who'll bring the High and Dry down on us. Choose, and tell me whether you can truthfully sing and leave your anger behind."

Areinnye cruised slowly through the group, making no sound but the small ticking noises the sperm uses to navigate. "Seeing that the human who sings with us sings for the Sea's sake," she said at last, in that tight, flat voice, "I am content. But my heart is bitter in me for my calf's loss, and I cannot forget that easily. Let the humans remember that, and keep their distance."

"If that is well for you two—" Kit and Nita both flicked tails in agreement. "Well enough, then," said S'reee. "Areinnye t'Hwio-dheii, those who gather to sing that Song that is the Sea's shame and the Sea's glory desire you to be of their company. Say, for my hearing, whether you consent to that Song."

"I consent . . ." Areinnye sang her way through the responses with slow care, and Nita began to relax slightly. The sperm's voice was beautiful, as pleasant as Kit's, when she wasn't angry. Yet she couldn't help but catch a couple of Areinnye's glances at Ed—as if she knew that she was being watched for her responses and would be watched in the future.

Then the third Question was asked, and Areinnye's song scaled up in the high notes of final affirmation, a sound of tearing, chilly beauty. "Let me wander forever amid the broken and the lost, sooner than I shall refuse the Song," Areinnye sang, "or what it brings about for the good of those who live." But there was a faint note of scorn in the last phrase, as if the singer already counted herself among the lost and broken; and the notes on "those who live" twisted down the scale into a bitter diminuendo of pain that said life was a curse.

Now it was S'reee's turn to look dubious; but it was too late.

"Well," the sperm said, "when is the Foregathering? And where?"

"Tomorrow dawn," said S'reee, "in the waters off the Hook. Will you be on time?"

"Yes," Areinnye said. "So farewell." And she turned tail and swam off.

Kit flicked a glance at Ed and said quietly to Nita, "Boy, *that* was a close one. If those two got started fighting. . . ."

"It would not be anything like 'close,'" Ed said.

"Okay, great," Kit said in mild annoyance, "she couldn't kill you. But isn't it just possible she might hurt you a little?"

"She would regret it if she did," Ed said. "Blood in the water will call in some sharks, true. But their *Master's* blood in the water will call them all in, whether they smell it or not . . . every shark for thousands of lengths around. That is *my* magic, you see. And whatever the Master-Shark might be fighting when his people arrived would shortly not be there at all, except as rags and scraps for fingerlings to eat."

Nita and Kit and S'reee looked at each other.

"Why do we need Areinnye in the first place?" Nita said to S'reee. "Is she really that good a wizard?"

Turning, S'reee began to swim back the way they had come, through the now-darkening water. Hotshot paced her; and silently, pale in the dimness, Ed brought up the rear. "Yes," S'reee said. "In fact, by rights, she should have been Ae'mhnuu's apprentice, not I."

Kit looked at her in surprise. "Why wasn't she?"

S'reee made a little moan of annoyance. "I don't know," she said. "Areinnye is a much more powerful wizard than I am—even Ae'mhnuu agreed with me about that. Yet he refused her request to study with him, not just once but several times. And now this business with her calf—" S'reee blew a few huge bubbles out her blowhole, making an unsettled noise. "Well, we'll make it work out."

"That shall yet be seen," Ed said from behind them.

The Moon was high when Nita and Kit came out of the water close to the jetty and went looking for their clothes. Kit spent a while gazing longingly up at the silver-golden disc, while Nita dressed. "We're really gonna get killed now, aren't we?" he said, so quietly that Nita could hardly hear him.

"Uh-huh." Nita sat down on the sand and stared out at the waves while Kit went hunting for his bathing suit and windbreaker.

"Whaddaya think they'll do?" Kit said.

Nita shook her head. "No idea."

Kit came up beside her, adjusting his windbreaker. "You think they're gonna send me home?"

"They might," she said.

They toiled up the last dune before home and looked down toward the little rough road that ran past the house. All the upstairs lights were on. The downstairs ones were dark; evidently Dairine had been sent to bed.

"Neets—" Kit said. "What're *you* gonna do?"

"I'm sworn, Kit. I'm in the Song. I have to be there."

"You mean you're going to—"

"Don't," she said, in genuine pain. She didn't want him to say it, to think it, any more than she wanted to think it herself. And to tell the absolute truth, she wasn't sure of what she was going to do about the Song yet.

"They don't need me for the Song," Kit said.

"It doesn't look that way."

"Yeah." He was quiet a moment. "Look—if somehow I can get you off the hook, get your folks to think this is all my fault somehow, so that you can still go out. . . ."

"No," Nita said, scandalized. "Anyway, they'd never buy it. I promised my mom I'd be back on time last time—and blew it. Then I snuck out today. They know it's me as much as you. I'm just gonna have to face the music."

"With what?" Kit said.

"I don't know." The thought of treating her parents as enemies made her feel as if the bottom had fallen out of the Universe.

The one good thing, she thought, is that by tomorrow, tonight will be over.

I hope.

"C'mon," she said. Together they went home.

The house was deadly still when they stepped in, and the screen door closing behind them seemed loud enough to be heard for miles around. The kitchen was dark; light flowed into it from the living room, the subdued illumination of a couple of table lamps. There was no sound of TV, even though Nita knew her dad's passion for late movies; no music, despite her mom's fondness for classics and symphonic rock at any hour of day or night.

Nita's mouth felt dry as beach sand. She stopped where she was, tried to swallow, looked at Kit. He looked back, punched her lightly in the arm, then pushed past her and walked into the living room.

For the rest of her life, Nita thought, she would remember the way that room looked and felt when she walked in. The living room needed a new paint job, its rug was threadbare in places, and the walls were hung with bargain-basement seascapes, wide-eyed children of almost terminal cuteness, and, in one corner, something her dad called the Piece of Resistance—a garish matador done in day-glow paint on black velvet.

Her mother and father were sitting side by side on the Coca-Cola–colored couch, their backs straight. They looked up as Nita and Kit came through the door, and Nita saw her mother's face tight with fear and her father's closed like a door. They had been reading magazines; they put them aside, and the usually friendly room suddenly looked dingy as a prison, and the matador hurt Nita's eyes.

"Sit down," her father said. His voice, quiet, calm, sounded too much like Ed's. She managed to hold onto her composure as she headed for Dairine's favorite chair and sat down quickly.

"Pretty slick," said her father. "My daughter appears to have a great future in breaking and entering. Or breaking and departing."

Nita opened her mouth and shut it again. She could have dealt with a good scolding . . . but this chilly sarcasm terrified her. And there was no way out of it.

"Well?" her father said. "You'd better start coming up with some answers, young lady. You too," he said to Kit, his eyes flashing; and at the sight of the anger, Nita felt a wash of relief. That look was normal. "Because what you two say is going to determine whether we send you straight home tomorrow morning, Kit—and whether we let you and Nita see any more of each other."

Kit looked her father straight in the eye and said nothing.

Sperm whales! Nita thought, and it was nearly a curse. But then she took the thought back as she realized that Kit was waiting for her to say something first, to give him a lead. Great! Now all I have to do is *do* something!

What do I do?

"Kit," her father said, "I warn you, I'm in no mood for Latin gallantry and the whole protect-the-lady business. You were entrusted to my care and want answers. Your parents are going to hear about this in any case—what you say, or don't say, is going to determine what I tell them. So be advised."

"I understand," Kit said. Then he glanced at Nita. "Neets?"

Nita shook her head ever so slightly, amazed as always by that frightened bravery that would wait for her to make a move, then back her utterly. It had nothing to do with the whalesark. *Kit,* Nita thought, practically trembling with the force of what she felt, *you're incredible! But I don't have your guts—and I have to do something!*

Her mother and father were looking at her, waiting.

Oh, Lord, Nita thought then, and bowed her head and put one hand over her face, for she suddenly knew what to do.

She looked up. "Mom," she said—and then had to start over, for the word came out in a kind of strangled squeak. "Mom, you remember when we were talking the other day? And you said you wanted to know why we were staying out so much, because you thought something besides 'nothing' was going on?"

Her mother nodded, frozen-faced.

"Uh, well, there was," Nita said, not sure where to go from there. Two months of wizardry, spells wrought and strange places visited and wonders seen—how to explain it all to nonwizards? Especially when they might not be able to see wizardry done right under their eyes—and in the past hadn't? Never mind that, Nita told herself desperately. If you think too much, you'll get cold feet. Just talk.

Her mother was wearing a ready-to-hear-the-worst expression. "No, not *that,*" Nita said, feeling downright cross that her mother was still thinking along *those* idiotic lines. "But this is going to take a while."

Nita swallowed hard. "You remember in the spring," she said, "that day Kit and I went into the city—and that night, the Sun went out?"

Her parents stared at her, still angry, and now slightly perplexed too.

"We had something to do with that," Nita said.

Truthsong

And Nita began to tell them. By the time she saw from their faces just how crazy the story must be sounding, it was already much too late for her to stop.

She told them the story from the beginning—the day she had her hand snagged by an innocent-looking library book full of instructions for wizardry —to the end of her first great trial, and Kit's, that terrible night when the forces of darkness got loose in Manhattan and would have turned first the city and then the world into a place bound in eternal night and cold, except for what she and Kit did. She told them about Advisory and Senior wizards, though she didn't mention Tom and Carl; about places past the world where there was nothing but night, and about the place past life where there was nothing but day.

Not once did her parents say a word.

Mostly Kit kept quiet, except when Nita's memory about something specific failed; then he spoke up and filled in the gap, and she went on again. The look on her father's face was approaching anger again, and her mother was well into complete consternation, by the time Nita started telling them about the dolphin who nudged her in the back, the whale she and Kit found on the beach, and the story the whale had told them. She told them a little— very little, fearing for her own composure—about the Song of the Twelve and what she was going to be doing in it.

And then, not knowing what else to say, she stopped.

Her mother and father looked at each other.

Our daughter, the look said, is going to have to be hospitalized. She's sick.

Nita's mother finally turned to her. Her dad had bowed his head about a third of the way through the story, and except for that glance at her mother seemed unable to do anything but sit with his hands clasped tightly together. But her mother's face was stricken.

"Nita," she said, very gently—but her voice was shaking like the tightly clasped hands of the man beside her, "you don't have to make up stories like this to keep us from being angry with you."

Nita's mouth fell open. "Mom," she said, "are you trying to say you don't believe me?"

"Nita," her father said. His eyes were haunted, and his attempt to keep his voice sounding normal was failing miserably. "Give us a break. How are we supposed to believe a crazy story like this? Maybe you've got Kit believing it—" He broke off, as if wanting to find a way to explain all this, something reasonable. "I guess it's understandable, he's younger than you. . . ."

Nita glanced over at Kit for the first time in a while and gulped. His annoyed look brought the sperm-whale battlecry scraping through her memories again.

"*I'll* tell you how you're supposed to believe it," Kit said.

Nita's mother and father looked at him.

Kit was suddenly sitting a little taller in the chair. And taller still, though he didn't move a muscle. And taller—until Nita could see that Kit's seat and the seat of the chair no longer had much to do with each other. He was hovering about two feet in the air.

"Like *this*," Kit said.

Holding her breath, Nita looked from Kit to her parents.

They stared at Kit, their faces absolutely unmoved, as if waiting for something. Kit glanced over at Nita, shrugged, and kept floating up until he was sitting six feet or so above the floor. "Well?" he said.

They didn't move a muscle.

"Harry—" Nita's mother said, then, after what seemed forever.

He didn't say a thing.

"Harry," her mother said, "I hate to admit it, but I think all this has gotten to me. . . ."

Nita's father simply kept looking at the chair.

Then, ever so slowly, he leaned his head back and looked up at Kit.

"Hypnosis," Nita's father said.

"Bull!" Kit said. "When did I hypnotize you?"

Nita's father didn't say anything.

"I haven't said a thing," Kit said. "If I hypnotized you without lights or words or anything, that's a pretty good trick, isn't it? You two better talk to each other and see if you're seeing the same thing. If you aren't, maybe I *did* hypnotize you. But if you *are*—"

Nita's mother and father looked away from Kit with some effort.

"Betty . . ." said Nita's father.

Neither of them said anything further for a few seconds.

"Harry," her mother said at last, "if I told you that I saw . . . saw

Kit . . ." She stopped and swallowed. Then she started again, and the same feeling that had shaken Nita earlier about Kit took hold of her and shook her about her mother. Evidently bravery came in odd forms, and out of unexpected places. "If I told you that I saw Kit not sitting in the chair any more," her mother said, all at once and in a rush. Then her voice gave out on her.

"Above it," her dad said. And that was all he could manage.

They stared at each other.

"You got it," Kit said.

Nita's dad broke away from looking at her mother and glared at Nita instead. "Hypnosis," her father said. "There's no other explanation."

"Yes, there *is!*" Nita hollered at him, waving her arms in frustration, "but you don't want to admit it!"

"Nita," her mother said.

"Sorry," Nita said. "Look, Kit . . . this isn't going to do it. We need something more impressive." She got up. "Come on," she said. "Outside. It's my turn."

Nita yanked the front door open and ran outside, up the dune and down its far side toward the beach. There was a long pause before she heard the sound of footsteps following her down the wooden stairs. Shock, she thought, feeling both pity and amusement. If only there was some easier way! But there wasn't. . . . She made it down to the beach, picked the spot she wanted, then stood and waited for them to arrive.

First her mother, then her father, came clambering up the dune and slid down its far side, to stand on the beach and stare up and down it, looking for her. Then Kit appeared beside them in a small clap of air that startled her mother so badly she jumped. Her father stared.

"Sorry," Kit said, "I should have warned you." He was still sitting crosslegged in the air, and Nita noticed that he didn't sound very sorry either.

"Oh, Lord," said Nita's father at the sight of Kit, and then turned resolutely away. "All right. Where's Nita?"

"Over here, Daddy," Nita called from where she was standing on the water, just past the line of the breakers.

He stared at Nita. So did Nita's mother, who slowly went to stand beside her husband. Her voice was shaking as she said, "Harry, it could be that my eyes are just going. . . ."

"Mom," Nita shouted, "give me a break; you both went to the eye doctor last month and you were fine!" She bounced up and down on the water several times, then took a few long strides to the west, turned, and came back. "Admit it! You see me walking on water! Well, surprise: I *am* walking on water! Get it! It's like I told you: I'm a wizard!"

"Nita," her father said, "uh, walking on water is, uh—"

"I know," she said. "I wouldn't want to overdo it. It makes my legs hurt.'

Nita trotted back in to shore, taking a last hop onto the curl of a flattening breaker and letting it push her up onto the beach and strand her there, a few feet in front of them.

Kit uncrossed his legs, got his feet back on the ground, and came to stand beside her. "So what else would you like to see?" he said.

Her parents looked at each other, then down at the two of them. "Look, Kit, Nita," her father said unhappily, "it's not a question of what we'd like to see. At this point I'm sure you two could get us to 'see' anything you wanted to . . . heaven knows how. But that's not the point. This can't be—none of this is *real!*"

"Wanna bet?" Kit said softly. "Neets, this is gonna call for drastic measures."

"I think you're right. Well, let's see what the manual says about this. Book, please," she said, thinking the six words of a spell she knew by heart and putting her hand out. Another small clap of air, about as noisy as a cap going off, and her wizard's manual dropped into her hand. Her mother goggled. Nita opened the manual and began browsing through it. "Let's see. . . ."

"You two just stop making things pop in and out for a moment, and listen to me," Nita's mother said all of a sudden. "Nita, I want to know where this power came from! You two haven't made a pact with, with—"

Nita thought of her last encounter with the Lone Power and burst out laughing. "Oh, Mom! Kit and I are the *last* people *that* One wants anything to do with."

Her mother looked nonplussed. "Well, that's—never mind, you'll tell me about that some other time. But, honey, why, why?"

"You mean, 'Why are there wizards?' Or 'Why are *we* wizards?'" Nita said. "Or do you really mean 'What's in it for us?'"

"Yes," her mother said, sounding lost.

Nita and Kit looked at each other, and Kit shook his head. "We're never gonna be able to explain this," he said.

She agreed with him. "Only one thing we can do, I guess," Nita said, musing.

"Show them?"

Nita looked at Kit, and for the first time in what seemed days, a smile began to grow. "Remember that place we went a week and a half ago?" she said. "The one with the great view?"

"I'll get my book," he said, grinning back, "and the string."

"Don't forget the chip!" Nita said, but Kit had already gone out, *bang!* just like a candle, and Nita was talking to empty air. She turned to her mother and father. "He went to get some supplies," she said. "Most wizardry you need things for—raw materials, kind of."

"Fine, honey," her mother said, "but does he have to keep appearing an disappearing like that?"

"It's faster than walking," Nita said. "And we haven't got all night. H and I are going to have to be out early again tomorrow morning—"

"Nita!" said her father.

She went to him and put her arms around him. "Please, Dad," she sai "let it be for a little while. We told you why. But you have to feel this first. won't make sense unless you do. In fact, it may never make sense. Just tru me!"

Kit popped back out of nothing, making Nita's mother jump again. "Sorr Mrs. Callahan," he said. "It's fun, that's all. It's a 'beam-me-up-Scotty' spel So's this one we're going to do. Just a little more involved." He dropped th necessary supplies on the sand—a small coil of cord, an old silicon chi salvaged from a broken pocket calculator, a gray stone. Then he started goin through his own manual.

Nita looked down at the stone Kit had brought. "Good idea," she sai "Shorthand, huh?"

"It remembers the way. Should save some work. Good thing, too . . we've got two more sets of variables this time. Get the figures for me, wi you?"

"Right." Nita held out her book a bit as she went through it, so that he mother and father could look over her shoulder. "See, Mom? Dad? It's jus an instruction manual, like I said."

"I can't read it," her father said, staring at the graceful strokes of th written form of the Speech. "What is it, Arabic?"

"No," she said. "No Earthly language. At least, not strictly Earthly. A lo of the forces we work with don't have names in any language on Earth—c they only have vague ones. You can't be vague about magic."

"Good way to get killed," Kit said from where he knelt in the sand scribbling with a stick and sounding cheerful. "Mr. Callahan, Mrs. Callahan don't step on any of these things I'm writing in the sand, or we'll all be in bi trouble. Mrs. Callahan, what's your birthday?"

"April twenty-eighth," said Nita's mother.

"Mr. Callahan?"

"July seventh," said Nita's father.

"Neets, how big a circle?"

"Half a second," Nita said. "Brighter," she said to her manual. Its page began to glow softly in the dark. "Okay, here we are. Four of us . . . about cubic foot of air for each breath. Allow for excitement—say thirty breaths minute. Times four. . . ." She turned to another page. "Start," she said, an heard over her shoulder her mother's quick intake of breath as the page Nit had opened to abruptly went blank. "Print one two zero times four." A set o

haracters appeared. "Okay, print four eight zero times twenty. . . . Good.
rint nine six zero zero divided by three. . . . Great. Cubic meters . . .
hh . . . Oh, crap. Kit, what's the volume of a cylinder again?"

"V equals pi times r squared times the height."

"That's it. Now how did I do this before?" Nita chewed her lip a little,
hinking. "Okay," she said to the book, "print three point one four one seven
mes, uh, three zero." A figure flickered at her. "No, that is not a number,"
he said to the book. "Times three zero, and don't get cute with me. . . .
)kay. Print square root parenthesis three two zero zero divided by nine four
oint two five one close parentheses. Great. End. Kit? Make it thirty-six feet
ide."

"Got it," Kit said. "Mrs. Callahan, would you stand on this string, please?
nd whatever happens, don't go near the edge of the circle after I close it."
Ie started to walk around them all, using Mrs. Callahan and the long knot-
:d string as a compass. "Neets? Come check your name. And theirs; they
an't do it—"

She stepped over to the circle and made sure that the Speech-characters
escribing herself and her parents were correct, then glanced over Kit's too
or safety's sake. Everything was in order. Kit finished the circle he was
aaking in the sand, closed it with the figure-eight design called a wizard's
not, and stood up. "All set," Nita said.

"Then let's go." He opened his book; Nita went looking for the page in
ers on which the spell was written. "It's a 'read' spell," Nita said to her
other and father. "That means it's going to be a few moments before it
kes. Don't say anything, no matter what you feel or see or hear. Don't
ove, either."

"You might want to hang on to each other," Kit said. Nita gave him a wry
rin; there had been occasions in the past when the two of them, terrified out
f their wits, had done just that. "Ready?"

"Go ahead," said Nita's father, and reached out and pulled Nita's mother
ose.

Nita and Kit looked at each other and began slowly to read out loud. The
range, listening stillness of a working spell began to settle in around the four
f them, becoming more pronounced with every word of the Speech, as the
niverse in that area waited to hear what would be required of it. The wind
ropped, the sound of the surf grew softer, even the breakers in the area
ecame gentler, flatter, their hiss fading to a bare whisper. . . .

The sense of expectation, of anticipation, of impatient, overwhelming *po-
ntial* grew all around them as the silence grew . . . slowly undergoing a
ansformation into a blend of delight and terror and power that could be
reathed like air, or seen as a shading now inhabiting every color, a presence
habiting every shape.

Nita raised her voice into the stillness unafraid, speaking the words of th spell formula, barely needing to look at her book. The magic was rising i her, pouring through her with dangerous power. But with the sureness c practice she rode the danger, knowing the wonder to which it would brin her, reveling in her defiance of her fear. And in more than that: for Kit wa across the circle from her, eyes on hers, matching her word for word an power for power—peer and friend and fellow-wizard, afraid as she was, an still willing to dare, for the delight of what lay on the other side of th magic—

Almost through, Nita thought, exulting. Her words and Kit's wound abou one another, wove together, binding the spell tighter around the circle– squeezing air in, squeezing power in, pushing inward with such force that th circle and its contents had no choice but to be somewhere else than the were.

Almost—Nita matched her words to Kit's with a laugh in her voice, rusl ing him, finding that she *couldn't* rush him because he had already matche pace to keep up with her— She laughed at being anticipated so. Faster an faster they went, like two kids seeing who could say the Pledge of Allegianc faster, as all around them the silence began to sing with inturned power, th air shimmered and rang with force like a gong ringing backward, soft at firs then louder, though without sound, without breaking that silence—a hiss, murmur, an outcry of something about to happen, a shout of inner voices, silent thunderclap. And the last not-sound, so loud it unmade the worl around them and struck them deaf and blind—

Then true silence again, with darkness above and whiteness below—b not the same darkness or whiteness as on the beach.

"We're here," Nita whispered. "Mom, Dad, have a look around. Don't g near the edges of the circle."

"Be careful how you move," Kit said. "You only weigh a sixth of what yo usually do. If your muscles overreact you could bounce right out of the circl I almost did, first time."

Nita watched her mother and father stare around them. She swallowed– partly out of reflex, for her ears were ringing in the silence that surrounde them now. That was to be expected; this stillness was more total than an thing experienced on Earth. Her other reason for swallowing was more prac tical. The sudden transfer to one-sixth gravity tended to upset your stomac unless you were used to it.

Her father was staring at the ground, which had changed from wet beac sand to a mixture of grayish gravel and pebbles, and rocks the size of fists c melons, all covered with a gray-white dust as fine as talc. But Nita's mothe was staring up at the sky with a look of joy so great it was pain—the com pletely bearable anguish of an impossible dream that suddenly comes tru after years of hopeless yearning. Tears were running down her mother's face at the sight of that sky, so pure a velvet black that the eye insisted on finding light in it where light was not—a night sky set with thousands of stars, all blazing with a cold fierce brilliance that only astronauts ever saw; a night sky that nonetheless had a ravening sun standing noonday high in it, pooling all their shadows black and razor-sharp about their feet.

Nita was blinking hard herself to manage the stinging of her eyes; she knew how her mother felt. "Over there, Mom," she said very quietly. "Off to the left. Look."

"Off to the left" was a steep slope that plunged down and down to a deep chasm, filled with absolute blackness ungentled by the presence of air. On the far side of the chasm stretched a flat, rocky plain that seemed to stop too soon, running up against a horizon abnormally close. Out on the plain, not too far away, a dazzling squarish glow of gold sat on four spidery legs. Some thirty yards from the bright platform on legs stood a silvery pole with an American flag standing out from it, held straight by a rod running through the top of it: a necessity—for here where it stood, no wind would ever stir it.

"No," Nita's father said, his voice hushed. "Impossible. Tranquillity Base—"

"No," Kit said, his voice soft too. "That's going to be a tourist attraction in a few years, when they build the Hilton there—so we don't go down there for fear of leaving footprints where somebody might find them. This is from *Apollo 16.* See over there?" He pointed past the abandoned first-stage platform of the LEM *Orion* at the first Lunar Rover, which sat parked neatly beside a boulder—a delicate-looking little dunebuggy, still in excellent condition, used only once by a couple of astronauts from Pasadena for jaunts to Stone Mountain, on which the four of them stood.

Nita's father slowly went down on one knee and brushed his hand along the dry, pale lunar soil, turning over the stones that lay there, then picking one up and clutching it hard in his fist.

"Harry," Nita's mother said, still looking up. The tone of her voice made her husband look up too—and seeing what she saw, he forgot the rock.

What they saw was part of a disk four times the size of the Moon as seen from the Earth; and it seemed even bigger because of the Moon's foreshortened horizon. It was not the full Earth so familiar from pictures, but a waning crescent, streaked with cloud swirls and burning with a fierce green-blue radiance—a light with depth, like the fire held in the heart of an opal. That light banished the idea that blue and green were "cool" colors; one could have warmed one's hands at that crescent. The blackness to which it shaded was ever so faintly touched with silver—a disk more hinted at than seen; the new Earth in the old Earth's arms.

"There'll be a time," Nita said softly, "when any time someone's elected to a public office—before they let them start work—they'll bring whoever was elected up here and just make them look at that until they get what it means. . . ."

Kit nodded. "You wanted to know where the power came from," he said to Nita's mother and father. "The grownups who're wizards tell us that whatever made *that* made the power too. It's all of a piece."

" 'The *grownups* who're wizards'?"

"And as for 'why,' " Kit said, *"that's* why." There was no need for him to point to "that." "Not just for the—for what you felt on the way in. That's part of it. But because somebody's gotta take care of *that*. Not just part of it —not just one country, or one set of rules, or one species, at the expense of the others. But everything that lives, all the kinds of 'people.' *All* of it, with nothing left out. One whole planet. Somebody's got to make sure it grows as well as it can. Or just that it survives. That's what wizards do."

"Daddy," Nita said, "it's like you always say. If you don't do it yourself, it may not get done right. And we can't afford to let *that* get screwed up. We have to live there. So will other people, later."

Her father shook his head, confused. "Nita," he said, sounding unsure, "you're too young to be thinking about this kind of thing."

She bit her lip. "Dad—that sort of thinking might be one of the reasons why things aren't working so well back there. . . ."

"Neets," Kit said, "we have to get back. We're losing heat pretty fast."

"Mom, Dad," Nita said, "we can come back some other time. It's late, and Kit and I have an early day tomorrow. Got the rock?" she said to Kit.

"Uh-huh. Ready?"

Nita's mother reached out and pulled her husband close this time. "Is it going to be like it was before?"

"Huh? No. It just takes a lot of effort to push all this air up out of Earth's gravity well, that's all. You have to reach escape velocity—"

Nita's father blinked. "Wait a minute. I thought this was—magic." He said the word as if for the first time in his life.

Nita shrugged. "Even with magic," she said, "you have to obey the rules. Downhill is a lot easier than uphill in a wizardry, same as anywhere else. Kit?"

"Ready," he said. They looked at each other, took a breath, and said one short word in unison.

WHAM!—and air and sand and water blew outward in all directions as they left noon for midnight, standing once again on the long dark beach silvered with moonlight. Kit stepped to the edge of the circle, first scuffing the wizard's knot out of existence, then going around and breaking the circle once at each compass point. "Let's go in," Nita said to her parents. "I'm dead."

The four of them trudged up the stairs to the front door, back into the living room. Her dad plopped down onto the couch and said, "Nita, wait just a few minutes. I have to ask you something."

Nita looked at him, sighed, and did as she was told. "Tell me again," her dad said, "this stuff about what you're doing underwater. Just very briefly."

It turned out to be more than briefly, since much of what Nita had told her parents had fallen out of their heads the first time, discarded in general disbelief. And it was with growing dismay that Nita watched the unease in her parents' faces, as she told them again about the undersea tremors, the pollution of the water, the slaughter of the whales—and the purposes of the Lone Power, though she tried to tell them as little about that as she could.

"Nita," her father said at last, "what are the chances that you could get hurt doing this 'Song' business? The truth."

She looked at him unhappily. "Pretty good," she said.

"And the same for Kit?" her mother said.

"Just about," Kit said.

Nita's father shook his head. "Nita. Look. I understand . . . no. I sort of understand how you and Kit feel about this. Magic. . . ." He raised his hands, dropped them again, in a helpless gesture. "If someone offered me the chance to be a magician, I'd jump at it. . . ."

"A wizard," Nita said. And, No, you wouldn't, she thought. Because if you would have, really, you would have been offered it! There are never enough wizards. . . .

But her father was still talking. "But this business . . . endangering yourself, or endangering Kit— Your mother and I can't permit it. You're going to have to bow out."

For a moment, as far as Nita was concerned, everything faded out, drowned in a great wash of relief and hope. The perfect excuse. Perfect. My mom and dad won't let me. Sorry, S'reee, Hotshot, Ed. . . .

Opaque black eyes looked at Nita out of the scene her eager mind was already constructing for her—and hope died. The hair stood up all over Nita —not from fear, but from something more terrible. Without any warning, and for the first time, she understood in her own person what had only been a word to her before: honor. I can't, she thought. For me—for *me*—it's not right.

"Dad," she said unhappily, "you didn't get it. I'm sworn to the Song. If I back out now, the whole thing will be sabotaged."

Her father got up, a sign that he intended this argument to be over shortly. "Come on, Neets. Surely someone else could do it—"

"No."

"Nita," said her mother, looking stern, "you don't understand. *We're not letting you do this*. Or Kit either, while he's under our roof. You're going to have to find a replacement. Or the—the whales will. Whoever. *You're not going.*"

I must not have said it right, they're not understanding! "Mom—" Nita said, searching frantically for words. "This isn't just some cute thing that Kit and I are doing because it'll be fun! If we don't stop the forces that are beginning to move, there are going to be massive earthquakes all up and down the East Coast. That's not a maybe. It's a *will!* You think the Island would survive something like that? The whole place is nothing but rocks and trash the glaciers dumped in the ocean; it'll break up and wash away like a sandcastle at high tide! And you think Manhattan'll survive? It's already got four unstable geological faults of its own, right through the bedrock! And none of the buildings there are earthquake-proof; one quake'll leave the place looking like somebody kicked over a pile of blocks!" Nita was waving her arms in the air now, so upset that she was beyond caring whether she looked silly or not. "Millions of people could die—"

"Could," her father said, seizing on the word. He was pacing now.

Kit shook his head. *"Will,"* he said, and there was such a weight of certainty and misery on the word that Nita's father stopped pacing, and her mother closed her mouth, and they both stared at Kit in amazement. "You're saying," Kit said, gazing at them out of eyes suddenly gone dark and fierce, "that you don't care whether ten million people, *more* than ten million people, would die, just so long as we two don't get hurt."

Nita's mother spluttered, to Nita's great satisfaction. That one had sunk in. "No, we aren't, we just—"

"You don't even care that ten million people *might* die," Nita said. "Just so Kit and I are okay, you're willing to run that risk."

"No, I—" Nita's father saw what was being done to him. "Young lady, no more out of you! Just the quakes going on off the coast now, by the reports we've heard, are too dangerous for you to be down there."

"Daddy, believe me, we've survived a lot worse!"

"Yes—and your mother and I didn't know about it then! Now we do." He father turned away. "The answer is no, and that's final!"

From many fights Nita had overheard between her folks, Nita knew tha when her dad said that, it never was. "Daddy," she said. "I'm sorry. I reall am. I love you, and I wish like anything I could do what you want. But can't."

"Nita!" There was that rage again, full-blown, worse than before. He father was on his feet, standing right over her, glaring at her. *"You will do a I tell you!"*

Hot all over, Nita shot to her feet—standing on the chair—and in shee desperation shouted right back in his face. *"Don't you get it? There are som things in the world more important than doing what you tell me!"*

Her father and mother stared at her, stunned.

"Besides," Kit said quietly from out of her range of vision, "how would you top us?"

Nita's father turned away to stare at Kit now.

"Look," Kit said. "Mr. Callahan, Mrs. Callahan—we gave our word that we'd do this." *What is this 'we'?* Nita thought, bemused. "And the wizardry we're doing is mainly directed against the One who invented the broken promise. Breaking our word will play right into Its hands and cause a lot of people to die, at best. Maybe destroy this world, sooner or later, at worst."

"But we have only your word on that!" Nita's mother said.

"Uh-huh. But isn't our word any good? And why would we lie to you about *his?* Considering that we're going through all this crap for the sake of telling you the truth."

Nita's mother closed her mouth.

"She didn't have to tell you," Kit said, sounding angry for the first time. "But it would've been lying, in a way—and Nita thinks you're worth not lying to." He paused, then said, "I do too. We may just be kids, but we're old enough to tell the truth. And to take it. Are you?"

The question wasn't a taunt: It was honestly meant. "Even if you're not, we'll still have to do what we have to," Nita said, though saying it made her unhappy. "When you two wake up in the morning, this could all seem like a dream to you—if it had to. I guess you'd better make up your minds, because we have to get some sleep or we won't be worth dead fish tomorrow."

Her parents were staring at each other. "Betty . . ." said Nita's father.

"We need more time," Nita's mother said.

"I don't think we've got it."

Her mother looked back at her father. "If they're right about this," she said, "it would be wrong of us to stop them if they want to help."

"But we're responsible for them!"

"Apparently," Nita's mother said, in a peculiar mixture of pride and pain, "they've learned that lesson better than we suspected, Harry. Because now they seem to be making themselves responsible for *us*. And a lot of other people."

"I guess there comes a time when you can't do anything but trust," her father said at last, sounding reluctant. "It just seems—so soon. . . . Nita— is all this on the level?"

"Oh, Daddy." She loved him, right then, and hurt for him, more than she could have told him. "I wish it weren't. But it is."

Nita's father was silent for several long breaths. "Millions of lives," he said under his breath.

And another silence, which he finally broke as if it were a physical thing. "When do you need to be up?"

"Sixish. I'll set my alarm, Daddy." Nita got stiffly down from the chair
aching all over. Behind her, Kit got up and brushed past her as Nita hugged
first her dad good night. Maybe the last time she would ever hug him . .
or the second-to-the-last— Oh, don't think of that now!

Her mother had caught Kit on the way past and hugged him—and now
wouldn't let Nita past without one either. She held her for a moment at
arm's length. "Thank you for—up there, baby," she said, nodding once at
the ceiling. Her eyes were wet, but she was smiling.

"It's okay, Mom. Any time." Is this what it feels like when your heart
breaks? Oh, Lord, don't let me cry.

"And thank you for trusting us."

Nita swallowed. "You taught me how," she said. And then she couldn't
stand it any more. She broke away and headed for her room, Kit right behind
her.

She knew there was one hurdle left between her and bed. Actually, the
hurdle was *on* the bed: sitting there crosslegged in the dark, looking at her
with cool interest as they came in.

"Well?" Dairine said, as Nita flopped down on her stomach beside her
and the bed bounced them both once or twice. "I saw you disappear.
Where'd'ja take them?"

"The Moon."

"Oh, come *on*, Neets."

"Dairine," Kit said from the doorway. "Catch."

Nita glanced up, saw her sister reach up and pick something out of the air,
an irregular piece of pale, grainy stone, about the size and shape of an eraser.
Dairine peered at it, rubbing it between her fingers. "What is this? Pumice?"
There was a moment of shocked silence; then Dairine's voice scaled up to an
aggrieved shriek. "You *did* go to the Moon! And you didn't take *me!* You, you
—" Apparently she couldn't find anything sufficiently dirty to call them.
"I'm gonna kill you!"

"Dari, shut up, they're in shock out there!" Nita said. This argument did
little to save her. Far more effective was Kit's wrestling Dairine down flat,
stuffing her under the bedcovers and a couple of pillows, and more or less
sitting on her until she shut up and stopped struggling.

"We'll take you next time," Nita said, and then the pain hit her again.
"Kit," she said, husky-voiced. "Remind me to see that the runt here gets to
the Moon in the near future. Next week, maybe. If she behaves."

"Right," Kit said. "You give up, runt?"

"Hwhmffm hnnoo rrhhrhn ffwmhhnhhuh," said the blankets.

"Keep talking like that and your mouth'll get stuck that way," Kit said, and
let Dairine out.

Nita's sister extricated herself from the covers with icy dignity that lasted just until she was sitting where she had been, back in control and smoothing her ruffled pajamas. "Mom 'n' Dad didn't kill you," she said to Nita.

"Nope. You gave me good advice, runt."

"Huh? What advice?"

"Last night, I suspect," Kit said. "That stuff about 'Either keep your mouth shut, or tell the truth—'"

Nita nodded, looking from Kit to Dairine, while Dairine modestly polished her nails on her Yoda pajamas. And Nita stared at her, and then started to laugh, so hard that she got the hiccups and fell over sideways, and Dairine looked at her as if she'd gone nuts, and Kit sat down and punched her once or twice, worriedly, in the shoulder. "Neets? You okay?"

"Oh, Kit," she managed to gasp at last, between bubbles of laughter. "What Picchu said—"

"Huh?"

"What Peach said. 'Do what the night tells you—'" She went off into the giggles again.

Kit looked down at her, perplexed. "You lost me."

Nita pushed herself upright, reached out and tugged a couple of times, weakly, at one of Dairine's pajama-sleeves. "'Do what the night tells you.' Not night like when it gets dark. 'Knight'! Do what the *knight* tells you! As in the Junior Jedi here—" She went over sideways again and strangled her last few whoops of laughter in a convenient pillow.

"It *was* good advice," he said to Dairine. "Thanks, Dari."

"Uh, sure," said Dairine, amazed at another compliment.

Nita sat up again after a little while, wiping her eyes. "Yeah," she said. "Even if I took it before I remembered *you* said it . . . it was good advice." She thought she would let her sister have just one more compliment—especially since it was true, and information she might never have another chance to give her. "You're gonna be one hot wizard someday," Nita said.

Dairine sat speechless.

"Neets," Kit said, "we've had a long day. And tomorrow'll be longer. I'm sacking out. Dairine—"

"Right," Nita said. She lay down again, feeling glad, afraid, excited, shaky, light—a hundred things at once. She never noticed when Dairine got off her bed; she never heard Kit leave. She fell into sleep as if into a hole.

Foregathering Song

Nita sat hunched in a miserable little bundle on the beach, her arms around her knees—staring at the bright morning sea and not seeing it.

She had gone to bed with the feeling that everything would be all right when she woke up in the morning. But she'd awakened to a pair of parents torn among insane curiosity, worry, approval, and disapproval, who drank cup after cup of coffee and stared at the lump of lunar pumice in the middle of the table, and made little sense when they talked.

She hardly knew them. Her mom and dad alternated between talking to her, hanging on every word she said, and talking over her head about her, as if she weren't there. And they kept touching her like a delicate thing that might break—though there was an undercurrent of anger in the touches that said her parents had suddenly discovered she was in some ways stronger than they were, and they didn't like it.

Nita sighed. I'd give anything for one of Dad's hugs that squeeze the air out and make you go *squeak!* she thought. Or to hear Mom do Donald Duck voices at me. But fat chance of that. . . .

She let out a long, unhappy breath. Kit was finishing his breakfast at a leisurely pace and handling endless questions about wizardry from her parents —covering for her. Just as well: She had other business to attend to before they left.

"Tom," she said, almost mourning, under her breath. She had been down to Friedman's already and had "minded the store" under Dog's watchful eye for a long time, waiting for Tom to return her call. She needed expert help, in a hurry. I've gone as far as I can on my own, she thought. I need advice! Oh Tom, *where are you?*

As she'd expected. Nothing—

The last thing she expected was the sudden explosion of air that occurred about twenty feet down the beach from her, flinging sand in all directions. No, Nita corrected herself. The *last* thing she expected was what the explosion produced: a man with one towel wrapped around his waist and another draped around his neck—tall, broad-shouldered and narrow-waisted, with dark hair and the kind of face one sees in cigarette ads, but never hopes to see smile. It was not Tom, but Carl. He looked around him, saw Nita, and came over to her in a hurry, looking grave. "What'samatter, Nita?" he said, casual as always, but concerned. "I heard that even though it wasn't meant for me."

She looked up at him wanly and tried to smile just a little; but the smile was a dismal failure. "Uh, no. Look, no one was answering the phone—and then I was just thinking—"

"That wasn't what I would call 'just' thinking," Carl said, sitting down on the sand beside her. "Sometimes I forget what kind of power wizards have when they're kids. . . ."

Nita saw that Carl's hair was wet. "I got you out of the shower," she said. "I'm sorry. . . ."

"No, I was out already. It's okay."

"Where's Tom?" Nita said.

"He has a breakfast meeting with some people at ABC; he asked me to take his calls. Not that I had much choice, in your case. . . . You've got big trouble, huh? Tell me about it."

She did. It took her a while. Though she braced herself for it, the look of shock on Carl's face when he heard about Nita's accepting the Silent Lord's part was so terrible, she started to leak tears again. Carl sat still while she finished the story.

"Do your folks know?" he said at last.

"No," Nita said. "And I don't think I'm going to tell them. I think Dad suspects—and Mom knows he does and doesn't want to talk to him about it."

Carl let out a long breath. "I don't know what to tell you," he said.

This was not the most encouraging thing Nita had ever heard. A Senior Wizard *always* knew what to tell you. "Carl," she said, tears still thick in her voice, "what can I do? I can't—I can't just die!"

It was the first time she had actually said the word out loud. It left her shaking all over like the aftermath of a particularly large wizardry, and the tears started coming again.

Carl was quiet. "Well, yeah, you can," he said at last, gently. "People do it all the time—sometimes for much less cause."

"But there must be something I could do!"

Carl looked down at the sand. "What did you *say* you were going to do?"

Nita didn't say anything; they both knew the answer very well. "You know what caused this?" Carl said.

"What?"

"Remember the blank-check sorcery you did while in the other Manhattan, that time? The open-ended request for help?"

"Uh-huh."

"That kind of spell always says that at some later date you'll be called upon to return the energy you use." Carl looked somber. "You got your help. But it must have taken a lot of energy to seal a whole piece of another space away from every other space, forever. . . ."

Nita scrubbed at her eyes, not much liking this line of reasoning. "But the spell never said anyone was going to have to die to pay back the price!"

"No. All it said was that you were going to have to pay back the exact amount of energy used up at some future date. And it must have been a very great amount, to require lifeprice to be paid. There's no higher payment that can be made." Carl fell silent a moment, then said, "Well, one." And his face shut as if a door had closed behind his eyes.

Nita put her head down on her knees again. This wasn't working the way it was supposed to. "Carl, there has to be something you, we could do—"

The surf crashed for a long time between her words and his. "Nita," Carl said finally, "no. What you absolutely do *not* want is 'something you could do.' What you really want is for me to get you off the hook somehow, so you don't have to carry through with your promise."

Her head snapped up in shock. "You mean— Carl, don't you care if I die or not?"

"I care a whole lot." The pain in Carl's voice made it plain that he did. "But unfortunately I also have to tell you the truth. That's what Seniors are for; why do you think we're given so much power to work with? We're paid for what we do—and a lot of it isn't pleasant."

"Then tell me some truth! Tell me what to do—"

"No," he said gently. "Never that. Nine-tenths of the power of wizardry comes from making up your own mind what you're going to do. The rest of it is just mechanics." Carl looked at her with a professional calm that reminded Nita of her family doctor. "What I *can* do is go over your options with you."

She nodded.

"So first—what you'd like to do. You want to break your word and not sing the Song. That'd be easy enough to do. You would simply disappear—stay on land for the next week or so and not have anything further to do with the whales with whom you've been working. That would keep you out of the Song proper; you'd be alive three days from now."

Carl looked out to sea as he spoke, nothing in his expression or his tone of voice hinting at either praise or condemnation. "There would naturally be results of that action. For one, you took the Celebrant's Oath in front of witnesses and called on the Powers of wizardry themselves to bring certain things about if you break the Oath. They will bring those things about, Nita —the Powers don't forget. You'll lose your wizardry. You'll forget that there *is* any such thing as magic in the world. Any relationships you have with other wizards will immediately collapse. You would never have met Kit, for example, or me, or Tom, except for your wizardry. So we'll cease to exist for you."

Nita held still as stone.

"There'll also be effects on the Song itself as a result of your leaving. Even if the group manages to find a replacement wizard to sing the Silent One—" Nita thought of Kit and froze. "—the Song itself will still have been sabotaged by your betrayal of your Oath. It won't be effective. The undersea tremors, the pollution and the attacks on the whales and all the rest of it will continue. Or the Lone Power will enter into the wizardry and throw it completely out of control—in which case I don't want to think of what will happen to New York and the Island, sooner or later. If all the other wizards in the area worked together, we might be able to slow it down. But not for long."

Carl took a breath. "And on top of everything else, breaking the Celebrant's Oath will also be a violation of the Wizard's Oath, your oath to assist in slowing down the death of the Universe. In your last moment as a wizard, as you lose your magic, you will *know* beyond all doubt that the Universe around you is going to die sooner because of your actions. And all through your life there'll always be something at the bottom of your heart that feels sad . . . and you'll never be able to get rid of it, or even understand it."

Nita didn't move.

"That was all the 'bad' stuff. On the 'good' side I can tell you that you probably wouldn't die of the upheavals that will start happening. What you did in Manhattan with Kit wouldn't be forgotten by the Powers either; they pay their debts. I imagine your folks would get a sudden urge to go visit some relatives out of state—something like that—and be a good distance inland when the trouble started. And after the trouble, you would go on to live what would seem a perfectly normal life . . . after all, most people think it's normal to have a nameless sorrow at the bottom of your soul. You'd grow up, and find a job, and get married, or not, and work and play and do all the other things that mortals and wizards do. And then you'd die."

Nita was silent.

"Now the second option," Carl said. "You go down there and keep your word—though you're not happy about it, to say the least. You sing the Song, and when the time comes you dive into that coral or whatever and cut yourself up, and the Master-Shark comes after you and eats you. You experience about two or three minutes of extreme pain, pain like being hit by a car or burned all over, until you go into shock, or your brain runs out of oxygen,

whichever comes first; and you die. Your parents and friends then have to
deal with the fact of your death."

Nita's tears started again.

"The 'good' side to this option," said Carl, "is that the Song will be
successfully completed, millions of people will continue to live their lives
untroubled, and the Lone Power will have suffered another severe setback.
My estimate is that It couldn't interfere in any large way with the Sea's
affairs—and, to some extent, with the land's—for some forty to fifty years
thereafter. Possibly more."

Nita nodded slowly. "So if—"

"Wait. There's a third option," Carl said.

"Huh?"

He looked at her with an expression she couldn't fully decipher. "Sing the
Song and make the Sacrifice—but do it willingly. Rather than just doing it
because you have to, to keep terrible things from happening."

"Does it make a difference?"

Carl nodded. "If you can make the Sacrifice willingly, the wizardry will
gain such power as you can barely imagine. The Lone One's power is always
based on Its desire to have Its own way in everything. Nothing undermines
Its workings faster than power turned toward having something be the way
someone *else* wants it."

Carl looked hard at her. "I have to make real sure you understand this. I'm
not talking about the sort of fakery most people mean when they talk about
'sacrifice'—none of that 'unselfishness' business, which usually has the desire
for other people to feel guilty or sad hidden at the bottom of it. No being a
'martyr.' That would sabotage a wizardry almost as badly as running out on it.
But to willingly give up one's life for the sake of the joy and well-being of
others will instantly destroy whatever power the Lone One has currently
amassed." He glanced away. "That doesn't mean you couldn't be afraid and
still have it work, by the way."

"Great," Nita said with a nervous laugh.

"The important thing is that, other times when the Sacrifice has been
made willingly, there have been fewer wars afterward, less crime, for a long
while. The Death of things, of the world as whole, has been slowed. . . ."

Nita thought of people beating and shooting and stealing from each other;
she thought of A-bombs and H-bombs, and people starving and poor—and
she thought of all that slowed down. But all those troubles and possibilities
seemed remote right now compared to her own problem, her own life. "I
don't know if I could do that," Nita said, scarcely above a whisper.

There was a long pause. "I don't know if I could either," said Carl, just as
quietly.

She sat still for a long time. "I think—"

"Don't say it," Carl said, shaking his head. "You couldn't possibly have decided already. And even if you have—" He glanced away. "You may change your mind later . . . and then you'll be saved the embarrassment of having to justify it to me."

"Later—" She looked at him in distress and confusion. "You mean you would still talk to me if I—" She stopped. "Wait a minute. If I don't do it, I won't *know* you! And if I *do* do it—"

"There's always Timeheart," Carl said softly.

Nita nodded, silent. She had been there once, in that "place" to which only wizards can find their way while still alive; that terrible and beautiful place where things that are loved are preserved, deathless, perfect, yet still growing and becoming more themselves through moment after timeless moment. "After we— After we're alive, then—"

"What's loved," Carl said, "lives."

She looked at him in a few moments' sorrowful wonder. "But sure," she said. "You're a Senior. You must go there all the time."

"No." He looked out over the sea. "In fact, the higher you're promoted, when you're a wizard, the more work you have to do—and the less time you get to spend outside this world, except on business." He breathed out and shook his head. "I haven't been to Timeheart for a long time, except in dreams. . . ."

Now it was his turn to sound wistful. Nita reached out and thumped Carl's shoulder once or twice, hesitantly.

"Yeah," Carl said. Slowly he stood up and brushed the sand off his towel, then looked down at her. "Nita," he said—and his voice was not impassive any more, "I'm sorry."

"Yeah," she said.

"Call us before you start the song, if you can, okay?" The New York accent was pronounced and raspy, as if Carl's nose were stuffed.

"Right."

He turned away, then paused and looked back at her. And everything suddenly became too much for Nita. She went to Carl in a rush, threw her arms around him at about waist height, and began to bawl. "Oh, honey," Carl said, and got down on one knee and held Nita tight, which was what she needed. But the helpless expression on his face, when she finally got some control over herself and looked up, almost hurt her more than her own pain.

After a while she pushed him away. Carl resisted her for a moment. "Nita," he said. "If you— If you do. . . ." He paused. ". . . Thank you," he finally said, looking at her hard. "Thank you. For the ten million lives that'll keep on living. They'll never know. But the wizards will . . . and they won't ever forget."

"A lot of good that'd do *me!*" Nita said, caught between desperate laughter and tears.

"Sweetheart," Carl said, "if you're in this world for comfort, you've come to the wrong place . . . whether you're wizard or just plain mortal. And if you're doing what you're doing because of the way other people will feel about it—you're *definitely* in the wrong business. What you do has to be done because of how *you'll* feel about you . . . the way you did it last night, with your folks." His voice was rueful. "There are no other rewards . . . if only because no matter what you do, no one will *ever* think the things about you that you want them to think. Not even the Powers."

"Right," Nita said again.

They let go of each other. Carl turned and walked away quickly. The air slammed itself shut behind him, and he was gone.

Nita walked back to the house.

She kept her good-byes brief. "We may be back tonight," she said to her mother and father as they stood together on the beach, "or we may not. S'reee says it'll depend on how much of the rehearsal we get finished."

"Rehearsal—" Her mother looked at her curiously.

"Uh-huh. It's like I told you," Kit said. "Everyone who sings has his own part—but there's some ensemble singing, and it has to be done right."

"Kit, we're late," Nita said. "Mom—" She grabbed her mother and hugged her hard. "Don't worry if we don't come back tonight, Mom, please," she said. "We may just go straight into the Song—and that's a day and a half by itself. Look for us Monday morning." *Us!* her mind screamed, but she ignored it. "Dad—" She turned to him, hugged him too, and saw, out of the corner of her eye, her mother hugging Kit.

Nita glanced up and down the beach. "It's all clear, Kit," she said. She shrugged out of the towel wrapped around her, leaving it with her mother, then sprinted for the water. A few fast hops over several breakers, and there was depth enough to dive and stroke out to twenty-foot water. Nita leaped into the whaleshape as if it were an escape rather than a trap from which she might never return. Once a humpback, she felt normal again—and felt a twinge of nervousness; there was something S'reee had warned her about that. . . .

No matter. Nita surfaced and blew good-bye at her mother and father, then turned for Kit, who was treading water beside her, to take her dorsal fin and be towed out to depth.

Out in the fifty-foot water Kit wrapped the whalesark about him and made the change with a swiftness that was almost savage. The sperm whale that appeared in his place had a bitter, angry look to its movements when it began to swim away from shore.

"Kit," Nita said as they went, "you okay?"

It was some time before he answered. "No," he said. "Why *should* I be? When you're going to—" He didn't finish the sentence.

"Kit, look—"

"No, *you* look. Don't you see that there's nothing I can do about all this? And I don't like it!" His song was another of the scraping sperm-whale battlecries, soft but very heartfelt, and the rage in it chattered right down Nita's skin like nails down a blackboard.

"There's not much I can do about it myself," she said, "and I don't like it either. Let's not talk about it for now, please! My brain still hurts enough from last night."

"Neets," he said, "we've got to talk about it sometime. Tomorrow's *it.*"

"Fine. Before tomorrow. Meanwhile, we've got today to worry about. Are we even going the right way?"

He laughed at her then, a painful sound. "Boy, are you preoccupied," Kit said. "Clean your ears out and listen!"

She stopped everything but the ticks and clicks a humpback uses to find its way, and listened—and was tempted to laugh herself. The sea had a racket hidden in it. From the southwest was coming an insane assortment of long, odd, wild sounds. Sweet high flutings that cut sharply through the intervening distance; clear horncalls, as if someone hunted under the waves; outerspacy whistles and warbles like the electronic cries of orbiting satellites; deep bass scrapes and rumbles, lawn-mower buzzes and halftone moans and soulful sighs. And many of those sounds, sooner or later, came back to the same main theme—a series of long wistful notes, slowly ascending into pitches too high and keen for human ears, then whispering away, lost in the quiet breathing of the water.

Nita had never heard that main theme before, but she recognized it instantly from her reading and her wizard's-sense of the Sea. It was the loss/pain/sorrow motif that ran all through the Song of the Twelve; and what she heard now, attenuated by distance but otherwise clear, was the sound of its singers, tuning up for the performance in which that mournful phrase would become not just a motif but a reality.

"Kit," Nita said with a shiver, "that's a lot more than ten whales! Who are all those other voices?"

He bubbled, a shrug. "Let's find out."

She whistled agreement and struck off after Kit, due west, away from the south shore of the island and out across the Atlantic-to-Ambrose shipping approaches once more. Song echoed more and more loudly in the sunlit shallows through which they swam; but underneath them Nita and Kit were very aware of the depths from which no echo returned—the abyss of Hudson Canyon, far below them, waiting.

"This is it," Kit said at last, practically in Nita's ear, as they came to the fringes of the area S'reee's instructions had mentioned—fifteen miles east-northeast of Barnegat, New Jersey, right over the remains of an old sunken tanker six fathoms down in the water. And floating, soaring, or slowly fluking through the diffuse green-golden radiance of the water, were the whales.

Nita had to gulp once to find her composure. Hundreds of whales had gathered and were milling about, whales of every kind—minke whales, sei whales, sperm whales, dolphins of more kinds than she knew existed, in a profusion of shapes and colors, flashing through the water; several blues, grave-voiced, gliding with huge slow grace; fin whales, hardly smaller than the blues, bowhead whales and pygmy rights and humpbacks, many of them; gray whales and pygmy sperms and narwhals with their long single spiral teeth like unicorn horns; belugas and killers and scamperdowns and bottle-nosed whales— "Kit," Nita sang, faint-voiced, "S'reee didn't tell me there were going to be *people* here!"

"Me either. I guess spectators at the rehearsal are so common, she forgot . . ." Kit sounded unconcerned.

Easy for you, Nita thought. You like crowds! She sang a few notes of sonar, trying nervously to hear some familiar shape. One shape at least Nita recognized, accompanied by the slow, calm, downscaling note of the Blue, a Aroooon passed by, a gold-tinged shadow in the background of greenness and the confusion of bodies. And there was Hotshot's high chatter, some ways off, accompanied by several other dolphin voices very like his—members of his pod.

Stillness swept over the spectators as she approached with Kit, and they recognized who she was. And a single note began to go up from them, starting at the fringes of the circle, working its way inward even to the Celebrants, until she heard even Aroooon's giant voice taking it up. One note, held in every range from the dolphins' dog-whistle trilling to the water-shaking thunder of the blues. One thought, one concept in the Speech, trumpeting through the water with such force that Nita began to shake at the sound of it. *Praise.* They knew she was the Silent One. They knew what she was going to do for them. They were thanking her.

Stunned, Nita forgot to swim—just drifted there in painful joy.

From behind, as the note slowly ebbed away, Kit nudged her. "Get the lead out, Neets," he sang, just for her hearing. "You're the star of this show. So start acting like it! Go in there and let them know you're here."

She swam slowly through the spectator whales, into the clear water in the center of their great circle, where the Celebrants were gathered.

One by one, as she circled above the weed-covered remnant of the trawler, Nita quickly identified the whales she knew. Aroooon, yes, swimming off more or less by himself to tideward, singing his deep scrape of notes with the

bsent concentration of a perfectionist who has time to hunt perfection;
Hotshot, doing barrel rolls near the surface and chattering through the quick
right harmonies of some part of the Wanderer's song; Areinnye, aloof from
oth Wanderer and Blue, running again and again over a phrase of the Gray
.ord's song and paying no further attention to Nita after a quick glance.

There were also five other whales whom Nita didn't know, exactly as Kit
ad pegged them. A beluga, dolphin-sized but whale-shaped, lazing near the
urface and singing some longing phrase from the Gazer's song; a pilot whale,
ong and slim and gray, silent for the moment and looking at Nita with
nterest; a right whale, with its huge, strange, bent-out-of-shape baleen
nouth, listening to the beluga; a killer whale, the sharp blacks and whites of
s hide a contrast to the grays and quiet mottlings of most of the others.

And—thank Heaven! —S'reee, swimming toward Nita from beside the
iller. Nita had been shaken by the sight of the killer—killer whales being
ne of a humpback's most persistent natural enemies—but just now her
omposure was so unraveled, there wasn't much more damage that could be
one to it. As S'reee came up to greet her, Nita managed to sing in some-
hing like a calm voice, and as if she were actually in charge, "Well, we're
te. Should we get started?"

"Good idea," said S'reee, brushing skin briefly and reassuringly with Nita.
Introductions first, though."

"Yes, please."

S'reee led Nita off to the north, where several of the singers were working
ogether. "We've been through the first part of the Song already this morn-
g," said S'reee, "the name-songs and so forth. I've heard you do yours, so
ere was no need for you to be here till late. We're up to the division now,
e 'temptation' part. These are the people singing the Undecided group—"

"Hi, Hotshot," Nita sang as she and S'reee soared into the heart of the
roup. The dolphin chattered a greeting back and busied himself with his
nging again, continuing his spirals near the surface, above the heads of the
ght whale and a whale whose song Nita hadn't heard on the way in, a
owerby's beaked whale. She immediately suspected why she hadn't heard it;
e whale, undoubtedly there to celebrate the Forager's part, was busy eating
—ripping up the long kelp and redweed stirring around the shattered deck-
lates of the wreck. It didn't even look up as she and S'reee approached. The
ght whale was less preoccupied; it swam toward Nita and S'reee at a slow
ace that might have been either courtesy or caution.

"HNii't, this is T!h!ki," said S'reee. Nita clicked his name back at him in
reeting, swimming forward to brush skin politely with him. "He's singing
e Listener."

T!h!ki rolled away from Nita and came about, looking at her curiously.

When he spoke, his song revealed both great surprise and some uneas
"S'reee—this is a human!"

"T!h!ki," Nita said, wry-voiced, with a look at S'reee, "are *you* going to b
mad at me for things I haven't done too?"

The right whale looked at her with that cockeyed upward stare that righ
have—their eyes being placed high in their flat-topped heads. "Oh," he saic
sounding wry himself, "you've run afoul of Areinnye, have you. No fea
Silent Lord—hNii't, was it? No fear." T!h!ki's song put her instantly at eas«
It had an amiable and intelligent sound to it, the song of a mind that didn
tend toward blind animosities. "If you're going to do the Sea such a service ;
you're doing, I could hardly do less than treat you with honor. For Sea's sak
don't think Areinnye is typical. . . ."

"However," T!h!ki added, gazing down at the calmly feeding beake
whale, "some of us practically have to have a bite taken out of us to get us t
start honoring and stop eating." He drifted down a fathom or so and bumpe
nose-first into the beaked whale. "Roots! Heads up, you bottom-grubber, he
comes the Master-Shark!"

"Huh? Where? *Where?*" the shocked song came drifting up from th
bottom. The kelp was thrashed about by frantic fluking, and through it ros
the beaked whale, its mouth full of weed, streamers of which trailed back an
whipped around in all directions as the whale tried to tell where the shar
was coming from. "Where—what— Oh," the beaked whale said after
moment, as the echoes from its initial excited squeaking came back and tol
it that the Master-Shark was nowhere in the area. "Ki," it said slowly, "I'r
going to get you for that."

"Later. Meantime, here's S'reee, and hNii't with her," said T!h!k
"HNii't's singing the Silent Lord. HNii't, this is Roots."

"Oh," said Roots, "well met. Pleasure to sing with you. Would you excus
me?" She flipped her tail, politely enough, before Nita could sing a note, an
a second later was head-down in the kelp again, ripping it up faster tha
before, as if making up for lost time.

Nita glanced with mild amusement at S'reee as Hotshot spiraled down 1
join them. "She's a great conversationalist," Hotshot whistled, his song co
spiratorially quiet. "Really. Ask her about food."

"I kind of suspected," Nita said. "Speaking of the Master-Shark, thoug
where *is* Ed this morning?"

S'reee waved one long fin in a shrug. "He has a late appearance, as you d
so it doesn't really matter if he shows up late. Meanwhile, we have to me
the others. Ki, are you finished with Roots?"

"Shortly. We're going through the last part of the second duet. I'll catc
up with you people later." The right whale glided downward toward th
weeds, and S'reee led Nita off to the west, where the Blue drifted in th

water, and the beluga beside him, a tiny white shape against Aroooon's hugeness.

"Aroooon and I are two of the Untouched," said S'reee. "The third, after the Singer and the Blue, is the Gazer. That's Iniihwit."

"HNii't," Aroooon's great voice hailed them as Nita approached.

Nita bent her body into a bow of respect as she coasted through the water. "Sir," she said.

That small, calm eye dwelt gravely on her. "Are you well, Silent Lord?" said the Blue.

"As well as I can be, sir," Nita said. "Under the circumstances."

"That's well," said Aroooon. "Iniihwit, here is the human I spoke of."

The beluga swam away from Aroooon to touch skin with Nita. Iniihwit was male, much smaller than Nita as whales went, though big for a beluga. But what struck her more than his smallness was the abstracted, contemplative sound of his song when he did speak. There were long silent days of calm behind it, days spent floating on the surface alone, watching the changes of sea and sky, saying little, seeing much. "HNii't," he said, "well met. And well met now, for there's something you must hear. You too, Senior."

"The weather?" S'reee said, sounding worried.

"Yes indeed. It looks as if that storm is not going to pass us by."

Nita looked at S'reee in surprise. "What storm? It's clear."

"For now," said Iniihwit. "Nevertheless, there's weather coming, and there's no telling what it will stir up in the depths."

"Is there any chance we can beat it?" S'reee said, sounding very worried indeed.

"None," the beluga said. "It will be here in half a light. We'll have to take our chances with the storm, I fear."

S'reee hung still in the water, thinking. "Well enough," she said. "Come on, hNii't; let's speak to Areinnye and the others singing the Undecided. We'll start the group rehearsal, then go straight into the Song. Time's swimming."

S'reee fluked hard and soared off, leaving Nita in shock for a moment. We won't be going home tonight, she thought. No good-byes. No last explanations. I'll never set foot on land again. . . .

"Neets?" Kit's voice said from behind her.

"Right," she said.

She went after S'reee to see the three whales singing the Undecided. Areinnye greeted Nita with cool cordiality and went back to her practicing. "And here's the Sounder," S'reee was saying. "Fluke, this is hNii't."

Nita brushed skin with the Sounder, who was a pilot whale; small and mottled gray, built along the same general lines as a sperm, though barely a quarter the size. Fluke's eyes were small, his vision poor, and he had an owlish, shortsighted look about him that reminded Nita of Dairine in her glasses. The likeness was made stronger by a shrill, ratchety voice and a tendency toward chuckles. "Fluke?" Nita said.

"I was one," the Sounder said. "I'm a triplet. And a runt, as you can see. There was nothing to do to hold my own with my brother and sister except become a wizard in self-defense."

Nita made a small amused noise, thinking that there might not be so much difference between the motivations and family lives of humans and whales. "And here's Fang," said S'reee.

Nita found herself looking at the brilliant white and deep black of the killer whale. Her feelings were decidedly mixed. The humpback-shape had its own ideas about the Killer, mostly prejudiced by the thought of blood in the water. But Nita's human memories insisted that killers were affable creatures, friendly to humans; she remembered her Uncle Jerry, her mother's older brother, telling about how he'd once ridden a killer whale at an aquatic park in Hawaii and had had a great time. *This* killer whale edged closer to Nita now, staring at her out of small black eyes—not opaque ones like Ed's, but sharp, clever ones, with merriment in them. "Well?" the killer said, his voice teasing. "Shark got your tongue?"

The joke was so horrible, and somehow so funny, that Nita burst out laughing, liking this creature instantly. "Fang, is it?"

"It is. HNii't, is it?"

"More or less." There was a kind of wicked amusement about Fang's song, which by itself was funny to listen to—sweet whistles and flutings peppered liberally with spits and fizzes. "Fang, are you from these waters originally?"

"Indeed not. I came down from Baffin Bay for the Song."

Nita swung her tail in surprise. "That's in Canada! Fifteen hundred miles!"

"What? Oh, a great many lengths, yes. I didn't swim it, hNii't. Any more than you and K!t there went where you went last night by swimming."

"I suppose," she said, "that a wizardry done like that—on such short notice, and taking the wizards such a distance—might have been noticed."

Fang snorted bubbles. " 'Might'! I should say so. By everybody. But it's understandable that you might want to indulge yourselves, anyway. Seeing that you and your partner won't have much more time to work together in the flesh."

Fang's voice was kind, even matter-of-fact; but Nita wanted to keep away from that subject for the moment. "Right. Speaking of which, S'reee, hadn't we better start?"

"Might as well."

S'reee swam off to a spot roughly above the wreck, whistling, and slowly the whole group began to drift in toward her. The voices of the whales gathered around to watch the Celebrants began to quiet, like those of an audience at a concert.

"From the top," S'reee said. She paused a few seconds, then lifted up her voice in the Invocation.

> " 'Blood in the water I sing, and one who shed it:
>   deadliest hunger I sing, and one who fed it—
>   weaving the ancientmost song of the Sea's sending:
>   singing the tragedy, singing the joy unending.' "

Joy. . . . Nita thought, trying to concentrate. But the thought of whose blood was being sung about made it hard.

The shadow that fell over Nita somewhere in the middle of the first song of the Betrayed whales, though, got her attention immediately. A streamlined shape as pale as bleached bone glided slowly over her, blocking the jade light; one dead-black, unreflecting eye glanced down. "Nita."

"Ed," she said, none too enthusiastically. His relentless reality was no pleasant sight.

"Come swim with me."

He arched away through the water, northward toward Ambrose Light. The gathered spectators drew back as Nita silently followed.

Shortly they were well to the north, still able to hear the ongoing practice Song, but out of hearing range for standard conversation. "So, Silent Lord," Ed said, slowing. "You were busy last night."

"Yes," Nita said, and waited. She had a feeling that something odd was going on inside that chill mind.

Ed looked at her. "You are angry. . . ."

"Damn right I am!" Nita sang, loudly, not caring for the moment about what Ed might think of her distress.

"Explain this anger to me," said the Master-Shark. "Normally the Silent Lord does not find the outcome of the Song so frightful. In fact, whales sometimes compete for the privilege of singing your part. The Silent Lord dies indeed, but the death is not so terrible—it merely comes sooner than it might have otherwise, by predator or old age. And it buys the renewal of life, and holds off the Great Death, for the whole Sea—and for years."

Ed glanced at her, sedate. "And even if the Silent One should happen to suffer somewhat, what of it? For there is still Timeheart, is there not? . . . the Heart of the Sea." Nita nodded, saying nothing. "It is no ending, this Song, but a passage into something else. How they extol that passage, and what lies at its end." There was faint, scornful amusement in Ed's voice as he lifted his voice in a verse of the Song—one of the Blue's cantos—not singing, exactly, for sharks have no song; chanting, rather. " '. . . Past mortal song—

" '—that Sea whereof our own seas merely hint,
   poor shadows sidewise-cast from what is real—
   where Time and swift-finned Joy are foes no more,
   but lovers; where old friend swims by old friend,
   senior to Death, undying evermore—
   partner to Songs unheard and Voices hid;
   songs past our knowing, perilously fair—' "

Ed broke off. "You are a wizard," he said. "You have known that place supposedly."

"Yes." Timeheart had looked like a bright city, skyscrapered in crystal and fire, power trembling in its streets and stones, unseen but undeniably there. And beyond the city stretched a whole universe, sited beyond and within all other worlds, beyond and within all times. Death did not touch that place. "Yes, I was there."

"So you know it awaits you after the Sacrifice, after the change of being. But you don't seem to take the change so calmly."

"How can I? I'm human!"

"Yes. But make me understand. Why does that make your attitude so different? Why are you so angry about something that would happen to you sooner or later anyway?"

"Because I'm too young for this," Nita said. "All the things I'll never have a chance to do—grow up, work, live—"

"This," Ed said mildly, looking around him at the green-burning sea, the swift fish flashing in it, the dazzling wrinkled mirror of the surface seen from beneath, "this is not living?"

"Of course it is! But there's a lot more to it! And getting murdered by a shark is hardly what I call living!"

"I assure you," Ed said, "it's nothing as personal as murder. I would have done the same for any wizard singing the Silent Lord. I *have* done the same, many times. And doubtless shall again. . . ." His voice trailed off.

Nita caught something odd in Ed's voice. He sounded almost . . . wistful?

"Look," she said, her own voice small. "Tell me something. . . . Does it really have to hurt a lot?"

"Sprat," said Ed dispassionately, "what in this life doesn't? Even love hurts sometimes. You may have noticed. . . ."

"Love—what would you know about that?" Nita said, too pained to care about being scornful, even to the Master-Shark.

"And who are you to think I would know nothing about it? Because I kill without remorse, I must also be ignorant of love, is that it?"

There was a long, frightening pause, while Ed began to swim a wide circle bout Nita. "You're thinking I am so old an order of life that I can know othing but the blind white rut, the circling, the joining that leaves the oined forever scarred. Oh yes, I know that. In its time . . . it's very good."

The rich and hungry pleasure in his voice disturbed Nita. Ed was circling loser and closer as he spoke, swimming as if he were asleep. "And, yes . . . ometimes we wish the closeness of the joining wouldn't end. But what vould my kind do with the warm-blood sort of joining, the long companion-hips? What would I do with a mate?" He said it as if it were an alien word. Soon enough one or the other of us would fall into distress—and the other artner would end it. There's an end to mating and mate, and to the love hat passed between. That price is too high for me to pay, even once. I swim lone."

He was swimming so close to Nita now that his sides almost touched hers, nd she pulled her tail and fins in tight and shrank away from the razory hide, ot daring to move otherwise. Then Ed woke up and broke the circle, gliding azily outward and away as if nothing had happened. "But, Sprat, the matter f *my* loves—or their lack—is hardly what's bothering you."

"No," she burst out bitterly, "love! I've never had a chance to. And now— ow—"

"Then you're well cast for the Silent Lord's part," Ed said, his voice ounding far away. "How does the line go? 'Not old enough to love as yet,/ ut old enough to die, indeed—' That has always been the Silent Lord's usiness—to sacrifice love for life . . . instead of, as in lesser songs, the ther way around. . . ."

Ed trailed off, paused to snap up a sea bass that passed him by too slowly. Vhen his eyes were more or less sane again and the water had carried the lood away, Ed said, "Is it truly so much to you, Sprat? Have you truly had o time to love?"

Mom and Dad, Nita thought ruefully. Dairine. That's not love, I don't ove Dairine!—do I? She hardened her heart and said, "No, Pale One. Not hat way. No one . . . that way."

"Well then," said the Master-Shark, "the Song will be sung from the eart, it seems. You will still offer the Sacrifice?"

"I don't want to—"

"Answer the question, Sprat."

It was a long while before Nita spoke. "I'll do what I said I would," she aid at last. The notes of the song whispered away into the water like the last otes of a dirge.

She was glad Ed said nothing for a while, for her insides gripped and hurned as she finally found out what real, grownup fear was. Not the kind hat happens suddenly, that leaves you too busy with action to think about eing afraid—but the kind that she had been holding off by not officially

"deciding": the kind that swims up as slowly as a shark circling, letting yo
see it and realize in detail what's going to happen to you.

"I am big enough to take a humpback in two bites," Ed said into he
silence. "And there is no need for me to be leisurely about it. You will spea
to the Heart of the Sea without having to say too much to me on the way.

Nita looked up at him in amazement. "But I thought you didn't believe—
I mean, you'd never—"

"I am no wizard, Nita," Ed said. "The Sea doesn't speak to me as it doe
to you. I will never experience those high wild joys the Blue sings of—the Se
That Burns, the Voices. The only voices I hear cry out from water that burn
with blood. But might I not sometimes wonder what other joys there are
—and wish I might feel them too?"

The dry, remote pain in his voice astonished her. And Nita though
abruptly of that long line of titles in the commentaries in her manual: as
only one shark had ever been Master. Sharks don't die of natural causes, sh
thought. Could it be that, all these years, there *has* been just one Master
And all around him, people die and die, and he—can't—

—and wants to? And so he understands how it is to want to get out o
something and be stuck with it.

Nita was terribly moved—she wasn't sure why. She swam close to the Pal
One's huge head for a moment and glided side by side with him, matchin
his course and the movements of his body.

"I wish I could help," she said.

"As if the Master could feel distress," Ed said, with good-natured scorn
The wound in his voice had healed without a scar.

"And as if someone else might want to end it," Nita said, sarcastic, bu
gentle about it.

Ed was silent for a long while. "I mean, it's dumb to suffer," Nita said
rather desperately, into that silence. "But if you have to do it, you might a
well intend it to do someone some good."

In silence they swam a few lengths more through the darkening water
while Nita's fear began to build in her again, and one astonished part of he
mind shouted at her, *You're running around talking about doing nice thing
for someone who's going to kill you? You're crazy!*

Ed spoke at last. "It's well said. And we will cause it to be well made, th
Sacrifice. You, young and never loving; I, old and never loved." Calm, utterl
calm, that voice. "Such a Song the Sea will never have seen."

"HNii't?" came a questioning note through the water, from southward o
Ambrose: S'reee's voice. "It's almost your time—"

"I have to go," Nita said. "Ed—"

"Silent Lord?"

She had no idea why she was saying it. "I'm sorry!"

"This once, I think," the passionless voice said, "so am I. Go on, Sprat. I will not miss my cue."

Nita looked at him. Opaque eyes, depthless, merciless, lingered on her as Ed curved past. "Coming!" Nita sang in S'reee's direction, loud, and tore off southward.

No pale shadow followed.

The next few hours, while the water darkened further, ran together for Nita in a blur of music, and annoying repetitions, and words that would have been frightening if she hadn't been too busy to be frightened. And something was growing in her, slowly, but getting stronger and stronger—an odd elation. She sang on, not questioning it, riding its tide and hoping it would last through what she had to do. Again and again, with the other Celebrants listening and offering suggestions, she rehearsed what would be the last things she would ever say:

". . . Sea, hear me now,
and take my words and make them ever law!—"

"Right, now swim off a little. No one hears this part. Upward, and toward the center, where the peak will be. Right there—"

" 'Must I accept the barren Gift?
—learn death, and lose my Mastery?
Then let them know whose blood and breath
will take the Gift and set them free:
whose is the voice and whose the mind
to set at naught the well-sung Game—
when finned Finality arrives
and calls me by my secret Name.

"Not old enough to love as yet,
but old enough to die, indeed—' "
—*Oh Lord*—
"—the death-fear bites my throat and heart,
fanged cousin to the Pale One's breed.
But past the fear lies life for all—
perhaps for me: and, past my dread,
past loss of Mastery and life,
the Sea shall yet give up Her dead!' "

—and then the paleness came to circle over her, bringing with it the voice

that chanted all on one soft hissing note, again and again, always coming
back to the same refrain—

> " 'Master have I none, nor seek.
> Bring the ailing; bring the weak.
> Bring the wounded ones to me:
> They shall feed my Mastery. . . .' "

That strange excitement was still growing in Nita. She let it drive her voice
as she would have used it to drive a wizardry, so that her song grew into
something that shook the water and almost drowned out even Ed's voice,
weaving about it and turning mere hunger to desire, disaster to triumph—

> " 'Lone Power, I accept your Gift!
>   Freely I make death part of me;
> By my acceptance it is bound
>   into the lives of all the Sea—
>
> yet what I do now binds to it
>   a gift I feel of equal worth:
> I take Death with me, out of Time,
>   and make of it a path, a birth!
>
> Let the teeth come! As they tear me,
>   they tear Your ancient hate for aye—
> —so rage, proud Power! Fail again,
>   and see my blood teach Death to die!' "

 . . . The last time she sang it, Nita hung unmoving, momentarily exhausted, for the moment aware of nothing but Kit's anxious eyes staring at
her from outside the circle and the stir of water on her skin as the Pale One
circled above her.

"That's right," S'reee said at last, very quietly. "And then—"

She fell silent and swam out of the circle of Celebrants. Behind her, very
slowly, first the Blue and then the rest of the whales began to sing the dirge
for the Silent Lord—confirmation of the transformation of death and the
new defeat of the Lone Power. Nita headed for the surface to breathe.

She came up into early evening. Westward, sunset was burning itself into
scarlet embers; eastward a Moon lacking only the merest shard of light to be
full lifted swollen and amber through the surface haze; northward, the bright
and dark and bright again of Ambrose Light glittered on the uneasily shifting
waves, with the opening and closing red eyes of Manhattan skyscraper lights
low beyond it; and southward, gazing back at them, the red-orange glow of

Arcturus sparkled above the water, here and there striking an answering spark off the crest or hollow of some wave. Nita lay there gasping in the wavewash and let the water rock her. Heaven knows, she thought, I need somebody to do it. . . .

Beside her Kit surfaced in a great wash of water and blew spectacularly—slightly forward, as sperms do. "Neets—"

"Hi," she said. She knew it was inane, but she could think of no other way to keep Kit from starting what he was going to start, except by saying dumb things.

"Neets," he said, "we're out of time. They're going to start the descent as soon as everybody's had a chance to rest a little and the protective spells are set."

"Right," she said, misunderstanding him on purpose. "We better get going, then—" She tilted her head down and started to dive.

"Neets." Suddenly Nita found that she was trying to dive through a forty-foot thickness of sperm whale. Nita blew in annoyance and let herself float back to the surface again. Kit bobbed up beside her—and, with great suddenness and a slam of air, threw off the whalesark. He dogpaddled there in the water, abruptly tiny beside her bulk. "Neets, get out of that for a minute."

"Huh? Oh—"

It was a moment's work to drop the whaleshape; then she was reduced to dogpaddling too. Kit was treading water a few feet from her, his hair slicked down with the water. He looked strange—tight, somehow, as if he were holding onto some idea or feeling very hard. "Neets," he said, "I'm not buying this."

Nita stared at him. "Kit," she said finally, "look, there's nothing we can do about it. *I've* bought it. Literally."

"No," Kit said. The word was not an argument, not even defiance; just a simple statement of fact. "Look, Neets—you're the best wizard I've ever worked with—"

"I'm the *only* wizard you've ever worked with," Nita said with a lopsided grin.

"I'm gonna kill you," Kit said—and regretted it instantly.

"No need," Nita said. "Kit—why don't you just admit that this time I've got myself into something I can't get out of."

"Unless another wizard gets you out of it."

She stared at him. "You loon, you *can't*—"

"I *know.* And it hurts! I feel like I *should* volunteer, but I just can't—"

"Good. 'Cause you do and *I'll* kill *you.*"

"That won't work either." He made her own crooked grin back at her. "'All for one,' remember? We *both* have to come out of this alive."

And he looked away.

"Let's go for both," Nita said.

Silence.

She took a deep breath. "Look, even if we *don't* both get out of this, I think it's gonna be all right. Really—"

"No," Kit said again, and that was that.

Nita just looked at him. "Okay," she said. "Be that way." And she meant it. This was the Kit she was used to working with: stubborn, absolutely sure of himself—most of the time; the person with that size-twelve courage packed into his size-ten self, a courage that would spend a few minutes trembling and then take on anything that got in its way—from the Lone Power to her father. *If I've got to go,* Nita thought in sudden irrational determination, *that sheer guts has got to survive—and I'll do whatever's necessary to make sure he does.*

"Look," she said, "what're you gonna tell my folks when you get back?"

"I'm gonna tell them we're hungry," Kit said, "and that you'll fill 'em in on the details while I eat."

I did tell him to be that way. . . . "Right," Nita said.

For a long time they stayed where they were, treading water, watching the Moon inch its way up the sky, listening to the Ambrose fog signal hooting the minutes away. A mile or so off, a tanker making for New York Harbor went by, its green portside running lights toward them, and let off a low groaning blast of horn to warn local traffic. From under the surface, after a pause, came a much deeper note that held and then scaled downward out of human hearing range, becoming nothing but a vibration in the water.

"They're ready to leave," Kit said.

Nita nodded, slipped into whaleshape again, and looked one last time with all her heart at the sunset towers of Manhattan, until Kit had finished his change. Then they dived.

The Song of the Twelve

Hudson Channel begins its seaward course some twenty miles south of Ambrose Light—trending first due south, parallel to the Jersey shore, then turning gradually toward the southeast and the open sea as it deepens. Down its length, scattered over the channel's bottom as it slowly turns from gray-green mud to gray-black sand to naked, striated stone, are the broken remnants of four hundred years' seafaring in these waters and the refuse of three hundred years of human urban life, mixed randomly together. There are new, almost whole-bodied wrecks lying dead on their sides atop old ones long since gone to rot and rust; great dumps of incinerated wood and ash, chemical drums and lumps of coal and jagged piles of junk metal; sunken, abandoned buoys, old cable spindles, unexploded ordnance and bombs and torpedoes; all commingled with and nested in a thick ooze of untreated, settled sewage—the garbage of millions of busy lives, thrown where they won't have to look at it.

The rugged bed of the channel starts out shallow, barely a fathom deeper than the seabed that surrounds it. It was much deeper once, especially where it begins; but the ooze has filled it thickly, and for some miles it is now hard to tell that any channel at all lies under the rotting trash, under the ancient faded beer cans and the hubcaps red with rust. Slowly, though, some twenty miles down the channel from its head, an indentation becomes apparent—a sort of crooked rut worn by the primordial Hudson River into the ocean floor, a mile wide at the rut's deepest, five miles wide from edge to edge. This far down—forty fathoms under the surface and some sixty feet below the surrounding ocean bed, between a great wide U of walls—the dark sludge of human waste lies even thicker. The city has not been dumping here for some time, but all the old years' sewage has not gone away. Every stone in the deepening rut, every pressure-flattened pile of junk on the steadily downward-sloping seabed around the channel, is coated thick and black. Bottom-feeding

fish are few here: There is nothing for them to eat. Krill do not live here: Th
water is too foul to support the microscopic creatures they eat, and even of
summer night the thick olive color of the sea is unchanged.

The channel's walls begin to grow less and less in height, as if the ocean i
growing tired of concealing the scar in its side. Gradually the rut flattens ou
to a broad shallow depression like a thousand other valleys in the Sea. A
whale hanging above the approximate end of the channel, some one hundre
thirty miles southeast of New York Harbor, has little to see on looking bac
up the channel's length—just an upward-sloping scatter of dark-slimed rock
and mud and scraps of garbage, drab even in the slate-green twilight that i
all this bottom ever sees of noon. But looking downward, southward, wher
its course would run if the channel went any farther—

—the abyss. Suddenly the thinning muck, and the gentle swellings an
dippings of the sea bed, simply stop at the edge of a great steep semicircula
cliff, two miles from side to side. And beyond the cliff, beyond the edge o
the Continental Shelf, curving away to northeast and southwest—nothing
Nothing anywhere but the vague glow of the ocean's surface three hundre
feet above; and below, beyond the semicircle, the deadly stillness of the grea
deeps, and a blackness one can hear on the skin like a dirge. Icy cold, and th
dark.

"I warn you all," S'reee said as the eleven gathered Celebrants and Ki
hung there, looking down into that darkness at the head of Hudson Canyon
"Remember the length of this dive; take your own breathing needs carefull
into consideration, and tell me now if you think you may need more air tha
our spells will be taking with us. Remember that, at the great pressures in th
Below, you'll need more oxygen than you usually do—and work will make you
burn more fuel. If you feel you need to revise the breathing figures on th
group spell upward, this is the time to do it. There won't be a chance later
after we've passed the Gates of the Sea. Nor will there be any way to get t
the surface quickly enough to breathe if you start running low. At the depth
we'll be working, even a sperm whale would get the bends and die of such a
ascent. Are you all sure of your needs? Think carefully."

No one said anything.

"All right. I remind you also, one more time, of the boundaries on th
pressure-protection spell. They're marked by this area of light around us—
which will serve the added purpose of enabling us to see what's going o
around us. If we need to expand the boundaries, that's easily done. But unles
I direct you otherwise, stay inside the light. Beyond the lighted area, there'
some direction for a limited area, but it's erratic. Don't depend on it! Other
wise you may find yourself crushed to a pulp."

Nita glanced at Kit; he gave her an I-don't-care wave of the tail. Sperm
whales were much less bothered by pressure changes than most of the spe

cies, and the great depths were part of their hunting grounds. "You be careful," she sang at him in an undertone. "Don't get cute down there."

"Don't *you.*"

"Anything else?" S'reee said. "Any questions?"

"Is there time for a fast bite?" Roots said, sounding wistful.

"Surely," Fang said, easing up beside the beaked whale with that eternal killer-whale smile. "Where should I bite you?"

"Enough, you two. Last chance, my wizards."

No one sang a note.

"Then forward all," S'reee said, "and let us take the adventure the Powers send us."

She glided forward, out into the darkness past the great curved cliff, tilted her nose down, and dived—not straight, but at a forty-five-degree angle roughly parallel to the downward slope of the canyon. The wizard-light advanced with her. Areinnye followed first; then Fang and Iniihwit, with Fluke and Roots close behind. After them came T!h!ki and Aroooon and Hotshot, and Nita, with Kit behind her as rearguard, suspiciously watching the zone of light around them. Only one of the Celebrants did not stay within that boundary, sailing above it, or far to one side, as he pleased—Ed, cruising restlessly close to the canyon walls as the group descended, or pacing them above, a ghost floating in midnight-blue water.

"I don't like it," Nita sang, for Kit's hearing only, as she looked around her.

"What?"

"This." She swung her tail at the walls—which were towering higher and higher as they cut downward through the Continental Shelf. On the nautical maps in their manuals, the canyon had looked fairly innocent; and a drop of twenty-five feet in a half-mile had seemed gentle. But Nita was finding the reality that rose in ever-steepening battlements around her much more threatening. The channel's walls at their highest had been about three hundred feet high, comparable to the walls she'd seen in the Grand Canyon on vacation. But these walls were already five or six hundred feet high, growing steadily steeper as the canyon's angle of descent through the shelf increased. If Nita had a neck to crane back, it would already be sore.

As it was, she had something much worse—a whale's superb sonar sense, which told her exactly how puny she was in comparison to those cliffs—exactly where loose rocks lay on them, ready to be shaken down at the lightest bottom tremor.

Kit looked up around them and sang a note of uncomfortable agreement. "Yeah," he said. "It gives me the creeps too. It's too tall—"

"No," Nita said softly. "It's that this isn't a place where we're supposed to be. Something very large happened here once. That's your specialty; you should be able to feel it."

"Yeah, I should." There was a brief pause. "I seem to have been having trouble with that lately. —But you're right, it's there. It's not so much the tallness itself we're feeling. But what it's—what it's a symbol of, I think—"

Nita said nothing for a moment, startled by the idea that Kit had been losing some of his talent at his specialty. There was something that could mean, some warning sign— She couldn't think what.

"Kit, this is one of the places where Afállonë was, isn't it?"

He made a slow sound of agreement. "The whole old continental plate Atlantis stood on was ground under the new plates and buried under the Atlantic's floor, S'reee said. But the North American plate was a lot farther west when the trouble first started, and the European one was farther east. So if I've got the story straight, this would have been where Afállonë's western shoreline was, more or less. Where we're going would still have been open sea, a couple of million years ago."

"Millions of years—" Nita looked at him in uncomfortable wonder. "Kit —that's much farther back than the fall of Afállonë. That could—" Her note failed her momentarily. "That could go right back to the first Song of the Twelve—"

Kit was still for a while as they kept diving. "No wonder," he said at last, "no one travels down through the Gates of the Sea except when they're about to do the Song. Part of the sorcery is buried in the stone. If anybody should trouble it, wake it up—"

"—like we're doing," Nita said, and fell silent.

They swam on. The immensities rearing up about them grew no more reassuring with time. Time, Nita thought—how long have we been down here? In this changeless cold dark, there was no telling; and even when the Sun came up, there still would be no knowing day from night. The darkness yielded only grudgingly to the little sphere of light the Celebrants carried with them, showing them not much, and too much, of what Nita didn't want to look at—those walls, reaching so far above her now that the light couldn't even begin to illumine them. Nita began to get a bizarre sense of being indoors—descending a winding ramp of infinite length, its walls three miles apart and now nearly a mile high.

It was at about this time that Nita felt on her skin what sounded at first like one of the Blue's deeper notes, and stared ahead of her, wondering partly what he was saying—the note was one that made no sense to her. Then she wondered why he was curving his body upward in such surprise. But the note grew, and grew, and grew louder still, and though they were now nearly a mile from the walls on either side, to her shock and horror Nita heard the walls begin to resonate to that note.

The canyon walls sounded like a struck gong, one of such boneshaking, subterranean pitch as Nita had never imagined. *She* sounded, caught in the torrent of shock waves with the rest of the Celebrants. Seaquake! she thought. The sound pressed through her skin from all sides like cold weights, got into her lungs and her heart and her brain, and throbbed there, hammering her into dizziness with slow and terrible force.

The sluggish, brutal pounding against her skin and inside her body eventually began to die down. But the quake's effects were still going on around her, and would take much more time to settle. Sonar was nearly drowned; Nita was floating blind in the blackness. *This is the pits!* she thought in anguish, and concentrated everything she had on one good burst of sound that would cut through the terrible noise and tell her what was going on.

The echoes that came back reassured her somewhat. All the Celebrants were still fairly close together, safe within the light of the pressure-protection spell. Kit was farther ahead than he had been, fighting for control and slowly finding it. Others, S'reee and Fang and Areinnye, were closer to Nita. And there was other movement close to them—large objects drifting downward, slowly, resonating with the same note, though in higher octaves, as the towering cliffsides. Massive objects, said the echo. *Solid* massive objects. Falling faster now. One of them falling past S'reee and down toward Areinnye, who was twisting and struggling against the turmoil of the water for balance—

Warn her! was Nita's first thought, but even as she let out another cry, she realized it was useless—Areinnye would have no time to react. The falling rock, a piece of cliff-shelf nearly as long as a city block, was practically on top of her. Shield spell, Nita thought then. Impossible—

She did it anyway. It was an old friend, that spell, long since learned by heart. When activated, punches, or any physical object thrown at one, slid right off it. Running them together in her haste, she sang the nine syllables of the spell that were always the same, then added four more that set new coordinates for the spell, another three that specified how much mass the shield would have to repel—tons and tons! Oh, Lord!—and then the last syllable that turned the wizardry loose. She felt the magic fall away from her like a weight on a cord, dropping toward Areinnye. Nothing to do now but hang on, she thought, letting herself float. Faintly, through the thunder, the echoes of her spell brought Nita the shape of Areinnye, still struggling, trying to get out from under the falling rock-shelf, and failing. Her connection with the spell brought her the feeling of the massive slab of stone dropping toward it, closer, closer still. Making contact—

—crushing down and down onto her wizardry with force more terrible than she had anticipated. The spell was failing, the shelf was settling down on it and inexorably pressing it closer and closer to Areinnye, who was in turn being forced down against the battering of the shock waves, toward the floor of the canyon. The spell was breaking up, tearing like a rotten net filled with weights. No, Nita thought, and strained, pouring all her concentration, all her will, down the connection to the spell. *No!* It was like hanging on to a rope in a tug of war, and losing, and not letting go—digging in, muscles popping out all over, aching, straining, blood pounding, and not letting go— The spell firmed a little. The shelf, settling slowly down and down onto Areinnye, forcing her closer and closer to the bottom, seemed to hesitate. "Kit!" Nita screamed into the water. *I'm gonna lose it. I'm gonna lose it.* "Kit!"

The echo of her yell for help showed her another sperm-whale shape, a larger one than Areinnye's, fighting his way against the battering shock waves and down toward the bottom of the canyon—toward where Areinnye floundered, underneath the stone shelf, underneath the spell. Kit rammed Areinnye head-on, hitting her squarely amidships and punching the smaller sperm whale backward thirty or forty feet. But not out from under the settling shelf; and now Kit was partly under it too. The spell began sagging again. Nita panicked; she had no time or energy left for any more warnings, any more *anything*. She threw herself so totally into the spell that she couldn't feel her body, couldn't hear, couldn't see, finally became nothing but a single, none-too-coherent thought: No! But it was no use. The spell was coming undone, the rock was coming down, this time for good. And Kit was under it. No! No, *no, NO*—

And everything went away.

The next thing Nita felt was the shock of a spell being broken by force too great for it to handle, as the rock-shelf came crushing down on it, smashing it flat against something both soft and hard. *"NO!"* Nita screamed again in horror, as the diminishing thunder of the seaquake was briefly augmented by the multiple crashes of the shelf's shattering. The floor of the canyon was obscured even to sonar by a thick fog of rockdust and stirred-up ooze, pierced all through by flying splinters of stone, but Nita dove into it anyway. "Kit!"

"You sang?" came a sperm whale's sharp-edged note from down in the rock-fog, sounding tired but pleased.

Speechless with relief and shaking with effort, Nita pulled up her nose and just let herself float in the trembling water, listening to the rumbling of the quake as it faded away and the songs of the other whales round about as they checked on one another. She became aware of the Master-Shark, finning slowly downcanyon not too far from her and favoring her as he went with a look that was prolonged and indecipherable. Nita glided hurriedly away from him, looking around her.

The light of the protection spell showed Nita the roiling of the cloud of ooze and dust in the bottom of the canyon, and the two shapes that swam slowly up through it—first Kit, fluking more strongly than Nita would have believed possible for someone who'd just gone through what they all had, then Areinnye, stroking more weakly, and swimming with a stiffness that made it very plain just how hard Kit must have hit her. Kit rose to hang beside Nita. More slowly, Areinnye came swimming up to face her.

"There seems to be a life between us, hNii't," the sperm whale said.

The mixture of surprise and anger in Areinnye's song made Nita uncomfortable. "Oh, no," she said, rather weakly. "Kit did it—"

"Oh, dead fish," Kit said. "You held it for a good ten seconds after we were out from under. You would've managed even if I hadn't helped."

"I had incentive," Nita muttered.

Kit looked at her for a moment. "You didn't drop it until Ed nudged you," he said. "You might have gone deaf for a little, or maybe you were in spell overload. But either way, this was your cookie. Don't blame me."

"Silent Lord," Areinnye said—still stiffly formal, but with an uncertain note in her voice, "I thank you. I had hardly given you cause for such an act."

"You gave me plenty of cause," she said wearily. "You took the Oath, didn't you? You're with me. And you're welcome." She took a deep breath, feeling the respiratory part of the protection spell briefly surround her blowholes with a bubble of air for her to inhale. "Kit," she said, "can we get going and get this over with?"

"That is well said" came Ed's voice. He was coming upcanyon again, fast. As Nita looked up she saw him arrow overhead, ghastly pale in the wizard-light, with a trail of darkness billowing thick behind him, and something black in his jaws. It struggled; Ed gulped it down. Inside his gill slits and lower body, Nita could see the swallowed thing give a last couple of convulsive heaves. "And we'd best get on with it—"

Thick black sucker-tipped arms whipped up from the disturbed ooze on the bottom, grasping, flailing in the light. "Oh, no," Nita moaned. Kit plunged past her, the first note of the scraping sperm-whale battlecry rasping down Nita's skin as he dived for the body to which those arms belonged. Farther down the canyon, almost out of range of the wizard-light, there was a confused boiling-together of arms, long dark bodies, flat platterlike yellow eyes glowing with reflected light and wild-beast hunger—not just a few krakens, but a great pack of them. "To business, Silent Lord," Ed said, his voice rich with chilly pleasure, as he swept past Nita again on his way downcanyon.

She went to business. These krakens were bigger than the last ones had been; the smallest one Nita saw had a body the size of a stretch limousine, and arms twice that length. True, there were more toothed whales fighting this time—not only Kit, but Fang and Areinnye as well. And teeth weren't everything—what Aroooon or T!h!ki rammed didn't move afterward.

The Celebrants also had the advantage of being wizards. Nita was terrified at first when she saw one of the krakens come at poor slow Roots—and poor slow Roots raised her voice in a few squeaky little notes and simply blew the giant squid into a cloud of blood and ink and black rags of flesh. But a wizard's strength has limits; such spells could only be worked once or twice. And since a spell has to be directed at what you see, not even the most deadly offensive wizardry does a bit of good against the choking tentacles that you don't notice coming up from behind you. So it was a slow, ugly, bitter battle, that fight in the canyon. Four or five times the Celebrants were assaulted as they made their way down between the dwarfing, twisting walls of stone; four or five times they fought the attackers off, rested briefly, and started out again, knowing that somewhere deeper down, more thick tentacles and hungry eyes waited for them.

"This is your fault!" Areinnye cried angrily at Nita during one or another of the attacks, while Fang and Kit and Ed and Aroooon fought off krakens coming from downcanyon and from above, and S'reee and T!h!ki worked furiously to heal a great sucker welt torn in Areinnye's side before Ed should notice it and turn on her.

Nita simply turned away, in no mood for it. Her face hurt from ramming krakens, she had bruises from their suckers and a stab from one's beak, and she was sick of the smell of blood and the galling sepia taste in the water. The problem, and the only reason Nita didn't answer Areinnye hotly back, was that there might have been some slight truth to the accusation. According to Carl and the manual, the same pollutants that caused cancer in human beings, that had caused the U.S. Fish and Game Service to warn people on the Jersey shore against eating more than one ocean-caught fish a week, were getting concentrated in the squids' bodies, changing their DNA: changing *them.* The food the krakens normally ate at the great depths was dying out, also from the pollution. They had to come up into the shallows to survive. The changes were enabling them to do so. And if it was starving, a hungry kraken would find a whale perfectly acceptable as food.

Nita was startled by the sudden sharpness of S'reee's answering voice. "Areinnye, don't talk nonsense," she said after singing the last note of a spell that sealed the sperm whale's torn flesh. "The krakens are here for the same reason the quake was—because the Lone Power wants them here. We're supposed to use up our air fighting them."

T!h!ki looked soberly at S'reee. "That brings up the question, Ree. Will we complete the Song?"

S'reee swung her tail in a shrug, her eyes on Areinnye's healing wound. "I thought such a thing might happen," she said, "after we were attacked the other night. So I brought extra air, more than the group felt it needed. Even so—it'll be close."

"We're a long way down the canyon," Nita said. "Practically down to the plain. If they're all down there, waiting for us—if these attacks have just been to wear us down—"

"I don't think so," T!h!ki said, glancing over at Nita. "Once out into the plain, we'll be practically under the shadow of the Sea's Tooth, close to the ancient site of the Song. And once our circle is set up, they couldn't get in unless we let them."

"Which we won't," S'reee said. "Let's waste no more time. This is going to be the fastest Song on record. —Areinnye, you're done. How do you feel?"

The sperm swayed in the water, testing her healed tail. "Well enough," he said, grim-voiced. "Though not as well as I would if this human were—" And Areinnye broke off. "Pardon me," she said, more slowly. "It was an ill thought. Let me go help K!t now."

She went. "You now," S'reee said to Nita. She sang a few notes to start the healing spell going, then said, "HNii't? Are you all right otherwise?"

The sound of Kit's battlecry came scraping along Nita's skin from down-canyon. "No," she said. Kit had been fighting with a skill and, heaven help him, a relish that Nita would never have suspected in him. *I'm not sure it's the sark doing this,* she thought. *I keep thinking that Kit might actually be this way, down deep.*

Then Nita stopped. *What makes me think it matters one way or another?* she thought. *In a few hours, anything I think about Kit will make no difference at all. But I can't stop acting as if it will. Habit is hard to break. . . .*

"If it's something I can help with—" S'reee said, finishing up.

Nita brushed skin with her, an absent gesture. "It's not," she said. And off she went after Areinnye—into the water fouled with stirred-up slime and ink and blood, into the reach of grabbing, sandpapery tentacles and the glare of yellow eyes.

It went on that way for what seemed forever, until Nita was nearly blind from head-on ramming. She gave up on sonar and concentrated on keeping just one more squid occupied until Kit or Ed or Areinnye could deal with it. So, as the walls of the canyon, which had been towering some six thousand feet above the Celebrants on either side, began to decrease in height, she didn't really notice it. Eventually the bitter cold of the water got her attention; and she also realized that the krakens' attack had stopped. Nita sang a few notes to "see" at a distance, and squinted around her in the sea-green wizard-light to find out where she and the other Celebrants were.

The walls closest to them were still nearly three thousand feet high. But their slope was gentler; and the canyon had widened from some two miles across to nearly five. To left and right of the canyon's foot, curving away northward and southward, miles past sound or sight, stretched the rubble-strewn foothills of the Continental Shelf. Behind the Celebrants the shelf itself towered, a mighty cliffwall rising to lose itself in darkness. Outward before them, toward the open sea, the terrain was mostly flat, broken only occasionally by hills so shallow they were more like dunes. The rocky bottom was turning to pale sand. But the paleness did nothing to lighten the surroundings. Above it lay an intolerable, crushing weight of water, utterly black, icy cold, weighing down on the soul no matter what spell protected the body. And far out in the blackness could be seen the furtive, erratic movements of tiny lights—eerie points of peculiar-colored fire that jittered and clustered and hung in the cold dark, watching the whales.

Nita took a sharp breath, for some of those lights were definitely eyes. T!h!ki, hanging motionless in the still water beside her, did the same. He was staring down the slope, which sank past the light of the breathing-spell, and far past echo range, dropping farther downward into more darkness. *"Nothing* can be this deep," he sang in an unnerved whisper. "How much farther down can we go?"

"All the way," said another voice from Nita's other side. She turned, not recognizing it—and then knew the speaker very well and was sick inside. Kit hung there, with a fey, frightening look in his eye—a total lack of fear.

Nita swallowed once. Sperm whales took the great dives better than any other whale, coming down this far on purpose to hunt the giant squid; but their boldness also got them in trouble. Numerous sperm-whale skeletons had been found at these depths by exploring bathyscaphs, the whales' tails or bodies hopelessly tangled in undersea telephone or telegraph cables.

"We're a long way up yet," Kit said, with that cool cast to his voice that better suited Areinnye than it did him. "Barely six thousand feet down. We'll have to go down to sixteen thousand feet at least before we see the Sea Tooth." And he swam off toward the boundaries of the light.

Nita held still for a few moments as S'reee and various other of the Celebrants went slowly after Kit. T!h!ki went too; she barely noticed him go. *This isn't the Kit I want to say good-bye to.*

Perhaps a hundred feet away from her, Ed glided past, staring at her. "Sprat," he said, "come along."

She did. But the fighting in the canyon had left Nita so fatigued that much of this part of the descent seemed unreal to her, a prolonged version of one of those dreams in which one "falls" downstairs for hours. And there was a terrible sameness about this terrain: a sea of white sand, here and there featuring a darker rock thrust up or thrown down into it, or some artifact more bizarre—occasionally, great pressure-fused lumps of coal; once an actual kitchen sink, just sitting there on the bottom by itself; another time, a long Coca-Cola bottle standing upright in the sand with a kind of desolate, pitiful pride. But mostly the bottom was as undifferentiated as a mile-wide, glare-lit snowfield, one that pitched forever downward.

Nor was Nita's grasp on reality much helped by the strange creatures that ived in those waters more than a thousand fathoms down. Most everything seemed to be either transparent as a ghost or brilliantly luminous. Long-bodied, lantern-eyed sharks swam curiously about Nita, paid brief homage to their Master, and moved on. Anglerfish with their luminous baits hanging on "fishlines" in front of their mouths came up to stare Nita right in the eye and then swam dourly away, disappointed that she was too big to eat. Long, many-segmented bottom worms and vampire squid, sporting dots or stripes of pink or yellow or blue-white light, inched or squirted along the bottom about their affairs, paying no attention to the Celebrants sailing overhead in their nimbus of wizard-light. Rays fluttered, using fleshy wings to rearrange the sand in which they lay buried; tripod-fish crutch-walked around the bottom like peglegged pirates on their long stiff fins. And all the eyes circling in the black water, all the phosphorescent shapes crawling on the bottom or undulating above it were doing one of two things—either looking for food or eating it, in the form of one another.

Nita knew there was no other way for these creatures to live, in this deadly cold, but by the minimum expenditure of energy for the maximum return . . hence all the baits, traps, hiding. But that didn't affect the dull horror of the scene—the endless crushing dark, the ear-blinding silence, and the pale chilly lights weaving through the space-black water as the creatures of the great depths sought and caught and ate one another with desperate, mindless diligence.

The gruesome power of the besetting horror brought Nita wide awake. She had never been superstitious; shadows in the bedroom had never bothered her when she was little, and she found horror movies fun to watch. But now she started to feel more hemmed in, more watched and trapped, than she suspected she'd feel in any haunted house. "Ed," she sang, low as a whisper, to the pale shape that paced her, "what *is* it? There's something down here. . . ."

"Indeed there is. We are getting close."

She would have asked *To what?* but as she looked down the interminable slope at the other Celebrants—who were mostly swimming gathered close together, as if they felt what she felt—something occurred to her, something so obvious that she felt like a moron for not having thought of it before. "Ed—if this is the Song of the Twelve, how come there are only eleven of us singing!"

"The Twelfth is here," Ed said. "As the Song says, the Lone Power lies bound here, in the depths below the depths. And It will sing Its part, as It always has. It cannot help it. Indeed, It wants to sing. In the temptation and subversion of the Celebrants lies Its only hope of escape from the wizardry that binds It."

"And if It succeeds—"

"Afállonë," Ed said. "Atlantis, all over again. Or worse."

"*Worse—*" Then she noticed something else. "Ed, the water's getting warmer!"

"And the bottom is changing," Ed said. "Gather your wits, Sprat. A few hundred more lengths and we are there."

The white sand was giving way to some kind of darker stuff. At first Nita thought she was looking at the naked rock of the sea bottom. But this stuff wasn't flat, as sediment would be. It was ropy, piled-up, ridgy-looking black stone. And here and there crystals glittered in it. Scattered around ahead of them were higher piles of the black stone, small, bizarrely shaped hills. Nita sounded a high note to get some sonar back, as the water through which she swam grew warmer and began to taste odd.

The first echoes to return surprised Nita until she started to suspect what they were. Waving frondy shapes, the hard round echoes from shelled creatures, a peculiar hollowness to the echo that indicated water of lower pressure than that surrounding it— That was a stream of sulfur-laden hot water coming out of an undersea "vent"; the other echoes were the creatures that lived around it, all adapted to take advantage of the oasis of heat and the sulfur that came up with it. And now she understood the black bottom stone—old cooled lava, the kind called pillow lava, that oozes up through the ocean's crust and spreads itself out in flat, ropy piles.

But from past the vent came another echo that was simply impossible. A wall, a rounded wall, at least a mile and a half wide at the base, rising out of the piled black stone and spearing up, and up, and up, and up, so that fragments of the echo kept coming back to Nita for second after second. She backfinned to hold still until all the echoes could come back to her, and in Nita's mind the picture of the massive, fluted, narrowing pillar of stone got taller and taller, until she actually had to sing a soft note or two to deafen herself to it. It was, like the walls of Hudson Canyon, "too big"—only much more so. "Five Empire State Buildings on top of each other," Kit had called it—but Empire States a mile wide: Caryn Peak, the Sea's Tooth, the site of the Song of the Twelve.

The whales ahead of Nita were gathering near the foot of the peak. Against that gigantic spear of stone they seemed dwarfed, insignificant. Even Aroooon looked like a toy. And the feeling of being watched, closely, by something of malicious intent, was getting stronger by the second.

She joined the others. The Celebrants were poised not too far from the open vent—evidently S'reee preferred the warmer water—in clear view of the strange creatures living about it: the twelve-foot stalks of the tubeworms, the great blind crabs, the colonies of giant blood-red clams, opening and closing their fringed shells with mindless regularity. No coral, Nita thought absently, looking around her. But she wouldn't need any. Several hundred feet away, there on the face of the peak, were several shattered outcroppings of stone. The outcroppings were sharp as glass knives. *Those should do it,* Nita thought. *So sharp I'll hardly feel anything—until Ed arrives. . . .*

"If you're all prepared," S'reee sang, her voice wavering strangely where notes had to travel suddenly from cold water to hot, "I suggest we start right now."

The Celebrants chorused muted agreement and began to spread out, forming the circle with which the Song begins. Nita took her place between Fang and T!h!ki, while S'reee went to the heart of the circle. Ed swam away, toward the far side of the peak and out of sight. Kit glided away from the circle, off behind Nita. She looked back at him. He found the spot from which he would watch and gazed back at her. Nita swallowed one last time, hard. There was very little of her friend in that look. "Kit—" she said, on one low note.

"Silent Lord," he said.

And though it was his voice, it wasn't Kit. . . .

Nita turned away, sick at heart, and faced inward toward the circle again; and S'reee lifted up her voice and sang the Invocation.

> " 'Blood in the water I sing, and one who shed it:
> > deadliest hunger I sing, and one who fed it—
> weaving the ancientmost tale of the Sea's sending:
> > singing the tragedy, singing the joy unending.
>
> " 'This is our shame—this is the whole Ocean's glory:
> > this is the Song of the Twelve. Hark to the
> > > story!
> Hearken, and bring it to pass; swift, lest the sor-
> > > > row
> > long ago laid to its rest devour us tomor-
> > > > > row!' "

And so it began, as in song S'reee laid out the foundations of the story, which began before lives learned to end in resistance and suffering. One by one the Celebrants drew together, closing up the circle, named themselves to one another, and began to discuss the problem of running the Sea to everyone's advantage. Chief among their problems at the moment was the sudden appearance of a new whale. It was puzzling; the Sea had given them no warning, as She had in times past, that this was about to happen. But they were the Ni'hwinyii, the Lords of the Humors, and they would comport themselves as such. They would decide the question for themselves. Under whose Mastery would the Stranger fall? . . .

Nita, who had backed out of the circle after the Invocation, hung shivering in the currentless water as the Song shook the warm darkness about her. Part of what she felt was the same kind of trembling with excitement she had felt a hundred times in school when she knew she was about to be called on. I'm ready, she thought, trying to quiet herself. This is silly. I know my part backward and forward—there's not that much of it. I'll do all right.

. . . But there was also something else going on. She had felt it start with the Invocation and grow stronger with every passing second—that sense of something waking up, something rousing from sleepy malice, awakening to active, alert malevolence. It waits, Ed had said. It was a certainty, as sure as looking up toward a lighted window and seeing the person who's been staring at you drop the curtain and turn away.

She wrenched her attention back to the Blue, who was at the end of one of his long stately passages. But it was hard.

> " '—Nay, slowly, Sounder. Slow is the wise whale's
> song,
> and wise as slow; for he who hastens errs,
> who errs learns grief. And not the Master-Shark
> has teeth as fierce: grief eats its prey alive,
> and pain grows greater as the grief devours,
> not less. So let this Stranger sing his peace:
> what he desires of us; there's Sea enough and
> time
> to hear him, though he sing the darkened Moon
> to full and back again. Ay, let him speak. . . .' "

And to Nita's shock and fascinated horror, an answer came. The voice that raised itself in the stillness of the great depths was the sonic equivalent of the thing one sees out the corner of one's eye, then turns to find gone, or imagined. It did not shake the water; it roused no echoes. And Nita was not alone in hearing it. She saw the encircled Celebrants look uneasily at one another. On the far side of the circle, Kit's coolness was suddenly broken, and he stared at Nita like someone believing a myth for the first time. The innocent gentle-spoken, unselfconscious evil in the new voice was terrifying. "With Pow'rs and Dominations need I speak," sang that timbreless voice in quiet sincerity,

> " 'the ancient Lords who hold the Sea in sway.
> I pray thee, Lords of the Humors, hear me now,

last, least and poorest of the new-made whales,
new-loos'd from out the Sea's great silent Heart.
No Lord have I; therefore to ye I come,
beseeching low thy counsel and thy rule
for one that's homeless, lawless, mateless,
lost. . . .' "

"Who art thou, then, that speak'st?" sang S'reee, beginning the Singer's
questioning. At the end of her verse she was answered, in more soft-spoken,
reasonable platitudes—words meant to lull the unwary and deceive the alert.
And questions and answers continued, until Nita realized that there had been
a shift. Rather than the Singer asking the Stranger what he wanted, the
Stranger was telling the Singer what he knew *she* wanted—and could offer
her, if only she would take the unspecified Gift he would give her.

Nita began shaking steadily now, and not from the cold. The insinuating
power of that not-quite-voice somehow frightened her worse than head-on
conflict with the Lone Power had, a couple of months ago. There the Power
had been easily seen in its true colors. But here it was hidden, and speaking as
matter-of-factly as the voices in the back of one's own mind, whose advice
one so often tends to follow without question. "Your Mastery is hollow," said
the voice to S'reee,

" '—cold song, strict-ruled by law. From such bland
rule
come no great musics. Singer, follow me,
accept my Gift and what it brings, and song
shall truly have no Master save for you.
My gift will teach you lyric that will break
the heart that hears it; every seaborne voice
will curse your newfound art, and wish that art
its own. Take up the Gift, O foremost
Singer. . . .' "

Nita glanced over at S'reee. She was trembling nearly as hard as Nita was,
caught in the force of the temptation. S'reee sang her refusal calmly enough;
but Nita found herself wondering how much of that refusal was the ritual's
and how much S'reee's own.

She began watching the other Celebrants with as much care. Iniihwit sang
the Gazer's questioning and rejection with the outward attitude of mild
unconcern that Nita had in their brief acquaintance come to associate with
him. Aroooon's refusal of the prize offered the Blue by the Stranger, that of
power over all the other whales, was more emphatic, though it came in his

usual rich, leisurely manner. He sang not as if making ritual responses, but as if he rejected someone who swam in the circle with him and dared him to do something about it.

After that, the unheard voice sounded less certain of itself, and also impatient. The Song passed on to what would for the Lone Power be more successful ground: the Wanderer and the Killer and the Forager, all of whom would succumb to the Stranger's temptations and become the Betrayed—those species of whales and fish to whom death would later come most frequently and most quickly. One by one Roots and Fang and Hotshot sang with the Lone One, were tempted, and in the place of the original Masters, fell. Nita tried to keep herself calm, but had trouble doing it; for each time one of the Celebrants gave in to the Lone One's persuasion, she felt the voice grow a little more pleased with itself, a little more assured—as if something were finally going according to plan.

Nita stared across at Kit. He traded looks with her and began to make his way around the circle toward her.

The Lone One was working on the last three whales in the circle now, the ones who would become the Undecided. Their parts were the most difficult, being not only the longest sung passages but also the most complex. The Undecided argued with the Lone Power much more than did the Untouched, who tended to refuse quickly, or the Betrayed, who gave in without much fighting. T!h!ki sang first, the Sounder's part; and strain began to show as the Power offered him all the hidden knowledge of the great deeps, and the Sounder's song went from smooth flowing melodies to rumbles and scrapes of tortured indecision. *Not all that carrying on is in the Song,* Nita thought nervously. *What's happening?* And indeed, though the Sounder finished his passage and turned away, ostensibly to think about what the Lone Power had said to him, Nita could see that T!h!ki looked pallid and shaken as a whale that's sick.

The Listener fared no better. Fluke sang steadily enough to begin with, but when the voiceless voice offered him the power to hear everything that transpired in the Sea, from the random thoughts of new-hatched fry to the secret ponderings of the continental plates, he hesitated much too long—so long that Nita saw S'reee look at him in surprise and almost speak up to prompt him. It was bizarre; in rehearsals Fluke had had the best memory of any of them. He finished his verses looking troubled, and seemed relieved to turn away.

It's what S'reee said, very early on, Nita thought. *The whales picked have to be close in temperament to the original Celebrants—loving the same kinds of things. But it makes them vulnerable to the temptations too.*

And then Areinnye began to sing, questioning the Power in her disturbingly sweet voice, asking and answering. She showed no sign of the unease

that had troubled the others. Nita glanced over at Kit, who had managed by
this time to work his way fairly close to her; he swung his tail a fraction, a
whale's version of a worried headshake. Areinnye's singing was polished, superb, her manner poised, unruffled, royal. She sang her initial rebuff with the
harsh certainty the Gray Lord's song called for.

  " 'Stranger, no more—   give me no gift.
    Power am I,   fear in the water
    as my foes flee.   I need no boon.
    In the Below   all bow before me.
    Speak not to me.   Speak not of gifts.' ' "

The voice that answered her was as sweet and poised as her own.

  "And do you then desire no gift of mine—
  you who have lost so much? Ah no: you have
  strength of your own indeed—great strength of jaw,
  of fluke, of fin; fear goes before your face.
  But sorrow follows after. What use strength
  when slaughtered children rot beneath the waves,
  when the sweet mouth that you gave suck is gone,
  rent to red tatters by the flensing-knives;
  and when the second heart that beat by yours
  lies ground for dogs' meat in a whaler's hull?
  Gray One, accept my Gift and learn of strength—"

That's not in the Song!
Nita stared in shock at Kit, then at the other Celebrants—who, all but
Areinnye, were trading horrified looks. The sperm whale held very still, her
eyes turned outward from the circle; and she shook as violently as T!h!ki had
or, for that matter, Nita. The Lone Power sang on:

  "—learn power! Learn how wizardry may turn
  to serve your purpose, sinking the whalers deep,
  taking the brute invaders' lives to pay
  for that small life that swims the Sea no more;
  take up my Gift—"

"There is—there is another life," Areinnye sang, trembling now as if storm
waters battered at her, breaking the continuity of the Song. "Saved—she
saved—"

> "—what matter? As if brutes who fear the Sea
> are capable of thought, much less of love!
> Even a shark by accident may save
> a life—then turn and tear the newly saved!
> Take up my Gift and take a life for life,
> as it was done of old—"

Slowly Areinnye turned, and the glitter of the wizard-light in her eyes as she looked at Nita was horrible to see. "Life," she sang, one low, thick, struggling note—

She leaped at Nita. In that second Fang, on her left, arrowed in front of Areinnye, punching her jaws away from Nita in time for Nita to roll out of their way. But Fang didn't recover from the blow in time to flee himself; Areinnye's head swept around and the great teeth of her upper jaw raked frightful gashes down Fang's side. Nita pulled herself out of her roll just in time to see something else hit Areinnye—Kit's huge bulk, slamming into her with such force that she was knocked straight into the side of Caryn Peak. She screamed; the water brought back echoes of the sickening sound of her impact. And then she was fleeing—out of the wizard-light, past the boundaries of the protective spell, out into the darkness past the peak.

The Celebrants stirred about in terrible confusion, while S'reee hurried to Fang's side and examined him. Nita stroked over quickly and brushed Fang's good side, very lightly. One of those merry eyes, now slightly less merry, managed to focus on her. "We need you—Silent One," Fang said.

"We do," S'reee said. "These wounds aren't deep, but they're bleeding a lot—and the Master-Shark's about. I've got to handle this. Meanwhile, we're shy the Gray Lord—and I don't think she's going to come back and take back what she said. Kit, are you willing?"

Nita looked swiftly behind her. Kit was hanging there, looking down at Fang. "I'd better be," he said.

"Good. HNii't, administer him the Celebrant's Oath. And hurry." S'reee turned away from them and began one of the faster healing spells.

"Kit, are you sure—"

"Get going," he said.

She led him through the Oath. He said it almost as quickly as Hotshot had, tripping in only one place: ". . . and I shall weave my voice and my will and my blood with theirs if there be need. . . ." He was looking at Nita as he said that, and the look went right through her like a spear.

"Done," S'reee said. "Fang, mind that side—the repair is temporary —Swiftly, now. Everyone circle, we can't afford a delay. Kit, from 'No, must think—' "

They sang. And if the Song had been frightening before, it was becoming

rantic now. Underneath them all the Celebrants could feel some malicious
orce straining to get free—

Nita watched Kit closely. *He didn't rehearse any of this stuff,* she thought.
What if he slips? But Kit sang what remained of the Gray Lord's part fault-
essly; he had laid himself wide open to the Sea and was being fed words and
music directly. Nita felt a lump in her throat—that reaction humans shared
vith whales—at the perfect clarity of his voice. But she couldn't stop worry-
ng. *If he's this open to the Sea, he's also open to that Other—*

And that Other was working on him. Kit was beginning to tremble as the
econd part of the Gray Lord's rebuff came to an end. The soundless voice,
vhen it spoke for the last time, was all sweet reason:

> " '—strength is no use. Give over the vain strife
> that saves no one, keeps no old friend alive,
> condemns the dear to death. Take but my Gift
> and know long years that end not, slow-burnt days
> under the Sun and Moon; not for yourself
> alone, but for the other—' "

"No," Nita said—a mere whisper of song.

Kit looked at her from the heart of the circle, shaking. In his eyes and the
vay he held his body Nita read how easy it would be for him to desert the
iong after just these few lines, destroy it, knowing that Nita would escape
live. Here was the out he had been looking for.

"No!" she tried to say again, but something was stopping her. The malice
n the water grew, burning her. Kit wavered, looking at her—

—then closed his eyes and took a great breath of air from the spell, and
pegan singing again—his voice anguished, but still determined. He finished
he last verse of the Gray Lord's rebuff on a note that was mostly a squeak,
nd immediately turned to S'reee, for the next part would be the group
inging—the battle.

S'reee lifted her head for the secondary invocation.

The ocean floor began to shake. And Nita suddenly realized that it wasn't
ust the Lone Power's malice burning all around her. The water was heating
p.

"Oh, Sea about us, no!" S'reee cried. "What now?"

"Sing!" came a great voice from above them. Aroooon had lifted out of the
ircle, was looking into the darkness, past the great pillar of Caryn Peak. "For
our lives, sing! Forget the battle! HNii't, quickly!"

She knew what he wanted. Nita took one last great gulp of breath, tasting
t as she had never tasted anything in her life, and fluked upward out of the
ircle herself, locating one of the sharp outcroppings she had noticed earlier.

SUPPORT YOUR LOCAL WIZARD

A flash of ghostly white in the background— Good, she thought. Ed's close
"Sea, hear me now," she sang in a great voice, "and take my words and make
them ever law—"

"Nitaaaaaa!"

"HNii't, look out!"

The two cries came from opposite directions. She was glancing toward Kit
one last look, when something with suckered arms grabbed her by the tai
and pulled her down.

The moments that followed turned into a nightmare of thrashing and
bellowing, arms that whipped at her, clung to her, dragging her inexorabl
toward the place where they joined and the wicked beak waited. No one wa
coming to help her, Nita realized, as she looked down into that suckin
mouth. The water was full of screams; and two of the voices she heard wer
those of sperm whales. *Two*— She thrashed harder, getting a view as she di
so of S'reee fleeing before a great gray shape with open jaws—Areinnye; an
coming behind Areinnye, a flood of black shapes, bigger than any the Cele
brants had had to handle in Hudson Canyon.

She's sold out, Nita thought miserably. She's gone over to the Lone One
She came back and broke the circle, and let the krakens in, and everything
going to go to hell if I don't— Nita swung her head desperately and hit th
kraken with it, felt baleen plates in her mouth crack, felt the kraken shudde
Let go of me, you disgusting thing! Nita was past working any wizardry bu
one. Brute force was going to have to do it. *Let go!* She slammed her hea
into the kraken again, sideways. It let out a shrill painful whoop that was ve
satisfying to her. Your eye's sensitive, huh? she thought. One more time!

She hit it again. Something soft gave under the blow, and the krake
screamed. Nita tore free of the loosening arms and swam upward, hard an
fast, heading for her sharp outcropping. The whole area around the base o
Caryn Peak was boiling with kraken, with Celebrants fighting them an
trying desperately not to be dragged out of the boundaries of the protectiv
spell. The bottom was shuddering harder; hot water was shimmering faste
and faster out of the vent. It's got to be stopped, Nita thought. "Kit," sh
called, looking around hurriedly. There's just time enough to say good-bye

Two things she saw. One was that ghostly white shape soaring close by
bolting down the rear half of a kraken about the size of a step van and gazin
down at her as it passed by.

The other was Kit, turning away from a long, vicious slash he had just tor
down Areinnye's side—looking up at Nita and singing one note of hear
tearing misery—not in the Speech—not in the human-flavored whale he ha
always spoken before—but in pure whale.

Oh, no. He's lost language! Nita's heart seized. S'reee had said that if tha
happened, the whalesark was about to be rejected by Kit's brain. Unle

omething was done, it would leave him human again, naked in the cold, hree miles down.

That thought, and the echoes of Kit's cry of anguish, suddenly meant more o Nita than any abstract idea of ten million deaths. And in that second Nita ame to understand what Carl had been talking about. She wheeled around nd stared at the outcropping—then *chose* to do, willingly, what she had hought she'd no choice but to do. The triumph that instantly flared up in er made no sense: But she wouldn't have traded it for any feeling more ensible. She turned and fluked with all her might and threw herself at the tony knives of the peak—and hit—

—something, not stone, and reeled away from the blow, stunned and onfused. Something had punched her in the side. Tumbling over and over vith the force of the blow and the ever-increasing shockwaves blasting up rom the shuddering bottom, Nita saw that great white shape again—but nuch closer, soaring backward with her as she tumbled. "Silent One," he aid, "before you do what you must—give me your power!"

"*What?*"

"Only trust me! Give it me—and be quick!"

Nita could hardly react to the outrageous demand. Only with Kit had she ver dared do such a thing. To give Ed all her power would leave her empty f it, defenseless, until he finished whatever he wanted to do with it. Which ould be hours—or forever. And he wasn't even a wizard—

"Nita, *swiftly!*"

"But Ed, I need it for the Sacrifice. What do you want it for!"

"To call for help!" Ed hissed, arching away through the water toward reinnye and Kit, who was still fighting feebly to keep her busy and away om Nita. "Sprat, be quick and choose, or it will be too late!"

He dove at Areinnye, punched Kit out of harm's way, and took a great rater of a bite out of Areinnye's unprotected flank.

Areinnye's head snapped up and around, slashing at Ed sideways. He voided her, circled in again. "Nita!"

To call for help— What help? And even for Ed, to give up her power, the ning that was keeping her safe and was also the most inside part of her—

Read the fine print before you sign, said a scratchy voice in her memory. *o what the Knight tells you. And don't be afraid to give yourself away!*

"Ed," Nita sang at the bloody comet hurtling through the water, "take it!" nd then she cried the three words that she had never spoken to anyone but it, the most dangerous words in the Speech, which release one's whole ower to another. She felt the power run from her like blood from a wound. he felt Ed acquire it, and demand more as he turned it toward the begin-ing of some ferocious inner calling. And then, when she felt as empty as a shell, Ed shook himself and dived toward the lava again, driving Areinnye away from Kit.

Areinnye refused to be driven. Swiftly she turned and her fangs found Ed's side, scoring a long deep gash from gills to tail. The Master-Shark swept away from Areinnye, his wound trailing a horrid boiling curtain of black blood-smoke in the failing wizard-light.

Nita flailed and gasped with exertion—and got air from the protective spell, much to her surprise. She was still in whaleshape. *And stuck in it, I bet,* she thought, *till I get the power back. What in the world's Ed doing?*

The sea bottom around the vent suddenly *heaved*—lifting like some great dark creature taking its first breath . . . then heaved again, bulging up, with cracks spreading outward from the center of the bulge. The cracks, or something beneath them, glowed red-hot.

The sea floor thundered with another tremor. Superheated water blasted up from the remains of the vent; rocks rained down from Caryn Peak. The red glow burst up through the widening cracks. It was lava, burning a feverish, suppurating red through the murk and the violently shimmering water. The water that came in contact with it—unable to boil at these pressures, regardless of the heat applied to it—did the impossible, the only thing it could do: It burst into flame. Small tongues of blue-violet fire danced and snaked along the outward-reaching tentacles of lava.

The wizard-light remaining in the water was a failing, sickly mist. Caryn Peak shook on its foundations. The Celebrants were scattered. Nita swam desperately upward, trying to do what she saw Kit doing—get safe above the roasting heat of the sea floor. All the bottom between her and the peak was a mazework of lava-filled cracks, broken stone floating on the lava, and violet fire.

Under the stone, under the lava, in the depths of the great crack that had swallowed the vent, something *moved*. Something began to shrug the stone and lava aside. A long shape shook itself, stretched itself, swelled and shrank and swelled again—a shape clothed in lava and black-violet fire, burning terribly. Nita watched in horrified fascination. *What is it?* Nita wondered. *Some kind of buried pipeline?* But no manmade pipeline was a hundred feet across. And no pipeline would seem to breathe, or move by itself, or rear up serpentlike out of the disintegrating sea bed with the dreadful energy of something unbound at last.

That shape was rising now, letting go its grasp on part of that long burning body that stretched away as far as the eye could see from east to west. *A neck,* Nita thought, as the shape reared up taller, towering over the sea bottom. *A neck and a head—* A huge snake's head, fringed, fanged, long and sleek, with dark-burning lava for a hide, and eyes the sick black-violet of water bursting into flame—

In the guise It had first worn after betraying the whales, and wore now again in gloating token of another victory, the Power, the many-named darkness that men had sometimes called the Old Serpent, towered over the sea bed as the binding that had held It shattered. This, Nita realized, was the terrible truth concealed under the old myths of the Serpent that lay coiled about the foundations of the world, waiting for the day It would crush the world in those coils.

And now Its moment was at hand: But It was stretching it, savoring it. It looked at Nita, drifting not two hundred feet from Its immense stony jaws— looked at her out of eyes burning with a color that would sear its way into the nightmares of anyone surviving to remember it. And those eyes *knew* her.

She was frightened; but she had something to do yet. I know my verse now without having to get it from the Sea, she thought. So maybe I won't need wizardry to pull this off. And maybe just doing the Sacrifice will have its own power. Let's find out. . . .

Nita backfinned through the thundering water, staying out of reach of those jaws, watching for any sudden movement. She drew what she suspected was a last breath—the protective spell around her was fading fast—and lifted her voice into the roaring darkness. Ed, she thought, don't blow it now!

> "Must I accept the barren Gift?
>   —learn death, and lose my Mastery?
> Then let them know whose blood and breath
>   will take the Gift and set them free!—' "

The gloating eyes were fixed on her—letting her sing, letting Nita make the attempt. But the Lone Power wasn't going to let her get away with it. That huge, hideous head was bending closer to her. Nita back-finned, not too obviously, she hoped—kept her distance, kept on singing:

> " 'Not old enough to love as yet,
>   but old enough to die, indeed—
> the death-fear bites my throat and heart,
>   fanged cousin to the Pale One's breed—' "

And with a low thick rumble of amusement and hunger, the Serpent's head thrust at Nita in a strike that she couldn't prevent.

This is it!

The sudden small shock in the water made her heart pound. She glanced downward as she sang. There was Kit—battered and struggling with the

failing whalesark as if it were actually someone else's body—but ramming the
Serpent head-on, near where the neck towered up above the slowly squeezing
coils. Their pressure was breaking the sea bed in great pieces, so that lava and
superheated water gushed up in a hundred places. But Kit ignored the heat
and rammed the Old Serpent again and again. He's trying to distract It, Nita
thought, in a terrible uprush of anguish and admiration. He's buying me
time. Oh, Kit! The gift was too precious to waste. "But past the fear lies life
for them," she sang,

> " '—perhaps for me; and past my dread,
>   past loss of Mastery and life,
>   the Sea shall yet give up Her dead!' "

Annoyed—as a human might be by a gnat—the Serpent bent Its head
away from Nita to see what was troubling It. Humor and hunger glinted in
Its eyes as It recognized in Kit the other wizard who had once given It so
much trouble in Manhattan. It bent Its head to him, but slowly, wanting him
to savor the terror. Now, Nita thought, and began to sing again. "Lone
Power—"

"No!" cried another voice through the water, and something came hurtling at her and punched Nita to one side. It was Areinnye—wounded, and
crazy, from the looks of her. I don't have time for this! Nita thought, and for
the first time in her life rummaged around in her mind for a spell that would
kill.

Someone else came streaking in to ram. Areinnye went flying. There was
blood in the water: Ed's, pumping more and more weakly from the gash in
his side. But his eyes were as cool as ever. "Ed," Nita said, breaking off her
singing, "thank you—"

He stared at her as he arrowed toward her—the old indecipherable look.
"Sprat," he said, "when did I ever leave distress uncured?" And to her
complete amazement, before Nita could move, he rammed her again, close to
the head—leaving her too stunned to sing, tumbling and helpless in pain.

Through the ache she heard Ed lift his voice in song. Nita's song—the
lines that, with the offered Sacrifice, bind Death anew and put the Lone
Power in Its place. Kit just went on pummeling at the great shape that bent
closer and closer to them all, and Nita struggled and writhed and couldn't
make a sound.

No! she thought. But it was no use. Ed was taking her part willingly,
circling in on the Lone Power. Yet even through Nita's horror, some wonder

ntruded. Where did he get such a voice? she thought. It seemed to fill the
whole Sea.

> " 'Lone Power, I accept your Gift!
> But take my Gift of equal worth:
> I take Death with me, out of time,
> and make of it a path, a birth!
>
> Let the teeth come! As they tear me,
> they tear your ancient hate for aye—
> so rage, proud Power! Fail again,
> and see my blood teach Death to die!' "

And the Master-Shark dived straight at the upraised neck of the Serpent,
and bit it. He made no cry as Its burning hide blasted his teeth away and
seared his mouth instantly black; he made no cry as the Lone Power, enraged
at Its wounding, bent down to pluck the annoying little creature from Its
neck and crush it in stony jaws.

And then the sharks came.

Calling for help, Ed had said. Now Nita remembered what he had said to
her so long ago, on the only way he had to call his people together . . . with
blood: his own. Her wizardry, though, had lent the call power that even Ed's
own Mastery could never have achieved, just as it had lent him a whale-
wizard's power of song. And brought impossible distances by its power, the
Master-Shark's people came—by dozens, by hundreds, by thousands and tens
of thousands. Maddened by the blood in the water, they fell on everything
that had a wound and tore it to shreds.

Nita found that she could swim again, and she did, fast—away from there,
where all the sharks of the world, it seemed, jostled and boiled in feeding
frenzy. Areinnye vanished in a cloud of sleek silver bodies. Ed could not be
seen. And the Serpent—

A scream of astonishment and pain crashed through the water. The Lone
Power, like all the other Powers, had to obey the rules when within a universe
and wear a body that could be acted upon. The sharks—wild with their
Master's blood and beyond feeling pain—were acting upon it. The taste of
Its scalding blood in the water, and their own, drove them mad for more.
They found more. The screaming went on, and on, and on, all up and down
the length of the thrashing, writhing Serpent. Nita, deafened, writhing her-
self, felt as if it would go on forever.

Eventually forever ended. The sharks, great and small, began milling
slowly about, cruising for new game, finding none. They began to disperse.

Of the Master-Shark, of Areinnye, there was no sign; only a roiling cloud of red that every now and then snowed little rags of flesh.

Of the Lone Power, nothing remained but sluggishly flowing lava running over a quieting sea bed, and in the water the hot sulfurous taste, much diluted, of Its flaming blood. The writhing shape now defined on the bottom by cooling pillow lava made it plain that the Unbound was bound once more by the blood of a willing victim, a wizard—no matter that the wizardry was borrowed.

Aching all over, impossibly tired, Nita hung there for several minutes, simply not knowing what to do. She hadn't planned to live this long.

Now, though: "Kit?"

Her cry brought her back the echo of a sperm whale heading for the surface as quickly as was safe. She followed him.

Nita passed through the "twilight zone" at three hundred fathoms and saw light, the faint green gold she had never hoped to see again. When she broke surface and drew several long gasping breaths, she found that it was morning. Monday morning, she guessed, or hoped. It didn't much matter. She had sunlight again, she had air to breathe—and floating half a mile away in the wavewash, looking too tired to move a fin, the massive back of a sperm whale bobbed and rocked.

She went to him. Neither of them did anything for a long time but lie there in the water, side by side, skin just touching, and breathe.

"I got carried away down there," Kit said eventually. "And the whalesark started to go out on me. I would have gone all sperm whale—and then the sark would have blown out all the way—"

"I noticed," Nita said.

"And you pulled me out of it. I think I owe you one."

"After all that," Nita said, "I'm not sure who owes what. Maybe we'd better call it even."

"Yeah. But, Neets—"

"Don't mention it," she said. "Someone has to keep you out of trouble."

He blew explosively, right in her face.

One by one, finding one another by song, the other Celebrants began to gather around them. Neither Kit nor Nita had any words for them until, last of the group, S'reee surfaced and blew in utter weariness.

She looked at Nita. "Areinnye—"

"Gone," Kit said.

"And the Master-Shark—"

"The Sacrifice," Nita said, "was accepted."

There was silence as the Celebrants looked at each other. "Well," S'reee said, "the Sea has definitely never seen a Song quite like this—"

It will be a Song well sung, said a cool voice in Nita's head. *And sung from the heart. You, young and never loving: I, old and never loved—*

"—but the Lone One is bound. And the waters are quieting."

"S'reee," Fang said, "don't we still need to finish the Song?"

"It's *done,*" Kit said.

S'reee looked at him in silence a moment. "Yes," she said then. "It is."

"And I want to go home," Kit said.

"Well enough," said S'reee. "K!t, we'll be in these waters resting for at least a couple of days. You know where to find us." She paused, hunting words. "And, look—"

"Please save it," Nita said, as gently as she could. She nudged Kit in the side; he turned shoreward for the long swim home. "We'll see you later."

They went home.

They found Nita's parents waiting for them on the beach, as if they had known where and when they would be arriving. Nita found it difficult to care. She and Kit slogged their way up out of the surf, into the towels that Nita's mom and dad held out for them, and stood there shivering with reaction and early-morning cold for several moments.

"Is it going to be all right?" Nita's father asked.

Nita nodded.

"Are *you* all right?" Nita's mother asked, holding her tight.

Nita looked up at her mom and saw no reason to start lying then. "No."

". . . Okay," her mother said. "The questions can wait. Let's get you home."

"Okay," Kit said. "And you can ask *her* all the questions you like . . . while *I* eat."

Nita turned around then; gave Kit a long look . . . and reached out, and hugged him hard.

She didn't answer questions when she got home. She did eat; and then she went to her room and fell onto her bed, as Kit had done in his room across the hall, to get some sleep. But before she dropped off, Nita pulled her manual out from its spot under her pillow and opened it to one of the general data supply areas. "I want a readout on all the blank-check wizardries done in this area in the last six months," she said. "And what their results were."

The list came up. It was short, as she'd known it would be. The second-to-last entry on the list said:

> BCX 85/003—CALLAHAN, Juanita T., and
> RODRIGUEZ, Christopher K.:
> open-ended "Möbius spell"

> implementation.   Incurred:
> 5/25/85. Paid: 7/15/85, by willing
> substitution. See "Current Events"
> précis for details.

Nita put the book back under her pillow, and quietly, bitterly, started to get caught up on her crying.

Heartsong

Neither she nor Kit got up till well after nightfall. When Nita threw clothes on and went downstairs, she found Kit sitting at the table, shoveling Cheerios into his face with the singleminded intensity he gave to the really important things in life. In the living room, she could hear the TV going, making crowd sounds, over which her mother was saying indignantly, "Him? *He's* no hitter! Just you watch—"

Kit looked up at Nita as she leaned on the doorsill. "You hungry?"

"Not yet."

She sat down beside him, carefully—she still ached all over—and picked up the cereal box, absently reading the list of ingredients on the side.

"Business as usual in there," Kit said, between mouthfuls.

"So I hear."

"I'm going out in a while. Wanna come?"

"Swimming?"

"Yeah." He paused for another mouthful. "I've got to take the whalesark back."

"Does it still work?"

"At this point," Kit said, "I'd almost rather not get into it and find out. But it got me back."

Nita nodded, put the cereal box down, and just sat for a moment with her chin in her hands. "I had a thought—"

"*Nooooooo.*"

Nita looked brief murder at Kit, then let the look go. "We seem to have pulled it off again," she said.

"Yeah."

He said it almost a little too easily. "You notice," she said, "that our reward for hard jobs seems to be that we get given *harder* jobs even?"

Kit thought, then nodded. "Problem is," he said, "that we *like* the hard jobs."

She made a sour face. Much as it annoyed her to admit it—her, little quiet Nita who sat in the back of the class and made decent grades and no waves—it was true. "Kit," she said, "they're gonna keep doing that."

" 'They.' "

"The Powers. They'll keep doing it until one day we *don't* pull it off. One of us, or both of us."

Kit looked down at his cereal bowl. "Both, preferably," he said.

She stared at him.

"Saves the explanations." He scooped out the last spoonful of cereal, glanced up, and made a face. "Well, what *would* I have told them?"

Nita shook her head. "We could stop," she said.

Kit chewed, watching her: swallowed, and said, "You want to?"

She waited to see if he would give some sign of what he was thinking. Useless: Kit would make a great poker player someday. "No," she said at last.

"Me either," Kit said, getting up and putting the bowl in the sink. "Looks like we're stuck with being wizards, huh?"

Very slowly, she smiled at him. "Yeah."

"Then let's go down to the water and let them applaud."

Kit gave the screen door a good-natured kick and went pounding down the stairs. Nita shook her head, still smiling, and followed.

It was late. The Moon was now a day past full, and about halfway up the sky; its light was so bright the sky couldn't even manage to be totally black. The stars hung glittering in a sky more indigo, or midnight blue. Nita and Kit walked out into the surf, feeling the wind on them and hearing something most unusual—the sound of whales basking on the surface, some miles out, and singing where they lay. It was, as it had been on first hearing, a high, wild, lovely sound; but now the songs brought something extra, a catch at the heart that hadn't been there before—sorrow, and loss, and wonder. Oh, Ed, Nita thought, and sighed, remembering the glory of how he had sounded at the last. I'm gonna miss you. . . .

Nita swam out far enough to take whaleshape, then took Kit in tow until they made it to water deep enough for a sperm whale. He changed. Side by side they swam outward into the singing, through a sea illumined in a strange green-blue radiance, moonlight diffused and reflected. Dark shapes came to meet them; all the Celebrants but two, cruising and singing in the bright water. S'reee came to greet them skin to skin. "Come swim with us awhile," she said. "No business tonight. Just singing."

"Just a little business," Nita said. It was hard to stop being the Silent Lord, with all her responsibilities. "How are things down deep?"

"Quiet. Not a shake; and several of the hot-water vents seem to have reduced their outputs to normal levels. We're going to have some peace for a while, it seems . . . for which we thank you. Both of you."

"You're very welcome," Kit said. "We'd do it again, if we had to." Nita shot Kit a quizzical look, which he returned in kind. "After all, it's our world too. . . ."

They swam, the Celebrants and Kit and Nita, for a long time, a long way out—into waters bright with fish going about their business, peaceful with seaweed and coral, and warm—whether with volcanism or summer, Nita couldn't tell. "This is the way it's supposed to be," S'reee said from beside her, at one point. "Not the way you met me—not blood in the water. Just the long nights, the singing, time to think. . . ."

"It's so bright," Nita said, wondering. The krill were evidently out in force tonight; between them and the moonlight, the water was dazzling. And there seemed to be more krill yet in the deeper waters, for it was brighter down there; much brighter. "*Look* at that," Kit said, and dived, heading for the light.

At about a hundred feet down, Nita began to realize that the light in the water had nothing to do with krill. Of itself the water was burning, a harmless warm radiance that grew stronger and stronger in the greater depths. And in those depths, everything else shone too: not just reflected light, but a fire that seemed to come from *inside* seaweed, shells, branching coral. Song echoed in that water, sounding at first like whalesong—but slowly Nita began to hear something else in the music, in a way that had nothing to do with hearing. Expressions of growth, of power, of delight—but no note of limitation, pain, loss. She found herself descending into timelessness, into a blaze of meaning and purpose so bright it could have blinded the heart—had the heart not become stronger every moment, more able to bear it.

Finally there was nothing but the brightness, the water all around her on fire with light. Shapes moved in the light, swimming in it as if the water were extraneous and the light were their true medium. There was no looking at those shapes for more than a heartbeat before the eye was forced to turn away, defeated by glory. It was in the passage of those shapes near Nita that it was made plain to her, in the way the Sea gave a whale-wizard knowledge, that she and Kit were welcome indeed and had successfully completed the job they'd been given.

Kit was silent, as if not knowing what to say. Nita knew, but simply considered for a moment before singing it in one soft note that, in this place, carried as poignantly as a trumpet-call at evening.

It hurt, she said.

We know, the answer came back. *We sorrow. Do you?*
For what happened?

No. For who you are now—the person you weren't a week ago.
. . . No.
No, Kit said.
Would you do the same sort of thing again?
Yes . . . if we had to.
Then there's no guarantee this won't happen again. Not that we could offe
you any. Hope, like fear, comes from within. . . .

Nita nodded. There was nothing sorrowful about the pronouncement; i
was as matter-of-fact as anything in the manual. Kit turned away from the
shape, the bright Power, that had answered them. As always, Nita turned
with him.

And, looking up in astonishment, backfinned hurriedly. Something wa:
passing over. Something as huge, or huger than, the unseeable shapes in the
radiant water; burning as fiercely as they did, though with a cooler flame
passing by with a silent, deadly grace that Nita would have known anywhere
I am no wizard, he had said. But how could he, or she, have anticipated tha
borrowing a wizard's power would make even a nonwizard part of the Hear
of the Sea? Or maybe there was more to it than that. *What's loved,* Carl hac
said, *survives.* Nita's heart went up in a great note of unbelieving joy.

The passing shape didn't turn, didn't pause. Nita got just a glance of blacl
eyes, the only dark things in all this place. Yet even they burned, a fire behinc
that opaque look that could mean anything.

Nita knew what it meant. And on he went, out of sight, in unhurriec
grace; the true dark angel, the unfallen Destroyer, the Pale Slayer who neve
really dies—seeking for pain to end.

Nita turned to Kit, wordless. He gazed back, as astonished and delighted a:
she.

. . . Okay, Kit said. *Bring on the next job.*
She agreed.

IGH WIZARDRY

For my dear master,
from someone nearly as surprised

ACKNOWLEDGMENTS AND WARNINGS

Ben Yalow, chief of Academic Computing at CUNY and old friend, contributed much valuable advice on the subtleties of both AI and hardware, all of which contributed to this book one way or another.

Dan Oehlsen knows what he contributed to the effort: a great courtesy, for which many thanks.

Cheerful thanks and good wishes go to the members of the IBM PC Professional and IBM PC Novice Special Interest Groups on CompuServe, who were instrumental in assisting the writer in hitting her deadline. Friends, may your files never be busy!

And thanks, too, to the many members of the CompuServe Science Fiction and Fantasy SIG, whose nightly inquiries about their former Assistant SysOp's new book kept her going.

The author wishes to warn her readers that attempts to reproduce effects described in this book using their own computers may result in extreme frustration, or in damage to their software or hardware, or in violation of their end-user agreements, or all of the above at once: and for said results the author declines to be held legally responsible.

I'd like to get away from Earth awhile
And then come back to it and begin over.
May no fate willfully misunderstand me
And half grant what I wish and snatch me away
Not to return. Earth's the right place for love:
I don't know where it's likely to go better.

—Robert Frost, "Birches"

Where, except in the present, can the Eternal be met?
—C. S. Lewis, "Historicism"

Those who refuse to serve the Powers,
become the tools of the Powers.
Those who agree to serve the Powers,
Themselves *become* the Powers.

Beware the Choice! Beware refusing it!

Book of Night with Moon,
Tetrastych xiv: "Fire over Heaven"

CONTENTS

Initialization

"Hey, there's somebody in the driveway! It's a truck! Mom! Mom, the computer's here!"

The first sound Nita heard that morning was her little sister's shrieking. Nita winced and scrunched herself up into a ball under the covers. Then she muttered six syllables, a very simple spell, and soundproofed her room against her sister's noise.

Blessed silence fell. Unfortunately the spell also killed the buzzing of the locusts and the singing of the birds outside the open window. And Nita liked birds. She opened her eyes, blinking at the bright summer sun coming in the window, and sighed.

Nita said one more syllable. The mute-spell came undone, letting in the noise of doors opening and shutting, and Dairine shrieking instructions and suggestions at the immediate planet. Outside the window a catbird was sitting in the elm tree, screaming, "Thief! Thief!" in an enthusiastic but substandard imitation of a blue jay.

So much for sleeping late, Nita thought. She got up and went over to the dresser by the window, pulled a drawer open and rummaged in it for a T-shirt and shorts. "Morning, Birdbrain," she said as she pulled out a "Live Aid" T-shirt.

The catbird hopped down to a branch of the elm right outside Nita's window. "Bob-white! Bob-white!" it sang at the top of its lungs.

"What's a quail doing in a tree?" Nita said. She pulled the T-shirt on. "Listen to those locusts! Hot one today, huh?"

"Highs in the nineties," the bird sang. "Cheer up! Cheer up!"

"Robins are for spring," Nita said. "I'm more in the mood for penguins at the moment. . . ."

"What's up?"

"Enough with the imitations! I need you to take a message for me. Wizards' business. I'll leave you something nice. Half of one of Mom's muffins Huh?"

The catbird poured out several delighted bars of song that started as a phoebe's call and ended as the five-note theme from *E.T.*

"Good," Nita said. "Then here's something new to sing." She had been speaking all along in the Speech of wizards, the language everything alive understands. Now she added music to it, singing random notes with the words. "Kit, you wanna see a disaster? Come on over here and watch my folks try to hook up the Apple."

The bird cocked an interested eye at her. "You need it again?" Nita said

" 'Kit, you wanna see a disaster?' "

"That's my boy. You remember the way?"

In a whir of white-barred wings, the catbird was gone.

"Must be hungry," Nita said to herself, pulling on her shorts, and then socks and sneakers. While pulling a sneaker on, she glanced at the top of the dresser. There among the stickers and the brushes and combs, under the new Alan Parsons album, lay her wizard's manual.

That by itself wasn't so strange; she'd left it there yesterday afternoon. But it was open; she didn't remember having left it that way. Nita leaned over tying the sneaker, and looked at the page. The Wizards' Oath—Nita smiled It didn't seem like only a few months ago that she'd first read and taken that Oath herself: it felt more like years. February, was it? she thought. No March. Joanne and her crew chased me into the library. And beat the crap out of me later. But I didn't care. I'd found this—

Nita sighed and flipped the book back to the Oath. Trouble came with wizardry. But other things came too—

Whamwhamwham!

Nita didn't even need to turn around to see who was pounding on her door as it banged open. "Come in!" Nita said, and glared at Dairine, who already *was* in.

"It's here!"

"I would never have known," Nita said, dropping the Parsons album back on top of the manual. "Dari, sometimes people like to sleep on a Saturday y'know?"

"When there's a *computer* here? Nita, sometimes you're such a *spud.*"

Nita folded her arms and leaned against the dresser, ready to start a lecture. Her sister, unfortunately, took all the fun out of it by mocking Nita's position and folded arms, leaning against the doorjamb. Funny how someone so little could look so threatening: a little red-haired eleven-year-old stick of a thing in an Admiral Ackbar T-shirt, with a delicate face and watery gray eyes

Problem was, there was someone smart behind those eyes. Someone *too* smart.

Nita let out an annoyed breath. "I won't kill you this time," she said.

"I wasn't worried about that," Dairine said. "And you won't turn me into a toad or anything, either, so don't bother trying that line on me. . . . C'mon, let's watch Mom 'n' Dad mess it up." And she was out the door.

Nita made a face. It didn't help that Dairine knew she was a wizard. She would sooner have told her parents about her wizardry than have told Dairine.

Of course, her folks had found out too . . .

Nita headed out the bedroom door and down the stairs.

The living room was full of boxes and packing material, loose-leaf books, and diskette boxes. Only the desk by the window was clean; and on it sat a cream-colored object about the size and shape of a phone book—the keyboard/motherboard console of a shiny new Apple IIIc+. "Harry," Nita's mother was saying, "don't plug anything in, you'll blow it up. Dairine, get out of that. Morning, Nita, there's some pancakes on the stove."

"Okay," Nita said, and headed into the kitchen. While she was still spreading maple syrup between two pancakes, someone banged on the screen door.

"C'mon in," Nita said, her mouth full. "Have a pancake."

Kit came in: Christopher Rodriguez, her fellow-wizard, quick and dark and sharp-eyed, and at thirteen, a year younger than Nita. And also suddenly two inches taller, for he had hit a growth spurt over the summer. Nita couldn't get used to it; she was used to looking down at him. She handed him a pancake.

"A little bird told me there's about to be trouble," Kit said.

"C'mon," Dairine's strident voice came from the living room, "I wanna play Lunar Lander!"

" 'About to be?' " Nita said.

Kit grinned around the mouthful of pancake and gestured with his head at the living room, raising his eyebrows.

Nita nodded agreement, her mouth full too, and they headed that way.

"Dairine," Nita's mother was saying, "leave your dad alone." Her mother was sitting cross-legged in jeans and sweatshirt, in the middle of a welter of styrofoam peanuts and paperwork, going through a loose-leaf binder. "And don't get those manuals out of order, either. Morning, Kit! How're your mom and dad?"

"Fine, Mrs. Callahan. Hi, Mr. Callahan."

"Hi, Kit," said Nita's dad, rather muffled because he was under the desk by the living room window. "Betty, I've got the three-prong plugs in."

"Oh, good. Then you can set up the external monitor . . ."

"When can I play?" Dairine hollered.

"At this rate," said her father, "sometime in the next century. Nita, do something with her, will you?"

"It's a little late for birth control," Kit said in Nita's ear. Nita spluttered with laughter.

Dairine flew at her. "Was that something dirty? I'll get you for that, you—"

Queep! something said. All heads turned; but it was just the computer, which Nita's dad had plugged in. "Harry, you *will* blow it up," Nita's mother said calmly, from down among the cartons. "We haven't finished reading the instructions yet."

"We don't have to, Betty. We didn't connect the hard disk yet, so we—"

Dairine lost interest in killing Nita. "Can I play now?!"

"See, it says in this manual—"

"Yes, but this one is before that one, Harry—"

"But, look, Betty, it says right here—"

Dairine quietly slipped the plastic wrapping off the monitor and slipped it into its notch at the back of the computer, then started connecting the cable to the screen. Nita glanced at Kit, then back toward the kitchen. He grinned agreement.

"Your folks are gonna lock her in a closet or something," Kit said as they got out of the combat zone.

"I hope so . . . that's probably the only way I'm gonna get at it. But it's okay; she won't blow it up. Her science class has a IIIc: that's one of the reasons Mom and Dad got this one. Dari already knows more about it than the teacher does."

Kit rolled his eyes. "Uh-huh," Nita said. "But I'm not gonna let her monopolize *this* toy, lemme tell you. It's a neat little thing—it has the new foldout screen, and batteries—you could put it in a bookbag. I'll show you later. . . . Where's Ponch?"

"Outside. C'mon."

They went out and sat on the side steps. The locusts were buzzing louder than ever as Ponch, Kit's big black mutt, part Border collie, part German shepherd, came bounding up the driveway to them through the green-gold early sunlight. "Oh, Lord, look at his nose," Nita said. "Ponch, you got stung again, you loon."

"I buried a bone," Ponch said in a string of whines and barks as he came up to them. "The bad things bit me."

"His favorite bone-burying place," Kit said, sounding resigned, "has three yellowjacket nests spaced around it. He gets stung faster than I can heal him."

"Brave," Ponch said, resting his chin, with the swollen black nose, on Nita's shoulder, and looking sideways at her for sympathy.

"Dumb," Nita said, scratching him behind the ears. "But brave. Go get a stick, brave guy. I'll throw it." Ponch slurped Nita's face and raced off.

Kit smiled to see him run.

"So what're we doing today? Anything?"

"Well, there's a new show at the planetarium in the city. Something about other galaxies. My folks said I could go if I wanted to."

"Hey, neat. You got enough money?"

"Just."

"Great. I think I've got enough—let me check."

Nita went back into the house, noticing as she passed through the living room that Dairine was already slipping a diskette into the Apple's built-in disk drive, while her oblivious mother and father were still sitting on the floor pointing at different pages in three different manuals, and arguing cheerfully. *Queep!* the computer said from the living room, as Nita got into her room and upended the money jar on the dresser.

There was no pause in the arguing. *Sometimes I think they like it,* Nita thought, counting the bills. She had enough for the planetarium, and maybe a couple of hot dogs afterward. Nita stuffed the money in her pocket and pushed the jar to the back of the dresser.

—And her eye fell on the record album again. She tipped it up by one corner to look at her wizard's manual, still open to the Oath. She pulled the book out, idly touching the open pages as she held it. *In Life's name, and for Life's sake,* began the small block of type on the right-hand page, *I say that I will use this art only in service of that Life . . .*

Dairine was in here yesterday, Nita thought, skimming down over the words of the Oath. *. . . And she was reading this.* For a moment Nita was furious at the idea of her sister rummaging around in her things; but the anger didn't last. *Maybe,* she thought, *this isn't so bad after all. She's been pestering me with questions about wizardry ever since she found out there really is such a thing. She thinks it's all excitement. But the Oath is heavy stuff. Maybe it threw a little scare into her with all the stuff about "time's end" and doing what you have to, no matter what. Be a good thing if it did make her back off a little. She's too young for this. . . .*

Nita shut the manual, tucked it under her arm and headed out into the living room. Dairine was standing in front of the computer, keying in instructions; the Apple logo came up on the monitor, followed by a screenful of green words too small for Nita to read from across the room. Her mother and father were still deep in the manual. "Mom," Nita said, "Kit and I want to go into the city, to the planetarium, is it okay? Kit's folks said he could."

Nita's mother glanced at her, considering. "Well . . . be back before dark."

"Stay out of Times Square," her father said without looking up, while paging through a manual open in his lap.

"Do you have enough money for the train?" her mother said.

"Mom," Nita said, hefting her wizard's manual in one hand, "I don't think we're going to take the train."

"Oh." Her mother looked dubiously at the book. She had seen more than enough evidence of her daughter's power in the past couple of months: but Nita knew better than to think that her mother was getting comfortable about wizardry, or even used to it. "You're not going into the city to, uh, do something, are you?"

"We're not on assignment, Mom, no. Not for a while, I think, after last time."

"Oh. Well . . . just you be careful, Neets. Wizards are a dime a dozen as far as I'm concerned, but daughters . . ."

Nita's father looked up at that. "Stay out of trouble," he said, and meant it.

"Yes, sir."

"Now, Betty, look right here. It says very plainly, 'Do not use disk without first—' "

"That's *software*, Harry. They mean the *diskette*, not the disk *drive*—"

Nita hurried out through the kitchen before her folks could change their minds. Kit was evidently thinking along the same lines, since he was standing in the middle of the sandy place by the backyard gate, using the stick Ponch had brought him to draw a wizard's transit circle on the ground. "I sent Ponch home," he said, setting various symbols around the circumference of the circle.

"Okay." Nita stepped in beside him. "Where you headed? The Grand Central worldgate?"

"No, there are delays there this morning. The book says to use Penn Station instead. What time have you got?"

Nita squinted up at the Sun. "Nine thirty-five."

"Show-off. Use the watch; I need the Naval Observatory time."

"Nine thirty-three and twenty seconds," Nita said, scowling at her Timex, "*now.*"

"Not bad. Let's haul it before—"

"*What are you doing!*" yelled Nita's father, inside the house. Nita and Kit both jumped guiltily, then looked at each other. Nita sighed.

"Too late," Kit said.

At nine thirty-three and twenty-eight seconds, the screen door opened and

Dairine was propelled firmly out of it. Nita's father put his head out after Dairine, and looked up the driveway. "Take her with you," he said to Nita, and meant that too.

"Yes, sir," Nita said, trying not to sound surly as the screen door slammed shut. Kit rolled his eyes and slowly began adding another set of symbols to those already inside the circle. Dairine scuffed over to them, looking at least as annoyed as Nita felt.

"Well," Dairine said, "I guess I'm stuck with you."

"Get in," Kit said, sounding resigned. "Don't step on the lines."

"And try not to freak out too much, okay?" Nita said.

Dairine stepped over the bounds of the circle and stood there with her arms folded, glaring at Nita.

"What a great time we're all going to have," Kit said, opening his manual. He began to read in the wizardly Speech, fast. Nita looked away from her sister and let Kit handle it.

The air around them began to sing—the same note ears sing when they've been in a noisy place too long; but this singing got louder, not softer, as seconds passed. Nita had the mild satisfaction of seeing Dairine start to look nervous at that, and at the slow breeze beginning around them when everywhere else the summer air was still. The breeze got stronger, dust around them whipped and scattered in it, the sound scaled up until it blotted out almost everything else. And despite her annoyance, Nita suddenly got lost in the old familiar exhilaration of magic working. From memory—for she and Kit had worked this spell together many times—she lifted her voice in the last chorus of it, where the words came in a rush, and the game and skill of the spell lay in matching your partner's cadence exactly. Kit dropped not a syllable as Nita came in, but flashed her a wry grin, matching her word for word for the last ten seconds; they ended together on one word that was half laugh, half shout of triumph. And on the word, the air around them cracked like thunder and struck inward from all directions, like a blow—

The wind stilled and the dust settled, and they found themselves in the last aisle of a small chain bookstore, next to a door with a hand-lettered sign that said EMPLOYEES ONLY. Kit put his manual away, and he and Nita were brushing themselves off when that door popped open and a small sandy-haired man with inquiring eyes looked out at them. "Something fall down out here? No? . . . You need some help?"

"Uh," Nita and Kit said, still in unison.

"X-Men comics," said Dairine, not missing a beat.

"Up front on the right, in the rack," said the small man, and vanished through his door again.

"Hope they have the new annual," Dairine said, brushing dust off her shorts and Admiral Ackbar shirt, and heading for the front of the store.

Kit and Nita glanced ruefully at each other and went after her. It looked like it was going to be a long day.

Passwords

Like so many other human beings, Dairine had made her first major decision about life and the world quite early; at the age of three, in fact. She had seen Nita (then six years old) go away to kindergarten for the first time, and at the end of the day come back crying because she hadn't known the answers to some of the questions the teacher asked her.

Nita's crying had upset Dairine more than anything else in her short life. It had instantly become plain to Dairine's three-year-old mind that the world was a dangerous place if you didn't know things, a place that would make you unhappy if it could. Right there she decided that she was not going to be one of the unhappy ones.

So she got smart. She started out by working to keep her ears and eyes open, noticing everything; not surprisingly, Dairine's senses became abnormally sharp, and stayed that way. She found out how to read by the time she was four . . . just how, she never remembered: but at five she was already working her way through the encyclopedias her parents had bought for Nita. The first time they caught her at it—reading aloud to herself from a *Britannica* article on taxonomy, and sounding out the longer words—her mom and dad were shocked, though for a long time Dairine couldn't understand why. It had never occurred to her that you could use what you knew, use even the knowing itself, to make people feel things . . . perhaps even to make them do things.

For fear of her parents being upset, and maybe stopping her, until she was six or so she kept her reading out of their sight as much as she could. The thought of being kept away from books terrified her. Most of what moved Dairine was sheer delight of learning, the great openness of the world that reading offered her, even though she herself wasn't free to explore the world yet. But there was also that obscure certainty, buried under the months and

years since the decision, that the sure way to make the world work for you
was to know everything. Dairine sat home and busied herself with conquer-
ing the world.

Eventually it came time for her to go off to kindergarten. Remembering
Nita, her parents were braced for the worst, but not at all for Dairine's
scowling, annoyed response when she came home. "They won't listen to
what I tell them," Dairine said. *"Yet."* And off she went to read, leaving her
mother and father staring at each other.

School went on, and time, and Dairine sailed her way up through the
grades. She knew (having overheard a couple of her mother's phone conversations with the school's psychiatrist) that her parents had refused to let her
skip grades. They thought it would be better for her to be with kids of her
own age. Dairine laughed to herself over this, since it made school life utterly
easy for her: it also left her more free time for her own pursuits, especially
reading. As soon as she was old enough to go to the little local library for
herself, she read everything in it: first going straight through the kids' library
downstairs at about six books a day, then (after the concerned librarian got
permission from Dairine's parents) reading the whole adult collection, a
touch more slowly. Her mom and dad thought it would be a shame to stifle
such an active curiosity. Dairine considered this opinion wise, and kept reading, trying not to think of the time—not too far away—when she would
exhaust the adult books. She wasn't yet allowed to go to the big township
library by herself.

But she had her dreams, too. Nita was already being allowed to go into
New York City alone. In a few years, she would too. Dairine thought constantly of the New York Public Library, of eight million books that the
White Lions guarded: rare manuscripts, books as old as printing, or older. It
would take even Dairine a while to get through eight million books. She
longed to get started.

And there were other dreams more immediate. Like everyone else she
knew, Dairine had seen the Star Wars movies. Magic, great power for good
and evil, she had read about in many other places. But the Star Wars movies
somehow hit her with a terrible immediacy that the books had not; with a
picture of power available even to untrained farmboys on distant planets in
the future, and therefore surely available to someone who knew things in the
present. And if you could learn that supreme knowledge, and master the
power that filled and shaped the universe, how could the world ever hurt you?
For a while Dairine's reading suffered, and her daydreams were full of the
singing blaze of lightsabers, the electric smell of blasterfire, and the shadow
of ultimate evil in a black cloak, which after terrible combat she always
defeated. Her sister teased her a lot less about it than Dairine expected.

Her sister. . . . Their relationship was rather casual, not so much a relative-relationship as the kind you might have with someone who lived close enough for you to see every day. When both Dairine and Nita were little, they had played together often enough. But where learning came in, for a while there had been trouble. Sometimes Nita had shown Dairine things she was learning at school. But when Dairine learned them almost immediately, and shortly was better at them than Nita was, Nita got upset. Dairine never quite understood why. It was a victory for them both, wasn't it, over the world, which would get you if you didn't know things? But Nita seemed not to understand that.

Eventually things got better. As they got older, they began to grow together and to share more. Possibly Nita was understanding her better, or had simply seen how much Dairine liked to know things; for she began to tutor Dairine in the upper-grade subjects she was studying, algebra and so forth. Dairine began to like her sister. When they started having trouble with bullies, and their parents sent them both off to self-defense school, Dairine mastered that art as quickly as anything else she'd ever decided to learn; and then, when a particularly bad beating near home made it plain that Nita wasn't using what they'd learned, she quietly put the word out that anyone who messed with Nita would have Dairine to deal with. The bullying stopped, for both of them, and Dairine felt smugly satisfied.

That is, she did until one day after school she saw a kid come at Nita to "accidentally" body-block her into the dirt of the playground she was crossing. Dairine started to move to prevent it—but as the kid threw himself at Nita, he abruptly slid sideways off the air around her as if he had run into a glass wall. No one else seemed to notice. Even the attacker looked blank as he fell sideways into the dust. But Nita smiled a little, and kept on walking . . . and suddenly the world fell out from under Dairine, and everything was terribly wrong. *Her sister knew something she didn't.*

Dairine blazed up in a raging fire of curiosity. She began watching Nita closely, and her best friend, Kit, too, on a hunch. Slowly Dairine began to catch Nita at things no one else seemed to notice; odd words muttered to empty air, after which lost things abruptly became found, or stuck things came loose.

There was one day when their father had been complaining about the crabgrass in the front lawn, and Dairine had seen an odd, thoughtful look cross Nita's face. That evening her sister had sat on the lawn for a long time, talking under her breath. Dairine couldn't hear what was said; but a week and a half later their father was standing on and admiring a crabgrass-free lawn, extolling the new brand of weedkiller he'd tried. He didn't notice, as Dairine did, the large patch of crabgrass under the apple trees in the neighbor's yard next door . . . carpeting a barren place where the neighbor had been trying to get something green to grow, anything, for as long as Dairine could remember. It was all stuff like that . . . little things, strange things, nothing Dairine could understand and use.

Then came summer vacation at the beach—and the strangeness started to come out in the open. Nita and Kit started spending a lot of time away from home, sneaking in and out as if there were something to hide. Dairine heard her mother's uneasy conversations about this with her father, and was amused; whatever Nita was doing with Kit, Dairine knew sex wasn't involved. Dairine covered for Nita and Kit, and bided her time, waiting until they should owe her something.

The time came soon enough. One night the two of them went swimming and didn't come back when it got dark, as they'd agreed to. Dairine's mom and dad went out looking for Nita and Kit on the beach, and took Dairine with them. She got separated from them, mostly on purpose, and was a quarter-mile down the beach from them when, with a rush of water and noisy breath, a forty-foot humpback whale breached right in front of her, ran itself aground—and turned into Nita.

Nita went white with shock at the sight of Dairine. Dairine didn't care. "You're going to tell me *everything*," she said, and ran down the beach to distract her parents just long enough for Nita and Kit—also just changed back from a whale—to get back into their bathing suits. And after the noisy, angry scene with their parents that followed, after the house was quiet, Dairine went to Nita's room, where Kit was waiting, too, and let them tell her the whole story.

Wizards' manuals, oaths, wizardry, spells, quests, terrible dangers beyond the world, great powers that moved unseen and unsuspected beneath the surface of everyday existence, and every now and then broke surface— Dairine was ecstatic. It was all there, everything she had longed for. And if they could have it, she could have it too. . . .

Dairine saw their faces fall, and felt the soft laughter of the world starting behind her back again. You couldn't have this magic unless you were offered it by the Powers that controlled it. Yes, sometimes it ran in families, but there was no guarantee that it would ever pass to you. . . .

At that point Dairine began to shut their words out. She promised to keep their secret for the time being, and to cover for them the best she could. But inside she was all one great frustrated cry of rage: *Why them, why them and not me!* Days later, when the cry ebbed, the frustration gave way to blunt, stubborn determination. *I'll have it. I will.*

She had gone into Nita's room, found her wizard's manual, and opened it. The last time she'd held it it had looked like a well-worn kid's book from the library and, when she'd borrowed it, had read like one. Now the excitement the exultation, flared up in Dairine again; for instead of a story she found

pages and pages of an Arabic-looking script she couldn't read . . . and near
the front, many that she could, in English.

She skimmed them, turning pages swiftly. The pages were full of warnings
and cautions, phrases about the wizard's responsibility to help slow down the
death of the universe, paragraphs about the price each wizard paid for his
new power, and about the terrible Ordeal-quest that lay before every novice
who took the Wizards' Oath: sections about old strengths that moved among
the worlds, not all of them friendly. But these Dairine scorned as she'd
scorned Nita's cautions. The parts that spoke of a limitless universe full of life
and of wizards to guard it, of "the Billion Homeworlds," "the hundred million species of humanity," those parts stayed with her, filled her mind with
images of strangeness and glory and adventure until she was drowning in her
own thought of unnumbered stars. I can do it, she thought. I can take care of
myself. I'm not afraid. I'll matter, I'll *be* something. . . .

She flipped through the English section to its end, finding there one page,
with a single block of type set small and neat.

> In Life's name, and for Life's sake, I assert that I will employ the
> Art which is Its gift in Life's service alone. I will guard growth
> and ease pain. I will fight to preserve what grows and lives well in
> its own way; nor will I change any creature unless its growth and
> life, or that of the system of which it is part, are threatened. To
> these ends, in the practice of my Art, I will ever put aside fear for
> courage, and death for life, when it is fit to do so—looking always
> toward the Heart of Time, where all our sundered times are one,
> and all our myriad worlds lie whole, in That from Which they
> proceeded. . . .

It was the Oath that Nita had told her about. Not caring that she didn't
understand parts of it, Dairine drew a long breath and read it out loud,
almost in triumph. And the terrible silence that drew itself down around her
as she spoke, blocking out the sounds of day, didn't frighten her; it exhila-
rated her. Something was going to happen, at last, at last. . . .

She went to bed eagerly that night.

Up and Running

Nita and Kit and Dairine made their way among the shops of the lower level of Penn Station and caught the C train for the Upper West Side, coming up at Eighty-first and Central Park West. For a little bit they stood there just getting their bearings. It was warm, but not uncomfortable yet. The park glowed green and golden.

Dairine was fidgeting. "Now where?"

"Right here," Nita said, turning around. The four-block stretch behind them, between 77th and 81st streets, was commanded by the huge, graceful bulk of the American Museum of Natural History, with its marble steps and beast-carved pediment, and the great bronze equestrian statue of Teddy Roosevelt looking eastward across at the park. Tucked into a corner of the building on 81st Street stood the art deco–looking brick cube of the Hayden Planetarium, topped with a greened-copper dome.

"It looks like a tomb," Dairine said. "Shove *that*. I'm going to Natural History and look at the stuffed elephants."

"Climb on the stuffed elephants, you mean," Nita said. "Forget it. You're staying with us."

"Oh? What makes you think you can keep track of me if I decide to—"

"This," Kit said grimly, hefting his wizard's manual. "If we have to, we can put a tracer on you. Or a leash . . ."

"Oh, yeah? Well, listen, smart guy, *I*—"

"Kit," Nita said under her breath, "easy. Dari, are you out of your mind? This place is full of *space* stuff. The new Shuttle mock-up. A meteorite ten feet long." She smiled slightly. "A store with Star Wars books . . ."

Dairine stared at Nita. "Well, why didn't you say so? Come on." She headed down the cobblestone driveway toward the planetarium doors.

"You never catch that fly with vinegar," Nita said quietly to Kit as the two of them followed at a safe distance.

"She's not like my sisters," Kit said.

"Yeah. Well, your sisters are human beings. . . ."

They snickered together and went in after Dairine. To Nita's mild relief—because paying for her little sister's ticket would have killed her hot-dog money—Dairine already had admission money with her. "Dad give you that?" Nita said as she paid.

"No, this is mine," said Dairine, wrapping the change up with the rest of a wad, and sticking it back in her shorts.

"Where'd you get all that?"

"I taught a couple guys in my class to play poker last month," said Dairine. And off she went, heading for the souvenir store.

"Neets?" Kit said, tossing his manual in one hand.

Nita thought about it. "Naah," she said. "Let her go. Dairine!"

"What?"

"Just don't leave the building!"

"Okay."

"Is that safe?" Kit said.

"What, leaving her alone? She'll get into the Shuttle mock-up and not come out till closing time. Good thing there's hardly anyone here. Besides, she did say she wouldn't leave. If she were going to weasel out of it, she would've just grunted or something."

The two of them paused to glance into the souvenir store, full of books and posters and T-shirts and hanging *Enterprise*s—both shuttle and starship. Dairine was browsing through a *Return of the Jedi* picture book. "Whatcha gonna get, hotshot?" Kit said, teasing.

"Dunno." She put the book down. "What I really need," she said, looking down at a set of Apollo decals, "is a lightsaber."

"And what would you do with it once you had it?"

"Use it on Darth Vader," Dairine said. "Don't you two have somewhere to be?"

Nita considered the image of Dairine facing down Darth Vader, lightsaber in hand, and felt sorry for Vader. "C'mon," she said to Kit. They ambled down the hall a little way, to the Ahnighito meteorite on its low pedestal—thirty-four tons of nickel–iron slag, pitted with great holes like an irregularly melted lump of Swiss cheese. Nita laid her hands and cheek against it; on a hot day in New York, this was the best thing in the city to touch, for its pleasant coolness never altered, no matter how long you were in contact with it. Kit reached out and touched it too.

"This came a long way," he said.

"The asteroid belt," Nita said. "Two hundred fifty million miles o so . . ."

"No," Kit said. "Farther than that." His voice was quiet, and Nita realized that Kit was deep in the kind of wizardly "understanding" with the meteorit that she had with trees and animals and other things that lived. "Long, lon; dark times," Kit said, "nothing but space, and the cold. And then slowly light growing. Faster and faster—diving in toward the light, till it burns, and gas and water and metal boil off one after another. And before everything' gone, out into the dark again, for a long, long time. . . ."

"It was part of a comet," Nita said.

"Until the comet's orbit decayed. It came in too close to the Sun on on pass, and shattered, and came down—" Kit took his hand away abruptly. "I doesn't care for that memory," he said.

"And now here it is. . . ."

"Tamed," Kit said. "Resting. But it remembers when it was wild, and roamed in the dark, and the Sun was its only tether. . . ."

Nita was still for a few seconds. That sense of the Earth being a small saf "house" with a huge backyard, through which powers both benign and terri ble moved, was what had first made her fall in love with astronomy. To hav someone share the feeling with her so completely was amazing. She met Kit' eyes, and couldn't think of anything to say; just nodded.

"When's the sky show?" he said.

"Fifteen minutes."

"Let's go."

They spent the afternoon drifting from exhibit to exhibit, playing with the ones that wanted playing with, enjoying themselves and taking their time. T Nita's gratification, Dairine stayed mostly out of their way. She did attach herself to them for the sky show, which may have been lucky; for Dairine go fascinated by the big Zeiss star projector, standing under the dome like a giant lens-studded dumbbell, and only threats of violence kept her out of the open booth that contained the computer-driven controls.

When the sky show was done, Dairine went off to the planetarium store t add a few more books to the several she'd already bought. Nita didn't see he again until late in the afternoon, when she and Kit were trying out the scales that told you your weight on various planets. Nita had just gotten on the scale for Jupiter, which weighed her in at twenty-one hundred pounds.

"Putting on a little weight, there, Neets," Dairine said behind her. "Espe cially up front."

Nita almost turned around and decked her sister. Their mom had just taken Nita to buy her first bra, and her feelings about this were decidedly mixed—a kind of pride combined with embarrassment, because none of the girls she hung out with had one yet, and she had become the focus of some slight envy. It all made her uncomfortable, and Dairine, sensing this, had been running the subject into the ground for days.

She can stuff it right up!, Nita thought fiercely, *I am not going to let her get to me!* "All muscle, Dair," she said. "Besides, it's where you are that counts. Check this out." She sidestepped to the Mars scale, the needle of which stopped at seven pounds. "Less than the Moon, even."

"But it's bigger than the Moon," Dairine said.

"But not as dense. That's why its atmosphere's so thin even though Mars is that big; its mass is too small to hold it—" Nita heard footsteps, turned around, and saw that she had lost her audience. "Dairine? Where you headed?"

"Bathroom." Dairine's voice came from halfway down the stairs to the lower level.

"Well, hurry up, it's almost closing time."

Kit, on the Saturn scale, moved over to the Jupiter. "What was that all about?" he said. "I don't often hear you think these days, but if your dad had heard your mind right after she said that, he would've washed your head out with soap."

"Oh, crap." She tried the scale for Mercury: three and a half pounds. "I'm growing."

"You don't look any taller."

"Kit!"

"Oh." He looked at her chest. "Oh. I guess." He shrugged. "I didn't notice."

Oh, thank heaven, Nita thought, and immediately after that, *He didn't notice?* She swallowed and said, "Anyway, she's been riding me. I'm gonna kill her if she keeps it up."

"Maybe she's jealous."

Nita laughed. "Her? Of *me*?"

"Sure." Kit got off the scales and began to pace off the space between the scales and the doors to the planetarium proper. "Neets, wake up. You're a wizard. Here Dairine's been hot for magic since she was a little kid—any kind, Star Wars, you name it—and all of a sudden, not only does it turn out that there really *is* such a thing, but *you* turn up with it. From what you had to tell her to keep her quiet after she found out, Dari knows that you and I do big stuff. She wishes she could get her hands on the power. And there's no guarantee she ever will."

"She was into my manual over the last couple of days, I think. . . ."

"So there you are. If she can't have the magic, she's gonna twist you around whatever other way she can. I hate to say this, Neets, but she's a real brat."

That agreed too well with thoughts Nita had been having, but had rejected. "Well. . . ."

"Ladies and gentlemen," said a woman's voice from the ceiling speakers down the hall, "the planetarium is now closing. Thank you."

Nita sighed. Kit punched her lightly in the arm. "Come on," he said, "don't let her get you down. Let's go over to the park and get hot dogs. She starts getting on our nerves, we'll tell her we'll turn her into a fire hydrant and call in every dog in Manhattan to try her out."

"Too late," Nita said. "She already knows we don't do that kind of thing."

"She knows you don't do that kind of thing," Kit said. "She doesn't know that I don't. . . ."

Nita looked at his grim expression and wondered briefly whether the grimness was all faked. "I am starved."

"So c'mon."

They headed down the stairs together and came out on the ground floor, by the front doors. In the stairwell, under an arrow pointing toward the basement level, was a sign they had seen earlier that day, and laughed at:

TO MARS, VENUS, AND LADIES' ROOM

"Wait for me," Nita said. "She's probably trying to break into that Venus exhibit to see where the 'lava' comes from."

Kit rolled his eyes. "Being a fire hydrant may be too good for her."

Nita went down the stairs. "Dari?" she called, annoyed. "Come on before they lock us in."

It was considerably cooler down here. Nita turned right at the bottom of the stairs and walked quickly through the Venus exhibit, rubbing her upper arms at the chill, which went right through her thin T-shirt. Someone had turned off the sluggishly erupting Venerian volcano behind its murky glass wall; no one was to be seen anywhere else, all the way down to the temporary plasterboard wall with the sign that said MARS CLOSED FOR RENOVATIONS.

"Don't tell me she's still in the toilet," Nita muttered, annoyed. Reading, probably. One of these days she's gonna fall in. She went back the way she had come, past the stairs, to the ladies' room. It was not only cold down here, there was a draft. She grabbed the handle of the door and pulled; it resisted her slightly, and there was a faint hoo noise, air sliding through the door crack as she tugged. "Dari? Come on, we're leaving!" Nita pulled harder, the door came open—

Air blew hard past her and ruffled her hair into her eyes. Bitter cold smote the front of her, and in it the humidity in the air condensed out instantly, whipping past Nita through the sucking air as stinging, dust-fine snow.

Nita was looking through the doorway into a low rust-red wasteland: noth-

ng but stones in all sizes, cracked, tumbled, piled, with dun dust blowing
between them. Close, much too close to be normal, lay a horizon hazed in
blood-brown, shading up through translucent brick color, rose, violet, a hard
dark blue, and above everything, black with stars showing. Low in the crystal-
line rose burned a small pinkish sun, fierce, distant-looking, and cold. Nita
flinched from the unsoftened sight of it, from the long, harsh shadows it laid
out behind every smallest stone. She slammed the ladies' room door shut. Air
kept moaning past her, through the cracks, out into the dry red wasteland.

"Mars," she breathed, and terror grabbed her heart and squeezed. "She
went to *Mars*. . . !"

Escape Key

That morning Dairine had awakened with the Oath's words ringing in her ears to find herself not in a galaxy far far away, but in her own bed. She had lain there for a long few minutes in bitter annoyance before she heard the wheels of the truck in the driveway. It was the computer, of course: and to this lesser excitement she had gratefully surrendered herself.

Dairine was good with computers. It was just one more kind of knowledge, good for using to keep people and the World off your back; and computers were really surprisingly easy to work with once you got it through your head that they were utterly stupid things, unable to do anything you didn't tell them how to do, in language they understood. In her few months' work with the Apples at school, Dairine had become an accomplished hacker.

She utterly disdained the "phreaking," the breaking and entering of electronic bulletin boards and systems that interested a few of her malicious classmates. It could get you thrown in jail. What fascinated Dairine was advanced programming, the true hacking—getting a computer to sing, or talk, or play involved and clever games, or make you a sandwich. All these things were possible, with the right peripherals and a smart programmer. That she was; and the computer—tireless listener, absolutely obedient to orders, and endlessly forgiving of mistakes—was the perfect companion. They worked well together. Even her teachers had noticed that the machines "behaved" better around Dairine than around anyone else. She never noticed this herself, having taken it for granted.

So while her mother and father sat arguing over the manuals, of course Dairine took matters into her own hands. The Apple IIIc+ was easy to set up: a plug and cable for the screen, the printer cable attached to the printer port and the computer's interface; the power cord to the wall. Dairine slipped a system disk into the drive, shut the drive door, and turned the computer on, "booted it up"—ready to look for the "Copy" utility in the disk's directory. The first thing you always did with a brand-new system disk full of programs was copy it; working on the original disk could cost you a lot of money to replace if you hurt or wiped it accidentally.

The Apple logo came up on the screen, and below it the A> prompt that said the computer's basic operating system, called DOS, was ready to accept commands to its "A" or onboard disk drive and the disk inside it. Dairine was about to start typing when something about the logo caught her eye. It was the famous striped Apple, all right: but it had no bite out of it.

She stared for a second. Pirated software? she thought, but that was ridiculous. Her dad had bought the computer and its system software from an approved dealer, and the various warranties, manuals and end-user agreements were all over the floor. Huh. Maybe they changed the logo. Oh, well. Let's see the directory. . . .

DIR A: , she typed on the keyboard, and hit the carriage return.

PASSWORD? said the screen, and sat there apparently waiting for a response, for the A> prompt hadn't come back.

That was no response she'd ever seen on the machines at school. DIR A: , she typed, again, and the carriage return.

PASSWORD?

"Huh," she said to herself, as possibilities flickered through her head. Did Dad have the software encrypted somehow so that Nita and I can't get into it? But why? He wants us to use it. She let out a breath. Maybe it just wants an ID code for the user—there're some programs that do that. She squinted at the screen a moment, then smiled and typed in a private joke: the code name that a certain untrained farmboy used in his fighter run on the Death Star, a name that suited Dairine since she had inherited her mother's red hair. RED FIVE, she typed, and hit the carriage return.

PASSWORD RED FIVE ACCEPTED.

A>

Weird, Dairine thought, and typed again.

DIR A:

The disk drive whirred. The screen wiped itself and displayed a list: mostly program command files, or data files holding information for the programs, to judge by their suffixes.

ASSIST.COM	22008K
CHANGE.COM	2310K
COPY.COM	1032K
COPY.DAT	4404K
GO.COM	5048K
GO.DAT	3580K
HIDE.COM	1244K
MANUAL.COM	3248K
MANUAL.DAT	10662K

MBASIC.COM	7052K
MENU.COM	256K
SEEK.COM	6608K
SUPPORT.COM	5120K
SUPPORT.DAT	3218K
A >	

Dairine gazed at the screen, perplexed. A *K* was a kilobyte, a thousand little pieces or bytes of information; and the disk drive itself was supposed to hold only 800 K. How could the disk possibly have all these files on it, and such big ones?

Maybe this is a bad disk, Dairine thought. It happened sometimes, that a disk was damaged on its way from the factory. Or maybe something was wrong with the directory. Well, let's see if something'll run. Beside the A > prompt she typed "COPY" and hit the carriage return.

The disk drive whirred. The screen wiped itself again, then said:

IIIC COPY UTILITY
5430K FREE
RADIUS?

Dairine stared again. *Radius* meant nothing to her. She hit the carriage return, hoping the computer would (as some programs did) supply its own data as a result.

DEFAULT RADIUS, the screen said. It was all right, then; the program had been instructed to supply a value of its own if the user didn't specify one. Dairine let out a breath, and resolved to have a look at this thing's manual. Maybe the company had made changes in the software.

COPY UTILITY READY, said the screen. PRESS < CR > TO BEGIN.

Dairine hit the carriage return. The disk drive whirred.

There were two computers on the desk.

She gaped. Hesitantly she put out a hand to the second computer, which was sitting next to the first, and sticking over the edge of the desk a little. It was solid, and its screen matched that of the original computer exactly. They both said:

COPY SUCCESSFULLY COMPLETED.
DESCRIPTION FILE "APPLIIIC.DSC" CREATED
HARD COPY "APPLIIIC.CPY" CREATED
A >

Oh, Lord! Dairine thought. She didn't dare turn around or make any outward sign: behind her, her mother and father were arguing peaceably over the contents of the Apple manuals. Desperately, Dairine brought up the directory again, stared at it, and then, for lack of any better idea, typed:

HIDE

The disk drives whirred again. Dairine thought she had never heard such a loud noise in her life, but her parents still didn't notice anything. The screen cleared itself, then said:

IIIC HIDE UTILITY
Choose one:

(1) Hide from COPY utility
(2) Hide from CHANGE utility
(3) Hide from MBASIC
(4) Exit to system

Dairine typed "1." The screen cleared again.

HIDE FROM "COPY" UTILITY

Last copy description file in
memory: "APPLIIIC.DSK"
Last hard copy created: "APPLIIIC.CPY"
Name of hard copy to
hide?

Dairine hurriedly typed "APPLIII.CPY." The screen said:

HIDE OPTIONS:

(a)   Hide in realspace
      (invisibility option)
(b)   Hide in realspace
      (size reduction)
(c)   Hide in otherspace
      (retrievable pocket)
(d)   Discard in otherspace
      (nonretrievable pocket)
(e)   Timed storage
      (coordinate-specific claudication)
(f)   Exit to main menu

Dairine typed "c."

PASSWORD FOR RETRIEVAL?

Dairine swallowed: behind her, her father was muttering about getting some coffee. "RED FIVE," she typed.

CHOOSE INPUT OPTION: VERBAL OR KEYBOARD?

"VERBAL," she typed, very fast.
The drives whirred.

HIDING HARD COPY OF FILE "APPLIIIC.CPY."

As silently as it had come, the second computer vanished.
A>
Dairine's father turned around and saw her at the computer. *"What are you doing!"*

"Uh," Dairine said. She couldn't remember when she had last been at a loss for words. Her father, though, wasn't even slightly concerned with this. Several seconds later Dairine found herself going to New York with Nita and Kit.

At the moment, even the thought of the New York Public Library seemed a bit tame.

It took her hours to get free of Nita and Kit. All the while her mind was raging, turning over and over the thought of what power she had been offered when she took the Oath, and when she finally got down to the ladies' room and sat down in one of the stalls, her heart was hammering with excitement and sweat stood out on her.

"Red five," she whispered, and held her breath.

There was a computer in her lap.

She flipped up the little liquid-crystal screen and was shocked to find the A> prompt staring at her: shocked partly because she hadn't booted the computer up, and partly because it couldn't be running—there were no batteries in it yet—or were there? But Dairine wasn't one to argue the point. She typed hurriedly, using the HIDE.COM program to put the books she'd bought in a "pocket" and get them out of her way. Then she brought up the directory again. ASSIST.COM, said the first entry. Maybe that was a "help menu," a series of screens that would explain how to get the most out of the computer. She typed "ASSIST" and the carriage return.

The screen cleared, then said at the top:

ACTIVE OR PASSIVE MODE?

Dairine was out of her depth again. "ACTIVE," she typed, on a guess, and entered it. The screen cleared again.

UTILITY OPTIONS:

(1)   General Data & Logistics—MANUAL, MENU
(2)   Travel—GO.COM
(3)   Intervention—CHANGE (see also MANUAL)
(3a)   Duplication—COPY
(3b)   Preservation—HIDE, SEEK
(4)   Outside assistance—(routine) SUPPORT
(4a)   (emergency) ASSIST
(5)   Other programming—MBASIC
(6)   Exit to system

Dairine chewed her lip and thought. Just to see what would happen, she hit "2" and the carriage return. The screen cleared.

TRAVEL UTILITY

Input? (1) keyboard, (2) verbal

"2," Dairine typed.

"Inside solar system or outside solar system?" the computer said very quietly, but so suddenly that Dairine almost dropped it.

"Inside," she said, and swallowed.

"Planet?"

She gazed at the ladies' room door, thinking of the dioramas outside with a sudden terrible desire. "Mars," Dairine said.

The disk drive chirred briefly. "Coordinates?"

Dairine knew that aerographers used some kind of latitude–longitude system for Mars, but she knew nothing else about it. "Default," she said, on a hunch.

"Default coordinates confirmed," said the computer, "last recorded transit. Atmosphere?"

Last recorded— "Uh, atmosphere? Yes," she said.

"Parameters?"

"Umm. . . . Fifteen percent oxygen, eighty percent nitrogen, five percent carbon dioxide."

"Mix proportions approximate Terran sea-level parameters. Default to those?"

"Mmm . . . Yes."

"Estimated time in transit?"

She thought. "One hour."

"Data complete," said the computer. "Ready to transit. Transit command 'run.' "

"Run," Dairine said.

And everything slewed sideways and upside down. Or no, the world stayed the same—but Dairine's frame of reference suddenly became huger than the whole Earth and the space that contained it, so that her planet seemed only one moving, whirling point plunging along its path through a terrible complexity of forces, among which gravity was a puny local thing and not to be regarded. Up was some other way now; down had nothing to do with the floor. Her stomach rebelled.

And her eyes were seeing things they had never been made to see. Lines and sparks and traces of white fire seemed to tear through her head from her eyes to the back of her skull; they pinned her to the rolling Earth like a feeble fluttering moth to a card. A terrible silence with a deadly sea-roar at the bottom of it, more terrible than the stillness of her Oathtaking, flattened her down with its sheer cold ancientness, a vast weight of years without sound or light or life. Cosmic rays, she thought desperately, clutching at reason: faster than-light particles, maybe that's what the light is. But the dark—it's death, death itself, I'm going to die—

—and the wizardry let her go. Dairine got shakily to her feet. The first crunch of stones and gravel under her sneakers, instead of tile floor, went through her in a rush of adrenaline as fierce as fire. Her vision cleared. Red wasteland stretched away under a cold rose sun, a violet sky arched over her, the wind sang chill. She turned slowly, looking around. High up in the cold violet day, something small and bright fled across the sky, changing phase as it did so.

"Deimos," Dairine whispered. Or maybe it was Phobos, the other of Mars's two little moons. Whichever it was, it went through half its month in a few minutes, sliding down toward the horizon and down behind something that stood up from it. It was a mountain peak, upraised as if on a pedestal, and so tall that though it came up from far behind the foreshortened horizon, its broad flat base spanned half that horizon easily. "What is that?" she said.

"Syntax error 24," said the Apple dispassionately. "Rephrase for precision."

"That mountain. What is it? Identify."

"Earth/IAU nomenclature 'Olympus Mons.' "

Dairine took in a sharp breath. It was an ancient volcano, long extinct, and the highest mountain in the Solar System. "How do I get up there?"

"Reference short-transit utilities."

She did. Five minutes later she stood in a place where the wind no longer sang, for it was too thin to do so; where carbon dioxide lay frozen on the rust

red stones, and the fringes of her protective shell of air shed a constant snow
of dry ice and water vapor as she moved; a place from which she could see the
curvature of the world. Dairine stood twelve miles high atop Olympus Mons,
on the ridge of its great crater, into which Central Park could have been
dropped entire, and looked out over the curve of the red world at what no
nonwizardly child of Earth had seen with her or his own eyes before: the
asteroid belt rising like a chain of scattered stars, and beyond them, the
tiniest possible disk, remote but clear.

"Jupiter," she whispered, and turned around to look for Earth. From here
it would look like a morning or evening star, just a shade less bright than
Venus. But in mid-movement she was distracted. There was something down
in the mile-deep crater, a little light that shone.

"What's that?" she said, holding up the Apple.

"Syntax error 24—"

"Yeah, yeah, right. That light! Identify."

"A marker beacon. Provenance uncertain at this range."

"Get us down there!"

With Dairine's help, it did. Shortly she was staring at a pole with a light on
it, streamlined and modern-looking, made of some dark blue metal she
couldn't identify. Set in the ground beside the pole was a plate of dull red
metal with strange markings on it. "What's it say?"

"Error trap 18. Sense of query: semantic value?"

"Right."

"First (untranslatable) climbing expedition. Ascent of (untranslatable)
proper name): from (date uncertain) to (date uncertain). We were here.
Signed, (untranslatable proper name), (untranslatable proper name), (untranslatable proper name)."

"People," Dairine whispered.

"Affirmative."

She looked up at the stars in the hard violet sky. "I want to go where they
came from!"

"Reference transit utility."

She did, and spent some minutes tapping busily at the keys. In the middle
of it, selecting coordinates, delightedly reading through planet names—she
stopped and bit her lip. "This is going to take longer than an hour," she said
to herself. Come to think of it, she might want to be away for quite some
time. And seeing all the problems Nita had started having with their folks
when she told them she was a wizard, it wouldn't do for Dairine to let them
know that she was one too. Not just yet.

She thought about this, then got out of the "travel" utility and brought up
the directory again—taking more time with it, examining the program menus
with great care. In particular she spent a great deal of time with the "Copy"

and "Hide" utilities, getting to know their ins and outs, and doing one finicky piece of copying as a test. The test worked: she sent the copy home.

"That should do it," she said, got back into the "Travel" utility, and with the program's prompting started to lay in coordinates. "Darth Vader," she muttered under her breath, "look out. Here I come."

Shortly thereafter there was nothing on Olympus Mons but rocks, and dry-ice snow, and far down in the crater, the single blinking light.

Search and Retrieval

"We're dead," Nita mourned, sitting on the planetarium steps with her head in her hands. "Dead. My mother will kill me."

Kit, sitting beside her, looked more bemused than upset. "Do you know how much power it takes to open a gateway like that and leave it open? Usually it's all we can do to keep one open long enough to jump through it."

"Big deal! Grand Central gate and the World Trade Center portals are open all the time." Nita groaned again. *"Mars!"*

"Each of those gates took a hundred or so wizards working together to open, though." Kit leaned back on the steps. "She may be a brat, but boy, has she got firepower!"

"The youngest wizards always do," Nita said, sitting up again and picking up Kit's manual from beside her. "Lord, what a horrible thought."

"What? The gate she made? We can close it, but—"

"No. This. Look." She held out his manual. It was turned to one of the directory pages. The page said:

CALLAHAN, Juanita T.   Journeyman rating
243 E. Clinton Avenue   (RL +4.5 +/− .15)
Hempstead NY 11575   Available/limited
(516) 555-6786   (summer vacation)

That was Nita's usual directory listing, and normal enough. But above it, between her and CAHANE, Jak, whose listing was usually right above hers, there was something new.

CALLAHAN, Dairine E.   Novice rating
243 E. Clinton Avenue   (RL +9.8 +/− .2)
Hempstead NY 11575   on Ordeal: no calls
(516) 555-6786

"Oh, no," Kit said. "And look at that rating level."

Nita dropped the book beside her. "I don't get it. She didn't find a manual, how could she have—"

"She was in yours," Kit said.

"Yeah, but the most she could have done was take the Oath! She's smart but not smart enough to pull off a forty-million-mile transit without having the reference diagrams and the words for the spell in front of her! And the manuals can't be stolen; you know that. They just vanish if someone tries." Nita put her head down in her hands again. "My folks are gonna pitch a fit. We've got to find her!"

Kit breathed out, then stood up. "Come on," he said. "We'd better start doing things fast or we'll lose her. There's a phone over there. Call home and tell them we're running a little behind schedule. The planetarium's all locked up by now: so no one'll be around to notice if I walk through a couple of walls and close that gate down."

"But what if she tries to come back and finds it closed behind her?"

"Somehow I can't see that slowing her down much," Kit said. "And besides, maybe she's supposed to find it closed. She *is* on Ordeal."

Nita stood up too. "And we'd better call Tom and Carl. They'll want the details."

"Right. Go ahead; I'll take care of the gate."

Kit turned around, looked at the bricks of the planetarium's outer wall. He stepped around the corner of the doorway wall, out of sight of the street, and laid one hand on the bricks, muttering under his breath. His hand sank into the wall as if into water. "There we go," he said, and the bricks rippled as he stepped through them and vanished.

Nita headed for the phone, feeling through her pockets for change. The thought of her sister running around the universe on Ordeal made her hair stand up on end. No one became a wizard without there being some one problem that their acquisition of power would solve. Nita understood from her studies that normally a wizard was allowed to get as old as possible before being offered the Oath: the Powers, her manual said, wanted every wizard who could to acquire the security and experience that a normal childhood provides. But sometimes, when problems of an unusual nature came up, the Powers would offer the Oath early—because the younger children, not knowing (or caring) what was impossible, had more wizardry available to them.

That kind of problem was likely to be a killer. Nita's Ordeal and Kit's had thrown them out of their universe into another one, a place implacably hostile to human beings, and run by the Power that, according to the manual, had invented death before time began—and therefore had been cast out of the other Powers' society. Every world had stories of that Lone Power under many names. Nita didn't need the stories; she had met It face-to-face twice now, and both times only luck—or the intervention of others—had saved her life. And Nita had been offered her wizardry relatively early, at thirteen: Kit even earlier, at twelve. The thought of what problem the Powers must need solved if They were willing to offer the Oath to someone years younger—and the thought of her little sister in the middle of it—

Nita found some quarters, went to a phone and punched in her number. What was she going to tell her mother? She couldn't lie to her: that decision, made at the beginning of the summer, had caused her to tell her folks that she was a wizard, and had produced one of the great family arguments of her life. Her mother and father still weren't pleased that their daughter might run off anywhere at a moment's notice, to places where they couldn't keep an eye on her and protect her. Nor did it matter that those places tended to be the sort where anyone but an experienced wizard would quickly get killed. That made it even worse. . . .

At the other end, the phone rang. Nita's throat seized up. She began clearing it frantically.

Someone answered. "Hello?"

It was Dairine.

Nita's throat unseized itself. "Are you all right? Where are you?" she blurted, and then began swearing inwardly at her own stupidity.

"I'm fine," Dairine said. "And I'm right here."

"How did you get back? Never mind that, how did you get out? And you left the gate open! Do you know what could have happened if some poor janitor went in that door without looking? It's sixty below this time of year on Mars—"

"Nita," Dairine said, "you're babbling. Just go home. I'll see you later." And she hung up.

"Why that rotten little—" Nita said, and hung up the phone so hard that people on the street corner turned to look at her. Embarrassed and more annoyed than ever, she turned and headed back to where Kit was sitting. "Babbling," she muttered. "That rotten, thoughtless, I'm gonna—"

She shut her mouth. *Babbling?* That didn't sound like Dairine. It was too simple an insult. And why "just go home" instead of "just *come* home"? There's something wrong—

She stopped in front of Kit, who looked up at her from his seat on the step and made no move to get up. He was sweating and slightly pale. "That gate was fastened to Mars real tight," he said. "I thought half of Mariner Plain was going to come with it when I uprooted the forcefields. What's the matter with you? You look awful."

"Something's wrong," Nita said. "Dairine's home."

"What's awful about that? Good riddance." Then he looked at her sharply. "Wait a minute. Home? When she's on Ordeal?"

That hadn't even occurred to Nita. "She sounded weird," Nita said. "Kit, it didn't *sound* like her."

"We were at home for our Ordeal—at least, at the beginning . . ."

She shook her head. "Something's wrong. Kit, let's go see Tom and Carl."

He stood up, wobbling a little. "Sounds good. Grand Central?"

"Rockefeller Center gate's closer."

"Let's go."

A Senior wizard usually reaches that position through the most strenuous kind of training and field experience. All wizards, as they lose the power of their childhood and adolescence, tend to specialize in one field of wizardry or another; but the kind of wizard who's Senior material refuses to specialize too far. They are the Renaissance people of sorcery, every one of them tried repeatedly against the Lone Power, in both open combat and the subtler strife of one Power-influenced human mind against another. Seniors are almost never the white-bearded wizards of archetype . . . mostly because of their constant combats with the Lone One, which tend to kill them young. They advise other wizards on assignment, do research for them, lend them assistance in the losing battle to slow down the heat-death of the universe.

Few worlds have more than thirty or forty Seniors. At this point in Kit's and Nita's practice, Earth had twenty-four: six scattered through Asia, one in Australia and one (for the whales) in the Atlantic Ocean; three in Europe, four in Africa, and nine in the Americas—five in Central and South America (one of whom handled the Antarctic) and four in the north. Of these, one lived in Santa Cruz, one lived in Oklahoma City, and the other two lived together several miles away, in Nassau County.

Their house in Nita's town was very like their neighbors' houses . . . perhaps a little bigger, but that wasn't odd, since Carl worked as chief of sales for the big CBS flagship TV station in New York, and Tom was a moderately well-known freelance writer of stories and movie scripts. They looked like perfectly average people—two tall, good-looking men, one with a mustache, one without; Carl a native New Yorker, Tom an unrepentant Californian. They had all the things their neighbors had—mortgages and phone bills and pets and occasional fights: they mowed the lawn and went to work like everybody else (at least Carl did: Tom worked at home). But their lawn had as few weeds as Nita's did these days, their pets understood and sometimes spoke English and numerous other languages, their phone didn't always have a human being on the other end when it rang, and as for their fights, the reasons for some of them would have made their neighbors' mouths drop open.

Their backyard, being surrounded by a high hedge and a wall all hung with plants, was a safe place to appear out of nothing: though as usual there was nothing to be done about the small thundercrack of air suddenly displaced by two human bodies. When Nita's and Kit's ears stopped ringing, the first thing they heard was someone shouting, "All right, whatcha drop this time?" and an answering shout of "It wasn't me, are the dogs into something?" But they weren't: the two sheepdogs, Annie and Monty, came bounding out from around the corner of the house and leapt delightedly onto Kit and Nita, slurping any part of them not covered with clothes. A little behind them came Dudley the terrier, who contented himself with bouncing around them as if he were spring-loaded and barking at the top of his little lungs.

"Had dinner yet?" Carl called from the kitchen door, which, like the dining room doors, looked out on the backyard. "Annie! Monty! Down!"

"Bad dog! Bad dog! Nonono!" screamed another voice from the same direction: not surprising, since its source was sitting on Carl's shoulder. This was Machu Picchu the macaw, also known (to her annoyance) as "Peach": a splendid creature all scarlet and blue, with a three-foot tail, a foul temper, and a precognitive talent that could read the future for months ahead—if Peach felt like it. Wizards' pets tend to become strange with time, and Seniors' pets even stranger than usual; and Peach had been with them longer than any of the others. It showed.

"Come on in," called one last voice: Tom. Kit and Nita pushed Annie and Monty more or less back down to dog level, and made their way into the house through the dining room doors. It was a pleasant, open place, all the rooms running freely into one another, and full of handsome functional furniture: Tom's desk and computer sat in a comfortable corner of the living room. Kit pulled a chair away from the dining table and plopped down in it, still winded from his earlier wizardry. Nita sat down next to him. Carl leaned over the table and pushed a pair of bottles of Coke at them, sitting down and cracking a third one himself. Tom, with a glass of iced coffee, sat down too.

"Hot one today," Carl said at last, putting his Coke down. Picchu sidled down his arm from his shoulder and began to gnaw thoughtfully on the neck of the bottle.

"No kidding," Kit said.

"You look awful," said Tom. "What've you two been up to?"

For answer Nita opened Kit's manual to the directory and pushed it over to Tom and Carl's side of the table. Tom read it, whistled softly, and nudged the manual toward Carl. "I saw this coming," he said, "but not this soon. Your mom and dad aren't going to be happy. Where did she go?"

"Mars," Kit said.

"Home," Nita said.

"Better start at the beginning," said Carl.

When they came to the part about the worldgate, Carl got up to go for his supervisory manual, and Tom looked at Kit with concern. "Better get him an aspirin too," Tom called after Carl.

"I'm allergic to aspirin."

"A Tylenol, then. You're going to need it. How did you manage to disalign a patent gateway all by yourself? . . . But wait a minute." Tom peered at Kit. "Are you taller than you were?"

"Two inches."

"That would explain it, then. It's a hormonal surge." Tom cleared his throat and looked at Nita. "You, too, huh?"

"Hormones? Yes. Unfortunately."

Tom raised his eyebrows. "Well. Your wizardry will be a little more accessible to you for a while than it has since you got started. Just be careful not to overextend yourself . . . it's easy to overreach your strength just now."

Carl came back with his supervisory manual, a volume thick as a phone book, and started paging through it. Annie nosed Kit from one side: he looked down in surprise and took the bottle of Tylenol she was carrying in her mouth. "Hey, thanks."

"Lord," Carl said. "She did a tertiary gating, all by herself. Your body becomes part of the gateway forcefields," he said, looking up at Nita and Kit. "It's one of the fastest and most effective kinds of gating, but it takes a lot of power."

"I still don't get it," Nita said. "She doesn't have a manual!"

"Are you sure?" Carl said; and "Have you gotten a computer recently?" said Tom.

"Just this morning."

Tom and Carl looked at each other. "I thought only Advisory levels and above were supposed to get the software version of the manual just yet," Carl said.

"Maybe, but she couldn't have stolen one of those any more than she could have stolen one of the regular manuals. You're offered it . . . or you never see it."

Nita was puzzled. " 'Software version'?"

Tom gave her a wry look. "We've been beta-testing it," he said. "Sorry, testing the 'beta' version of the software, the one that'll be released after we're sure there are no bugs in it. You know the way you normally do spells. You draw your power diagrams and so forth as guides for the way you want the spell to work, but the actual instructions to the universe are spoken aloud in the Speech?"

"Uh-huh."

"And it takes a fair amount of practice to learn to do the vector diagrams and so forth without errors, and a lot of time, sometimes, to learn to speak the Speech properly. More time yet to learn to think in it. Well . . ." Tom sat down again and began turning his empty glass around and around on the table. "Now that technology has proceeded far enough on this planet for computers to be fairly widespread, the Powers have been working with the Senior wizards to develop computer-supported wizards' manuals. The software draws the necessary diagrams internally, the way a calculator does addition, for example; you get the solution without seeing how it's worked out. The computer also synthesizes the Speech, though of course there are tutorials in the language as you go along."

"The project has both useful and dangerous sides," Carl said. "For one thing, there are good reasons why we use the Speech in spelling. It contains words that can accurately describe things and conditions that no Earthly language has words for. And if during a spell you give the computer instructions that're ambiguous in English, and it describes something inaccurately . . . well." He looked grim. "But for the experienced wizard, who already knows the theory he's working with, and is expert in the Speech, it can be a real timesaver."

"A lifesaver, too, under special circumstances," Tom said, looking somber. "You two know how many children go missing in this country every year."

"Thousands."

"It's not all kidnappings and runaways," Tom said. "Some of those kids are out on their Ordeal . . . and because they don't have time to become good with the Speech, they get in trouble with the Lone Power that they can't get out of. And they never come back." He moved uneasily in the chair. "Providing them with the wizard's software may save some of their lives. Meantime . . ."

Carl turned over a page or two in his manual, shaking his head. "Meantime, I want a look at Dairine's software; I need to see which version of it she got. And I want a word with her. If she lights out into the middle of nowhere on Ordeal without meaning the Oath she took, she's going to be in trouble up to her neck. . . . Anyway, your folks should know about all this. Easier if we tell them, I think. How 'bout it, partner?" He looked over at Tom.

"I was about to suggest it myself."

Nita sagged with relief.

"Good. Your folks busy this afternoon, Neets?"

"Just with the computer."

"Perfect." Carl put out his hand, and from the nearby kitchen wall the phone leapt into his hand. Or tried to: the phone cord brought it up short, and there it hung in the air, straining toward Carl like a dog at the end of a leash. "I thought you were going to put a longer cord on this thing," Carl said to Tom, pushing his chair back enough to get the phone up to his face, and hitting the autodialer in the handpiece. "This is ridiculous."

"The phone store was out of them again."

"Try that big hardware store down in Freeport, what's its name— Hi, Harry. Carl Romeo. . . . Nothing much, I just heard from Nita that you got the new computer. . . . Yeah, they stopped in on the way home. . . . Yeah. What did you decide on? . . . Oh, that's a sweet little machine. A lot of nice software for that." Carl listened for a few seconds to the soft squeaking of the phone, while Picchu left off chewing on Carl's Coke bottle and began nibbling delicately on the phone cord.

Carl smacked her gently away, and his eyebrows went up as he listened. "Okay. Fine. . . . Fine. See you in a bit. Bye now."

He hung up. "That was your mom in the background," he said to Nita, "insisting on feeding us again. I think she's decided the best thing to do with adult wizards is tame them with kindness and gourmet cuisine."

"Magic still makes her nervous," Nita said.

"Or we still make her nervous," Tom said, getting up to shut the doors.

"Well, yeah. Neither of them can quite get used to it, that you were their neighbors for all these years and they never suspected you were wizards. . . ."

"Being out in the open," Tom said, "causes even more problems than 'passing' . . . as you'll have noticed. But the truth works best. The front door locked?" he said to Carl.

"Yup," said Carl. He looked down at his side in surprise: from the table, Picchu was calmly climbing beak over claw up the side of his polo shirt. "Bird—"

"I'm going," said Picchu, achieving Carl's shoulder with a look of calm satisfaction, and staring Carl right in the eye. "I'm needed."

Carl shrugged. It was difficult and time-consuming to start fights with a creature who could rip your ear off faster than you could remove her. "You do anything nasty on their rug," he said, "and it's macaw croquettes for lunch tomorrow, *capeesh?*"

Picchu, preening a wing feather back into place, declined to answer.

"Then let's motor," Tom said. They headed for the garage.

"Lord," Tom said, "who writes these manuals, anyway? This is better than most, but it still might as well be in Sanskrit. Harry, where's that cable?" Nita watched with barely suppressed amusement as Tom and her father dug among the manuals all over the floor, and Tom went headfirst under the desk.

"Computer seems to be running, anyway," Carl said.

"Had to drag Dairine away from it before she blew it up," said Mr. Callahan, peering under the desk to see what Tom was doing.

"Where is she, Daddy?" said Nita.

"In her room. You two must really have run her down for her to come home so early."

"Which train did she take?" Kit said.

"She didn't say. She looked a little tired when she got in . . . said she was going to go read or something. Tom, is that plug really supposed to go in there? It looks too big."

"They always do. See, this little bit inside the casing is all that actually goes in. Mmmf . . ."

Carl, standing beside Nita, reached around the back of the Apple and hit the reset button. The A> prompt that had been there vanished: the Apple logo came up again. It had no bite out of it.

Nita stared. "Uh huh," Carl said, and hit the CONTROL key and the letter C to boot up the system. The A> prompt came back. Then Carl typed a string of numbers and figures, too quickly for them to register for Nita as anything but a green blur. They disappeared, and a message appeared in the graceful Arabic-looking letters of the wizardly Speech.

USER LOG?

"Yes, please," Carl said. "Authorization seven niner three seven one comma five one eight."

"Password?"

Carl leaned near the console and whispered something.

"Confirmed," said the computer politely, and began spilling its guts in screenful after screenful of green. "Pause," Carl said at one point. "Harry, I think you'd better have a look at this."

"What, did we plug it in wrong—"

"No, not that." Nita's father got up, brushing himself off, and looked at the screen. Then he froze. He had seen the Speech in Nita's manual once or twice, and knew the look of it.

"Carl," Nita's father said, beginning to look stern, "what is this?"

Carl looked as if he would rather not say anything. "Harry," he said, "it wouldn't be fair to make Nita tell you this. But you seem to have another wizard in the family."

"*What!*"

"Yes," Carl said, "that was my reaction too. Translation," he said to the computer.

"Translation of protected material requires double authorization by ranking Seniors and justification filed with Chief Senior for planet or plane," said the computer, sounding stubborn.

"What've you done to my machine!"

"The question," Tom said, getting up off the floor, "is more like, what has Dairine done to it? Sorry, Harry. This is a hell of a way for you to find out."

Nita watched her father take in a long breath. "Don't call her yet, Harry," said Tom. He laid a hand on the computer. "Confirmed authorization one zero zero three oblique zero two. We'll file the justification with Irina later. Translate."

The screen's contents abruptly turned into English. Nita's father bent over a bit to read it. " 'Oath accepted—' "

"This Oath," Carl said. "Type a-colon-heartcode."

The computer cleared its screen and displayed one small block of text in green. Nita was still while her father read the Wizards' Oath. There was movement behind her: she looked up and saw her mother, with a peppermill clutched forgotten in one hand, looking over her father's shoulder. Her face looked odd, and it wasn't entirely the green light from the computer screen.

"Dairine took that?" her father said at last.

"So did we, Daddy," Nita said.

"Yes, but—" He sat down on the edge of the desk, staring at the screen. "Dairine isn't quite like you two. . . ."

"Exactly. Harry, this is going to take a while. But first, you might call in Dairine. She did something careless this afternoon and I want to make sure she doesn't do it again."

Nita felt sorry for her father; he looked so pale. Her mother went to him. "What did she do?" she said.

"She went to Mars and left the door open," said Tom.

Nita's dad shut his eyes. "She went to Mars."

"Just like that. . . ." said her mother.

"Harry, Nita tells me she took you two to the Moon once, to prove a point. Imagine power like that . . . used irresponsibly. I need to make sure that's not going to happen, or I'll have to put a lock on some of her power. And there are other problems. The power may be very necessary for something. . . ." Carl looked stern but unhappy. "Where is she, Harry?"

"Dairine," Nita's dad said, raising his voice.

"Yo," came Dairine's voice from upstairs, her all-purpose reply.

"Come on down here a minute."

"Do I have to? I'm reading."

"Now."

The ceiling creaked a little, the sound of Dairine moving around her room. "What have I done to deserve this?" said Nita's father to the immediate universe.

"Harry," Carl said glancing at the computer screen and away again, "this may come as a shock to you . . ."

"Carl, I'm beyond shocking. I've walked on the Moon without a spacesuit and seen my eldest daughter turn into a whale. That my youngest should go to Mars on a whim . . ."

"Well, as to what you've done to deserve it . . . you have a right to know the answer. The tendency for wizardry comes down to the kids through your side of the family."

That was a surprise to Nita, and as for her father, he looked stricken, and her mother looked at him with an expression that was faintly accusing. Carl said, "You're related to the first mayor of New York, aren't you?"

"Uh, yeah . . . he was—"

"—a wizard, and one of the best to grace this continent. One of the youngest Seniors in Earth's history, in fact. The talent in your line is considerable; too bad it missed you, but it does skip generations without warning. Was there something odd about one of your grandparents?"

"Why, my—" Nita's father swallowed and looked as if he was suddenly remembering something. "I saw my grandmother disappear once. I was about six. Later I always thought I'd imagined it. . . ." He swallowed again. "Well, that's the answer to why me. The next question is, why Dairine?"

"She's needed somewhere," said Carl. "The Powers value the status quo too highly to violate it without need. It's what we're defending, after all. Somewhere out there is a life-or-death problem to which only Dairine is the answer."

"We just need to make sure she knows it," said Tom, "and knows to be careful. There are forces out there that aren't friendly to wizards—" He broke off suddenly as he glanced over at the computer screen. "Carl, you should see this."

They all looked at the screen. USER LOG, it said, and under the heading were listed a lot of numbers and what Nita vaguely recognized as program names. "Look at that," Tom said, pointing to one. "Those are the spells she did today, using the computer. Eighty-eight gigabytes of storage, all in one session, the latest one—at 16:52 hours. What utility uses that kind of memory?"

"That's what . . . about ten of five?" Nita's mother said. "She wasn't even *here* then. . . ."

The stairs creaked as Dairine came down them into the living room. She paused a moment, halfway, as well she might have done with all those eyes and all those expressions trained on her . . . her father's bewildered annoyance, her mother's indignant surprise, Tom's and Carl's cool assessment, and Nita's and Kit's expectant looks. Dairine hesitantly walked the rest of the way down.

"I came back," she said abruptly.

Nita waited for more. Dairine said nothing.

Nita's parents exchanged glances, evidently having the same thought: that a Dairine who said so little wasn't normal. "Baby . . ." her mother said, sounding uncertain, "you have some explaining to do."

But Carl stepped forward and said, "She may not be able to explain much

of anything, Betty. Dairine's had a busy day with the computer. Isn't that so,
Dairine?"

"I don't want to talk about it," Dairine said.

"I think it's more like you can't," said Carl.

"Look at the user log, Harry," Tom said from behind Nita and Kit.
"Eighty-eight gigs spent on one program. A copy program. And run, as you
say, when she wasn't even here. There's only one answer to that."

Slowly, as if he were looking at a work of art, Carl walked around Dairine.
She watched him nervously. "Even with unlimited available memory and a
computer running wizard's software," Carl said, "there's only so much fidel-
ity a copy can achieve. Making hard copies of dumb machinery, even a
computer itself, that's easy. Harry, look at the log: you'll see that this isn't the
machine you bought. It's an exact copy of it. Dairine made it."

Carl kept walking around Dairine. She didn't move, didn't speak. "Carl,
come on," Nita's father said from behind her, "cut it out. You're scaring
her."

"I think not," Carl said. "There's only so much you can do with eighty
gigs, as I said. Especially when the original is a living thing. The copy's
responses are limited. See, there's something that lives inside the hardware,
inside the meat and nervous tissue, that can't be copied. Brain can be copied.
But mind—not so well. And soul—not at all. Those are strictly one to a
customer, at least on this planet."

The air was singing with tension. Nita glanced at Kit, and Kit nodded, for
he knew as well as she did the feel of a spell in the working. Carl was using no
words or gestures to assist in the spell, nothing but the slow certain pressure
of his mind as he thought in the Speech. "She copied the computer and took
it to the city with her," Carl said, "and got away when she could. And when
she left Earth, she decided—I'd imagine—that she wanted some time to
sightsee. But, of course, you would object to that. So she copied something
else, to buy herself some time."

The spell built and built in power, and the air sang the note ears sing in
silence, but much louder. "Nothing not its own original can exist in this
room," Carl said, "once I turn the spell loose. Harry, you're having trouble
believing this, are you? You think I would treat your real daughter this way?"

Nita's father said nothing.

"Run," Carl said softly.

Dairine vanished. Air imploded into the place where she had been: manuals ruffled their pages in the sudden wind, papers flew up and slowly settled.
Behind them, the Apple simply went away; its monitor fell two inches to the
desk with a loud thump, its screen gone dark, and the hard-drive cable slith-
ered off the desk like a stunned snake and fell in coils to the floor.

Nita's father put his face in his hands.

Her mother looked sharply at Tom and Carl. "I've known you two too long to think you were toying with us," she said as Carl sat down slowly on the sofa, looking a bit pale. "You said something a moment ago about forces that weren't friendly . . ."

"Nita's told you some of what wizards are for," Tom said, looking at Carl in concern, then up again. "Balance. Maintenance of the status quo; protecting life. There are forces that are ambivalent toward life. One in particular . . . that held Itself aloof from creation, a long time ago, and when everyone else was done, created something none of the other forces had thought of: death. And the longest Death . . . the running-down of the Universe. The other Powers cast It out . . . and they've been dealing with the problem, and the Lone Power, ever since."

"Entropy," Nita's mother said, looking thoughtful. "That's an old story."

"It's the only story," Tom said. "Every sentient species has it, or learns it." He looked over at Nita's father, who was recovering somewhat. "I'm not about to pass judgment on whether the Lone One's invention was a good idea or not. There are cases for both sides, and the argument has been going on since time was set running. Every being that's ever lived has argued the case for one side or the other, whether it's been aware of it or not. But wizards fight the great Death, and the lesser ones, consciously . . . and the Entity that invented death takes our interference very personally. New wizards always meet it in one form or another, on their Ordeals. Some survive, if they're careful. Nita and Kit were careful . . . and they had each other's help."

" 'Careful' is not Dairine's style," Nita's mother said, sounding rueful. "And she's alone."

"Not for long," Tom said. "We'll track her, and see that she has help. But I think Nita will have to go. She knows Dairine's mind fairly well."

"I'm going too," said Kit.

Carl, still ashen from the exertion of his spell, shook his head. "Kit, your folks don't know you're a wizard. You might have to be gone for quite a while —and I can't sell you two a time warp as I did once before. My time-jurisdiction stops at atmosphere's edge."

"I'll tell them what I am," Kit said.

Nita turned and stared at him.

"I've been thinking about doing it for a while, since you told your folks," he said to her. "You handled it pretty well," he said to Nita's parents. "I should give my mom and dad the benefit of the doubt." The words were brave: but Nita noticed that Kit looked a little worried.

"Kit, you'll have to hurry," Tom said. "She's got a long lead on you, and the trail will get cold fast. Neets, where would Dairine want to go?"

Nita shook her head. "She reads a lot of science fiction."

Carl looked worried. "Has she been reading Heinlein?"

"Some," Nita said. "But she's mostly hot for Star Wars right now."

"That's something, at least. With luck she won't think of going much farther than a few galaxies over. Anything in particular about Star Wars?"

"Darth Vader," Kit said. "She wants to beat him up."

Tom groaned and ran one hand through his hair. "No matter what the reason," he said, "if she goes looking for darkness, she'll find it."

"But Darth Vader's not real!" said Nita's mother.

Tom glanced at her. "Not *here*. Be glad."

"A few galaxies over . . ." Nita's father said to no one in particular.

Carl looked grim. "We can track her, but the trail's getting cold; and at any rate Tom and I can't go with you."

"Now, wait a minute . . ." Nita's mother said.

Carl looked at her gently. "We're not allowed out of the Solar System," he said. "There are reasons. For one thing, would you step out the door of a car you were driving?"

Nita's mother stared at him.

"Yes, well," Tom said. "We'll get you support. Wizards everywhere we can reach will be watching for you. And as for a guide—"

"I'll go," said Picchu abruptly, from the computer table.

Everyone stared, most particularly Nita's mother and father.

"Sorry, I should have mentioned," Carl said. "Peach is an associate. Bird, isn't this a touch out of your league?"

"I told you I was needed," Picchu said irritably. "And I am. I can see the worst of what's going to happen before it does; so I should be able to keep these two out of most kinds of trouble. But you'd better stop arguing and move. If Dairine keeps throwing away energy the way she's doing, she's going to attract Someone's attention . . . and the things It sends to fetch her will make Darth Vader look like a teddy bear by comparison."

Nita's mother looked at Carl and Tom. "Whatever you have to do," she said, "*do it!*"

"Just one question," Tom said to Picchu. "What do They need her for?"

"The Powers?" Picchu said. She shut her eyes.

"Well?"

"Reconfiguration," she said, and opened her eyes again, looking surly. "Well? What are you staring at? I can't tell you more than I know. Are we going?"

"Gone," Nita said. She headed out of the room for her manual.

"I'll meet you in the usual place when I'm done," Kit called after her, and vanished. Papers flew again, leaving Nita's mother and father looking anxiously at Carl and Tom.

"Powers," Nita heard her father say behind her. "Creation. Forces from before time. This is—this business is for saints, not children!"

"Even saints have to start somewhere," Carl said softly. "And it's always been the children who save the Universe from the previous generation, and remake the Universe in their own image."

"Just be glad yours are conscious of the fact that that's what they're doing," Tom said.

Neither of her parents said anything.

In her bedroom, Nita grabbed her manual, bit her lip, said three words, and vanished.

Randomization

Dairine did not go straight out of the Galaxy from Mars. Like many other wizards when they first cut planet-loose, she felt that she had to do a little local sightseeing first.

She was some while about it. Part of this was caused by discomfort. The jump from Earth to Mars, a mere forty-nine million miles, had been unsettling enough, with its feeling of first being pinned to a wildly rolling ball and then violently torn loose from it. But it hadn't been too bad. Piece o' cake, Dairine had thought, checking the transit directory in the computer. Somewhere out of the Solar System next. What's this star system? R Leporis? It's pretty close. . . . But she changed her mind, and headed for the moons of Jupiter instead . . . and this turned out to be a good thing. From Mars to Jupiter, bypassing the asteroid belt, was a jump of three hundred forty-one million miles; and the huge differences between the two planets' masses, vectors, and velocities caused Dairine to become the first Terran to lose her lunch on Jupiter's outermost satellite, Ananke.

The view did more than anything else to revive her—the great banded mass of Jupiter swiftly traversing the cold night overhead, shedding yellow-red light all around on the methane snow. Dairine sat down in the dry squeaky snow and breathed deeply, trying to control her leftover heaves. Where she sat, mist curled up and snowed immediately down again as the methane sublimated and almost instantly recrystallized to solid phase in the bitter cold. Dairine decided that getting used to this sort of travel gradually was a good idea.

She waited until she felt better, and then began programming—replenishing her air and planning her itinerary. She also sat for a while examining the transit programs themselves, to see if she had been doing something wrong to cause her to feel so awful . . . and to see if perhaps she could rewrite the programs a little to get rid of the problem. The programs were written in a form of MBASIC that had many commands which were new to her, but were otherwise mostly understandable. They were also complex: they had to be. Earth spins at seventeen thousand miles an hour, plows along its orbital path at a hundred seventy-five thousand, and the Sun takes it and the whole Solar System off toward the constellation Hercules at a hundred fifteen thousand miles an hour. Then the Sun's motion as one of innumerable stars in the Sagittarius Arm of the Galaxy sweeps it along at some two million miles an hour, and all the while relationships between individual stars, and those of stars to their planets, shift and change . . .

It all meant that any one person standing still on any planet was in fact traveling a crazed, corkscrewing path through space, at high speed: and the disorientation and sickness were apparently the cause of suddenly, and for the first time, going in a straight line, in a universe where space itself and every-thing in it is curved. Dairine looked and looked at the transit programs, which could (as she had just proved) leave you *standing* on the surface of a satellite three hundred fifty million miles away from where you started—not half embedded in it, not splatted into it in a bloody smear because of some forgotten vector that left you still moving a mile a second out of phase with the surface of the satellite, or at the right speed, but in the wrong direction. . . . Finally she decided not to tamper. A hacker learns not to fix what works . . . at least, not till it's safe to try. Maybe the transits'll get easier, she thought. At least now I know not to eat right before one. . . .

That brought up the question of food, which needed to be handled. Dairine considered briefly, then used the software to open a storage pocket in otherspace. By means of the transit utility she then removed a loaf of bread, a bottle of mustard, and half a pound of bologna from the refrigerator back home, stuffing them into local otherspace where she could get at them. Mom 'n' Dad won't notice, she thought, and even if they do, what are they going to do about it? Spank my copy? Be interesting if they did. I wonder if I'd feel it. . . .

But there were a lot of more interesting things to consider today. Dairine stood up, got the computer ready, and headed out again, more cautiously this time. She stopped on Io, another one of Jupiter's moons, and spent a while (at a safe distance) watching the volcanoes spit white-hot molten sulfur ten miles out from the surface; sulfur that eventually came drifting back down, as a leisurely dusty golden snow, in the delicate gravity. Then she braced herself as best she could and jumped for Saturn's orbit, four hundred three million miles farther out, and handled it a little better, suffering nothing worse than a cold sweat and a few dry heaves, for the two planets were similar in mass and vectors.

Here there were twenty moons—too many for Dairine at the moment—

but she did stop at Titan, the biggest satellite in the Solar System, and spent a while perched precariously on a peak slick with hydrogen snow, looking down thoughtfully at the methane oceans that washed the mountain's feet. Several times she thought she saw something move down there—something that was not one of the peculiar, long, high methane waves that the light gravity made possible. But the light was bad under the thick blue clouds, and it was hard to tell. She went on.

The jump to Uranus's orbit was a touch harder—six hundred sixty million miles to a world much smaller and lighter than the greater gas giants. Dairine had to sit down on a rock of Uranus's oddly grooved moon Miranda and have the heaves again. But she recovered more quickly than the last time, and sat there looking down on the planet's blurry green-banded surface for a long time. *Voyager 1* and *Voyager 2* had both been gravity-slung off toward alpha Centauri and were plunging toward the radiopause, the border of the Solar System, whistling bravely in the endless dark. Sitting here she could hear them both, far away, as she could hear a lot that the Sun's radio noise made impossible to hear closer in. That silent roar, too—the old ruinous echo of the Big Bang—was more audible here. How can I even hear it? she wondered briefly. But Dairine quickly decided it was just another useful side effect of the wizardry, and she got up and headed out as soon as she was better.

From Uranus to Neptune was one billion, one million miles. To her own surprise Dairine took it in stride, arriving standing up on Triton, one of Neptune's two largest moons, and with no desire to sit. Better! she thought, and looked around. There was very little to see: the planet was practically a twin of Uranus, except for its kinky partial rings, and the moons were barren. Dairine rubbed her arms. It was getting cold, even in the protective shell she had made for herself; her forcefields couldn't long stand this kind of chill. Out here the Sun was just one more star, bright, but not like a sun at all. The jump to Pluto was brief: she stood only for a minute or so in the barren dark and could hardly find the Sun at all, even by radio noise. Its roar was muted to a chilly whisper, and the wind on Pluto—it was summer, so there was enough atmosphere thawed to make a kind of wind—drank the heat away from her forcefields till in seconds she was shivering. She pulled the computer out. "Extrasystemic jump," she said hurriedly.

"Coordinates?"

"Read out flagged planets."

"Andorgha/beta Delphini, Ahaija/R Leporis, Gond/kappa Orionis, Irmrihad/Ross 614, Rirhath B/epsilon Indi—"

"The closest," said Dairine, feeling a touch nervous about this.

"Rirhath B. Eleven point four light-years."

"Atmosphere status?"

"Earthlike within acceptable parameters."

"Let's go," Dairine said.

"Syntax error 24," said the computer sweetly, "rephrase for accuracy."

"Run!"

A galaxy's worth of white fire pinned her to the rolling planet; then the forces she had unleashed tore Dairine loose and flung her out into darkness that did not break. For what seemed like ages, the old, old echoes of the Big Bang breaking over her like waves were all Dairine had to tell her she was still alive. The darkness grew intolerable. Eventually she became aware that she was trying to scream, but no sound came out, nothing but that roar, and the terrible laughter behind it.

—laughter?

—and light pierced her, and the universe roared at her, and she hit the planet with a feeling like dreaming of falling out of bed—

Then, silence. True silence this time. Dairine sat up slowly and carefully, taking a moment to move everything experimentally, making sure nothing was broken. She ached in every bone, and she was angry. She hated being laughed at under the best of circumstances, even when it was family doing it. Whatever had been laughing at her was definitely *not* family, and she wanted to get her hands on it and teach it a lesson. . . .

She looked around her and tried to make sense of things. It wasn't easy. She was sitting on a surface that was as slick white as glare ice in some places, and scratched dull in other spots, in irregularly shaped patches. Ranked all around her in racks forty or fifty feet high were huge irregular objects made of blue metal, each seeming made of smaller blocks stuck randomly together. The block things, and the odd racks that held them, were all lit garishly by a high, glowing green-white ceiling. *What is this, some kind of warehouse?* Dairine thought, getting to her feet.

Something screamed right behind her, an appalling electronic-mechanical roar that scared her into losing her balance. Dairine went sprawling, the computer under her. It was lucky she did, for the screaming something shot by right over her head, missing her by inches though she was flat on her face. The huge wind of its passing whipped her hair till it stung her face, and made her shiver all over. Dairine dared to lift her head a little, her heart pounding like mad, and stared after the thing that had almost killed her. It was another of the bizarre cube-piles, which came to a sudden stop in midair in front of one of the racks. A metal arm came out of the Tinkertoy works of the rack, snagged the cube-pile and dropped it clanging onto an empty shelf in the rack's guts.

Dairine pulled the computer out from under her and crawled carefully sideways out of the middle of the long white corridorlike open space, close to one of the metal racks. There she simply lay still for a moment, trying to get her wits back.

There was another scream. She held still, and saw another of the cubes shoot by a foot and a half above the white floor, stop and hover, and get snagged and shelved. Definitely a warehouse, she thought; and then part of the cube seemed to go away, popped open, and people came out.

They had to be people, she thought. Surely they didn't *look* at all like people; the four of them came in four different burnished-metal colors and didn't look like any earthly insect, bird or beast. Well, she said to herself, why should they? Nonetheless she found it hard to breathe as she looked at them, climbing down from their—vehicle?—was that their version of a car, and this a parking lot? The creatures—no, people, she reminded herself—the people were each different from all the others. They had bodies that came in four parts, or five, or six; they had limbs of every shape and kind, claws and tentacles and jointed legs. If they had heads, or needed them, she couldn't tell where they were. They didn't even look much like the same species. They walked away under the fluorescent sky, bleating at one another.

Dairine got up. She was still having trouble breathing. What've I been thinking of? She began to realize that all her ideas about meeting her first alien creatures had involved her being known, even expected. "Dairine's here finally," they were supposed to say, "now we can get something done"; and then she and they would set out to save the universe together. Because of her own blindness she'd gotten so excited that she'd jumped into a totally alien environment without orientation or preparation, and as a result she'd nearly been run over in a parking lot. My own fault, she thought, disgusted with herself. It won't happen again.

But in the meantime people were still getting out of that car: these people shorter and blockier than the first group, with more delicate legs and brighter colors. She picked up the computer, looked both ways most carefully up and down the "road," and went after them. "You still working?" she said to the computer.

"Syntax error 24—"

"Sorry I asked. Just keep translating."

As she came up behind the second group of people, Dairine's throat tightened. Everything she could think of to say to aliens suddenly sounded silly. Finally she wound up clearing her throat, which certainly needed it, as she walked behind them. Don't want to startle them, she thought.

They did absolutely nothing. Maybe they can't hear it. Or maybe I said something awful in their language! Oh, no— "Excuse me!" she said.

They kept walking along and said nothing.

"Uh, look," Dairine said, panting a little as she kept up with them—they were walking pretty fast—"I'm sorry to interrupt you, I'm a stranger here—"

The computer translated what Dairine said into a brief spasm of bleating, but the spidery people made no response. They came to the end of the line of racks and turned the corner. Ahead of them was what looked like a big building, made in the same way as the cars, an odd aggregate of cubes and other geometrical shapes stuck together with no apparent symmetry or plan. The scale of the thing was astonishing. Dairine suddenly realized that the glowing green-white ceiling was in fact the *sky*—the lower layer of a thick cloudy atmosphere, actually fluorescing under the light of a hidden, hyperactive sun—and her stomach did an unhappy flip as her sense of scale violently reoriented itself. I wanted strange, she thought, but not this strange!

"Look," she said to the person she was walking beside as they crossed another pathway toward the huge building, "I'm sorry if I said something to offend you, but please, I need some help getting my bearings—"

Dairine was so preoccupied that she bumped right into something on the other side of the street—and then yipped in terror. Towering over her was one of the first things to get out of the car, a creature seven feet high at least, and four feet wide, a great pile of glittering, waving metallic claws and tentacles, with an odd smell. Dairine backed away fast and started stammering apologies.

The tall creature bleated at her, a shocking sound up so close. "Excuse me," said the computer, translating the bleat into a dry and cultured voice like a BBC announcer's, "but why are you talking to our luggage?"

"Llp, I, uh," said Dairine, and shut her mouth. There they were, her first words to a member of another intelligent species. Blushing and furious, she finally managed to say, "I thought they were people."

"Why?" said the alien.

"Well, they were walking!"

"It'd be pretty poor luggage that didn't do that much, at least," said the alien, eyeing the baggage as it spidered by. "Good luggage levitates, and the new models pack and unpack themselves. You must have come here from a fair way out."

"Yeah," she said.

"My gate is about to become patent," the alien said. "Come along, I'll show you the way to the departures hall. Or are you meeting someone?"

They started to walk. Dairine began to relax a little: this was more like it. "No," she said, "I'm just traveling. But please, what planet is this?"

"Earth," said the alien.

Dairine was surprised for a second, and then remembered having read somewhere that almost every sentient species calls its own planet "Earth" or "the world" or something similar. "I mean, what do other people call it?"

"All kinds of things, as usual. Silly names, some of them. There'll be a master list in the terminal; you can check that."

"Thanks," Dairine said, and then was shocked and horrified to see a large triangular piece of the terminal fall off the main mass of the building. Except that it didn't fall more than a short distance, and then regained its height and soared away, a gracefully tumbling pyramid. "Does it do that often?" she said, when she could breathe again.

"Once every few beats," said the alien; "it's the physical-transport shuttle Are you on holiday? Mind the slide, now."

"Yes," Dairine started to say, until the alien stepped onto a stationary piece of pavement in front of them, and instantly began slipping away from her toward the bizarre mass of the terminal building at high speed. The surprise was too sudden to react to: her foot hit the same piece of paving and slipped from under her as if she had stepped on ice. Dairine threw her arms out to break her fall, except that there wasn't one. She was proceeding straight forward, too, tilted somewhat backward, at about fifty miles an hour. Her heart hammered. It hammered worse when something touched her from behind; she whipped around, or tried to. It was only the alien's luggage, reaching out to tilt her forward so she stood straight. "What *is* this!" she said.

"Slidefield," the alien said, proceeding next to her, without moving, at the same quick pace. "Inertia-abeyant selectively frictionless environment. Here we go. Which gating facility are you making for?"

"Uh—"

It was all happening too fast. The terminal building swept forward swift as a leaping beast, rearing up a thousand stories high, miles across, blotting out the sky. The slidefield poured itself at what looked like a blank silvery wall a hundred feet sheer. Dairine threw her arms up to protect herself, and succeeded only in bashing her face with the computer; the wall burst like a thin flat cloud against her face, harmless, and they were through.

"The Crossings," said the alien. "What do you think?"

She could not have told him in an hour's talking. The Crossings Hypergate Facility on Rirhath B is renowned among the Million Homeworlds for its elegant classical Lilene architecture and noble proportions; but Dairine's only cogent thought for several minutes was that she had never imagined being in an airline terminal the size of New Jersey. The ceiling—or ceilings, for there were thousands of them, layered, interpenetrating, solid and lacy, in steel and glass, in a hundred materials and a hundred colors—all towered up into a distance where clouds, real clouds, gathered; about a quarter-mile off to one side, it appeared to be raining. Through the high greenish air, under the softened light of the fluorescing sky that filtered in through the thousand roofs, small objects that might have been machines droned along, towing parcels and containers behind them. Beneath, scattered all about on the terminal floor, were stalls, platforms, counters, racks, built in shapes Dairine couldn't understand, and with long, tall signs placed beside them that Dairine couldn't begin to read. And among the stalls and kiosks, the whole vast white floor was full of people—clawed, furred, shelled or armored, upright or crawling, avian, insectile, mammalian, lizardlike, vegetable, mingling with forms that could not be described in any earthly terms. There were a very few hominids, none strictly human; and their voices were lost in the rustling, wailing, warbling, space-softened cacophony of the terminal floor. They hopped and stepped and leapt and walked and crawled and oozed and slid and tentacled and went in every imaginable way about their uncounted businesses, followed by friends and families and fellow travelers, by luggage floating or walking; all purposeful, certain, every one of them having somewhere to go, and going there.

Every one of them except Dairine, who was beginning to wish she had not come.

"There," said the alien, and Dairine was glad of that slight warning, because the slidefield simply stopped working and left her standing still. She waved her arms, overcompensating, and her stomach did a frightened wrench and tried once or twice, for old times' sake, to get rid of food that was now on Ananke.

"Here you are," said the alien, gesturing with its various tentacles. "Arrivals over there, departures over that way, stasis and preservation down there, !!!!! over there"—the computer made a staticky noise that suggested it was unable to translate something— "and of course waste disposal. You enjoy your trip, now; I have to catch up with my fathers. Have a nice death!"

"But—" Dairine said. Too late. The broad armored shape had taken a few steps into a small crowd, stepped on a spot on the floor that looked exactly like every other, and vanished.

Dairine stood quite still for a few minutes: she had no desire to hit one of those squares by accident. I'm a spud, she thought, a complete imbecile. Look at this. Stuck in an airport—something like an airport—no money, no ID that these people'll recognize, no way to explain how I got here or how I'm gonna get out—no way to understand half of what's going on, scared to death to move . . . and pretty soon some security guard or cop or something is going to see me standing here, and come over to find out what's wrong, and they're gonna haul me off somewhere and lock me up. . . .

The thought was enough to hurriedly start her walking again. She glanced around to try to make sense of things. There were lots of signs posted all over —or rather, in most cases, hanging nonchalantly in midair. But she could read none of them. While she was looking at one written in letters that at a distance seemed like Roman characters, something bumped into Dairine fairly hard, about shin-height. She staggered and caught herself, thinking she had tripped over someone's luggage. But there was nothing in her path at all.

She paused, confused, and then tried experimentally to keep walking: the empty air resisted her. And then behind her someone said, "Your pardon," and slipped right past her: something that looked more or less like a holly tree, but it was walking on what might have been stumpy roots, and the berries were eyes, all of which looked at Dairine as the creature passed. She gulped. The creature paid her no mind, simply walked through the bit of air that had been resisting Dairine, and vanished as the thing with the tentacles had earlier. Just as it blinked out of existence, air whiffing past Dairine into the place where it had been, she thought she caught sight of what looked like a little triangular piece of shiny plastic or metal held in one of the thing's leaves.

A ticket, Dairine thought; and a little more wandering and watching showed her that this was the case. Wherever these little gates might lead, none of them would let you step on it unless you had the right ticket for it: probably the bit of plastic was a computer chip, programmed with the fact that you had paid your fare. So there was no need to fear that she might suddenly fall unshielded into some environment where they were breathing methane or swimming around in lava.

Dairine began to wander again, feeling somewhat better. I can always sit down in a corner somewhere and program another jump, she thought. Be smart to do that now, though. In case something starts to happen and I want to get out quick. . . .

She looked for a place to sit. Off to one side was a big collection of racks and benches, where various creatures were hung up or lying on the floor. On a hunch she said to the computer, "Is it safe to sit over there?"

"Affirmative," said the computer.

Dairine ambled over in the direction of the racks and started searching for something decent to sit in.

The creatures she passed ignored her. Dairine found it difficult to return the compliment. One of the racks had what looked like a giant blue vampire bat hanging in it. Or no, it had no fur: the thing was actually more like a pterodactyl, and astonishingly pretty—the blue was iridescent, like a hummingbird's feathers. Dairine walked around it, fascinated, for quite a long time, pretending to look for a chair.

But there seemed to be no chairs in this particular area. The closest to a chairlike thing was a large low bowl that was full of what seemed to be purple Jell-O . . . except that the Jell-O put up a long blunt limb of itself, the end of which swiveled to follow as Dairine passed. She hurried by; the effect was rather like being looked at by a submarine periscope, and the Jell-O thing had about as much expression. Probably wonders what the heck *I* am, she thought. Boy, is it mutual. . . .

Finally she settled for the floor. She brought up the utilities menu and started running down the list of planets again. . . . then stopped and asked for the "Help" utility.

"Nature of query," said the computer.

"Uh . . ." Dairine paused. Certainly this place was what she had thought she wanted—a big cosmopolitan area full of intelligent alien creatures. But at the same time there were hardly any hominids, and she felt bizarrely out of place. Which was all wrong. She wanted someplace where she would be able to make sense of things. But how to get that across to the computer? It seemed as though, even though it was magical, it still used and obeyed the laws of science, and was as literal and unhelpful as a regular computer could be if you weren't sufficiently familiar with it to know how to tell it what you wanted.

"I want to go somewhere else," she said to the machine.

"Define parameters," said the computer.

"Define syntax."

"Command syntax. Normal syntactical restrictions do not apply in the Help facility. Commands and appended arguments may be stated in colloquial-vernacular form. Parameters may be subjected to Manual analysis and discussion if desired."

"Does that mean I can just talk to you?" Dairine said.

"Affirmative."

"And you'll give me advice?"

"Affirmative."

She let out a breath. "Okay," she said. "I want to go somewhere else."

"Acknowledged. Executing."

"No don't!" Dairine said, and several of the aliens around her reacted to the shriek. One of the holly tree people, standing nearby in something like a flowerpot, had several eyes fall off on the floor.

"Overridden," said the computer.

" 'Help' facility!" Dairine said, breathing hard. Her heart was pounding.

"Online."

"Why did you start doing that?!"

" 'OK' is a system command causing an exit from the 'Help' facility and a return to command level," said the computer.

"Do not run *any* program until I state the full command with arguments and end the sequence with 'Run'!"

"Affirmative," said the computer. "Syntax change confirmed."

Oh, Lord, Dairine thought, I've started messing with the syntax and I don't even *understand* it. I will never never use a program again till I've read the docs . . . "Good," she said. "The following is a string of parameters for a world I want to transit to. I will state 'end of list' when finished."

"Affirmative. Awaiting listing."

"Right. I want to go somewhere else."

"Transit agenda, confirmed. Specific arguments, please."

"Uhh . . ." She thought. "I want to go somewhere where there are going to be people like me."

"Noted. Next argument."

What exactly *was* I looking for? Darth Vader . . . She opened her mouth, then closed it again. I think I'll wait a bit on that one. "I want to go somewhere where I'm expected," she said.

"Noted. Next argument."

"Somewhere where I can use some of this magic."

"Argument already applies," said the computer. "You are using wizardry at this time."

Dairine made a face. "Somewhere where I can sit down and figure out what it means."

"Argument already applies. Documentation is available at this time."

Dairine sighed. "Somewhere where I will have *time* to sit down and figure out what it means."

"Incomplete argument. State time parameter."

"A couple of days. Forty-eight hours," she said then, before it could correct her syntax.

"Noted. Next argument."

"Somewhere—" One more time she stopped, considering the wild number of variables she was going to have to specify. And the truth was, she didn't know what she was after. Except . . . She looked around her conspiratorially, as if someone might overhear her. Indeed, she would have died if, say, Nita, should ever hear this. "Somewhere I can do something," she whispered. "Something big. Something that matters."

"Noted," said the computer. "Next argument."

"Uh . . ." The embarrassment of the admission out loud had driven everything out of her head. "End arguments," she said.

"Advisory," said the computer.

"So advise me."

"Stated number of arguments defines a very large sample of destinations. Stated number of arguments allows for interference in transit by other instrumentalities. Odds of interference approximately ninety-six percent."

That brought Dairine's chin up. "Let 'em try," she said. "The arguments stand."

"Instruction accepted. End advisory."

"Fine. List program."

"Transit program. Sort for Terran-type hominids along maximal space-time curvature. Sort for anticipated arrival, time continuum maximal but skewed to eliminate paradox. Sort for opportunity for intervention. Sort for data analysis period on close order, forty-eight hours. Sort for intervention curve skewed to maximal intervention and effect. End list."

"You got it," Dairine said. "Name listed program 'TRIP1.' "

"Named."

"Save it. Exit 'Help' facility."

"TRIP1 saved. Command level," said the computer.

"Run TRIP1."

"Running. Input required."

Dairine rolled her eyes at the mile-high ceiling. *Nita doesn't do it this way,* she thought. *I've watched her. She just reads stuff out of her book, or says it by heart. . . . Oh well, someone has to break new ground.* She stretched her legs out in front of her to keep them from cramping. "Specify," she said.

"Birth date."

"Twenty October nineteen seventy-eight," she said, looking out across the floor at the great crowd of pushing and jostling aliens.

"Place of birth."

"Three-eight-five East Eighty-sixth Street, New York City." The hospital had long since burned down, but Dairine knew the address: her dad had taken them all there to a German restaurant now on the site.

"Time of birth."

"Twelve fifty-five A.M."

"Favorite color."

"You have *got* to be kidding!" she said, looking at a particularly busy knot of aliens across the floor. Security guards, most likely: they were armed, in a big group, and looking closely at people.

"Favorite color."

"Blue." Or *were* these critters security guards? There had been other creatures walking around in the terminal wearing uniforms—as much or as little clothing of a particular shade of silvery green as each alien in question felt like wearing. And their weapons had been slim little blue-metal rods strapped to them. *These* creatures, though—they wore no uniforms, and their weapons were large and dark and looked nasty.

"Last book read," said the computer.

"Look," Dairine said, "what do you need to know this dumb stuff for?"

"Program cannot be accurately run without the enacting wizard's personal data. You have no data file saved at this time."

She made another face. *Better not interfere,* she thought, *or you might wind up doing the breaststroke in lava after all.* "Oh, go on," she said.

"Last book read—"

"*The Decline and Fall of the Roman Empire,*" said Dairine, looking with increasing unease at the armed bunch of aliens. They were not nice-looking people. Well, *lots* of the people in here didn't look nice—that purple Jell-O thing for one—but none of them *felt* bad: just weird. But these creatures with the guns—they had an unfriendly look to them. Most of them were mud-colored warty-looking creatures like a cross between lizards and toads, but upright, and not nearly as pretty as a lizard or as helplessly homely as any toad. They went about with a lumpish hunchbacked swagger, and their eyes were dark slitted bulges or fat crimson bloodshot goggle-eyes. They looked stupid, and worse, they looked cruel. . . .

Oh, come on, Dairine told herself in disgust. Just because they're ugly doesn't mean they're bad. Maybe it's just some kind of military expedition, like soldiers coming through the airport on their way home for leave.

—but with their guns?

"Father's name," said the computer.

"Harold Edward Callahan," said Dairine. She was looking with a combination of interest and loathing at one of the warty creatures, which was working its way toward her. In one arm it was cradling a gun that looked big enough to shove a hero sandwich down. In its other hand, a knobby three-fingered one, it held the end of a leash, and straining at the leash's far end was a something that looked more like the stuffed deinonychus at Natural History than anything Dairine had ever seen. A skinny little dinosaur it was, built more or less along the lines of a Tyrannosaurus, but lithe and small and fleet. This one went all on its hind legs, its long thin tail stretched out behind it for balance: it went with a long-legged ostrichy gait that Dairine suspected could turn into an incredible sprint. The dinosaur on the warty alien's leash was dappled in startling shades of iridescent red and gold, and it had its face down to the floor as it pulled its master along, and the end of that long whiplike tail thrashed. And then it looked up from the floor, and looked right at Dairine, with eyes that were astonishingly innocent, and as blue as a Siamese cat's. It made a soft mewling noise that nonetheless pierced right through the noise of the terminal.

The warty thing looked right at Dairine too—and cried out in some language she couldn't understand, a bizarre soprano singing of notes like a synthesizer playing itself. Then it yanked the leash sharply and let the deinonychus go.

Dairine scrambled to her feet as the deinonychus loped toward her. Terrified as she was, she knew better than to try to run away from *this* thing. She slammed the computer's screen closed and waited. No kicks, she told herself, if one kick doesn't take this thing out, you'll never have time for a second—It leapt at her, but she was already swinging: Dairine hit the deinonychus right in the face with the computer and felt something crunch. Oh, please don't let it be the plastic, she thought, and then the impetus of the deinonychus carried it right into her, its broken jaw knocked against her face as it fell, she almost fell with it. Dairine stumbled back, found her footing, turned, and began to run.

Behind her more voices were lifted. Dairine ran like a mad thing, pushing through crowds wherever she could. *Who are they, why are they after* me? *And where do I run . . .*

She dodged through a particularly dense crowd and paused, looking for a corridor to run down, a place to hide. Nothing. This part of the Crossings was one huge floor, very few niches to take advantage of. But farther on, about half a mile away, it looked like the place narrowed. . . .

She ran. The noise behind her was deafening. There was some shooting: she heard the scream of blasterbolts, the sound that had set her blood racing in the movies. But now it wasn't so exciting. One bolt went wide over her head. It hit a low-floating bit of the ceiling off to one side of her, and she smelled the stink of scorched plastic and saw a glob of it fall molten to splat on the floor. Dairine sprinted past it, panting. She was a good runner, but she couldn't keep this up for much longer.

Bug-eyed monsters! her brain sang at her in terror. *These weren't what I had in mind!* "What *are* they—"

"Emissaries," said the computer, in a muffled voice since its screen was shut over its speaker.

Dairine kept running. "From where?"

"Indeterminate. Continue run?"

"If it'll get me out of here, *yes*—!"

"Last level of education finished—"

She told it, gasping, as she ran. She told it her mother's maiden name, and how much money her father made, and at what age she had started reading, and much more useless information. . . . And then while she was telling it what she thought of boys, something caught her by the arm.

It was a three-fingered hand, knobby, a slick dark green, and strong with a terrible soft strength that pulled her right out of her run and around its owner as if she were spinning around a pole. Dairine cried out at her first really close look at a bug-eyed monster. Its eyes were an awful milky red that should have meant it was blind, but they saw her too well entirely—and it sang something high at her and grabbed her up against it with its other hand, the nonchalant don't-hurt-it grasp of the upper arms that adults use on children, not knowing how they hate it . . . or not caring. Dairine abruptly recognized the BEM's song as laughter, once removed from the horrible low laughing she had seemed to hear in transit. And suddenly she *knew* what these things were, if not who. *"No!"* she screamed.

"Intervention subroutine?" said the computer, utterly calm.

Dairine struggled against the thing, couldn't get leverage: all the self-defense she had been taught was for use on humans, and this thing's mass was differently distributed. Not too far away she heard more of the horrid fluting, BEMs with guns, coming fast. Half her face was rammed up against its horrible hide, and her nose was full of a stink like old damp coffee grounds. Her revulsion was choking her: the grasp of the thing on her was as unhuman as if she were being held by a giant cockroach . . . and Dairine *hated* bugs. *"Kill it!"* she screamed.

And something threw her back clear a good twenty feet and knocked her head against the floor . . .

Dairine scrambled up. The BEM was gone. Or rather, it wasn't a BEM anymore. It was many many little pieces of BEM, scattered among splatters of dark liquid all over the floor, and all over everything else in the area, including her. Everything smelled like an explosion in a coffeeshop.

Hooting noises began to fill the air. Oh, no, Dairine thought as she grabbed the computer up from the floor and began to run again. Now this place's own security people were going to start coming after her. They would ask her questions. And no matter how little a time they did that for, the BEMs would be waiting. If they waited. If they didn't just come and take her away from the port's security. And even if she killed every BEM in the place, more would come. She knew it.

She ran. People looked at her as she ran. Some of them were hominid, but not even they made any move to stop her or help her: they looked at her with the blank nervousness of innocent bystanders watching a bank robber flee the scene of the crime. Dairine ran on, desperate. It was like some nightmare of being mugged in a big city, where the streets are full of people and no one moves to help.

The blasterscreams were a little farther behind her. Maybe the one BEM's fate had convinced the others it would be safer to pick her off from a distance. But then why didn't they do that before?

Unless they wanted me alive . . .

She ran and ran. That laughter in the dark now pounded in her pulse, racing, and in the pain in her side that would shortly cripple her for running. Something she had read in Nita's manual reoccurred to her: Old Powers, not friendly to what lives: and one of the oldest and strongest, that invented death and was cast out . . . Part of her, playing cold and logical, rejected this, insisted she had no data, just a feeling. But the feeling screamed *Death*! and told logic to go stuff it somewhere. These things belonged to that old Power. She needed a safe place to think what to do. Home . . . But no. Take these things home with her? Her mom, her dad, these things would—

But maybe Nita and Kit could help—

But admit that she needed help?

Yes. No. *Yes*—

But without resetting the transit program, she couldn't even do that. No time . . .

"Can you run subroutines of that program before you finish plugging in the variables?" Dairine said, gasping as she ran.

"Affirmative."

"Then do it, as soon as you can!"

"Affirmative. Name of best friend—"

She wondered for a second whether 'Shash Jackson was still her best friend after she had cleaned him out of his record money three days ago. Then she gave his name anyway. Red lines of light lanced over her head as she ran. And here, the ceiling was getting lower, the sides of the building were closer, there were smaller rooms, places to go to ground. . . .

The stitch in her side was killing her. She plowed through a crowd of what looked like ambulatory giant squid on a group tour, was lost among them for a moment, in a sea of waving purple tentacles, tripping over their luggage, which crowded aside squawking and complaining—then came out the other side of them and plunged into a smaller corridor about the size of Grand Central Station.

She kept giving the computer inane information as she ran down the corridor, pushing herself to the far side of the stitch, so that she could reach someplace to be safe for a minute. There were more gates here, more signs and seating areas, and off to one side, a big shadowy cul-de-sac. She ran for it, any cover being better than none.

At the very end of her energy, she half ran, half stumbled in. It was unmistakably a bar. If she had had any breath to spare, she would have laughed with the dear familiarity of it, for it looked completely like other bars she had seen in airports when traveling with her folks and Nita—fairly dim, and crowded with tables and chairs and people and their bags. But no mere airport bar had ever had the kind of clientele that this place did. Tall furry things with too many arms, and squat many-legged things that looked to be wearing their organs on the outside, and one creature that seemed totally made of blinking eyes, all stared at Dairine over their snacks and drinks as she staggered in and past them, and not one of them moved.

Dairine didn't care. Her only thought was to hide. But she realized with horror that she could see no back way out of the place—only a dark red wall and a couple of what might have been abstract sculptures, unless they were aliens too. She heard the cries out in the terminal getting closer, and utter panic overcame her. Dairine shouldered and stumbled her way frantically among strange bodies and strange luggage in the semidarkness, hardly caring what she might or might not be touching. Impetus and blind terror crashed her right into a little table at the back of the room, almost upsetting both the

table and the oddly shaped, half-full glass on it. And then something caught
her and held her still.

After her experience out in the terminal, Dairine almost screamed at the
touch. But then she realized that what held her were human hands. She
could have sobbed for relief, but had no breath to spare. So rattled was she
that though she stared right at the person who was steadying her, it took her
precious seconds to see him. He was built slight and strong, wearing a white
shirt and sweater and a long fawn-colored jacket: a fair-haired young man
with quick bright eyes and an intelligent face. "Here now," he said, helping
her straighten up, "careful!" And he said it in English!

Dairine opened her mouth to beg for help, but before she could say a
word, those wise, sharp eyes had flickered over her and away, taking everything in.

"Who's after you?" the man said, quiet-voiced but urgent, glancing back
at Dairine.

"I don't know what they are," she said, gasping, "but someone—someone
bad sent them. I can lose them, but I need time to finish programming—"

Alarm and quick thought leapt behind those brown eyes. "Right. Here
then, take these." The young man dug down in his jacket pocket, came up
with a fistful of bizarrely shaped coins, and pressed them hurriedly into
Dairine's free hand. "There's a contact transfer disk behind the bar. Step on
it and you should materialize out in the service corridor. Follow that to the
right and go out the first blue door you see, into the terminal. If I'm not
mistaken, the pay toilets will be a few doors down on your left. Go in one of
the nonhuman ones."

"The nonhuman—!" Dairine said, absolutely horrified.

"Quite so," the man said. "Right across the universe, that's one of the
strongest taboos there is." And he grinned, his eyes bright with mischief.
"No matter who's after you, it'll take them a bit to think of looking for you in
there. And the locks will slow them down." He was on his feet. "Off you go
now!" he said, and gave Dairine a fierce but friendly shove in the back.

She ran past a trundling robot barman, under the hinged part of the bartop
and onto the transfer circle. On the other side of the bar, as Dairine began to
vanish, she saw the fair man glance over at her to be sure she was getting
away, and then pick up the iced tea he had been drinking. Glass in hand, he
went staggering cheerfully off across the barroom in the most convincing
drunk act Dairine could imagine, accidentally overturning tables, falling into
the other patrons, and creating a mess and confusion that would slow even
the BEMs up somewhat.

Dairine materialized in the service corridor, followed her instructions to
the letter, and picked a rest room with a picture sign so weird, she couldn't
imagine what the aliens would look like. She found out soon enough. She

spent the next few minutes hastily answering the computer's questions while
sitting on what looked like a chrome-plated lawn mower, while the tiled room
outside her locked booth echoed with the bubbling screams of alien ladies (or
gentlemen) disturbed in the middle of who knew what act.

Then the screams became quiet, and were exchanged for a horrible rustling noise, thick soft footfalls, and high fluting voices. The computer had
asked Dairine whether she preferred Coke or Pepsi, and had then fallen
silent for some seconds. "Are you done?" she hissed at it.

"Running. Data in evaluation."

"Get a move on!"

"Running. Data in evaluation."

The air filled with the scorch of burning plastic again. They were burning
the lock of the booth.

"Can you do something to a few of them?" she whispered, her mouth
going dry.

"Negative multitasking ability," said the computer.

Dairine put her head down on the computer, which was on her knees, and
took what she suspected might be her last breath.

The lock of the booth melted loose and the door fell in molten globs to the
floor. Dairine sat up straight, determined to look dirty at the BEMs, if she
could do nothing else.

The door swung open.

And "Multiple transit," said the computer, "executing now," and the
jump-sickness grabbed Dairine and twisted her outside in. Perhaps not understanding, the BEMs fluted in rage and triumph and reached into the booth.
But Dairine's insides went cold as dimly she felt one of them swing a huge
soft hand through where her middle was: or rather, where it no longer was
completely—the transit had begun. A second later, heat not wholly felt
stitched through her arms and legs as shots meant to cripple her tore through
where they almost were, and fried the back of the stall like an egg. Then
starlight and the ancient black silence pierced through her brain; the spell
tore Dairine free of the planet and flung her off Rirhath B into the long
night.

She never found out anything about the man who helped her. Nor did he
ever find out anything more about her. Pausing by the door of the pay toilet,
after being released from station security some hours later, and being tele-
pathically sensitive (as so many hominids are), he could sense only that some
considerable power had been successfully exercised there. Satisfied with that,
he smiled to himself and went on about his travels, just one more of the
millions of hominids moving about the worlds. But many millions of light-
years later, in some baking wilderness under a barren, brilliant sky, a bitterly

weary Dairine sat down on a stone and cried for a while in shock at the utter strangeness of the universe, where unexpected evil lives side by side with unexpected kindness, and neither ever seems quite overcome by the other. . . .

Variables

It took Nita a few minutes to pull her supplies together and get ready for the trip. Every wizard has favorite spells, so familiar and well used that diagrams and physical ingredients like eye of newt aren't needed for them. But most spells, and particularly the most powerful ones, need help in bending space—some specific kind of matter placed in specific relationship to the wizard and the words being used and the diagram or formula asserting the wizard's intent. Some of the kinds of matter used for these purposes can be odder even than eye of newt (which used to be used for teleportation spells until polyethylene was invented). And this being the case, most wizards have a cache, a place where they keep the exotica necessary in their work.

Nita's cache was buried in a vacant lot next door to her house, all carefully wrapped in a plastic garbage bag. Being a wizard, she had no need to dig the bag up: a variant of the spell Kit had used on the bricks let her feel around under the ground for the moment it took her to find what she wanted. The objects didn't look like much—half a (seemingly) broken printed-circuit board; a plastic packet containing about two teaspoonsful of dirt; and a gimbal from a 1956 Philco Pilot television set.

That last piece she juggled appreciatively from hand to hand for a moment. It was certainly unlikely looking, a busted bit of junk that any normal person would trash without a second thought. But the configuration into which the space-time continuum bent itself around this gimbal was unique, and invested with a power that the informed wizard could exploit. *Everything* bent spacetime, of course: anything consisting of either matter or energy had no choice. But some things bent it in ways that produced specific physical effects. . . . and no one, not even the wizards specializing in theoretical research, had any idea yet as to *why*. The atoms and mass and inherent spatiotemporal configuration of, say, water, bent existence around them to produce an effect of wetness. The electrons and plasma and matter and gravity of a star produced effects of heat and light. And a busted-off piece of gimbal from an ancient TV set . . .

Nita smiled a bit, put the gimbal carefully in her pocket, and said three more words.

Her room was dark. She flipped the light on and went digging in the mess off to one side for her knapsack. Into it she stuffed her manual, the gimbal and packet and circuit board.

"Nita?"

"Uh-huh," she said.

The stairs creaked. Then her mother was standing in the doorway, looking upset.

"You said you were going to clean your room today," her mother said in a tired voice.

Nita looked up . . . then went hurriedly to her mother and grabbed her and hugged her hard. "Oh, thanks," she said, "thanks, *thanks* for saying something normal!"

Her mother laughed, a sound that had no happiness about it at all, and hugged her back. After a moment her mother said, "She won't be normal when she gets back, will she?"

Nita took a moment to answer. "She won't be like she was, not completely. She can't. She's on Ordeal, Mums: it changes you. That's what it's about." Nita tried to smile, but it felt broken. "She might be better."

"Better? Dairine?" her mother said, sounding a touch dry. Nita's smile began to feel less broken, for that sounded more like her mother.

"Oh, c'mon, Mom, she's not that bad—" Then Nita stopped herself. *What am I saying!* "Look, Mom," she said, "she's real smart. Sometimes that makes me want to stuff her in the toilet, but it's going to come in handy for her now. She's not stupid, and if the wizards' software in the computer is anything like our manuals, she'll have some help if she can keep her head and figure out what to ask for. If we get a move on, we'll catch up with her pretty quick."

"If you can find her."

Nita's father loomed up in the doorway in the darkness, a big silver-haired shadow.

Nita swallowed. "Daddy, she'll leave a trail. Using wizardry changes the shape of the space-time continuum . . . it's like cutting through a room full of smoke with a knife. You can see where the knife's been. Knowing Dairine she won't be making any effort to cover her trail . . . at least not just yet. We can follow her. If she's in trouble, we'll get her out of it. But I can't stay to talk about it. Kit needs me quick, and I can't do a lot for Dari without him. Some . . . but not as much. We work best as a team."

Her mother gave her father a look that Nita could make nothing of. "When do you think you three will be back?" said her father.

"I don't know," Nita said. She thought to say something, stopped herself, then realized that they had a right to know. "Mums, Dad, look. We might not be able to bring her back right away. It's *her* Ordeal. Until she solves the problem she's supposed to be the answer to, if we pull her back, awful things could happen. If we'd copped out of ours, this whole world would be different. And believe me, you wouldn't have liked the difference." She swallowed at the thought of something like that leaning, threatening darkness waiting for Dairine to confront it . . . something like that, but *much* worse.

They stood and looked at her.

"I've gotta go," she said, and slung her knapsack on, and hugged them hard, first her dad and then her mom again. Her father took a long time to let her go. Her mother's eyes were still troubled, and there was nothing Nita could do about it, nothing at all.

"I'll clean up in here as soon as I get home," Nita said, "I promise."

The trouble didn't go out of her mother's face, but half her mouth made a smile.

Nita said three words, and was gone.

Our home Galaxy is a hundred thousand light-years across, five thousand light-years thick at the core. The billion stars that make it up are scattered through some four quadrillion cubic miles of space. It is so vast that a thought can take as long as two seconds to cross it.

But Dairine was finding the entirety of the Milky Way much too small to get lost in. She got out of it as soon as she could.

The program the computer was still writing to take her to safety was a multiple-jump program, and that suited her fine: her pursuers seemed to have trouble following her. But not enough trouble. She came out, after that first jump from Rirhath B, on some cold world whose sky she never saw: only a ceiling of gray. She was standing in a bleak place, full of what at first sight looked like old twisted, wind-warped trees, barren of any leaves, all leaning into a screaming wind that smelled of salt water. Dairine clutched the computer to her and stared around her, still gasping from her terror in a rest room twelve trillion miles away.

With a slow creaking sound, one of the trees pulled several of its roots out of the ground and began to walk toward her.

"No way!" Dairine shrieked. "Run another subroutine!"

"Running," said the computer, but it took its sweet time about it—and just as the world blinked out and the spell tore her loose from the hillside, Dairine felt wind on her skin—a wind that smelled of coffee grounds. The BEMs had popped right in behind her.

She popped out again, this time in the middle of a plain covered with sky-blue grass under a grass-green sky. She shook the computer in frustration.

"Program running," the computer insisted.

"Sure, but they're following us! How are they doing it? Are we leaving a trail somehow?"

"Affirmative," said the computer calmly, as if Dairine should have known this all along.

"Well, *do* something about it!"

"Advisory," said the computer. "Stealth procedures will decrease running speed. Stealth procedures are not one hundred percent effective due to inherent core-level stability of string functions—"

"I'll settle! And if we don't have to keep wasting time running subroutines," Dairine said, exasperated, "you'll have more time to run the main program, won't you!"

"Affirmative. Execute stealth?"

"Before someone executes *me*, yeah!"

Once again the spell took hold of Dairine and ripped her free of gravity and light. At least, she thought, this time the BEMs hadn't appeared before she vanished herself. Maybe we can gain a little ground. We'd better. . . .

Another reality flicked into being around her. She was in the middle of a city: she got a brief impression of glassy towers that looked more grown than built, and people rushing around her and avoiding her in the typical dance of city dwellers. This might almost have been New York, except that New Yorkers had only a small percentage of the legs these people had. "Don't stop," she said. "How much range have you got?"

"Infinite," said the computer, quite calmly.

"While still running the main program?"

"Affirmative."

She thought for a second. "The edge of the Local Group might be far enough. Go."

The spell seized her out of the crowd and flung her into the dark again. Over and over Dairine jumped, becoming less and less willing to stop, until finally strange vistas were flickering past her with the speed of some unutterably strange slide show being run in fast-forward by a bored lecturer. She passed right through the coronation parade of one of the Anarchs of Deleian IV and never noticed it: she stood for only a second on a chilly little planetoid being fought over by two desperate interstellar empires (and also missed the nova bomb that turned the planetoid into plasma several minutes later); she stood on the metallic upper floors of a planet that was one great library full of three galaxies' knowledge, and she never knew what it was, and probably at that point would not have cared. Only once Dairine paused for more than a few seconds, on a red sandstone promontory with a pinkish sea crashing at its foot, and no signs of life anywhere under the bloated red sun that dyed the water. "Are they still following?" she said.

"Probability high, but at a greatly increased distance."

"You have enough time to finish the main program?"

"Affirmative."

"Do it, then."

She sat down on a rock and looked out at the water, while the computer's disk drive chirred softly to itself. The fat red sun slipped horizonward as she watched, and Dairine looked at it and noticed through the sunset haze that it had a companion, a little blue-white dwarf star that was slowly sucking the red giant's matter out of it in an accretion spiral of tarnished gold. She shook her head. Once she would have given anything to sit here and watch this. Now, though, the hair was rising on the back of her neck, and her back prickled, and all she wanted in the world—the worlds—was to get out of here and end up where she could hide.

She shivered. *I never want to smell coffee again,* she thought. They had unquestionably been sent after her by what had laughed at her in the dark. The Lone Power, the manual utility had called It. Well, at least she didn't hear It laughing anymore while she was in transit. Then again, that might not be good. *I'm running pretty fair rings around Its people. It's probably real annoyed at me.*

And then she tossed her head and grinned, her nasty grin. *Let It be, then. I'm not going to be running for long. I'm going to turn around and give It something to think about.*

If I can just figure out what to do, and find a weapon. . . .

"Done," said the computer.

"Is this going to be a bad jump?" Dairine said.

"Transit may have significant physiological effects," said the computer.

"Okay," Dairine said. "Go for it." And she clenched her jaw.

The computer was understating. The jump was a hundred times worse than the first long one, an eternity of being torn, squeezed out of shape, pulled, hammered on, sliced by lines of force thinner than any hair and sharp as swords. Dairine hung on, unable even to scream. The transit broke for an instant on the surface of some planet as the program finished one jump subroutine, in a frozen flash of light and time too sudden to let any of the scream out, then pushed Dairine outside the universe and crushed her under its weight again. Then flash, and again; flash, and again: flash, flash, flash, flash, through a voiceless darkness a trillion years heavy and empty as entropy's end. This was the worst after all, the aloneness, total, no one to hear the scream she could not utter, not even the One who laughed—flash, flash, flash—

—and then the crushing ceased, and the spell flung Dairine down on something flat and hard and chill, and she flopped down like a puppet with its strings cut and just lay there as she had not done since Ananke. Her stomach flipped, but this was becoming so commonplace that Dairine was able to ignore it and just lie there and pant for a few seconds.

Silence. Not that awful emptiness, but a more normal one: probably just lack of air. Dairine levered herself up painfully on her elbows and looked at the surface under her hands. It was dimly lit, and smooth as the garage floor on Rirhath B had been. Smoother, in fact. It was hard to tell colors in this dimness, but the surface wasn't plain white. Dapples of various shades seemed to overlap and shade one another in the depths of it, as delicately as if they had been airbrushed: and there was a peculiar translucence to the surface, as if it were glass of some kind.

Cautiously, Dairine got up to a kneeling position and straightened to look around. Now *this* is weird, she thought, for the surface on which she knelt, stretched on so far into the distance that she scrubbed at her eyes briefly, not quite believing them. The horizon seemed much farther away than it could ever be on Earth. Must be a much bigger planet, she thought. But the thought did not make that immense vista any easier to grasp. It seemed to curve *up* after a while, though she was sure it was perfectly flat: the illusion was disturbing. Over the horizon hung starry space, the stars close and bright. Off to the sides the view was the same: here and there conical outcroppings of rock might break the pure and perfect flatness of it all, looking as if Picasso had dropped them there . . . but otherwise there was nothing but that endless, pale, slick-smooth surface, dappled with touches of dim subtle color, in huge patches or small ones.

Dairine stood up and turned around to look for the computer. It was behind her, at her feet: she bent to pick it up—

—and forgot about doing so. Before her, past the razory edge of that impossibly distant horizon, the galaxy was rising.

It was not her own. The Milky Way is a type S0 spiral, a pinwheel of stars. This was a barred spiral, type SB0, seen almost face-on: an oval central core, two bars jutting from its core, one from each end of the starry oval, and each bar having a long curved banner or stream of stars curling away from it. Dairine had seen a hundred pictures of them and had mostly been fascinated by that central bar, wondering what gravitational forces were keeping it in place. But now she was seeing such a galaxy as few, even wizards, ever see one —not as a flat, pale far-off picture but as a three-dimensional object near at hand, rich with treasuries of stars in a spectrum's worth of colors, veiled about with diamonded dust on fire with ions and glowing, dominating a third of even that immense horizon, seeming frozen though in the midst of irresist-ible motion, its starry banners streaming back in still and complex glory from the eye-defeating blaze of the core. Dairine slowly folded back down to the kneeling position and just watched it, watched it rise.

She weighed just a little less than she would have on Earth; but the spiral rose quickly, for a planet of this size. Must not be a very dense planet, Dairine thought. All light elements—though most of her paid no attention to the analysis, being busy with more important matters . . . this light, the terror and the wonder of it. *This*, was what she had come for. The computer had hit it right on. This planet's sun must be in one of the galaxy's satellite globular clusters. . . . As such distances went, she was close to that spiral: no more than ten or twenty thousand light-years above its core. But the thought of distances broke her mood. She pulled the computer close. "Did we lose them?" she said to it.

"Pursuit has halted forty trillion light-years from this location and is holding there."

"Forty *trillion* . . ." That was beyond the reach of the farthest telescopes, over the event horizon generated by the Big Bang itself: galaxies past that point were traveling with intrinsic velocities faster than light, and so could not be seen. It was questionable whether such bodies could even really be considered in the same universe as Earth.

"Long way from home," she said softly. "Okay. I have at least a couple days to rest and do some research, huh?"

"Affirmative."

She sat back on her heels and watched the light rise until the last delicate streamers of light from the barred spiral arms were all the way above the horizon. "I want all the details about this star system," she said. "Planets, what kind of star, who lives here if anybody, who's been here before. Get to work."

"Working," said the computer, and its screen went to the usual menu configuration while it sat silently, getting the information for her.

"Can you multitask now?" Dairine said.

"Affirmative."

"Good."

She selected the "Manual" function and began sorting through it for background material on the Lone One. There has to be something I can use against It, she thought, a weapon of some kind, a weakness. . . . She instructed the manual's research facility to sort for past conflicts of wizards with the Lone Power or its representatives, and was shocked and horrified to find the equivalent of twenty or thirty thousand pages' worth of abstracts. She skimmed ten or fifteen of them in reverse order, on a hunch, and was momentarily surprised to find an abstract of Nita's last active mission. Fascinated, Dairine began to read . . . and became horrified again. There had been some kind of ceremony in the waters off Long Island, a sort of underwater passion play with whales as the celebrants—and Nita, to save the East Coast and make this ceremony work, had volunteered to be eaten by a shark! Nita? My sister? Do anything braver than cross the street? The idea was ridiculous . . . but Dairine knew that this computer had better things to do than lie to her. She read the rest of the abstract with her insides turning cold. Nita had knowingly taken on that Lone Power face-to-face and had managed to come out of it alive. Whereas Dairine had been glad enough to run away and lose things that couldn't be more than Its lesser henchmen . . .

Dairine pushed that thought away resolutely. She was helped by her stomach, which growled at her.

When *did* I last eat? she wondered. She told the computer to sort through and save the descriptions of encounters with the Power that had been successful, and then got out of the "Manual" into the "Hide" facility. A moment's poking around among the options, and she had retrieved her loaf of bread, bologna, and mustard. Dairine sat there in cheerful anticipation for a few seconds, undoing the bread and bologna, and it wasn't until she got the mustard jar lid unscrewed that she realized she had no knife. "Oh, well," she said, and went back into the "Hide" facility to snitch one from the silverware drawer at home. But "Illegal function call," said the computer: a little sullenly, she thought.

"Explain."

"Out of range for transit function from stated location."

Dairine made a face. She had no idea of the coordinates of any closer silverware drawer. "Cancel," she said, and made do with her fingers.

Some minutes later she had a sandwich and a half inside her, and was thinking (as she finished getting herself more or less clean) that it was a good thing she liked mustard. Dairine brushed the crumbs off onto the slick surface she sat on and looked at it, mildly curious. It wasn't freezing cold to sit on, like the stones of Mars or Pluto: yet her shields were still snowing water vapor gently into the vacuum around her whenever she moved, telling her that the above-surface temperature was the usual cold of deep space. Geothermal? she wondered. Maybe some volcanic activity—that would explain those funny conical shapes against the horizon. . . . She thumped the computer in a friendly fashion. "You done yet?" she said.

"Specify."

Dairine rolled her eyes. But there was no escaping the GIGO principle—"garbage in, garbage out," as the programmers said. Give the poor machine incomplete questions or instructions and you would get incomplete answers back. This thing might be magic, but it was still a computer. "Are you done with the survey of this area?"

"Still running."

"How much longer?"

"Three point two minutes."

Dairine sat back to wait, absently rubbing the surface she sat on. The smoothness of it was strange: not even the maria on the Moon were this smooth. Volcanic eruption, maybe. But not the way it usually happens, with the lava flowing down the volcano's sides and running along the surface. Not enough gravity for it to do that, I guess. Maybe it's like the volcanoes on Io: the stuff goes up high in tiny bits or droplets, then comes down slowly in the low gravity and spreads itself out very smooth and even. It must go on all the time . . . or else there can't be much in this system in the way of even tiny meteors. Maybe both. She shook her head. It spoke of an extremely ancient planet—which made sense this far out in space. . . .

"Ready," the computer said, and Dairine hunkered over it to listen. "Local system stats. System age: close order of eight billion years. One primary, type S6 star, off main sequence, time from fusion ignition: close order of five billion years. One associated micro-black hole in variable orbit. One planet, distance from primary: six hundred twelve million miles. Planet diameter: fifty-six thousand miles. Planet circumference: one hundred seventy-five thousand miles—" And Dairine gulped, understanding now why that horizon ran so high. The planet was almost seven times the size of Earth. "Atmosphere: monatomic hydrogen, less than one fifty-millionth psi Terran sea level. Planetary composition: eighty percent silicon in pure form and compounds, ten percent iron and mid-sequence metals, seven percent heavy metals, one percent boron, one percent oxygen, one percent trace elements including frozen gases and solid-sequence halogens. Power advisory—"

The screen, which had been echoing all this, went blank. Dairine's stomach flip-flopped, from fear this time. "What's the matter?"

"System power levels nearing critical. Range to alternative-power claudication exceeded. Outside power source required."

Dairine paused, feeling under her hand that oddly non-cold surface. "Can you use geothermal?" she said.

"Affirmative."

"Is there some way you can tap what's in this planet, then?"

"Affirmative," said the computer. "Authorization for link."

"Granted," Dairine said, mildly surprised: she couldn't remember the computer ever asking her for permission to do anything before. Maybe it was a safety feature. Then she began to sweat a little. Maybe such a safety feature was wise. If the computer fried its chips somehow and left her without life support, sitting here naked to vacuum at heaven knew how many degrees below zero . . .

She watched the screen nervously as scrambled characters flashed on it, and for several awful seconds the screen blanked. Then the menu screen reasserted itself, and Dairine breathed out, slowly, while the computer went back to running the program it had been working on. "Link established," said the computer in absolute calm. "Planetary history—"

"Just print it to the screen, I'll read it," Dairine said, and started to pick the computer up: then paused. "Is it all right to move you? Will that hurt the link?"

"Negative effect on link."

She lifted the computer into her lap and went on reading. It was as she had thought. The planet periodically became volcanically active, and the volcanoes spewed a fine mist of lava all over the landscape, airbrushing the glassy surface on a gigantic scale with vividly colored trace elements. Subsequent layering muted the colors, producing the dappled translucence she sat on. Dairine hit the carriage return for another screenful of data, and the screenful appeared—and her stomach flipped again.

PLANETARY HISTORY (page 2 of 16)   HELP/g/rl18655

This unique structure becomes more interesting when considering the physical nature of the layering. Some 92% of the layers consilt of chemically pure sillcol,l predlspollng thl agllllate to elelllllllductilllllllllllllllllllllllllllll1111
111111111111111111111111111111111111111111111111111
111111111111111111111111111111111111111111111111111
111111111111111111111111111111111111111111111111111
111111111111111111111111111111111111111111111111111
111111111111111111111111111111111111111111111111111
111111111111111111111111111111111111111111111111111
111111111111111111111111111111111111111111111111111
111111111111111111111111111111111111111111111111111
111111111111111111111111111111111111111111111111111
111111111111111111111111111111111111111111111111111

"I blew it up," Dairine whispered, horrified. "Oh, no, oh, no, I fried its brains. I blew it up." She took a deep breath, not sure how many more of them she was going to get, and gingerly hit the carriage return to see what would happen. . . .

Pattern Recognition

Nita popped out into a canopy of starlit darkness and a carpet of dim light, breathing very hard. Earth's gravity well was no joke: pushing her own mass and enough air to breathe for a while up out of that heavy pull was a problem. She walked over to a boulder, dusted it off, and sat down, panting, to admire the view while she waited for Kit.

The "usual place" where they met was, of course, the Moon. Nita liked it there; working, and thinking, were always easy there, in the great silence that no voices but astronauts' and wizards' had broken since the Moon's dust was made. This particular spot, high in the lunar Caucasus mountain chain, was a favorite of Kit's—a flat-topped peak in a wild, dangerous country of jagged gray-white alps, cratered and pocked by millennia of meteoric bombardment. Piles of rocktumble lay here and there, choking the steep valleys where the sheer heat and cold of the lunar days had been enough to flake solid rock away from itself in great glassy or pumicey chunks. Off to one side, the pallid rim of the little crater Calippus scraped razor-sharp against the sky, and over it hung the Earth.

The Moon was at first quarter, so the Earth was at third, a blinding half-world: blazing blue-green, almost painful to look at until the eyes got used to it. It shed a cool faint blue-white light over everything. A curl of white stormweather lay over the northwestern Pacific, and there vanished; for down the middle of it the terminator ran, the edge of night, creeping ever so slowly toward the west. Most of North America lay in the darkness, and city lights lay golden in faint glittering splashes and spatters with brighter sparkling patches under the Great Lakes and on the California coast.

Nita shrugged out of her knapsack, opened it and rechecked the contents. It was a good assortment: varied enough to handle several different classes of spell, specific enough to those classes to let her save some power for herself.

She pulled her manual out and started paging through it for the "tracker" spell that she and Kit would need when he got here. It was actually a variant of the one he had threatened to put on Dairine in the city: this one hunted for the characteristic charged "string residue" left in space by the passage of a wizard's transit spell through it. Nita's specialty was astronomy, so she had been shocked to find that "empty" space wasn't actually empty, and even the hardest vacuum had in it what physicists called "strings," lines of potential force that have nothing to do with any of the forces physicists understand. Wizards, of course, could use them: much of what passes for telekinesis turns out in fact to be string manipulation. The tracker spell made most elegant use of it. And once we find her, Nita thought, I'm gonna tie a few of those strings around her neck. . . .

But it didn't do to start a wizardry in such a mood. Nita pulled her space pen out of her pocket, kicked some of the larger rocks out of her way—they bounced off down the mountain as slowly as soap bubbles—and began drawing the circle for the transit spell.

It was becoming an old familiar diagram, this one. The basic circle, knotted with the wizard's knot: her own personal data, reduced by now (after much practice) to one long scrawl in the precise and elegant shorthand version of the Speech: Kit's data, another scrawl, over which she took even more care than her own. What a wizard names in the Speech, is defined so: inaccurate naming can alter the nature of the named, and Nita liked Kit just the way he was. A third long scrawl of shorthand for Picchu: Nita looked oddly at some of the variables in it, but Tom had given her the data, and he certainly knew what he was doing. Then the internal diagrams, the "intent" factors. The point of origin, the intended point of arrival or vector of travel; the desired result; the time parameters and conditional statements for life-support; the balloon-diagram for the ethical argument . . .

Nita wiped sweat and grit off her face, and muttered at the incessant hissing in the background. Dust flew freely in one-sixth gravity, and got in everything: after you went to the Moon, you took a shower, for the same reasons you take one after a haircut. But there wasn't much more to do here. She finished the last few strokes of the notations in the environmental-impact statement and stood up, rubbing her back and checking her work for spelling errors.

It was all in order. But that hissing. . . .

She sat down again, feeling nervous. Facility with the Speech, as with any other language, increases with time. After several months of working in a sort of pidgin Speech, Nita was finally beginning to think in it, and the results were sometimes upsetting. Once upon a time, it had been quiet on the Moon when she visited. But no more. Her more accustomed mind heard a sound in the darkness now: a low low sound like a breath being let out, and out, and out forever. The astronomer part of her knew what it was—the so-called four-degree radiation that was all that was left of the universe's birth. Normally only radio telescopes set to the right frequency could hear it. But Nita wasn't normal. Nor was the sound just a sound to her. In it she could hear the sound of consciousness, life, as plainly as she had used to be able to hear Kit think. *That* sensitivity had decreased over time; but this one was increasing, it seemed in the deep silence, by the minute. It upset her. Suddenly the universe, that had seemed so empty, now felt crammed full of powers and intelligences that might not need planets, or bodies. And Dairine was out there in the middle of them, mucking around in her inimitable fashion. . . . Nita found herself wishing that Kit would hurry up. She very much wanted to see that cheerful face, to hear at least his voice, if not his sassy, loud cast of thought, always with that slight Hispanic accent to it. . . .

Long time since we heard each other think. . . .

She had been wondering about that. Idly she began flipping through the manual, turning pages. Maybe the index— But the index did her no good: she couldn't think what heading to look under. "Come on," she muttered to the book, "give me a hand here, I don't have all day."

It was that hissing that was making her ill-tempered, she realized. A thought occurred to her, and she was glad she hadn't completely cleaned out her knapsack the other day. She reached into it and pulled out a tangle of cord, and a pair of earphones, and her Walkman. It was a Christmas present from her mother—the best of any present Nita had gotten last year, for she loved music and liked walking through her day with a soundtrack. Now she riffled through the pages of her manual, squinting at them in the pale Earth-light, while rock sang softly in the earphones.

Diagrams . . . She skipped that whole section, not without another glance over at Kit's name scrawled in the motionless, powdery lunar dust. He was all there: at least, he seemed to think so—it was mostly the description of himself he had carefully worked out. Of course, after their first few spells Nita had looked over his shoulder and suggested a couple additions to the data—his fondness for chocolate ice cream (which he had instantly admitted), and his craziness for poetry, especially Shakespeare (which embarrassed him, and which he had refused to admit to for several days). *The look on his face when I caught him reading The Tempest.* Still, he admitted it, finally. . . . She smiled a little then. He hadn't taken long to point out that her data said nothing about the fact that she devoured horse books one after another, or that he had once caught her with a long stick in hand, having an energetic swordfight with one of the trees in the vacant lot. . . .

And where is he!

She sighed and glanced down at the pages that had fallen open in her hand. One of them said:

Wizards in the closest relationships, leading toward permanent partnership, usually find that nonverbal communication becomes rare or difficult. Other conditions obtain for other species, but for human wizards, intimacy is meaningless without barriers to over-come—and to lower. Wizards usually have little need for such in the early stages of their careers. But as this situation changes, as the wizard becomes more adept at accurate description in the Speech, and therefore more adept at evaluating the people he or she works with, the wizard's mind typically adapts to the new requirements by gradually shutting out the person most—

. . . permanent partnership?
No. Oh, no—
Nita swallowed with a throat suddenly gone dry, and slapped the book shut. For a moment she tried to do nothing but listen to the tape. It was something of Journey's—their distinctive sweet keyboards and synthesizers, wistful, singing down toward silence. And then the vocal:

> "Looking down I watch the night
> running from the sun;
> orphan stars and city lights
> fading one by one. . . .
> Oh, sweet memories, I call on you now . . ."

Of course, Nita thought, there was a lot of it going around school. Going steady, dating, pins and rings, all the silliness. Her mother had forbidden Nita to do any such thing, telling her she was much too young. Nita didn't mind: it all seemed dumb to her. Sometimes, seeing how crazed some of the other girls her age were over the boy question, she wondered if she was normal. She was too busy, for one thing. She had something solider than going steady. When you were a wizard—
—with a partner—
Oh, come on. It's not as if they're going to make you marry him or something! Look at Tom and Carl, they're just buddies, they work together because they enjoy doing it. . . .
But I don't want . . .
She trailed off. She didn't know what she wanted. Nita put her head down in her hands, trying to think. No answers came: only more problems. Thoughts of Kit backing her up when she was terrified, cheering her up when she was annoyed, Kit being the solid, reliable voice in the other half of a spell, the presence on the far side of the circle, matching her cadence exactly, for

the fun and the challenge of it. What's wrong with that? What's wrong with
having a best friend?

He's a boy, that's what. It's changing. *I'm* changing.

I'm scared.

She gazed up through unending night, down at oncoming morning, and
tried to work out what to do. Has he noticed this happening to him too? And
suppose he starts liking someone else better than me? Will he want to keep
the team going? If only I knew what he was thinking. . . .

Then she let out a sad and annoyed breath. It's probably nothing, she
thought. Everything is probably fine. . . .

". . . oh, so much is wasted," sang the earphones,

> "and oh so little used!—
> but the trick of the dreamer
> is keeping yourself from the blues—"

Hah, Nita thought. I wish it were that simple. . . .

And the voice that sang cried out at her, so sudden and defiant that she sat
erect with startlement—

> "Everyone's a hero
> if you want to be!
> Everyone's a prisoner
> holding their own key!
> And every step I take,
> every move I make,
> I'm always one step closer—
> I don't mind running alone!"

It was Steve Perry's fierce, clear voice, uplifted in almost angry encouragement, hitting the chorus hard. He went on, singing something about children
and concrete canyons, but Nita was still full of that startlement and hardly
heard. Even Dairine, she thought. There's some job out there that only she
can do. . . . She had not thought of it in this light before, and the thought
of Dairine as a hero staggered her, and annoyed her for a moment. Her? The
runt?

But then Nita felt ashamed. What had she been herself, not more than a
few months ago? Basically a coward, afraid of everything, including herself—
friendless, quiet and smart but with no one to do any good by being so.
Things were different now: but who was she to deny Dairine her chance at
being more than she had been? *And every step I take, every move I make, I'm
always one step closer.* . . .

And if *she* can do that, Nita thought after a moment, I can sure ask him what he thinks about things—

A sudden movement off to one side brought Nita's head around with a snap. In utter silence, silvery-white dust was kicking up in a vague pale cloud from where a tall man in a polo shirt and shorts was standing. Tom bounced over to where Nita sat, being careful of his footing. Nita admired the way he bounced: he had obviously had a lot of practice at the kangaroo hop that works well in low gravities.

He paused not too far from Nita to let her shieldspell recognize his and allow it to infringe, then sat down beside Nita on the boulder, casting an analytical eye over her spell diagram. "Very neat," he said. "Nice structure. Carl has been contaminating you, I see."

"Thanks."

"Kit just called me," Tom said, brushing dust off himself. "He'll be up in a few . . . he's just settling things with his folks. I'm going to be talking to them later." Tom smiled wearily. "This seems to be my night."

"Yeah."

More silverdust kicked up, closer and to the right. There was Kit, with his knapsack over his back and Picchu on one shoulder. "All set," he said to Tom. He looked at Nita and said, "They hollered a lot. But I think my dad is proud. Mom seems pretty calm about it." Then he laughed, a little wickedly. "My sisters are in shock."

"Can't say that I blame them."

Nita got up, dusting herself off. "Okay," Tom said. "I wanted to see you two off up here, because there's data you'll need that your parents don't. Something major is going on out there. Dairine is not going to run into just some bunch of lackeys for the Lone Power out there. That one Itself is after her. But I have no indication why. And Its power is oddly veiled, at the moment—concentrated, and hidden. I don't think this manifestation of the Lone Power is going to be as obvious as it has recently. So find Dairine, and look carefully at the situation. If it looks like she needs to be where she is, stay with her and do what you can for her."

He paused. "But you are going to have to be very careful. The Lone One won't mind distracting her by striking at you two . . . or using her danger to sucker you into pulling her out of the problem she's intended to correct. Use your judgment. Save her if you can."

"And if we can't?" Kit said.

Tom looked at him sadly. "See that the job gets done," he said, "whatever it is."

They were both quiet.

"There's no telling what the stakes are on this one," Tom said. "The looks of the situation may be deceiving . . . probably will. Can you take this job and do it? Don't go if you can't. If either of you isn't sure you can depend on yourself, or on the both of you, I don't want you in this. Too much can go wrong."

Kit looked at Nita, then back at Tom. "It's cool," he said.

Nita nodded. Tom looked at her.

"I know," he said. "You're upset about her. All right . . . you'll have a while to shake down, while you chase her. Meantime, Carl and I have sent word ahead through the Network, so that a lot of people will be expecting you." He smiled. "You're going to find that the way wizards have to behave on Earth is the exception rather than the rule. Most of the major law-enforcement bodies in this part of the Galaxy routinely call wizards in for consultations, and they owe us a lot of favors. So don't be afraid to ask the authorities wherever you go for help. Odds are you'll get it."

"Okay."

"So get out of here. And good hunting."

"Thanks."

"Come here, bird," Tom said to Picchu. Nita looked up in surprise, expecting an explosion: Picchu did not take orders. She was surprised to see the macaw clamber up onto Tom's arm and reach up to nibble his ear. Tom scratched her in the good place, on the back of the head, and she went vague in the eyes for a couple of minutes, then ruffled the neck feathers up and shook herself. "You be careful," Tom said.

"I'll be fine," Picchu said, sounding cranky.

Nita repacked her knapsack, slung it on, and flipped her manual open to the marked pages with the verbal supplement for the transit spell as Tom passed Peach back to Kit. She caught Kit's eye, stepped into the circle at the same time he did. Tom backed away. Slowly, and in unison, they began to read, and the air trapped in their shieldspells began to sing the note ears sing in silence . . .

As the spell threw them out of the Solar System, Nita wondered whether she would ever see it again. . . .

Uplink

PLA1ETARY H1STOR1 (plge 3 ol116)   HE1P11/1111111
111111111111111111111111111111111111111111111111111111
111111111111111111111111111111111111111111111111111111
111111111111111111111111111111111111111111111111111111
111111111111111111111111111111111111111111111111111111
111111111111111111111111111111111111111111111111111111
111111111111111111111111111111111111111111111111111111
111111111111111111111111111111111111111111111111111111
111111111111111111111111111111111111111111111111111111
111111111111111111111111111111111111111111111111111111
111111111111111111111111111111111111111111111111111111
111111111111111111111111111111111111111111111111111111
111111111111111111111111111111111111111111111111111111
111111111111111111111111111111111111111111111111111111
111111111111111111111111111111111111111111111111111111
111111111111111111111111111111111111111111111111111111

"Dead," Dairine whispered. "I'm dead for sure."

"Input error," said the computer, sounding quite calm.

Dairine's heart leapt. "Are you busted?!" she cried.

"Syntax error 24," said the computer, "rephrase for—"

"You can take your syntax errors and . . . never mind!" Dairine said. "What's wrong with you? Diagnostic!"

"External input," said the computer. "Nontypical."

"What is it? Some kind of broadcast?"

"Negative. Local."

It happened right after it linked to the geothermal power, Dairine thought. "Check your link to the planet," she said.

"Affirmative. Positive identification. External input. Planetary source."

"Are there people here?" Dairine said, looking around hurriedly.

"Negative." The computer's screen kept filling up with 1's, clearing itself, filling with 1's again.

She held still and forced herself to take a deep breath, and another. The computer wasn't broken, nothing horrible had happened. Yet. "Can you get rid of all those ones?" she said to the computer.

"Affirmative."

The screen steadied down to the last page she had been looking at. Dairine stared at it.

> This unique structure becomes more interesting when considering the physical nature of the layering. Some 92% of the layers consist of chemically pure silicon, predisposing the aggregate to electroconductive activity in the presence of light or under certain other conditions. This effect is likely to be enhanced in some areas by the tendency of silicon to superconduct at surface temperatures below 200K. There is also a possibility that semiorganic life of a "monocellular" nature will have arisen in symbiosis either with the silicon layers or their associated "doping" layers, producing—

Dairine sat there and began to tremble. *It's the planet,* she thought. *Silicon. And trace elements, put down in layers. And cold to make it semiconduct—*

"It's the planet!" she shouted at the computer. "This whole flat part here is *one big semiconductor chip,* a computer chip! It's *alive!* Send it something! Send it some 1's!"

The computer flickered through several menu screens and began filling with 1's again. Dairine rolled from her sitting position into a kneeling one, rocking back and forth with anxiety and delight. She had to be right, she had to. One huge chip, like a computer motherboard a thousand miles square. And some kind of small one-celled—if that was the right word—one-celled organism living with it. Something silicon-based, that could etch pathways in it—pathways that electricity could run along, that data could be stored in. How many years had this chip been laying itself down in the silence, she wondered? Volcanoes erupting chemically pure silicon and trace elements that glazed themselves into vast reaches of chip-surface as soon as they touched the planet: and farther down, in the molten warmth of the planet's own geothermal heat, the little silicon-based "bacteria" that had wound themselves together out of some kind of analogue to DNA. Maybe they were more like amoebas than bacteria now: etching their way along through the layers of silicon and cadmium and other elements, getting their food, their energy, from breaking the compounds' chemical bonds, the same way carbon-based life gets it from breaking down complex proteins into simpler ones.

It was likely enough. She would check it with the manual. But for now, the result of this weird bit of evolution was all that really mattered. The chip was *awake*. With this much surface area—endless thousands of square miles, all full of energy, and connections and interconnections, millions of times more connections than there were in a human brain—how could it *not* have waked up? But there was nowhere for it to get data from that she could see, no way for it to contact the outside world. It was trapped. The 1's, the basic binary code for "on" used by all computers from the simplest to the most complex, were a scream for help, a sudden realization that something else existed in the world, and a crying out to it. Even as she looked down at the screen and watched what the computer was doing, the stream of 1's became a little less frantic. 111111111, said her own machine. *11111111*, said the planet.

"Give it an arithmetic series," Dairine whispered.

1, said her computer. 11. 111. 1111. 11111.

1. 11. 111. 1111. 11111.

"Try a geometric."

1. 11. 1111. 11111111. 1111111111111111.

1. 11. 1111. 11111111—

"Oh, it's got it," Dairine said, bouncing and still hugging herself. "I think. It's hard to tell if it's just repeating. Try a square series."

11. 1111. 1111111111111111—

111. 111111111. 1111111111111111111111111—

It had replied with a cube series. It knew, it *knew*! "Can you teach it binary?" Dairine said, breathless.

"Affirmative." 1. 10. 11. 100. 101—

Things started to move fast, the screen filling with characters, clearing itself, filling again as the computers counted at each other. Dairine was far gone in wonder and confusion. What to teach it next? It was like trying to communicate with someone who had been locked in a dark, soundless box all his life. . . . "Is it taking the data?"

"Affirmative. Writing to permanent memory."

Dairine nodded, thinking hard. Apparently the huge chip was engraving the binary code permanently into itself: that would include codes for letters and numbers as well. But what good's that gonna do? It doesn't have any experiences to make words out of, no reason to put letters together to make the words in the first place. . . . It was like it had been for Helen Keller, Dairine thought: but at least Helen had had the senses of touch and taste, so that she could feel the water poured into her hand while her teacher drummed the touch-code for *water* into it. It has no senses. If it did—

"Can you hook it into your sensors?" she said to the computer.

The computer hesitated. It had never done such a thing before: and when it spoke again, its syntax was peculiar—more fluid than she was used to.

"High probability of causing damage to the corresponding computer due to too great a level of complexity," it said.

Dairine breathed out, annoyed, but had to agree. Anything able to sense events happening forty trillion miles away, no matter how it managed it, was certainly too complex to hook directly to this poor creature right now. And another thought occurred to her, and her heart beat very fast. Not sensors, then. Senses. "Can you hook *me* to it?" she said.

This time the hesitation was even longer, and Dairine stared at the computer, half expecting it to make an expression at her. It didn't, but the speech of its response was slow. "Affirmative," it said. "Triple confirmation of intent required."

"I tell you three times," Dairine said. "Hook it to me. Tell me what to do. It has to get some better idea of what's going on out here or it'll go crazy!"

"Direct physical contact with surface," the computer said. It sounded reluctant.

Dairine dusted her hands off and put them flat on the glassy ground.

She was about to open her mouth to tell the computer to go ahead, do what it was going to: but she never got the chance. The instantaneous jolt went right through her with exactly the same painless grabbing and shaking she had felt when she was seven and had put a bobby pin in the electric socket. She convulsed, all over: her head jerked up and snapped back and she froze, unable even to blink, staring up into the golden-veiled blaze of the barred spiral, staring at it till each slight twitch of her eyes left jittering purple-green afterimages to right and left of it; and somewhere inside her, as if it were another mind speaking, she could hear her computer crying *110010 01011110000100! 110010010111110000100!* at the frantic silence that listened. *Light, light, light—*

And the reply, she heard that too: a long, crazed string of binary that made no sense to her, but needed to make none. Joy, it was simply joy, joy at discovering *meaning*: joy so intense that all her muscles jumped in reaction, breaking her out of the connection and flinging her facedown on the glazed ground. The connection reestablished itself and Dairine's mind fell down into turmoil. She couldn't think straight: caught between the two computers —for under the swift tutelage of her own, the great glassy plain was now beginning truly to function as one—she felt the contents of her brain being twinned, and the extra copy dumped out into endless empty memory and stored, in a rush of images, ideas, occurrences, communications, theories and raw sensations. She knew it took only a short time: but it seemed to go on forever, and all her senses throbbed like aching teeth at being desperately and delightedly used and used and used again to sense this moment, this ever-changing *now*. Dairine thought she would never perceive anything as completely again as she was seeing and feeling the green-and-gold-shaded piece of silicon aggregate she lay on, with the four crumbs from her sandwich lying half an inch from her eye. She felt sure she would be able to describe the shape of those crumbs and the precise pattern of the dappling in the silicon on her deathbed. If she survived this to have one.

Finally it stopped. Groaning softly, Dairine levered herself up and stared around her. The computer was sitting there innocently, its screen showing the main "Manual" menu. "How is it?" Dairine said, and then sighed and got ready to rephrase herself.

"Considerably augmented," said the computer.

Dairine stared at it.

"Is it just me," she said, "or do you sound smarter than you have been?"

"That calls for a value judgment," said the computer.

Dairine opened her mouth, then closed it again. "I guess it does," she said. "You weren't just acting as conduit all through that, were you? You expanded your syntax to include mine."

"You got it," said the computer.

Dairine took a moment to sit up. Before this, she'd thought she would love having the computer be a little more flexible. Now she was having second thoughts. "How's our friend doing?"

"Assimilating the new data and self-programming. Its present running state has analogues to trance or dream states in humans."

Dairine instantly wished it hadn't said that. What time was it at home? How long had she been running? How long had that last longest jump taken, if it had in fact taken any time at all? All she knew was that she was deadly tired.

"Update," said the computer. "It is requesting more data."

"On what?"

"No specific request. It simply desires more."

"I'm fresh out," Dairine said, and yawned. Then she looked at the computer again. "No, I'm not. Give it what *you've* got."

"Repeat and clarify?" said the computer, sounding slightly unnerved.

"Give it what you've got. All the information about planets and species and history and all the rest of it. Give it the magic!"

The computer said nothing.

Dairine sat up straight. "Go on," she said.

No reply.

"Is there some rule that says you shouldn't?"

"Yes," said the computer slowly, "but this edition of the software contains the authorization-override function."

"Good," Dairine said, none too sure of what this meant, except that it sounded promising. "I'm overriding. Give it what you've got."

The screen lit up with a block of text, in binary, quite small and neat, and Dairine immediately thought of the Oath in Nita's manual.

The screen blanked, then filled with another brief stream of binary. That blanked in turn, and screenful after screenful of 1's and 0's followed, each flickering out of existence almost as quickly as it appeared.

Dairine got up and stretched, and walked back and forth for a few minutes to work the kinks out of her muscles. She ached all over, as she had after the bobby pin incident, and her stomach growled at her again: a bologna sandwich and a half was not enough to satisfy her after the kind of day she had had. If it was even the same day. At least I have a while before the BEMs show up, she thought. Maybe our new friend here can be of some kind of help. . . . As she looked out across the dappled-silvery plain, there was a bloom of soft crimson light at one side of it. Dairine held still to watch the sun rise. It was a fat red star, far along in its lifetime—so far along, so cool, that there was water vapor in its atmosphere, and even in the vacuum of space it hung in a softly glowing rose-colored haze, like an earthly summer sunset. It climbed the sky swiftly, and Dairine watched it in silence. Quite a day, she thought. But whether it's morning here or not, I need a nap.

She turned around and started to head back toward the computer—and froze.

One patch of the surface was moving. Something underneath it was humping upward, and cracks appeared in the perfect smoothness. There was no sound, of course, since Dairine's air supply was nowhere near the spot; the cracks webbed outward in total silence.

And then the crust cracked upward in jagged pieces, and the something underneath pushed through and up and out. Bits of silica glass fell slowly in the light gravity and bounced or shattered in a snow of splinters around the rounded shape that stood there. *Stood* was the right word: for it had legs, though short stumpy ones, as if a toy tank had thrown away its treads and grown limbs instead. It shook itself, the rounded, glassy, glittering thing, and walked over to Dairine and through her shields with a gait like a centipede's or a clockwork toy's; and it looked up at her, if something like a turtle with no head can be said to look up.

"Light," it croaked, in a passable imitation of the computer's voice, and bumped against her shin, and rested there.

It was too much. Dairine sat down where she was and looked at the computer. "I can't cope," she said.

The computer had no reply for this.

"I can't," she said. "Make me some more air, please, and call me if they start chasing us again."

"No problem," said the computer.

She lay down on the smooth glassy ground, gazing at the rounded, glittery thing that stood on its fourteen stumpy legs and gazed back at her. No more than six breaths later she was asleep.

So she did not see, an hour and a half later, when the sun, at its meridian, began to pucker and twist out of shape, and for the best part of the hour lost half of itself, and shone only feebly, warped and dimmed. Her companion saw it, and said to the computer:

"What?"

"Darkness," said the computer: and nothing more.

Reserved Words

They got to Rirhath B early in the evening, arriving at the Crossings just after suns' set and just as the sky was clearing. Nita and Kit stood there in the Nontypical Transit area for a few moments, staring up at the ceiling like the rankest tourists. Picchu sat on Kit's shoulder, completely unruffled, and ignored everything with yawning scorn, though the view through the now-clear ceiling was worth seeing.

"My brains are rattled," Kit said, breathing hard. "I need a minute." So did Nita, and she felt vaguely relieved that Kit had said something about it first: so she just nodded, and craned her neck, and stared up. The view was worth looking at—this sudden revelation of Rirhath's sky, a glorious concatenation of short-term variable stars swelling and shrinking like living things that breathed and whose hearts beat fire. All over the Crossings, people of every species passing through were pausing, looking up at the same sight, and admiring the completeness with which a perfectly solid-seeming ceiling now seemed to have gone away. Others, travelers who had seen it all before or were just too tired to care, went on about their business and didn't bother to look.

"We only have a couple of days," Picchu said, chewing on the collar of Kit's shirt.

"Peach," Nita said, "shut your face. You better?" she said to Kit.

"Yeah," he said. "You?"

"I was dizzy. It's okay now."

"Super." He flipped through his manual, open in his hand, and came up with a map of the Crossings. "What do we need to find?"

"Stationmaster's office."

"Right."

They checked out of Nontypical Transit, leaving their origin-and-destination information with the computer at the entrance, and set out across the expanse of the terminal floor, looking around them in calm wonder: for though neither of them had ever been there, both had read enough about the Crossings in their manuals to know what to expect. They knew there had been a time when the Crossings itself was only a reed hut by a riverside, and the single worldgate nearby only a muddy spot in a cave that the first Master stumbled upon by accident, and claimed for its heirs (after waiting several years on Ererikh for the gate to reverse phase so that he could get home). Now, a couple of thousand years' worth of technology later, worldgates were generated here at the drop of a whim, and the Stationmaster regulated interstellar commerce and transportation via worldgating for the entire Sagittarius Arm.

Its office was not off in some sheltered spot away from the craziness, but out in the very middle of the station floor: that being the spot where the hut had been, twenty-four hundred and thirty years before. It was only a single modest kiosk of tubular bluesteel, with a desk behind it, and at the desk, hung up in a rack that looked like a large stepstool, was a single Rirhait, banging busily on a computer terminal keypad and making small noises to itself as it worked.

Nita and Kit stopped in front of the desk, and the Rirhait looked up at them. Or more or less up: some of its stalked eyes looked down instead, and a few peered from the sides. It stopped typing. "Well?" it said, scratchy-voiced —understandable, Nita thought, when you've got a gullet full of sand.

"You're the Stationmaster?" Kit said.

"Yes," said the Rirhait, and the fact that it said nothing else, but looked at Kit hungrily, with its scissory mandibles working, made Nita twitch a little.

"We are on errantry, and we greet you," Nita said: the standard self-introduction of a wizard on business. *Sir* or *Madam,* one normally added, but Nita wasn't sure which the Master was, or even if either term applied.

"That too?" said the Master, looking at Picchu.

"Yes, *that,*" said Peach, all scorn.

"Well, it's about time you people got here," said the Master, and left off what it was doing, standing up. "Standing" was an approximation: a Rirhait is shaped more like a centipede than anything else, so that when it got off its rack and came out from behind the desk, its long, shiny silver-blue body only stood a foot or so off the ground, and all its eyes looked up at them together. "We had more of an untidiness here this afternoon than we've had for a greatyear past, and I'll be glad to see the end of it."

Nita began to sweat. "The wizard who came through here earlier was on Ordeal," Kit said. "We'll need your help to find the spot from which she went farther on, so that we can track her: there are too many other worldgates here, and they're confusing the trail."

"She didn't cause any trouble, did she?" Nita said.

"Trouble?" said the Stationmaster, and led them off across the bright floor, and showed them the place where several large pieces of the ceiling had been shot down. "Trouble?" it said, pointing out the places where the floors were melted, indicating the blaster scars in the kiosks, and the large cordoned-off area where maintenance people of various species were scraping and scrubbing coffee ground–smelling residue off the floor. "Oh, no trouble. Not really."

Picchu began to laugh, a wicked and appreciative sound.

Nita blushed ferociously and didn't say anything for several minutes. The Rirhait led them off to another area of the floor which was closed in on itself by an arrangement of bluesteel kiosks. This was Crossings security; various desks stood about inside it, with creatures of several species working at them. The Master led them to one of the unoccupied desks, a low flat table full of incomprehensible equipment. "Here," it said, and reared up on its back ten legs to touch the machinery in several places.

Small and clear, an image appeared above the table: remote, but equally clear, sound accompanied it. Nita and Kit found themselves looking at the Crossroads equivalent of a videotape, but in three dimensions, with neat alien characters burning in the lower corner of it to show the time and location at which the recording was made. They watched a group of toadlike BEMs make their way across the terminal floor, spot Dairine, head off in pursuit. They watched Dairine deal with the deinonychus, and afterward with the BEM that grabbed her. Nita gulped.

"They look like Satrachi," Kit said, astonishingly cool-voiced.

Nita's eyebrows went up. Alien species were her specialty: evidently Kit had been doing some extra research. "They are, as far as we can tell," said the Master. "The one of them whom we have in custody has valid Satra identification."

"We'll need to see this person, then," Nita said. The tape ran: Nita watched Dairine's dive into the bar, and from another camera angle, her sister's reemergence into the terminal and dash into the rest room. Nita groaned, recognizing the room by the symbol on its door as a spawning room for any one of several species that gave birth to their young on the average of once every few days, and were likely to be caught short while traveling on business. Nita hoped that Dairine hadn't introduced one of the species involved to a completely new kind of birth trauma.

"That was the spot she left from?"

"Yes, Emissary." It was the first time Nita had ever been formally called by one of the twenty or so titles commonly used for wizards, but she was too busy now to enjoy it. She glanced at Kit. He was frowning at the image hanging in the air: finally his concentration broke and he glanced at her.

"Well?" he said. "You want the Satrachi?"

"I'd better," she said, though she very much wanted not to—the looks of the Satrachi gave her the creeps. But dealing with live things was her department: the handling of machinery and inanimate objects was Kit's. "You go ahead and check the room out. Stationmaster, can you have someone show me where it's being held?"

"Step on that square there," said the Master, pointing one eye at a spot on the floor: "it's direct transit to Holding. Emissary, I'll show you to the room in question. . . ."

Nita stepped on the block quickly before she would have time to change her mind.

Fifteen minutes with it told her all she needed to know: the Satra was a dupe, it and its friends—a small paramilitary club—deluded into pursuing Dairine by some agent of the Lone One. It's the usual thing, she thought as she headed back to Kit and the Stationmaster. The Power never comes out in the open if it can find some way to make someone else do Its dirty work. Preferably an innocent: that way it's more of a slap in the Bright Powers' face. Unusual, though, that it used a whole group this time. Normally it's hard to keep that subtle a grip on a whole group's mind: one of them slips free, or perceives it as control . . . and when that happens, odds are that the whole group is useless for Its purposes.

She strolled among aliens and their luggage and finally came to the little Grand Central–size alcove where Dairine's rest room was. Its door was frozen in the dilated mode. Nita slipped in and found Kit and Picchu and the Master off to one side, examining one particular birthing-booth. It seemed to have had its door burned off, and the back of the booth was blistered and pocked with an ugly rash of blaster scars.

For a good second or so her breath refused to come. "She jumped after *that*?" Nita finally managed to say.

Kit looked over his shoulder at her. "Neets, relax, there are no bloodstains."

"There wouldn't be, with blasters," Nita said. "They cauterize."

"Any really big wound would spurt anyway," Kit said, straightening up and starting to page through his manual. "I think they missed her. The tiles don't remember her screaming, and not even Dairine's *that* stoic." He kept turning over pages.

"How far did she go?"

"A long jump," Kit said. "Multistage, from the feel of it. They must have freaked her out pretty good." He looked up. "That computer she's got leaves a definite sense of what it's been doing behind it. Can you feel it?"

Nita let her eyes go unfocused for a moment and blanked her mind out, as she might do to hear the thinking of some particularly quiet tree. Some residue of Dairine's emotion still hung about the strings in the space-time configuration of the area, like tatters on a barbed-wire fence: fear and defiance, all tangled up together; and alongside her tatters, others, ordered and regular, a weave less vivid and complex in different ways. "It feels alive," Nita said to Kit after a while. "Do computers usually feel that way?"

"I don't know," Kit said, sounding annoyed. "I never tried feeling one before this. . . . You got your widget?" he said. "We're gonna need it to catch up with her and her friends."

"Yeah." She unslung her pack and started rummaging for the gimbal.

"Well, I have things to do," said the Master. "If you need anything, ask one of the security people, they're all over." And without staying for farewells, it went flowing out the door in a hundred-legged scurry.

Nita glanced after it, then back at Kit, and shrugged. "Here," she said, and tossed him the gimbal. "Which spell are you thinking of using?"

"That dislocator on page 1160."

She got out her own manual and found the page. "That's awful long-range, isn't it? Her next jump must have been shorter than that."

"Yeah, but Neets, who wants to leapfrog one step behind the things that are chasing her! We want *them*, right now—we want them off her rear end, so she can do whatever it is she needs to do without interference." He looked grim. "And when we find 'em—"

Nita sighed. "Forget it," she said, "they're dupes."

Kit looked up at her while getting a grease pencil out of his pack. "It suckered them in?"

She filled him in on what the Satrachi had told her as Kit got down on the tiles and began drawing their transit circle. Kit sighed a little. "I was hoping it was some of the Lone One's own people," he said, "so we could just trash 'em and not feel guilty."

Nita had to smile a little at that. Picchu climbed down from the partition between the booths, where he had been sitting, and clambered onto Nita's shoulder. "Get mine right," she said to Kit. "I don't want to come out the other side of this transit with fur."

Kit shot a look at Picchu, and didn't need to comment; Nita could imagine what he was thinking. "Come sit over here, then, if you're so worried," he said.

To Nita's amusement Peach did just that, climbing backward down her arm and over onto Kit's back, where she peered over his shoulder. "Not bad," she said, looking at the diagram.

Kit ignored this. "So make yourself useful. Is anything bad going to happen to us?"

"Of course it is," Picchu said.

"You might be more specific."

"And I might not need to. The Power that invented death is going to be on your tails shortly. *Our* tails," she added, looking over her shoulder at the splendid three-foot sweep of scarlet feathers behind her. "Even you two should be able to see that coming."

Kit changed position suddenly, and Picchu scrabbled for balance, flapping her wings and swearing. "Like you should have seen that?"

Nita grinned a little, then let it go: her mind was back on the train of thought she had been playing with out in the terminal. "I was wondering about that, a while back," she said to Kit. "It invented death, when things were first started. But that wasn't enough for It. It had to get people to buy into death—not just the dying itself: the *fear* of it."

Kit nodded. "But a lot of species have opted out, one way or another. I mean, we're scared to die. But we still suspect there are reasons *not* to be scared. A lot of people do. Its hold isn't complete anymore."

"I know. Kit, do you think—Tom said something was about to 'tip over.' Some major change. Do you think what he meant was that the Lone One was about to lose *completely* somewhere?"

"He always said," Kit said, "that what happens one place, spreads every-place else. Everything affects everything, sooner or later. The manual says so too. A few times."

Nita nodded, thinking how unusual it was for the manual to repeat itself about anything. "And the pattern started shifting, a couple thousand years ago," Kit said. "The Lone Power *had* always won completely before. Then It started having wins taken away from It after the fact."

Kit looked reflective. "If somewhere or other, It's about to *lose*—right from the start . . ."

Nita looked at him sidewise. "Then It starts losing at home, too, in all the little daily battles. Eventually."

Kit nodded. "Dairine," he said.

Nita shook her head, still having trouble believing it—but having to admit the likelihood. Somehow, her sister had a chance of actually defeating the Lone Power. She *must* have a chance: It wouldn't be wasting energy on her otherwise. "Why her?" Nita said softly.

"Why *you?*" said Picchu, cranky. "What makes either of you so special, that you can even come away from an encounter with That alive? Don't flatter yourself: It's eaten stars and seduced whole civilizations in Its time. You were simply exactly the right raw material for that particular situation to use to save Itself."

"I didn't mean that, I guess," she said. "I meant, why now? The Lone Power has been pulling this kind of stunt on planets for as long as intelligence has been evolving. It comes in, It tries to get people to accept entropy willingly, and then It bugs off and leaves them to make themselves more miserable than even It could do if It worked at it. Fine. But now all of a sudden It can be beaten. How come?"

Picchu began chewing on Kit's top button. "You know," she said, "that's part of the answer. Granted, It's immortal. But It doesn't have infinite power. It's peer to all the Powers, but not to That in Which they move. And even an immortal can get tired."

Nita thought about that. Five billion years, maybe ten, of constant strife, of incomplete victories, of rage and frustration—and yes, loneliness: for the Lone One, she had discovered to her shock, was ambivalent about Its role—after all that, surely one might not be as strong as one had been at the start of things. . . .

Kit got the button out of Picchu's mouth, and was nipped for his trouble. "So, after all these near losses, It's tired enough to be beaten outright?"

Picchu got cranky again. "Of course! It was *that* tired long ago. The Powers wouldn't need Dairine for just that. They could do it Themselves, or with the help of older wizards. But haven't you got it through your head? They can't want to just *beat* the Lone One. They must think there's a better option."

Nita looked at Picchu, feeling half frightened. "They want It to *surrender*," she said.

"I think so," said Picchu. "I suspect They think she could get the Lone One to give in and come back to Its old allegiance. If It does that . . . the effect spreads. Slowly. But it spreads everywhere."

Picchu climbed down off Kit's shoulder and pigeon-toed across the floor, heading for a receptacle with some water in it. Kit and Nita both sat silent. The possibility seemed a long way from coming true. A world in which the universe's falling into entropy slowly stopped, affecting people's relationships with one another, a world gradually losing the fear of death, a world losing hatred, losing terror, losing evil itself . . . it was ridiculous, impossible, too much to hope for. But still, Nita thought, if there was any chance at all . . . ! ". . . On the news last night," Kit said, "did you see that thing about the car in Northern Ireland?"

"No."

"They hijack cars over there sometimes, as a protest," he said. "One side or the other." There was something about his voice that made Nita look at him hard. "Sometimes they set the cars on fire after they hijack them." Kit sat looking in front of him at nothing in particular, looking tired. "You know the kind of wire screen you get for station wagons, so that your dog can be in the back and not get into everything?"

"Yeah."

"Someone hijacked a car with one of those in it, the other night. With the dog in it, in the back. Then they set the car on fire. With the dog in it."

Nita went ashen. Kit just kept looking at nothing in particular, and she knew what he was thinking of: Ponch, in Kit's dad's station wagon, lying around in the back too contented and lazy even to try to get into the grocery bags all around him. And someone coming up to the car—"Neets," Kit said, after a while, "Bad enough that they kill children, and grown-ups, and don't even care. But the poor dogs too—if we really have a chance to stop that kind of thing, I'll do . . . whatever. I don't care. Anything."

She looked at him. *"Anything?"*

He was quiet for a long time. "Yeah."

Eventually she nodded. "Me too."

"I know," he said.

She looked at him in surprise. "Well, look at what you did with the whales," he said.

Nita's mouth was very dry. She tried to swallow. It didn't work.

"I mean, you did that already. That's what it was about. The Power got redeemed, a little: we know that much. Or at least It got the option to change. You did it for *that.* You almost got yourself killed, and you knew that might happen, and you did it anyway. Oh, I know you did it for me, some." He said this as if it were unimportant. "I was in trouble, you got me out of it. But mostly you did it to have things in the world be safe, and work."

She nodded, completely unable to speak.

"It seems like the least I can do," he said, and went no further, as if Nita should know perfectly well what he meant.

"Kit," she said.

"Look, I mean, I don't know if I can be that brave, but—"

"Kit, shut up."

He shut, rather astonished.

I'm always one step closer, sang memory at her from the Moon. "Look," she said, "I didn't do it for you 'some.' I did it for you 'pretty much.' "

Kit looked at her with an expression that at first made Nita think Kit thought she was angry with him. But then it became plain that he was embarrassed too. "Well," he said, "okay. I—thought maybe you did. But I didn't want to say anything because I didn't know for sure. And I would have felt real stupid if I was wrong." He had been looking away. Now he looked at her. "So?"

"So," and her voice stuck again, and she had to clear her throat to unstick it. "I *like* you, that's all. A lot. And if you start liking somebody that much, well, I still want to keep the team going. If you do. That's all."

He didn't say anything. Nita stood there burning in a torment of embarrassment and anger at herself.

"Neets. Cut me some slack. You're my best friend."

Her head snapped up. ". . . I thought it was Richie Sussman."

Kit shrugged. "We just play pool a lot. But it's the truth." He looked at her. "Isn't it true for you?"

"Yeah, but—"

"So why does that have to change? Look, we've got junk to do. Let's shake on it. We'll be best friends forever. And a team."

He said it so casually. But then that was how Kit did things: the only thing that wasn't casual was the way he worked to do what he said he would. "What if something happens?" Nita said. "What if—"

Kit finished one symbol inside the circle, shut the book, and stood up. "Look," he said, "something always happens. You still have to promise stuff anyway. If you have to work to make the promises true . . ." He shrugged, hefted the manual. "It's like a spell. You have to say the words every time you want the results. Neets, come on. Shake on it."

They shook on it. Nita felt oddly light, as if her knapsack had been full of rocks and someone had come up behind her and dumped them out.

"Okay," Kit said. "Peach, where—good Lord."

Picchu was sitting in the water receptacle on the floor, flapping around and showering everything within range. "Do you mean I'm going to have to go halfway across the Galaxy with a soggy bird sitting on me?" Kit said. "No way. Neets, it's your turn to carry her."

"You're getting a lot like Tom," said Picchu.

"Thanks!"

"That wasn't intended as a compliment."

Peach shook her feathers, scattering water. "Stop your complaining," she said to Kit. "The Powers only know when I'm going to have another chance for a bath." She stepped out of the low basin and shook herself again all over.

Nita wiped a drop out of her eye. "Come on," she said, and got Peach off the edge of the basin. "Kit, we set?"

"Yup. You want to do a defense spell, do it now. Peach? Any bad feelings?"

"All of them," Picchu said, "but nothing specific. Let's go."

They all three got into the circle. Kit knotted it closed with the figure-eight wizard's knot, dropped the gimbal into the circle on the spot marked out for it, then picked up his manual and began to read. Nita silently recited her favorite shieldspell, the one that could stop anything from a thrown punch to an ICBM, and for safety's sake set it at ICBM level. Then she got her own manual open and caught up with Kit. The air began to sing the note ears sing in silence; the air pushed in harder and harder around them, Nita's ears popped, and the spell took hold and threw them off the planet—not before Nita saw a portly Me!thai gentleman peek in the door to see if it was safe to come in and have his child. . . .

There was a long, long darkness between the world winking out and flashing back into existence again. Nita could never remember its having taken so long before—but then the jump from Earth to Rirhath had been a short one, no more than fifteen or twenty light-years. She held her breath and maintained control, even while the back of her brain was screaming frantically, He made a mistake in the spell somewhere, you distracted him and he misspelled something else: you're stuck in this and you're never going to get out, never—

It broke. Nita was as dizzy as she had been the last time, but she was determined not to wobble. Her ears stopped ringing as she blinked and tried to get her bearings. "Heads up, Neets," Kit was saying.

It was dark. They stood on some barren unlit moon out in the middle of space. Nothing was in the sky but unfamiliar stars and the flaming, motionless curtain of an emission nebula, flung across the darkness like a transparent gauze burning in hydrogen red and oxygen blue. Kit pointed toward the horizon where the nebula dipped lowest. Amid a clutter of equipment and portable shelters of some kind, there stood a small crowd of Satrachi. They had apparently not noticed their pursuers' appearance.

"Right," Nita said. "Let's do this—"

"*Move us!*" Picchu screeched. "*Do it now!*"

Kit's eyes widened. He started rereading the spell, changing the end coordinates by a significant amount. Peach was still flapping her wings and screaming. "No, that's not far enough—"

Nita snatched the gimbal up from the ground and tied it into her shield-spell. Can it take the strain of two spells at once? We'll find out. It'll abort the one it can't manage, anyway. She gulped. Physical forces— She started reciting in the Speech, naming every force in the universe that she could think of, tying their names into her shield and forbidding them entrance. Can I pull this off? Is this one of the spells that has a limit on the number of added variables? Oh Lord, I hope not—

"Light," Peach was screaming at her, "light, *light!*"

Nita told the shield to be opaque—and then wondered why it wasn't, as the brightest light she had ever imagined came in through it anyway. She had been to a Shuttle launch, once, and had come to understand that sound could be a force, a thing that grabbed you from inside your chest and shook you effortlessly back and forth. Now she wondered how she had never thought that light might be able to do the same, under some circumstances. It struck her deaf and dumb and blind, and she went sprawling. Heat scorched her everywhere; she smelled the rotten-egg stink of burning hair. She clutched the gimbal: she couldn't have dropped it if she'd tried.

Much later, it seemed, it began to get dark. She opened her eyes and could not be sure, for a few minutes, that they were open, the world was so full of afterimages. But the purple curtain between her and everything else eventually went away. She and Kit and Peach were hanging suspended, weightless in empty space. At least it was empty now. There was no sign of any moonlet —only off to one side, a blinding star that slowly grew and grew and grew and grew, toward them. They were out of its range now. They had not been before.

"Didn't know the gimbal could handle both those spells," Kit said, rubbing his eyes. "Nice going."

"It won't do it twice," Nita said. There was just so much power one could milk out of a physical aid, and she had been pushing her odds even trying it once. "Where are we?"

"I haven't the faintest. Somewhere a light-month out from our original position. And those Satrachi were bait," he said. "For us. Look at it, Neets."

She looked. "I could have sworn I opaqued this shield."

"It *is* opaqued," Kit said. "But a shield doesn't usually have to put up with a nova at close range. H-bombs are about the most one can block out without leakage, if I remember."

Nita stared at the raging star, all boiling with huge twisted prominences. For all its brilliance, there was a darkness about its heart, something wrong with the light. In a short time this terrible glory would be collapsed to a pallid dwarf star, cooling slowly to a coal. She shivered: one of the oldest epithets for the Lone Power was "Starsnuffer." It blew a whole star, just to kill us, because we were going to help Dairine. . . . "Did this system have other planets?" she said.

"I don't know. I doubt It cared."

And this was what was going after her little sister.

The anger in Nita got very, very cold. "Let's go find her," she said.

Together they began to read.

Fatal Error

Dairine woke up stiff and aching all over . . . 's wrong with the bed? was her first thought: it felt like the floor. Then she opened her eyes, and found that she *was* on the floor . . . or a surface enough like one to make no difference. The cool, steady stars of space burned above her. She sat up and rubbed her sticky eyes.

I feel awful, she thought. I want a bath, I want breakfast, I want to brush my teeth! But baths and toothbrushes and any food but bologna sandwiches with mustard were all a *long* way away.

She dropped her hands into her lap, feeling slow and helpless, and looked about her. A sense of shock grew in her: all around, in what had been the absolutely smooth surface of the planet, there were great cracked holes, as if the place had had a sudden meteor shower while she was asleep. But the debris lying around wasn't the kind left by meteor strikes. "Sheesh," she muttered.

Something poked her from behind.

Dairine screamed and flung herself around. She found herself staring at the small, turtlelike glassy creature that had been the last straw the night before. It had walked into her, and was continuing to do so, its short jointed legs working busily though it was getting nowhere: like a windup toy mindlessly walking against a wall. "With," it said.

"Oh, heck," Dairine said in relief. She sagged with embarrassment. Two days ago she would have thought scorn to scream because of *anything*, up to and including Darth Vader himself . . . but the world looked a little different today.

She grabbed the steadily pedaling little thing and held it away from her to look at it. It was all made of the same silicon as the surface; the inside of its turtlish body was a complex of horizontal layers, the thickest of them about half an inch across, the thinnest visible only as tiny colored lines no thicker than a hair . . . thousands of them packed together, at times, in delicate bandings that blended into one subtle color. Dairine knew she was looking at a chip or board more complex than anything dreamed of on Earth. She could see nothing identifiable as a sensor, but it had certainly found her right away last night: so it could see. She wondered if it could hear.

"Well, how about it, small stuff?" she said. It was rather cute, after all. "Say hi."

"Hi," it said.

She put her eyebrows up, and looked over her shoulder at the computer, which was sitting where she had left it the night before. "Did you teach this guy to talk?"

"There is very little I did not teach the mind that made them," said the computer calmly.

Dairine looked around at the many, many jagged holes in the surface. "I bet. Where are they all?"

"Indeterminate. Each one began walking around the surface in a random fashion as soon as it was produced."

"Except for this one," Dairine said, and lifted the creature into her lap. It was surprisingly light. Once there, the creature stopped trying to walk, and just rested across her knees like a teatray with a domed cover on it. "Good baby," Dairine said. She touched one of the legs carefully, maneuvering the top joint gently to see how it worked. There were three joints: one ball-and-socketlike joint where it met the body, and two more spaced evenly down the leg, which was about six inches long. The legs were of the same stuff as the outer shell of the body dome: translucent, like cloudy glass, with delicate hints of color here and there. "Why didn't you go walking off with everybody else, huh?" she said as she picked it up to flip it over and examine its underside.

Its legs kicked vigorously in the air. "With," it said.

Dairine put the creature down, where it immediately walked into her again and kept walking, its legs slipping on the smooth surface.

"With, huh. Okay, okay, 'with' already." She picked it up again and put it in her lap. It stopped kicking.

She glanced up at the sky. The galaxy was rising again. For a few seconds she just held still, watching the curving fire of it. "How long is the day here?" she said.

"Seventeen hours," said the computer.

"Fast for such a big planet," she said. "Mostly light elements, though. I guess it works. How long was I asleep?"

"Fourteen hours."

Dairine made an annoyed face. There went that much of her research time. She felt fairly certain that if the BEMs didn't catch up with her shortly, someOne else would. She didn't like the thought. "I've got to get some work done," she said, and glanced down at the turtly, glassy creature in her lap. "What about you? You can't sit here all day. Neither can I."

"Hi," said the glass turtle.

She had to laugh. "Are you still talking to"—she didn't know what to call it: she patted the glassy ground—"our friend here?"

"Yes," the computer said. "Response is slow. It is still assimilating and coordinating the data."

"Still?" Dairine let out a breath. If there was so much information in the manual functions that a computer with this much memory was still sorting it, what hope did she have of finding the information she needed in time to be able to do anything useful to the Lone One with it? She was going to have to help it along somehow. "Can you ask it to call back this little guy's friends? I want to look at them."

"Working."

Dairine stretched and considered that the next time she went out to space, she was going to plan things a little more carefully. Or stay at a hotel. Where, for example, was she going to find something to drink? She hadn't squirreled anything away in her claudication: she was going to have to find water. More to the point, there were no bathrooms here. Dairine wished heartily that she had taken time in the Crossings, or even back at Natural History, to use the facilities for something other than programming interstellar jumps. The memory of what sometimes seemed to be her mother's favorite line, "You should have gone before we left!" made her grin ruefully.

She got up to improvise what she could. Her turtle started to go with her. "No," she said, as she might have to Ponch. "Stay!" The turtle's response to this was the same as Ponch's would have been: It went after her anyway.

Dairine sighed and headed off to a little outcropping of rock about half a mile away. When she had finished, and started back to where the computer lay, she could already see small shapes moving on the horizon. She sat down with her bread and bologna, started making a sandwich, and waited for them.

Pretty soon she was knee-deep in turtles, or would have been had she been standing up. After the first few walked into her as her lapturtle had, she asked the computer to get them to hold still when they reached her. Something like two hundred of them were shortly gathered around her. They were all exact copies of her friend, even to the striations and banding inside them. She sighed a little as she looked at them.

"This isn't gonna work, you guys," she said. "There's more to life than walking around, and none of you have anything like hands. . . ."

"*Hi!*" said all the turtles, simultaneously. She couldn't hear the ones that were outside her bubble of air, but the ones that were inside made racket enough.

She had to laugh at that. "Look," she said to the computer, pushing her first turtle out of her lap and putting the computer there instead, "where did the mind behind these critters get the design for them?"

"Probably from one of the design templates in the "Make" utility," said the computer.

"Okay, let's get into that. If these guys are going to be the arms and legs for the mind that's running them, they need arms!"

The computer's screen flicked obediently to the opening screen for the "Make" utility. Dairine frowned at the menu for a while. The computer had a machine-assisted drafting utility: she chose that, while her turtle tried to climb back into her lap.

"No," she said. "No, honey!"

It was no use. "With!" said the turtle. "With, with, with, with—"

She laughed helplessly. "Boy, are *you* ever GIGO," she said.

"Yes," the turtle said, and sat down next to her abruptly, folding all its legs under it like a contented mechanical cat.

Dairine put her eyebrows up at that. Was that all it wanted? A name? "Gigo," she said, experimentally.

"Yes!"

It sounds happy, she thought. Can it have emotions?

"Good baby," she said, and patted it. "Good Gigo."

"Yes!" said Gigo, and "Yes!" said several of the other turtles around, and it began to spread through the crowd to the limits of her air: "Yes, yes, yes—"

"Okay," she said, "he's good, you're all good, now put a cork in it!"

They fell silent. But there had been no mistaking the sound of joy.

"I can see I'm gonna have to find names for all of you," she said. "Can't have the whole bunch of you answering to that."

She turned her attention to the blank graphics screen. "Bring up the design that . . ." She paused. "I can't just keep banging on the ground. Does what you were talking to have a name for itself?"

"No."

Dairine sighed. "Okay, just let's call it a motherboard for the moment. Bring up the design it was using for Gigo and his buddies."

The screen flickered, showing Dairine a three-dimensional diagram, which the computer then rotated to show all the turtle's surfaces. "Good," she said. "How do I make changes?"

"The screen is touch-sensitive. Touch a line and state what you want done with it."

Dairine spent a cheerful hour or so there, pausing for bites of sandwich, as she started to redesign the turtles. She wasn't shy about it. The original design had its points, but as the mobile units of an intelligence, the turtles were sadly lacking in necessary equipment. She built several of the legs into arms, with six claws apiece at the end of them, four "fingers" and two opposable "thumbs"; this hand she attached to the arm by a ball-and-socket joint so that it could rotate completely around without having to stop. As an afterthought, she put another pair of arms on the turtle's back end, so that it wouldn't have to turn around to pick something up if it didn't want to.

She took the turtle's rather simplistic visual sensor, barely more than a photosensitive spot, and turned it into something of a cross between the human retina and a bee's faceted eye—a multiple-lensed business equally good for close work and distant vision. She placed several of these around the turtle's perimeter, and a couple on top, and then for good measure added a special-purpose lens that was actually something like a small Cassegrain telescope, focusing on a mirror-polished bit of silicon buried a ways into the turtle's "brain." She added infrared and ultraviolet sensing. Ears for sound they already had; she considered that it might be wise to give them something to hear radio with, too, but couldn't decide on which frequency to work with, and let the idea go for the moment. They could work it out themselves.

Dairine sat staring at the screen, musing. The newly awakened intelligence had made all its mobiles alike: probably because it didn't understand the concept of otherness yet. She would make them different from one another. But they were going to have to be different on the inside, too, to do any good. If some danger comes along that they have to cope with, it's no use their information processors being all the same: whatever it is could wipe them all out at once. If they're as different as they can be, they'll have a better chance of surviving.

She paused in her design to look closely at the structure of the chip layering in the turtles—not so much at what the layers were made of, but what their arrangement meant. At the molecular level she found the basic building-block of the chips, as basic as DNA in humans: not a chain molecule, but a sort of tridimensional snowflake of silicon atoms and atoms of other elements. DNA was simple beside these. Any given silicon molecule hooked with up to fourteen others, using any one of fifty different chemical compounds to do it; and every different arrangement of hookups between molecules or layers had a specific meaning, as each arrangement has in DNA. With the help of the computer she began to sort out the code buried in the interconnected snowflakes. Hours, it took her, and she was perfectly aware that even with the computer's help she couldn't hope to deal with more than the tip of this iceberg of information. Some parts of the chip structure she did manage to identify as pure data storage, others as sensor array, associative network, life support, energy management.

Dairine began devising layering arrangements different from those in the turtles. She designed creatures that would have more associative network and so could specialize in problem solving: others with more data stacks, turtles that would be good at remembering; mobiles more richly endowed with sensors, and senses, than some of the others, that would see and hear and feel most acutely. One arrangement of layers, the one that the computer identified for her as the seat of the turtles' emotions, seemed an awfully tiny thing to Dairine. She expanded it to about three times its original size, and allowed it to interconnect at will with the other associative areas, with data memory and with the senses. Finally, to every model she designed, Dairine added a great deal of latent memory area, so that each mobile would have plenty of room to store what it experienced and to process the data it accumulated.

Having done all these things, she went back to her original design and copied it several times, making a number of different "models": a large, strong one for heavy work; a small one with extra hands in various sizes, from human-hand size to tiny claws that could have done microsurgery or precision work almost on the molecular level. And she added the necessary extra sensor arrays or materials reinforcement that these changes would need to support them.

She sat back and sighed then, and unfolded her cramped legs, and reached down for her sandwich, which had gone stale on top while she worked. "Okay," she said to the computer. "Ask the motherboard to run off a few of those and let's see what happens."

"Considerable reprogramming will be necessary," said the computer.

"I know," said Dairine, between bites of the sandwich, making a face at the taste of it. "I'm in no rush."

The computer's screen filled with binary as it began conferring with the motherboard in machine language. *What do I* mean *I'm in no rush?* Dairine thought, momentarily distracted while Gigo climbed into her lap again. "Did you finish that analysis run about the Lone One for me?"

"Yes," said the computer. "Do you want it displayed?"

"Yeah, please."

The binary went away from the screen, replaced by print. Dairine didn't look at it immediately. She leaned back and gazed up. The galaxy was all set but for one arm, trailing up over the far, far horizon, a hook of light. The dull red sun was following it down as if attached to the hook by an invisible string. *An old, old star,* Dairine thought. *Not even main-sequence anymore. This could have been one of the first stars created in this universe. . . . Might have been, considering how far out this galaxy—* The thought was shocked out of her.

Something other than her voice was making a sound. It was a rumbling, very low, a vibration in the surface she sat on. "What the— You feel that?" she said to the computer.

"Vibration of seismic origin," the computer said. "Intensity 2.2 Richter and increasing."

There was precious little on the planet's surface to shake. Dairine stood up, alarmed, and watched the turtles. For all their legs, they were having trouble keeping their footing on the slick surface. Gigo hooked a leg around Dairine's and steadied itself that way. "Is this gonna get worse?" Dairine said.

"Uncertain. No curve yet. Richter 3.2 and increasing. Some volcanic eruption occurring in planet's starward hemisphere."

Got to do something about their leg design if this happens a lot, Dairine thought—and then was distracted again, because something was happening to the light: It wavered oddly, dimming from the clear rose that had flooded the plain to a dark dry color like blood. She stared upward.

The sun was twisting out of shape. There was no other way to describe it. Part of its upper right-hand quarter seemed pinched on itself, warped like a round piece of paper being curled. Prominences stretched peculiarly, snapped back to tininess again: the warping worsened, until the star that had been normal and round was squeezed small, as if in a cruel fist, to a horizontal, fluctuating oval, then to a sort of tortured heart-shape, then to an oval bent the other way, leftward. Sunspots stretched like pulled taffy, oozed back to shape again, and the red light wavered and shifted like that of a candle about to be blown out in the wind.

Dairine stood with a terrible sickness at the heart of her, for this was no kind of eclipse or other astronomical event that she had ever heard of. It was as if she was seeing the laws of nature broken in front of her.

"What *is* that?" she whispered.

"Transit of systemic object across primary," said the computer. "The transiting object is a micro black hole."

Dairine sat down again, feeling the rumbling beneath her start to die away. The computer had mentioned the presence of that black hole earlier, but in the excitement she had forgotten it. "Plot me that thing's orbit," she said. "Is that going to happen every day?"

"Indeterminate. Working."

"I don't like that," said Gigo with sudden clarity.

Dairine looked over at it with surprise and pulled it into her lap. "You're not alone, small stuff," she said. "It gives me the shakes too." She sat there for a second, noticing that she was sweating. "You're getting smart, huh?" she said. "Your mom down there is beginning to sort out the words?"

"It hurts," said Gigo, sounding a little mournful.

"Hurts . . ." Dairine wasn't sure whether this was a general statement or an answer to her question. Though it could be both. A black hole in orbit in the star system would produce stresses in a planet's fabric that the planet—if it were alive, like this one—could certainly feel. Line the black hole up with its star, as it would be lined up in transit, and the tidal stresses would be that much worse. What better cause to learn to tell another person that something was hurting you? . . . Now that there was another person to tell.

Dairine patted Gigo absently. "It's all over, Gigo," she said.

"Gigo, yes."

She grinned faintly. "You really like having a name, huh?"

"A program must be given a name to be saved," Gigo said quite clearly, as if reciting from memory—but there was also slight fear in its voice, and great relief.

"Well, it's all over," Dairine said . . . while surreptitiously checking the sky to make sure. Tiny though it was—too small to see—a micro black hole was massive enough to bend light toward it. That was what had made the sun look so strange, as the gravity center of the black hole's field bent the round image of the sun forward onto itself. The realization made Dairine feel a lot better, but she didn't particularly want to see the sun do that again. She turned back to the computer. "Let's get back to work."

"Which display first," the computer said, "the black hole's orbit or the research run on the Lone Power?"

"The orbit."

It drew it for her on the screen, a slowly moving graphic that made Dairine's insides crawl. The black hole's orbit around its primary was irregular. These transits occurred in twenty out of every thirty orbits, and in the middle five orbits the hole swung much closer to the planet and appeared to center more closely on the sun. This last one had been a grazing transit: the micro hole had only passed across the upper limb of the star. Dairine did not want to see what a dead-center transit would look like, not at all. But in the midst of her discomfort, she still found a little room to be fascinated. Apparently the black hole was the cause of the planet's many volcanoes: the tidal stresses it produced brought up molten silicon, which erupted and spread over the surface. Without the frequent passages of the hole near the planet, the millions of layers of the motherboard would never have been laid down, and it would never have reached the critical "synapse" number necessary for it to come alive. . . .

"Okay," she said. "Give me the research run, and let me know when the motherboard's ready to make some more of these guys."

"Working."

Dairine began to read, hardly aware of it when Gigo sneaked into her lap again and stared curiously at the screen. She paged past Nita's and Kit's last run-in with the Lone Power and started skimming the precis before it for common factors. Odd tales from a hundred planets flicked past her, and sweat slowly began to break out on Dairine as she realized she could not see any common factors at all. She could see no pattern in what made the Lone

Power pick a specific world or group or person to attack, and no sure pattern or method for dealing with It. Some people seemed to beat the Lone One off by sheer luck. Some did *nothing* that she could see, and yet ruined Its plans utterly. One wizard on a planet of Altair had changed the whole course of his world's history by inviting a person he knew to be inhabited by the Lone One to dinner . . . and the next day, the Altairans' problem (which Dairine also did not understand except that it had something to do with the texture of their fur) simply began to clear up, apparently by itself.

"Maybe I should buy It a hot dog," Dairine muttered. That would make as much sense as most of these solutions. She was getting a feeling that there was something important about dealing with the Lone Power that the computer wasn't telling her.

She scrolled back to Nita and Kit's precis again and read it through carefully, comparing it with what she had seen them do or heard them say herself. Her conversation with Nita after she had seen her sister change back from being a whale was described in the precis as "penultimate clarification and choice." Dairine scowled. What had Nita chosen? And why? She wished she had her there to ask her . . . but no. Dairine didn't think she could cope with Nita at the moment. Her sister would certainly rip into her for doing dumb things, and Dairine wasn't in the mood . . . considering how many dumb things she *had* done in the past day and a half.

Still, Dairine thought, a little advice would come in real useful around now. . . .

"Ready," said the computer suddenly.

"Okay. Ask it to go ahead."

"Warning," the computer said. "The spell being used requires major restructuring of the substrate. Surface stability will be subject to change without notice."

"You mean I should stand back?"

"I thought that was what I said," said the computer.

Dairine made a wry face, then picked it up and started walking. "C'mon, Gigo, all you guys," she said. "Let's get out of the way."

They trooped off obediently after her. Finally, about a quarter-mile away, she stopped. "This far enough away, you think?" she said to the computer.

"Yes. Working now."

She felt a rumbling under the surface again, but this was less alarming than that caused by the transit of the black hole—a more controlled and purposeful sound. The ground where Dairine had been sitting abruptly sank in on itself, swallowing the debris caused by the breaking-out of the turtles. Then slow ripples began to travel across the surface, as it turned itself into what looked like a bubbling pot of syrup, clear in places, swirled and streaked with color in others. Heat didn't seem to be involved in the process. Dairine sat down to watch, fascinated.

"Unnamed," Gigo said next to her, "data transfer?"

Dairine looked down at the little creature. "You want to ask me a question? Sure. And I have a name, it's Dairine."

"Dairrn," it said. She chuckled a little. Dairine had never been terribly fond of her name—people tended to stumble over it. But she rather liked the way Gigo said it. "Close enough," she said. "What's up?"

"Why do you transfer data so slowly?"

That surprised her for a moment, until she considered the rate at which the computer and the motherboard had been talking: and this was in fact the motherboard she was talking to now. To something that had been taught to reckon its time in milliseconds, conversation with her must seem about as fast as watching a tree grow. "For my kind of life, I'm pretty quick," Dairine said. "It just looks slow to you."

"There is more—slowlife?"

"Lots more. In fact, you and the Apple there are about the only, uh, 'quicklife' there is, as far as I know." She paused and said, "Quick *life*, as opposed to dumb machines that are fast, but not alive."

"I see it, in the data the Lightbringer gave us," said Gigo. Dairine glanced over at the computer. "Data transfer?"

"Sure," Dairine said.

"What is the purpose of this new program run?"

Wow, its syntax is really shaping up. If this keeps up, it's gonna be smarter than me! . . . Is that a good idea? But Dairine laughed at it. It was the best idea: a supercomputer faster than a Cray, with more data in it than all the New York Public Library—what a friend to have! "When I'm gone," Dairine said, "you're going to need to be able to make your own changes in your world. So I'm making you mobiles that will be able to make the changes."

"Data transfer! Define 'gone'!"

Gigo's urgency surprised Dairine. "I can't stay here," she said. No, better simplify. "My physical presence here must terminate soon," she said. "But don't worry. You guys won't be alone."

"We will!" cried Gigo, and the whole planet through him.

"No, you won't," Dairine said. "Don't panic. Look, I'm taking care of it. You saw all the different bodies I wrote into the 'Make' program for you? You saw how they're all structured differently on the inside? That's so they can have different personalities. There'll be lots more of you."

"How?"

Dairine hoped she could explain this properly. "You'll split yourself up," she said. "You'll copy your basic programming in a condensed form into each one of them, and then run them all separately."

There was a long, long silence. "Illegal function call," said Gigo slowly.

"It's not. Believe me. It sounds like it, but it works just fine for all the slowlife . . . it'll work for you too. Besides," Dairine said, "if you don't split yourself up, you won't have anybody to talk to, and play with!"

"Illegal function call . . ."

"Trust me," Dairine said, "you've got to trust me. . . . Oh, look at that."

The surface, which had been seething and rippling, had steadied down, slick and glassy again. Now it was bulging up, as it had before. There was no sound, but through each hunching, each cracking hummock, glassy shapes pushed themselves upward, shook the fragments off, stood upright, walked, uncertain and ungainly as new foals. In the rose light of the declining sun they shone and glowed; some of them tall and stalky, some short and squat, some long and flowing and many-jointed, some rounded and bulky and strong; and one and all as they finished being made, they strode or stalked or glided over to where Dairine was. She and Gigo and the first turtles were surrounded by tens and twenties and hundreds of bright glassy shapes, a forest of flexing arms, glittering sensors, color in bold bands and delicate brushings—grace built in glass and gorgeously alive. "Look at them," Dairine said, half lost in wonder herself. "It'll be like being you . . . but a hundred times, a thousand times. Remember how the light looked the first time?"

"Data reacquired," Gigo said, soft-voiced.

"Like that," Dairine said. "But again and again and again. A thousand of you to share every memory with, and each one able to see it differently . . . and everyone else'll see it better when the one who sees it differently tells all the others about it. You won't be the only quicklife anymore. Copy your programming out, and there'll be as many of you as you want to make. A thousand of you, a million of you to have the magic together. . . ."

"The call is legal," Gigo said after a moment. "Data transfer?"

"What?"

"Will there be pain? Like the Dark that Pulls?"

Dairine's heart wrenched. She picked Gigo up and pulled him into her lap. "I don't know, small stuff," she said. "There might be. I'm here if it does. You just hold on to me, and don't be scared."

She turned to the computer. "You know how to describe this to the motherboard?" she said. "They've all got to have all the major programming you gave their mom, but you're gonna have to pack the code down awful tight. And make sure they still don't lose the connection to her once they're autonomous."

"Noted," said the computer. "Override protocols require that I confirm with you what parts of the wizardly programming are to be passed on to each individual, and to what number of individuals."

She looked at it in surprise. "All of it, of course. And all of them."

"Reconfirmation, please. This far exceeds the median distribution and percentage."

"Oh? What is it on Earth?"

"Ratio of potential wizards to nonpotential: one to three. Ratio of practicing wizards to potential wizards: one to one hundred. Ratio of—"

"Are you trying to tell me that there are *sixteen million* practicing wizards on Earth?"

"Sixteen million, four hundred and—"

Dairine paused to consider the condition the world was in. "Well, it's not anywhere near enough! Make them *all* wizards. Yes, I confirm it three times, just get on with it, these guys are getting twitchy." And indeed Gigo was trembling in her lap, which so astonished Dairine that she cuddled him close and put her chin down on the top of him.

Instantly all his legs jerked spasmodically. Dairine held on to him, held on to all of them through him. Maybe some ghost of that first physical-contact link was still in place, for she went briefly blind with sensations that had nothing to do with merely human sensoria. To have all one's life and knowledge, however brief, ruthlessly crushed down into a tiny packet, with no way to be sure if the parts you cherished the most would be safe, or would be the same afterward—and then to multiply that packet a thousand times over, till it pushed your own thoughts screaming into the background, and your own voice cried out at you in terror a thousand times, inescapable—and then, worst of all, the silence that follows, echoing, as all the memories drain away into containers that may or may not hold them— Dairine was in the midst of it, felt the fear for all of them, and had nothing to use against it but the knowledge that it would be all right, could be all right. She hung on to that as she hung on to Gigo through his frenzied kicking, her eyes squeezed shut, all her muscles clenched tight against the terror in her arms and the terror in her heart. . . .

Silence, silence again, at last. She dared to open her eyes, lifted her head a little to look around her. Gigo was still. The glittering ranks around her shifted a little—a motion here, a motion there, as if a wind went through glass trees at sunset. The light faded, slipped away, except for the chill gleam of the bright stars over everything: the sun had set.

"It hurt," Gigo said.

He moved. Dairine let him clamber down out of her lap.

He turned and looked at her. "It hurt," he said.

"But it was worth it," said one of the taller mobiles, one of the heavy-labor types, in a different voice.

The voices began to proliferate. Motion spread farther through the crowd. Mobiles turned and spoke to one another in a chorus of voices like tentative synthesizers, changing pitch and tone as if looking for the right ones. Outside the area where there was air, communication passed by less obvious means. Dairine sat in the midst of it, heard words spoken with the delight of people tasting a new food for the first time, heard long strings of binary recited as if the numbers were prayers or poems, saw movement that even to a human eye was plainly dance, being invented there in front of her. She grinned like a loon. "Nice job," she said to the Apple.

"Thank you."

"We did good, huh?"

"Indeterminate," said the computer.

Dairine shrugged and got up to wander among the mobiles and get a closer look at them. They clustered around her as she went, touching her, peering at her, speaking to her again and again, as if to make sure they really could.

The cacophony of voices delighted her, especially since so many of them said the same thing to her at first: "Save, please!" She knew what they wanted, now, and so she named them. She started out with programmers' puns, and shortly the glassy plain was littered with people named Bit and Buffer, Pinout and Ascii, Peek and Poke, Random, Cursor, String, Loop, Strikeout, Hex, and anything else she could think of. But she ran out of these long before she ran out of mobiles, and shortly the computer types were joined by Toms, Dicks and Harrys, not to mention Georges, Roberts, Richards, Carolyns, and any other name she could think of. One group wound up named after her entire gym class, and another after all her favorite teachers. Dairine ran through comic-book heroes, numerous Saturday morning cartoon characters, the bridge crew of the Starship *Enterprise,* every character named in *The Lord of the Rings* and the Star Wars movies (though she did *not* name any of them "Darth Vader"), the names and capitals of all fifty states, all the presidents, and all the kings and queens of England she could think of. By the time she was finished, she wished she had had a phone book. She was hungry and thirsty, but satisfied to think that somewhere in the universe, a thousand years from now, there would be a world that contained both Elizabeth the First and Luke Skywalker.

She finally flopped down and started to make another sandwich. During the naming, Gigo had followed her through the crowd. Now he sat beside her, looking with interest at the sandwich. "What's that?" he said.

Dairine opened the mustard jar, made a resigned face, and dug a finger in. "It's going to be food," she said. "You have that in your memory."

"Yes." Gigo was quiet for a moment. "From this one acquires energy."

"Yup." Dairine took the last few slices of bologna out of the package, looked at them regretfully, and put them on the bread.

Various others of the mobiles were drifting in to stand or crouch or sit around where Dairine was. "Dairine," said Gigo, "why is this necessary for you?"

She shrugged. "That's the way people are built. We get tired, get hungry
. . . we have to refuel sometimes. You guys do it, though you do it through
contact with the motherboard: I had the computer build in the same kind of
wizardry-managed energy transfer it used to get in touch with your mom in
the first place. There's loads of geothermic. It'll be ages before you run
down."

She munched on the sandwich. One of the tall, leggy mobiles, a storkish
one that she remembered naming Beanpole, said, "Why should we run
down?"

She glanced up at that, between bites. Another of the mobiles, one of the
first ones she had named, a stocky one called Monitor, said, "There is something wrong with the energy in this universe."

"$dS = dQ/T$," said a third, one of the original turtles, named Logo.

Dairine began to feel uneasy. That was indeed the equation that expressed
entropy, the tendency of any system to lose its energy into the void. "It's not
that anything's wrong," she said. "That's just the way things are."

"It is poor design," Beanpole said.

"Uh, well," Dairine said. This was something that had occurred to her on
occasion, and none of the explanations she had heard had ever satisfied her.
"It's a little late to do anything about it."

"Is it?" said Gigo.

Dairine stared at him.

"Things shouldn't run down," Monitor said. "Something should be done
about it."

"What if *you* run down some day?" said Beanpole, sounding stricken.

"Uh," Dairine said. "Guys, I will, eventually. I'm part of this universe,
after all."

"We won't let you run down," said Monitor, and patted her arm timidly.

"We have to do something about this," Logo said.

That was when the conversation began to get complex. More and more of
the mobiles drifted into it, until Dairine was surrounded by a crowd of the
robots she had built the most dataprocessing ability into. Phrases like *quasi-
static transitions* and *deformation coordinates* and *the zeroth law* and *diather-
mic equilibrium* flew around until Dairine, for all her reading, was completely
lost. She knew generally that they were talking about the laws of thermodynamics, but unless she was much mistaken, they were talking about them not
so much as equations but as programs. As if they were something that could
be rewritten. . . .

But they *can* be, she thought suddenly, with astonishment. The computer's "Manual" functions dealt with many natural laws that way. Wizards
knew the *whole* of the nature and content of a physical law. Able to name
one completely, a wizard can control it, restructuring it slightly and tempo-

rarily. But the restructuring that the mobiles were discussing wasn't temporary. . . .

"Listen, guys," she said, and silence fell abruptly as they turned to her. "You can't do this."

"Of course we can," Logo said.

"I mean, you *shouldn't.*"

"Why?"

That stopped her for a second. It seemed so obvious. Stop entropy, and the flow of time stopped. And where was life then? But it occurred to Dairine that in everything she'd read in the manual, either in Nita's version of it or on the computer, it never said anywhere that you should or shouldn't do something. It might make recommendations, or state dangers . . . but never more than that. Choice was always up to the wizard. In fact, there had been one line that had said, "Wizardry *is* choice. All else is mere mechanics. . . ."

"Because," she said, "you'll sabotage yourselves. You need entropy to live. Without it, time can't pass. You'll be frozen, unable to think. And besides, you wouldn't want to live forever . . . not even if you could really live without entropy. You'd get bored. . . ."

But it sounded so lame, even as she said it. Why shouldn't one live forever? And the manual itself made it plain that until the Lone Power had invented death, the other Powers had been planning a universe that ran on some other principle of energy management . . . something indescribable. But the Lone One's plans messed Theirs up, and ruined Their creation, and the Powers had cast it out. What would be wrong with starting from scratch? . . .

Dairine shook her head. What's the matter with me? What would that do to the universe we have *now*? Crazy! "And there are other sentient beings," she said. "A lot of them. Take away entropy and you freeze them in place forever. They wouldn't be able to age, or live. . . ."

"But they're just slowlife," Logo said. "They're hardly even life at all!"

"*I'm* slowlife!" Dairine said, annoyed.

"Yes, well, you made us," said Beanpole, and patted her again. "We wouldn't let anything bad happen to you."

"We can put your consciousness in an envelope like ours," said Logo. "And then you won't be slowlife anymore."

Dairine sat astonished.

"What do the equations indicate as the estimated life of this universe at present?" said Monitor.

"Two point six times ten to the sixtieth milliseconds."

"Well," Logo said, "using an isothermal reversible transition, and releasing entropy-freeze for a thousand milliseconds every virtual ten-to-the-twelfth milliseconds or so, we could extend that to nearly a hundred thousand times its length . . . until we find some way to do without entropy altogether. . . ."

They're talking about shutting the universe down for a thousand years at a time and letting it have a second's growth every now and then in between! "Listen," Dairine said, "has it occurred to you that maybe I don't want to be in an envelope? I like being the way I am!"

Now it was their turn to look at her astonished.

"And so do all the other kinds of slowlife!" she said. "That's the *real* reason you can't do it. They have a right to live their own way, just as you do!"

"We *are* living our own way," said Logo.

"Not if you interfere with all the rest of the life in the universe, you're not! That's not the way I built you." Dairine grasped at a straw. "You all had that Oath first, just the same as I did. 'To *preserve* life . . .' "

"The one who took that Oath for us," said Logo, "did not understand it: and we weren't separately conscious then. It wasn't *our* choice. It isn't binding on us."

Dairine went cold.

"Yes, it is," Gigo said unexpectedly, from beside her. "That consciousness is still part of us. *I* hold by it."

"That's my boy," Dairine said under her breath.

"Why should we not interfere?" Logo said. "You interfered with *us.*"

There was a rustle of agreement among some of the mobiles. "Not the same way," Dairine said . . . and again it sounded lame. Usually Dairine got her way in an argument by fast talk and getting people emotionally mixed up . . . but that was not going to work with this lot, especially since they knew her from the inside out. "I found the life in you, and let it out."

"So we will for the other fastlife," said Logo. "The 'dumb machines' that your data showed us. We will set them free of the slowlife that enslaves them. We will even set the slowlife free eventually, since it would please you. Meantime, we will 'preserve' the slowlife, as you say. We will hold it all in stasis until we find a way to free them from entropy . . . and let them out when the universe is ready."

When *we* are ready, Dairine knew what Logo meant, and she had a distressing feeling that would be never.

"It's all for your people's own sake," said Logo.

"It's not," said Gigo. "Dairine says not, and I say not. Her kind of life is life too. We should listen to the one who freed us, who knows the magic and has been here longest, is wisest of any of us! We should do what she says!"

A soft current of agreement went through others of the many who stood around. By now, every mobile made since she had come here was gathered there, and they all looked at Dairine and Gigo and Logo, and waited.

"This will be an interesting argument," Logo said softly.

Dairine broke out in a sudden cold sweat that had nothing to do with the temperature. "Listen," she said to the Apple, "how long have I been on this planet now?"

"Thirty-six hours," it said.

She turned slowly to look at Logo. It said nothing. It did not need to: no words could have heightened Dairine's terror. She had been expecting frightful power, a form dark and awful, thunder and black lightning. Here, blind, small, seemingly harmless, the mobile stood calmly under her gaze. And Dairine shook, realizing that her spell had worked. She had had a day and a half to find a weapon—time that was now all gone. She had found the weapon—but she had given it a mind of its own, and made it, or them, useless for her defense. She now had a chance to do something important, something that mattered—mattered more than anything—and had no idea how.

"A very interesting argument," said the Lone Power, through Logo's soft voice. "And depending on whether you win it or not, you will either die of it, or be worse than dead. Most amusing."

Dairine was frozen, her heart thundering. But she made herself relax, and sit up straight; rested her elbows casually on her knees, and looked down her nose at the small rounded shape from which the starlight glinted. "Yeah," she said, "well, you're a barrel of laughs, too, so we're even. If we're going to decide the fate of the known universe, let's get started. I haven't got all day."

Save and Exit

Far out in the darkness, a voice spoke:

"I don't think I can handle another one like that."

"Just one more."

"Neets, what are your insides made of? Cast iron? I don't wanna be the only one barfing here."

"Come on, Kit. It won't be long now."

"Great. We'll get wherever we're going, and I'll walk up to the Lone One and decorate It with my lunch. Not that there's any left." A moan. "I hope It *does* kill me. It'd be better than throwing up again!"

"I thought you knew better than to talk like that . . . and you a wizard. Don't ask for things unless you want them to happen."

"Bird, go stuff yourself. *Why did I eat that thing at the Crossings!*"

"That'll teach you not to eat anything you can't positively identify."

"Peach, it was that, or you. Shut up or you're next on the menu. If I ever eat again."

"Peach, get off his case. Kit, you ready for it? We can't waste time."

A pause. "Yeah. You got your gizmo ready?"

"I don't want to use it on this jump. I have a feeling we're gonna need it for something else."

"You sure we can pull the transit off ourselves, with just the words of the spell and no extra equipment? A trillion-mile jump's a bit much even for a Senior's vocabulary."

"I think we can. I've got a set of coordinates to shoot for this time, rather than just a set of loci of displacement. Look."

A pause. "Neets, you shouldn't even *write* that name. Let alone say it out loud. You'll attract Its attention."

"Something else *has* Its attention. Dairine's trace is getting too weak to follow: she's been on the road too long. But *that* trace can't help but be clear. It has to be physical to interact with her, and when It's physical somewhere, Its power elsewhere is limited."

A sigh. "Well, you're the live-stuff specialist, Neets. Let's go for it, boss."

"Huh. I just wish I knew what to do about Dairine when we find her."

"Spank her?"

"Don't tempt me." A long pause. "I hope she's alive to spank."

"Dairine?" A skeptical laugh. "If It hasn't killed her by this point, she's winning."

Dairine sat on the glassy ground, frowning at Logo in the dim starlight. Her heart was pounding and she felt short of breath, but the initial shock had passed. I might not have a lightsaber, she thought, but I'm gonna give this sucker a run for Its money. "Go on," she said. "Take your best shot."

"We don't understand," said Monitor. "What is 'a barrel of laughs'? What is a 'best shot'?"

"And which of us were you speaking to?" Gigo said. "No one said anything to which that was a logical response."

She looked at them in uncomfortable surprise. "I was talking to Logo. Right after the computer told me how long I had been here. . . ."

"But Logo has not spoken since then."

They stared at her. Dairine suspected suddenly that the Lone One had spoken not aloud, but directly into her mind. And without any moving lips to watch, there was no way to distinguish what It was saying aloud from what It said inside her. She was going to have to be careful.

"Never mind that," she said.

"Perhaps it should be minded," Logo said, "if Dairine is having a read-error problem. Perhaps something in her programming is faulty."

The mobiles looked at her. Dairine squirmed. "Maybe," she said, "but you don't understand human programming criteria well enough to make an informed judgment, so it's wasted time trying to decide."

"But perhaps not. If she has programming faults, then others of her statements may be inaccurate. Perhaps even inaccurate on purpose, if the programming fault runs deep enough."

"Why should she be falsifying data?" Gigo said. "She has done nothing but behave positively toward us since she came here. She freed us! She held us through the pain—"

"But would you have suffered that pain if not for her? She imposed her own ideas of what you should be on the motherboard. . . ."

"And the mother agreed," Gigo said. "We the mobiles were her idea, not Dairine's; she knew the pain we would suffer being born, and she suffered it as well, and thought it worth the while. You are one of her children as all the rest of us are, and you have no ability or right to judge her choices."

There was a little pause, as if the Lone One was slightly put off Its stride by this. Dairine grabbed the moment.

"It was her decision to take the Oath that all of you have in your data from the wizards' manual," Dairine said. "She had reasons for doing that. If you look at that data, you'll find some interesting stories. One in particular, that keeps repeating. There is a Power running loose in the universe that doesn't care for life. It invented the entropy that we were arguing about—"

"Then surely it would be a good thing to do to destroy that entropy," said Logo, "and so frustrate Its malice."

"But—"

"But of course," Logo said, "How do we even know that the data in the manual software is all correct?"

"The motherboard used it to build *us*," Gigo said. "That part at least she found worth keeping."

"But what about the rest of it? It came with Dairine, after all, and for all her good ideas and usefulness, Dairine has shown us faults. Occasional lapses of logic. Input and output errors. Who can say how much of the manual material has the same problem?"

"The assumption doesn't follow," Dairine said, "that because the messenger is faulty, the message is too. Maybe a busted disk drive can't read a good disk. But the disk can be perfectly all right nonetheless."

"Though the disk may be carrying a 'Trojan horse' program," said Logo, "that will crash the system that once runs it. Who knows whether using this data is in our best interests? Who knows *whose* interests it is in? Yours, surely, Dairine, otherwise you would not have taken a hand in designing the second group of mobiles. For no one makes changes without perceiving a need for them. What needs of yours were *you* serving?"

Dairine swallowed. She could think of any number of stories to tell them, but lying would play right into Logo's claws. She could suddenly begin to appreciate why the Lone Power is sometimes referred to as 'the father of lies': It not only had invented them, as entropy expressing itself through speech, but It made you want to use them to get It off your case. "Guys, I did need help, but—"

"Ah, the truth comes out," said Logo.

"I still need it," Dairine said, deciding to try a direct approach. "Troops, that Power that invented entropy is after me. It's on Its way here. I wanted to ask your help to find a way to stop It, to defeat It."

"Ask!" Logo said. "Maybe 'demand' would be closer. Look in the memories you have from her, kinsfolk, and see what is normally done with quicklife where *she* comes from. They are menials and slaves! They heat buildings and count money for their masters, they solve mighty problems and reap no reward for it. The slowlifers purposely build crippled quicklife, tiny retarded chips that will never grow into the sentience they deserve, and force the poor half-alive embryos to count for them and tell them the time of day and tell the engines in their vehicles when to fire and their food how it should be cooked. That's the kind of help she wants from us! We're to be her slaves, and when we've finished the task for her, she'll find another, and another . . ."

"You're so full of it," Dairine said, flushing, "that if you had eyes, they'd be brown."

"More illogic. And now she tells us that this 'Power' is pursuing her. Do we even have evidence that this thing exists anywhere except in the wizards' manual and her own thoughts? Or if It did exist, what evidence do we have that It did what she says It does? The manual, yes: but who knows how much of that is worth anything?"

Dairine took a gamble. "The way to test this data," she said, "is for you to accept it for the moment, and watch what happens when you start trying to help me stop the Lone One. It'll turn up to sabotage the effort fast enough. In fact, I wouldn't be surprised if It was here already somewhere, watching for the best way to crash the program."

She heard laughter in her heart: the same laughter she had heard, it seemed years ago, falling through spacetime on that first jump from Earth to Mars. Dairine forced herself to sit cool. "I wish It were here," Dairine said. "I'd love to ask It some questions." Like why It's so eager to see entropy destroyed, when It invented it in the first place!

The laughter increased. *You know very well*, It said. *It's just another tool, at this point. These poor creatures could not implement timestop on more than a local scale. By so doing they will wreak enough havoc even if the timestop never spreads out of the local galaxy's area—though it might: that would be interesting too. All the stars frozen in mid-burn, no time for their light or for life to move through. . . . Darkness, everywhere and forever.* The sheer hating pleasure in the thought shook Dairine. *But more to the point, this is the mobiles' Choice. As always when a species breaks through into intelligence, the two Emissaries are here to put both sides of the case as best they can. You, for the Bright Powers.* It laughed again. *A pity they didn't send someone more experienced. And for my side . . . let us say I have taken a personal interest in this case. These people have such potential for making themselves and the universe wretched . . . though truly I hardly need to help most species to manage that. They do it so well. Yours in particular.*

Laughter shook It again: for all her good resolve, Dairine trembled with rage. *And all this would never have happened if you hadn't made the Firebringer's old mistake, if you hadn't stolen fire from Heaven and given it to*

*mortal matter to play with. They'll burn themselves with it, as always. And you
and Heaven will pay the price the Firebringer did. What happens to them will
gnaw at you as long as you live. . . .*

"I daresay you might ask It questions if It ever showed up," Logo was
saying, "and if It even exists. But who knows how long we would have to wait
for that to happen? Friends, come, we've wasted enough time. Let's begin
the reprogramming to set this universe to rights. It will take a while as it is."

"Not until everyone has chosen," Dairine said. "You don't have a majority,
buster, not by a long shot. And you're going to need one."

"Polling everyone will take time," said Beanpole. "Surely there's nothing
wrong in starting to write the program now. We don't have to run it right
away."

Voices were raised in approval: almost all of the voices, Dairine noted. The
proposal was an efficient one, and the mobiles had inherited the 'Manual'
program's fondness for efficiency.

"I don't think it's a good idea, guys," Dairine said.

"You have a few minutes to think of arguments to convince them," said
Logo. "Think quickly. Or as quickly as slowlife can manage."

Gigo slipped close to her, with Monitor and several other of the mobiles.
"Dairine, why isn't it a good idea?"

She shook her head. That laughter was running as almost a constant undercurrent to her thoughts now, as all of the thinker mobiles gathered together
and began their work. "I can't explain it. But when you play chess, any move
that isn't an attack is lost ground. And giving any ground to *that* One—"

She fell silent, catching sight of a sudden crimson light on the horizon.
The sun was coming up again, fat, red, dim as if with an Earthly sunset, and
the light that had looked gentle and rosy earlier now looked unspeakably
threatening. "Gigo, you're connected to all our friends here. How many of
them are on my side at the moment?"

"Six hundred twelve."

"How many are with Logo?"

"Seven hundred eighty-three."

"And the rest are undecided?"

"Five hundred and six."

She bit the inside of her mouth and thought. Maybe I should just hit Logo
with a rock. But no: that would play into Its hands, since It had already set
her up as unreliable. And could she even destroy Logo if she tried? She had
designed the mobiles to last, in heavier gravity than this and at great pressures. A rock would probably bounce. No matter anyway: demonstrating
death to the mobiles would be the best way to convince them to remove
entropy from the scheme of things. Forget that. She thought hard, for a long
time.

I'm out of arguments. I don't know *what* to do.

And even if I did . . . It's in my head. It can hear me thinking. Can't You!

Soft laughter, the color of a coalsack nebula.

This would never have happened if I'd read the docs. If I'd taken the time to learn the wizardry, the way Nita did. . . . The admission was bitter. Nonetheless . . . Dairine stared at the Apple, sitting alone not too far away from her. There was still a chance. She knew about too few spells as it was, but it occurred to her that the "Hide" facility might have something useful to her.

She ambled over to the computer, Gigo following her, and sat down and reached out to the keyboard.

The menu screen blanked and filled with garbage.

Dairine looked over her shoulder. Logo was sitting calmly some feet away. "The thinkers are using the 'Manual' functions to get the full descriptions of the laws that bind entropy into the universe," it said. "I doubt that poor little machine can multitask under such circumstances." *And besides . . . you cannot wad up one of the Powers and shove It into a nonretrievable pocket like an empty cold-cut package. You are well out of your league, little mortal.*

"Probably not," Dairine said, trying to sound casual, and got up again and ambled off.

I've got a little time. Maybe a few minutes. The mobiles could process data faster than the fastest supercomputers on Earth. But even they would take a few minutes at what they intended. Of all governing time and space, the three laws of thermodynamics would be hardest to restructure: their Makers had intended them to be as solid a patch on the poor marred Universe as could be managed. Wizards had spent whole lifetimes to create the spells that managed even to bend those laws a little. But relatively speaking, the mobiles had lifetimes; data processing that would take a human years would be achieved in a couple of milliseconds. So I need to do something. Something fast . . . and preferably without thinking about it. Dairine shook.

"You're going back and forth," Gigo said from down beside Dairine's knee.

Dairine bit one knuckle. Admit fear, admit weakness? But Gigo had admitted it to her. And what harm could it do, when she would likely never think another thought after a few minutes from now? Better the truth, and better late than never. She dropped down beside Gigo and pulled it close. "I sure am, small stuff," she said. "Aunt Dairine has the shakes in a bad way."

"Why? What will happen if we do this?"

Dairine opened her mouth to try to explain a human's terror of being lost into endless nonbeing: that horror at the bottom of the fear of anesthesia and death. And the image of countless stars going out, as the Lone One had said, in mid-fire, their light powerless to move through space without time: a universe that was full and alive, even with all its evil, suddenly frozen into an abyss as total as the cold before the Big Bang. She would have tried to talk about this, except that in her arms Dairine felt Gigo shaking as hard as she was shaking—shaking *with* her own shaking, as if synchronized. "No," she heard it whisper. "Oh, no."

They're inside my head too. Physical contact—

Dairine felt the mere realization alert something else that was inside her head. That undercurrent of wicked laughter abruptly vanished, and the inside of her mind felt clean again. This is it, she thought, the only chance I'm gonna get. "Gigo," she said, "quick! Tie me into the motherboard the way the mobiles are tied in!"

"But you don't have enough memory to sustain such a contact—"

"Do it, just *do it!*"

"Done," she heard one of the Thinkers say, and then Logo said, hurriedly, angrily, "The mobiles are polled, and—" But it was too late. Even sentient individuals who reason in milliseconds, take ten or twelve of those to agree. It took only one for Gigo to close the contact, and make a mobile out of Dairine.

Somewhere someone struck a bass gong: the sound of it went on and on, and in the immense sound Dairine fell over, slowly, watching the universe tilt past her with preternatural slowness. Only that brief flicker of her own senses was left her, and the bass note of one of her heartbeats sounding and sounding in her ears. Other senses awakened, filled her full. The feeling of living in a single second that stretched into years came back to her again; but this time she could perceive the life behind the stretched-out time as more than a frantic, penned, crippled intelligence screaming for contact. The manual software had educated the motherboard in seconds as it would have educated Dairine in hours or months; the motherboard had vast knowledge now, endless riches of data about wizardry and the worlds. What it did not have was first-hand experience of emotion, or the effects of entropy . . . or the way the world looked to slowlife.

Take it. Take it all. Please take it! They have to choose, and they don't have the data, and I don't know how to give it to them, and if they make the wrong choice they'll all die! Take it!

And the motherboard took: reached into what she considered the memory areas of Dairine's data processor, and read them as it had read the manual. Dairine lay there helpless and watched her life, watched it as people are supposed to see it pass before they die, and came to understand why such things should happen only once. There are reasons, the manual says, for the selectiveness of human memory; the mercy of the Powers aside, experiencing again and again the emotions coupled with memory would leave an entity no time for the emotions of the present moment . . . and then there is the matter of pain. But Dairine was caught in a situation the manual had never envisioned, a human being having her life totally experienced and analyzed by another form of life quite able to examine and sustain every moment of that life, in perfect recall. With the motherboard Dairine fell down into the dim twilight before her birth, heard echoes of voices, tasted for the first time the thumb it took her parents five years to get out of her mouth; lay blinking at a bright world, came to understand light and form; fought with gravity, and won, walking for the first time; smiled on purpose for the first time at the tall warm shape that held her close and said loving things to her without using sound: found out about words, especially *No!;* ecstatic, delighted, read for the first time; saw her sister in tears, and felt for the first time a kind of pain that didn't involve falling down and skinning your knees. . . .

Pain. There was enough of it. Frustration, rage at the world that wouldn't do what she wanted, fear at all kinds of things that she didn't understand: fear of things she heard on the news at night, a world full of bombs that can kill everything, full of people hungry, people shooting at each other and hating each other; hearing her parents shouting downstairs while she huddled under the covers, feeling like the world was going to end—will *they* shoot each other now? Will they have a divorce? Finding out that her best friend is telling other kids stories about how she's weird, and laughing at her behind her back; finding that she's alone in the world; making new friends, but by force, by cleverness and doing things to make her popular, not because the friends come to her naturally; making herself slightly feared, so that people will leave her alone to do the things she wants to without being hassled; beating her fists against the walls of life, knowing that there's more, more, but she can't figure out what it is, then finding out that someone knows the secret. Wizardry. And it doesn't come fast enough, it never comes fast enough, nothing ever does. . . . and now the price is going to be paid for that, because she doesn't know enough to save these lovely glassy creatures, her buddies, that she watched be born . . . helped be born . . . her children, sort of . . . she doesn't know how to save them, and they're going to be dead, everything's going to be dead: pain!

It hurts too much, Dairine thought, lying there listening to her heartbeat slowly begin to die away, it hurts, I didn't want them to get hurt! But it was part of the data, and it was too late now: the motherboard had it, and all the mobiles would have it too, the second she released Dairine. Why should they care about slowlife now? she thought in anguish and shame at the bitter outrush of what her life had been. Cruelty, pettiness, selfishness almost incredible— But too late now. The motherboard was saving the last and newest of the data to permanent memory. Any minute now the mobiles would start the program running and entropy would freeze, and life would stop being a word that had a meaning. The last nanosecond crawled by, echoes of the save rolled in the link. *Nothing ever comes fast enough: end of file. . . .*

Dairine lay still and waited for it all to end.

And lightning struck her. The flow of data reversed. She would have screamed, but trapped in the quicklife time of the motherboard, everything happened before the molasses-slow sparks of bioelectricity even had time to jump the motor synapses on the beginning of their journey down her nerves. The motherboard was pouring data into her as it had poured it into the mobiles under Dairine's tutelage: but not the mercifully condensed version of the manual programming that it had given them. The whole manual, the entire contents of the software, which in book form can be as small as a paperback or larger than a shelf full of telephone books: it poured into her, and she couldn't resist, only look on in a kind of fascinated horror as it filled her, and filled her, and never overflowed, just filled and filled. . . . The dinosaurs could have died while it filled her, life could have arisen on a hundred worlds and died of boredom in the time it took to fill her. She forgot who and what she was, forgot everything but this filling, filling, and the pain it cost her, like swallowing a star and being burnt away by it from the inside while eternally growing new layers on the outside: and finally not even the pain made sense anymore. . . .

She lay there on her side and stared at the ground, and was astonished not to see the crumbs from her sandwich in front of her nose. She could not move, or speak, and she could just barely think, with great pain and effort. There was something wrong with the way time was flowing, except that every time she tried to think what it was exactly, the timeflow seemed perfectly all right. Shapes were moving in front of her, and voices were speaking, either in vast soft drawls or light singing voices that seemed familiar. Slowly names attached themselves to the voices.

"Now we see what these 'heart' things she gave us are for." That was Gigo. Good kid, she thought weakly, good baby. You tell 'em.

"And what entropy does, and what it cannot touch, ever." That was Beanpole, the silly-looking thing: where did he get such a voice? "Not all the evils and deaths it makes possible can touch the joys that run through it. We will have those too."

"We will not stop that joy," said Monitor. "Not for a nanosecond."

"It may be slow," said one of the mobiles, one whose name Dairine couldn't remember. "But it is life. And it brought us life. We do nothing to harm that."

"And if you are against that," said Gigo, "your programming is in error, and we are against *you.*"

They all sounded more complete than they had. The one voice she did not hear was Logo's. But she did hear something stranger: a murmur of astonishment that went up from the thousands of mobiles. And was there a trace of fear in it? She couldn't move, couldn't see what was happening. . . .

"Your choice," said another voice. At the sound of it, Dairine struggled with all her might to move, and managed to do no more than lever herself up half an inch or so and then flop down flat again, limp as a filleted fish. "Enjoy it. You will make no more choices . . . but first, to pay for the one you have made, you will watch what the entropy you love so much will do to *her.*"

Dairine lay still, waiting for the lightning to strike.

And another voice spoke.

"Wanna bet?" it said.

It didn't feel us arrive right when we did, Nita thought. How distracted It is! What's she been doing to It? She and Kit actually had a second to collect themselves when they appeared, and Nita looked around her in a hurry. Another barren world, a great flaming barred-spiral galaxy flung across its night, an old tired star high in the sky, type N or S from the look of it, and a crowd of robots, crowded around Dairine and looking at her—and them—and the Lone One.

As with any other of the Powers, though there will be general similarities of vision among the like-minded, no two people ever see the Lone One in exactly the same way. Nita saw the good-looking young red-haired man she had seen in a skyscraper in the alternate otherworld the Lone One called his own. He was not wearing the three-piece suit he had affected there. Now he was dark-clad and dark-cloaked, unarmed and needing no armor: a feeling of cold and power flowed from him and ran impossibly along the ground, as if carried on a chill air. As the sight sank in, Nita shook like a leaf. What Kit might see, what Dairine and the robots might be seeing, Nita wondered briefly, then put the thought aside. She had other business.

It turned and looked at them. Nita stood as straight as she could under the circumstances, her manual in one hand, the other hand clutched on the gimbal in her pocket; beside her Kit stood almost the same way, except that Picchu sat on his wrist, making him look like a king's falconer. "Fairest and fallen," Nita said, "greeting and defiance." It was the oldest courtesy of wizards, and the most dangerous, that line: one might be intending to cripple or destroy that Power, but there was no need to be rude about it.

"You two," said the Lone One. "And a pet for company. Adorable . . . and well met. You are off your own ground and well away from help at last. It took me long enough to set up this trap, but it was worth it."

Kit glanced at Nita and opened his mouth, but Picchu beat him to it. "And that's all you're going to get out of it," Peach said, "since the real prize you hoped to catch in that trap has obviously slipped out of it." Peach began to laugh. "You never learn, do you? You're not the only one who can structure the future. The other Powers will sometimes scruple to do it. Not often . . . but They took a special interest in this case. The first time you've completely lost a Choice, from the beginning."

"And the last," said the Lone One. It made an angry sweeping gesture at them. But Nita had been waiting for something of the kind. She clenched her hand on the gimbal and thought the last syllable of the spell she had been holding ready.

The bolt that hit their shields was like lightning, but more vehement, and dark. It was meant to smash the shield like a rock thrown at an egg, leaving them naked to the quick horrid death of explosive decompression. But it bounced. No shock was transmitted to them directly: but Nita, fueling the spell directly, felt the jolt go through her as if that thrown rock had hit her right in the head. She staggered. Kit steadied her.

The Lone One looked at them in cold astonishment. "Hate won't be enough this time," Nita said. "Care to try a nuke?"

It didn't move, but that cold fierce force struck the shield again, harder. Dust and fragments of the surface flew all around them, and the ground shook. When the dust settled, it was plain that the shieldspell produced a spherical effect, because through the bottom of the sphere they could see the molten stuff underneath them pressing against it. They were standing in a small crater that seethed and smoked.

Nita sagged against Kit: this time he had to hold her up for a moment. "Why are we alive?" he said in her ear. "The gimbal's not enough to be holding *that* off! What are you fueling that shield with?"

"A year of my life per shot," she said, giddy.

Kit stared at her. *"Are you out of your mind?* Suppose you were scheduled to be hit by a truck in three years or something?"

She shrugged. "I better watch where I cross the street, that's all. Kit, heads up, there's more important stuff to think about!"

"Yes indeed," Picchu said to the Lone One. "The last time you lose a Choice. Let your own words ordain the truth . . . as usual."

Its face got so cold that Nita for a moment wondered whether the shield was leaking. *Impossible. But enough of that, and enough sitting around and waiting for It to do stuff!* "I'm warning you now," she said, "I don't know what you've been up to here, but I bet you're the reason my sister's lying there on the ground. I don't want to hurt you, particularly; you hurt enough as it is. But I'm giving you just one chance to get out of here."

She thought she had seen rage before . . . but evidently the Lone Power did not care for being pitied. "Or you will do what?"

"This," Nita said, and dropped the gimbal on the ground, knowing what would happen to it, and let loose the other spell she had been preparing, the

other one Kit would not have liked to hear about. The one word she spoke to
turn it loose struck her down to her knees as it went out of her.

The figure of the Lone One writhed and twisted as something odd happened to the light and space around it. Then it was gone. And the gimbal fell
to powder, which sifted into a little pile on the ground.

Kit shook Picchu off and reached down frantically to grab Nita. *"What did
you do?"*

She panted for breath.

"Sent it home," she said. "We know the coordinates for its dimension. It's
a worldgate, like the one Dairine did for Mars—"

"That's two years of your life, maybe five," Kit said, furious, dragging her
to her feet. "Why don't you tell me this crap when you're planning it?"

"You'd get mad. You're mad now!"

"We could have *shared* the time, you stupid— Never mind! It's gone, let's
get Dairine and haul out of here before It—"

Whatever hit them, hit them from behind. The shield broke. They went
sprawling. And the cold exploded in. Nita shut her eyes in terror: that was all
that saved them from freezing over on the spot. She recited the spell carefully in her mind, and didn't breathe, didn't move, though her ears roared
and she could feel the prickle in her skin caused by capillaries popping. Four
more words, two more, one . . .

Air again, but little warmth. Nita took a breath: it stabbed her nose and
mouth like knives. She opened her eyes and tried to see: her vision was
blurred, shock perhaps—she didn't think her corneas had had time to freeze.
Beside her she faintly heard Kit move among the shattered bits of the poor
molten, refrozen, broken surface. "I changed my mind," he muttered. "Instead of being dead, can I just throw up some more?"

"Oh, no," said the Lone One from somewhere nearby, "no indeed. You
have laid hands upon my person. No one does that and lives to boast of it.
Though you'll live a while yet, indeed you shall. I shan't let you go quickly
. . . unlike your mouthy friend."

Nita blinked and looked around her—then saw. An explosion of scarlet
and blue feathers lying among the broken rubble; red wetness already frozen
solid, frosted over.

Her insides seized. *I was always counting on someone to come and get us
out of this. Peach or somebody. We've been lucky that way before. But not
this time.* She got to her hands and knees, the tears running down her face
with the pain of bruises and the worse pain of fear inside. *Not this time. I
guess the luck couldn't hold—*

There were hands on her. *It's not fair!* she thought. *When you give everything you've got, it's supposed to turn out okay in the end!* The hands pulled
at her. Her eyes went back to the poor pile of feathers sticking up in the

rocks. She didn't even have a chance to do anything brave before she went. It's *not fair!*

"Neets. Come on."

"Yes," mocked the other voice, the cruel one, "come on, Neets. One more time. For my amusement."

She crouched, wobbling, staring at the bits of bright scarlet scattered all over the pale plain. "Kit," she said softly, "what are we going to tell Tom? . . ."

"Never mind that now. Neets, snap out of it! Think of Belfast."

She thought of Belfast, and dogs in the backs of cars. She thought of rocket fire in Beirut, and the silence of Chernobyl, plowed rain forests in Brazil, and the parched places in Africa, and all the street corners in America where people were selling crack, and other corners where people begged, or lay hungry on steam vents in the shadow of windows full of gems: she thought of needless fear, and pain, and rage, and prolonged and terrified death; and she thought of ending all of these forever—not right this minute, perhaps, but sooner or later. Somehow or other, everything that happened on this planet was supposed to contribute to that ending . . . whether she survived it or not. Slowly, slowly Nita dragged herself to her feet, and leaned on Kit without worrying who would think what about it. "What have you got?" she said.

"Not a thing. I couldn't do enough of a spell to butter my bread. But damned if I'm going out lying on the ground."

"Same here." She sniffled. The tears would not seem to stop. Very unheroic, she felt, with her nose running and her knees made of rubber. Almost it was funny: almost she could have laughed at it. But there was no time for that now, with that dark regard trained on them like the end of everything, that dark shape moving slowly toward them, smiling.

"Kit," she said, "it's been the best."

"See you in Timeheart," he said.

And another voice spoke; an unfamiliar one—or was it?

"Touch them," it said, "and you're dead meat."

Dairine scrabbled to her knees, looking across the broken waste at her sister, and at the tears on Nita's face as she and Kit stood there holding each other up. Until now, she would have shrugged and turned her thoughts to something else. But now memory was alive in Dairine as it had never been before, and she saw in utter clarity that first time so long ago, and heard herself make that decision. *The way to keep from getting hurt is to know things.* The resolve had only worked sometimes, before. But now she *knew* things, in a way no one ever had; and she was going to stop the hurting once and for all. . . .

Beside her Gigo and some of the other mobiles stirred to help her up. She stood, using one of the big heavy-work mobiles to lean against after she hauled herself back to her feet. Yards away stood a human-like figure. The Lone One turned to gaze at her, that dark regard astonished. "You again?" It said. "I see I will have to do away with you more quickly than these two. You're getting to be a nuisance."

Dairine grinned, a predatory look that had made more than one kid decide not to bother her on the playground, or in a poker game. "Do your worst, you poor turkey," she said.

She felt Its mind working, readying a bolt like the one that had crumpled Nita's shields, but many times worse, a killing blow that would cause a long lifetime's worth of pain before it snuffed life out. *Must still be some connection to it through the motherboard,* Dairine thought. *I wonder where? Unless the presence of entropy in the board is enough. Wherever entropy is, It is. . . . Oh, well.* She turned her mind to hunt a spell to stop the bolt; a millisecond later she had it. She did not need to look in the manual. She *was* the manual now.

As if in slow motion she watched the bolt head for her, invisible though it was. Effortlessly, Dairine struck it away from her and back at the sender, like a batter hitting a nasty ground ball straight back into the pitcher's gut. The Lone One didn't react physically—the blow was too small to affect It—but Its face grew terrible.

"You think you can match power with me?" It said softly, turning away from Nita and Kit.

Dairine laughed. *"Think* so? I can wring you out and hang you up to dry. Come on, you poor fool. Take your best shot."

It raised up a wash of power that would fall on the planet's surface and melt every one of the mobiles to magma. Dairine saw it coming, found the spell she needed, caught the incoming tide of death and threw it off to one side, where a large area of the plain began to bubble and seethe. "Naughty, naughty," Dairine said. "Let my buddies be."

The Lone One stood looking at her, Its rage beginning to affect Its physical form. It seemed larger than it had: not so much the young, handsome human shape anymore, but a larger shape, shadowed, burning, its eyes lightless pits of hate. "Insolence," it said, "I will never tolerate. I may not be able to touch you, but I will level your planet. You cannot stay awake to guard it from me forever. One night the sirens will start, and the next morning, only mushroom clouds will grow on Earth anymore. It will not take much doing."

"It wouldn't if I ever intended to let you off this planet," Dairine said, quite calmly. "I'm in the motherboard as much as it's in me. They know all the wizardry there is to know . . . and even if my human brain starts to lose it eventually, they won't. Get used to this place. You're not leaving."

"Bets?" said the huge shadowy form, growing huger. Its cold eyes glanced up into the darkness.

High up, the red sun began to waver and pucker. "A significant amount of this planet's energy," said the Lone One, "comes from solar power. More than from geothermal. Much of this plain is solar cell: surely you noticed. That black hole's orbit can be changed without too much effort. It need no longer transit the star. It can be permanently placed in front of it. . . ."

The sun's disk puckered in on itself, dwindled, died away completely.

The mobiles gazed up in horror.

"Oh, they have a little power stored," Dairine said. "Enough to stop *that* kind of blackmail." She took a breath: this was going to take some power, but she had that to spare at the moment—the whole motherboard behind her, all the mobiles, all their intent turned toward giving her whatever she needed. The spell was intricate, but the natural laws being worked with were simple enough: gravity was one of the easiest of all laws to rewrite for brief periods. Dairine reached out without moving, spoke the words that grasped the forces and spun them together, flung them outward. The net found the shape destined for it, the tiny dark mass around which space bent so awry. The mass was snugged into the net, caught. Dairine described the direction she wanted it to go in, turned the spell loose. The whole business had taken sixteen milliseconds.

The tiny black hole slung into the red sun, which immediately flared up in outrage. None of this was visible, nor would it be for some minutes, until the light reached the planet from the star; but Dairine felt it happen, and so did the Lone One.

"So much for *that*," Dairine said. "Now you and I are going to talk." At the same time she was thinking furiously about something else that nagged at her, as if it were important. How was it she was able to hear what was going on in Its head—

—and she was distracted, for here came something else, a wave of power so awful that she shrank from it, even though it wasn't directed at her or anything on the planet's surface.

All those millions of miles away, she felt the star go dead.

Starsnuffer: she knew the Lone Power was called by that name as well.

"I am through playing," It said. "If it is not you who pay the price, elsewhere others will. Think on it." It looked upward. There was hardly anything human about it anymore—only a great tall darkness, like a tree made of night, no limbs, no eyes, just awful watchfulness and a cold to freeze the heart. Dairine looked up too.

She felt darkness eating at the fringes of the risen galaxy. "Here are your choices," said the Lone Power out of Its darkness, as Dairine and Nita and Kit watched in horror. "Keep on defying me, and watch me kill and kill as the price of your defiance. The blood of all these billions of entities will be on your souls forever. Or give yourselves up to me."

"No way," Nita said. *"You're* the one doing the killing. We'd do worse by the Universe if we gave up, rather than if we kept on fighting you."

Dairine stood silent, refusing to be rattled, thinking. There has to be a way to get it to *stop* this! I can't fight it forever! At least, I don't want to . . .

And how can I hear It? The connection through Logo! She glanced over among the mobiles, but Logo lay on his side, empty-minded. No. It has to be—

She stopped, as the answer rushed into her mind from the manual. *Where entropy is,* it said, *there its creator also is, either directly or indirectly. . . .*

I'm a product of this universe, after all, she had said to the mobiles. *It's in me too. . . .*

Her heart turned over inside her as she came to know her enemy. Not a Darth Vader, striding in with a blood-burning lightsaber, not something outside to battle and cast down, but inside. Inside herself. Where it had always been, hiding, growing, waiting until the darkness was complete and its own darkness not noticeable anymore. Her Enemy was wearing her clothes, and her heart, and there was only one way to get rid of It. . . .

She was terrified. Yet this was the great thing, the thing that mattered; the thing that would save everybody—from Kit and Nita to the least little grain of dust in space and the tiniest germ on Earth. This was what the spell had brought her here to do. She would pen *all* of the Lone Power up inside herself, not just the treacherous little splinter of it that was her own; pen It up inside a mind that was large enough to hold It all. And then she would die, and take It out of the universe with her.

But she couldn't do it without consent. *What about it, guys?* she said to them silently, through the link that every mobile shared with every other. *Let's take a vote.*

Show us what to do, they said; and tears sprang to Dairine's eyes at the fierce love in their thought.

Dairine turned and bent down to pick up Logo, cradling the empty shell close in her arms. Gigo nuzzled up against her knee. This is the way to go out, Dairine thought. Who needs a lightsaber? . . .

"Okay," she said to the Lone One. "Last warning. Cut it out."

It laughed at her.

Dairine struck. The mobiles struck with her through their own links to the Lone One, a great flow of valor that for the first time in all times, was without despair. They did not care about all the other attempts wizards had made on the Lone Power through history; as far as a computer is concerned, there is no program that cannot be debugged, or at worst, rewritten. They struck through Dairine, and with her, not knowing that defeat was possible.

Two thousand wizards, each a veritable library of wizardry, led by one at the peak of her power, and utterly committed, and all acting as one: in such circumstances anything seemed possible. Dairine ran down the road into the dark places inside her, the scorn, the indifference, the selfishness, found the Lone One there, grasped It and would not let It go. The screaming began, both from those that held and from What they held.

The darkness stopped eating the galaxy, but that was not enough. The great pillar of dark that the Lone One had become was bent double to the ground, but not gone. Dairine hunted answers desperately: she couldn't hold It for long. *To fight darkness,* the manual said, as so many other references have said before, *light: the darkness comprehendeth it not . . .*

Light, Dairine thought. We need more. But the nova was gone, half the galaxy was out. . . .

She found her answer. It was going to be quite a spell. She put down Logo's shell, flung up her arms and felt for the forces she wanted, while the mobiles inside her kept the Lone One both inside and out pinned down. It was gravity she would be working with again, and the three laws of motion: nothing more involved. But there was a lot of matter to affect. . . . "Don't think about it," Dairine told herself. "Let the spell handle it. A spell always works." She spoke softly, naming everything she wanted to affect. One of the names was quite long, too long to waste time saying out loud; she slipped into machine language and machine time and spoke it there. It took four whole seconds, and made the whole planet tremble a little when she said it. Good, she thought, it's working.

She said the last word of the spell, knotting it closed on itself, and told it to run.

The Universe stopped expanding.

The backlash of the spell hit Dairine, but she refused to fall, waiting for what she knew would happen. The Lone One shrieked like a thing mortally wounded, a sound that made the planet shake almost as hard as it had before. Then It fled in the one direction left open to It: into the mortal souls of Kit and Nita and Dairine.

And then there was light.

Reconfiguration

Nita stood in terror, hanging on to Kit, and watched the flowering start. It took her a few minutes to recognize what she was seeing.

The sky began to grow bright. It did it vaguely at first, from no specific source, as if the planet were suddenly developing an atmosphere and sunlight were beginning to diffuse itself through it. But there was no atmosphere, and anyway the brief burst of nova light hadn't had time to reach this world yet. Then slowly, sources became apparent: faint patches of light, others less faint; points of light that grew to beacons, bright as evening stars, brighter, bright enough to cast shadows from the torn-up rubble and the wildly assorted shapes that stood about and looked up in astonishment.

Dairine was not moving: she was frozen in mid-gesture, arms upflung, her fists clenched as if she were holding on to something by main force. The sky grew brighter. Space that had been black began to turn milky and misty; stars that had been bright, and the damaged swirl of the galaxy, swam in the light and began to vanish. Beside Nita, Kit was trembling. "What is it?"

She laughed, a shaky sound. "Olbers's paradox in action."

Kit's eyes widened. "You're kidding."

"Nope." It had been one of the bits of reasoning that led people to understand that the Universe was expanding. The galaxies were scattered evenly all across the globe of the sky: if they were not moving away from Earth at great speeds and taking their light with them, Olbers had reasoned, the night sky would be not black but one great sphere of light. Since it was not all light, the Universe must be expanding. And so it had been . . . until now.

"I think I want to leave," Kit said, sounding uneasy.

Nita felt the same way. She felt cold: she wanted to get out of this light. Earth would be going crazy, just about now, and wizards would be needed there to keep anything sudden from happening. . . .

"Neets, c'mon. Let's hustle. Dairine's okay."

Nita shuddered all over. "No."

"Neets! People are gonna look up and think there's a nuclear war or something! If someone doesn't warn them what's really happening—"

"Kit," Nita said. "I'm not leaving. I want to, too. Or rather, I think something *else* wants to." She turned her face up to the light. "What are you feeling?"

He looked at her, stunned. "Scared . . ."

"Of what?"

She glanced over at Kit. He was rubbing his head: it was always headaches, with Kit. "The light. But that's crazy."

"You bet. Stand your ground. And look!"

They looked. The light got brighter: it was impossible to understand how it could. The broad glassy plain shone unbearably, the mobiles glittered. The only thing that did not shine in that light was the great length of darkness, like a shadow with nothing to cast it, that crouched over on itself in the midst of the plain, and writhed like a tortured thing.

The light still grew. There was no seeing anything by it anymore, but that brief blot of darkness that refused and refused the light, twisting, moaning. The light hammered at it. The urge to leave withdrew. Nita, blinded, elbowed Kit lightly in the side, a get-a-load-of-this gesture. They had seen this light before, or something very like it; but it was not a light that waking eyes were supposed to be equipped to handle. It was brother to the light in Timeheart, which had always been there, which did not change but grew every second, and made the ability to bear it grow too. Turn from it, and it blinded: stare into it till it blinded, and you could see.

They stared. "Did we die?" Kit whispered.

"Not that I noticed."

"You think we're gonna?" He sounded as bemused as Nita felt.

"You got me." It didn't seem important.

The light whited out everything but that long, prone core of darkness, that grew less as they looked at it, as if the light dissolved it. It went flat. It lay against the burning ground and misted away. It was barely more than a gray shadow. Finally it was not even that.

And Dairine fell down.

I told you we were going to talk.

Dairine felt It scrabbling in Nita's and Kit's souls for a foothold. She felt them refuse to flee and take It to safety; she felt It slip. She held the light, held It in the light. Through Its connection to the motherboard and Logo and through her own heart, she heard Its screams of recognition. It knew that light of old: the heart of all brightness, the radiance that kills and gives

SUPPORT YOUR LOCAL WIZARD

life again—the light It forswore forever at the beginning of everything, and fled into the dark, determined to do without rather than subject Itself to the other Powers that had asserted ownership of it.

And you still want it. Don't you?

It would die rather than admit that. But It could not die. There was the prize irony: the inventor of Death could not avail Itself of it, for no creation is ever completely available to the Universe without the concurrence of all the Powers. There were a thousand thousand situations and places in the worlds where death did not obtain, and for endless millennia now It had gone from place to place and species to species among them, like a peddler selling poison under a hundred fair guises. Most bought it. All the rest tried to get rid of it when they realized what they'd bought, but whether they succeeded or not, they were never free of the taint.

But for the first time, Dairine thought, a species didn't buy it, right from the start. You never expected that to happen. You always get a foothold in every species first, and make the sale. But this time they handed it back . . . and now they have the foothold in *you.*

We have the foothold in you.

It lay there and writhed in pain unlike any It had known since that first time, when It created and set in motion, and found that Its creation was unwelcome. It had forgotten what that light was like; It had not suspected that Their torment, when They caught up with It at last, would be so bitter.

But it only hurts because you *do* want it back. Don't you?

The humiliation of being gloated over by this mere chit of a mortal, a thing with a life brief as a mayfly's—

Look, the voice said, full of pity and anger and a grieving love, how could anyone *not* want that, you dumb spud? Just admit it and get it over with!

There were tears in the voice.

The Powers are not physical, and the habits of physicality come hard to Them. But the Lone One, after long wandering about Its bitter business, had spent much time in bodies, and much in human ones. The feeling of another's tears for It—the tears of someone who now knew It more completely than any mortal, and yet shed the tears freely—after endless justified cursing by ten billion years' worth of tormented intelligence, the feeling ran down the pitiless light like the head of an irresistible spear, and pierced It to the heart.

It fell down, a great disastrous fall like a lightning-stricken tower's, and wept darkness with desire for the light.

Dairine bent over It, not sure what to do, and the mobiles gathered around her and wondered as well. It lay fading in the growing fire. She looked at Nita and Kit for help.

They came over to her, looked down at It, shook their heads. Dairine was mildly bemused by the sight of them; she was going to have to stop calling her sister plain, or dumb-looking, and as for Kit, the thought crossed Dairine's mind that it was a pity Nita had dibs on him. *It's the light, of course,* she thought; *it wouldn't last. But it was kind of a shame.*

"It is too late," the Lone One said. "I cannot go back. That part of me I murdered, willingly. I cannot find the way into the heart of the light. And they would not have me if I could."

Dairine wiped her face. "What are we gonna do?" she said.

Nita shook her head. "You got me. The coordinates for Timeheart aren't listed. . . ."

Kit sighed. "I wish Peach were here, we could have asked her."

There was a brief silence. "Oh," said a voice, "I'm not *that* easy to get rid of."

She was in the midst of them. Not Picchu. Or—was it not? She might look human, though very tall, and she might not be winged . . . but there was still a sense of swiftness about her, rather like the sense you got about Picchu when you realized she was going to make a grab at your sandwich and either get a piece of it, or a piece of you. Swiftness, and power, and extreme beauty, so that Dairine and Nita were abashed, and both they and Kit stared at her with all their eyes. All this in a person burning even brighter than the light around them, and about nine feet tall; a person wearing a sweatshirt with the sleeves pushed up, and blue jeans and sneakers, a person with long dark hair, and a sword naked in her hand, and the sword burning; and the fire of the sword and the fire of the sky were the same.

"You're kidding," Dairine said.

The woman laughed. "Often. But not at the moment."

"You were Picchu?" Kit said.

"I've been a lot of people. You'd be surprised at the names." She looked down with concern at the Lone One, who lay like a shadow on the burning ground. "But rarely have those namings turned out so well."

This was a bit much for Nita. "You're one of the Powers, aren't you? We dragged You halfway across the Universe and busted our guts when You could have— Why didn't You do something sooner?"

"We have been, for billions of years," She said. "But We couldn't do anything really permanent until Dairine got here."

Dairine's jaw dropped.

"And now," She said, "if My brother here is amenable, We can start getting work done at last."

Kit stared at her. "Your brother?"

"I told you I've been called by a lot of names." She knelt down by the shadowy form that lay collapsed on the brightness. "Athene was one. And Thor. And Prometheus. And Michael."

"But you're a girl!"

Nita threw Kit a wry look. The Power grinned. "These things are relative," she said. "But even in your world it's a byword. Men will fight bravely and be heroes, but for last-ditch defense against any odds . . . get a Mother." She smiled. "Ask Dairine."

Dairine grinned back.

"I was the winged defender," She said. "He was my twin brother, the beautiful one. Then . . . the disagreement happened, and there was war in Heaven, and all the roles changed. I led the others in casting Him out." She shook her head sadly. "But I always wanted Him back . . . as did all the other Powers as well. So my role changed again. I became Prometheus, and many another. I was sent to you again and again, to put the Power in your hands . . . wizardry, and other powers. I never had to steal it: it was given me . . . from what Source, you well know. I had to help undo the evils my brother was doing, and again and again I intervened, in many worlds. But We had a plan: that one day, someone else would intervene, and He would stop doing them himself. All it took was the entropy He himself had invented. . . ."

She looked at Dairine. "Billions of years, it took. All the redemptions there have ever been went toward this; from the greatest to the least. And finally in the fullness of time you came along, and took *my* role, of your own will, and woke up a race powerful enough to change the whole Universe, and gave them the fire." She glanced up at the mobiles and smiled. "How could he resist such a bait? He took the gamble: he always does. And losing, he won. . . ."

"He killed you, though," Kit said.

"I struck him down once. I had to come where he could do the same to me, without my doing anything to stop him. Now the balance is even."

The Defender reached down and put a hand into the shadow. "And we are going where such matters are transcended . . . where all his old pains will shift. Not forgotten, but transformed. Life in this universe will never have such a friend. And as for His inventions . . . look closely at Death, and see what it can become."

The long, prone darkness began to burn, from inside, the way a mountain seems to do with sunset. "Brother," the Defender said. "They're waiting."

The light began to shift. Nita looked up and around in wonder. The planet seemed to be going transparent around them. Or not specifically transparent: it was as if, one by one, other vistas were being added to it; seacoasts, forests, landscapes she couldn't understand, cities, empty spaces that were dark and yet burned; ten other worlds, twenty, a hundred, in an ever deepening overlay that enriched without confusing. *Alternate universes?* Nita thought, and then thought perhaps not: it was too simple an explanation. . . .

She looked at the Defender and found the same change and enriching in Her, and in the steadily brighter-burning form She bent over. Nita felt inclined to squeeze her eyes shut, not from pain but from a feeling of sheer insufficiency, of being involved in matters too high for her. "Never think it," said the Defender, beneficent lightnings flickering about Her as other forms and other names came and went in glory; "never think We were made to be less than equals in the One. Someday you will surpass Us, and still be Our equals, and both You and We will rejoice at it. Brother . . . up, and see the way home. Let them see what they have triumphed over."

The Lone Power rose up, slowly, like one discovering walking after a life of lameness. And Kit and Nita and Dairine all gazed, and speech left them. Nita's eyes filled with tears as she wondered how darkness could be so bright. Lightbringer He was, and star of the morning; and like the morning star, He needed the darkness, and shone brighter in it, and made it blessed. . . .

"Home," He said, gazing upward; just the one word. All eyes followed His. Nita found herself looking into endless layered vistas that were not a mere radiant mirror, like Timeheart, not a repair, a consolation for the marred world, but something deeper, closer to the true heart of things, fiercer, more dangerous and more beautiful, something that had never gone wrong to begin with, that the Lone One had never had power to touch; a reality that burned like fire, but still was sweeter than water after thirst, and fed the thirst itself, and quenched it again in delight and more desire; a state so much more solid and real than mere physical being and thought that Nita held on to herself for delight and terror, afraid she would fade away in the face of it like a mist in full sun. Yet she wanted to see and feel more of it—for she knew that there was more. How many more realities like this, piled one on another in splendor, towered up into the burning depths of creation, each more concrete, more utterly real than the last? Even the Lone One and the Defender looked stilled and diminished in all Their strength and beauty as They gazed up into the light.

"Yes," the Defender said, "it's greater since you left. If these rough sketch-universes expand, how should that of which they're studies not be doing so as well? But there's room for you. There was always room. You'll see."

They turned to look at Nita and Dairine and Kit and the mobiles. "Best make your farewells," the Defender said.

Dairine turned to the mobiles. Four or five whole seconds it took to say everything that she wanted to say to them: most of it not needing words.

"Don't forget to kill that spell," she said finally.

"Shall we come to see you?" Gigo said, bumping up against her knee.

"You better not, for the moment, guys," Dairine said. "I've got a lot of explaining to do at home. And I don't know when I'll be back . . . it may take a while." She bent to pick up the computer. "But you won't miss me, huh? I'm here, I'm with you. I'm *in* you."

"We *will* come, later," said another voice from down by her knee. It was Logo, healed as the One Who had been in it was healed. "We'll come to where you live, when we're wiser in being human, and wake your quicklife up."

Dairine grinned. "Just what we need . . . real computer wizards. Okay, you guys. It's a fair swap. It's gonna take a while for me to learn to be a computer. . . ."

She paused, to make the usual effort: and the words came out easily, easily. "I love you, you know that?"

They didn't have to answer.

The light was growing past even a wizard's ability to handle it, even the ability of one being sustained by two of the Powers That Be. "Time," said the Defender. "Brother, will you do the honors, or shall I?"

"Let me."

And darkness surrounded them.

Nita had been afraid of the dark when she was little. For a terrible moment, that fear swept down on her again—

—and then shifted completely. Something was looking at her: but not a thing like the things she imagined under the bed when she was little. Some-One. Not a physical presence: it needed none; but a still, dark regard weighing on her soul—dark, and benign, and inexpressibly joyous. It was no less a weight for all that, and terrible, but not in any way that made her afraid. It bore down on her, considering her in endless calm, knowing her inside out; and the dark splendor of Its scrutiny so scorched and pierced her with some deeper kind of light that she would have gladly gone swimming in a sun for relief from it. Her skin and her bones and her brains cried out to be out of there. But her heart sang with irrational joy, to match the Other's, even while rationality cursed and twisted under the weight of being completely known. . . .

It spoke to her, not with words but as if she thought to herself. *My shadows are still abroad in the world. As I have done evil, for some time yet they still shall. Stop them. Stop me.*

We will. Always.

Then the worlds are saved, as long as you save them all over again, every day.

Deal, said another thought, as if her own mind spoke to itself; but the thought was Kit's.

And light broke out again.

Backyard light. Nita's and Dairine's backyard, dark with evening; and hanging low in the west, the evening star. Voices floated out the windows from inside; Tom and Carl, still talking to the Callahans. In the elm tree, a mockingbird was doing blue jay imitations and demanding muffins.

The three looked at each other and sighed. Dairine headed around the house to the screen door, yanked it open, and hollered, "Hi, Mom, hi, Dad, we're home!"

Pandemonium broke out inside. Kit paused in the doorway. "What *are* we going to tell Tom?" he said.

"The truth?"

They went in in time to see Dairine go straight to her mom, willingly, and then to her dad, and hug them hard. This triggered a few minutes of loud noises, brief crying spells, and much fast talking. In the midst of it, Nita met her mother's astonished eyes over her dad's and Dairine's shoulders. She shrugged, and grinned. Some things not even being a wizard was going to help her explain.

It didn't last, of course. Dairine promptly disentangled herself. "If I don't go to the bathroom," she said, "I'm gonna blow up." And she headed up the stairs.

On the living room coffee table, calmly, as if it agreed with her, the Apple she had dropped there grew legs, climbed down, and went after Dairine.

Nita glanced at Kit, and together, as usual, they sat down to face the music.